The Sparkling Stories of

Phoebe and Her Unicorn

Complete Your Phoebe and Her Unicorn Collection

Phoebe and Her Unicorn
Dana Simpson

Unicorn on a Roll
Another Phoebe and Her Unicorn Adventure
Dana Simpson

Unicorn vs. Goblins
Another Phoebe and Her Unicorn Adventure
Dana Simpson

Razzle Dazzle Unicorn
Another Phoebe and Her Unicorn Adventure
Dana Simpson

Unicorn Crossing
Another Phoebe and Her Unicorn Adventure
Dana Simpson

Phoebe and Her Unicorn in
The Magic Storm
Dana Simpson

Unicorn of Many Hats
Another Phoebe and Her Unicorn Adventure
Dana Simpson

Phoebe and Her Unicorn in
Unicorn Theater
Dana Simpson

Unicorn Bowling
Another Phoebe and Her Unicorn Adventure
Dana Simpson

The Unicorn Whisperer
Another Phoebe and Her Unicorn Adventure
Dana Simpson

Camping with Unicorns
Another Phoebe and Her Unicorn Adventure
Dana Simpson

Virtual Unicorn Experience
Another Phoebe and Her Unicorn Adventure
Dana Simpson

Unicorn Famous
Another Phoebe and Her Unicorn Adventure
Dana Simpson

Unicorn Playlist
Another Phoebe and Her Unicorn Adventure
Dana Simpson

Unicorn Selfies
Another Phoebe and Her Unicorn Adventure
Dana Simpson

Unicornado
Another Phoebe and Her Unicorn Adventure
Dana Simpson

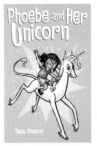

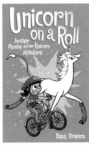

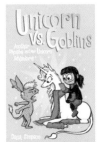

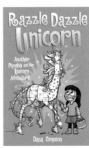

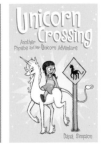

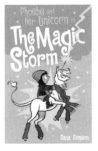

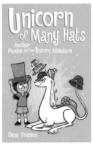

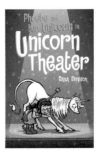

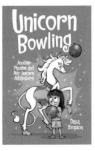

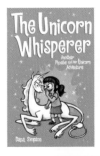

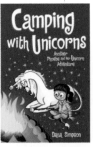

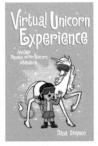

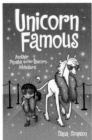

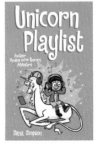

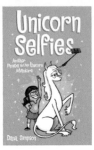

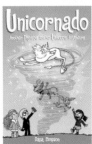

The Sparkling Stories of
Phoebe and Her Unicorn

Dana Simpson

Featuring comics from the original graphic novels
Phoebe and Her Unicorn in The Magic Storm and
Phoebe and Her Unicorn in Unicorn Theater

Andrews McMeel
PUBLISHING®

Phoebe and Her Unicorn is distributed internationally by Andrews McMeel Syndication.

Andrews McMeel Publishing
a division of Andrews McMeel Universal
1130 Walnut Street, Kansas City, Missouri 64106

www.andrewsmcmeel.com

23 24 25 26 27 SDB 10 9 8 7 6 5 4 3 2 1

ISBN: 978-1-5248-8090-3

Made by:
RR Donnelley (Guangdong) Printing Solutions Company Ltd.
Address and location of manufacturer:
No. 2, Minzhu Road, Daning, Humen Town,
Dongguan City, Guangdong Province, China 523930
1st Printing – 1/09/2023

Phoebe and Her Unicorn in The Magic Storm

Dana Simpson

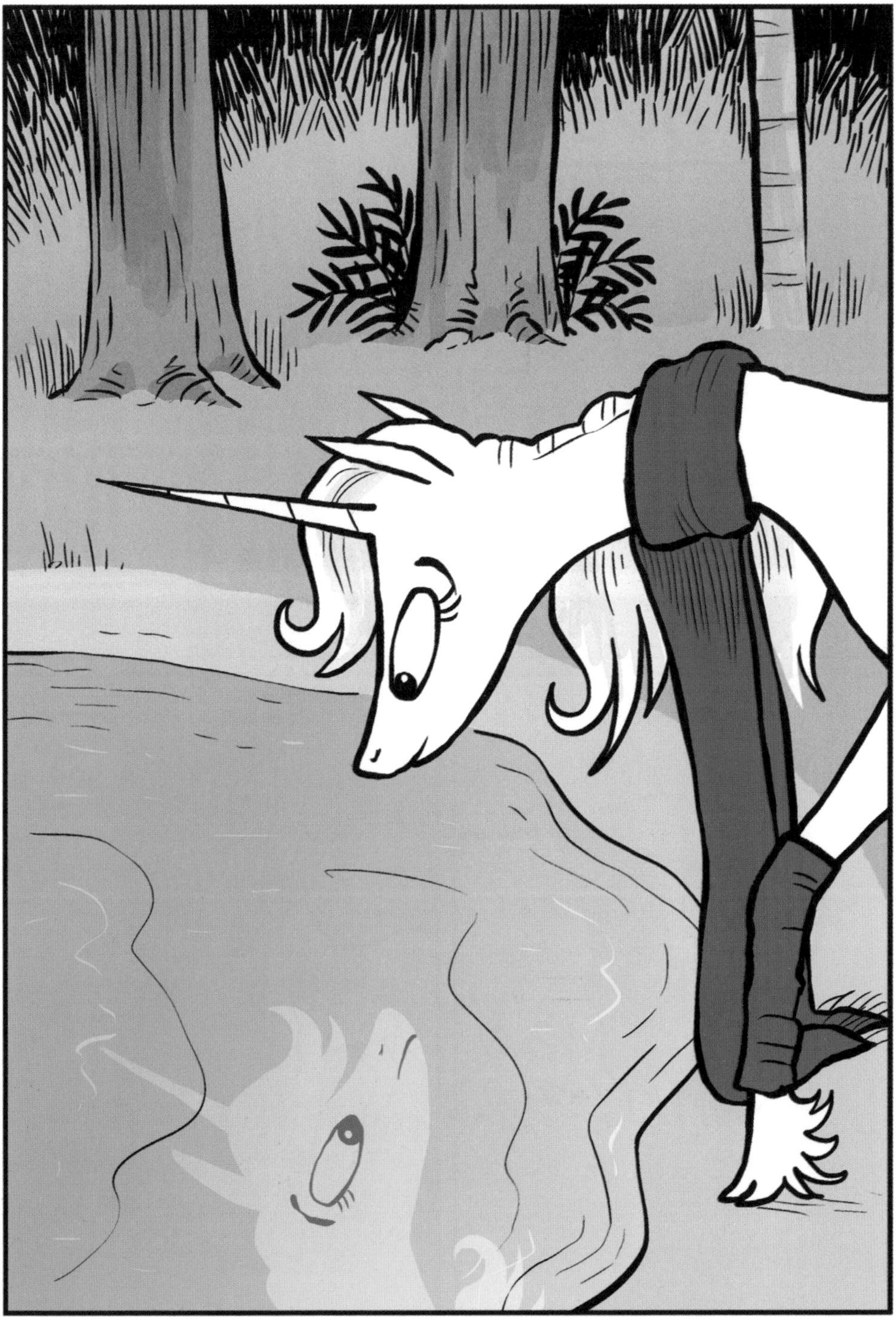

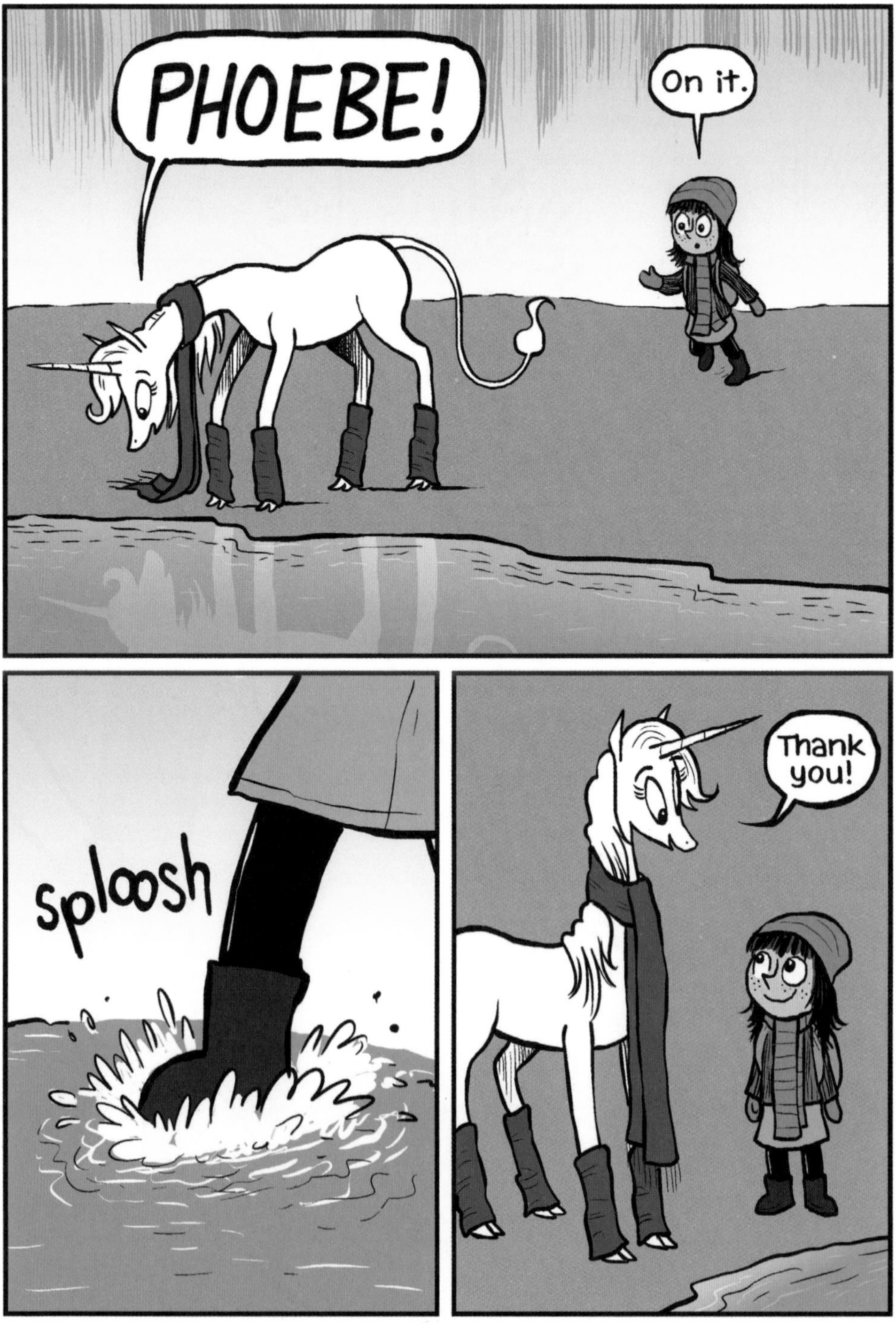
PHOEBE!
On it.
sploosh
Thank you!

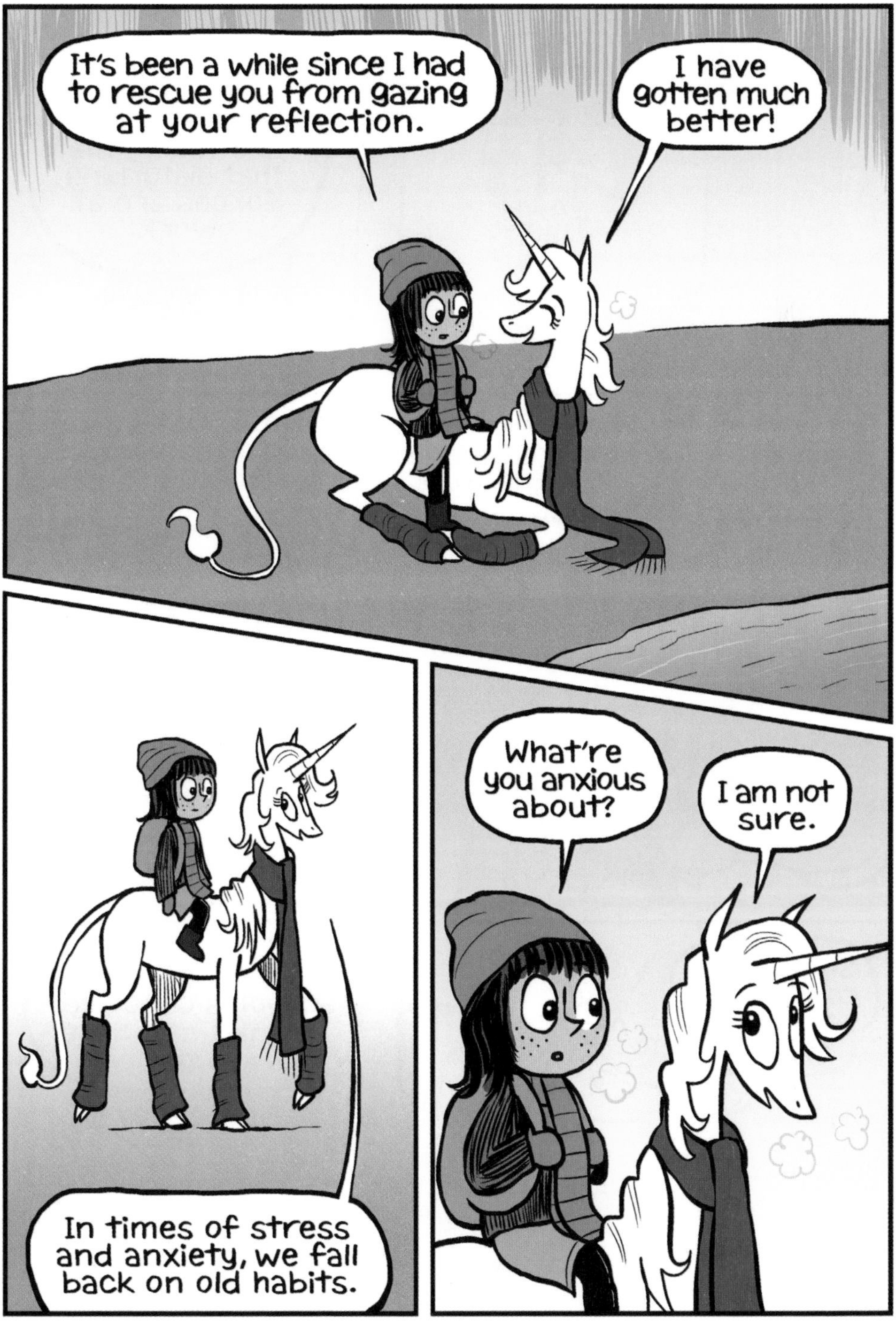
It's been a while since I had to rescue you from gazing at your reflection.
I have gotten much better!
In times of stress and anxiety, we fall back on old habits.
What're you anxious about?
I am not sure.

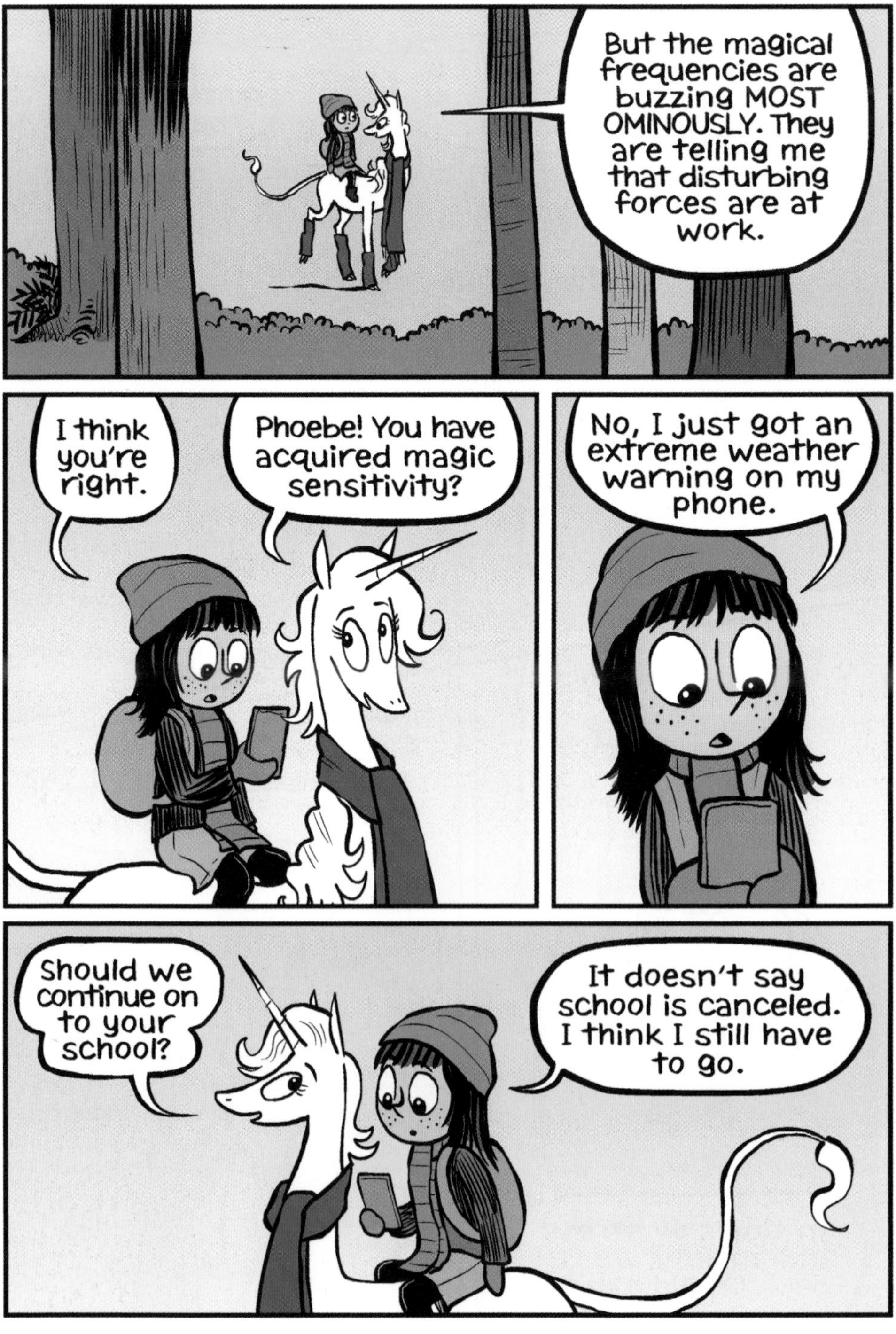
But the magical frequencies are buzzing MOST OMINOUSLY. They are telling me that disturbing forces are at work.
I think you're right.
Phoebe! You have acquired magic sensitivity?
No, I just got an extreme weather warning on my phone.
Should we continue on to your school?
It doesn't say school is canceled. I think I still have to go.

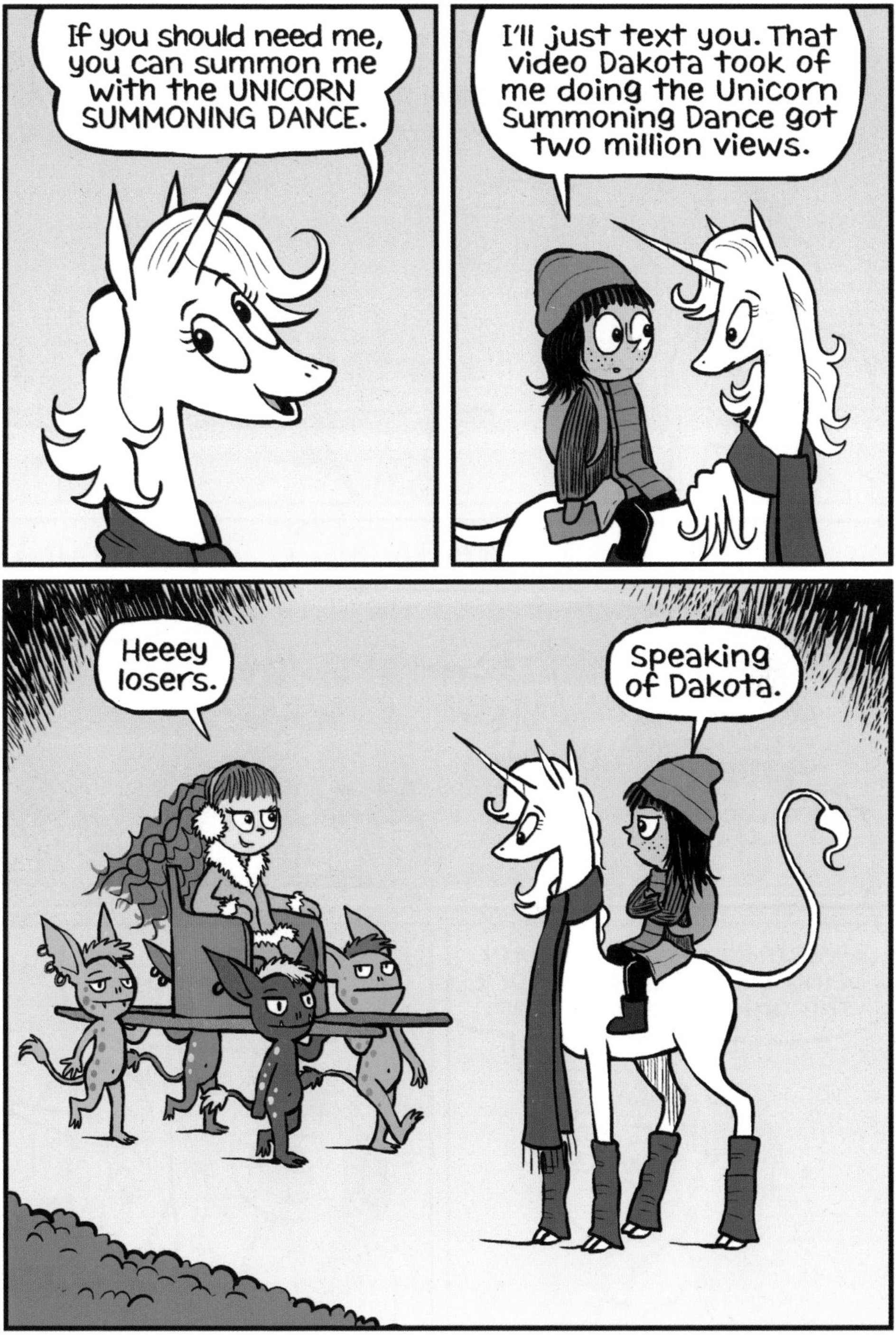
If you should need me, you can summon me with the UNICORN SUMMONING DANCE.
I'll just text you. That video Dakota took of me doing the Unicorn Summoning Dance got two million views.
Heeey losers.
Speaking of Dakota.

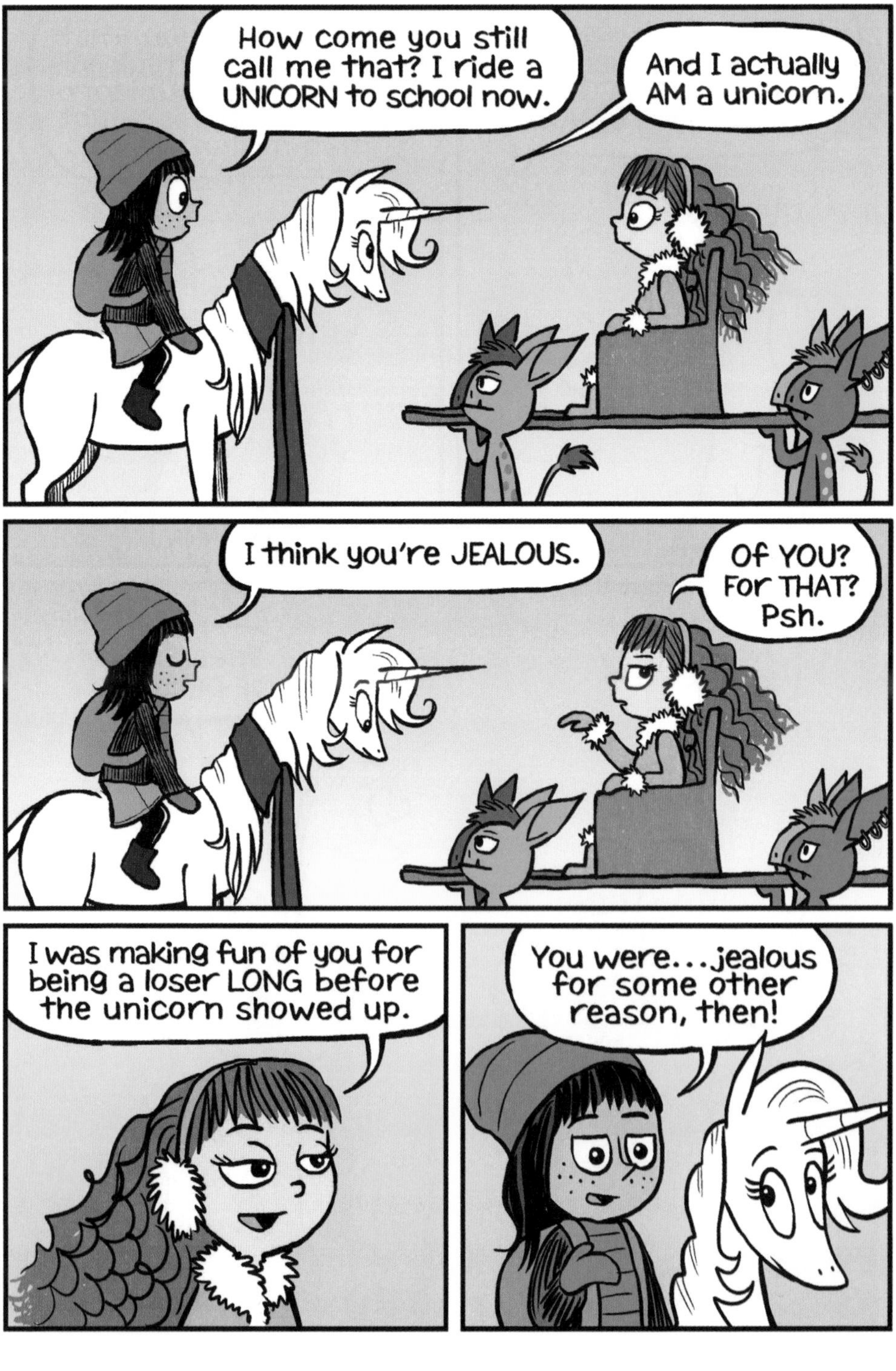
How come you still call me that? I ride a UNICORN to school now.
And I actually AM a unicorn.
I think you're JEALOUS.
Of YOU? For THAT? Psh.
I was making fun of you for being a loser LONG before the unicorn showed up.
You were...jealous for some other reason, then!

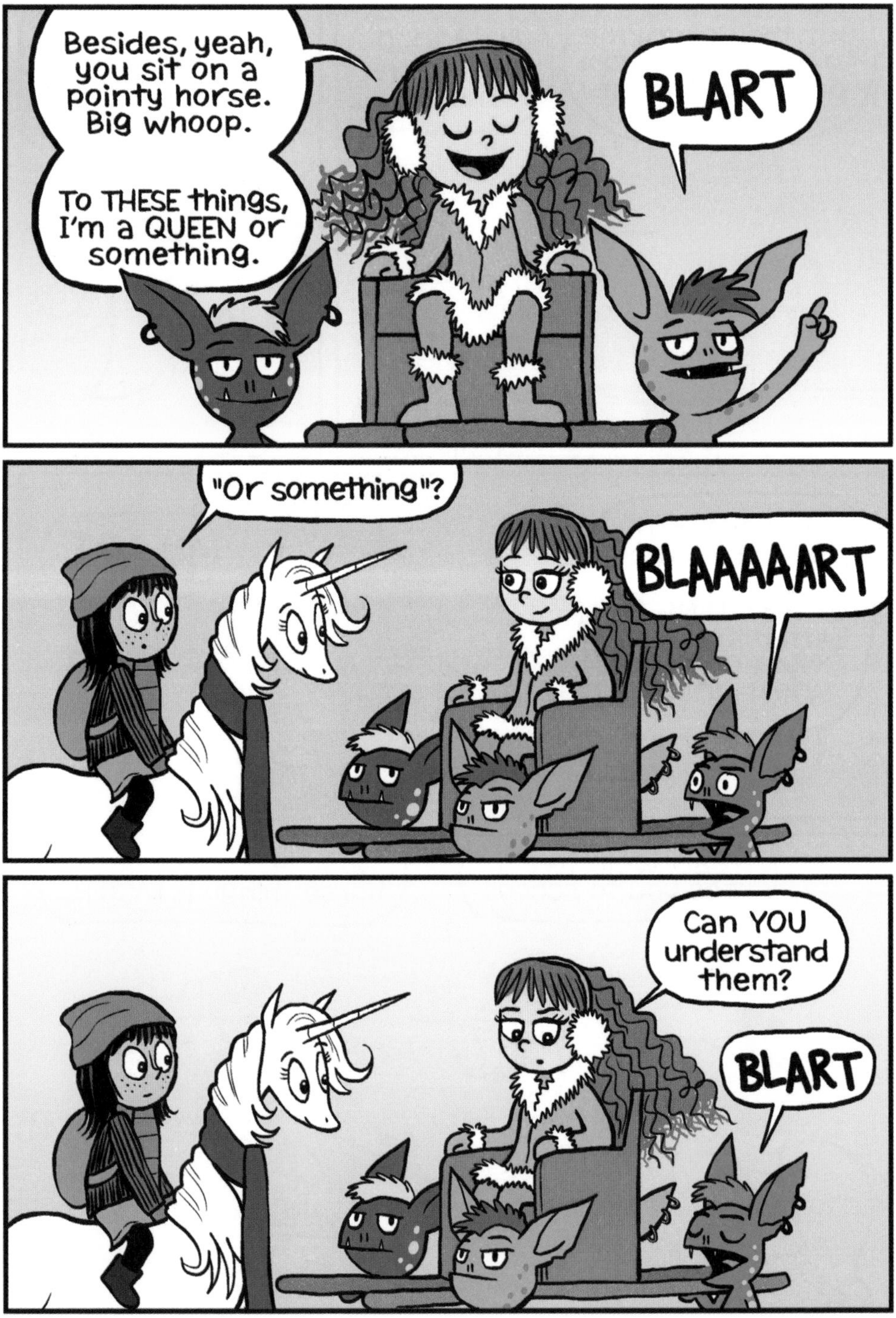
Besides, yeah, you sit on a pointy horse. Big whoop.
To THESE things, I'm a QUEEN or something.
BLART
"Or something"?
BLAAAAART
Can YOU understand them?
BLART

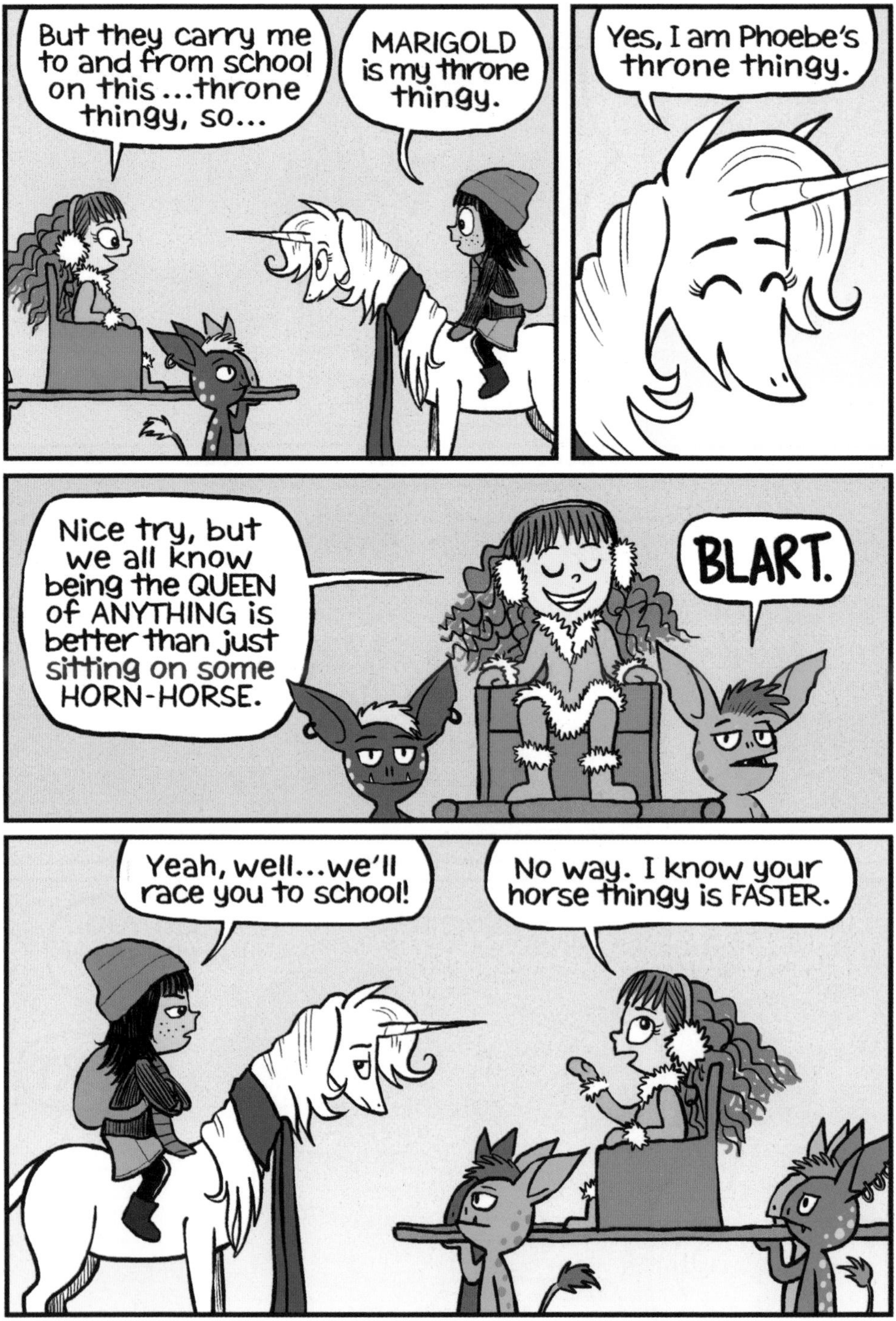
But they carry me to and from school on this...throne thingy, so...
MARIGOLD is my throne thingy.
Yes, I am Phoebe's throne thingy.
Nice try, but we all know being the QUEEN of ANYTHING is better than just sitting on some HORN-HORSE.
BLART.
Yeah, well...we'll race you to school!
No way. I know your horse thingy is FASTER.

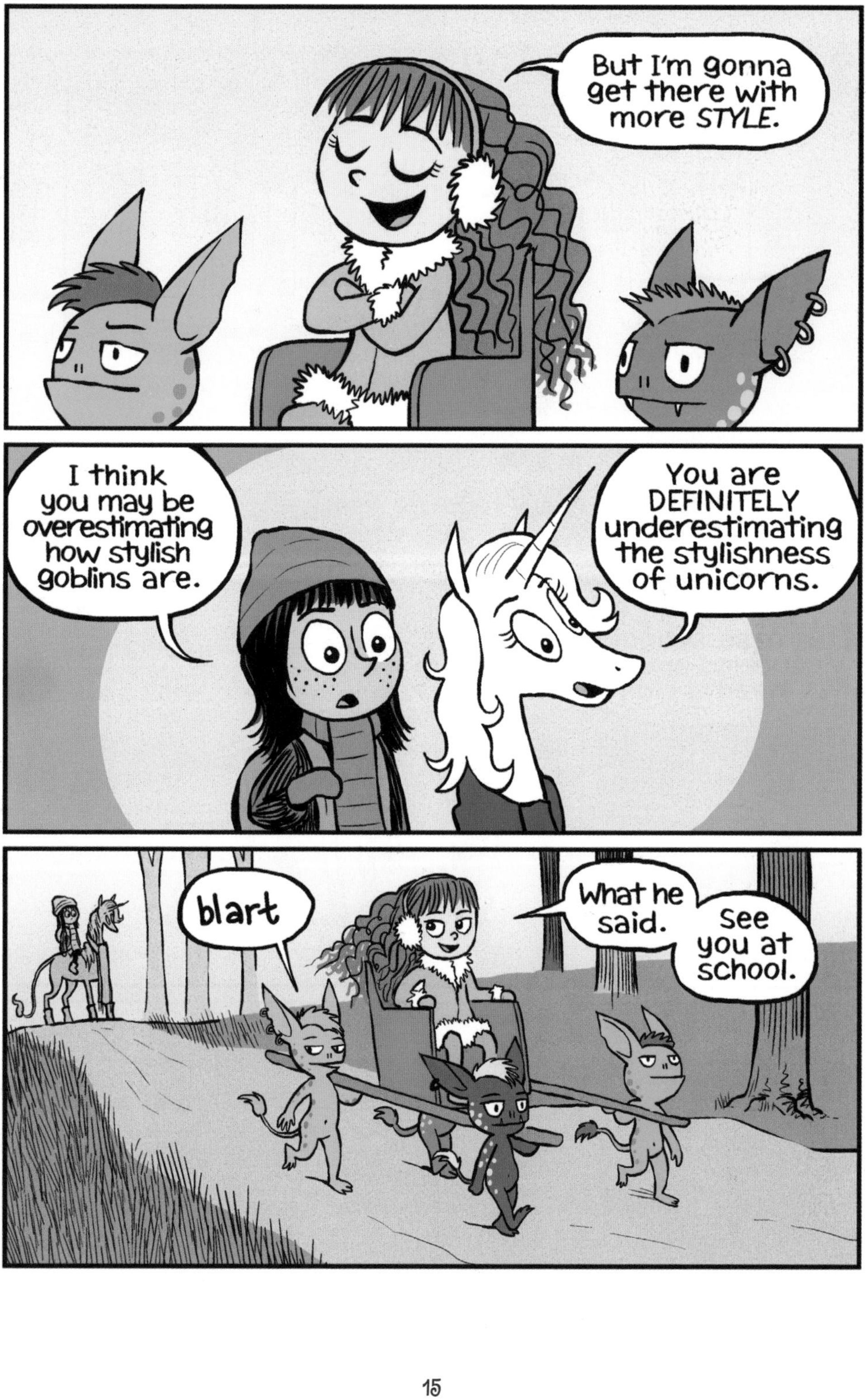

But I'm gonna get there with more STYLE.
I think you may be overestimating how stylish goblins are.
You are DEFINITELY underestimating the stylishness of unicorns.
blart
What he said.
See you at school.

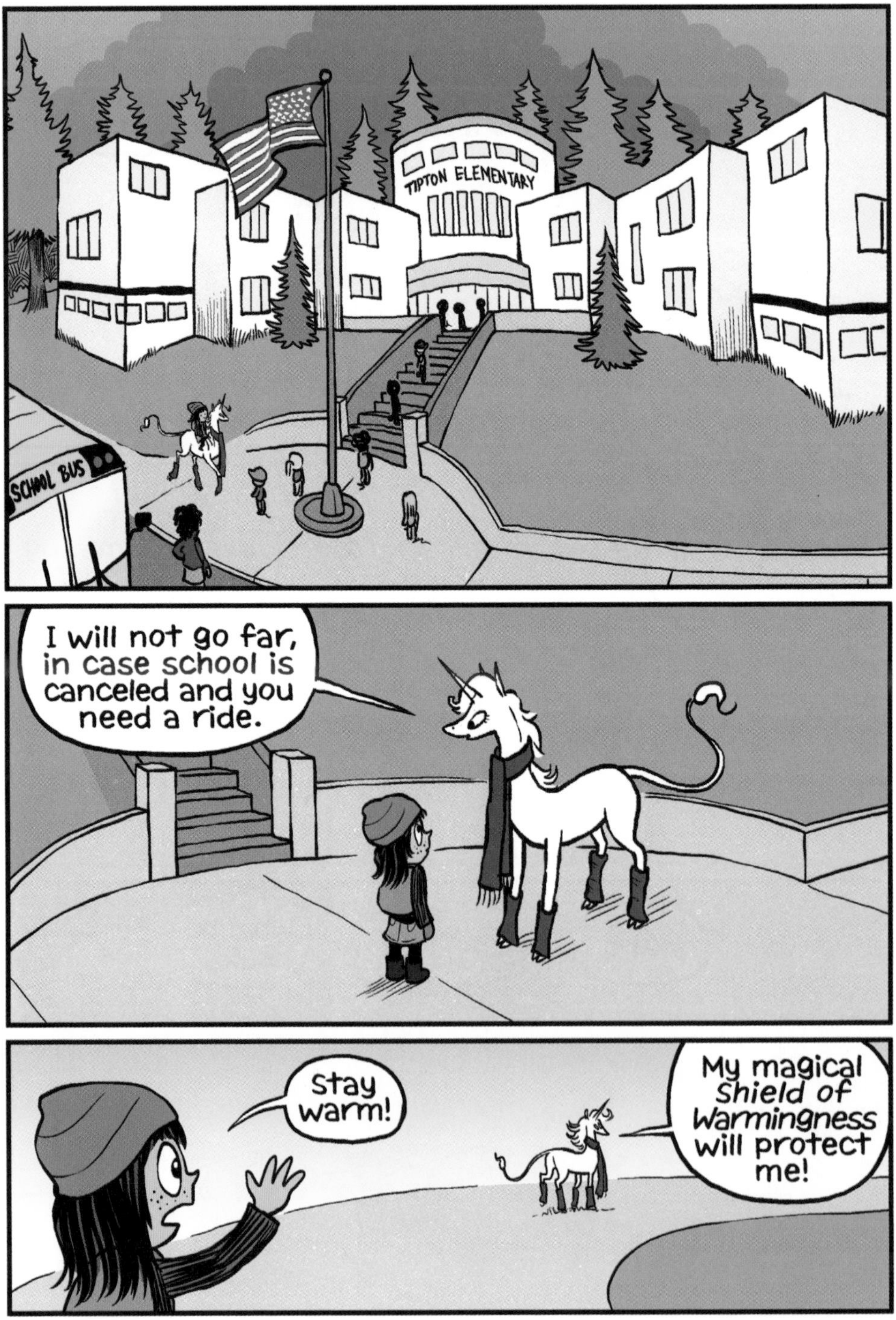
TIPTON ELEMENTARY
SCHOOL BUS
I will not go far, in case school is canceled and you need a ride.
Stay warm!
My magical Shield of Warmingness will protect me!

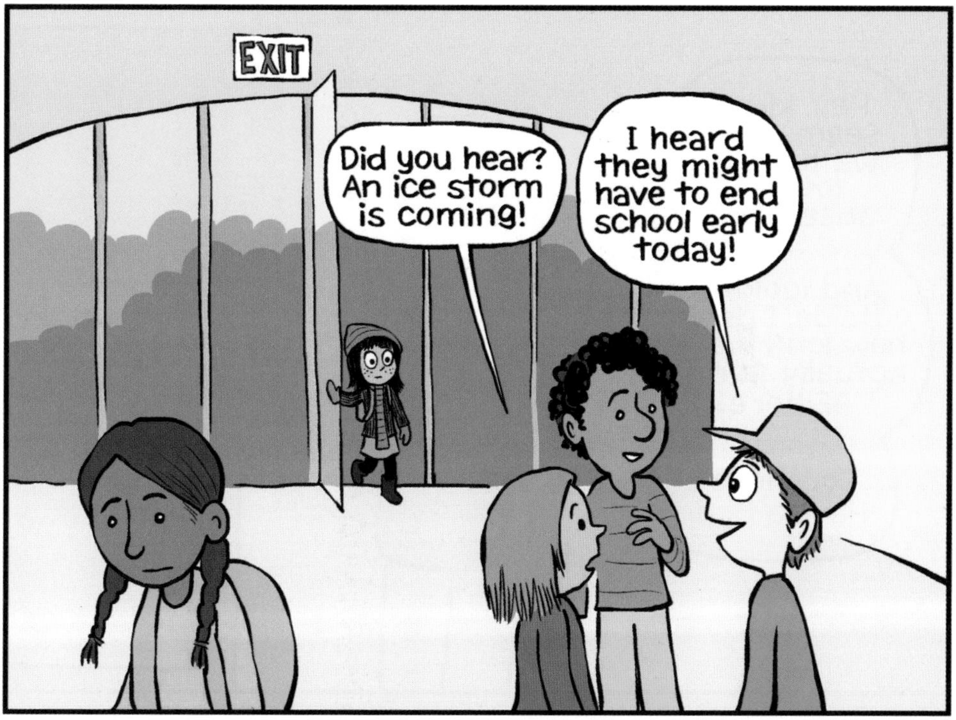
Did you hear? An ice storm is coming!
I heard they might have to end school early today!
EXIT

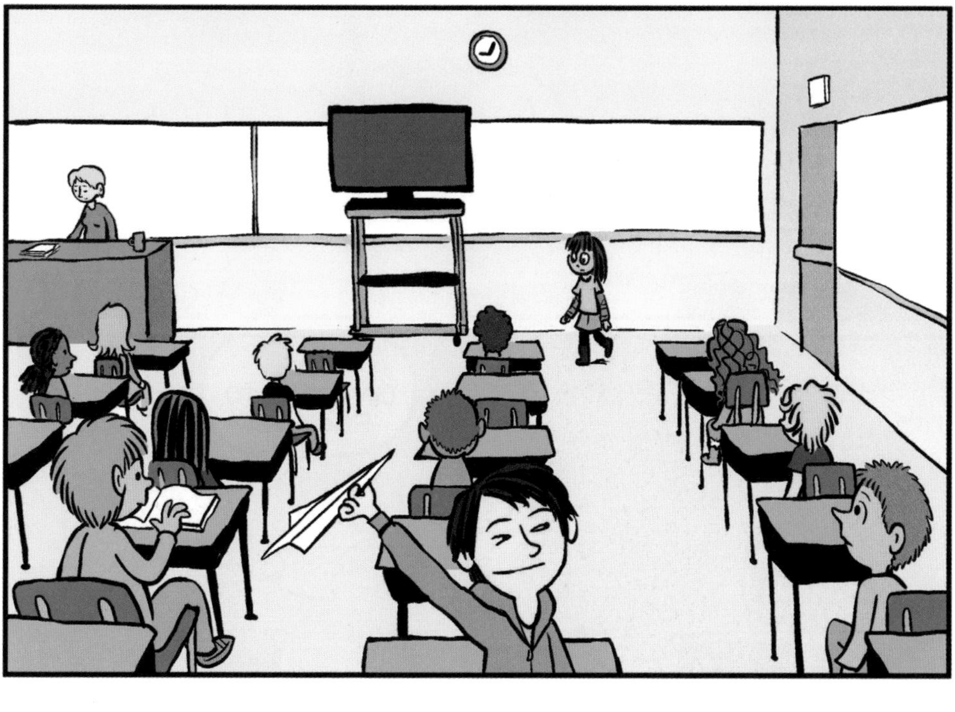

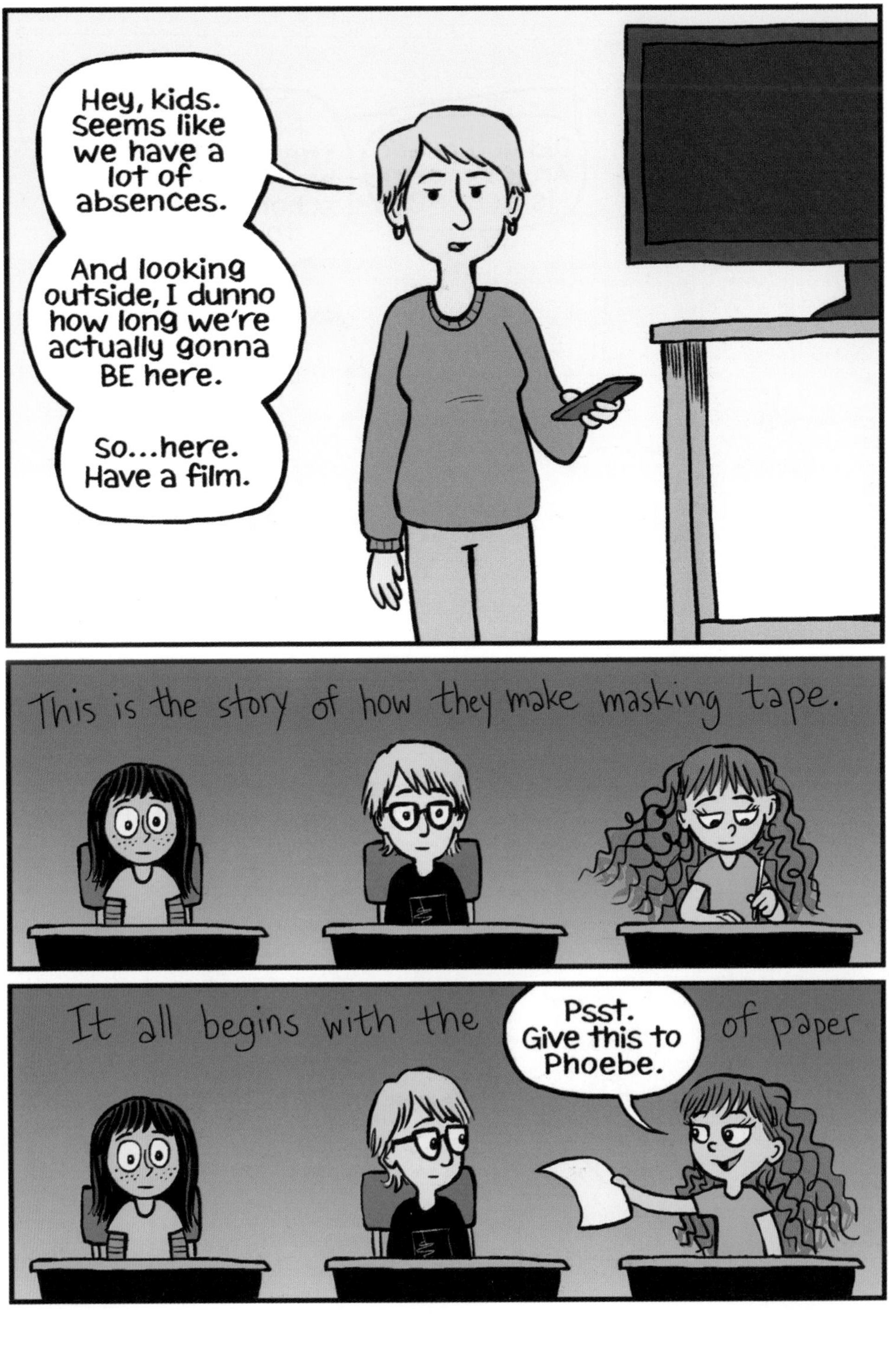
Hey, kids. Seems like we have a lot of absences.
And looking outside, I dunno how long we're actually gonna BE here.
So...here. Have a film.
This is the story of how they make masking tape.
It all begins with the
Psst. Give this to Phoebe.
of paper

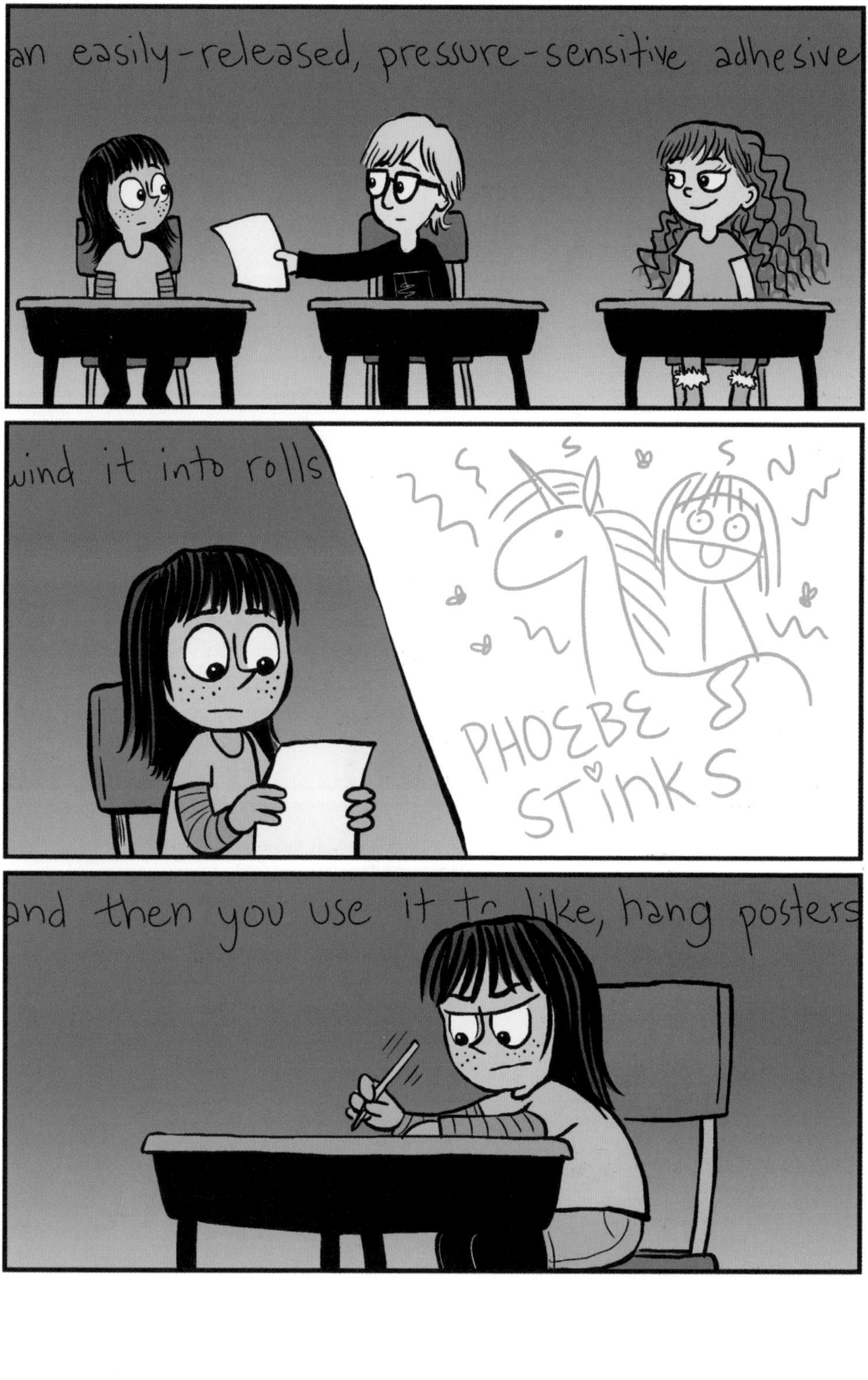
an easily-released, pressure-sensitive adhesive
wind it into rolls
PHOEBE STiNKS
and then you use it to like, hang posters

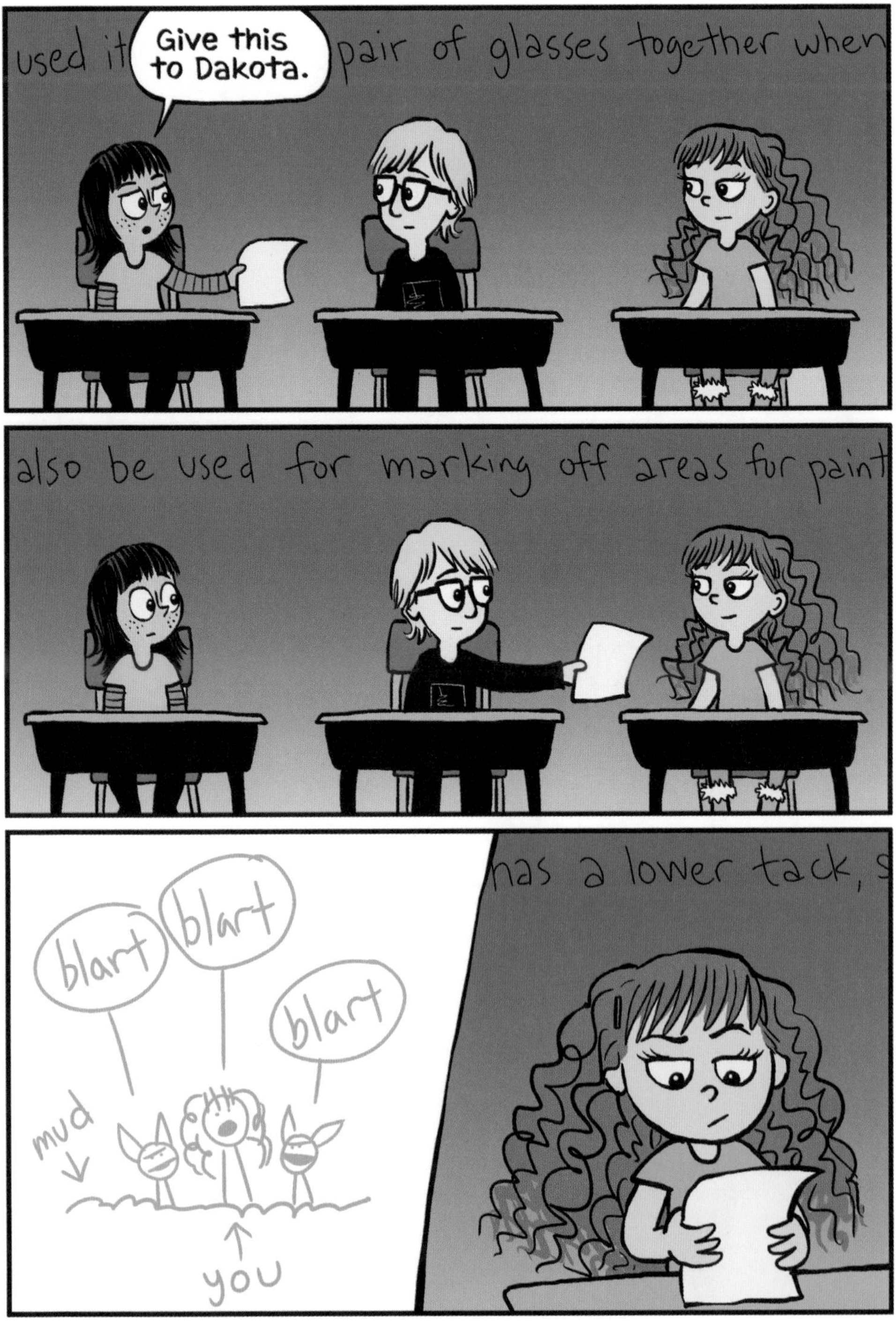
used it
Give this to Dakota.
pair of glasses together when
also be used for marking off areas for paint
has a lower tack, s
blart
blart
blart
mud
you

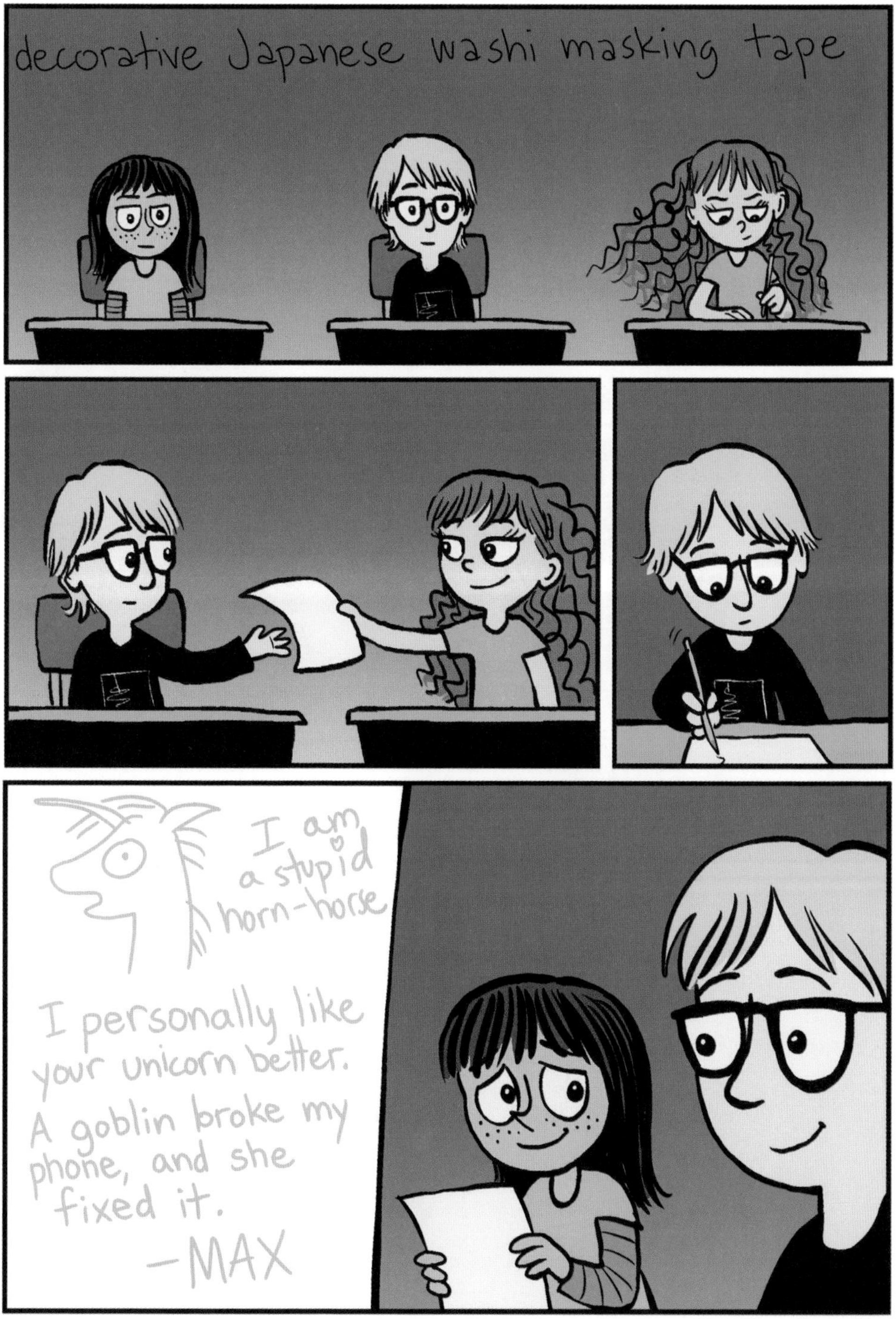
decorative Japanese washi masking tape
I am a stupid horn-horse
I personally like your unicorn better. A goblin broke my phone, and she fixed it. —MAX

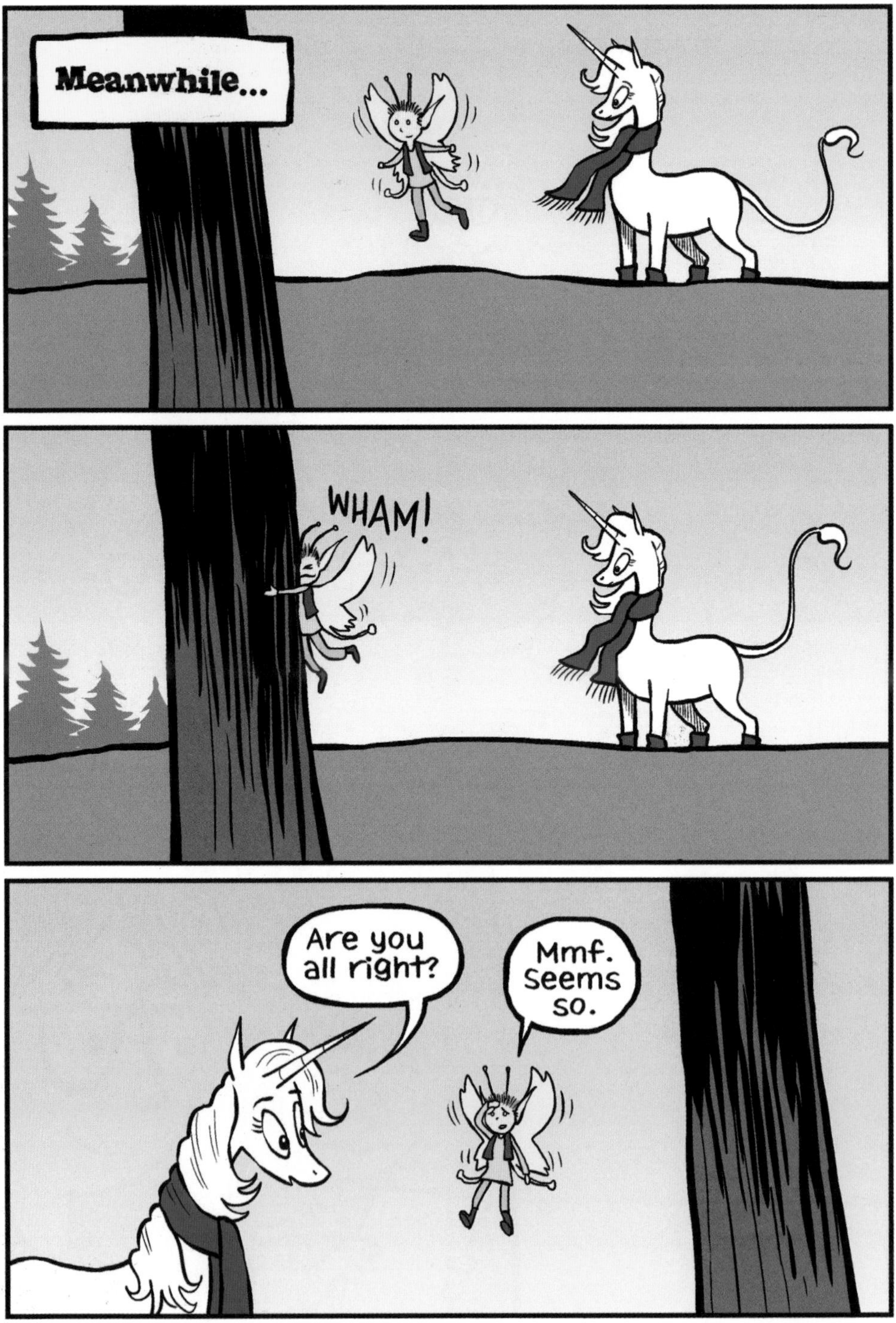
Meanwhile...
WHAM!
Are you all right?
Mmf. Seems so.

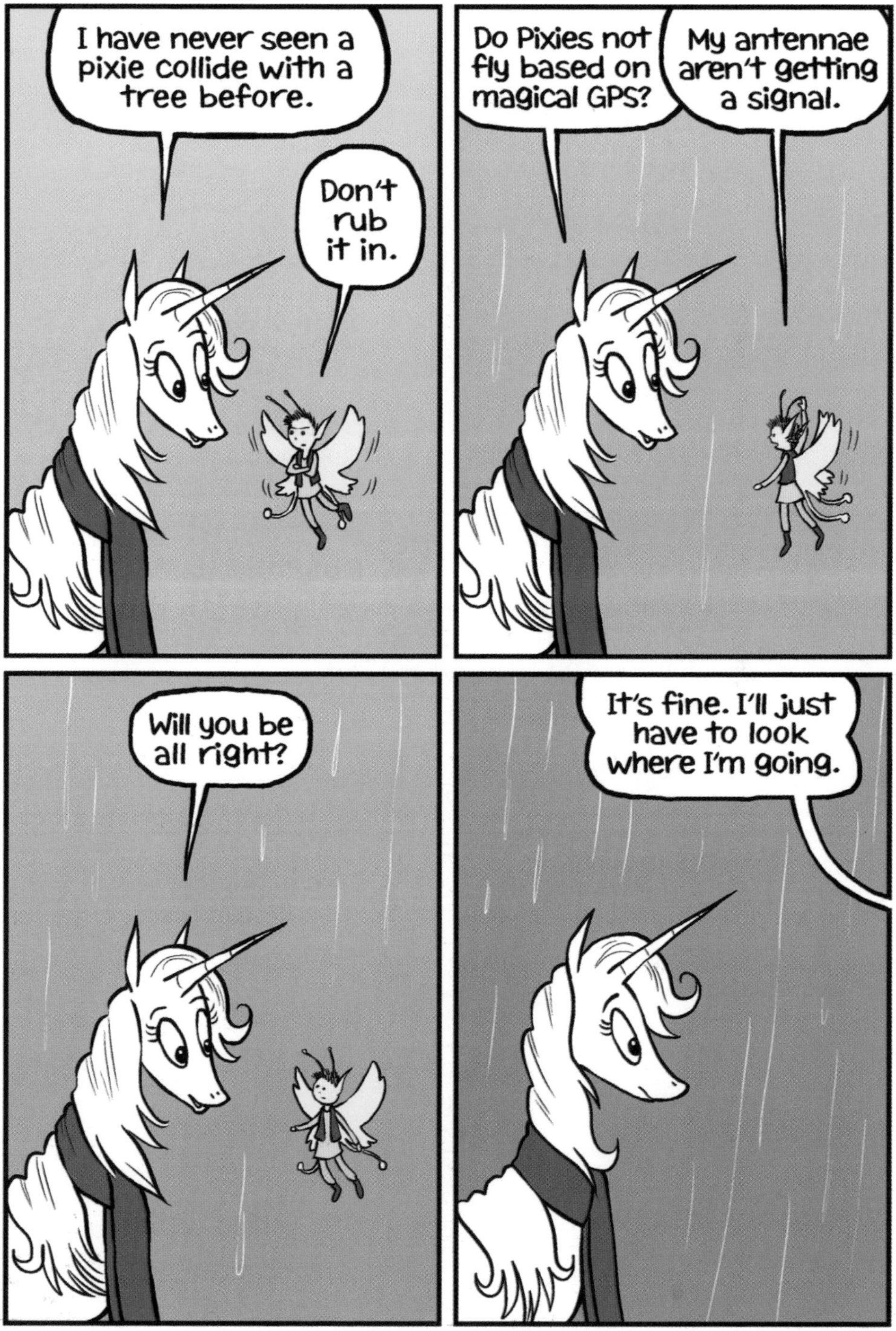
I have never seen a pixie collide with a tree before.
Don't rub it in.
Do Pixies not fly based on magical GPS?
My antennae aren't getting a signal.
Will you be all right?
It's fine. I'll just have to look where I'm going.

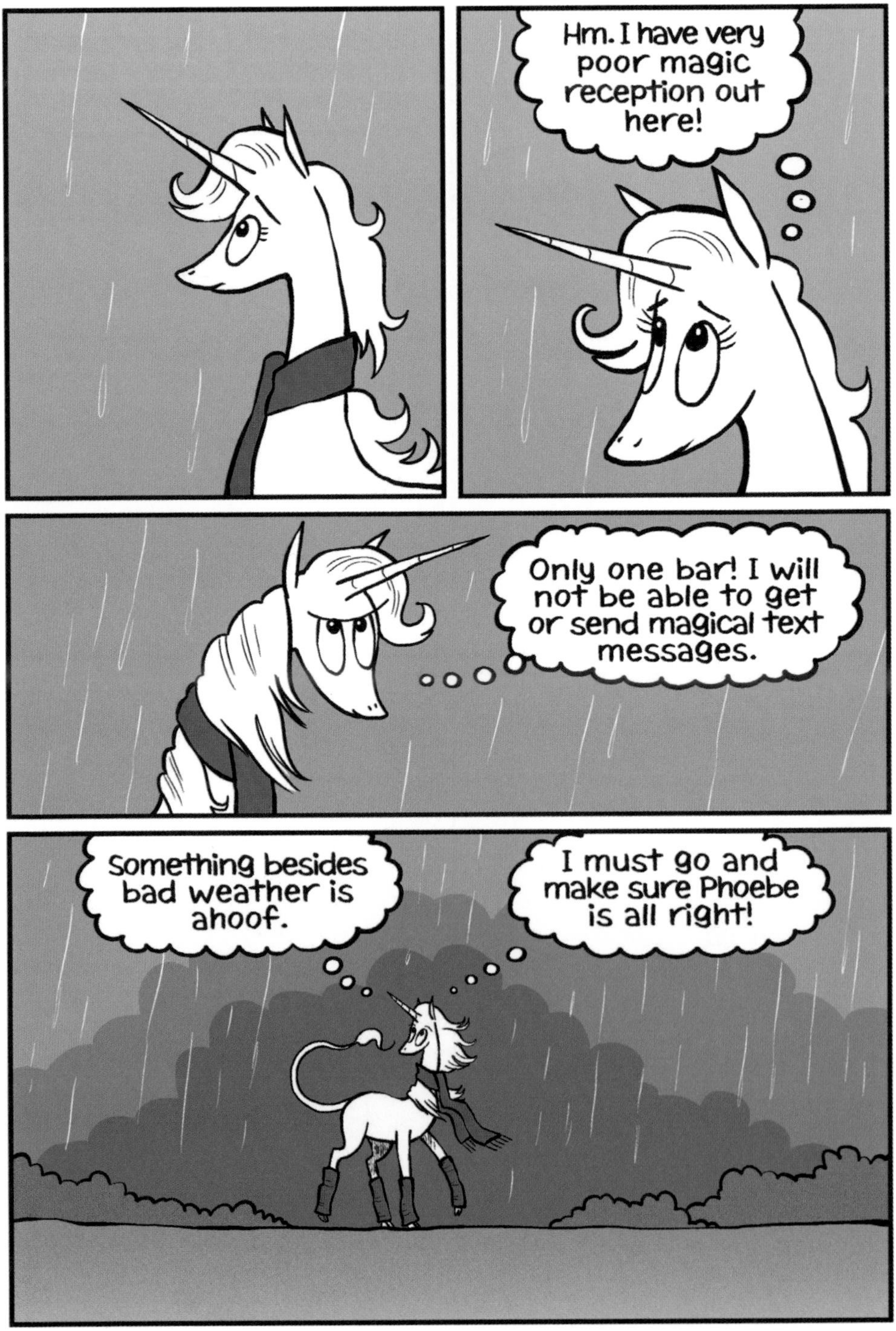
Hm. I have very poor magic reception out here!
Only one bar! I will not be able to get or send magical text messages.
Something besides bad weather is ahoof.
I must go and make sure Phoebe is all right!

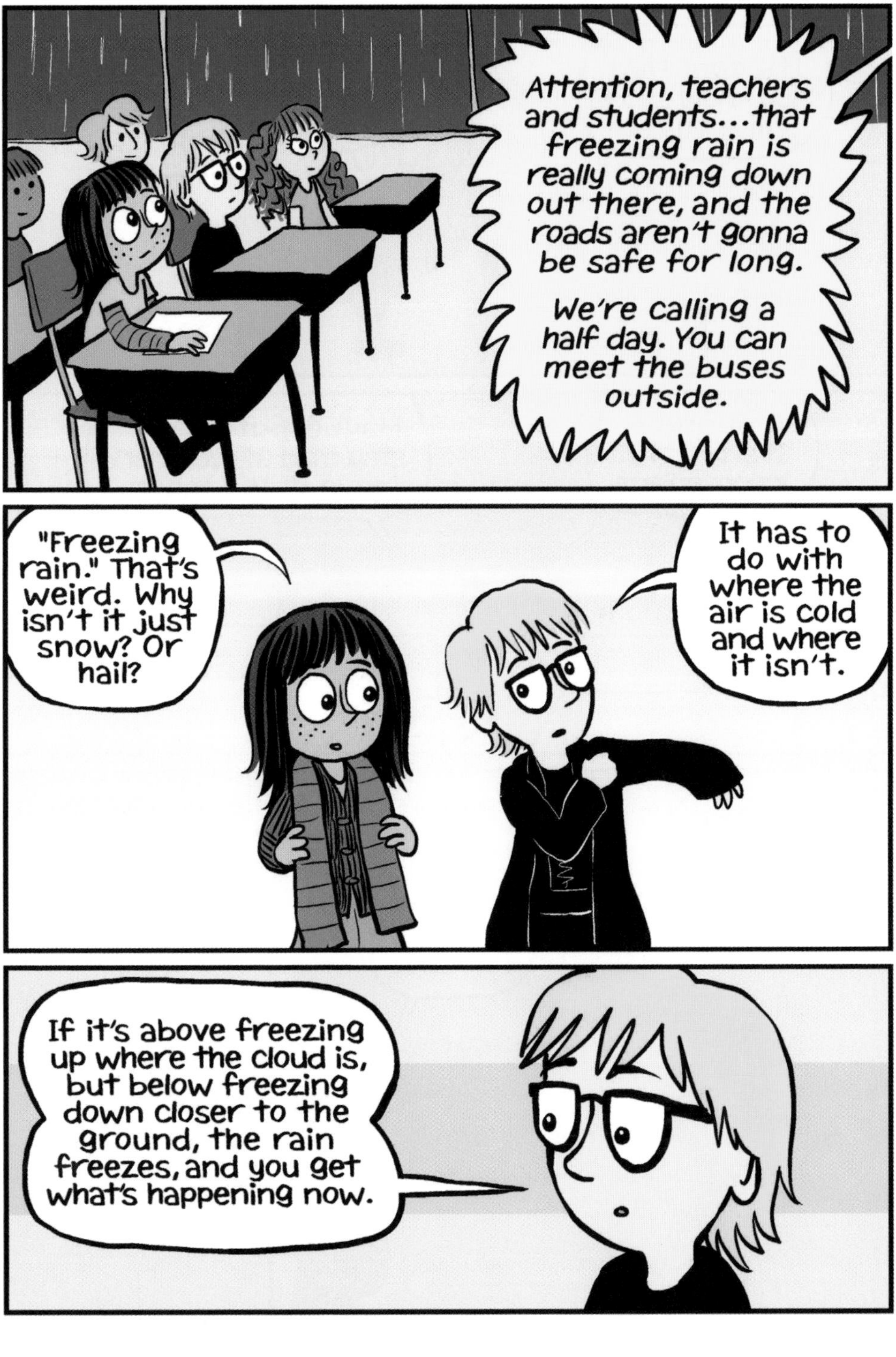
Attention, teachers and students...that freezing rain is really coming down out there, and the roads aren't gonna be safe for long.
We're calling a half day. You can meet the buses outside.
"Freezing rain." That's weird. Why isn't it just snow? Or hail?
It has to do with where the air is cold and where it isn't.
If it's above freezing up where the cloud is, but below freezing down closer to the ground, the rain freezes, and you get what's happening now.

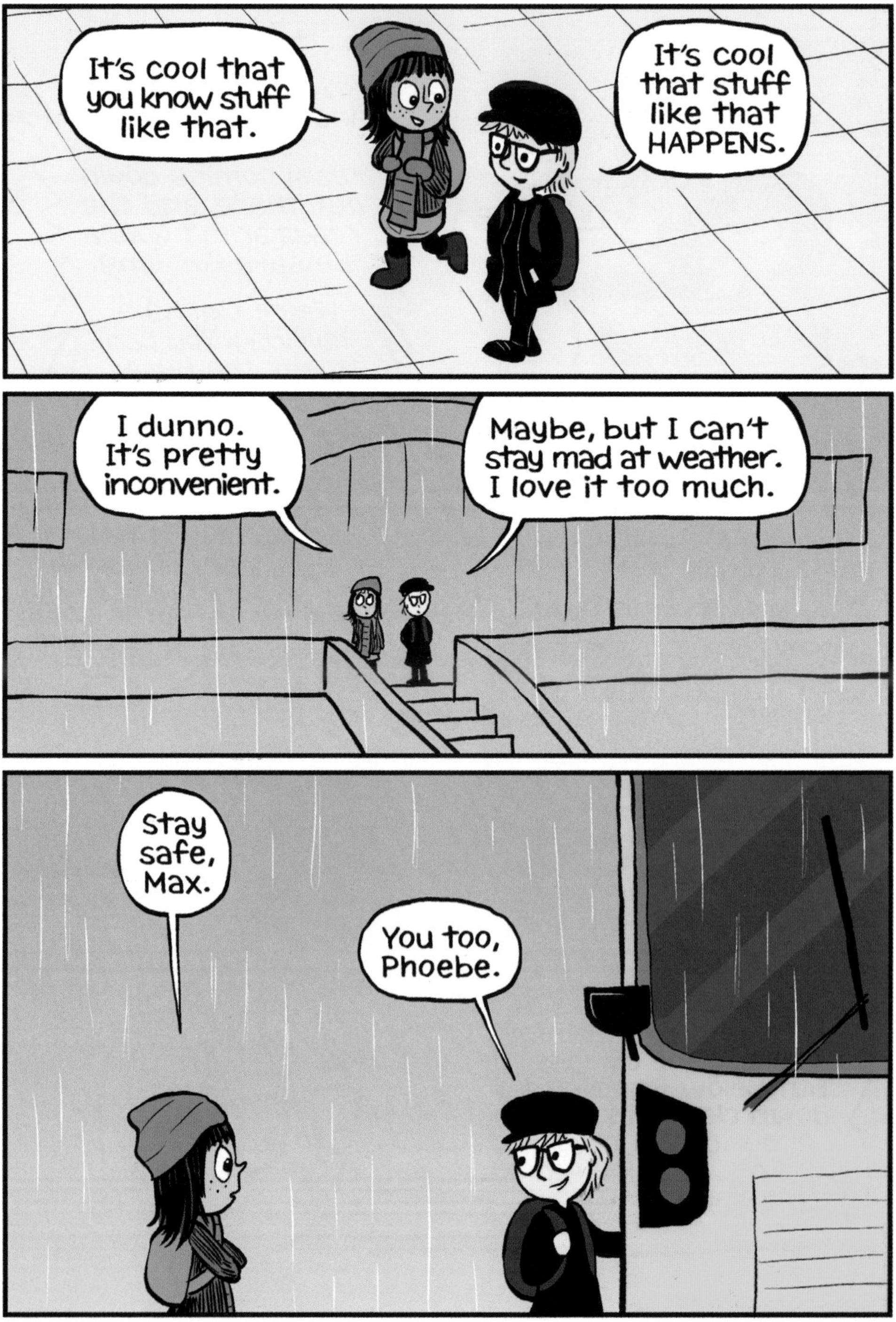
It's cool that you know stuff like that.
It's cool that stuff like that HAPPENS.
I dunno. It's pretty inconvenient.
Maybe, but I can't stay mad at weather. I love it too much.
Stay safe, Max.
You too, Phoebe.

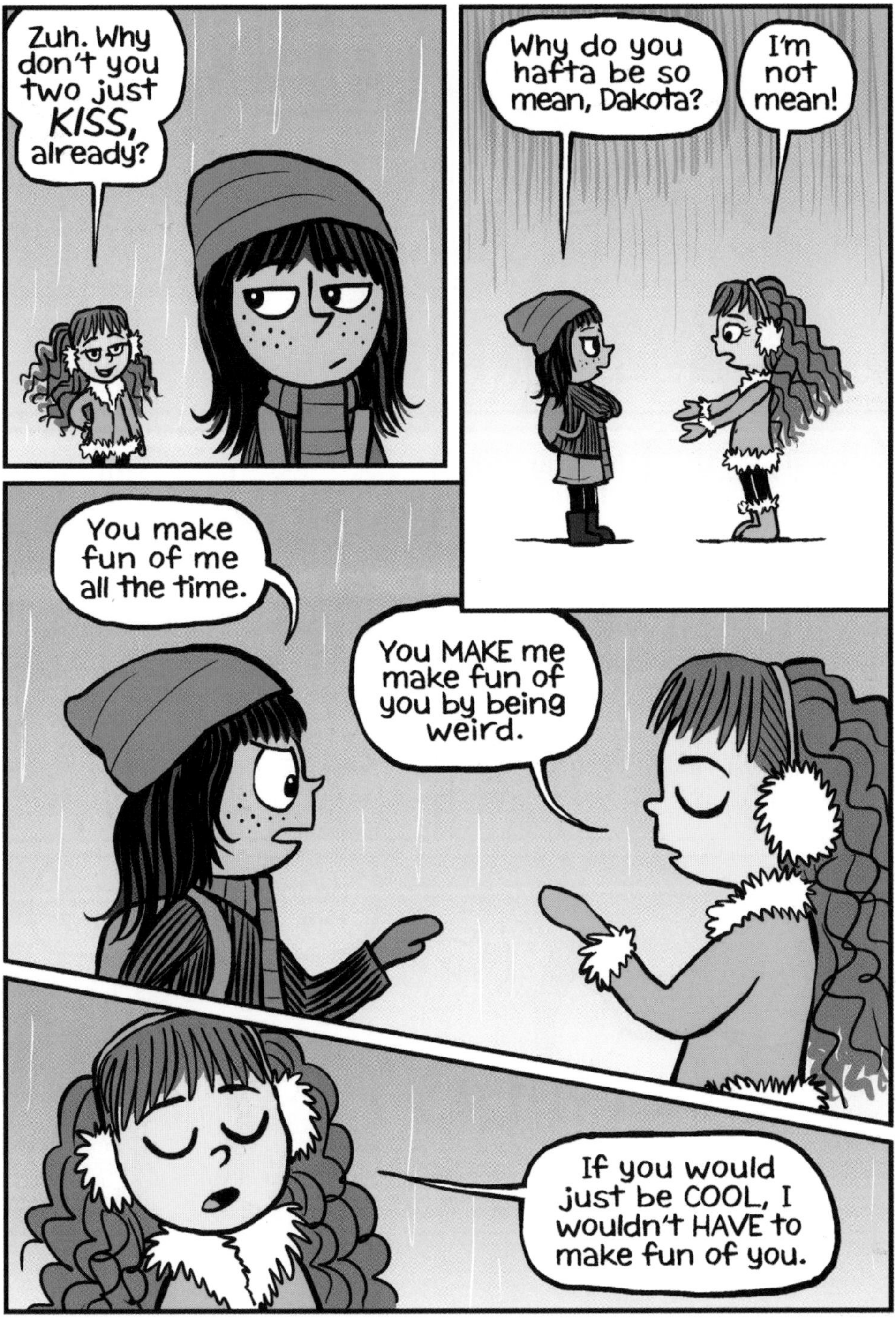
Zuh. Why don't you two just KISS, already?
Why do you hafta be so mean, Dakota?
I'm not mean!
You make fun of me all the time.
You MAKE me make fun of you by being weird.
If you would just be COOL, I wouldn't HAVE to make fun of you.

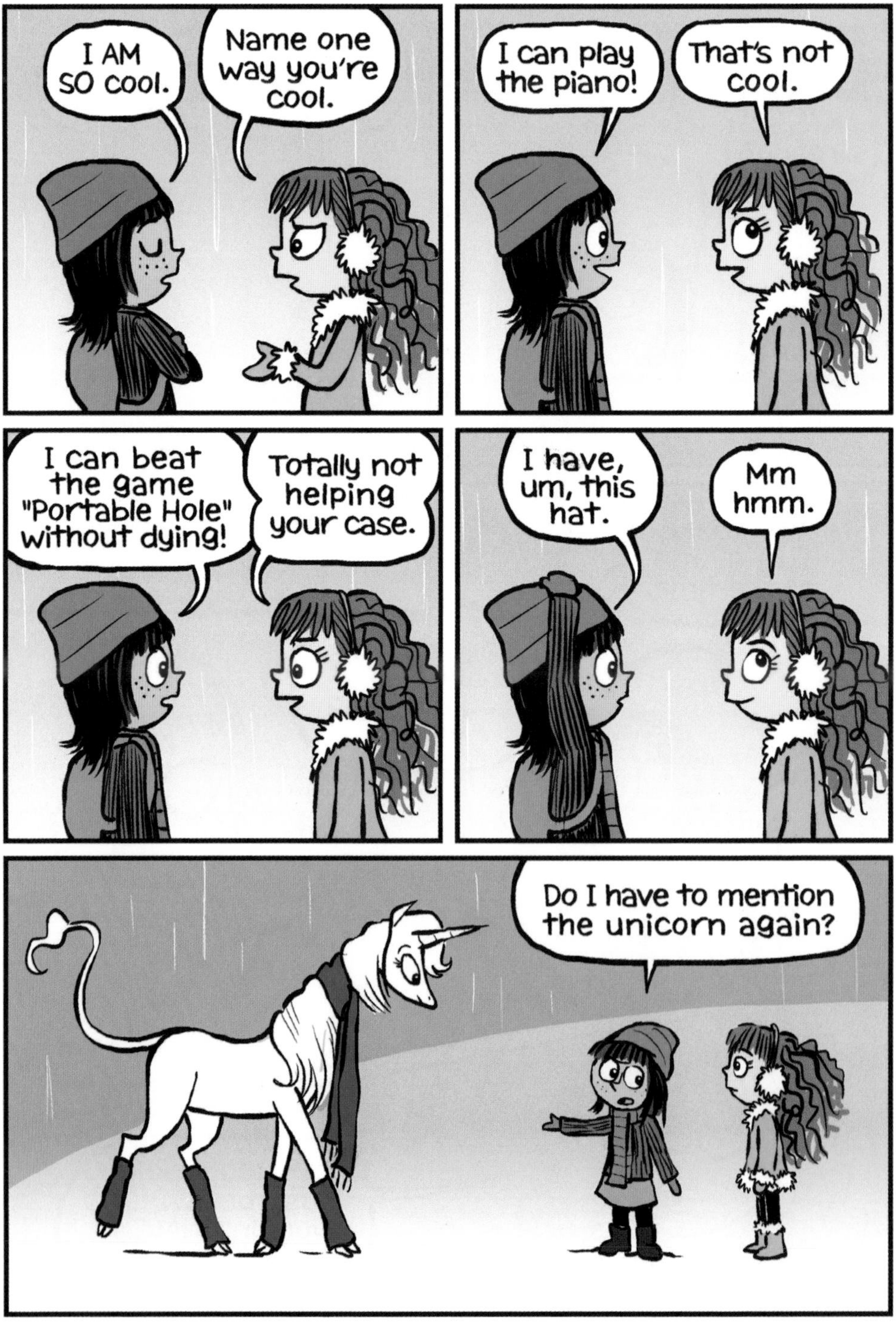
I AM SO cool.
Name one way you're cool.
I can play the piano!
That's not cool.
I can beat the game "Portable Hole" without dying!
Totally not helping your case.
I have, um, this hat.
Mm hmm.
Do I have to mention the unicorn again?

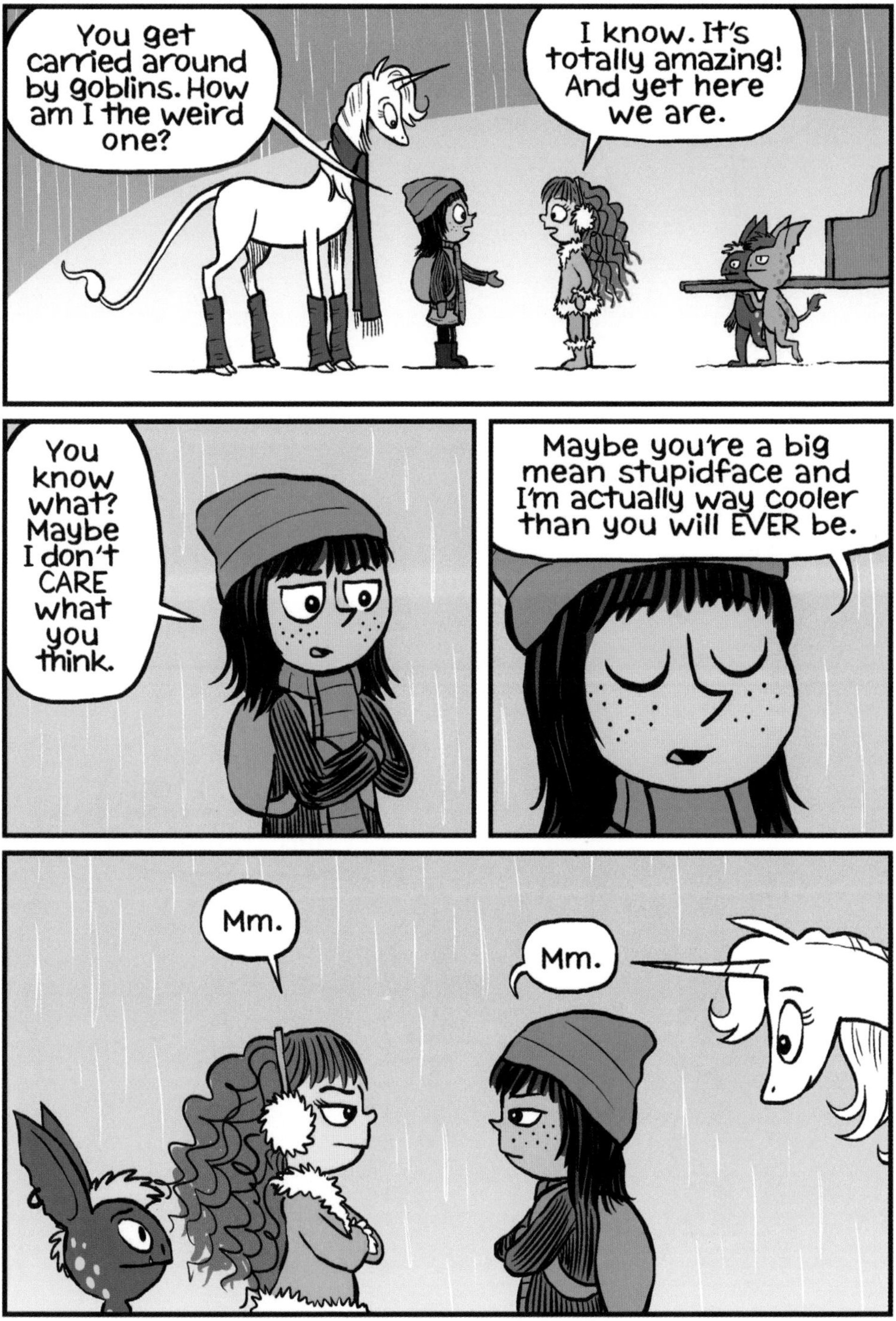
You get carried around by goblins. How am I the weird one?
I know. It's totally amazing! And yet here we are.
You know what? Maybe I don't CARE what you think.
Maybe you're a big mean stupidface and I'm actually way cooler than you will EVER be.
Mm.
Mm.

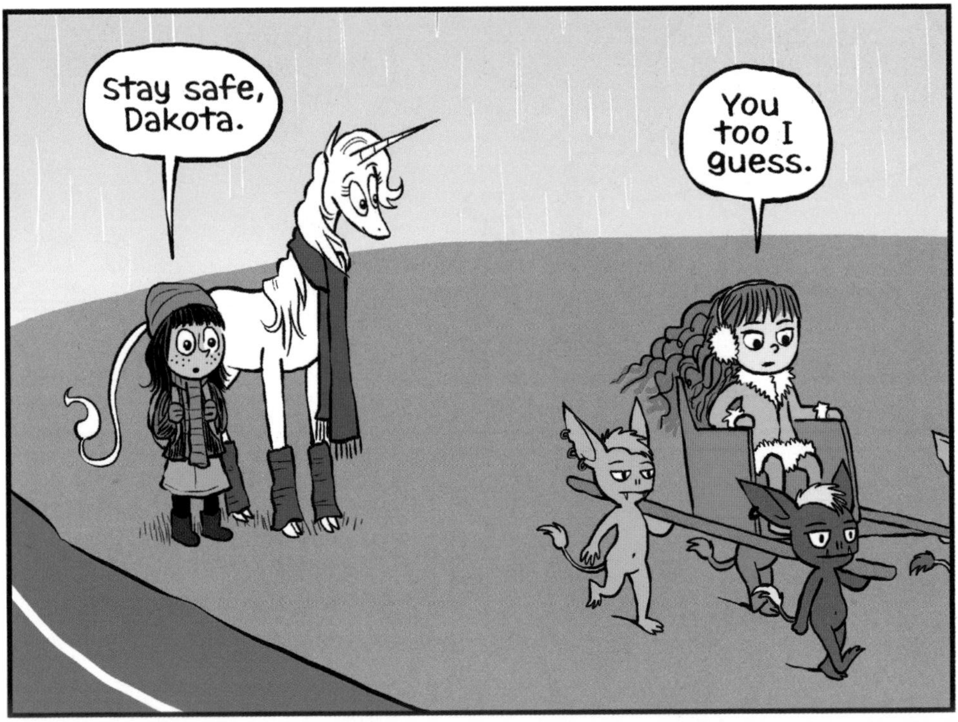
Stay safe, Dakota.
You too I guess.

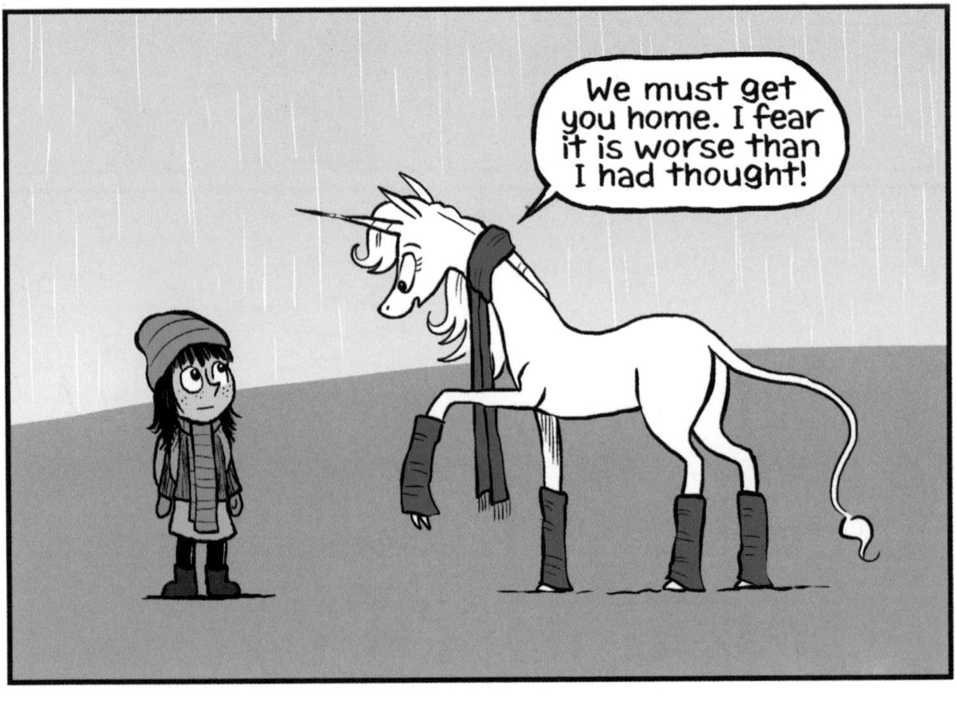
We must get you home. I fear it is worse than I had thought!

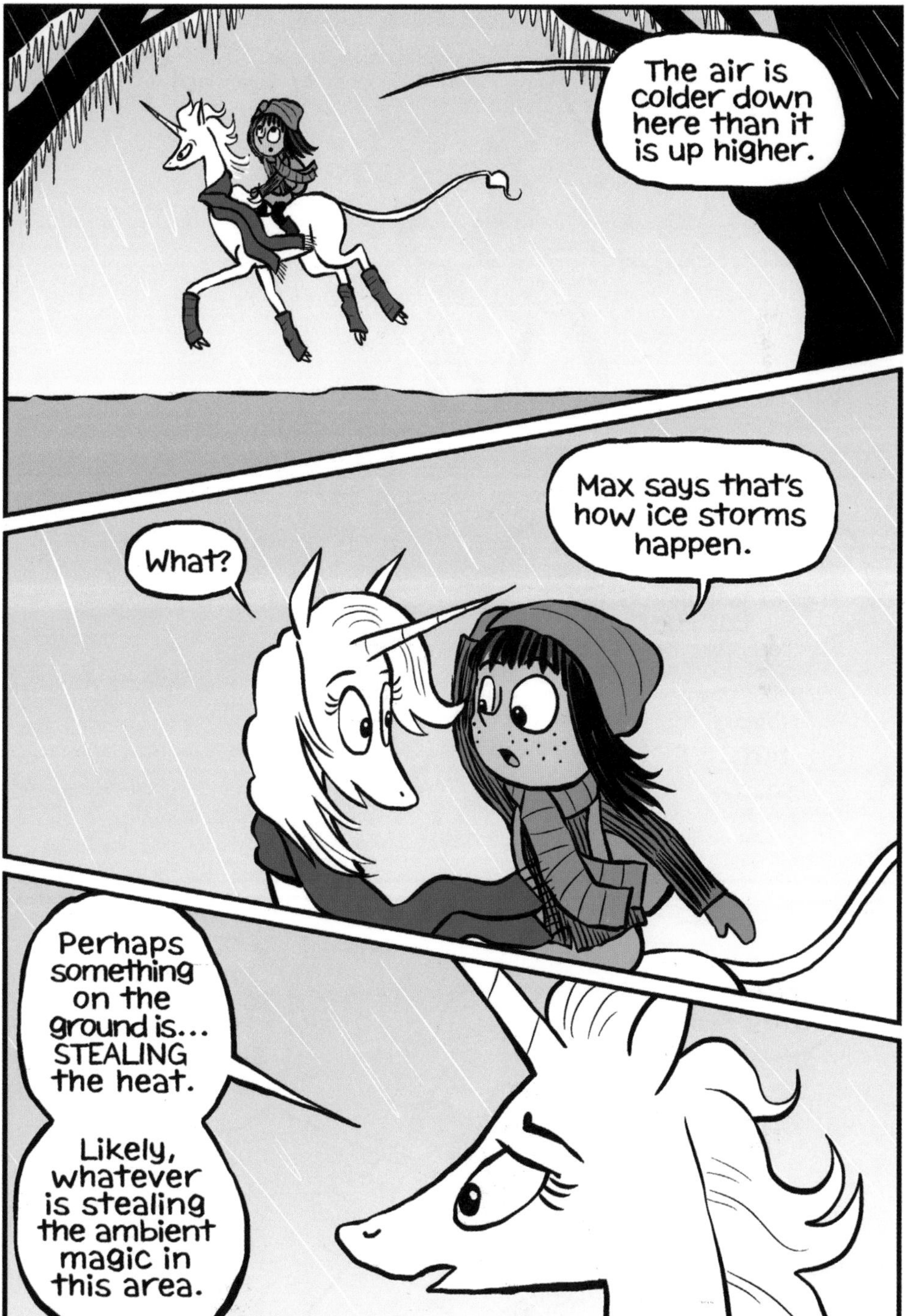
The air is colder down here than it is up higher.
Max says that's how ice storms happen.
What?
Perhaps something on the ground is... STEALING the heat.
Likely, whatever is stealing the ambient magic in this area.

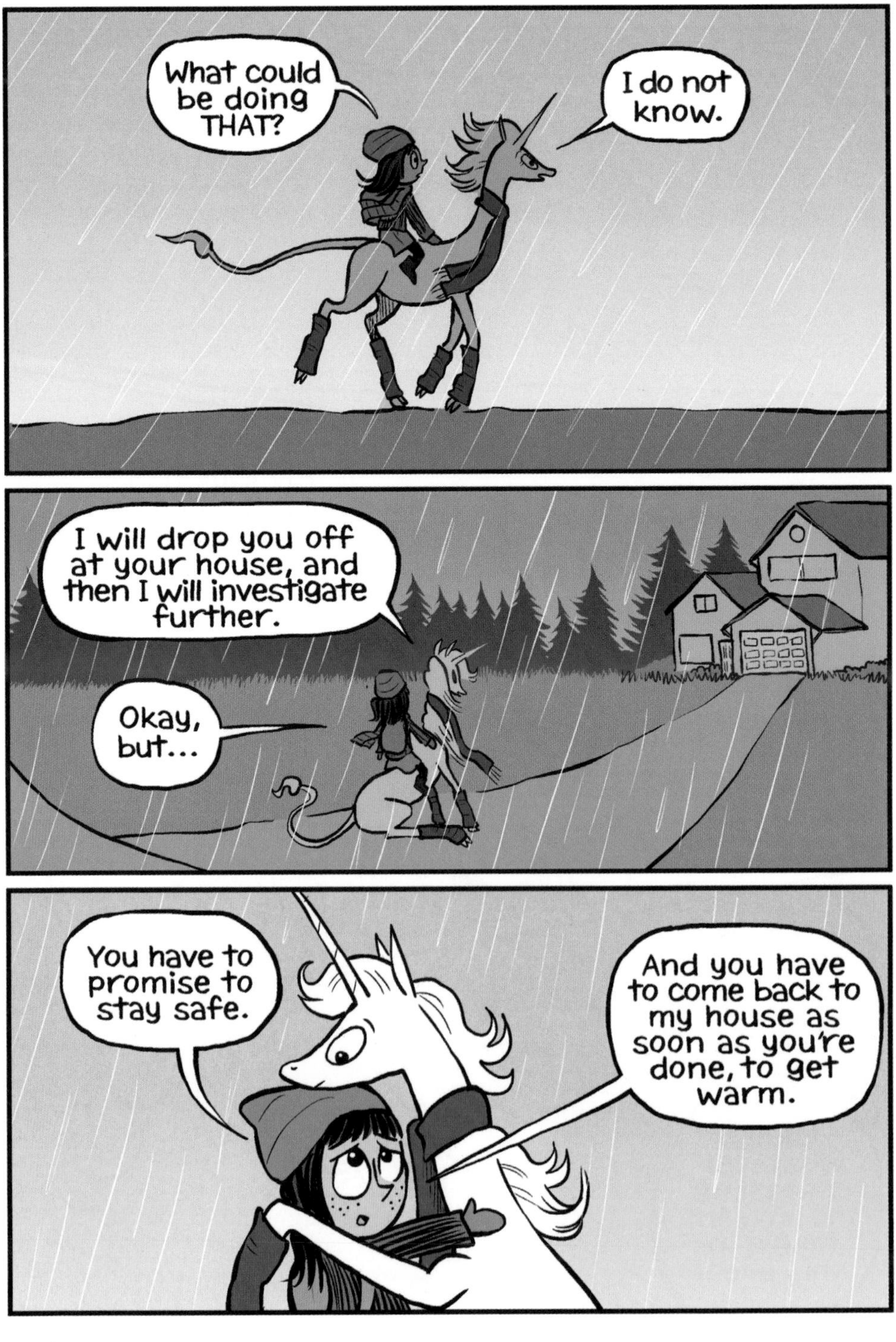
What could be doing THAT?
I do not know.
I will drop you off at your house, and then I will investigate further.
Okay, but...
You have to promise to stay safe.
And you have to come back to my house as soon as you're done, to get warm.

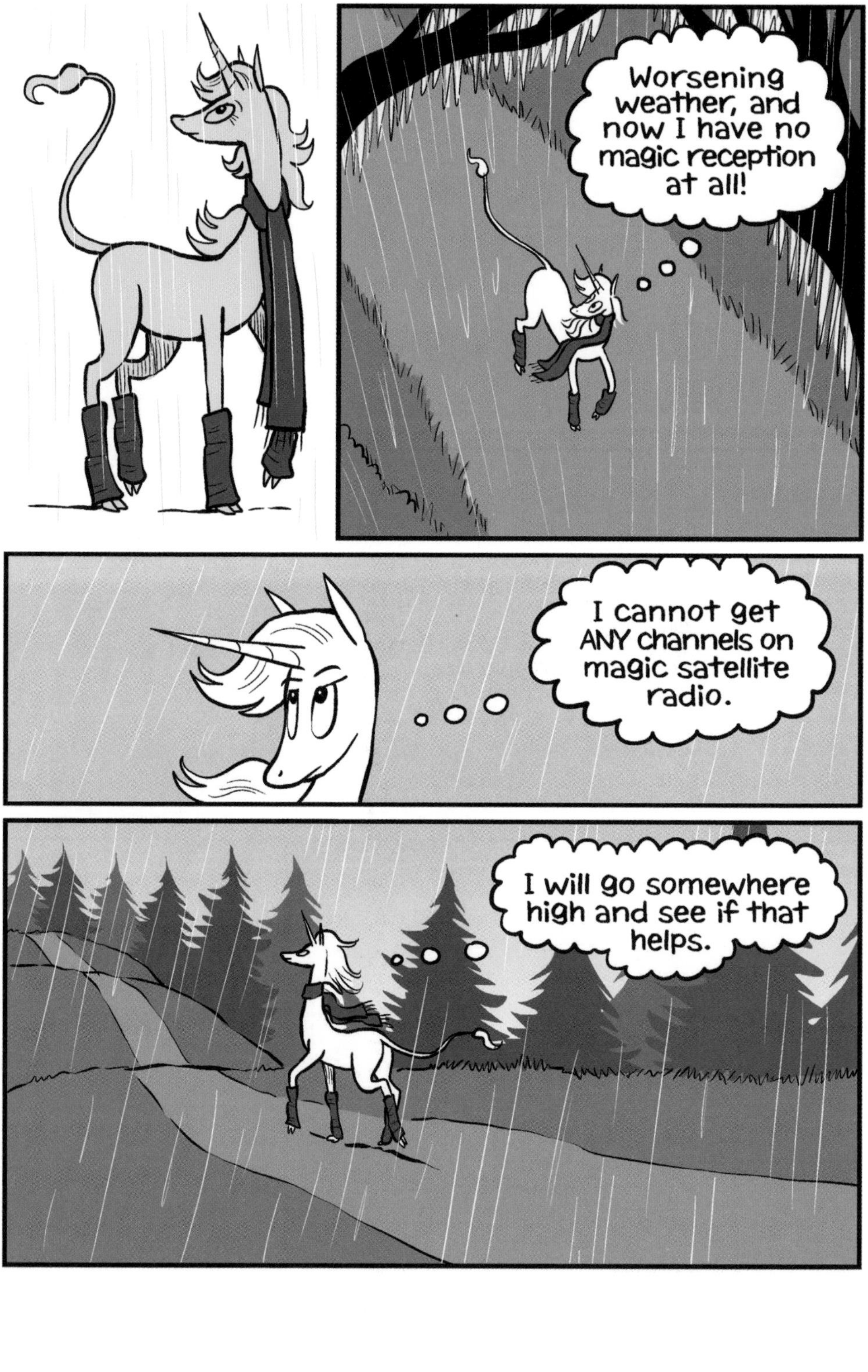
Worsening weather, and now I have no magic reception at all!
I cannot get ANY channels on magic satellite radio.
I will go somewhere high and see if that helps.

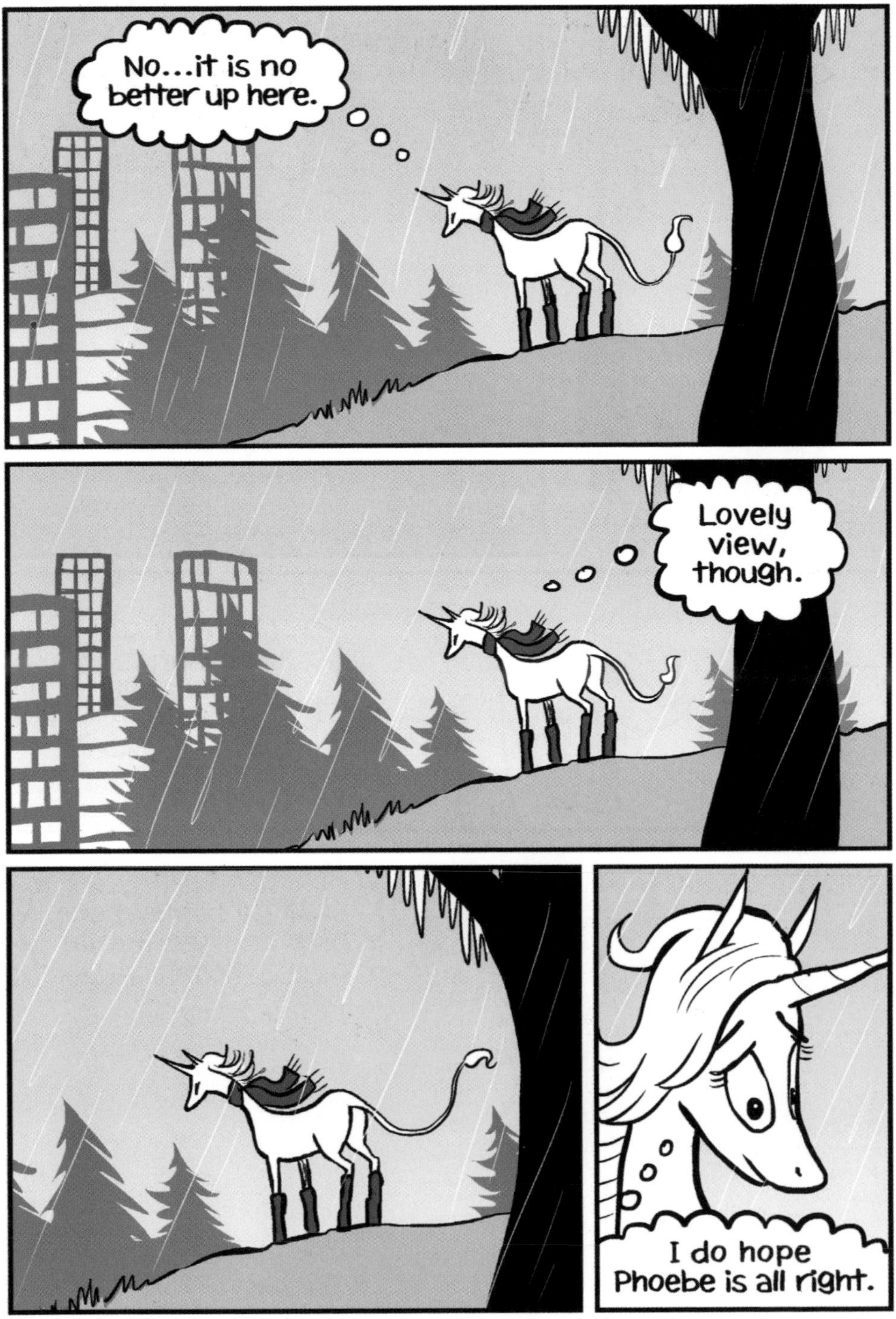
No...it is no better up here.
Lovely view, though.
I do hope Phoebe is all right.

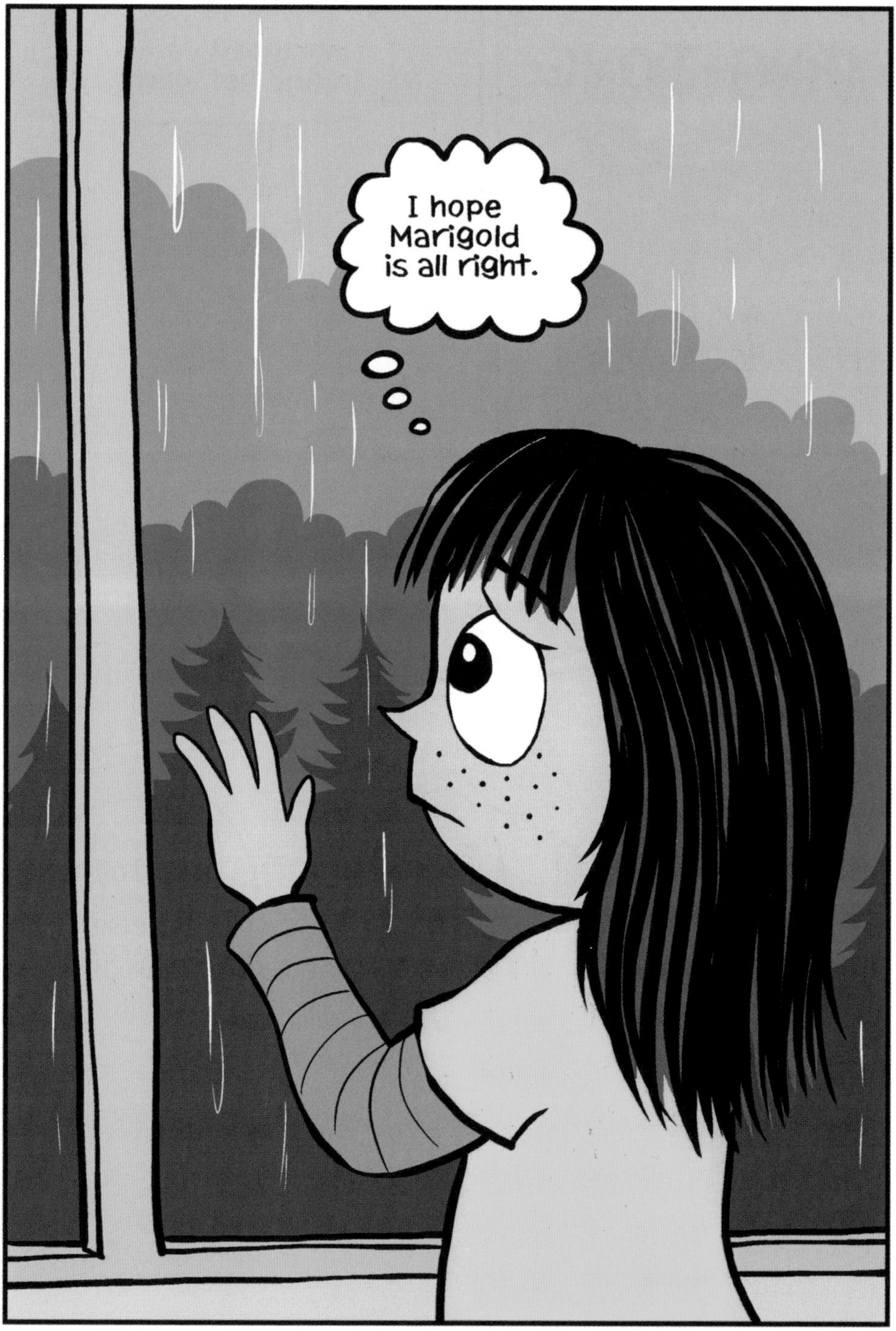
I hope Marigold is all right.

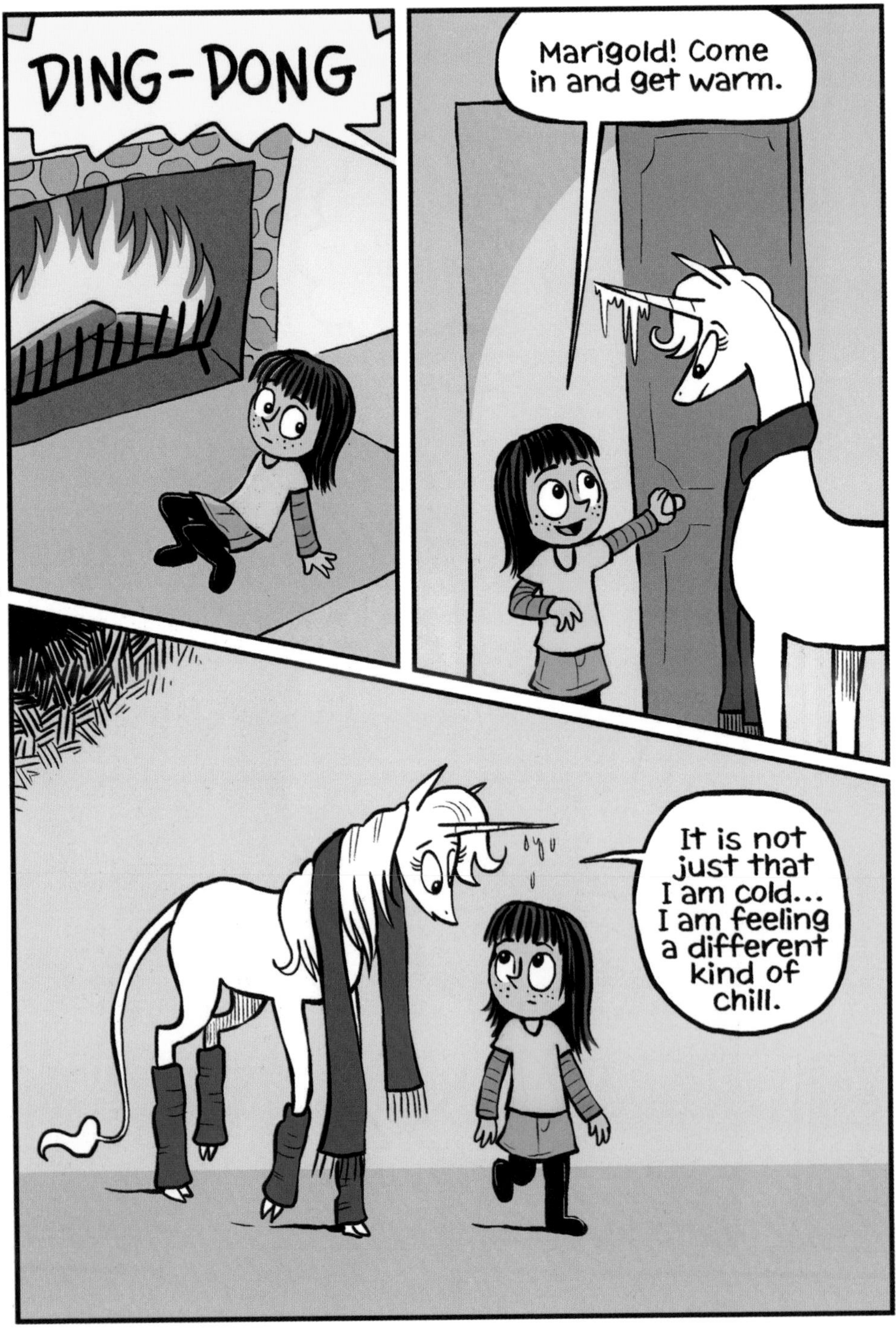
DING-DONG
Marigold! Come in and get warm.
It is not just that I am cold... I am feeling a different kind of chill.

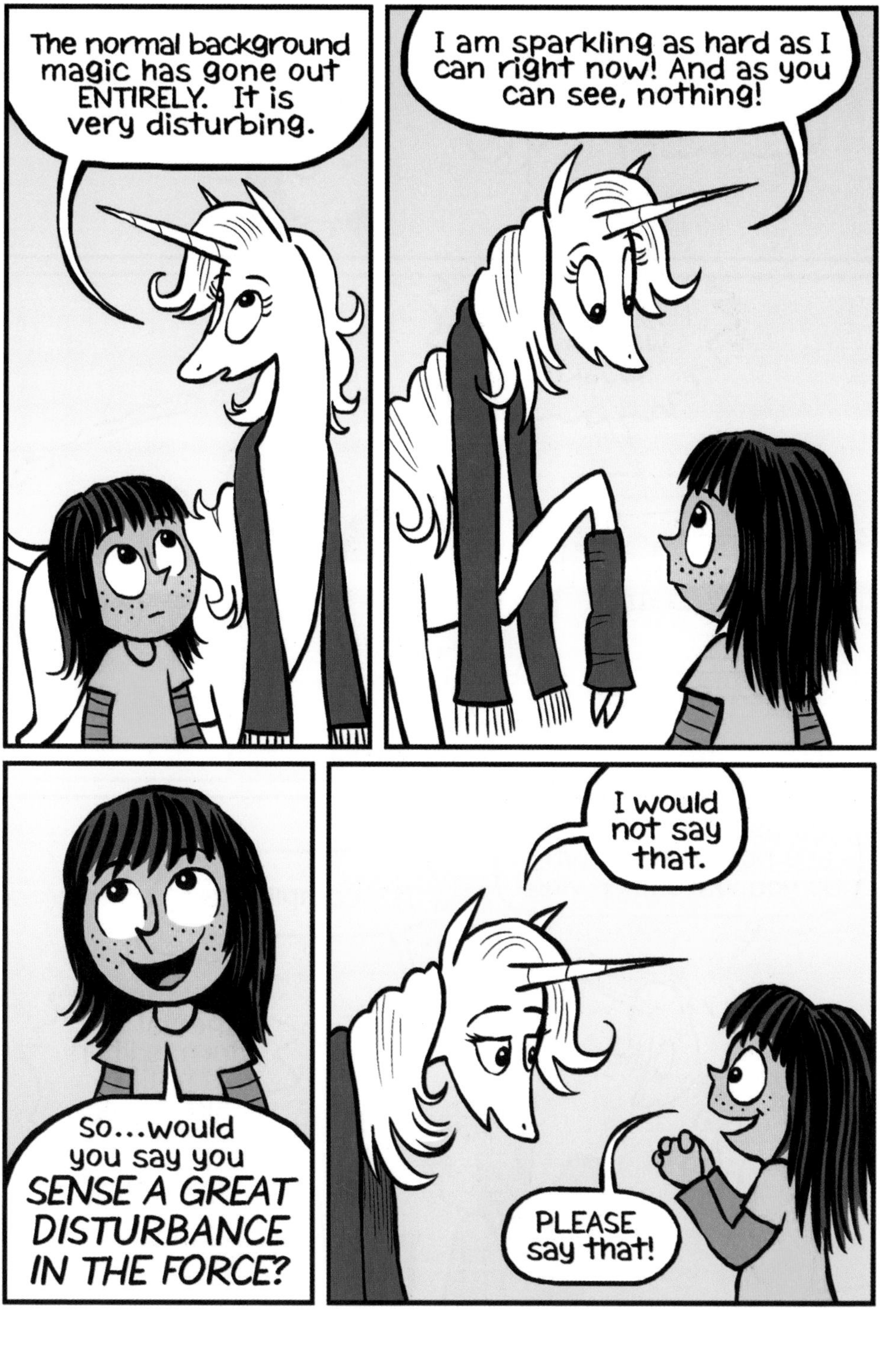
The normal background magic has gone out ENTIRELY. It is very disturbing.
I am sparkling as hard as I can right now! And as you can see, nothing!
So...would you say you *SENSE A GREAT DISTURBANCE IN THE FORCE?*
I would not say that.
PLEASE say that!

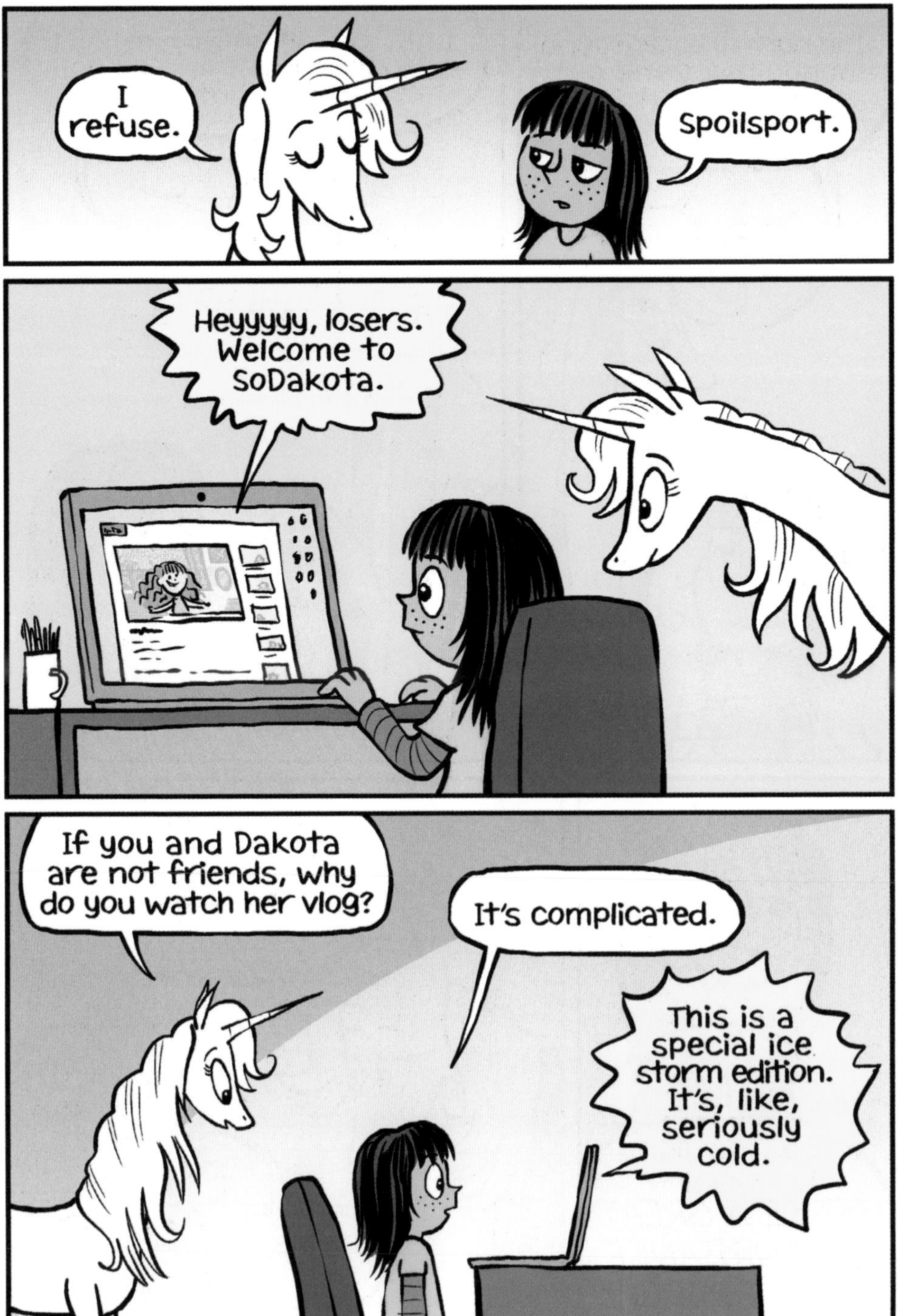
I refuse.
Spoilsport.
Heyyyyy, losers. Welcome to SoDakota.
If you and Dakota are not friends, why do you watch her vlog?
It's complicated.
This is a special ice storm edition. It's, like, seriously cold.

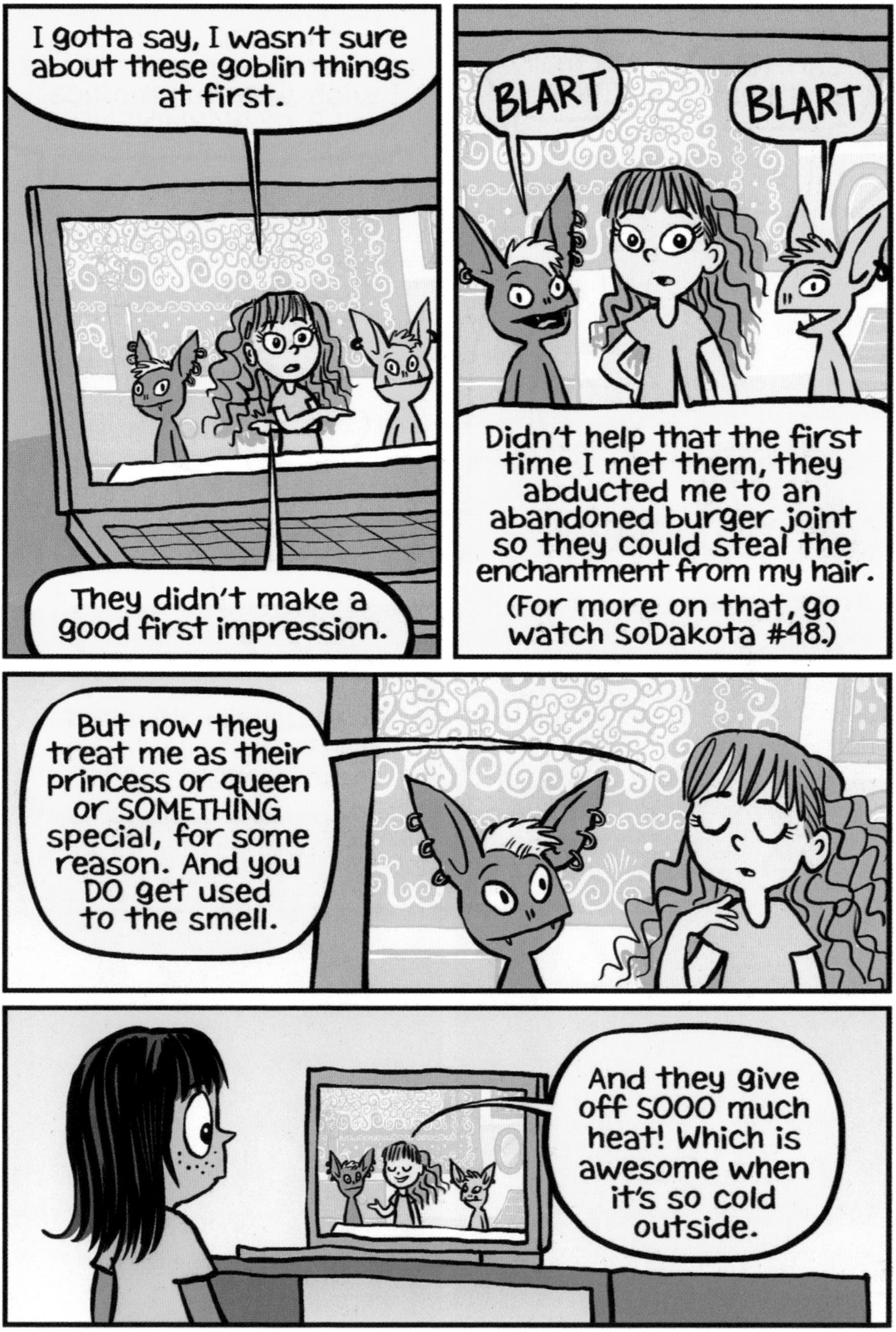
I gotta say, I wasn't sure about these goblin things at first.
They didn't make a good first impression.
BLART
BLART
Didn't help that the first time I met them, they abducted me to an abandoned burger joint so they could steal the enchantment from my hair.
(For more on that, go watch SoDakota #48.)
But now they treat me as their princess or queen or SOMETHING special, for some reason. And you DO get used to the smell.
And they give off SOOO much heat! Which is awesome when it's so cold outside.

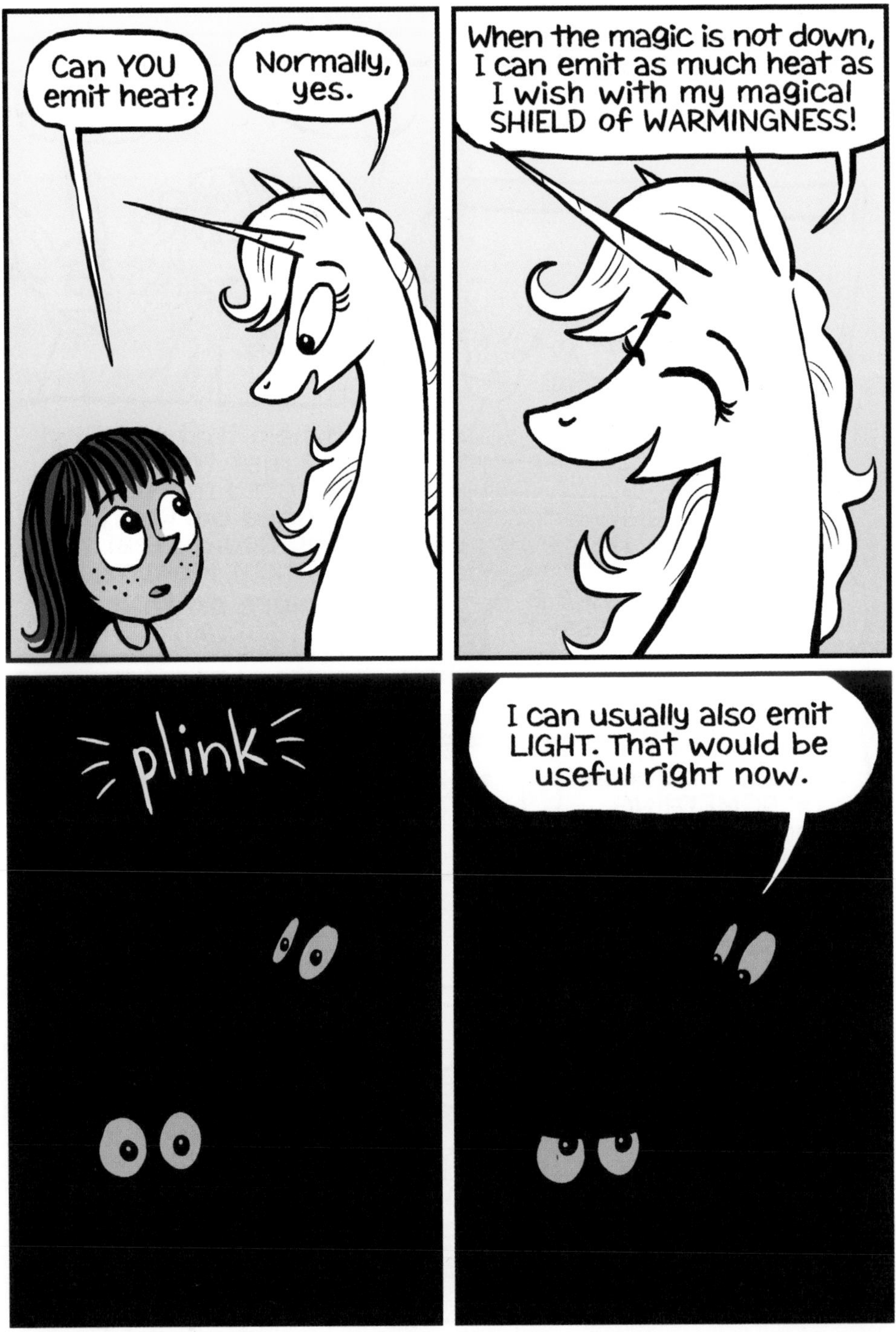
Can YOU emit heat?
Normally, yes.
When the magic is not down, I can emit as much heat as I wish with my magical SHIELD of WARMINGNESS!
plink
I can usually also emit LIGHT. That would be useful right now.

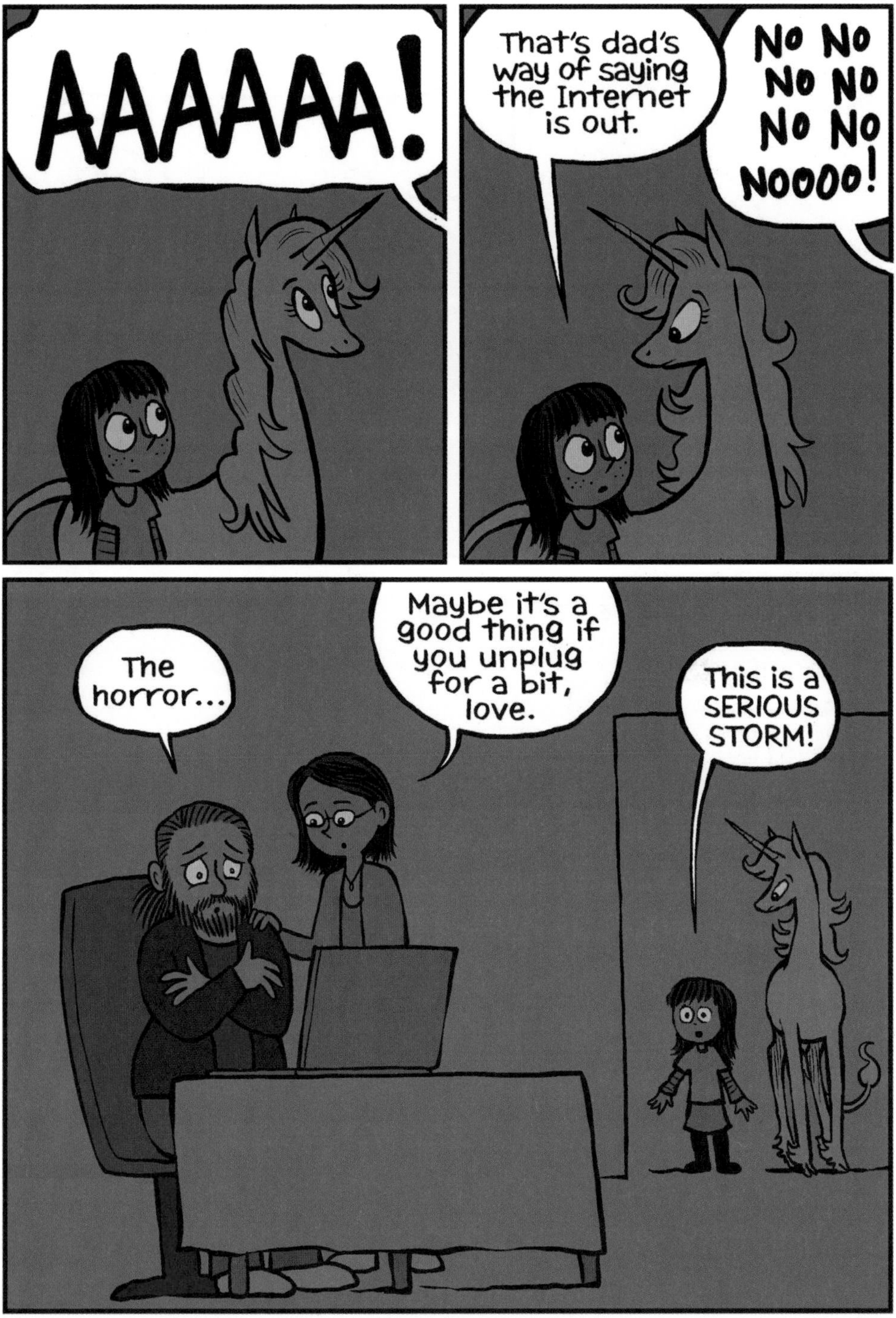
AAAAAA!
That's dad's way of saying the Internet is out.
NO NO NO NO NO NO NOOOO!
The horror...
Maybe it's a good thing if you unplug for a bit, love.
This is a SERIOUS STORM!

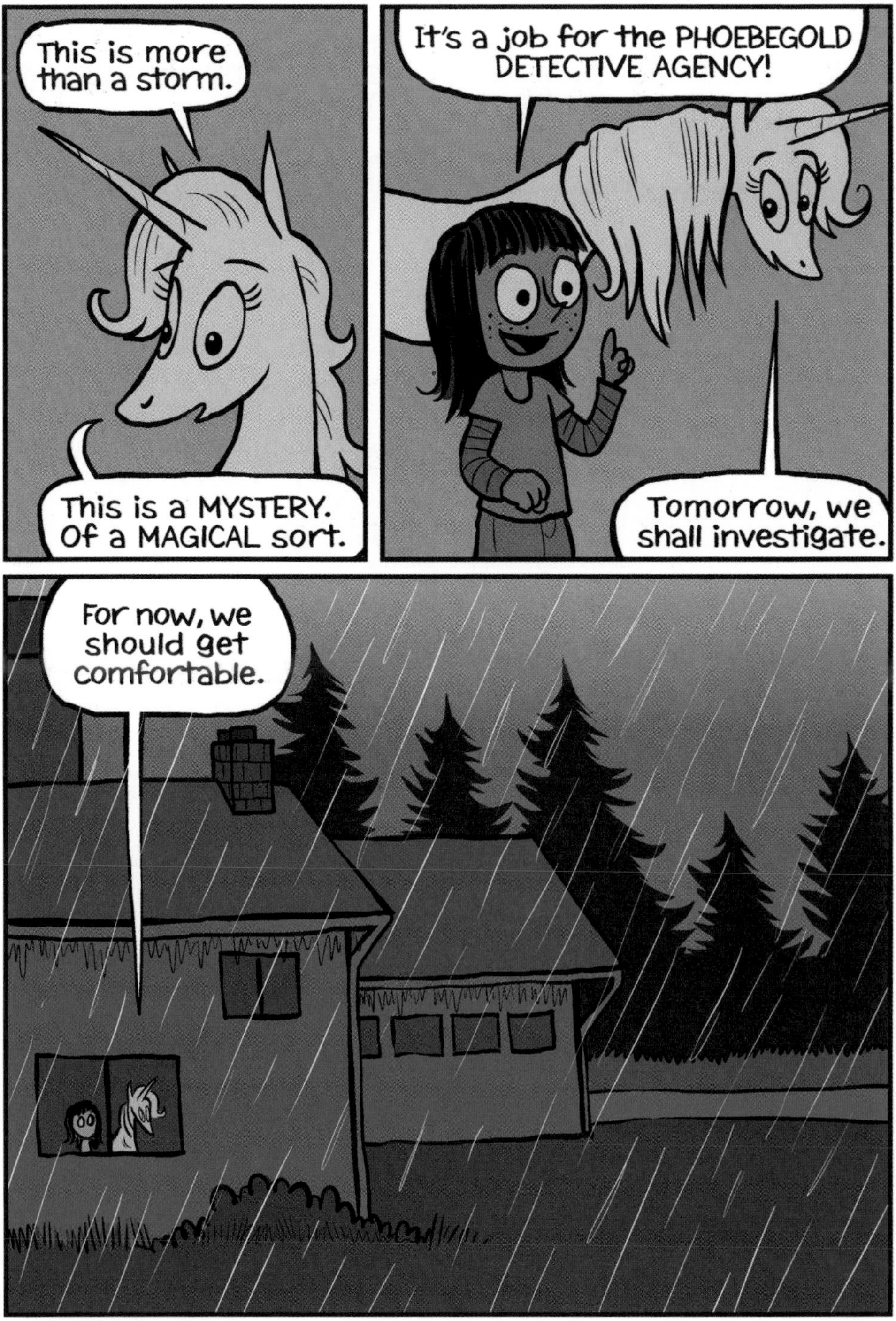
This is more than a storm.
This is a MYSTERY. Of a MAGICAL sort.
It's a job for the PHOEBEGOLD DETECTIVE AGENCY!
Tomorrow, we shall investigate.
For now, we should get comfortable.

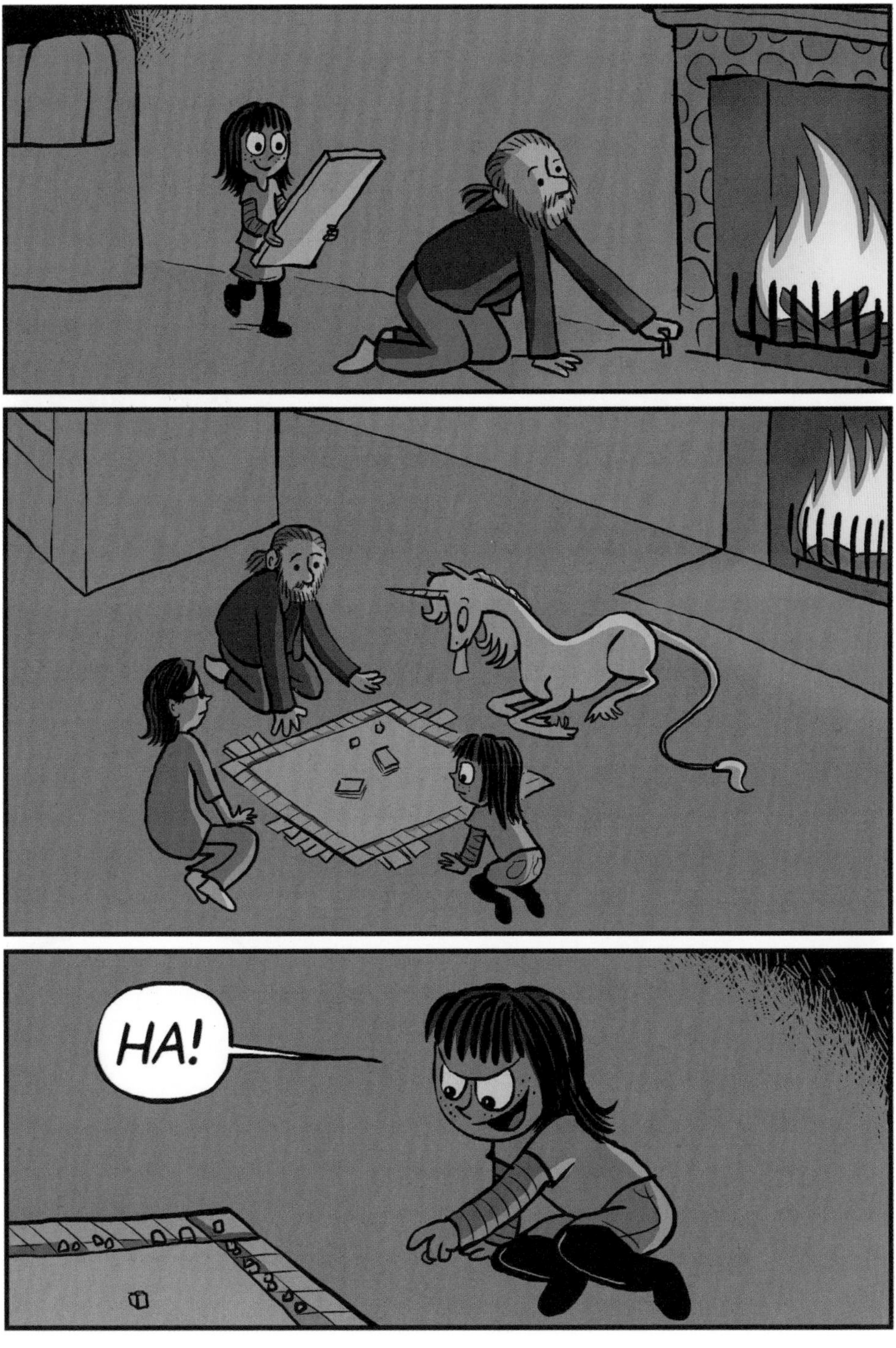
HA!

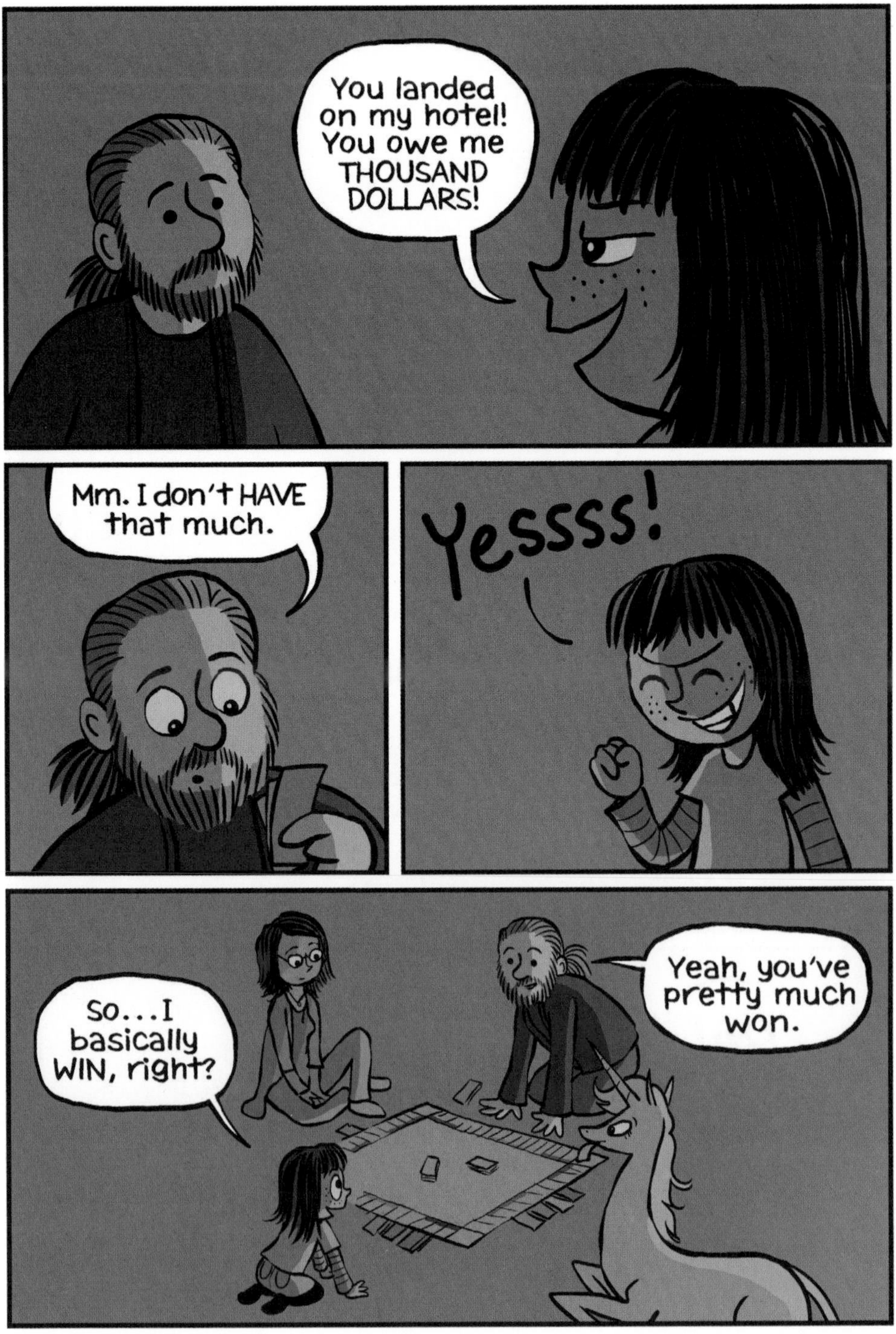
You landed on my hotel! You owe me THOUSAND DOLLARS!
Mm. I don't HAVE that much.
Yessss!
So...I basically WIN, right?
Yeah, you've pretty much won.

But the game isn't over?
Oh, not even close.
It's going to drag on for another few hours, while we start mortgaging everything and you bleed us dry.
Why?
Because it's a boring, Internetless wasteland, and our options are pretty limited.
ptoo

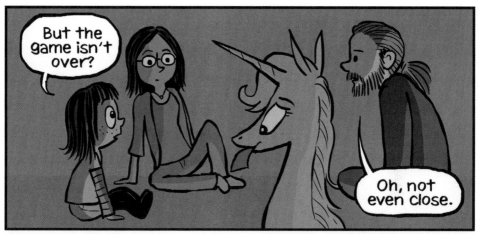

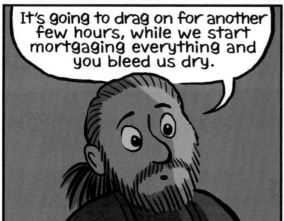

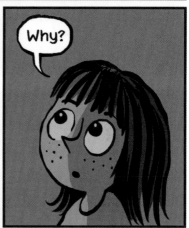

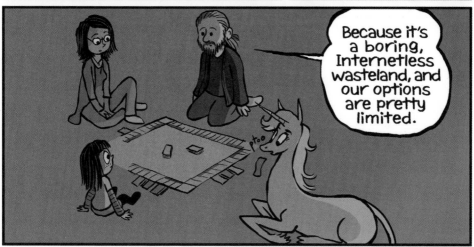

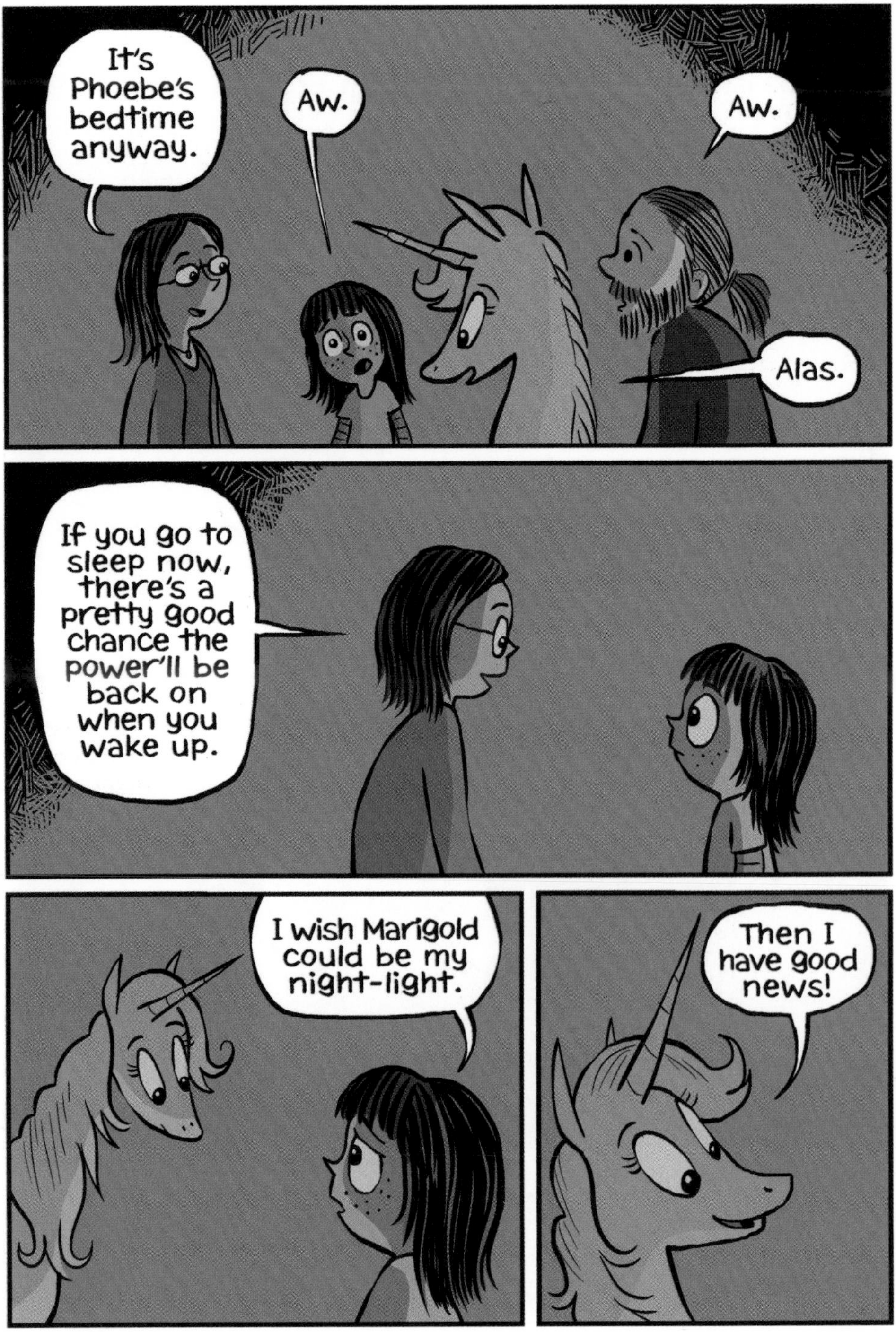
It's Phoebe's bedtime anyway.
Aw.
Aw.
Alas.
If you go to sleep now, there's a pretty good chance the power'll be back on when you wake up.
I wish Marigold could be my night-light.
Then I have good news!

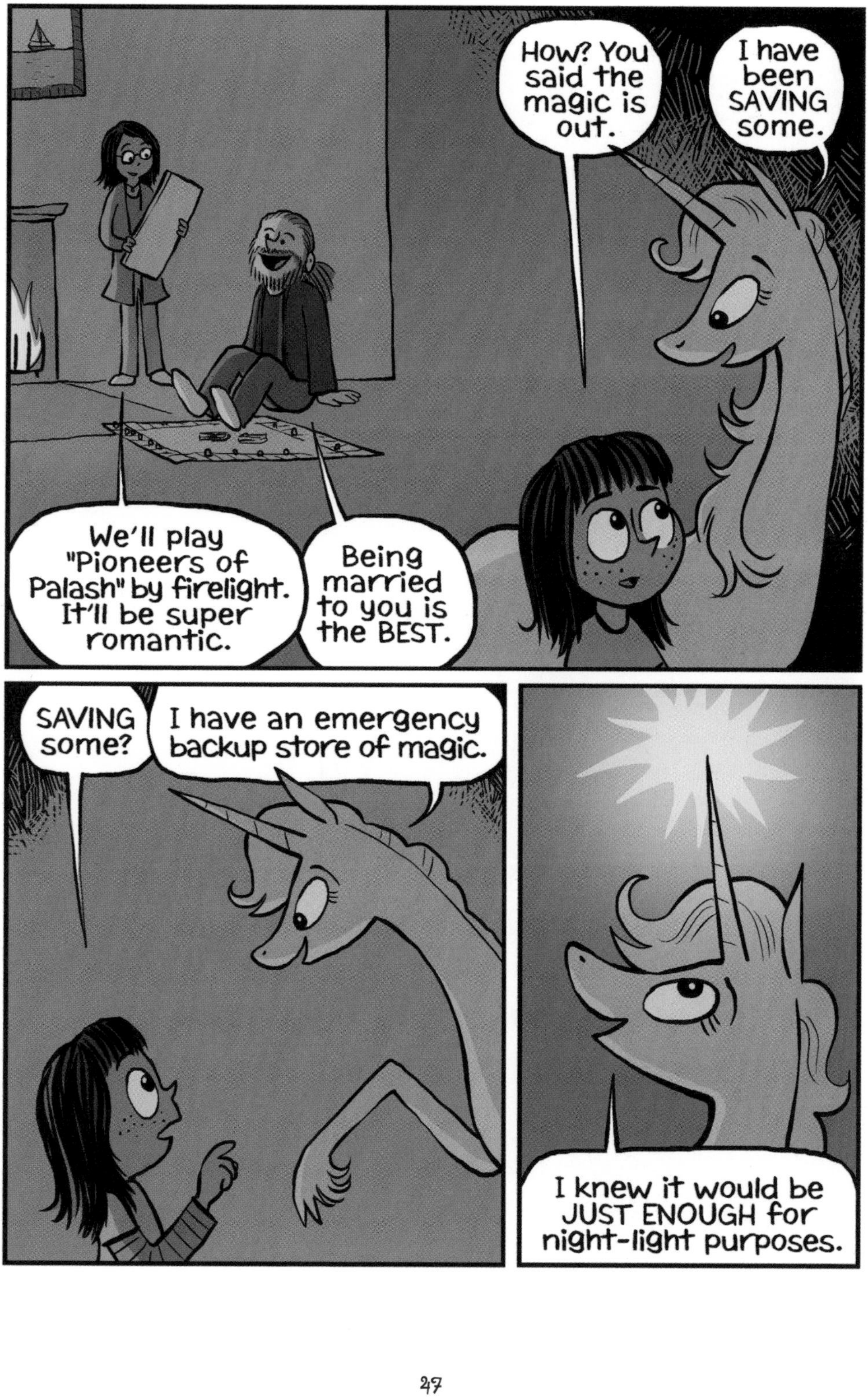
How? You said the magic is out.
I have been SAVING some.
We'll play "Pioneers of Palash" by firelight. It'll be super romantic.
Being married to you is the BEST.
SAVING some?
I have an emergency backup store of magic.
I knew it would be JUST ENOUGH for night-light purposes.

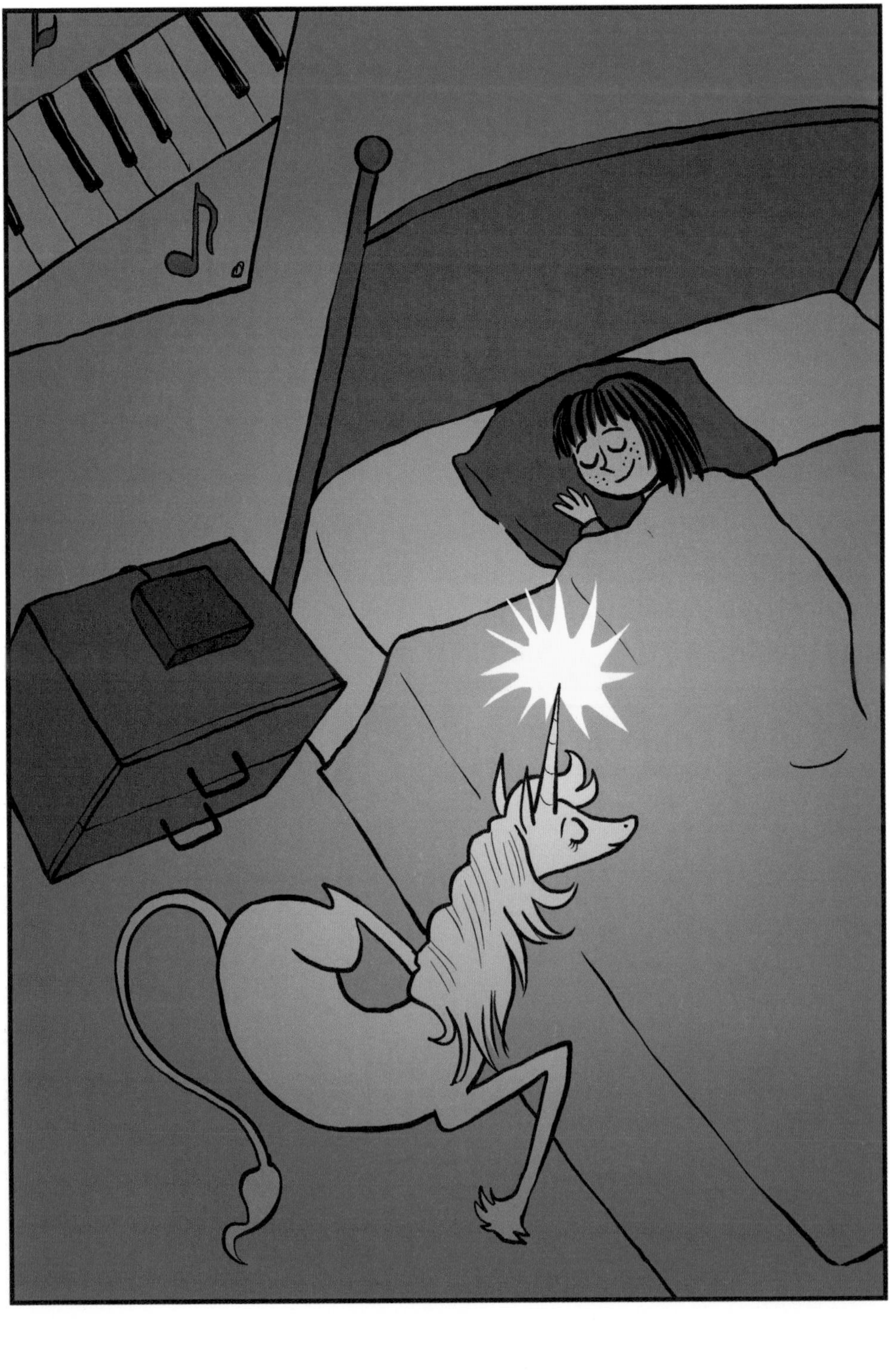

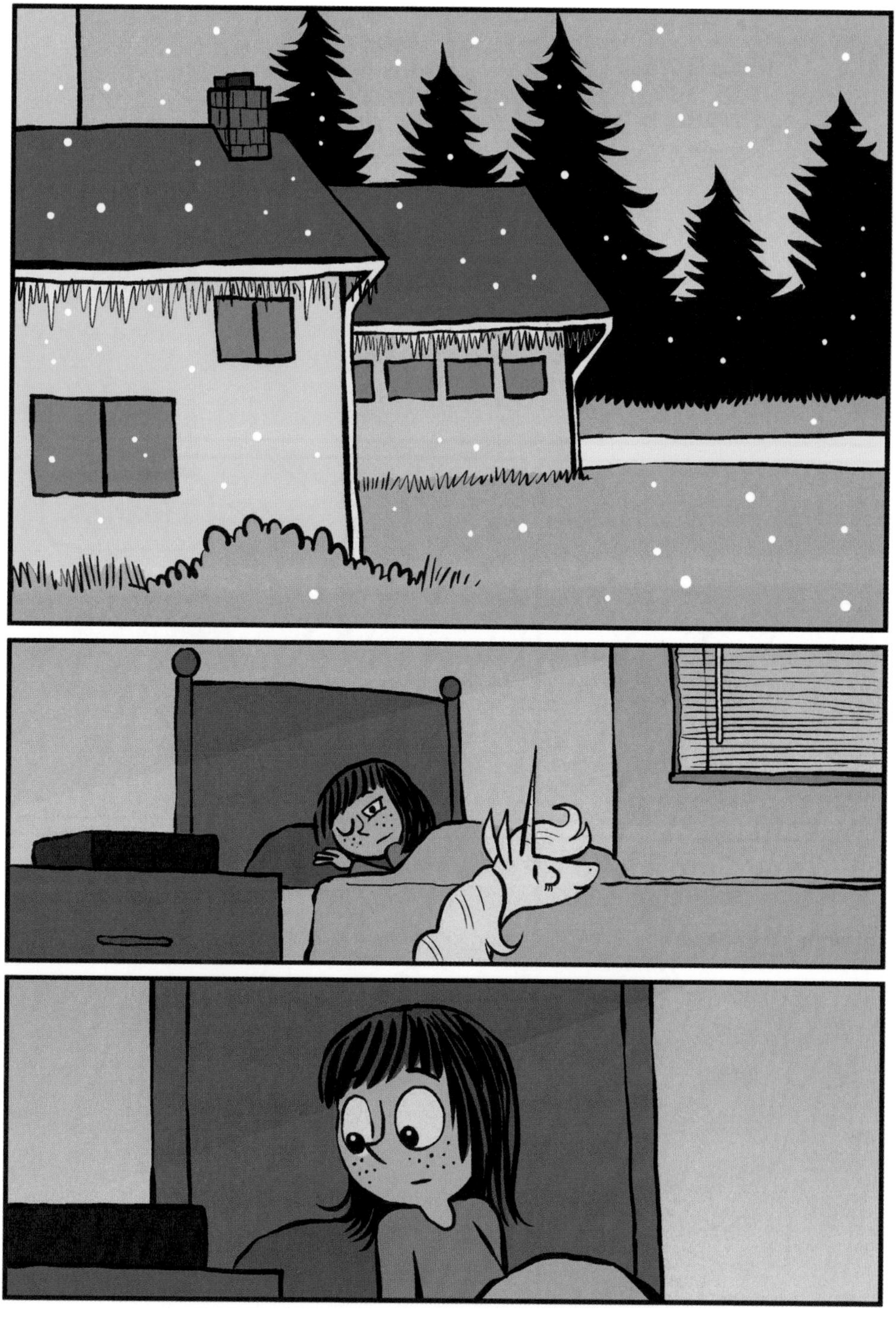

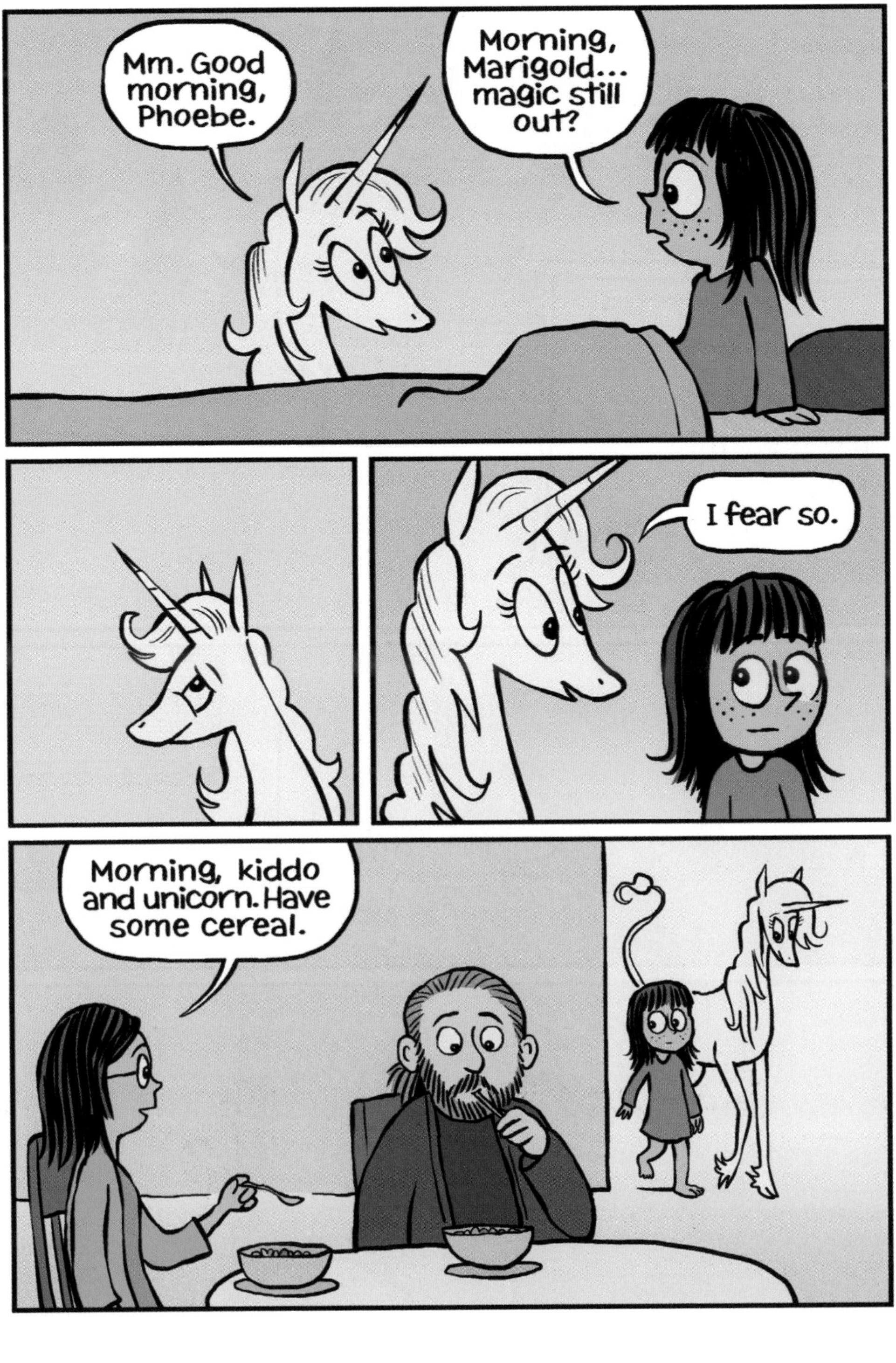
Mm. Good morning, Phoebe.
Morning, Marigold... magic still out?
I fear so.
Morning, kiddo and unicorn. Have some cereal.

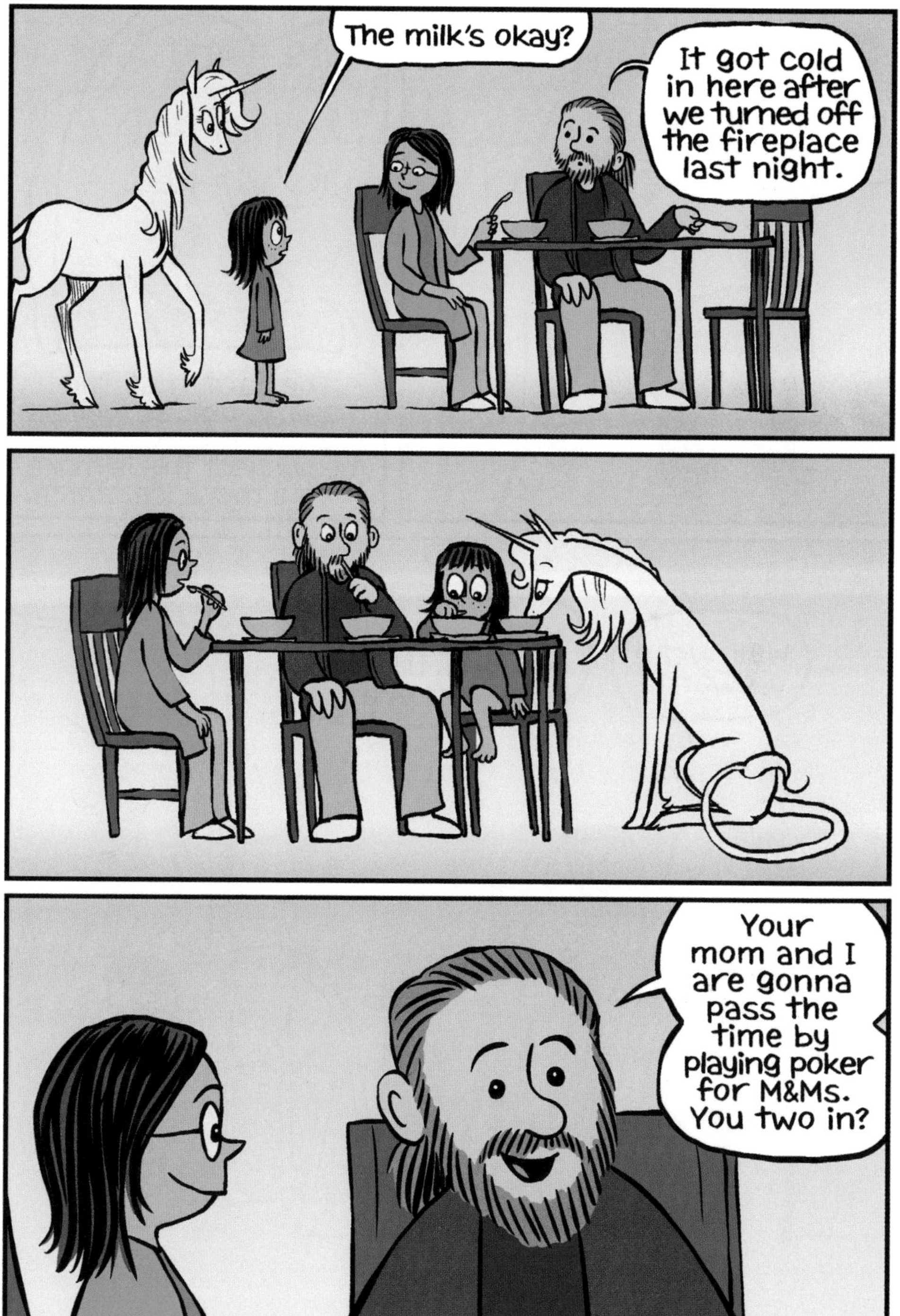
The milk's okay?
It got cold in here after we turned off the fireplace last night.
Your mom and I are gonna pass the time by playing poker for M&Ms. You two in?

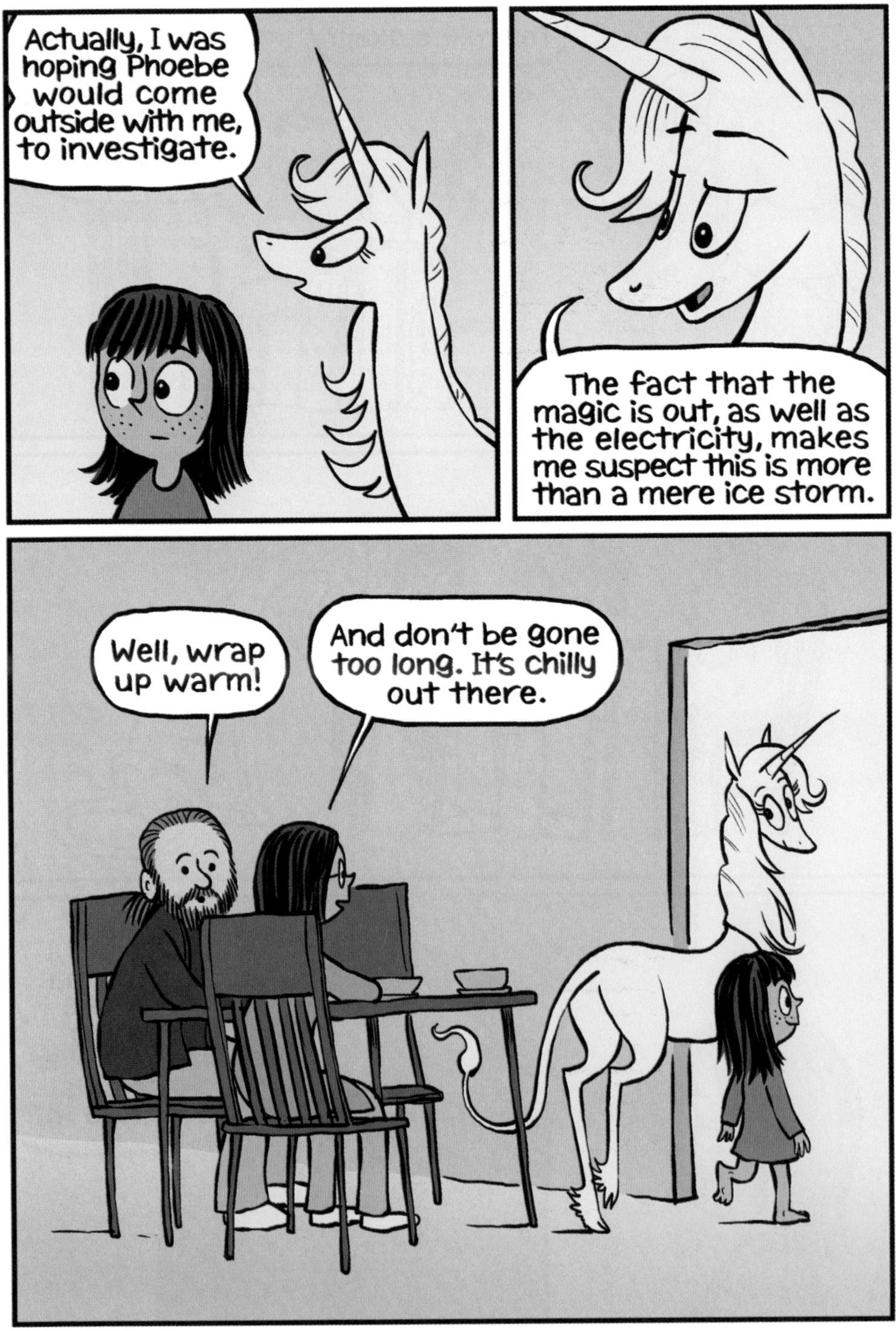
Actually, I was hoping Phoebe would come outside with me, to investigate.
The fact that the magic is out, as well as the electricity, makes me suspect this is more than a mere ice storm.
Well, wrap up warm!
And don't be gone too long. It's chilly out there.

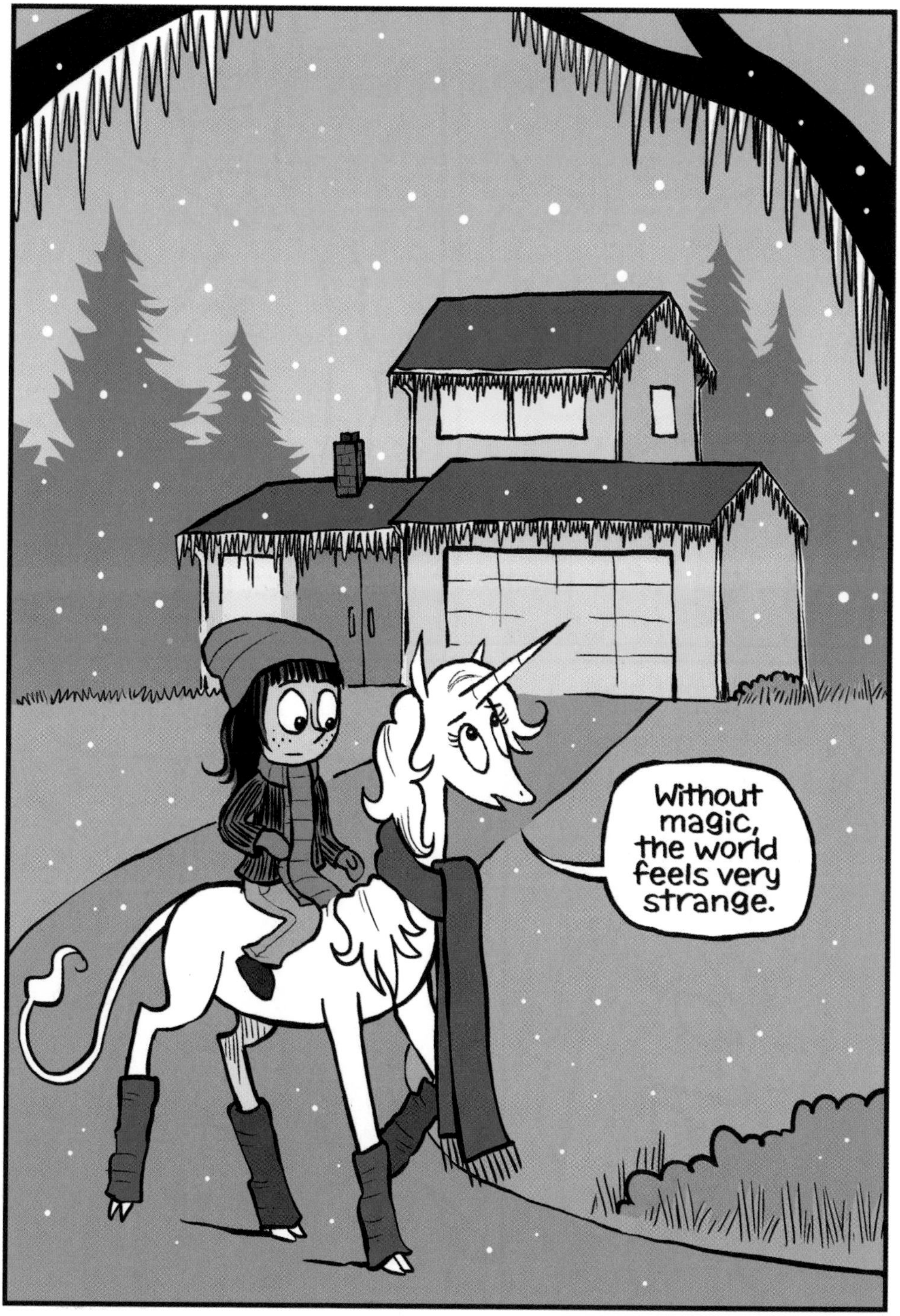
Without magic, the world feels very strange.

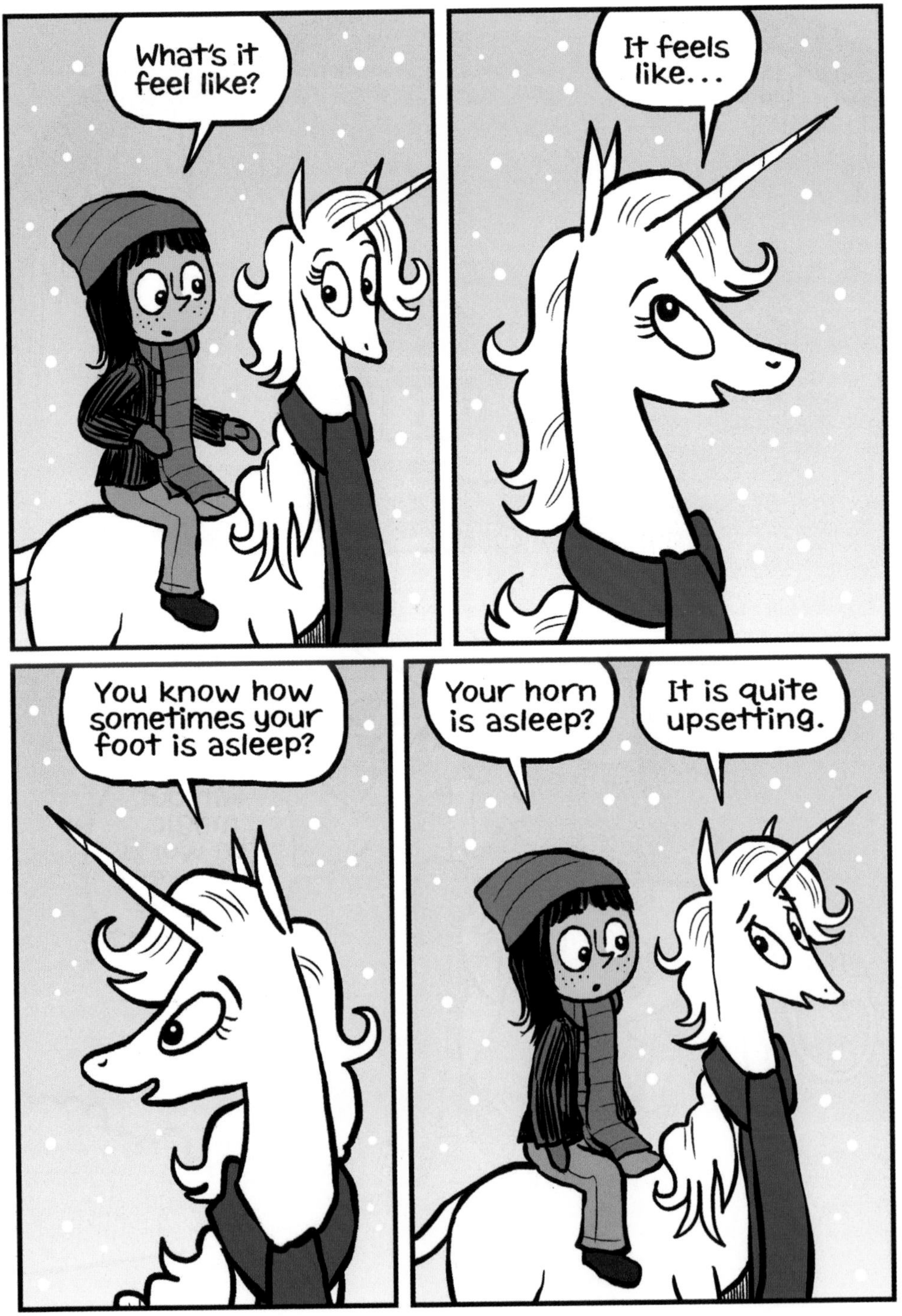
What's it feel like?
It feels like...
You know how sometimes your foot is asleep?
Your horn is asleep?
It is quite upsetting.

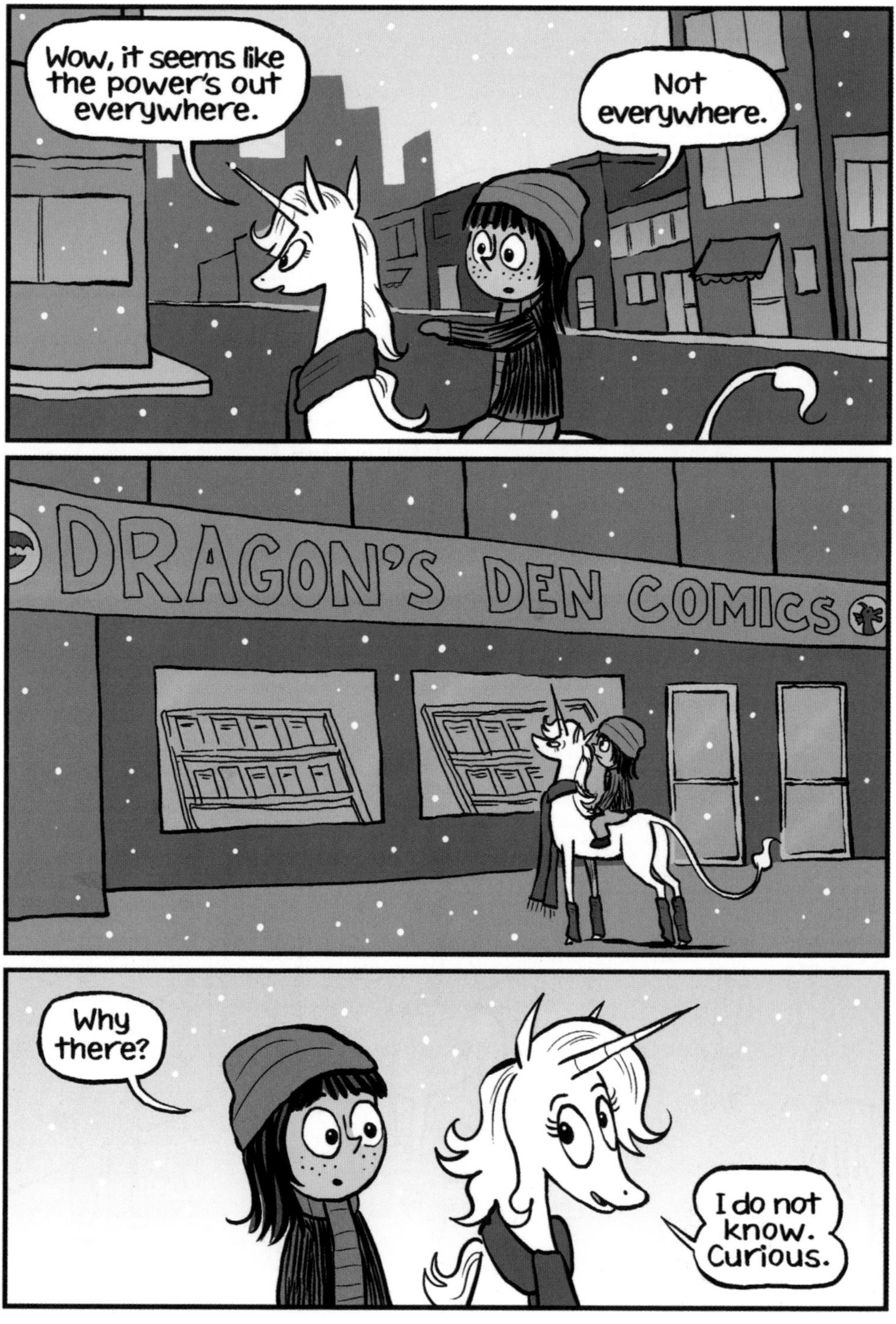
Wow, it seems like the power's out everywhere.
Not everywhere.
DRAGON'S DEN COMICS
Why there?
I do not know. Curious.

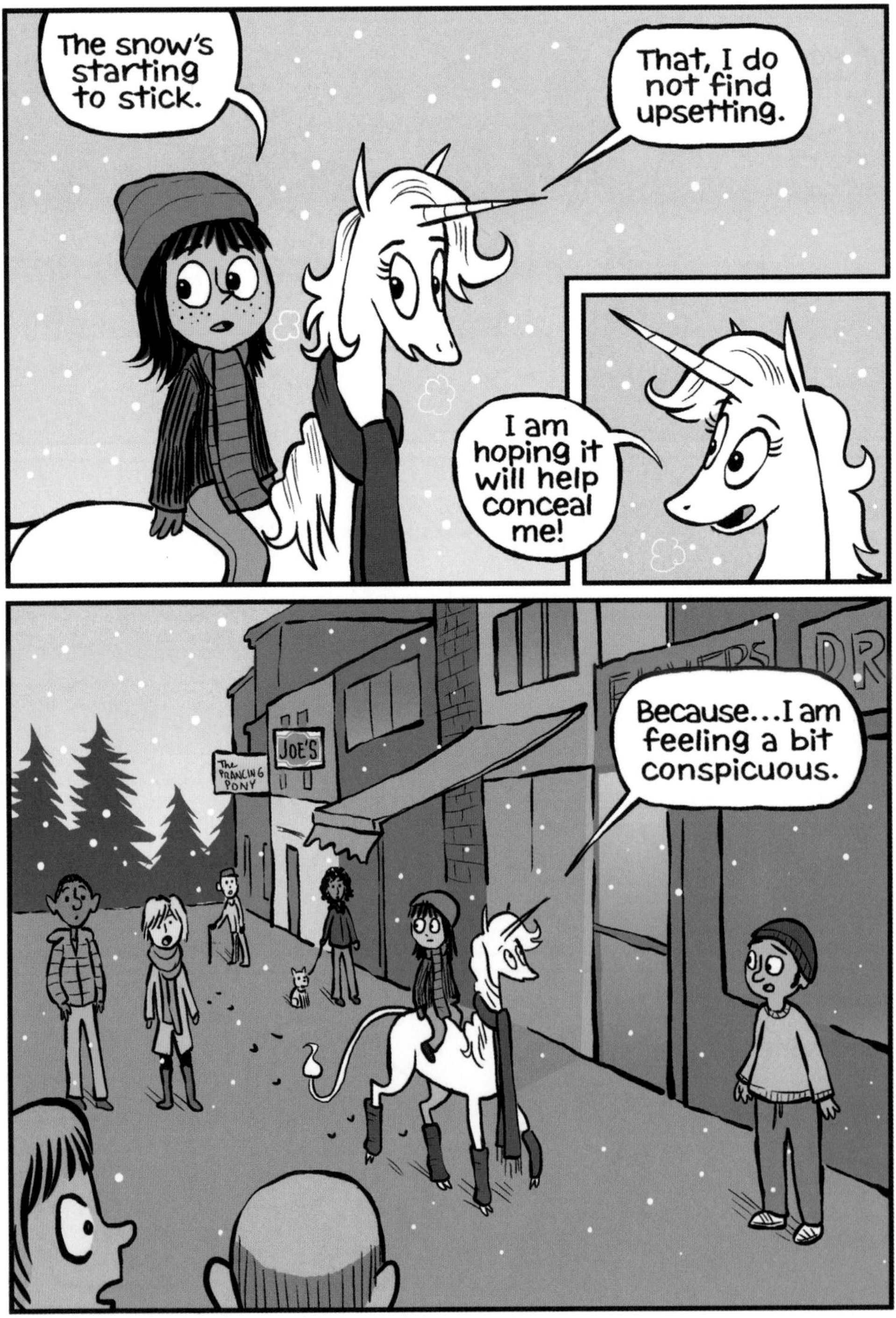
The snow's starting to stick.
That, I do not find upsetting.
I am hoping it will help conceal me!
The PRANCING PONY
JOE'S
Because...I am feeling a bit conspicuous.

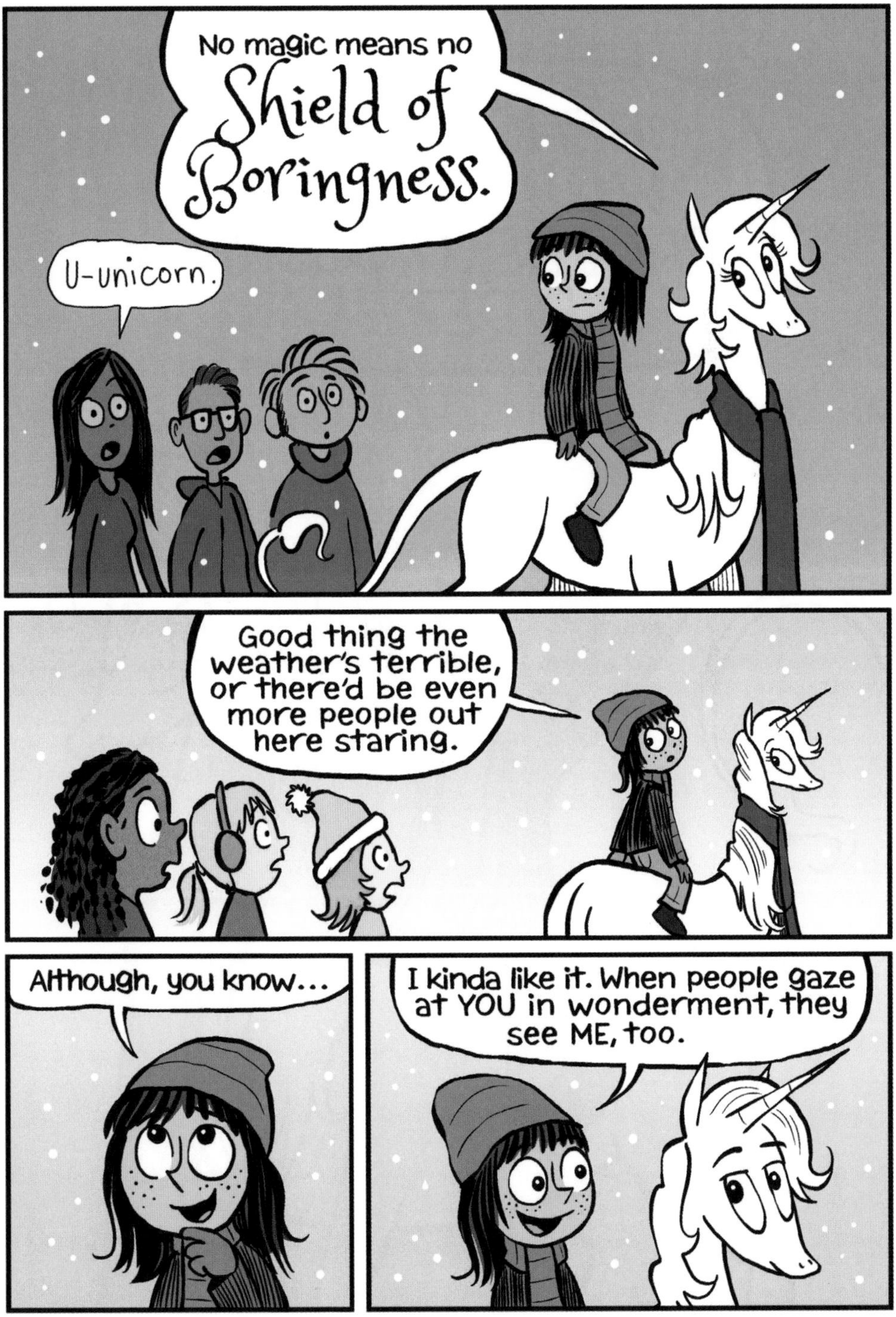
No magic means no Shield of Boringness.
U-unicorn.
Good thing the weather's terrible, or there'd be even more people out here staring.
Although, you know...
I kinda like it. When people gaze at YOU in wonderment, they see ME, too.

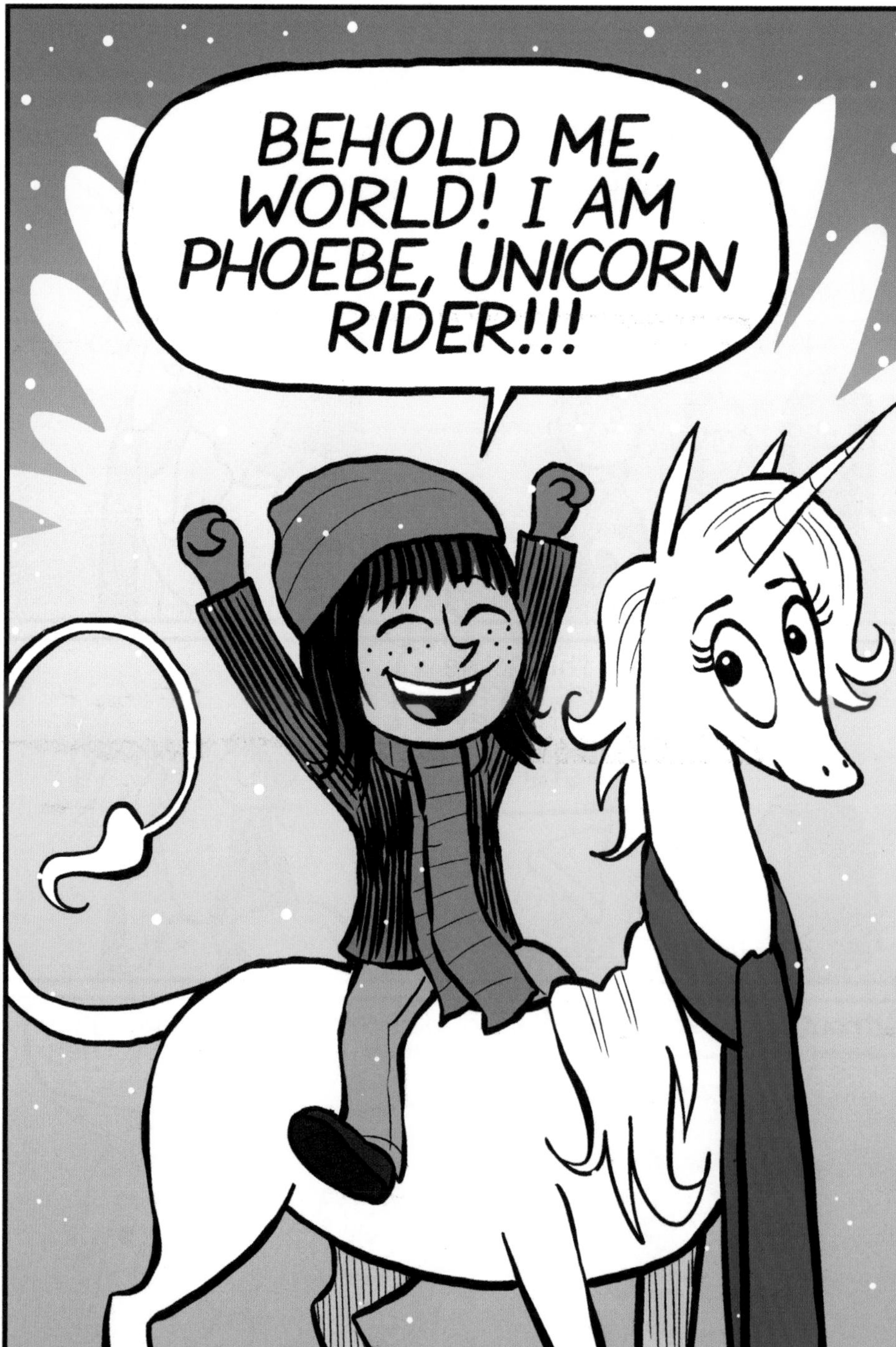
BEHOLD ME, WORLD! I AM PHOEBE, UNICORN RIDER!!!

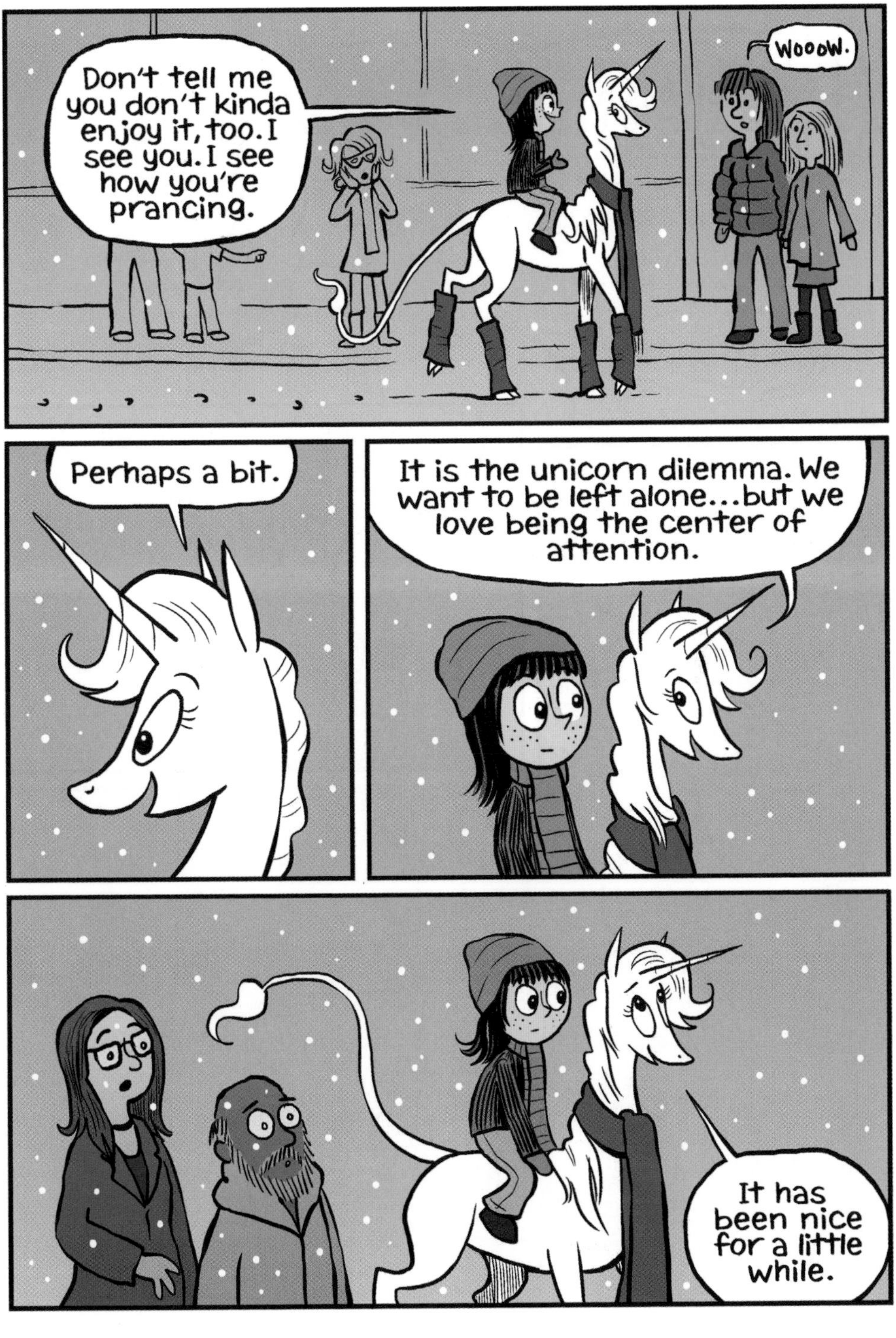
Don't tell me you don't kinda enjoy it, too. I see you. I see how you're prancing.
WOOOW.
Perhaps a bit.
It is the unicorn dilemma. We want to be left alone...but we love being the center of attention.
It has been nice for a little while.

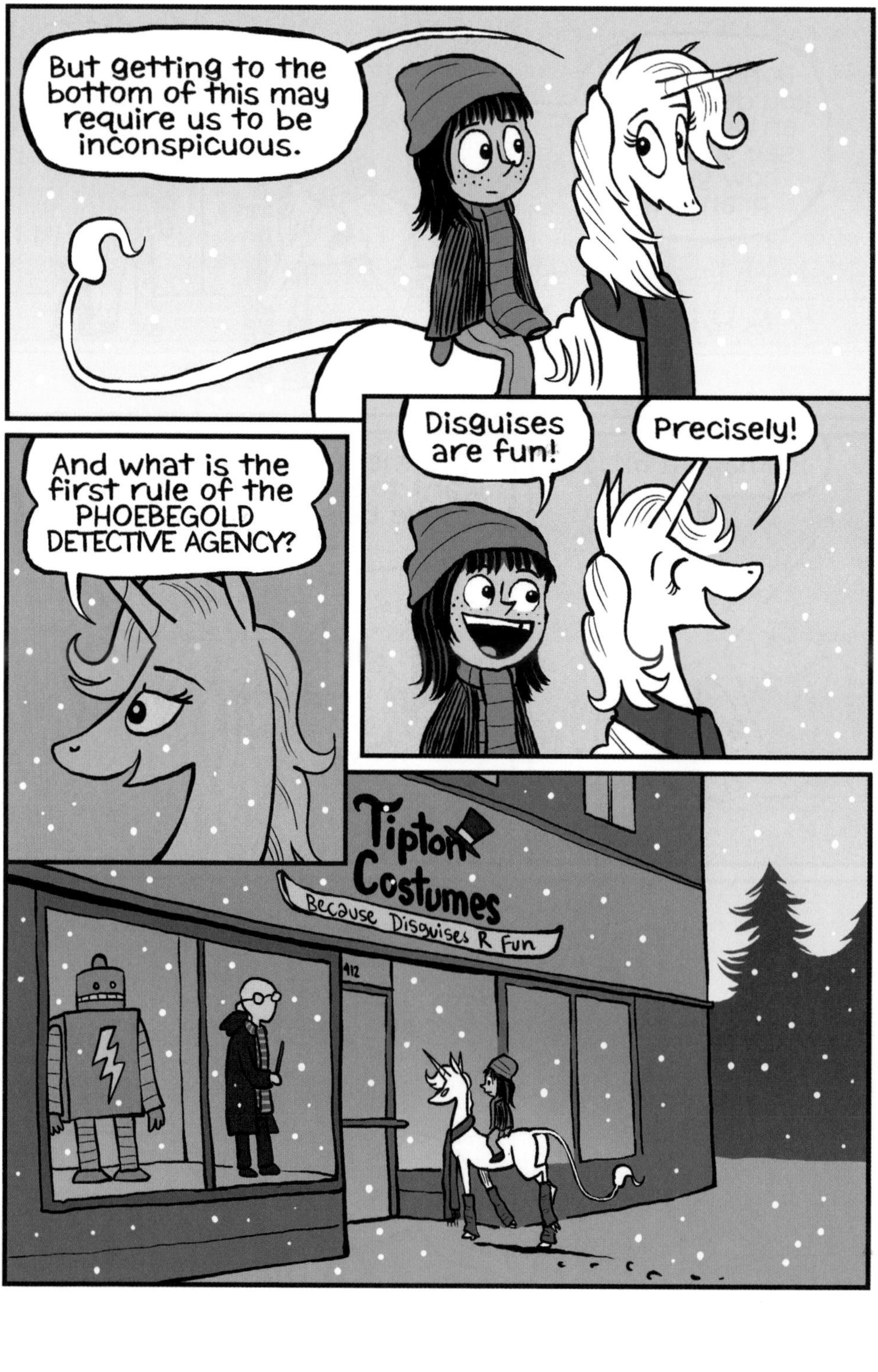
But getting to the bottom of this may require us to be inconspicuous.
And what is the first rule of the PHOEBEGOLD DETECTIVE AGENCY?
Disguises are fun!
Precisely!
Tipton Costumes
Because Disguises R Fun
412

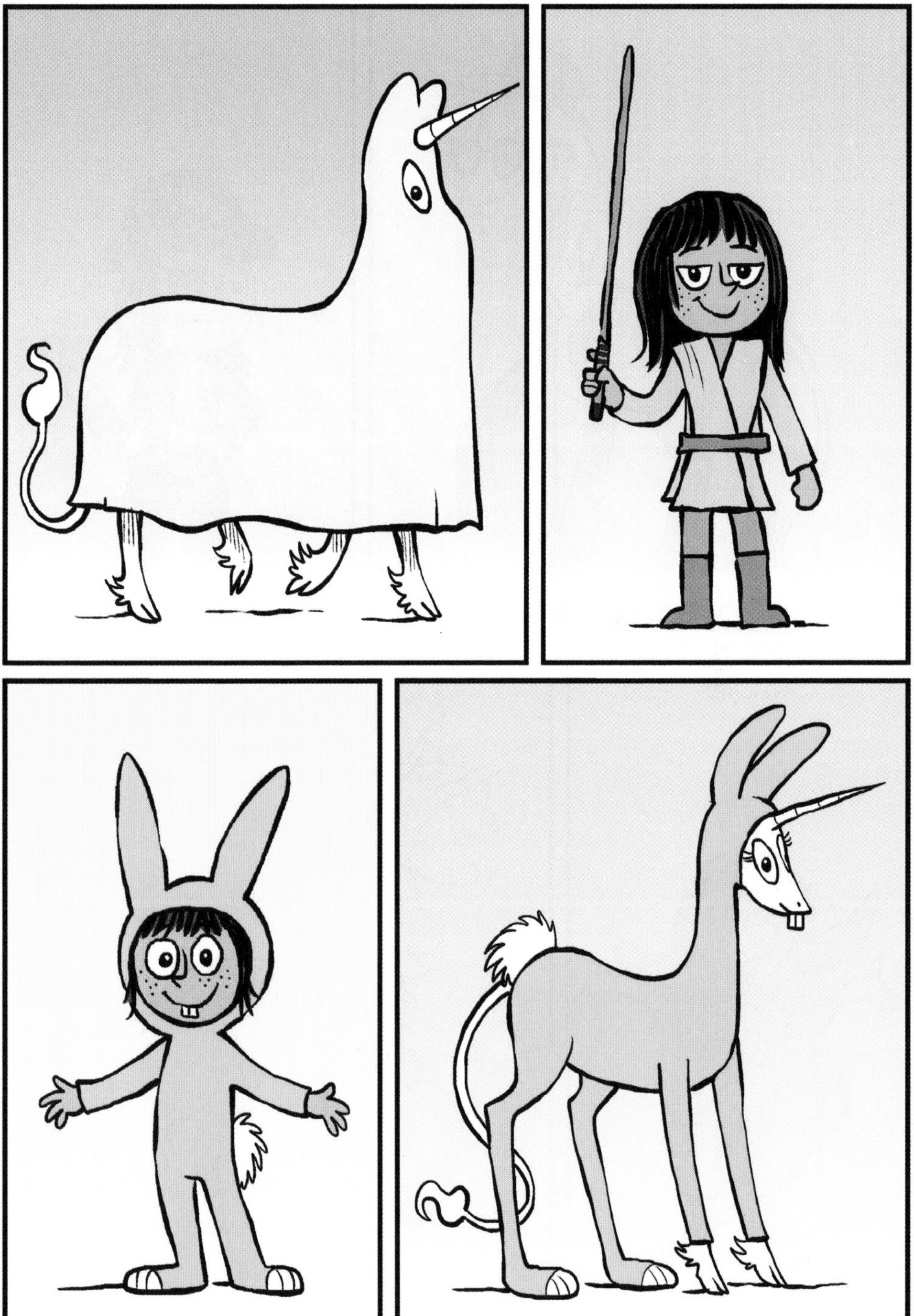

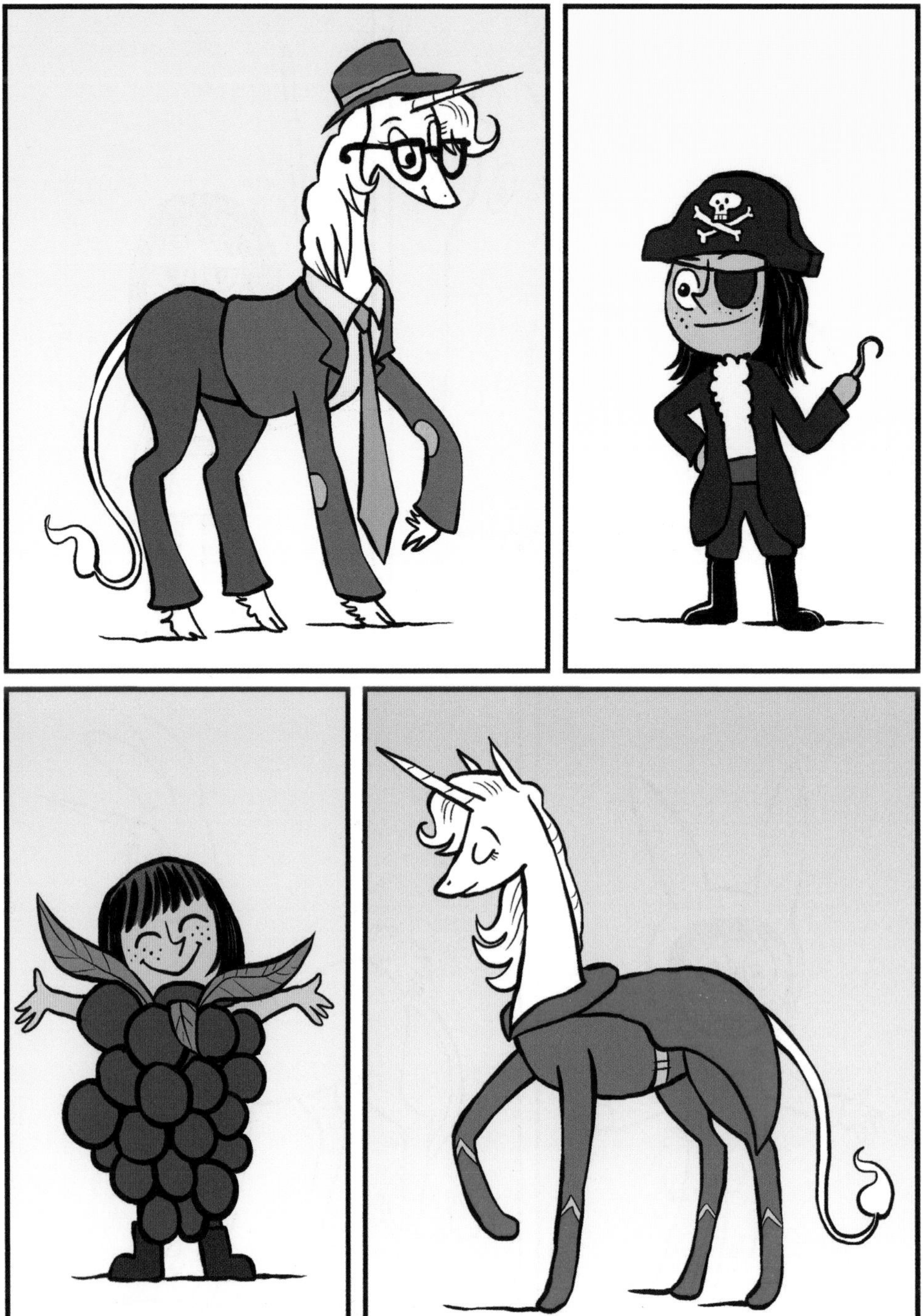

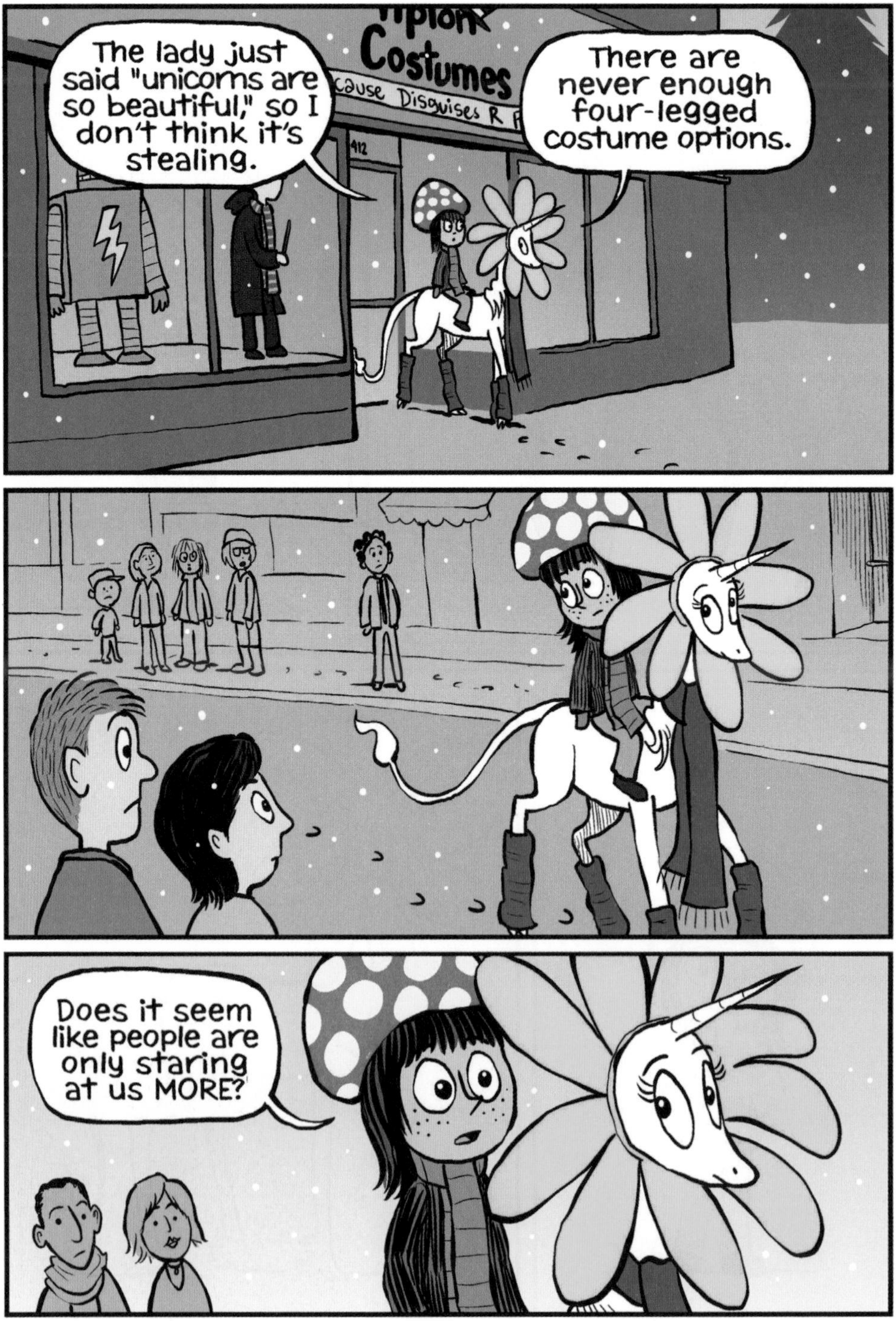
Costumes
Cause Disguises R
412
The lady just said "unicorns are so beautiful," so I don't think it's stealing.
There are never enough four-legged costume options.
Does it seem like people are only staring at us MORE?

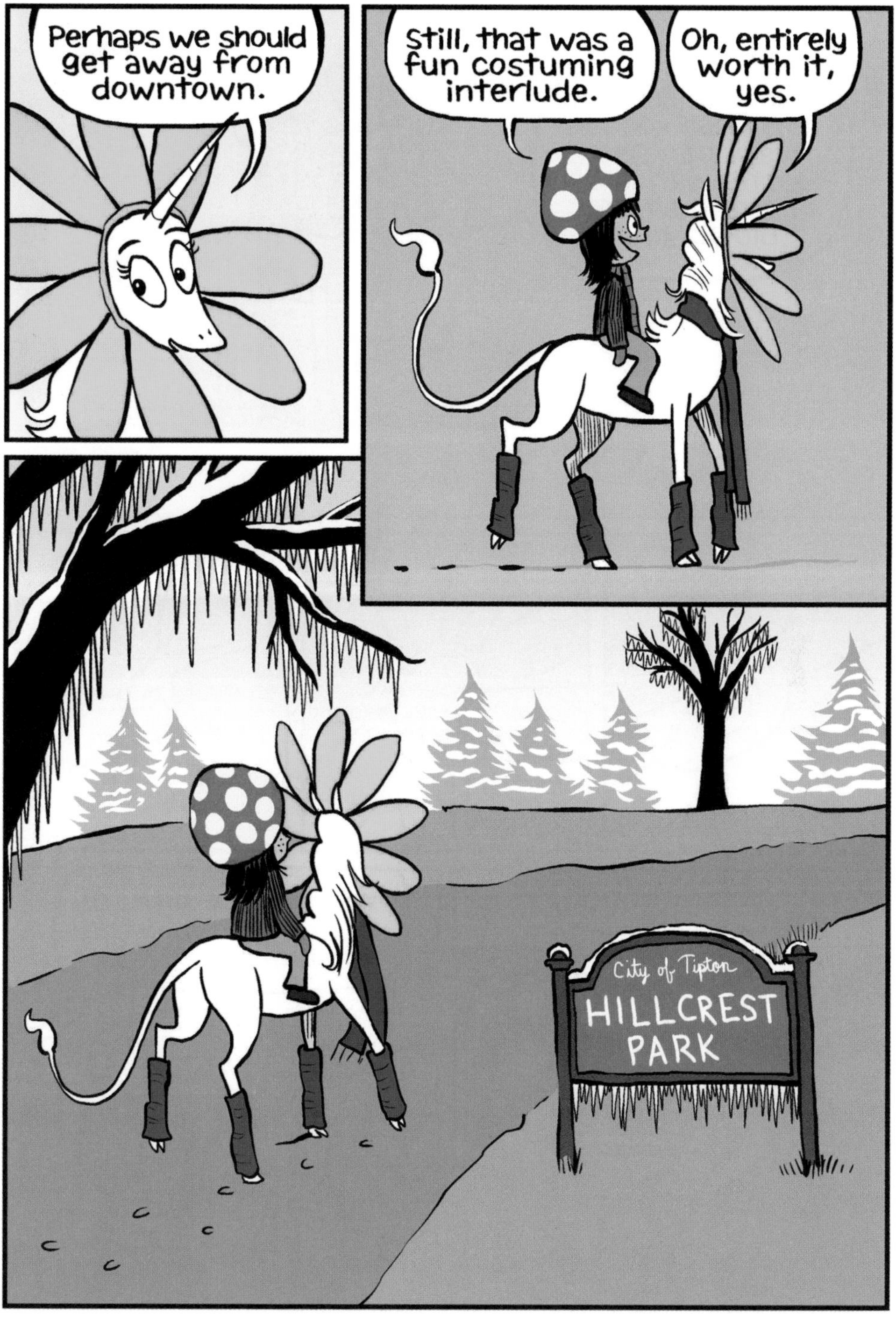
Perhaps we should get away from downtown.
Still, that was a fun costuming interlude.
Oh, entirely worth it, yes.
City of Tipton
HILLCREST PARK

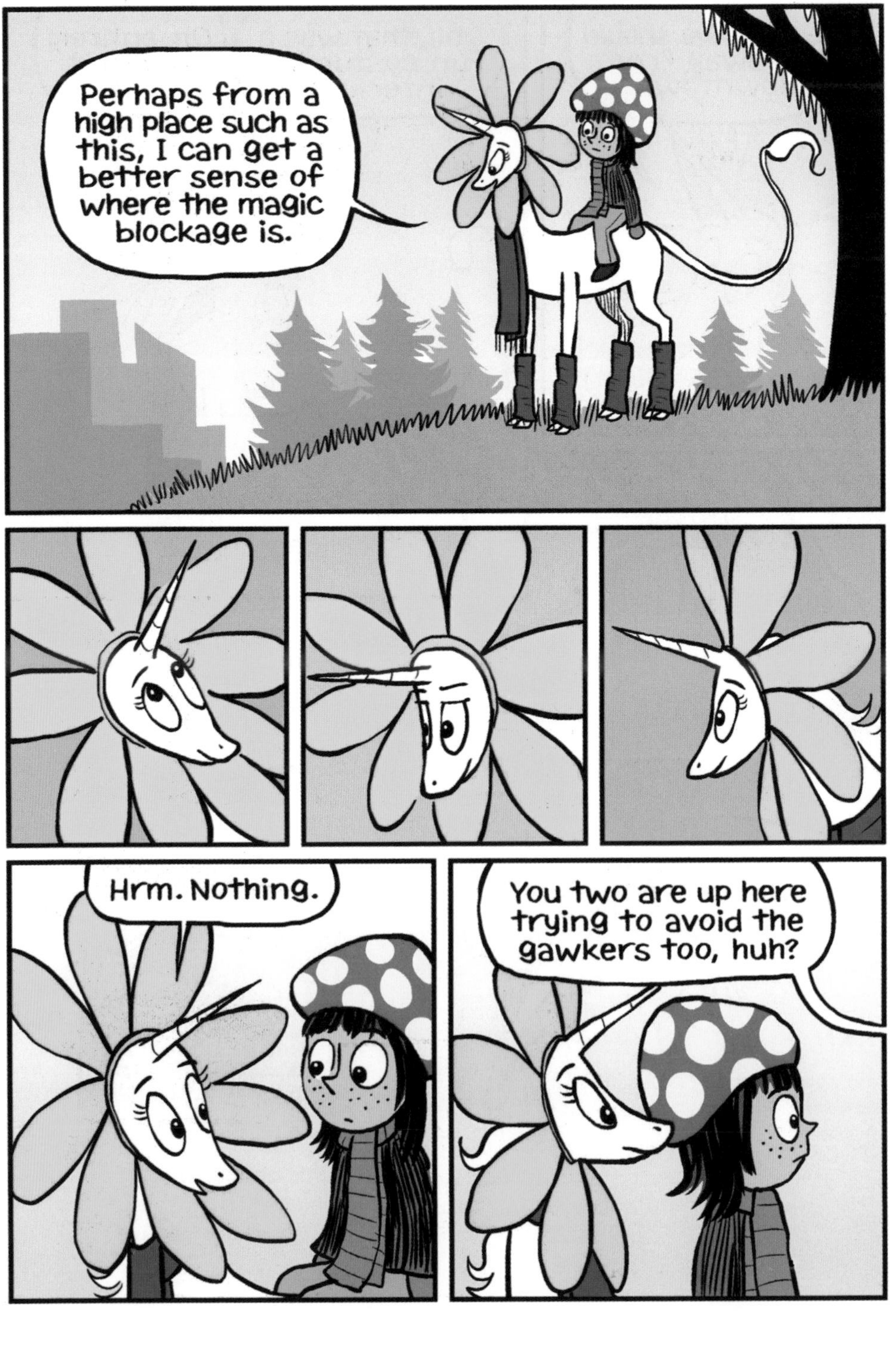
Perhaps from a high place such as this, I can get a better sense of where the magic blockage is.
Hrm. Nothing.
You two are up here trying to avoid the gawkers too, huh?

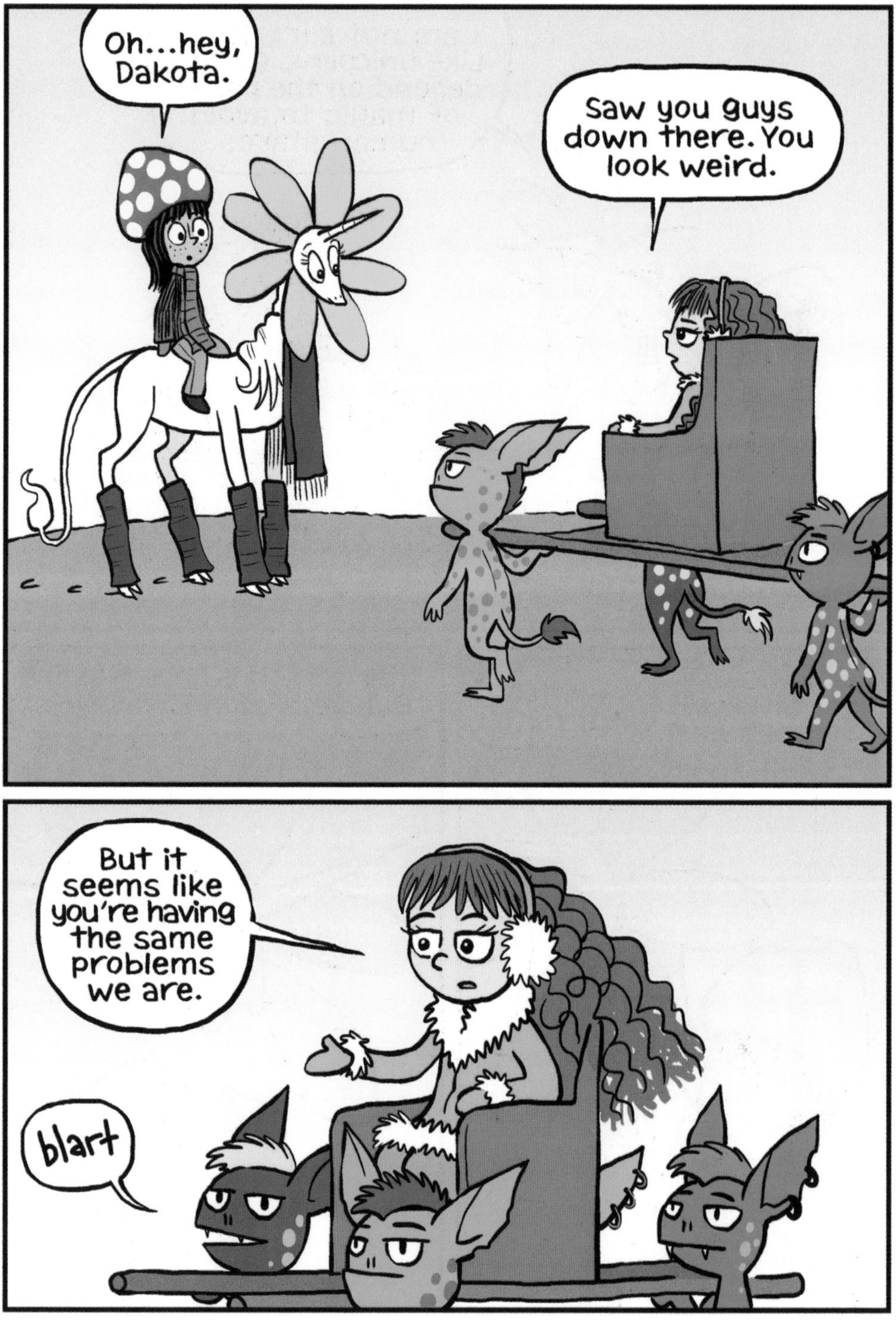
Oh...hey, Dakota.
Saw you guys down there. You look weird.
But it seems like you're having the same problems we are.
blart

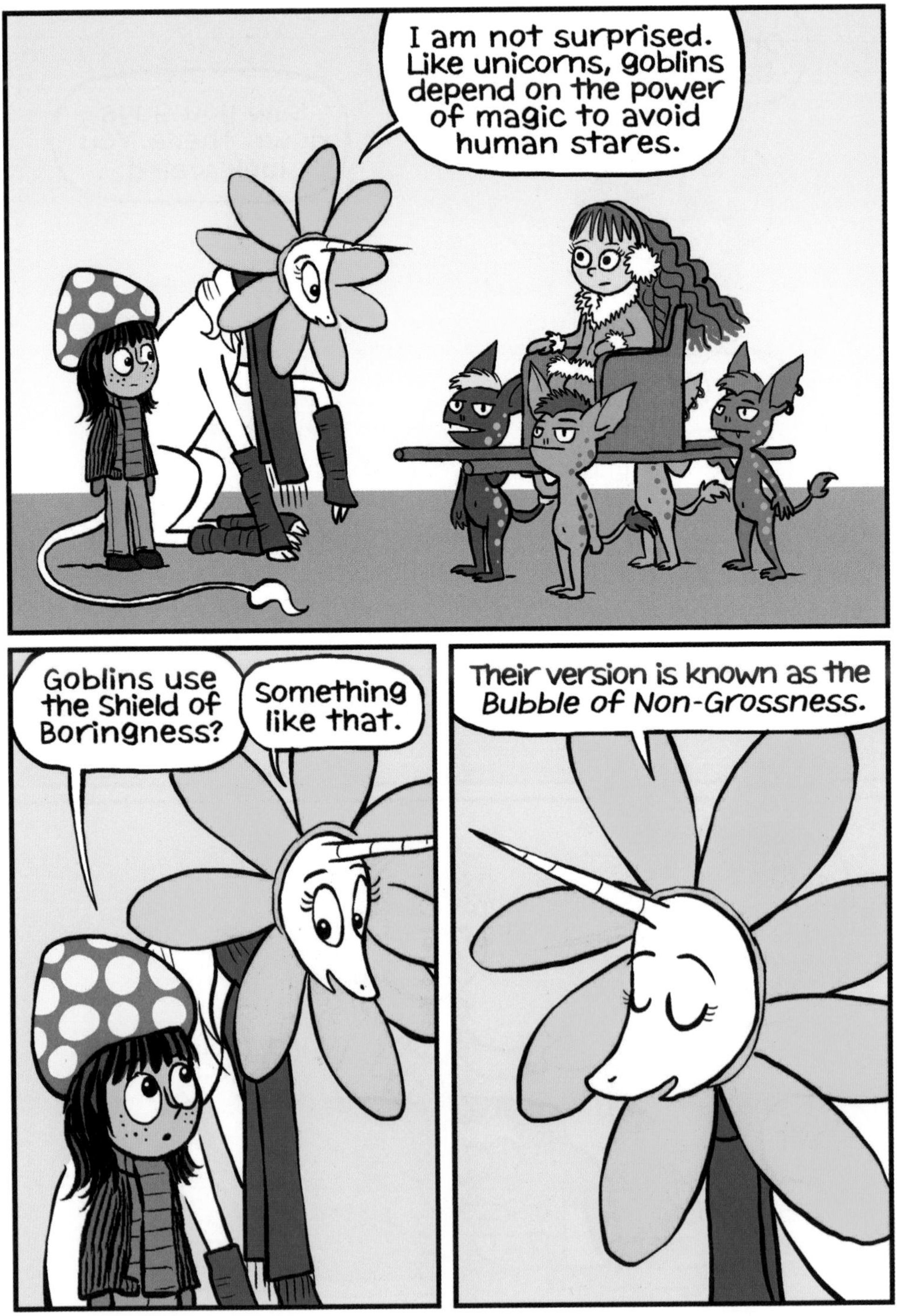
I am not surprised. Like unicorns, goblins depend on the power of magic to avoid human stares.
Goblins use the Shield of Boringness?
Something like that.
Their version is known as the *Bubble of Non-Grossness.*

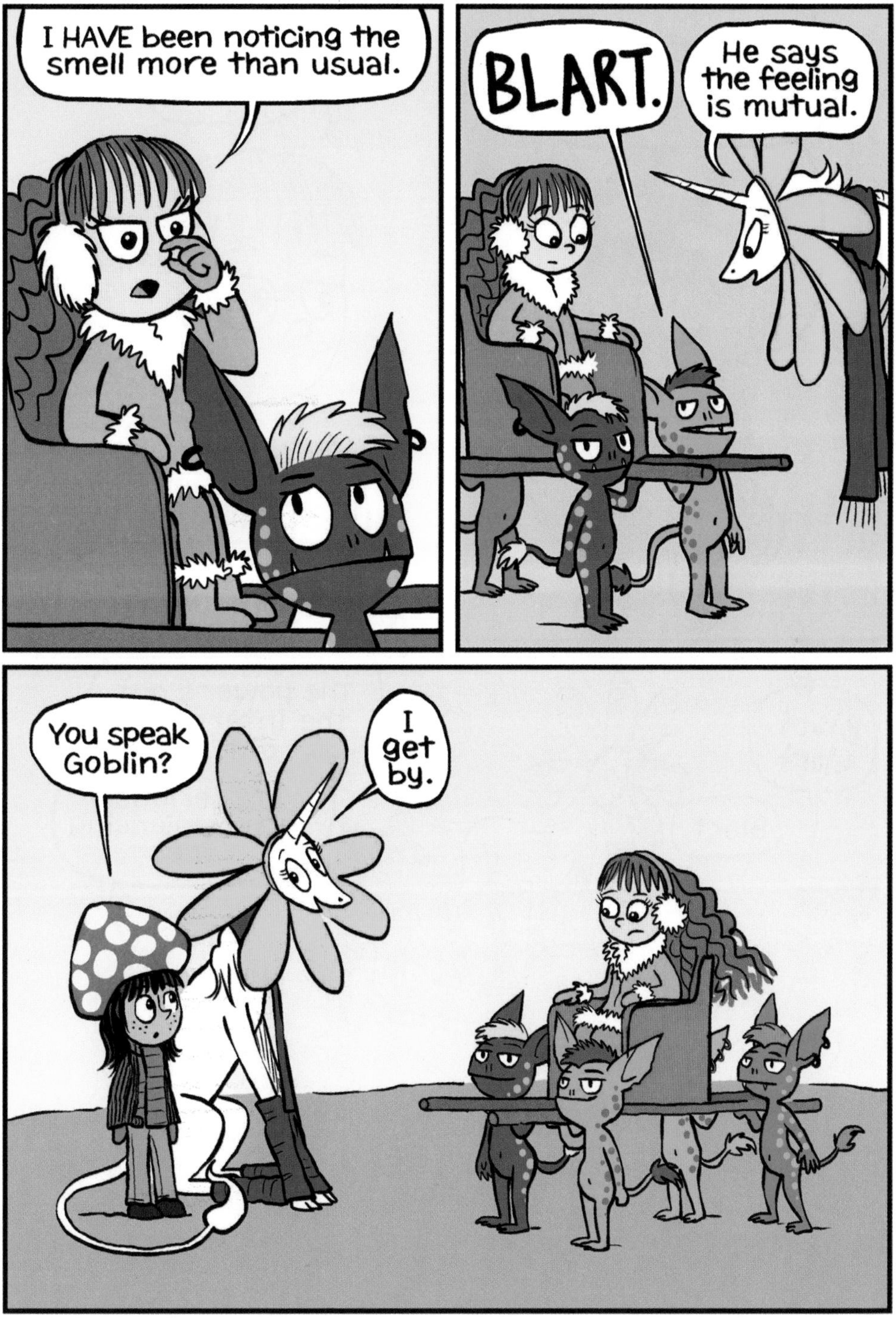
I HAVE been noticing the smell more than usual.
BLART.
He says the feeling is mutual.
You speak Goblin?
I get by.

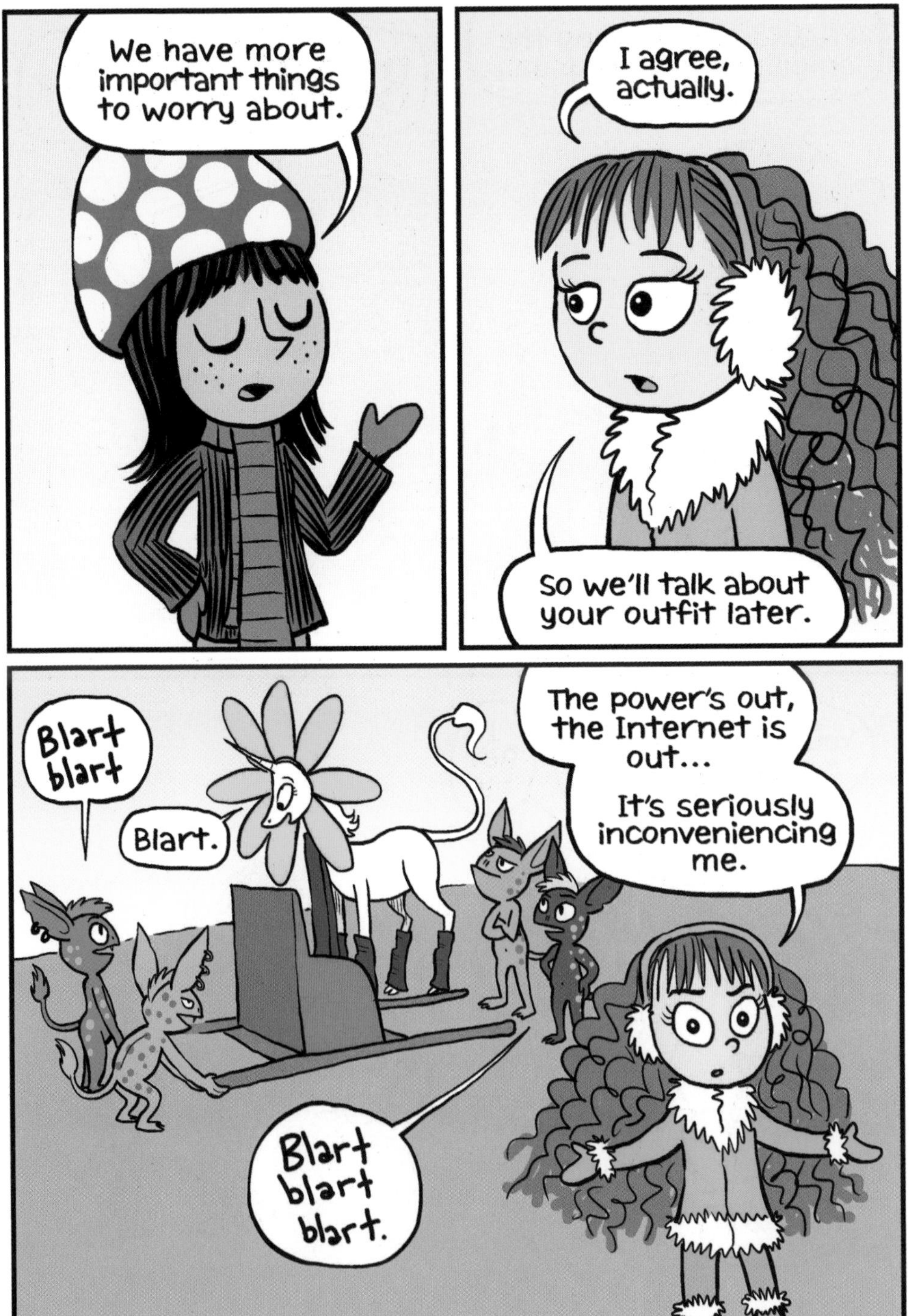
We have more important things to worry about.
I agree, actually.
So we'll talk about your outfit later.
Blart blart
Blart.
The power's out, the Internet is out...
It's seriously inconveniencing me.
Blart blart blart.

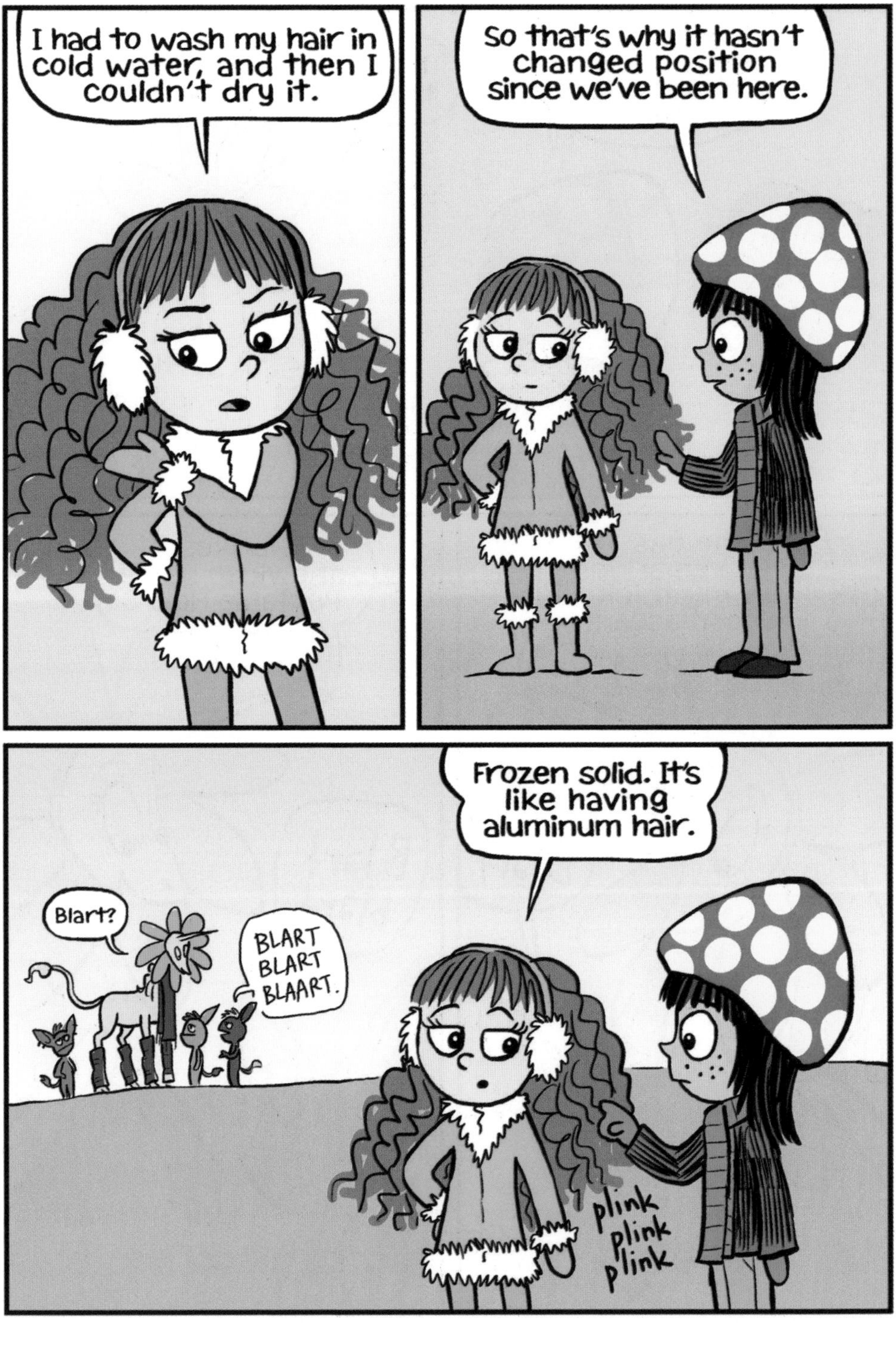
I had to wash my hair in cold water, and then I couldn't dry it.
So that's why it hasn't changed position since we've been here.
Frozen solid. It's like having aluminum hair.
Blart?
BLART BLART BLAART.
plink plink plink

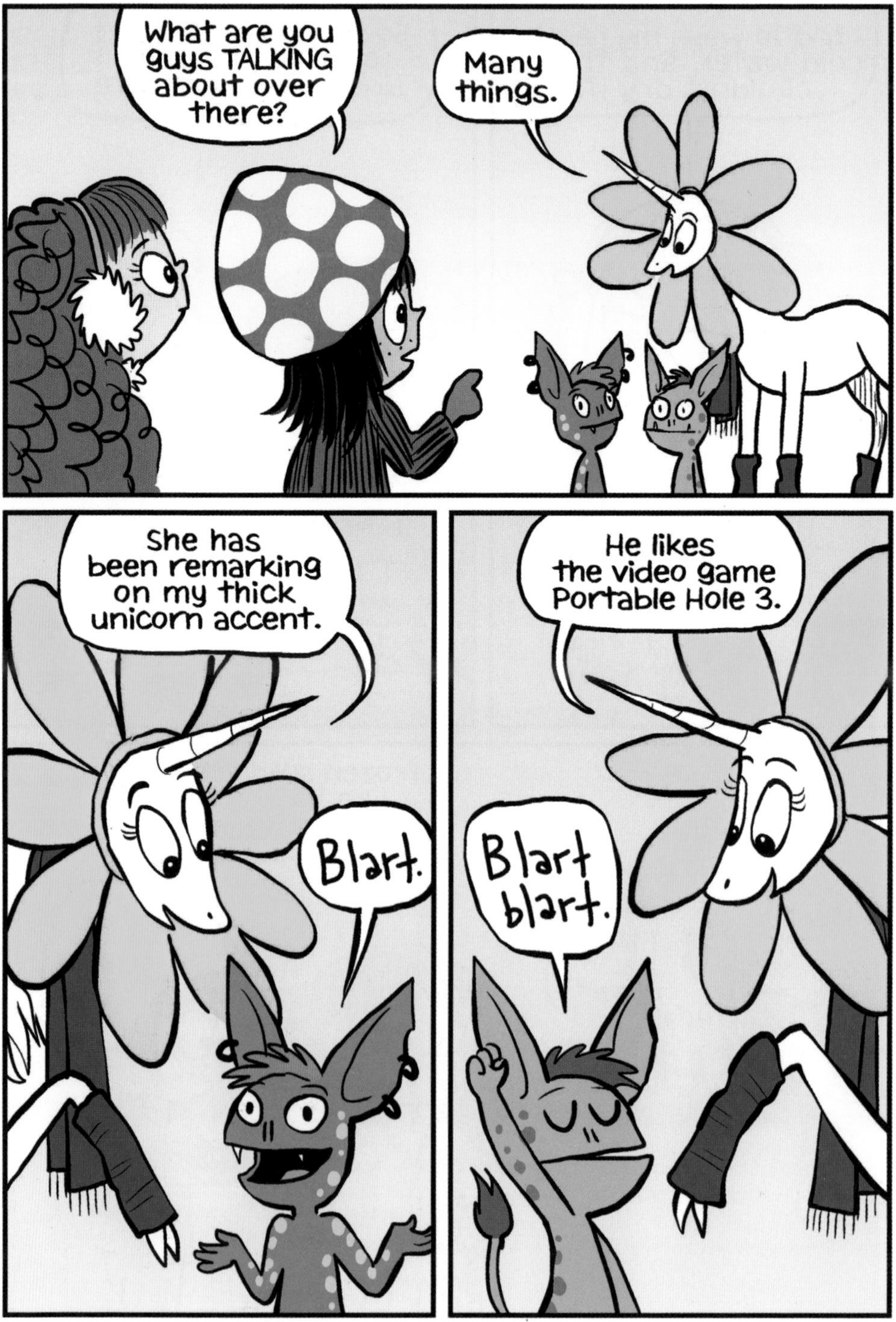
What are you guys TALKING about over there?
Many things.
She has been remarking on my thick unicorn accent.
Blart.
He likes the video game Portable Hole 3.
Blart blart.

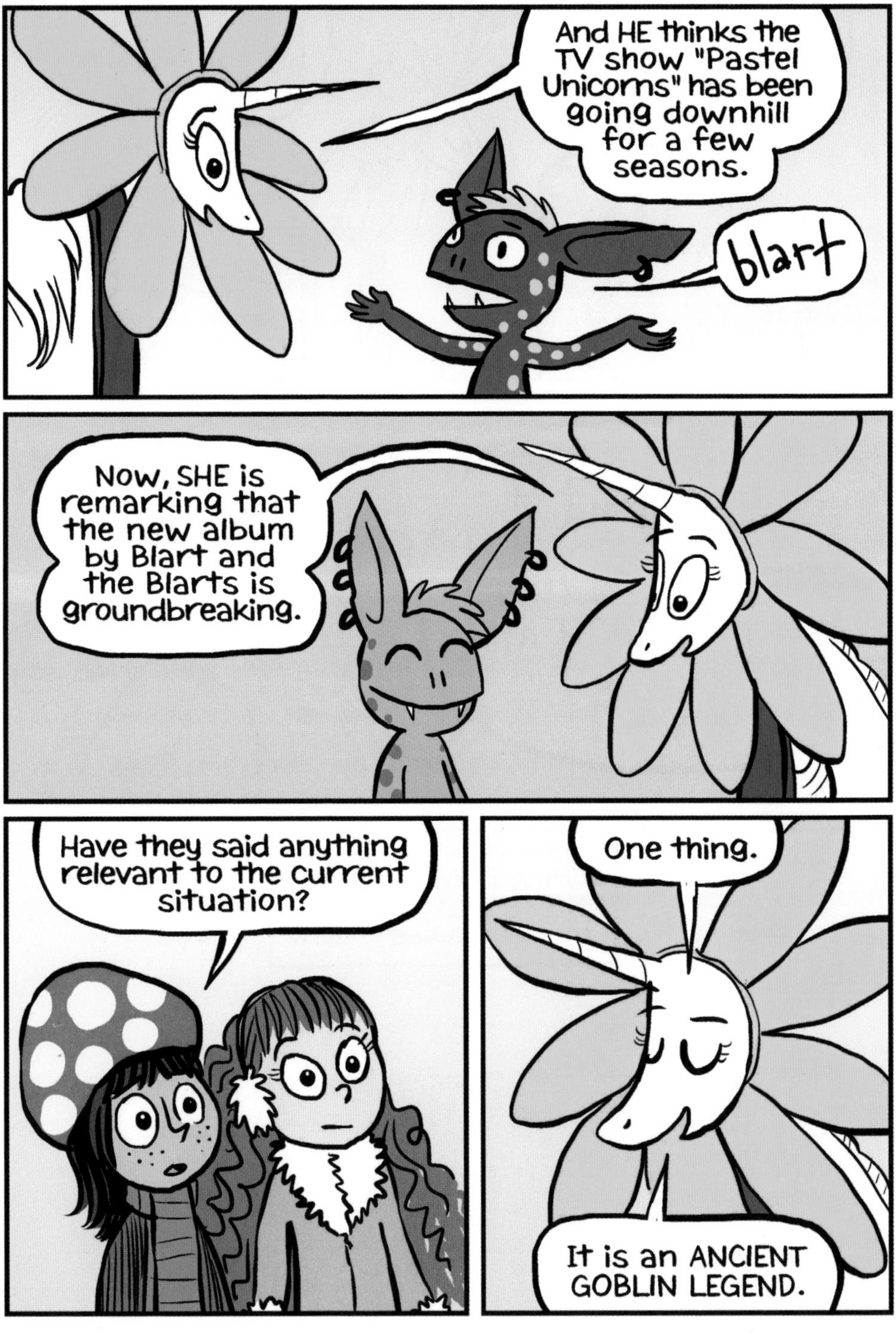
And HE thinks the TV show "Pastel Unicorns" has been going downhill for a few seasons.
blart
Now, SHE is remarking that the new album by Blart and the Blarts is groundbreaking.
Have they said anything relevant to the current situation?
One thing.
It is an ANCIENT GOBLIN LEGEND.

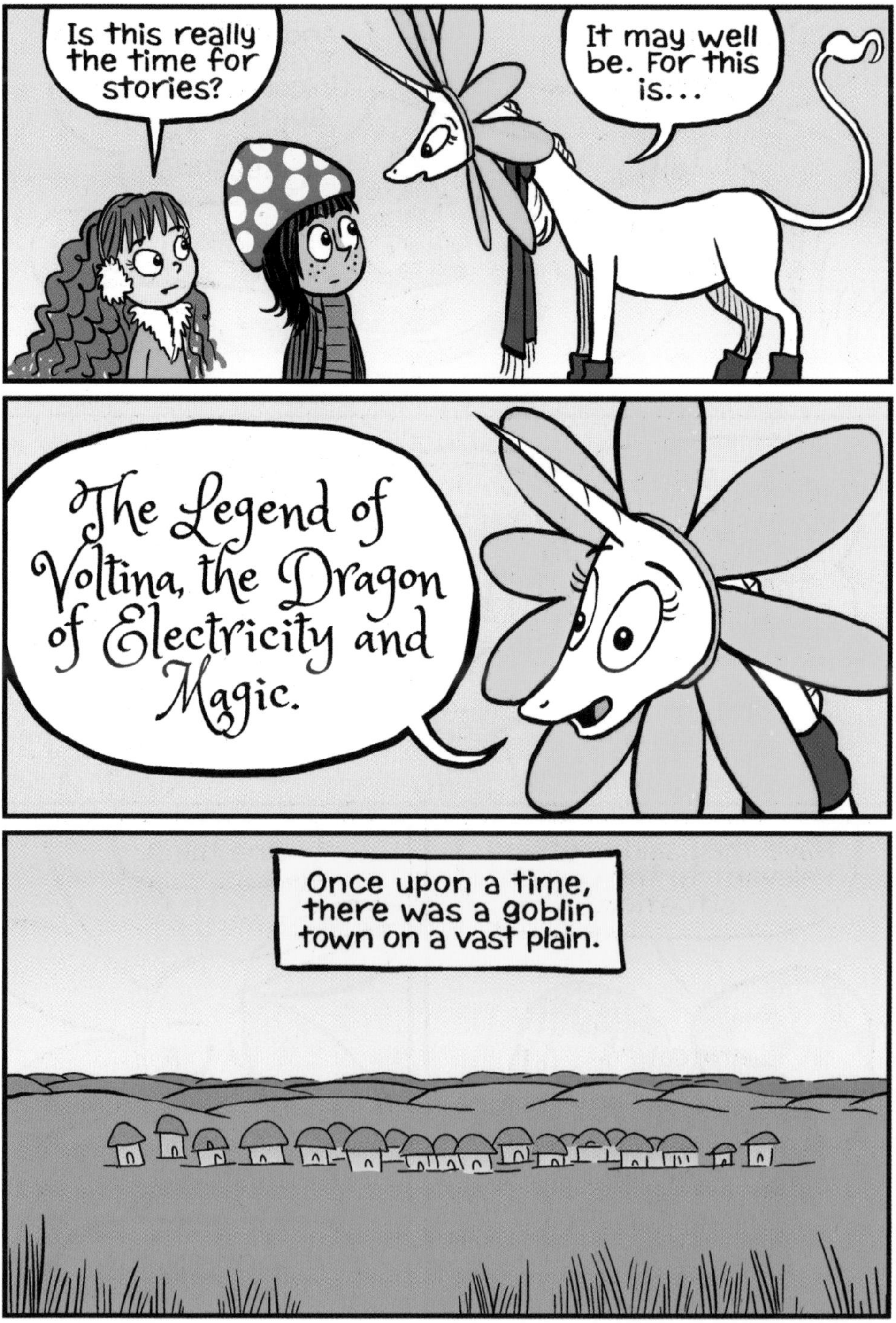
Is this really the time for stories?
It may well be. For this is...
The Legend of Voltina, the Dragon of Electricity and Magic.
Once upon a time, there was a goblin town on a vast plain.

And on a nearby hilltop there lived a dragon.

Her name was Voltina, and she was the sort of dragon who ATE LIGHTNING!

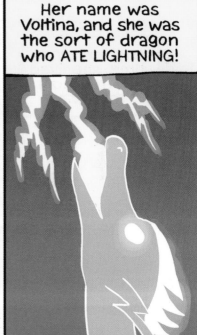

During storms, she would happily go outside for dinner.

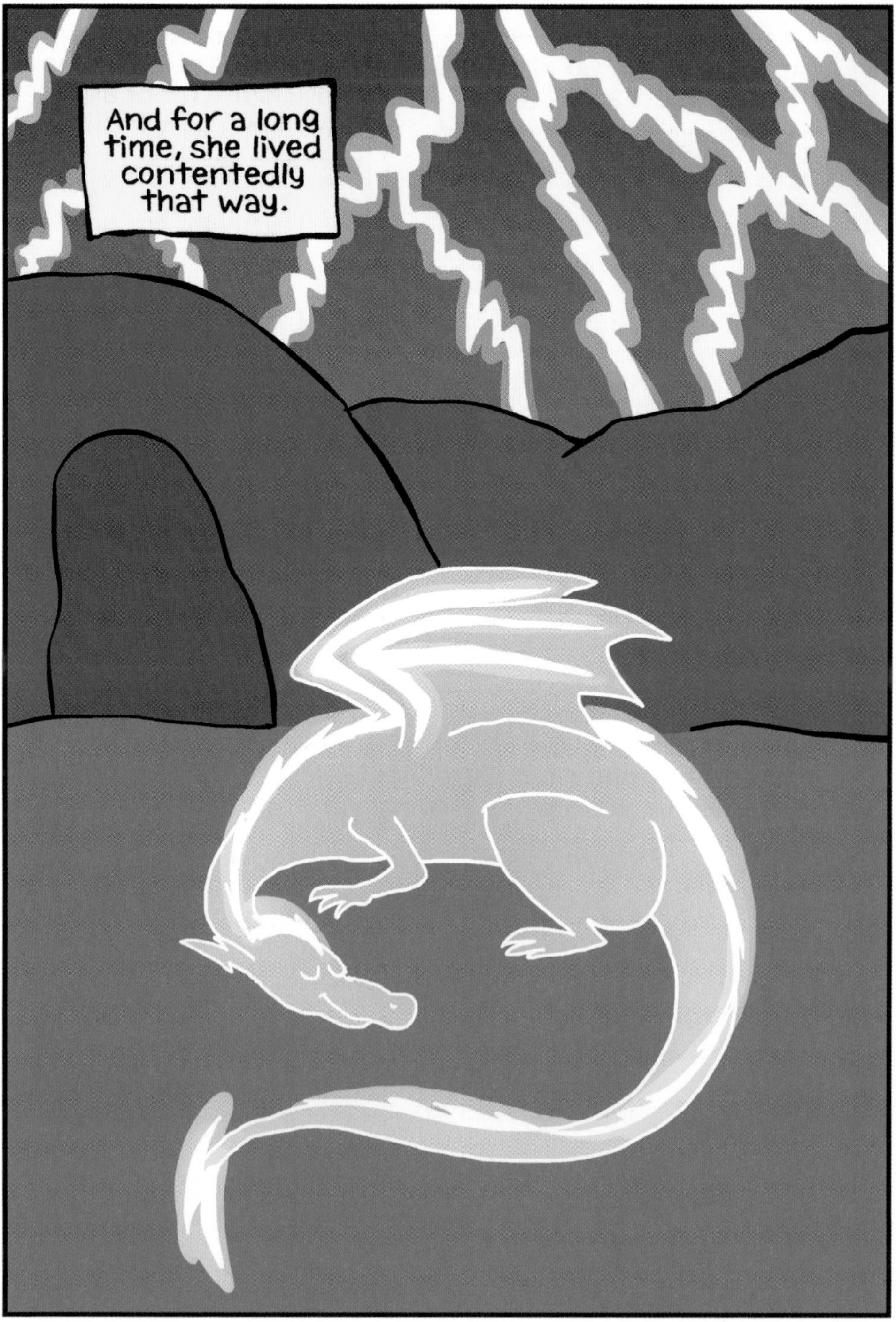
And for a long time, she lived contentedly that way.

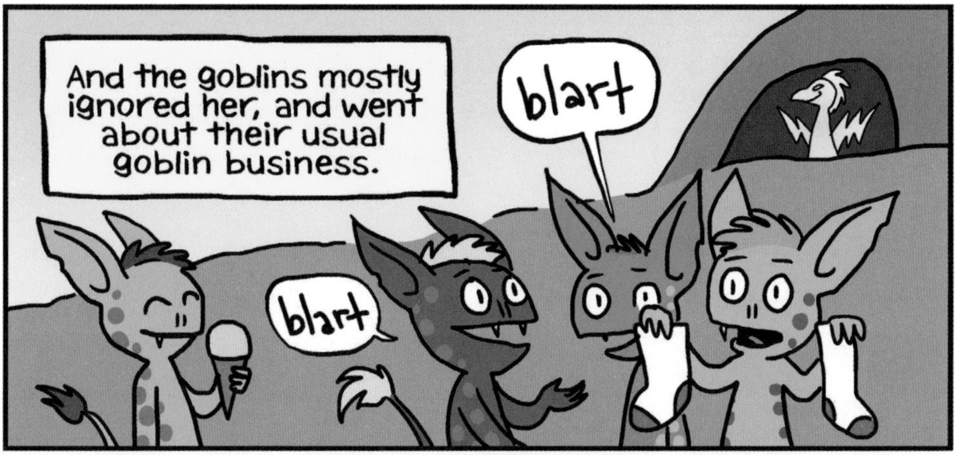
And the goblins mostly ignored her, and went about their usual goblin business.
blart
blart

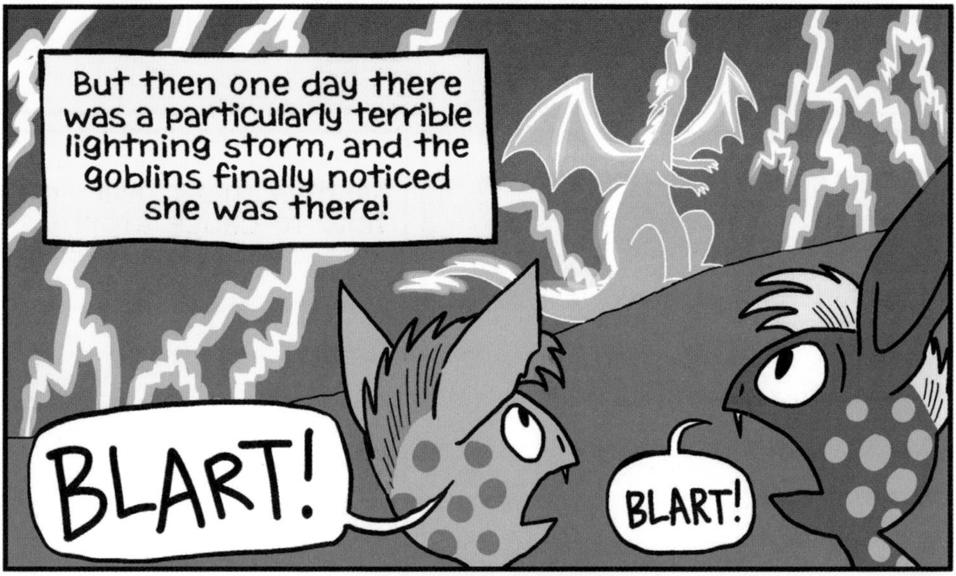
But then one day there was a particularly terrible lightning storm, and the goblins finally noticed she was there!
BLART!
BLART!

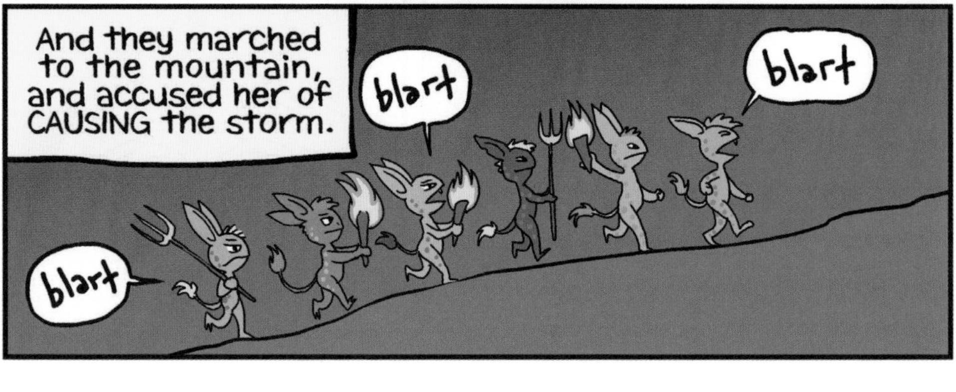
And they marched to the mountain, and accused her of CAUSING the storm.
blart
blart
blart

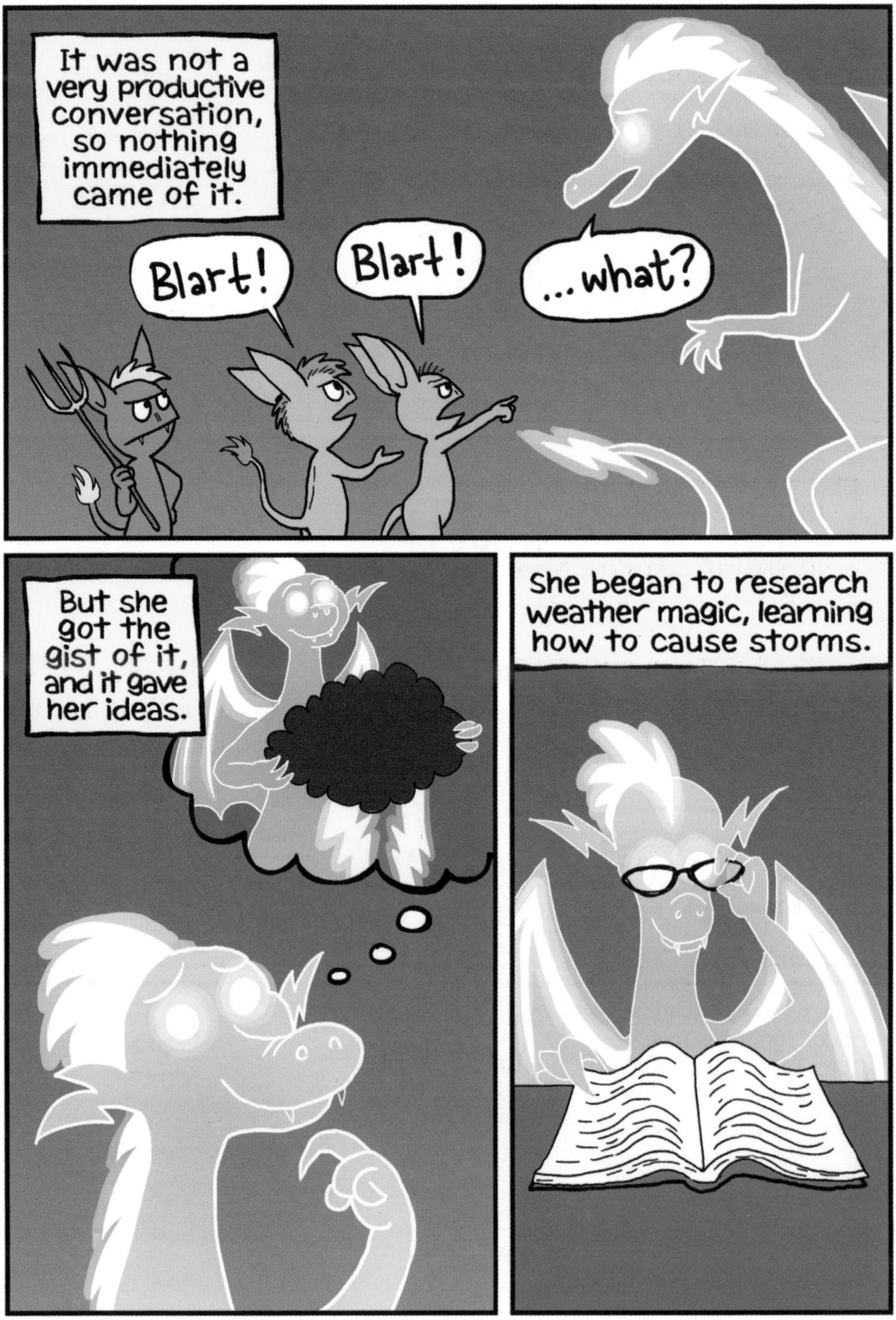
It was not a very productive conversation, so nothing immediately came of it.
Blart!
Blart!
...what?
But she got the gist of it, and it gave her ideas.
She began to research weather magic, learning how to cause storms.

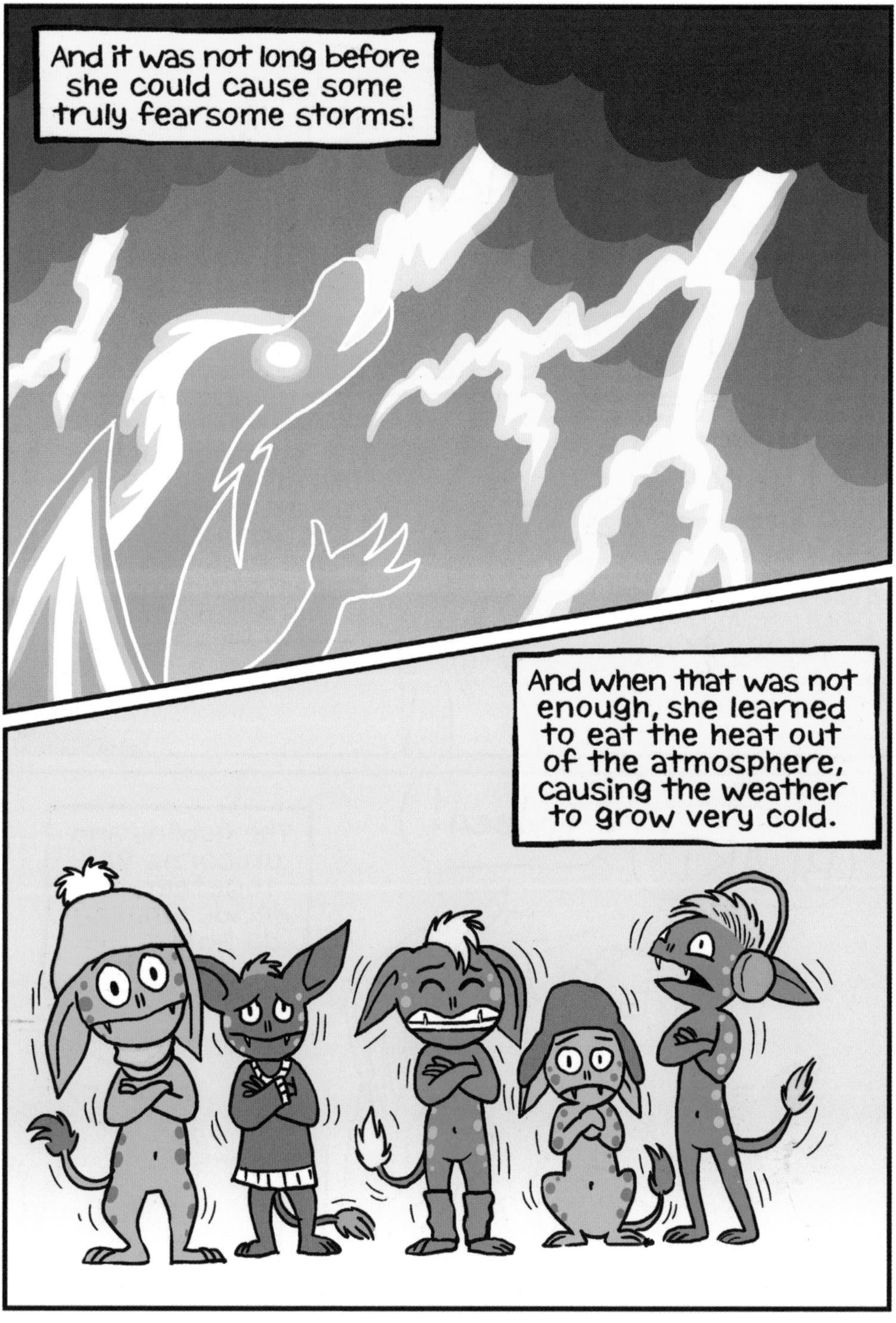
And it was not long before she could cause some truly fearsome storms!
And when that was not enough, she learned to eat the heat out of the atmosphere, causing the weather to grow very cold.

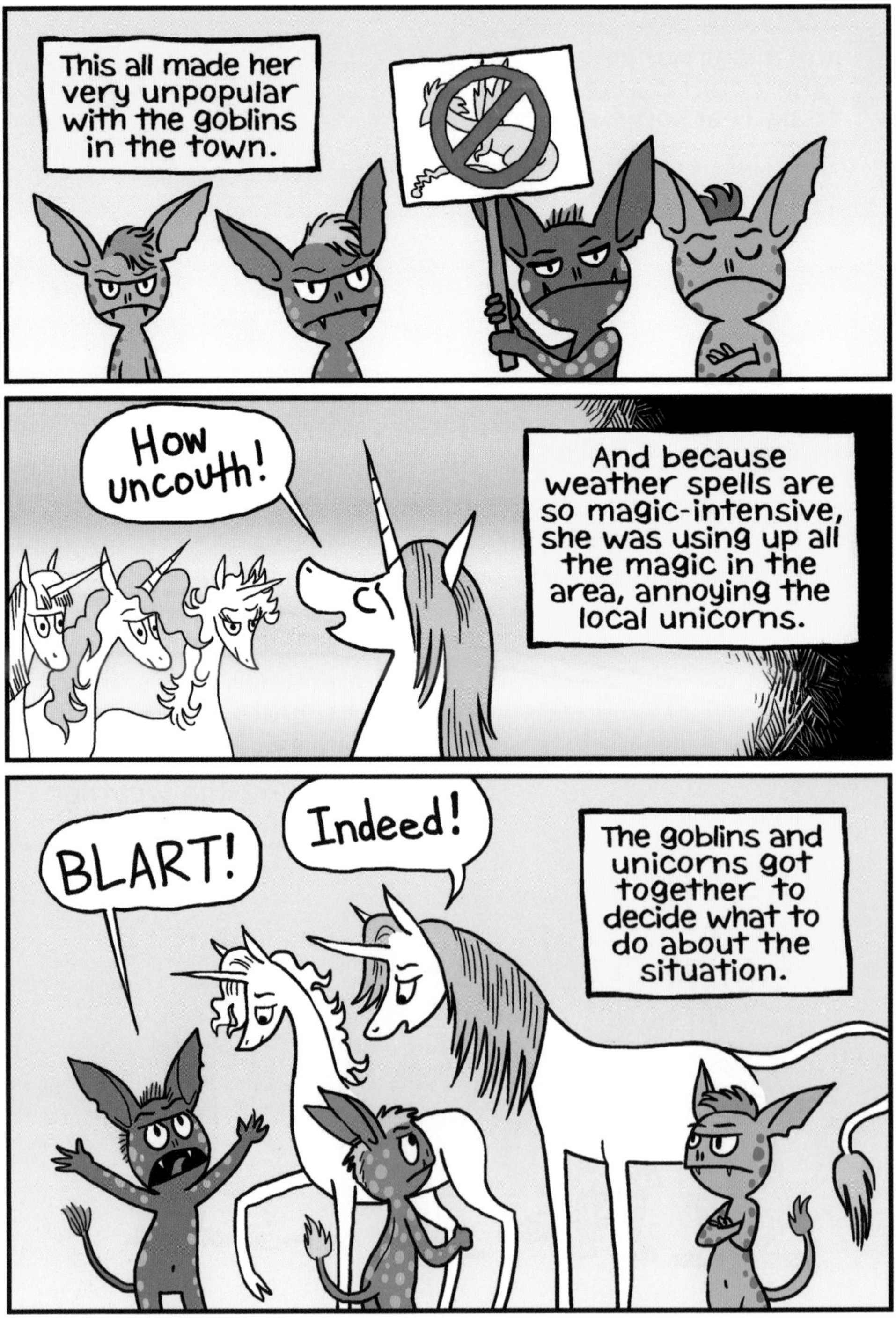

This all made her very unpopular with the goblins in the town.
How uncouth!
And because weather spells are so magic-intensive, she was using up all the magic in the area, annoying the local unicorns.
BLART!
Indeed!
The goblins and unicorns got together to decide what to do about the situation.

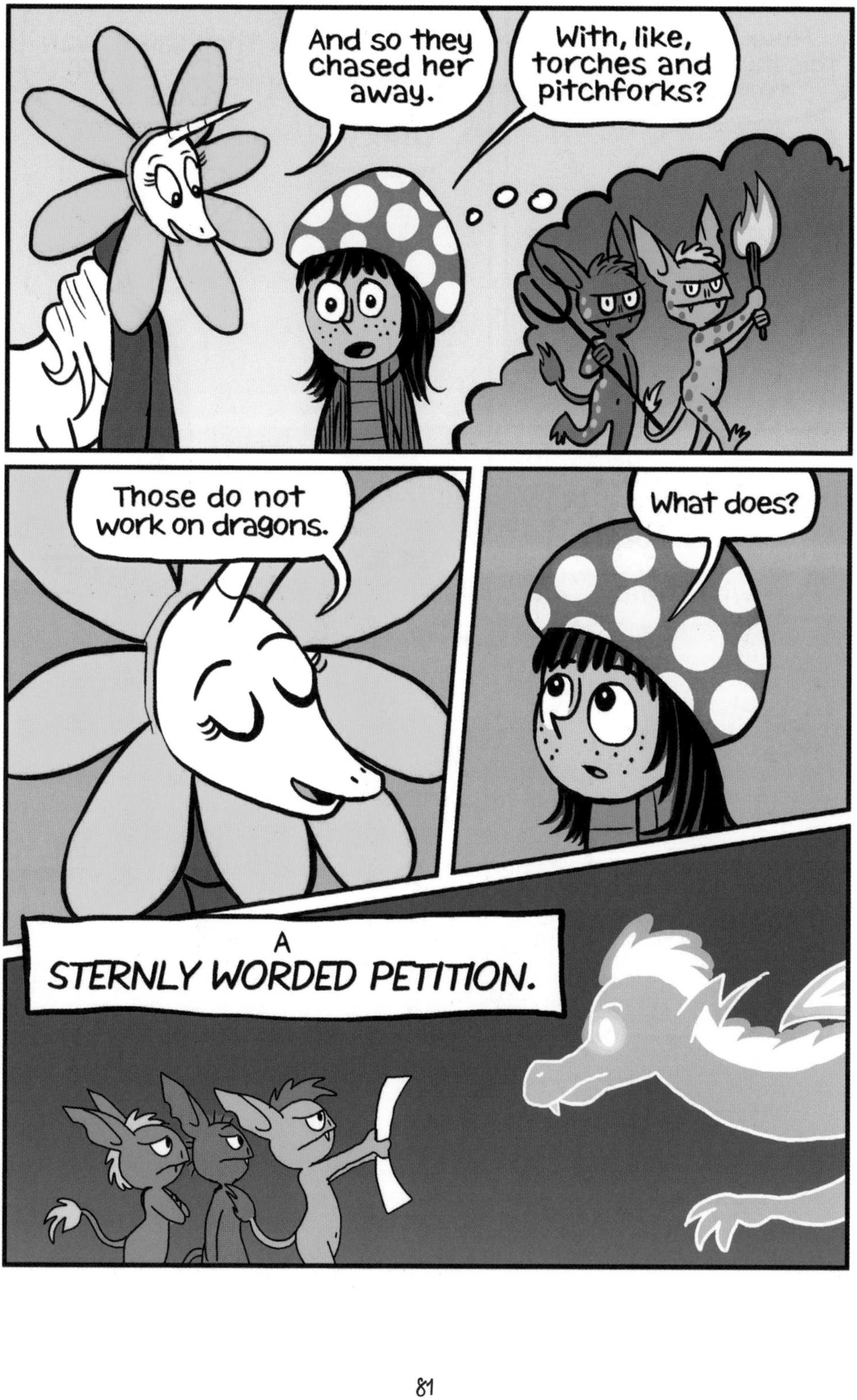
And so they chased her away.
With, like, torches and pitchforks?
Those do not work on dragons.
What does?
A STERNLY WORDED PETITION.

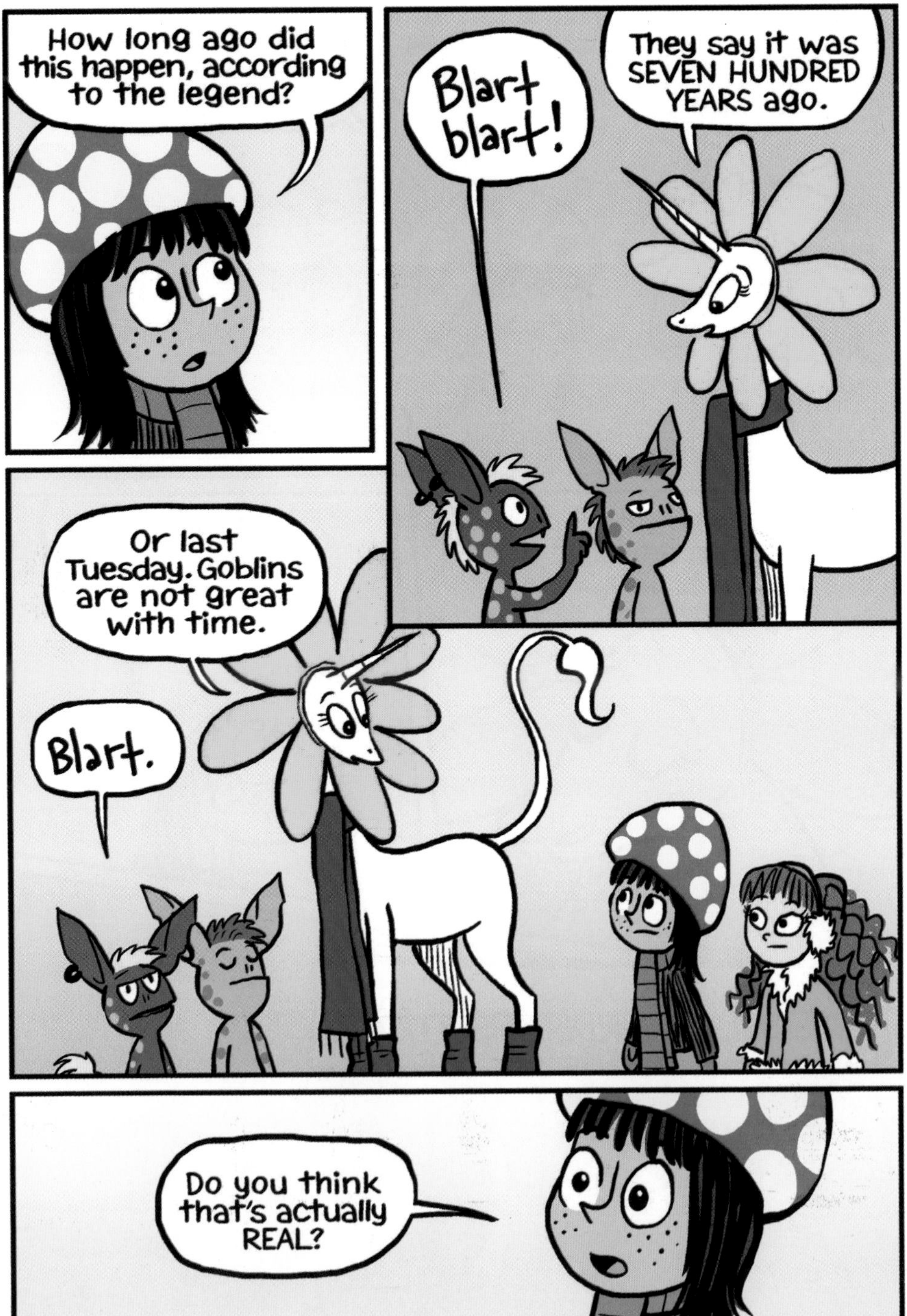
How long ago did this happen, according to the legend?
Blart blart!
They say it was SEVEN HUNDRED YEARS ago.
Or last Tuesday. Goblins are not great with time.
Blart.
Do you think that's actually REAL?

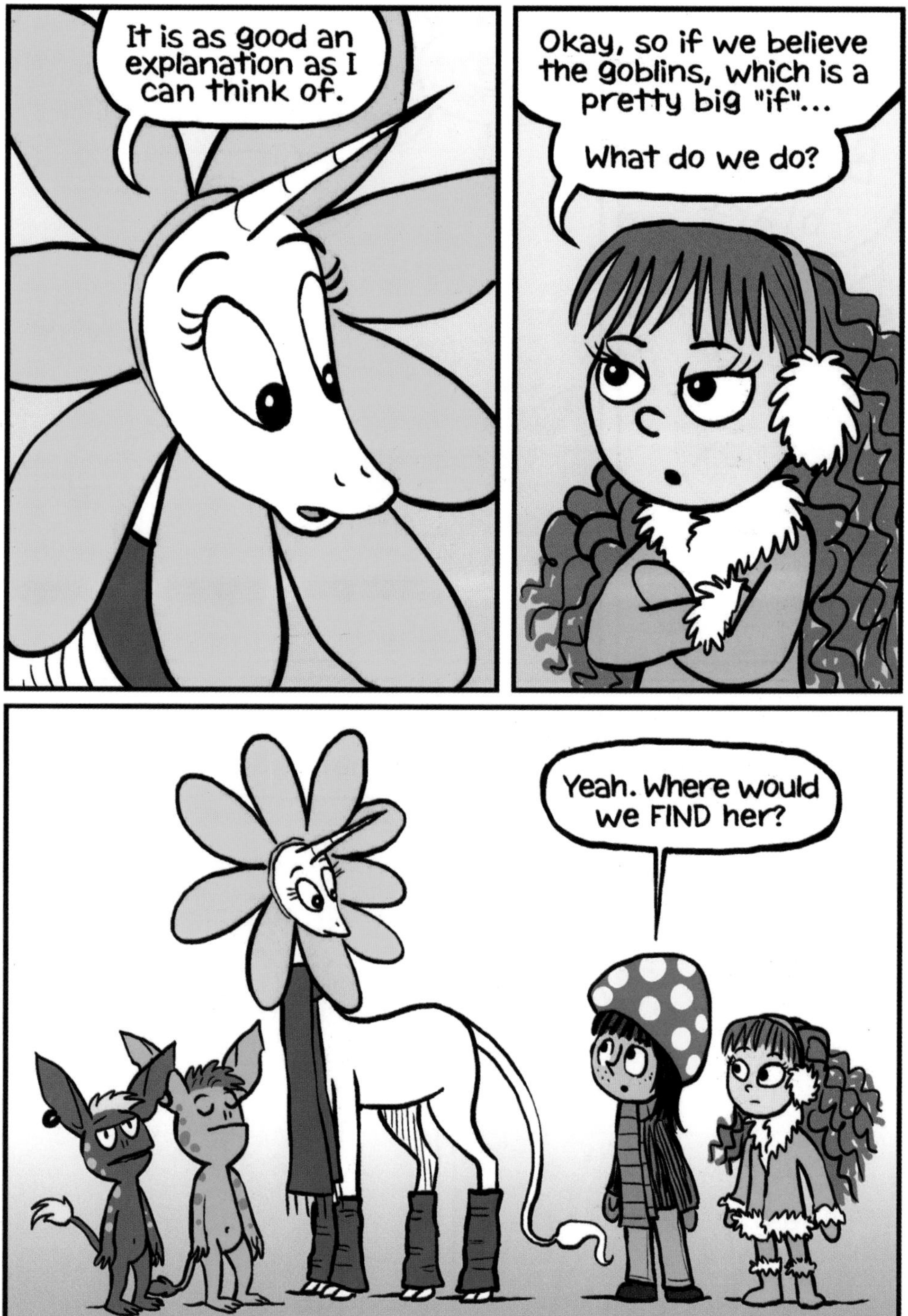
It is as good an explanation as I can think of.
Okay, so if we believe the goblins, which is a pretty big "if"...
What do we do?
Yeah. Where would we FIND her?

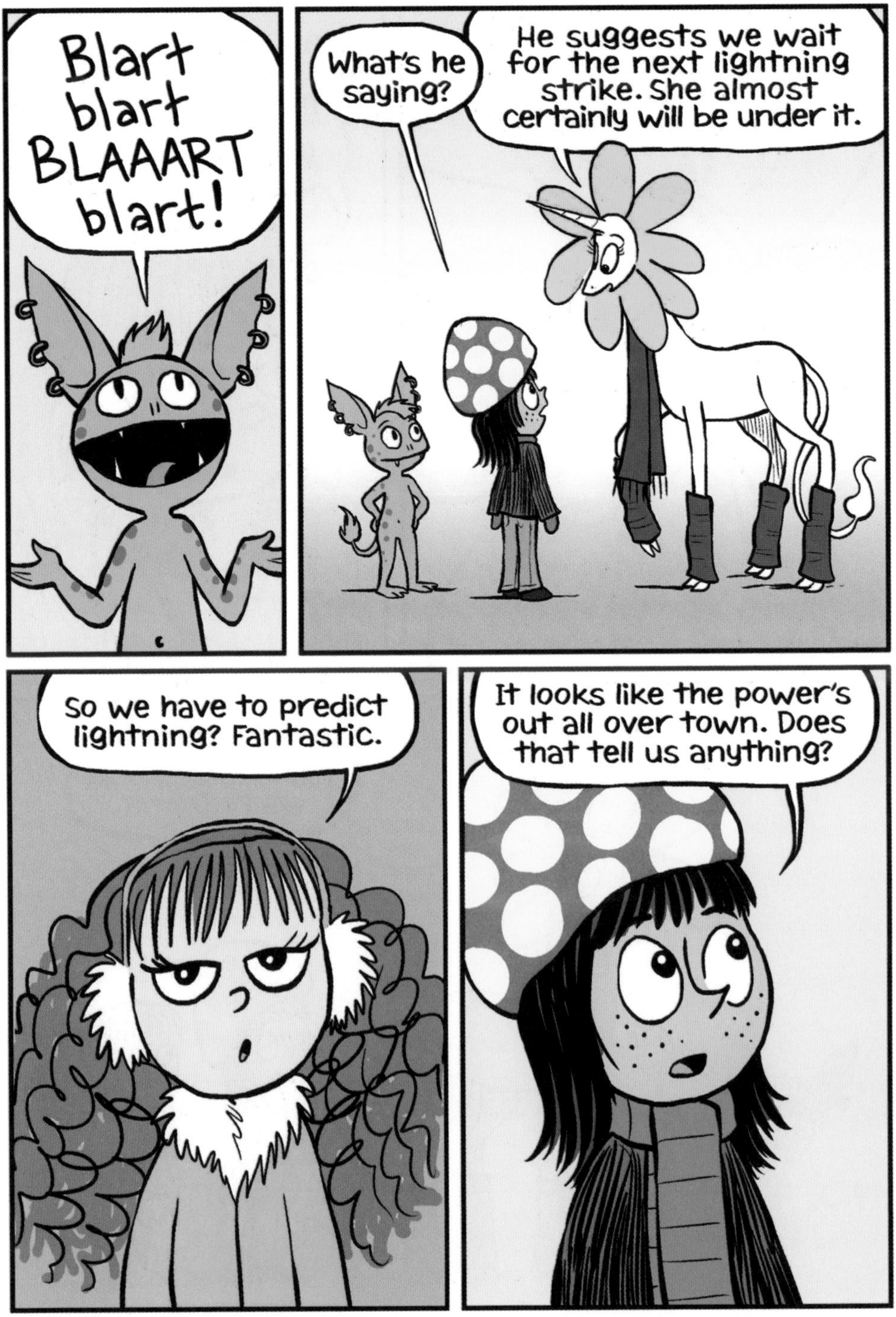
Blart blart BLAART blart!
What's he saying?
He suggests we wait for the next lightning strike. She almost certainly will be under it.
So we have to predict lightning? Fantastic.
It looks like the power's out all over town. Does that tell us anything?

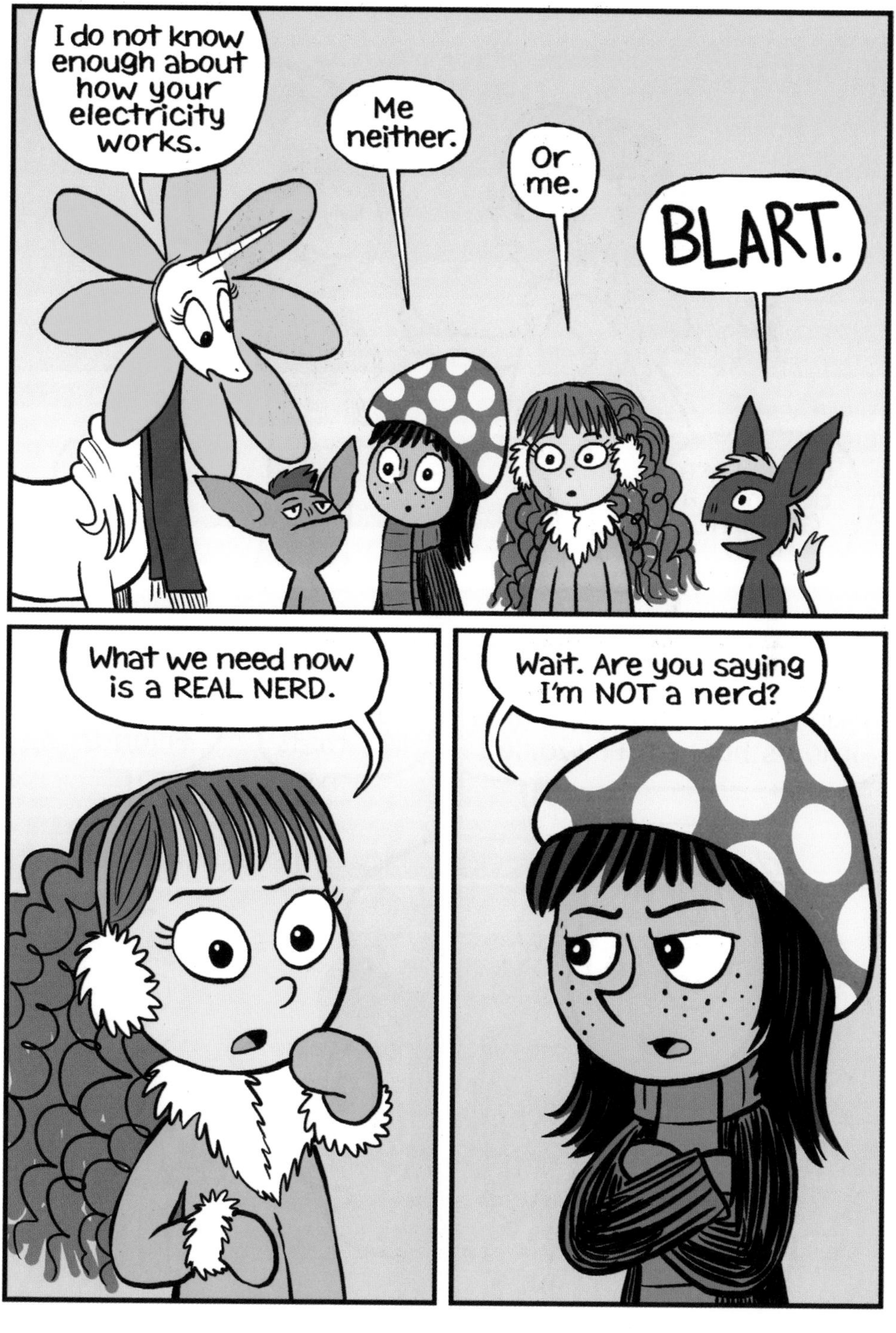
I do not know enough about how your electricity works.
Me neither.
Or me.
BLART.
What we need now is a REAL NERD.
Wait. Are you saying I'm NOT a nerd?

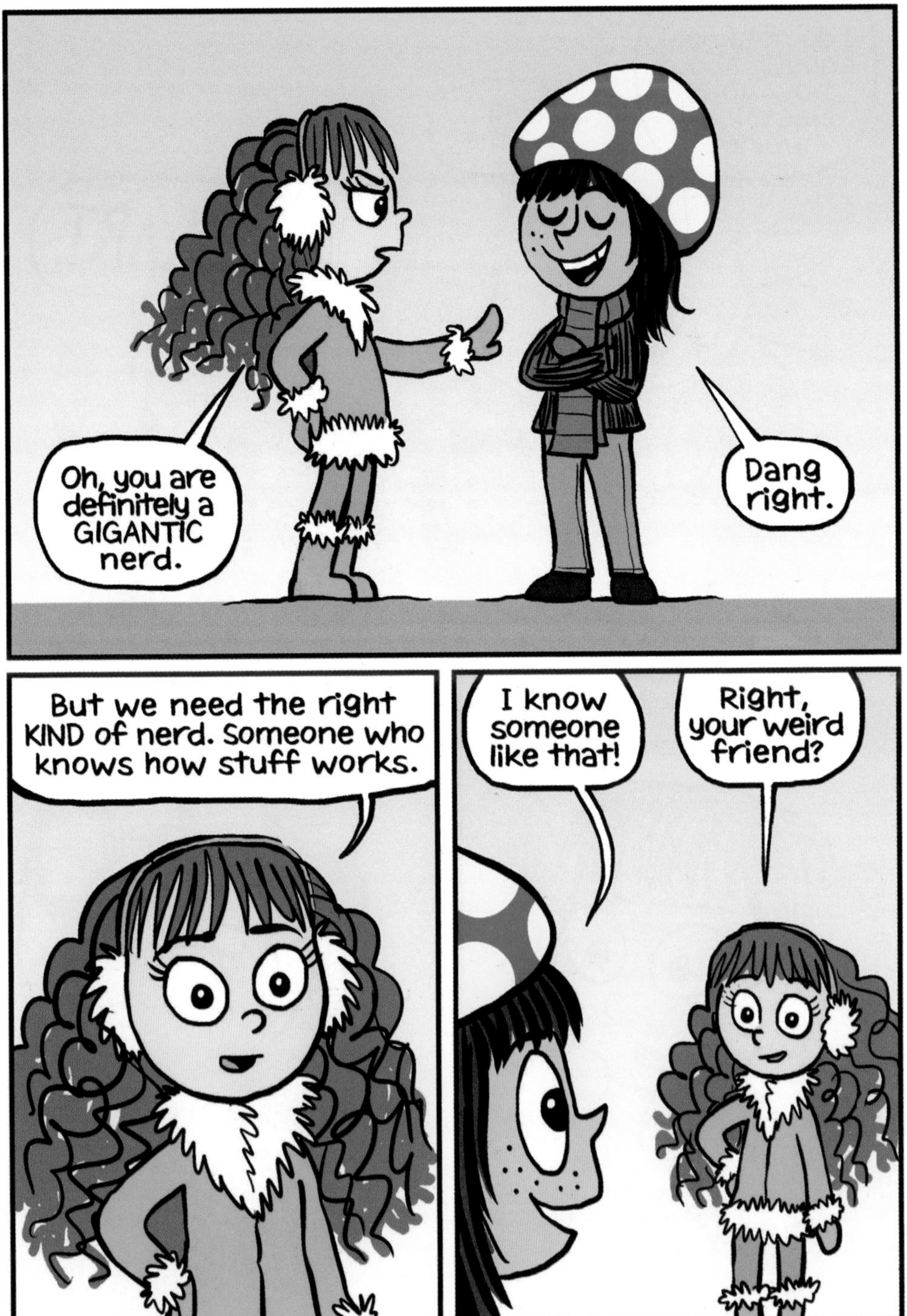
Oh, you are definitely a GIGANTIC nerd.
Dang right.
But we need the right KIND of nerd. Someone who knows how stuff works.
I know someone like that!
Right, your weird friend?

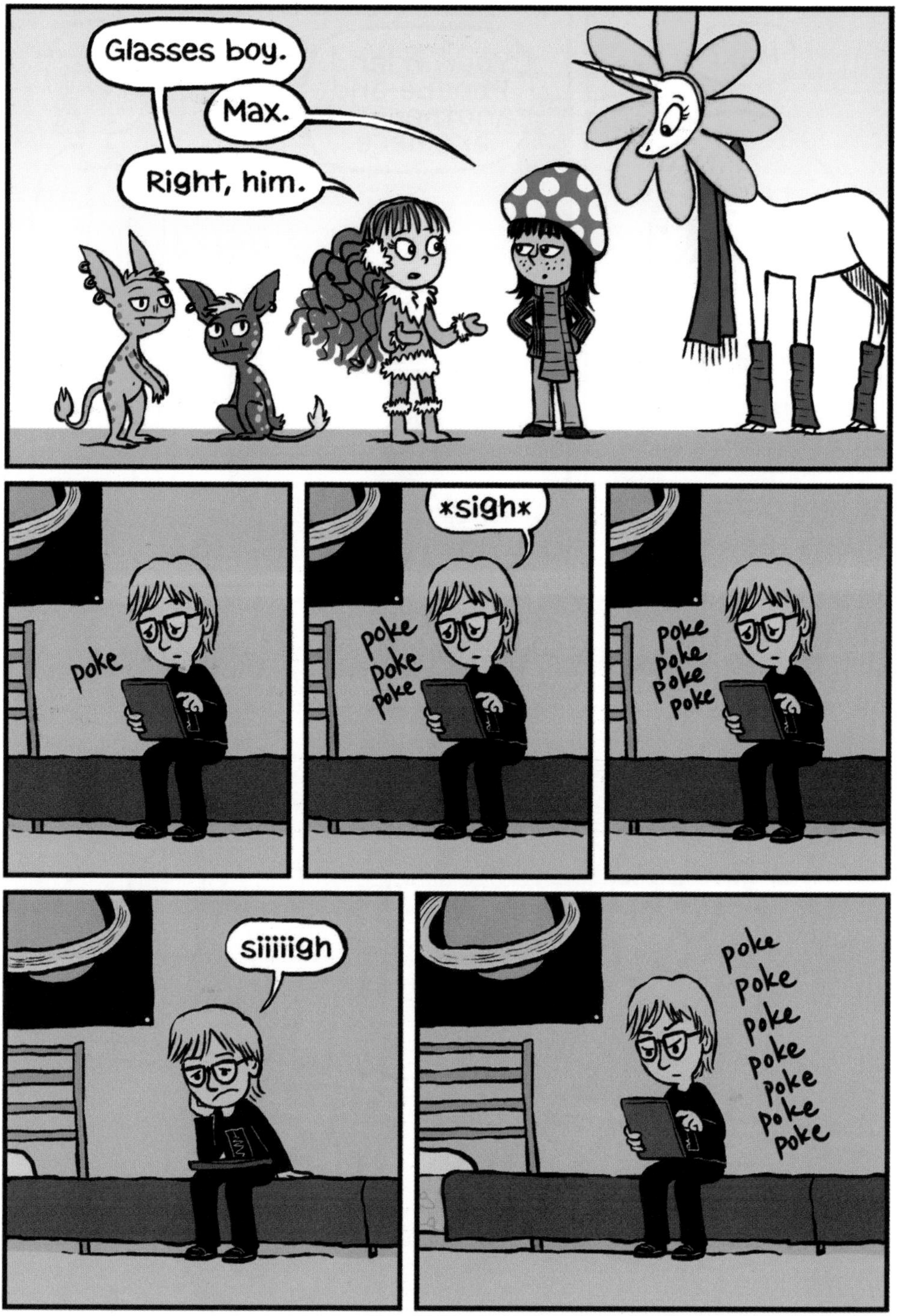
Glasses boy.
Max.
Right, him.
poke
sigh
poke poke poke
poke poke poke poke
siiiiigh
poke poke poke poke poke poke poke

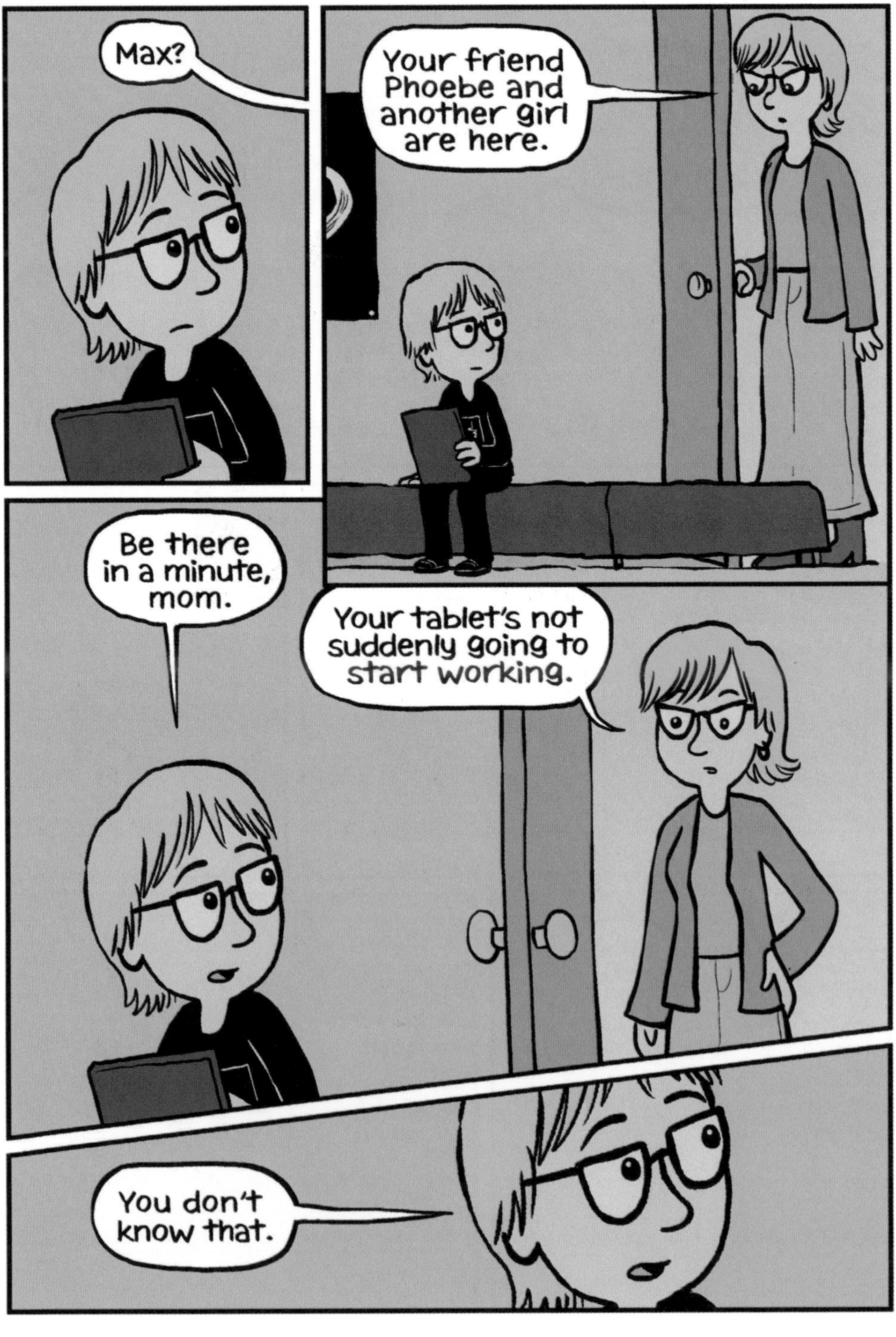
Max?
Your friend Phoebe and another girl are here.
Be there in a minute, mom.
Your tablet's not suddenly going to start working.
You don't know that.

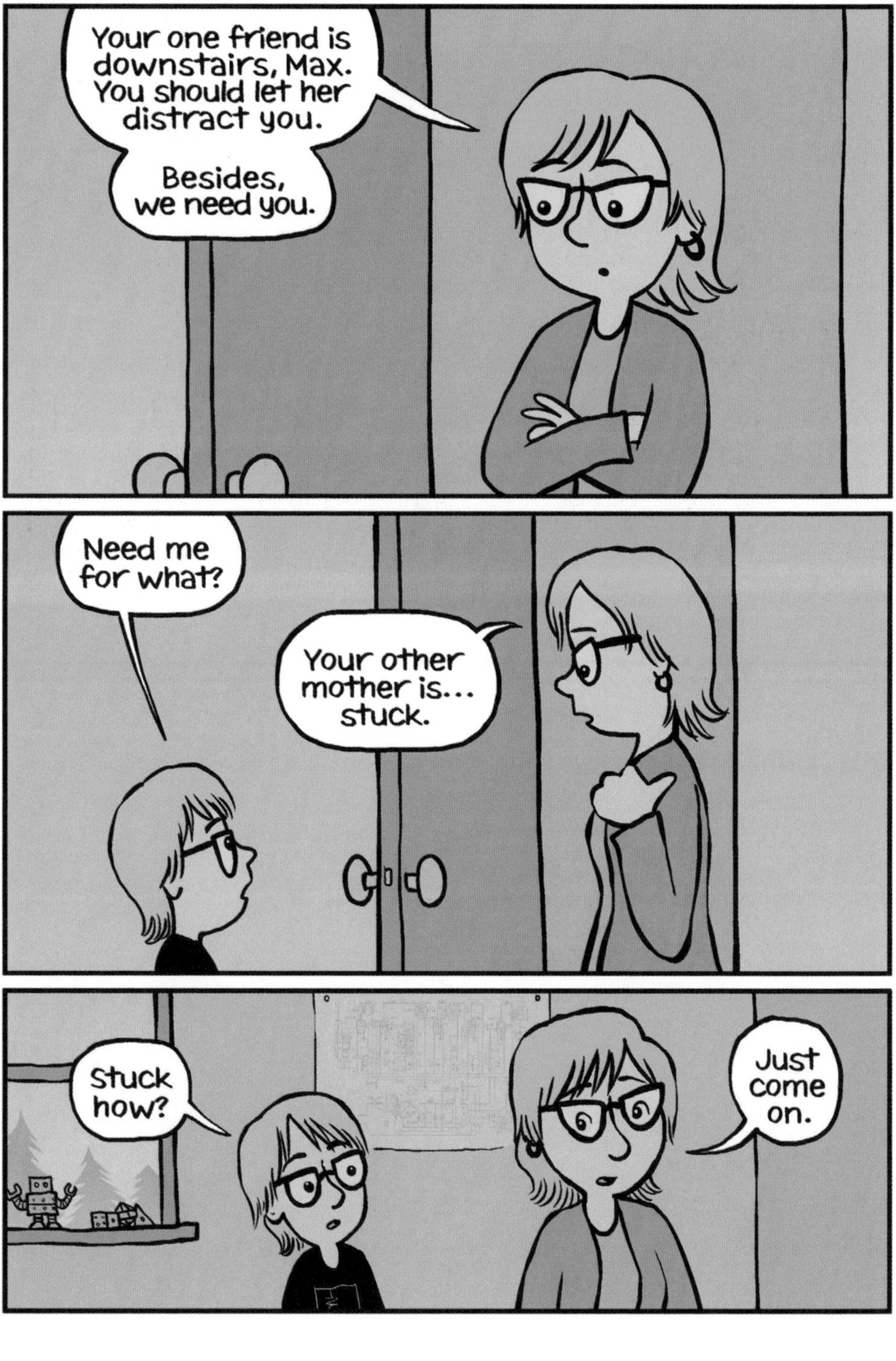
Your one friend is downstairs, Max. You should let her distract you.
Besides, we need you.
Need me for what?
Your other mother is... stuck.
Stuck how?
Just come on.

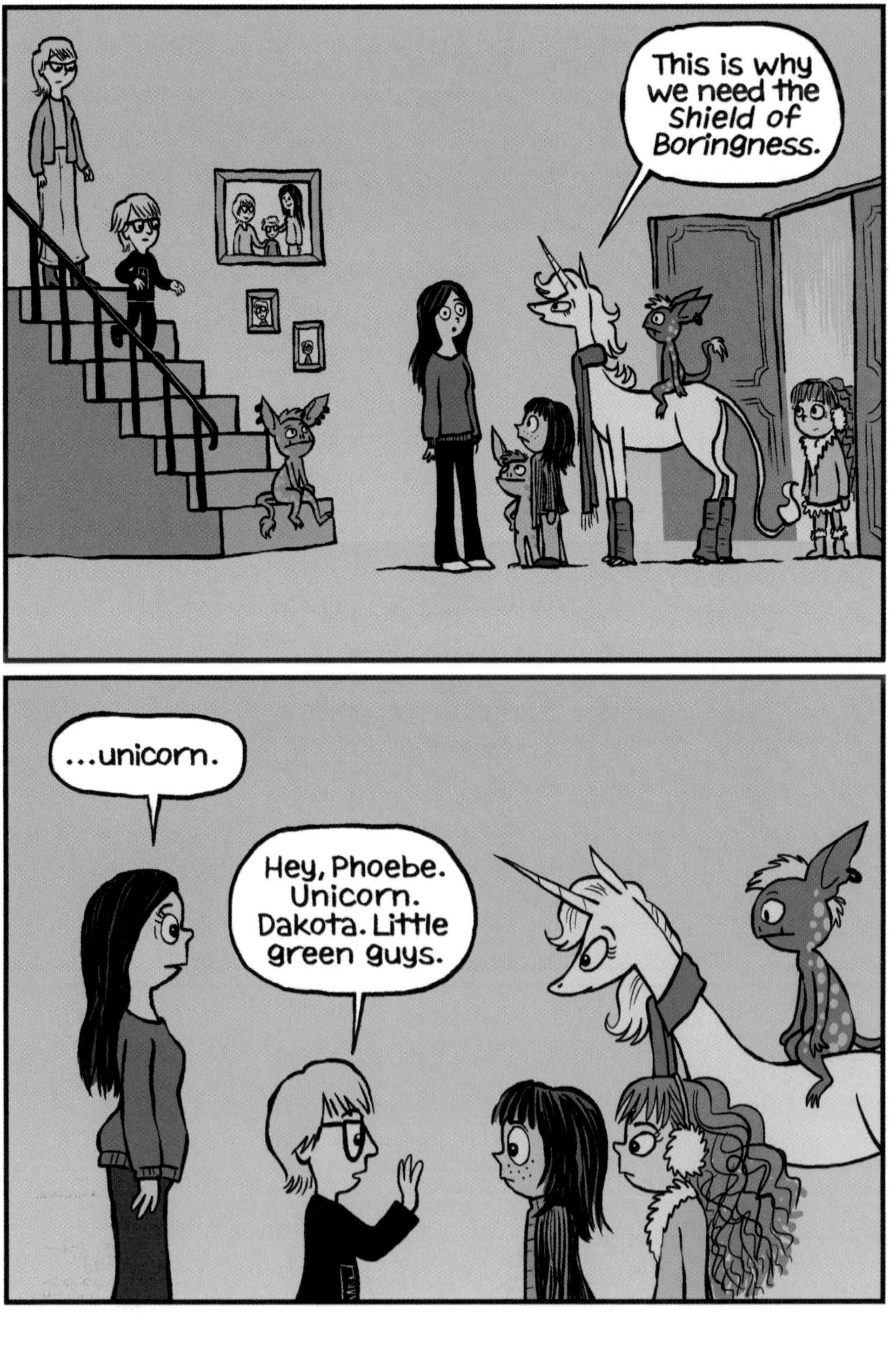
This is why we need the Shield of Boringness.
...unicorn.
Hey, Phoebe. Unicorn. Dakota. Little green guys.

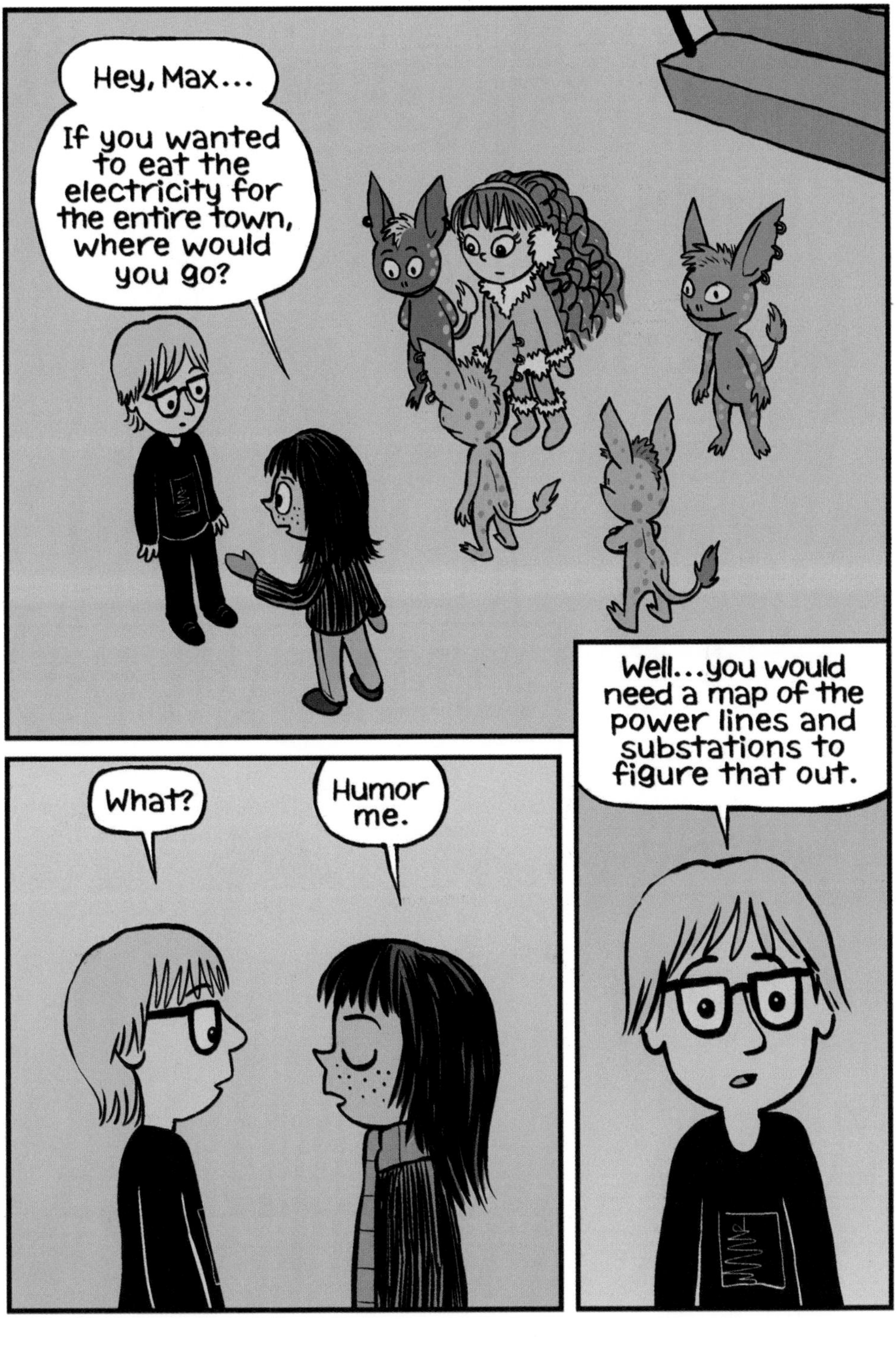
Hey, Max...
If you wanted to eat the electricity for the entire town, where would you go?
What?
Humor me.
Well...you would need a map of the power lines and substations to figure that out.

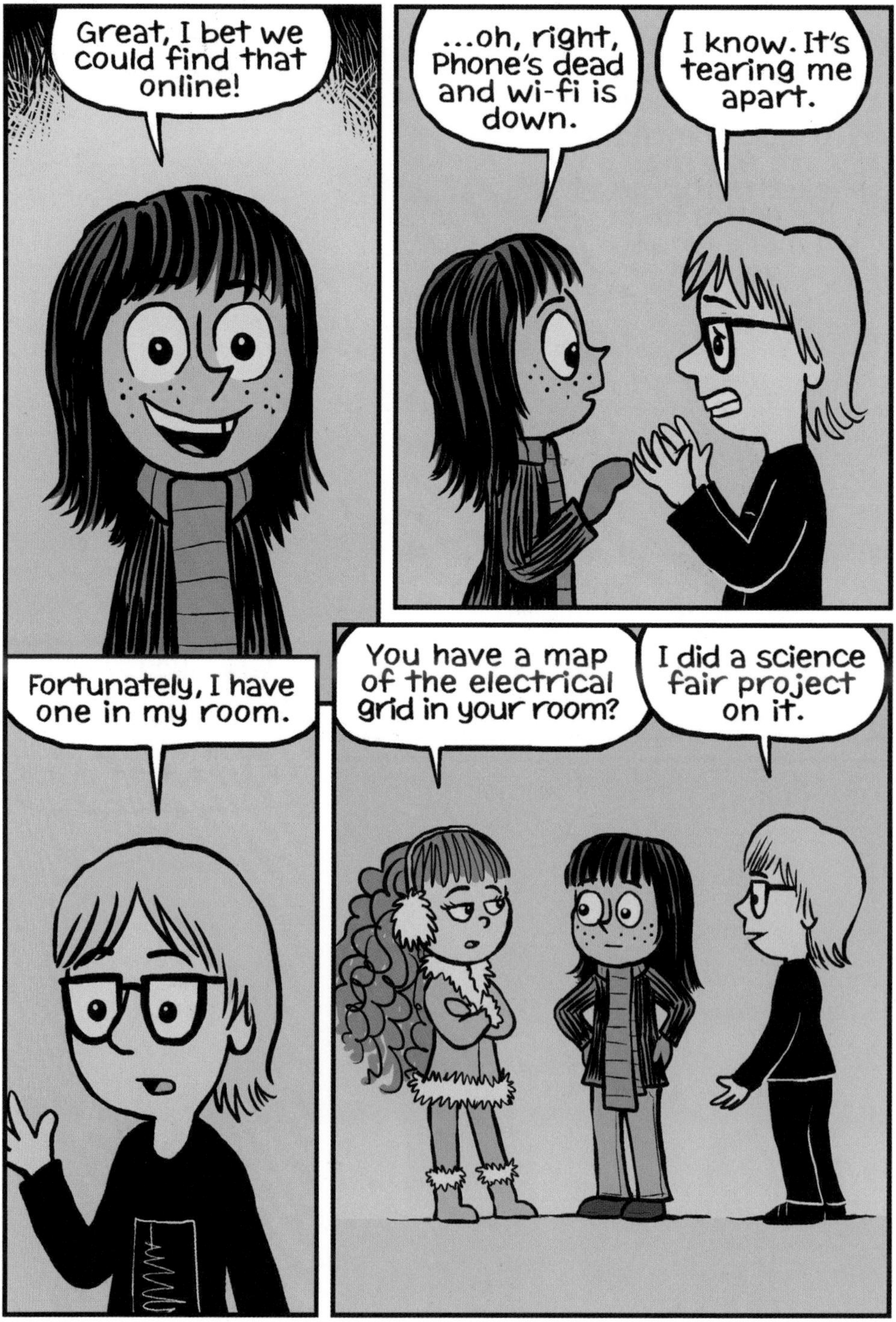

Great, I bet we could find that online!
...oh, right, Phone's dead and wi-fi is down.
I know. It's tearing me apart.
Fortunately, I have one in my room.
You have a map of the electrical grid in your room?
I did a science fair project on it.

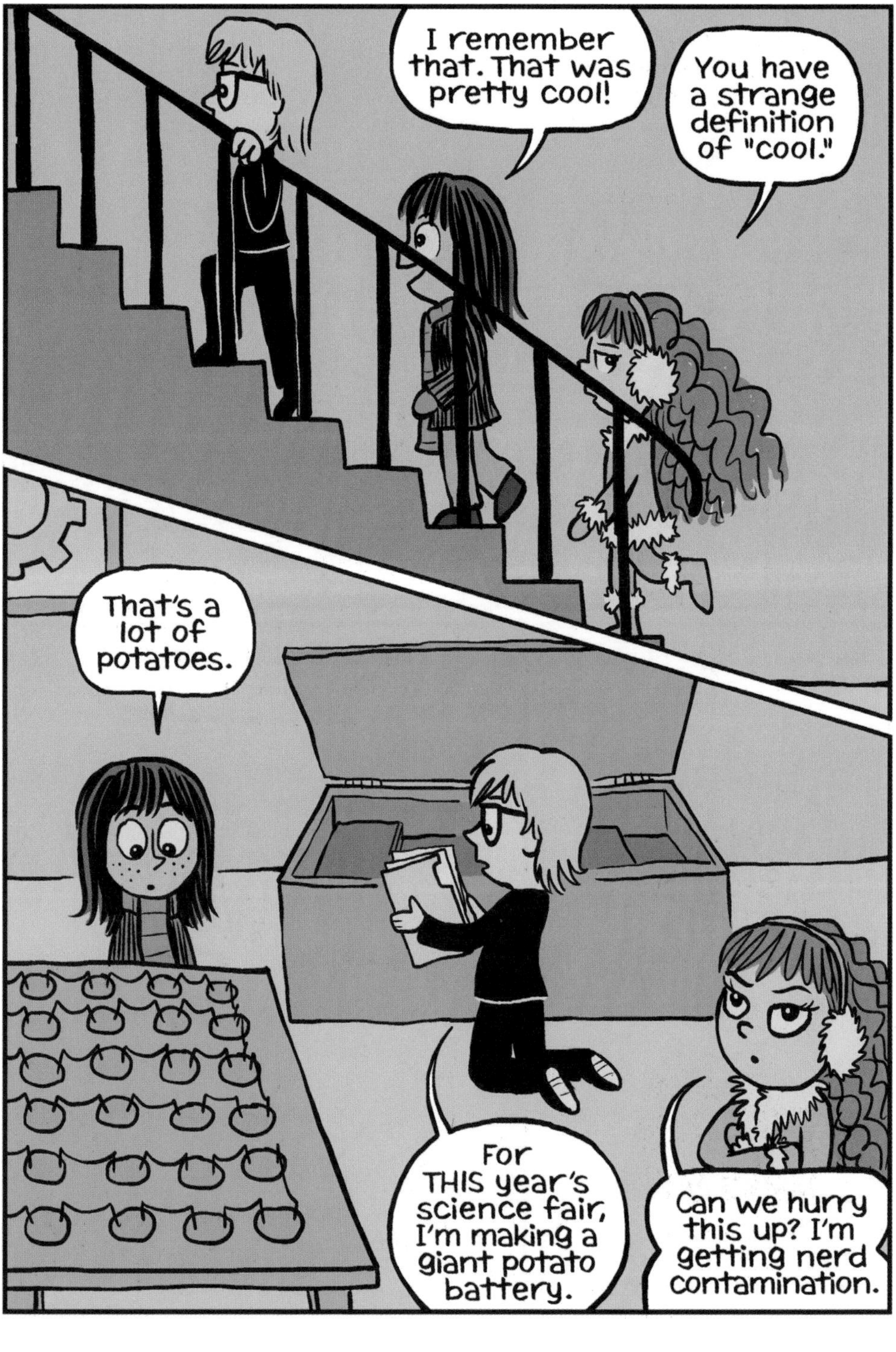
I remember that. That was pretty cool!
You have a strange definition of "cool."
That's a lot of potatoes.
For THIS year's science fair, I'm making a giant potato battery.
Can we hurry this up? I'm getting nerd contamination.

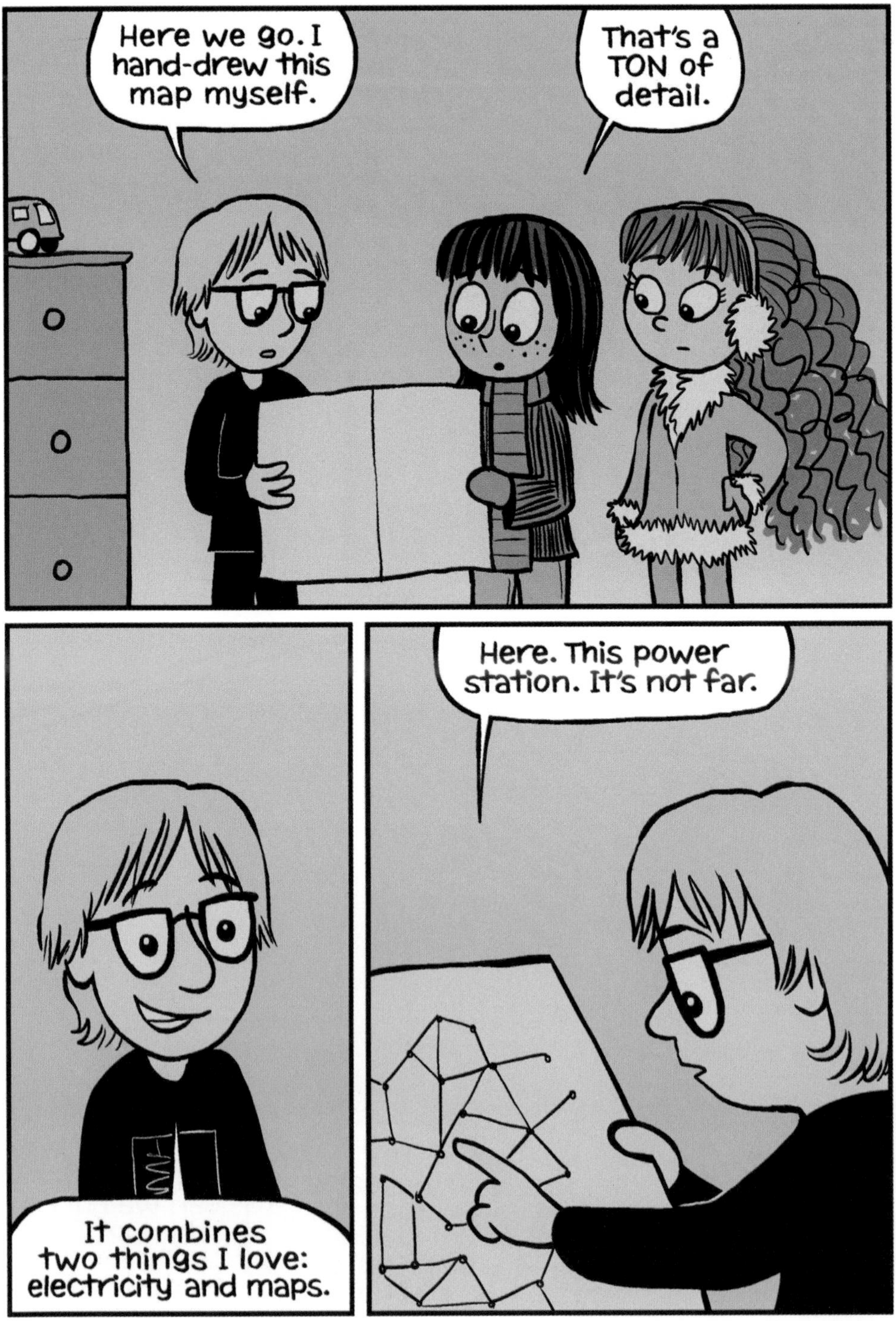

Here we go. I hand-drew this map myself.
That's a TON of detail.
It combines two things I love: electricity and maps.
Here. This power station. It's not far.

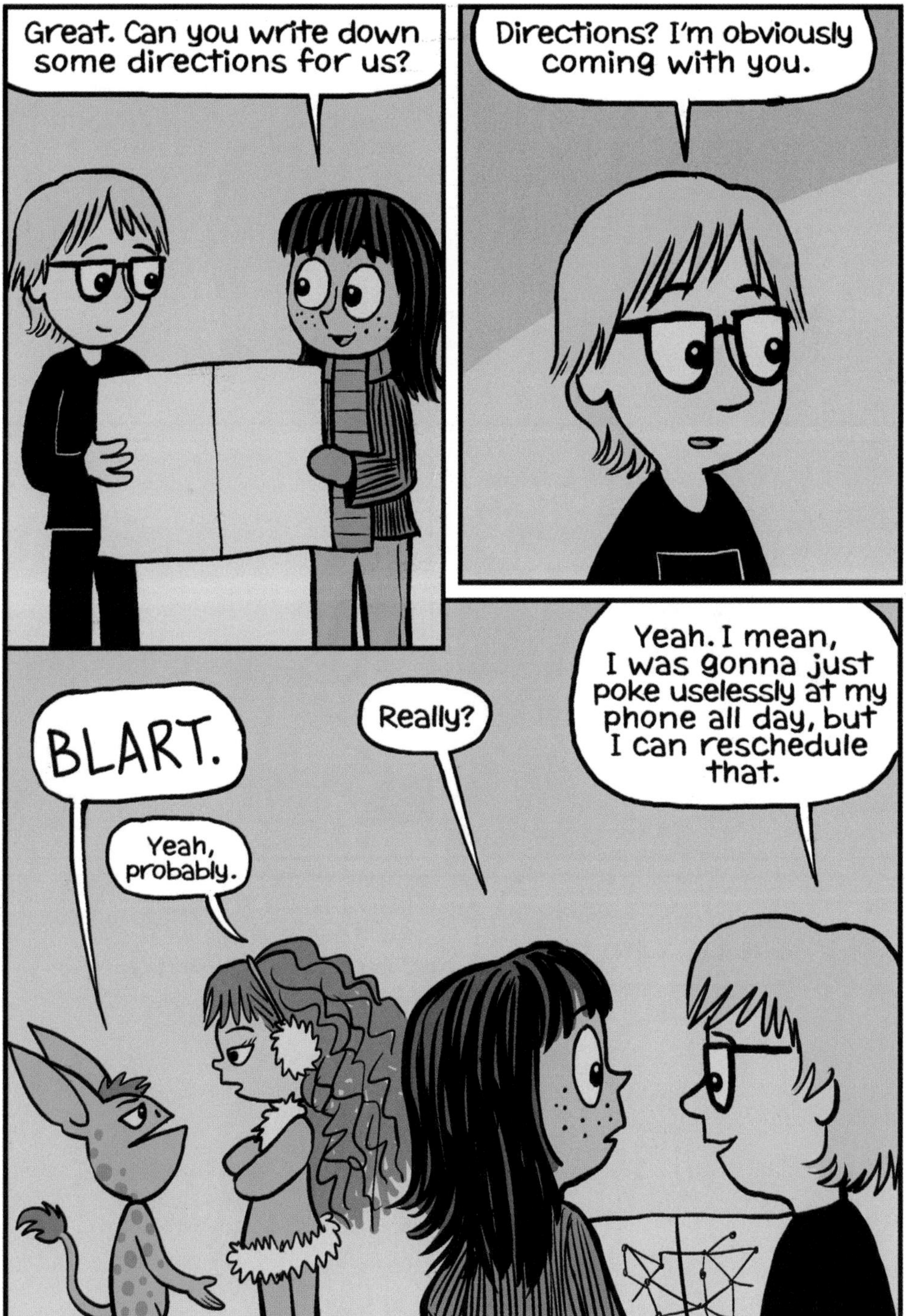
Great. Can you write down some directions for us?
Directions? I'm obviously coming with you.
BLART.
Yeah, probably.
Really?
Yeah. I mean, I was gonna just poke uselessly at my phone all day, but I can reschedule that.

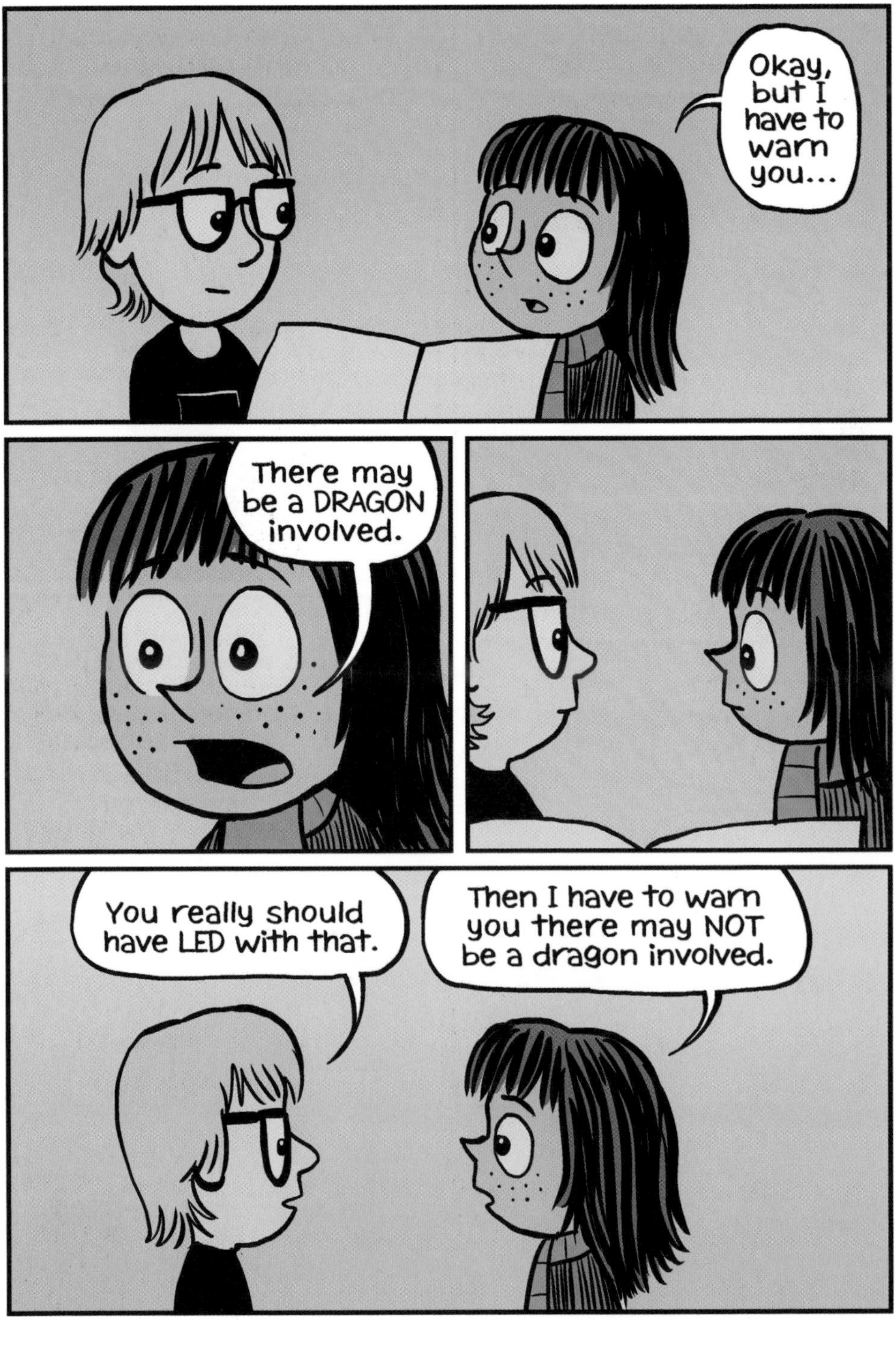
Okay, but I have to warn you...
There may be a DRAGON involved.
You really should have LED with that.
Then I have to warn you there may NOT be a dragon involved.

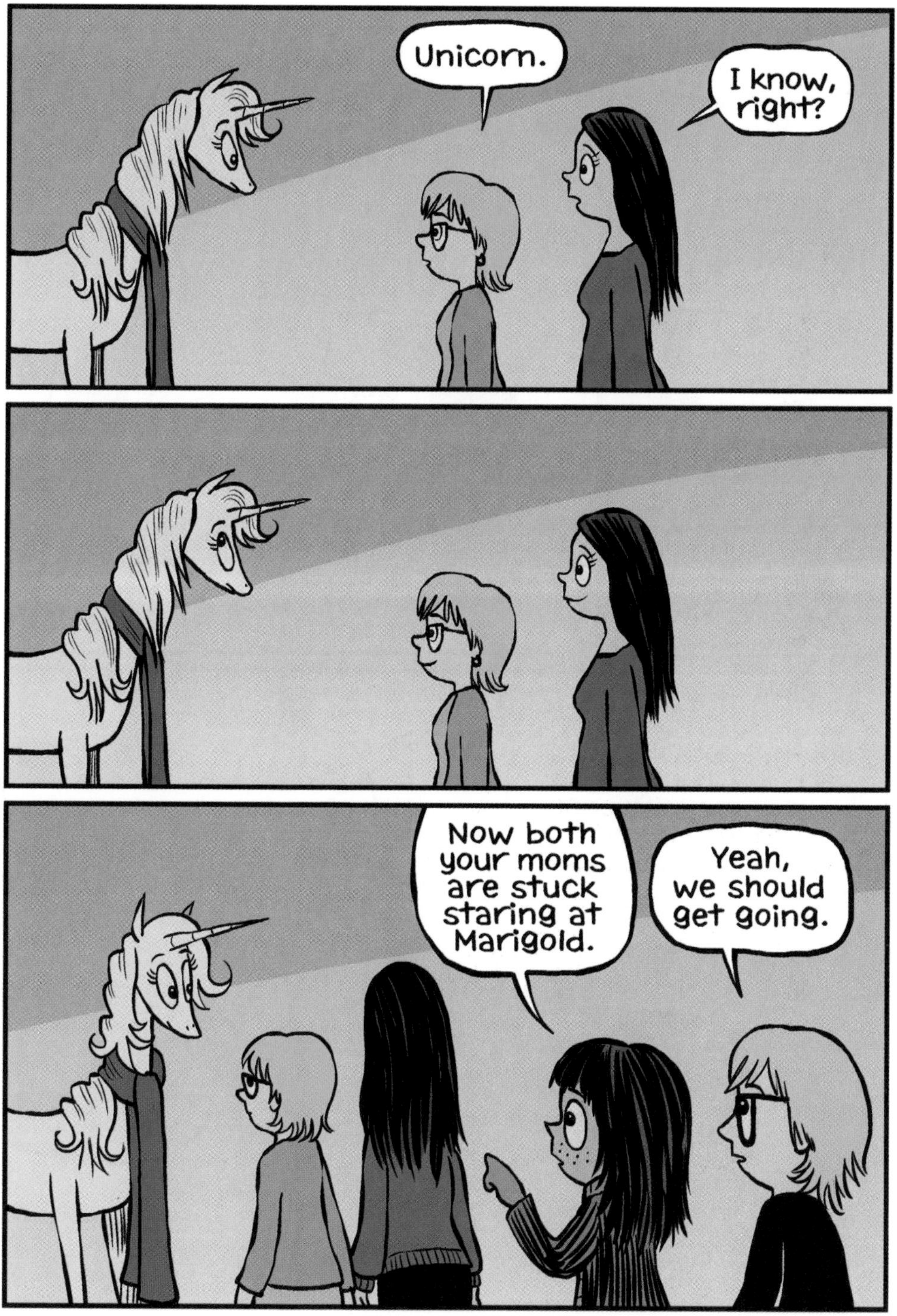
Unicorn.
I know, right?
Now both your moms are stuck staring at Marigold.
Yeah, we should get going.

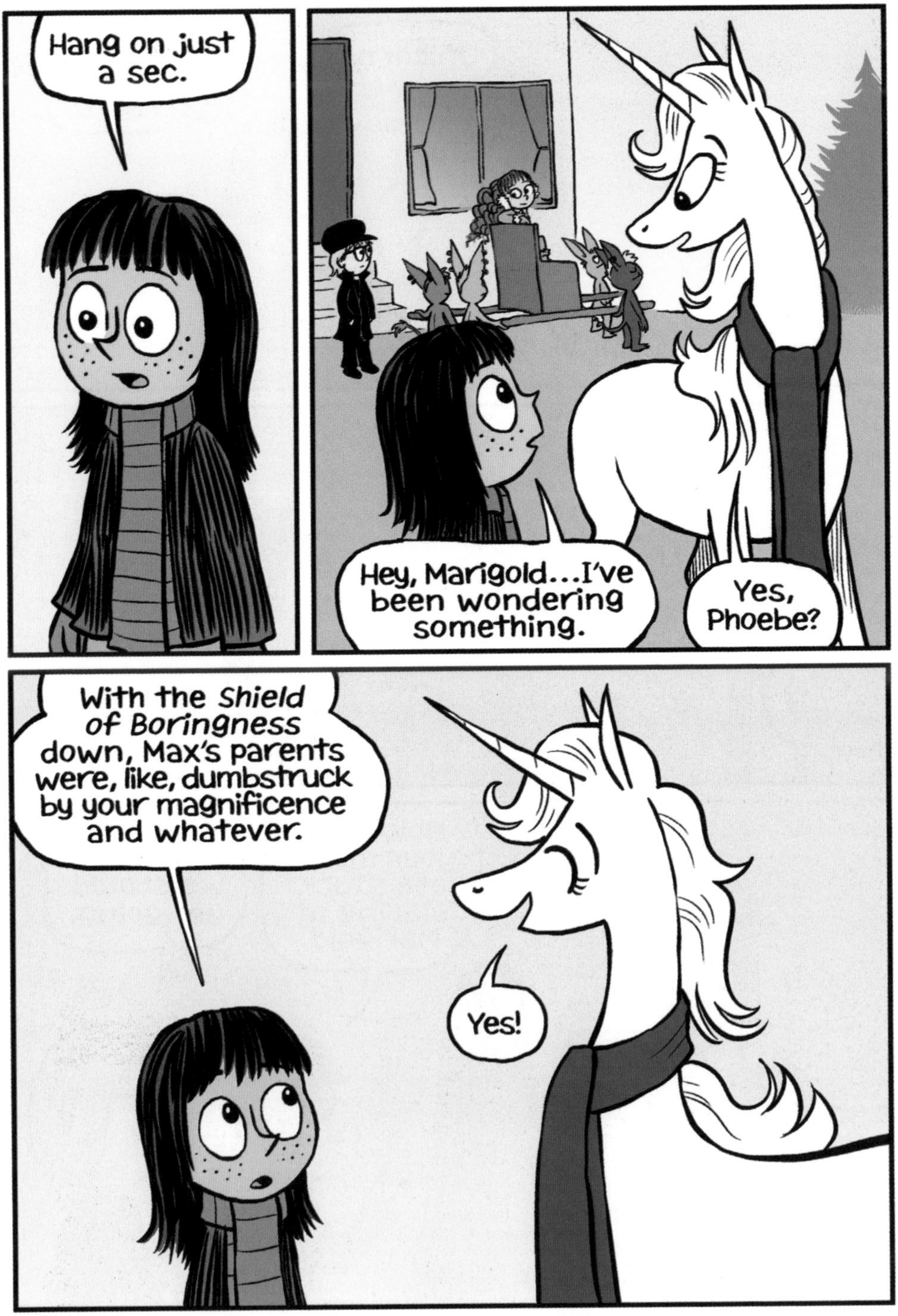
Hang on just a sec.
Hey, Marigold...I've been wondering something.
Yes, Phoebe?
With the *Shield of Boringness* down, Max's parents were, like, dumbstruck by your magnificence and whatever.
Yes!

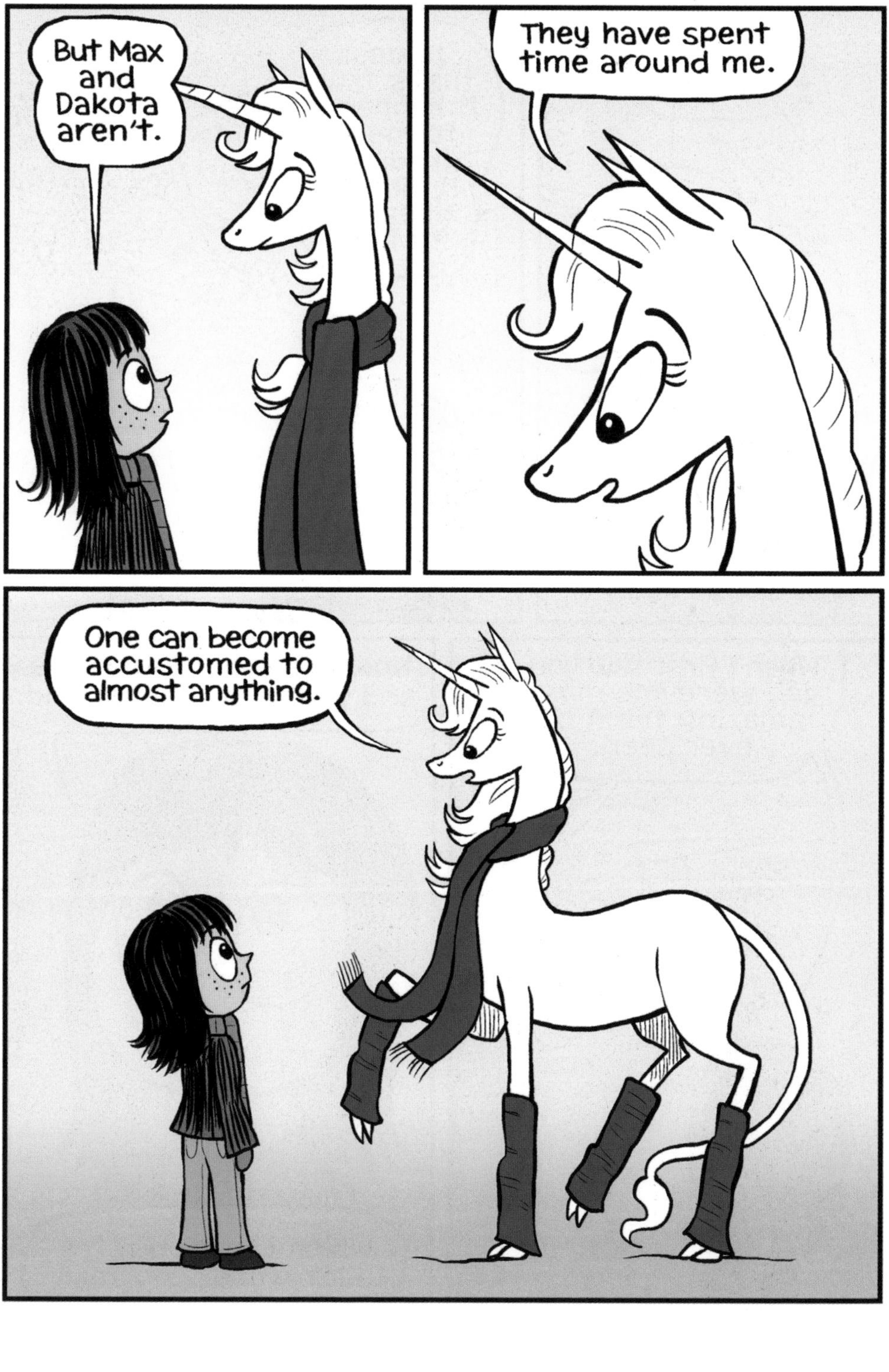
But Max and Dakota aren't.
They have spent time around me.
One can become accustomed to almost anything.

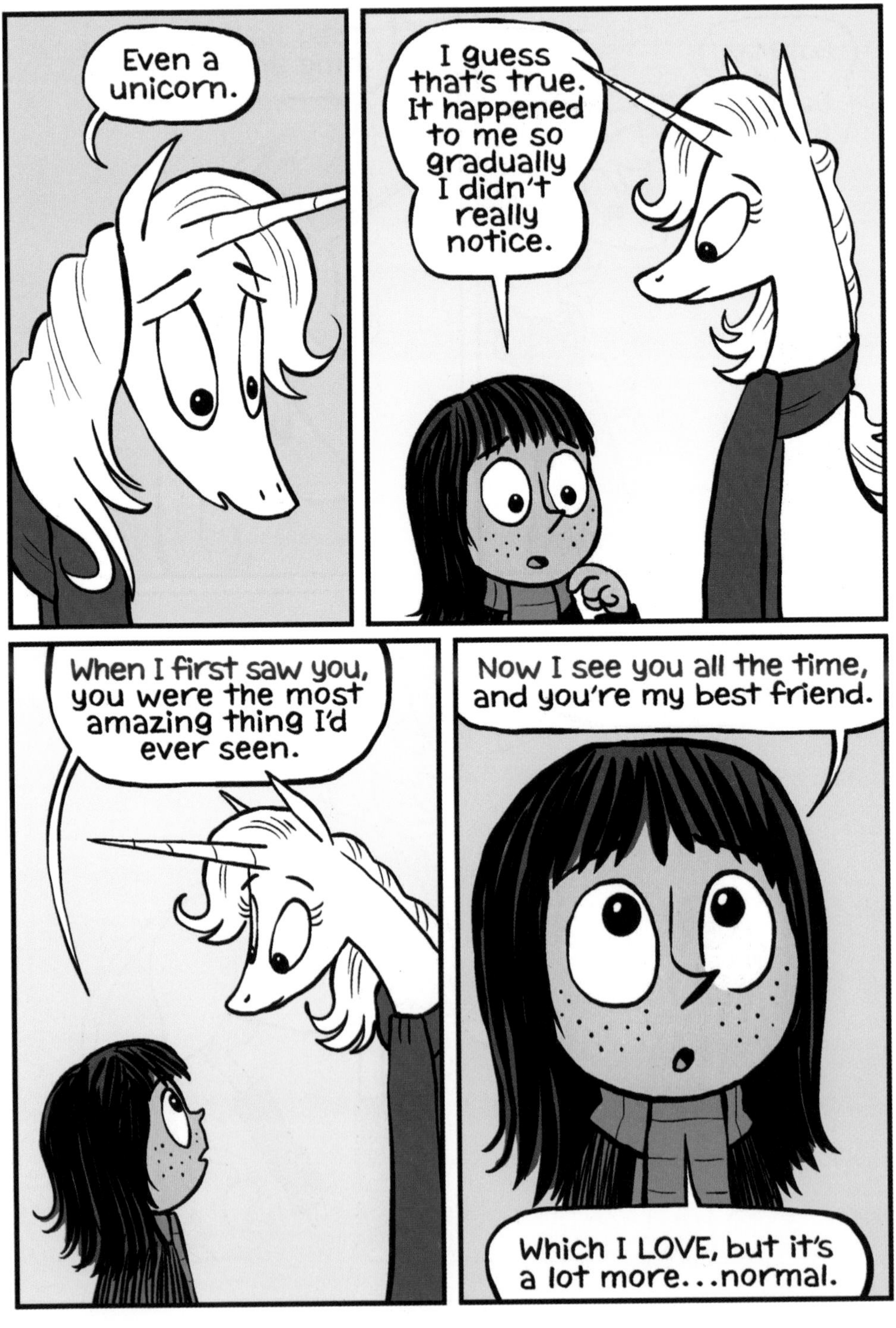
Even a unicorn.
I guess that's true. It happened to me so gradually I didn't really notice.
When I first saw you, you were the most amazing thing I'd ever seen.
Now I see you all the time, and you're my best friend.
Which I LOVE, but it's a lot more...normal.

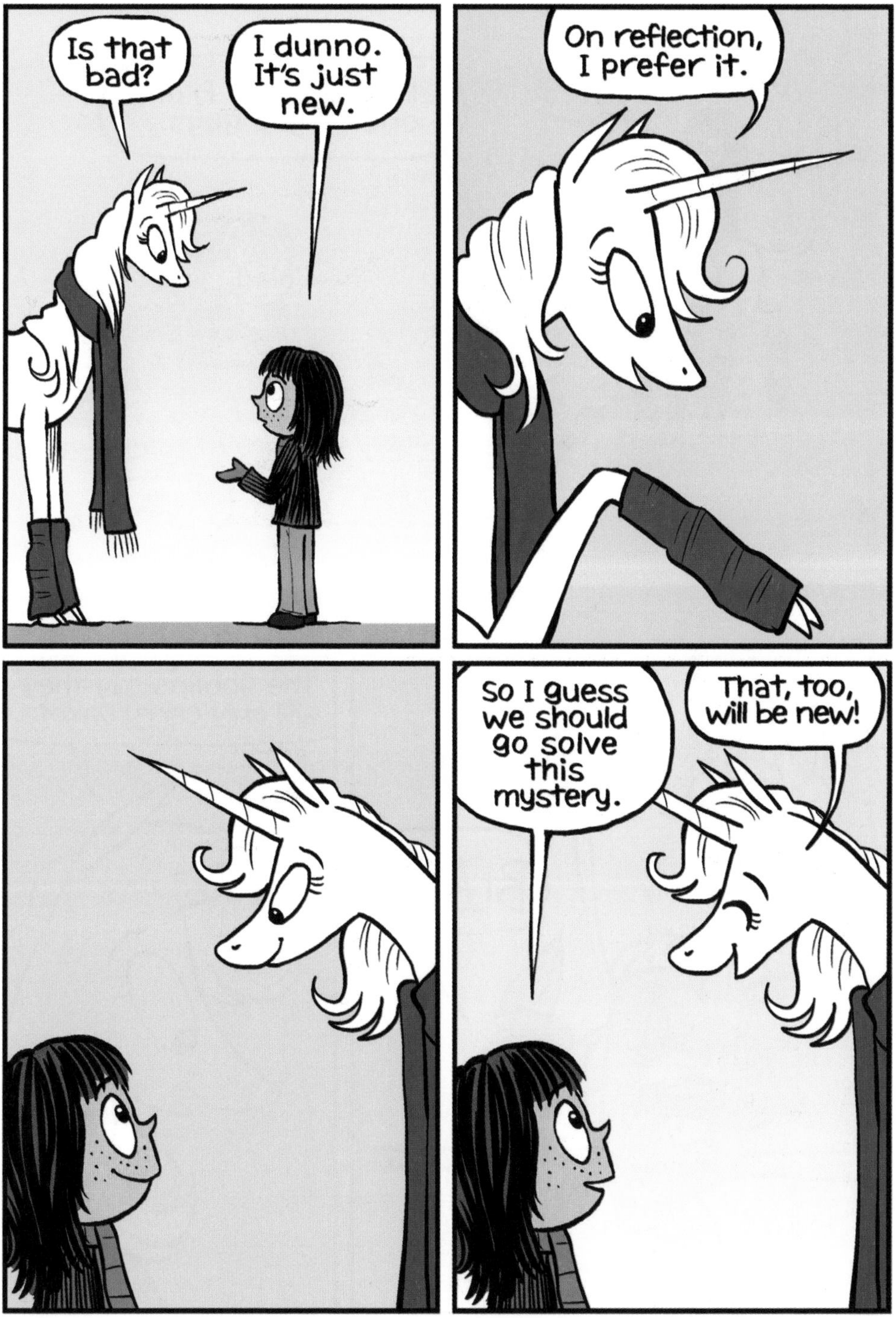

Is that bad?
I dunno. It's just new.
On reflection, I prefer it.
So I guess we should go solve this mystery.
That, too, will be new!

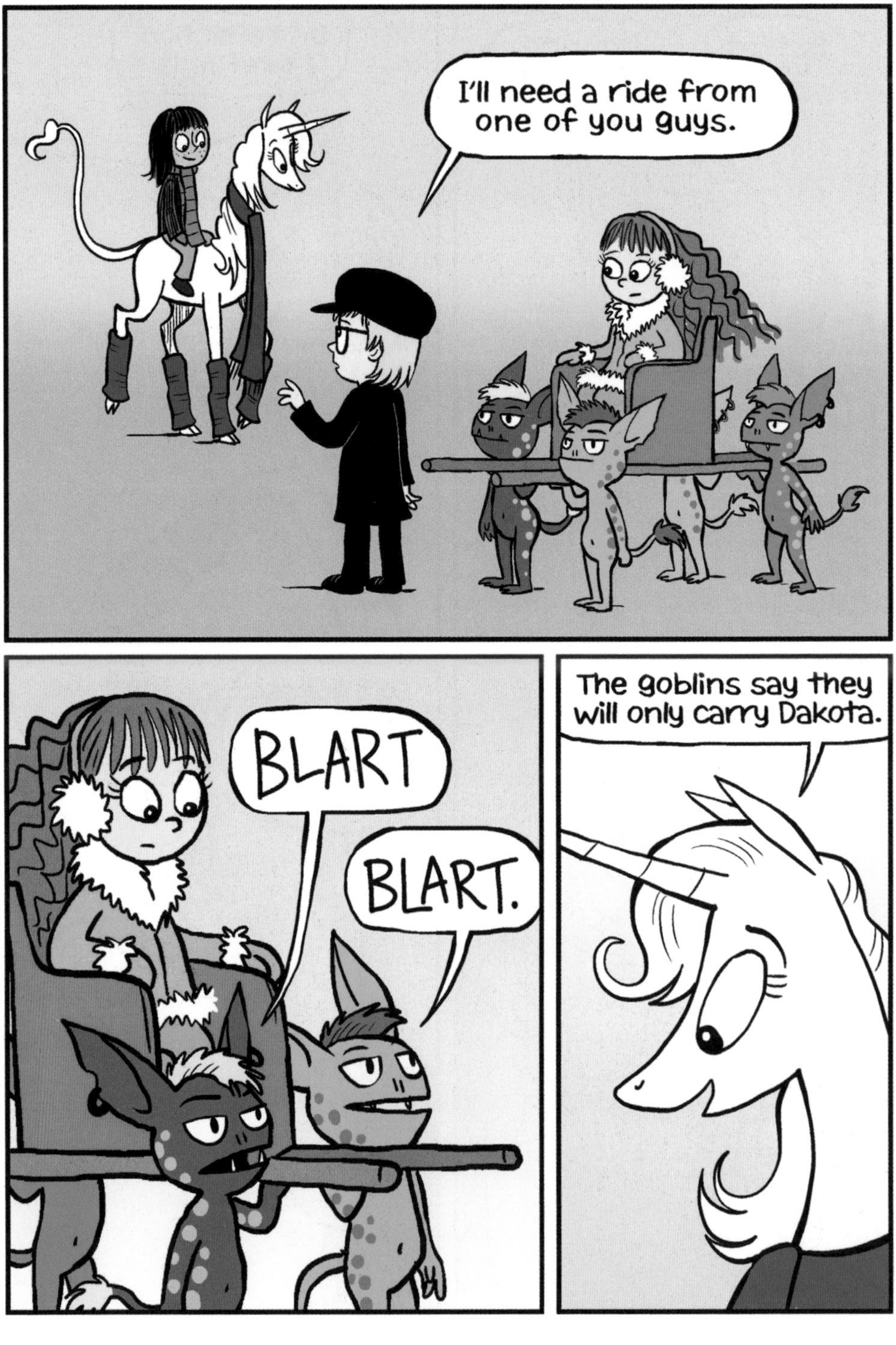
I'll need a ride from one of you guys.
BLART
BLART.
The goblins say they will only carry Dakota.

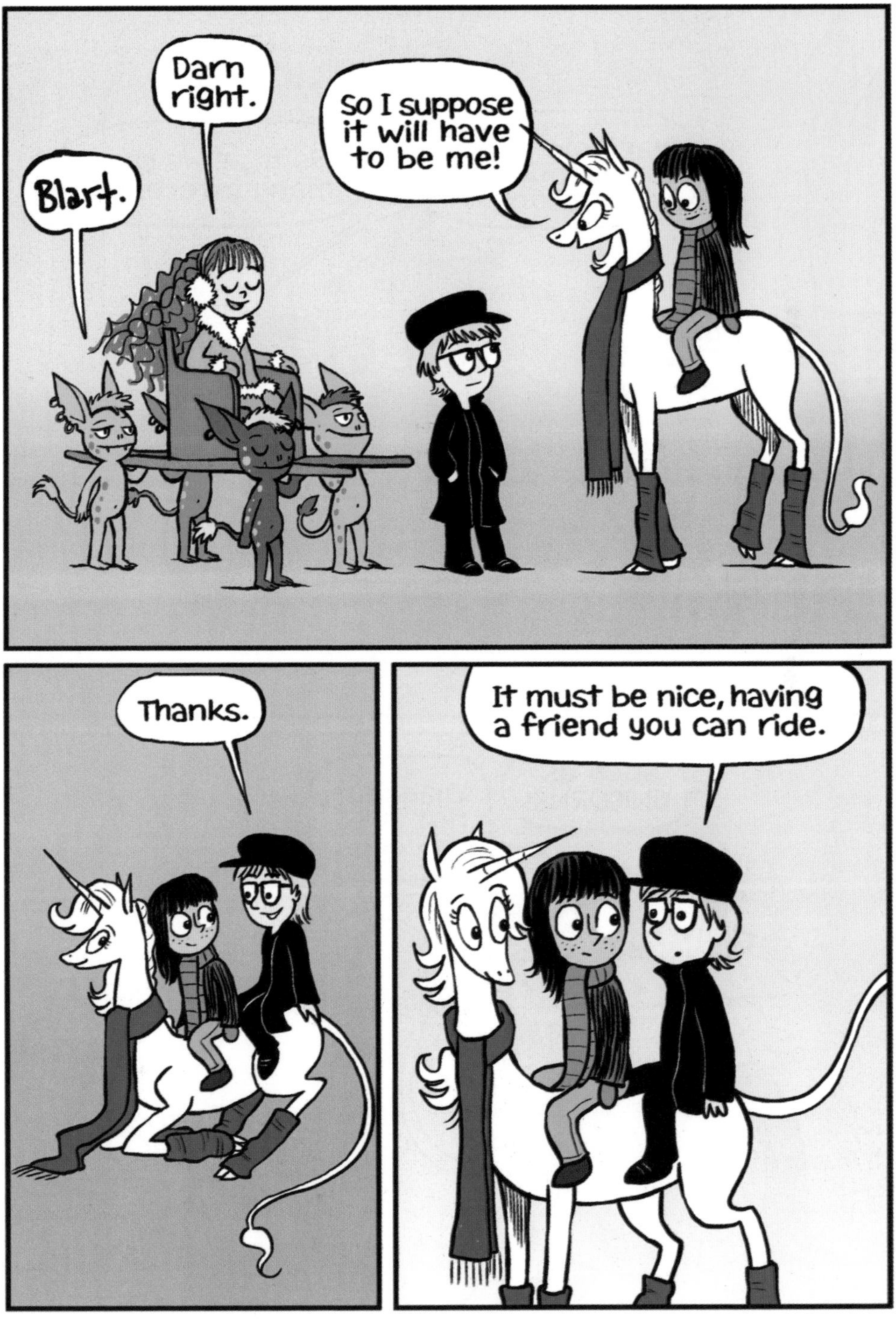
Blart.
Darn right.
So I suppose it will have to be me!
Thanks.
It must be nice, having a friend you can ride.

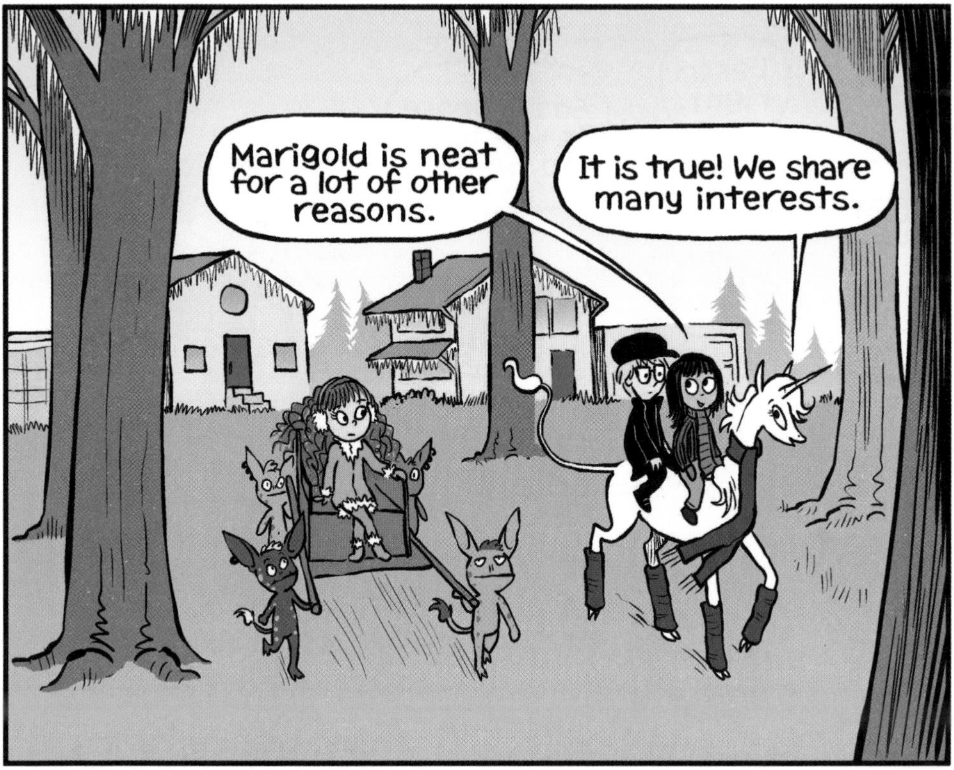
Marigold is neat for a lot of other reasons.
It is true! We share many interests.

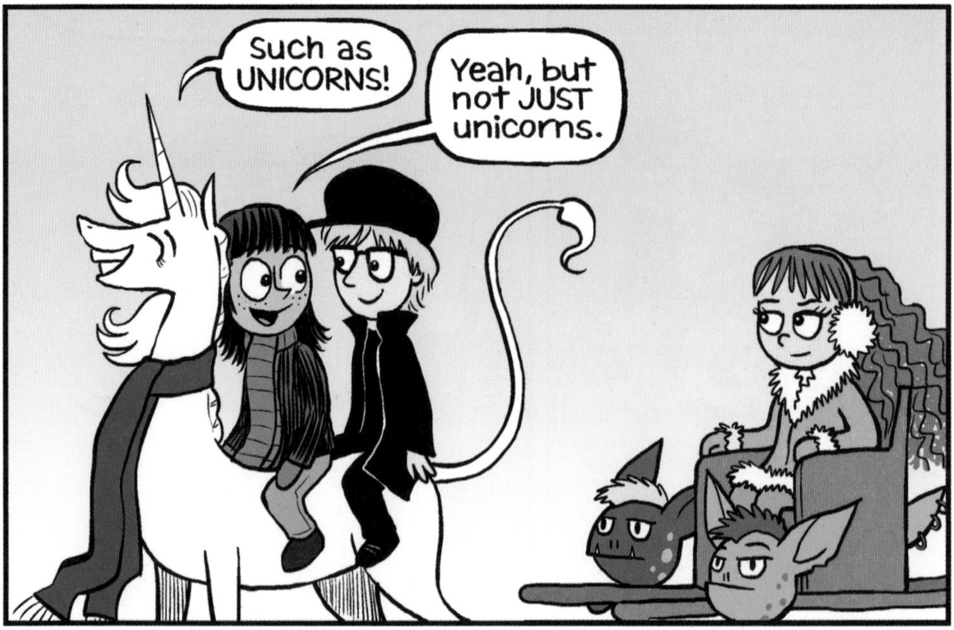
Such as UNICORNS!
Yeah, but not JUST unicorns.

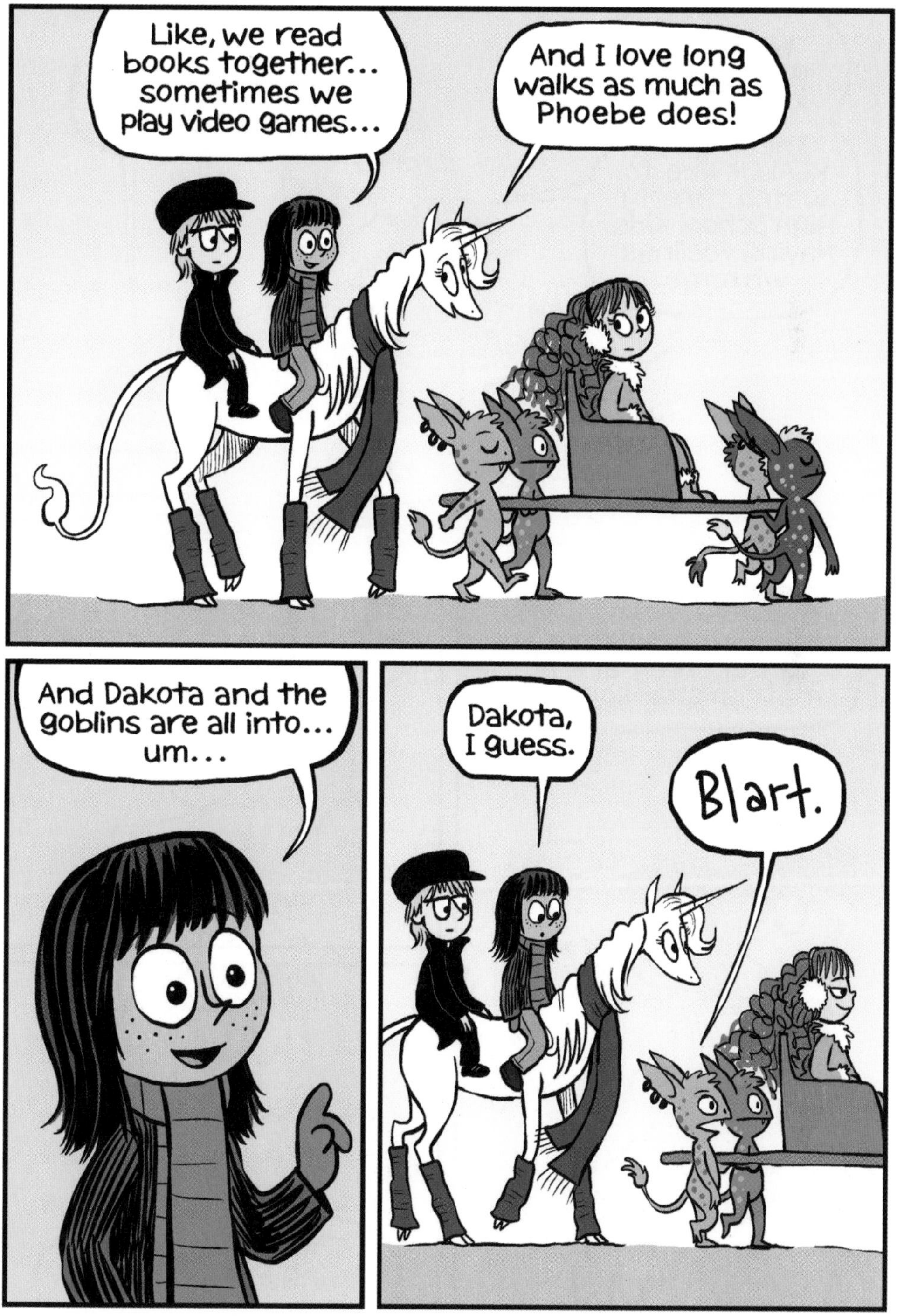
Like, we read books together... sometimes we play video games...
And I love long walks as much as Phoebe does!
And Dakota and the goblins are all into... um...
Dakota, I guess.
Blart.

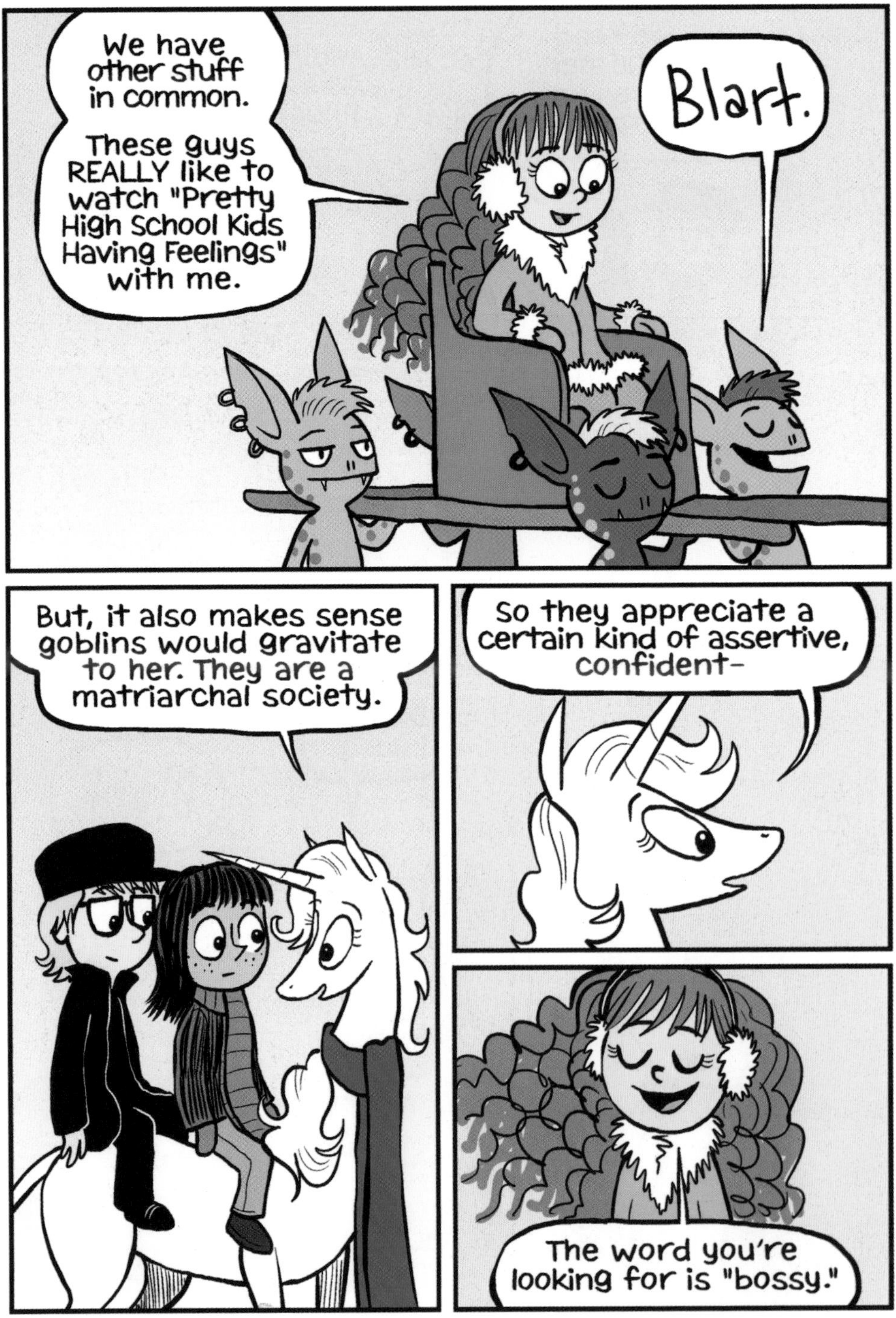
We have other stuff in common.
These guys REALLY like to watch "Pretty High School Kids Having Feelings" with me.
Blart.
But, it also makes sense goblins would gravitate to her. They are a matriarchal society.
So they appreciate a certain kind of assertive, confident-
The word you're looking for is "bossy."

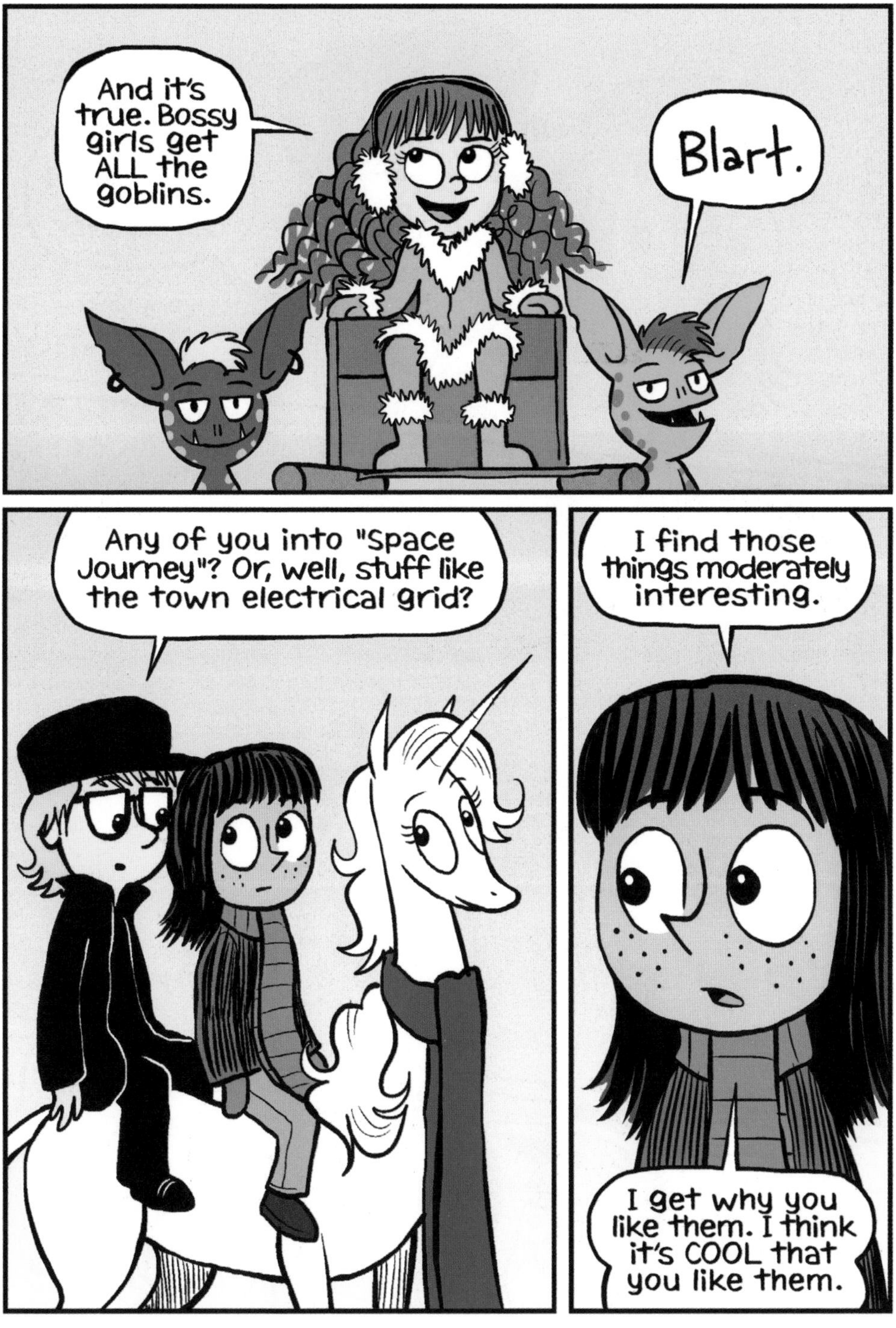
And it's true. Bossy girls get ALL the goblins.
Blart.
Any of you into "Space Journey"? Or, well, stuff like the town electrical grid?
I find those things moderately interesting.
I get why you like them. I think it's COOL that you like them.

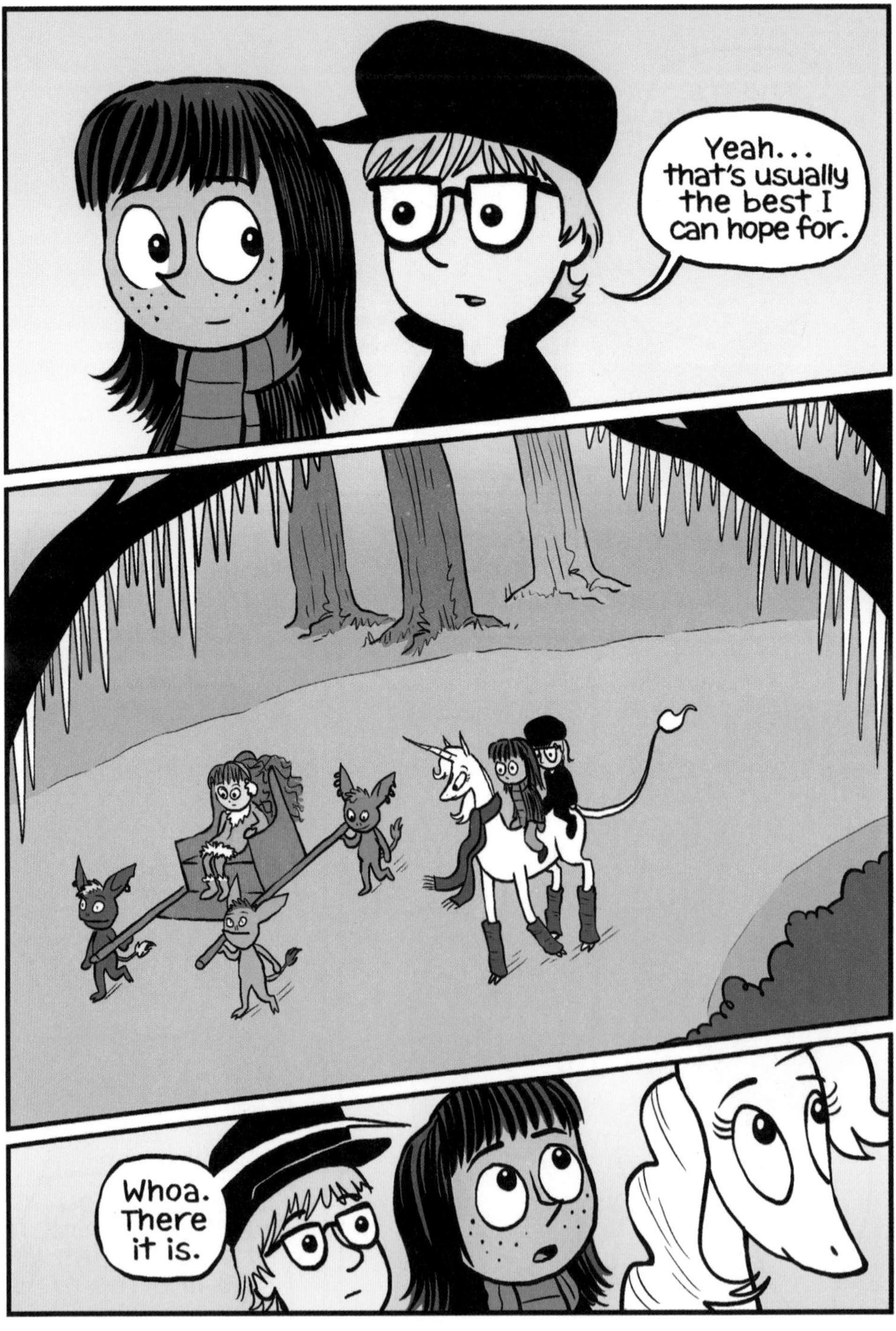
Yeah... that's usually the best I can hope for.
Whoa. There it is.

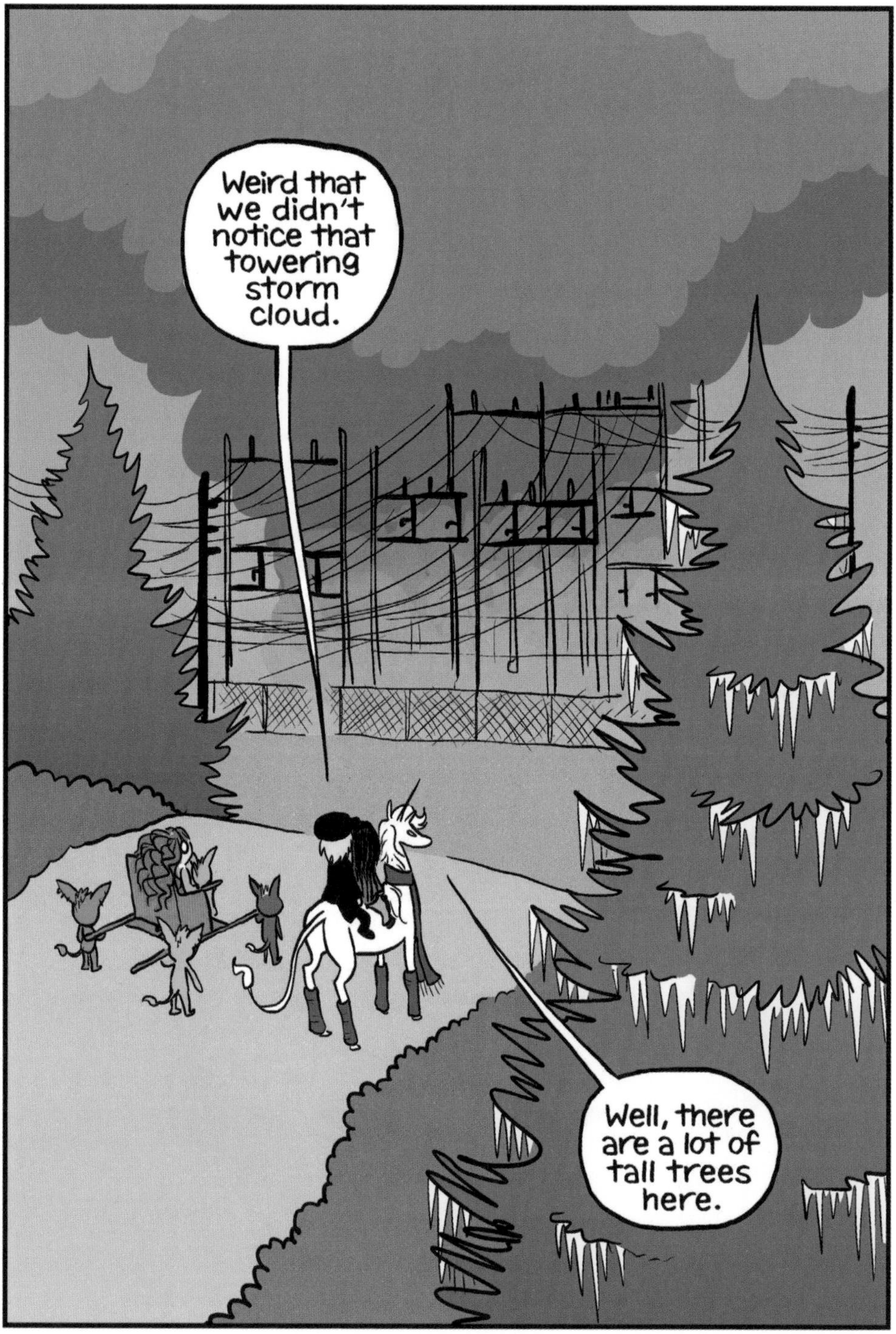
Weird that we didn't notice that towering storm cloud.
Well, there are a lot of tall trees here.

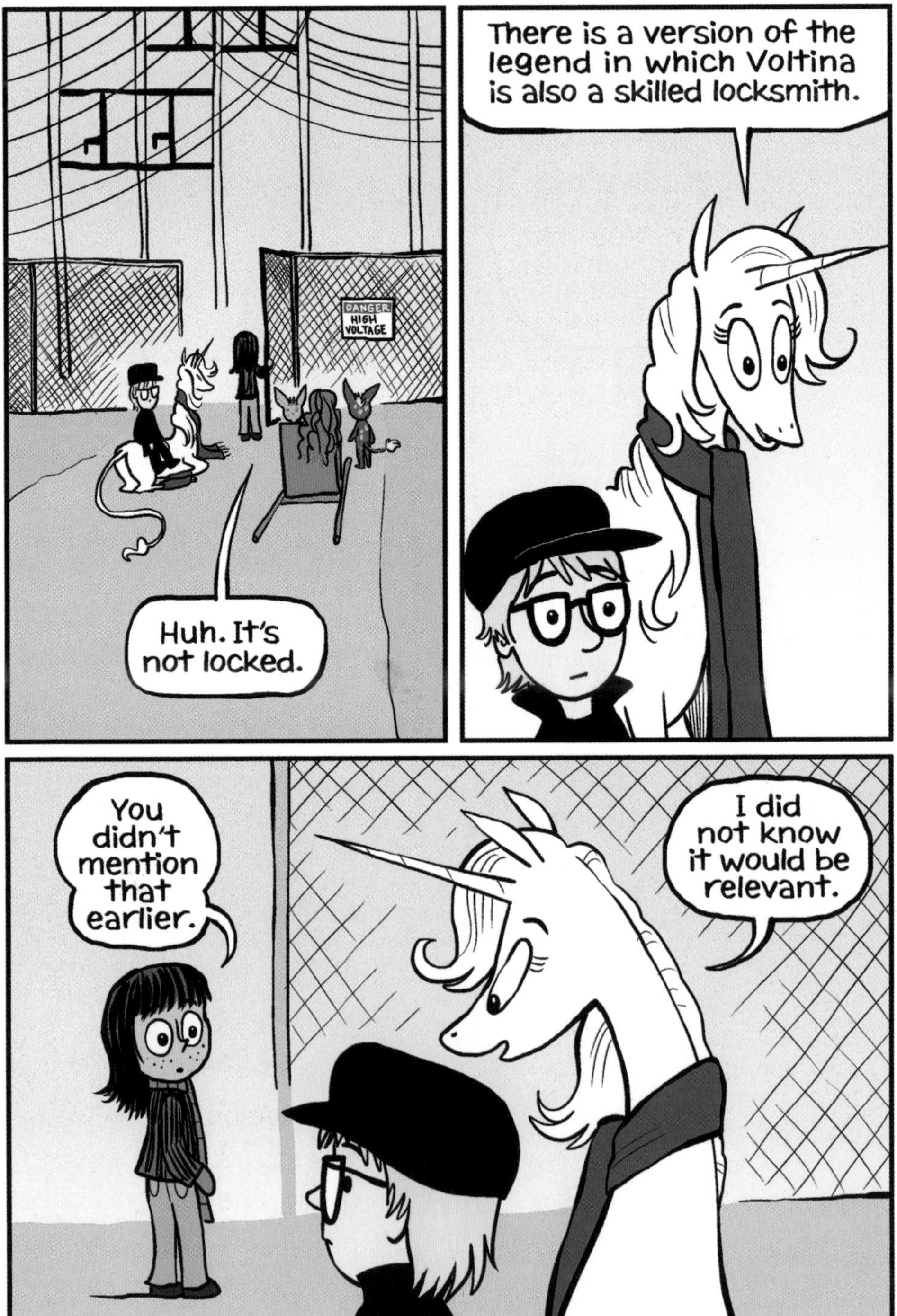

DANGER
HIGH VOLTAGE
Huh. It's not locked.
There is a version of the legend in which Voltina is also a skilled locksmith.
You didn't mention that earlier.
I did not know it would be relevant.

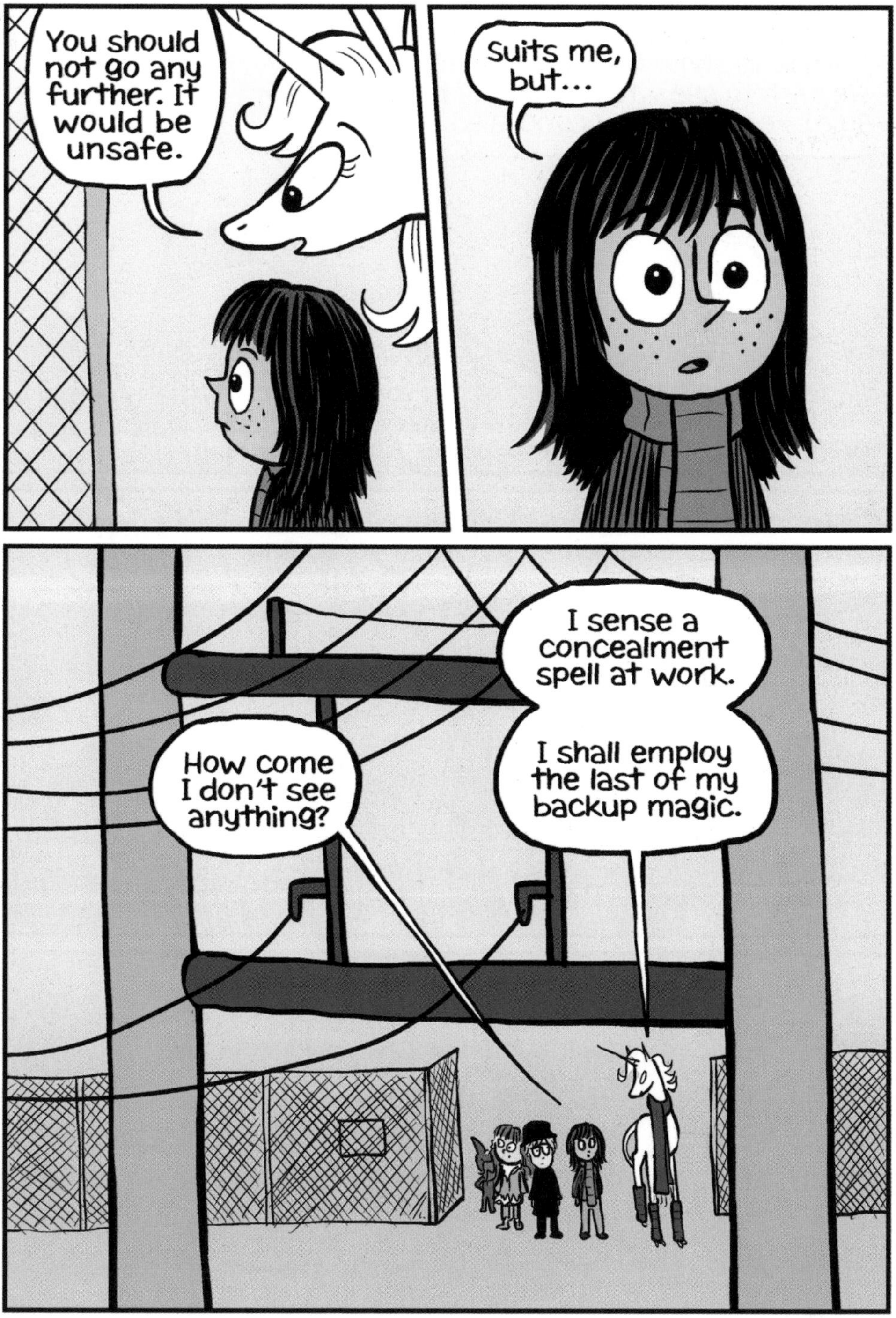

You should not go any further. It would be unsafe.
Suits me, but...
I sense a concealment spell at work.
I shall employ the last of my backup magic.
How come I don't see anything?

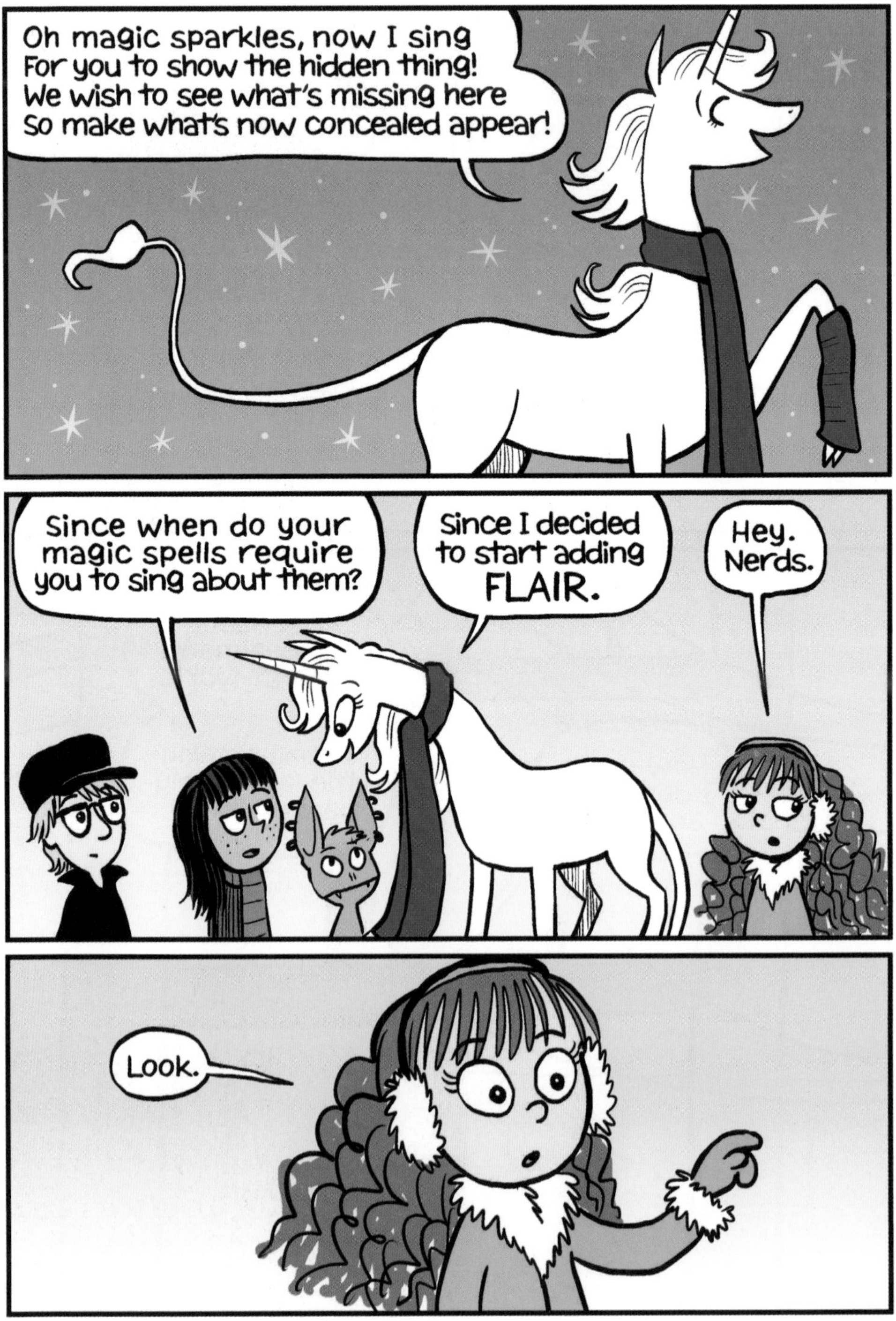
Oh magic sparkles, now I sing
For you to show the hidden thing!
We wish to see what's missing here
So make what's now concealed appear!
Since when do your magic spells require you to sing about them?
Since I decided to start adding FLAIR.
Hey. Nerds.
Look.

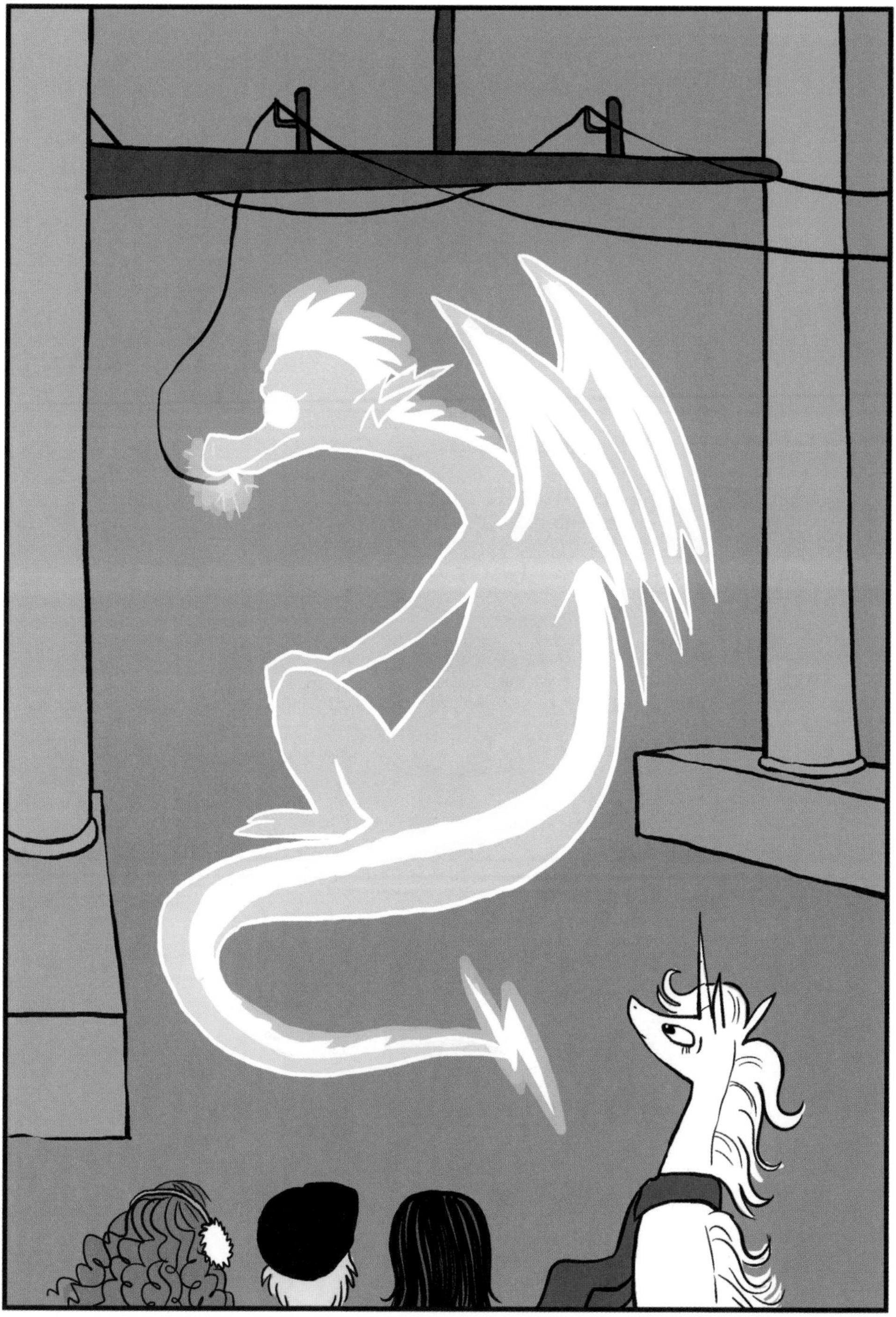

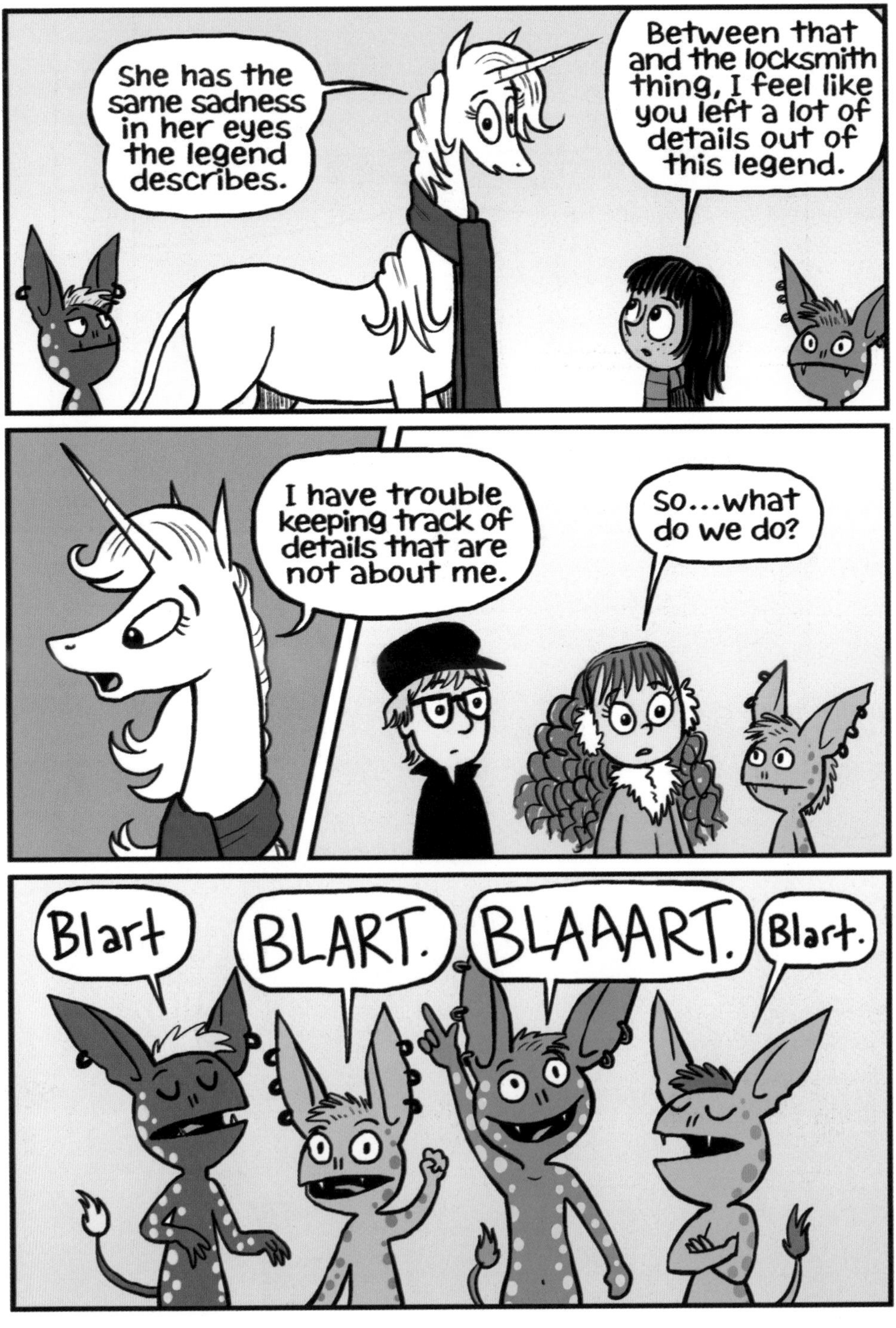
She has the same sadness in her eyes the legend describes.
Between that and the locksmith thing, I feel like you left a lot of details out of this legend.
I have trouble keeping track of details that are not about me.
So...what do we do?
Blart
BLART.
BLAAART.
Blart.

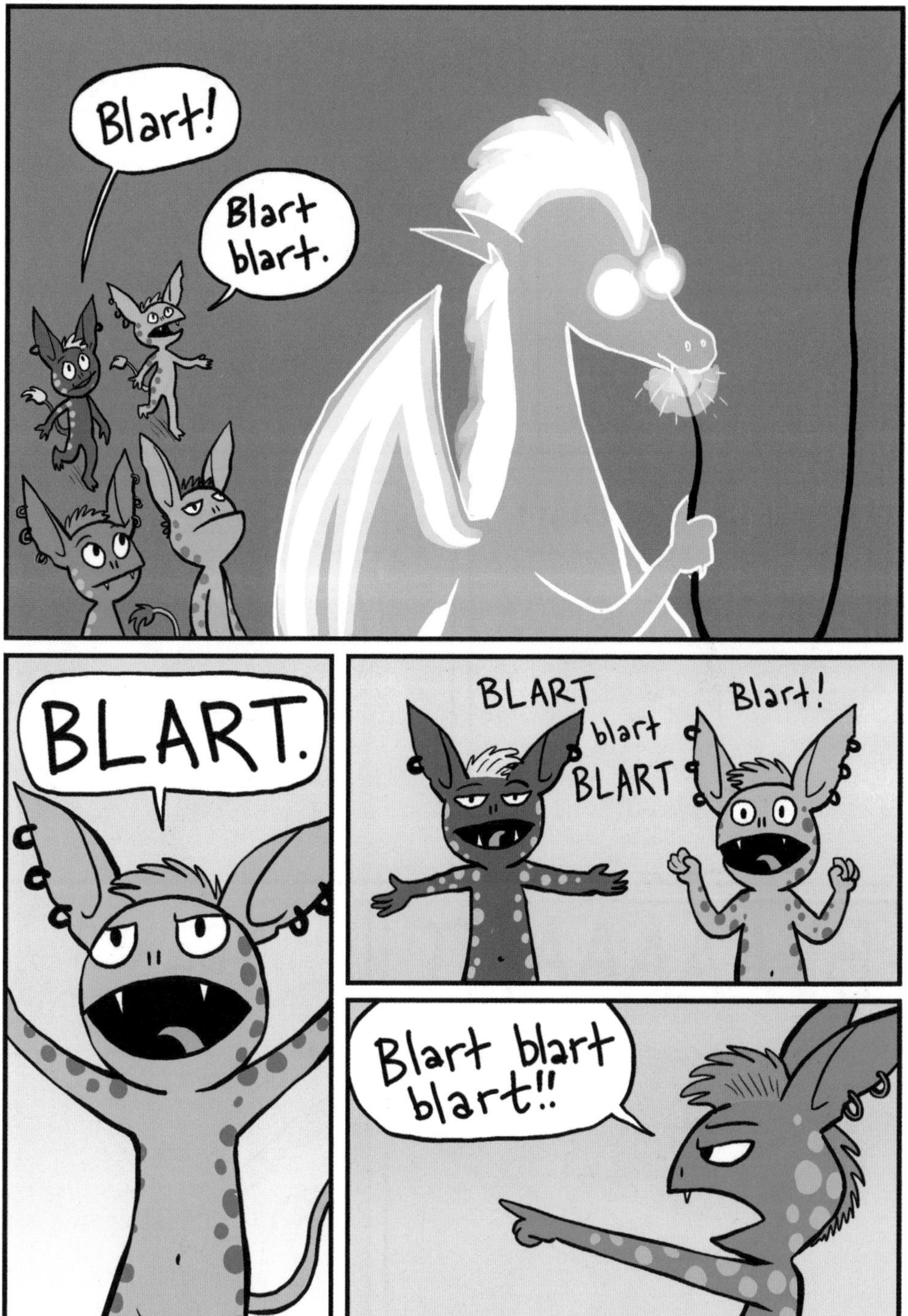
Blart!
Blart blart.
BLART.
BLART blart BLART
Blart!
Blart blart blart!!

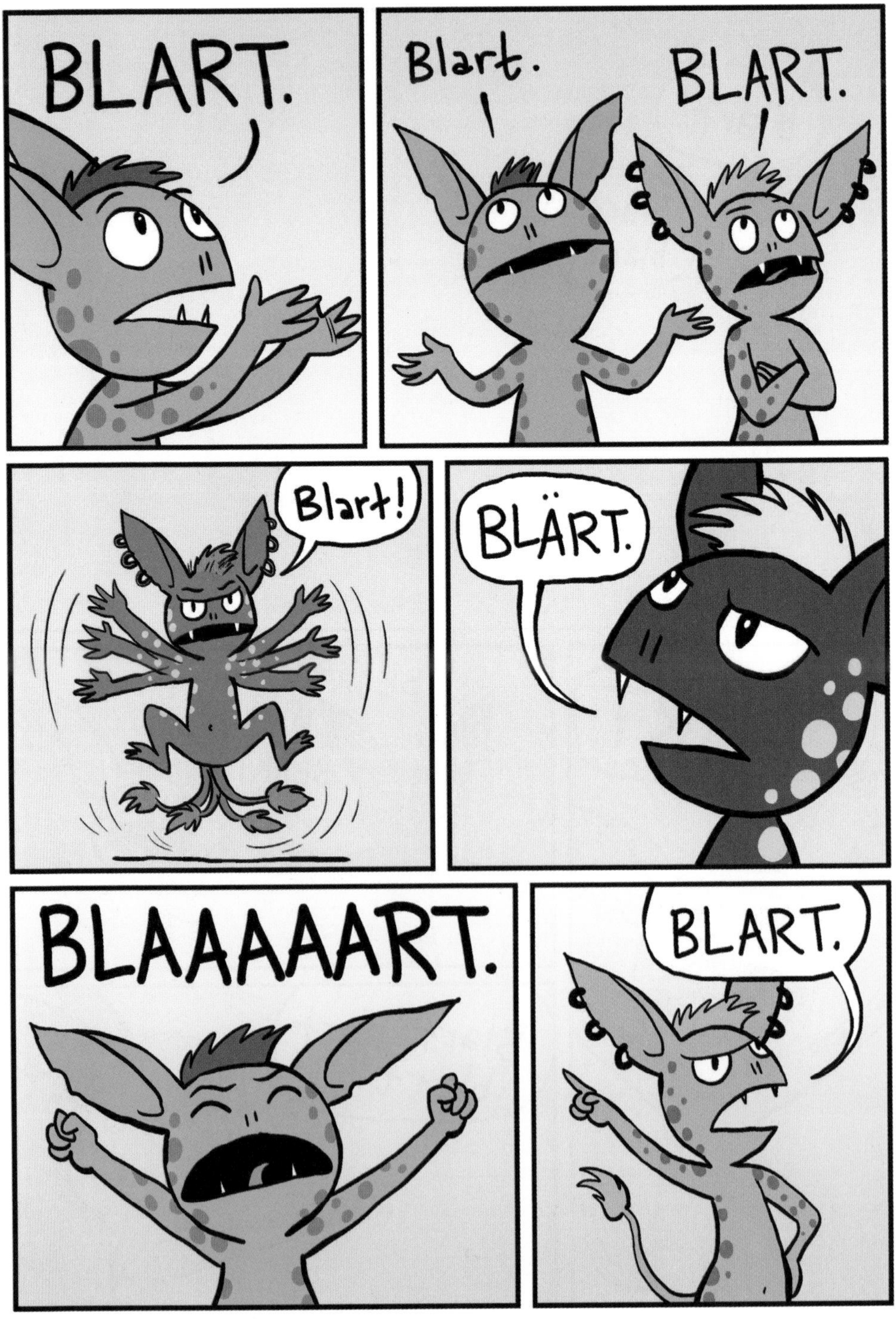
BLART.
Blart.
BLART.
Blart!
BLÄRT.
BLAAAAART.
BLART.

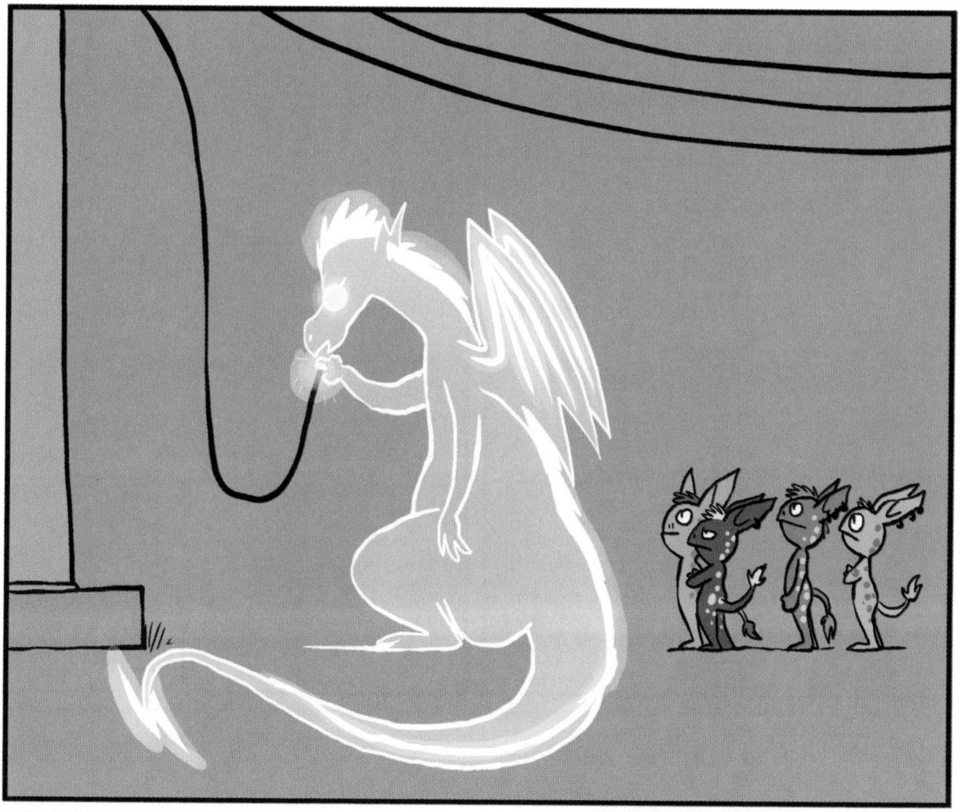

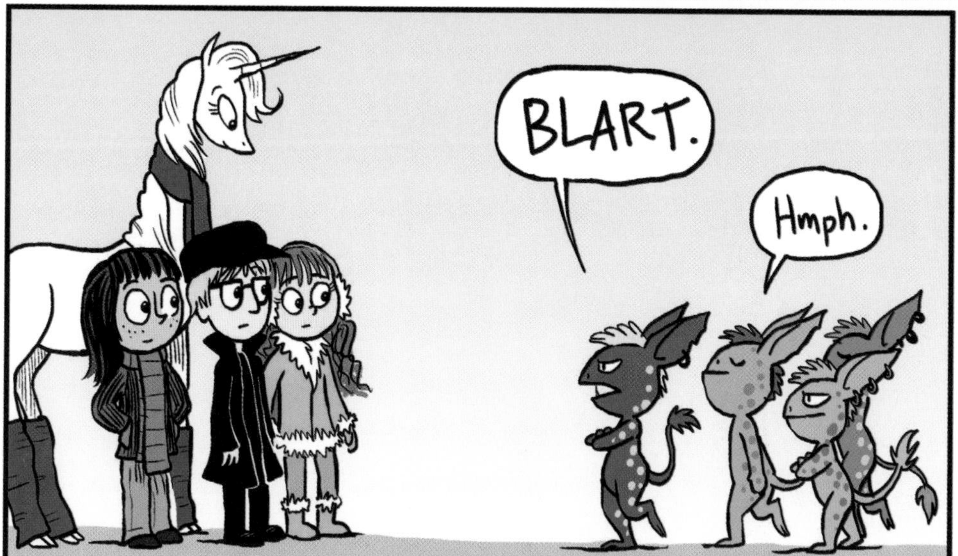
BLART.
Hmph.

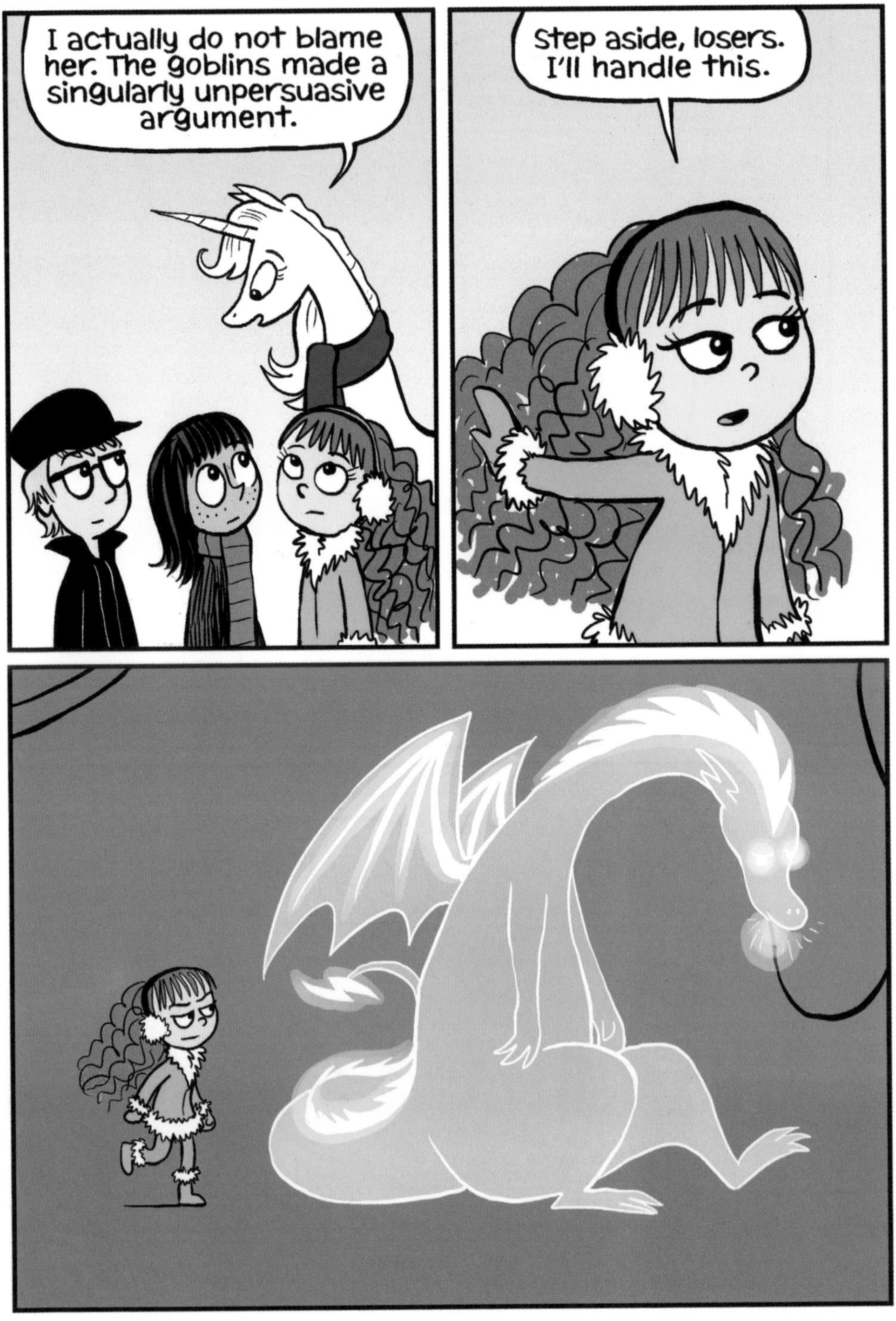
I actually do not blame her. The goblins made a singularly unpersuasive argument.
Step aside, losers. I'll handle this.

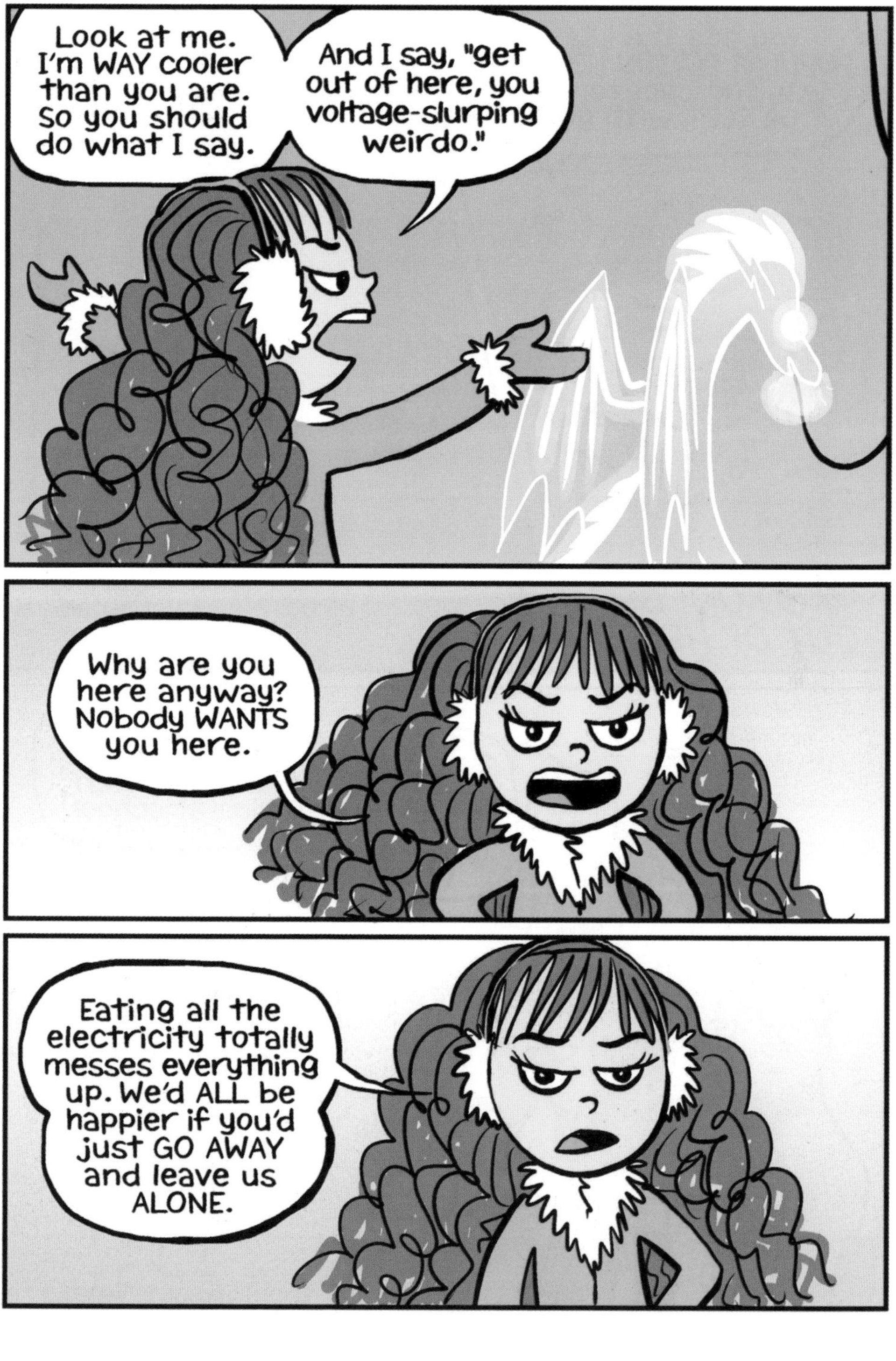
Look at me. I'm WAY cooler than you are. So you should do what I say.
And I say, "get out of here, you voltage-slurping weirdo."
Why are you here anyway? Nobody WANTS you here.
Eating all the electricity totally messes everything up. We'd ALL be happier if you'd just GO AWAY and leave us ALONE.

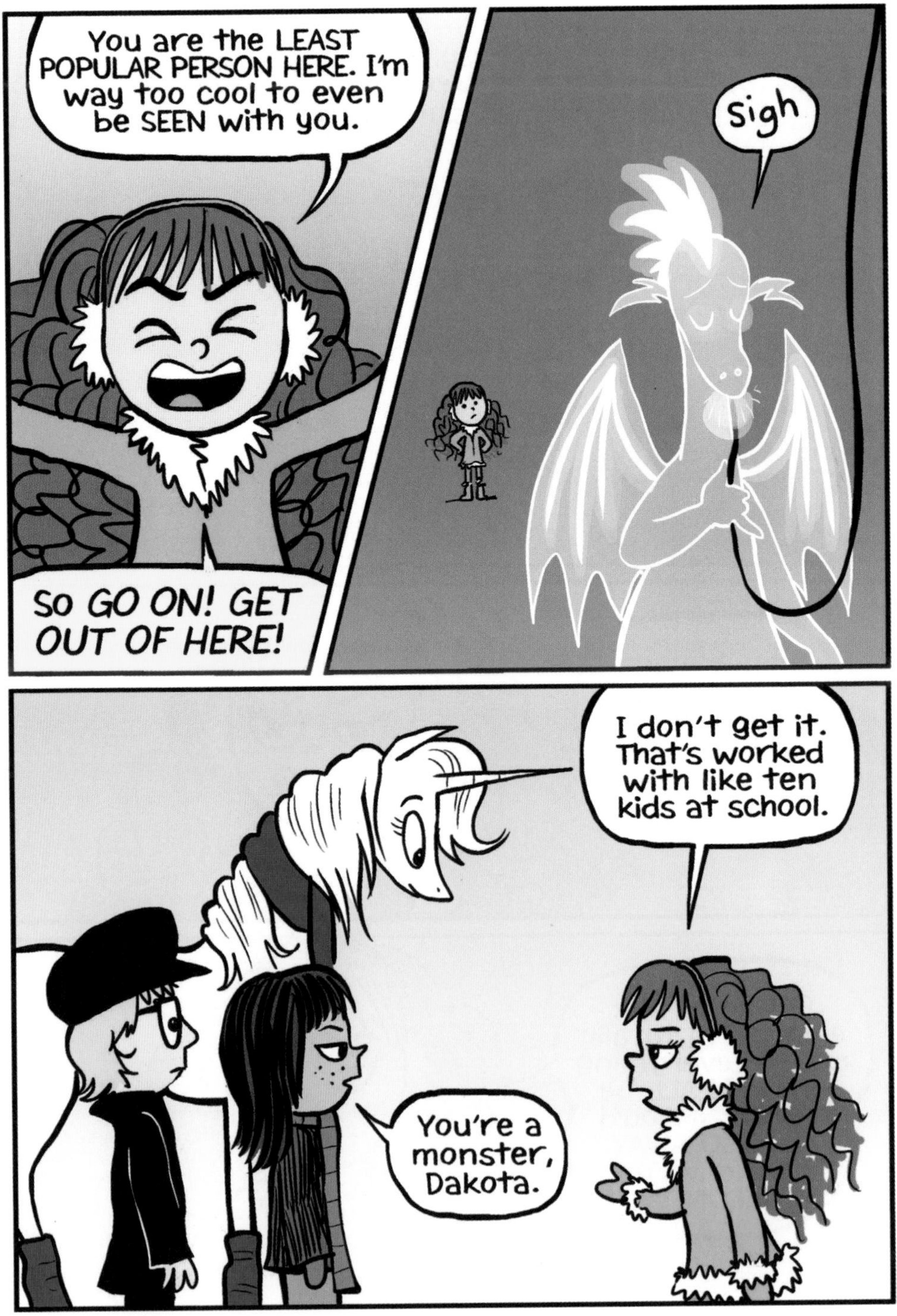
You are the LEAST POPULAR PERSON HERE. I'm way too cool to even be SEEN with you.
So GO ON! GET OUT OF HERE!
Sigh
I don't get it. That's worked with like ten kids at school.
You're a monster, Dakota.

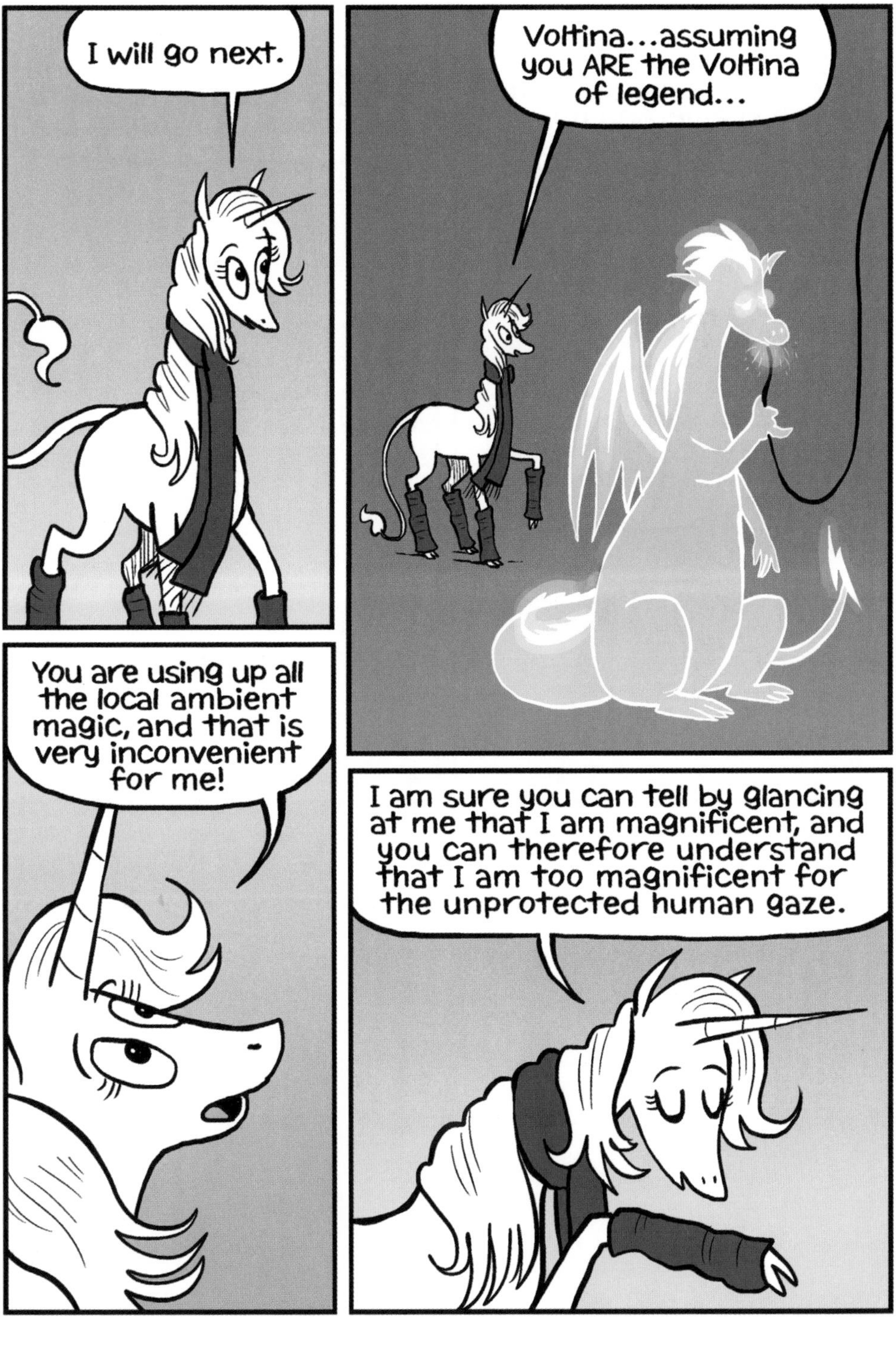
I will go next.
Voltina...assuming you ARE the Voltina of legend...
You are using up all the local ambient magic, and that is very inconvenient for me!
I am sure you can tell by glancing at me that I am magnificent, and you can therefore understand that I am too magnificent for the unprotected human gaze.

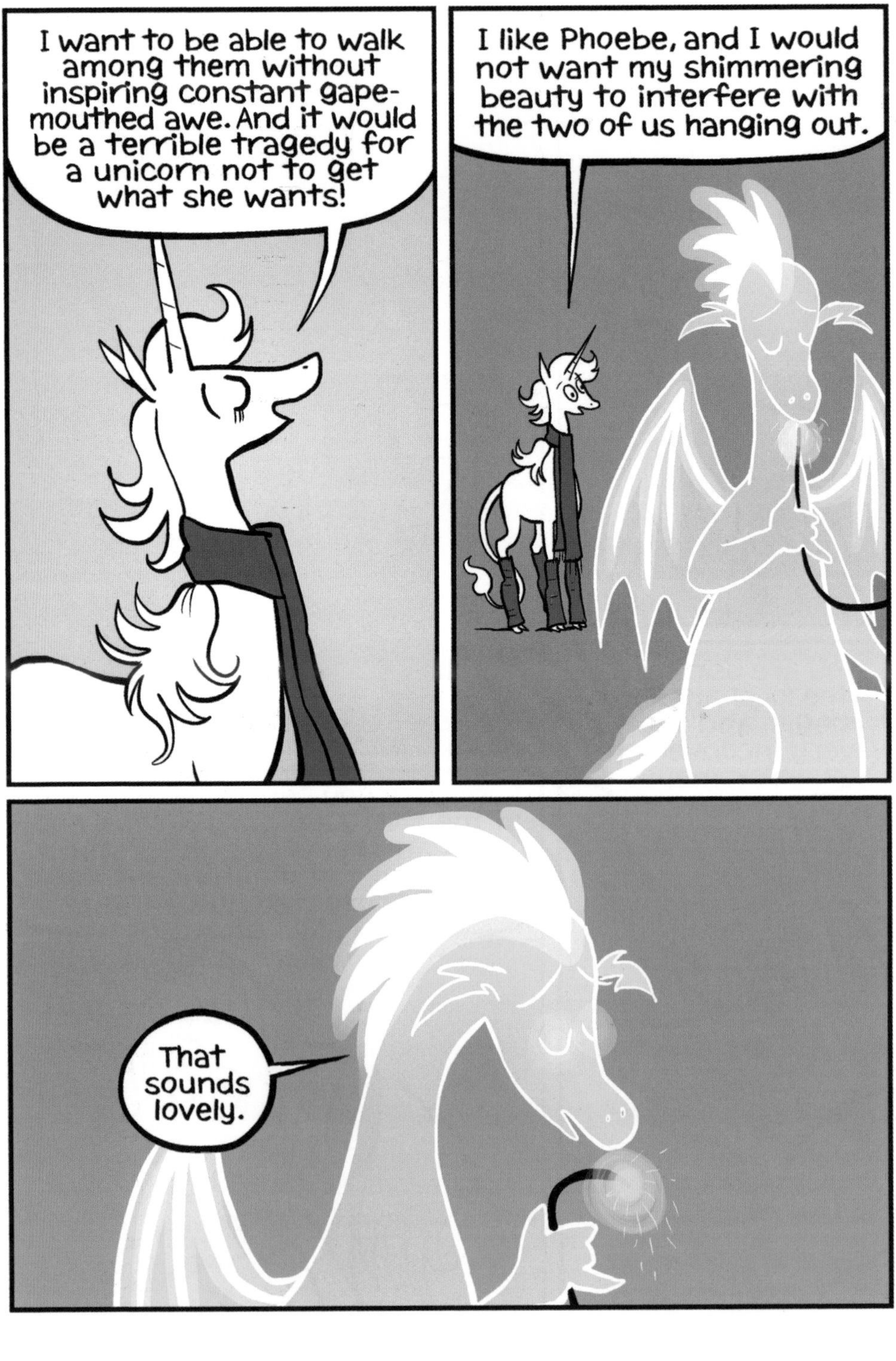
I want to be able to walk among them without inspiring constant gape-mouthed awe. And it would be a terrible tragedy for a unicorn not to get what she wants!
I like Phoebe, and I would not want my shimmering beauty to interfere with the two of us hanging out.
That sounds lovely.

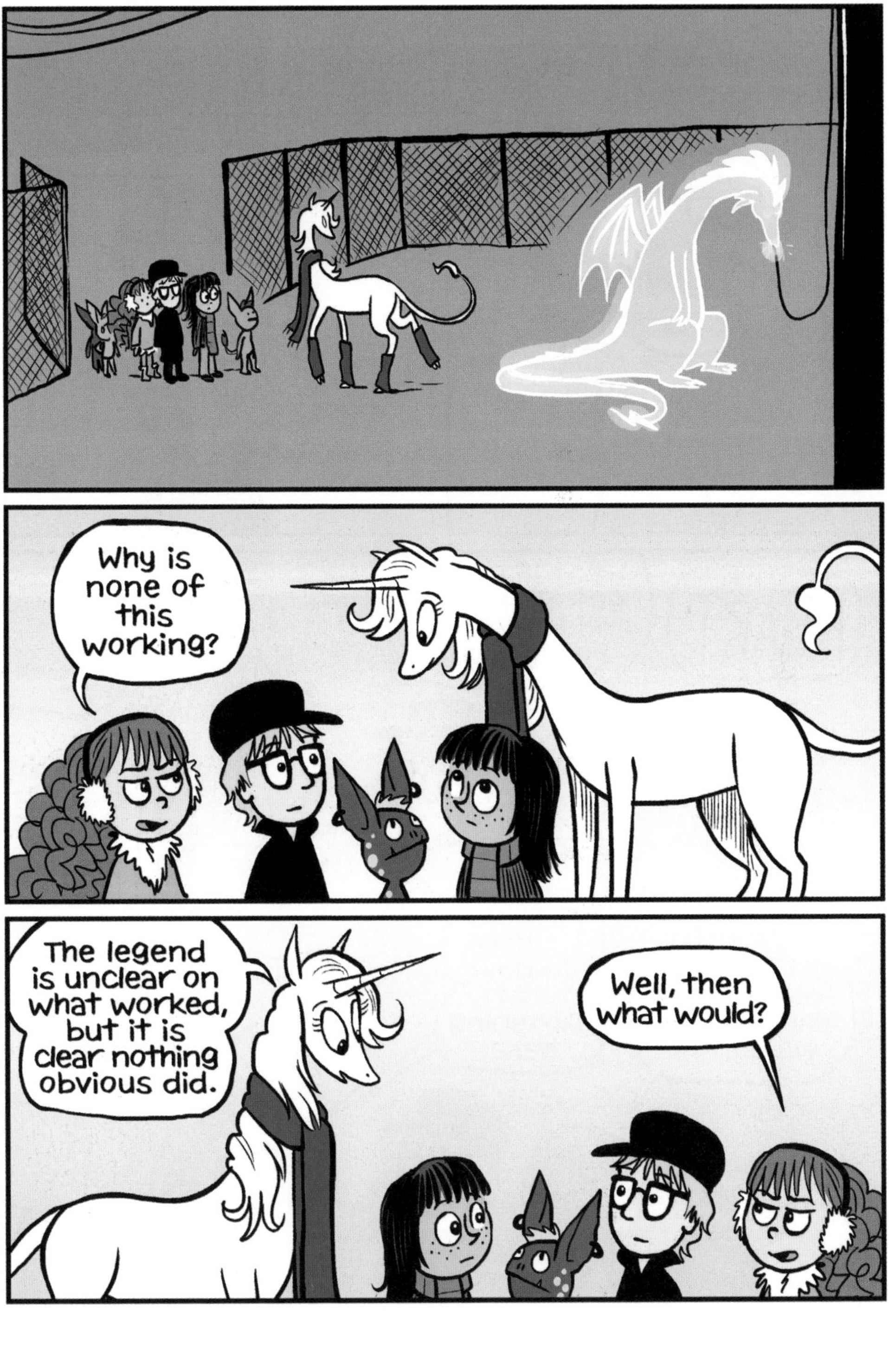
Why is none of this working?
The legend is unclear on what worked, but it is clear nothing obvious did.
Well, then what would?

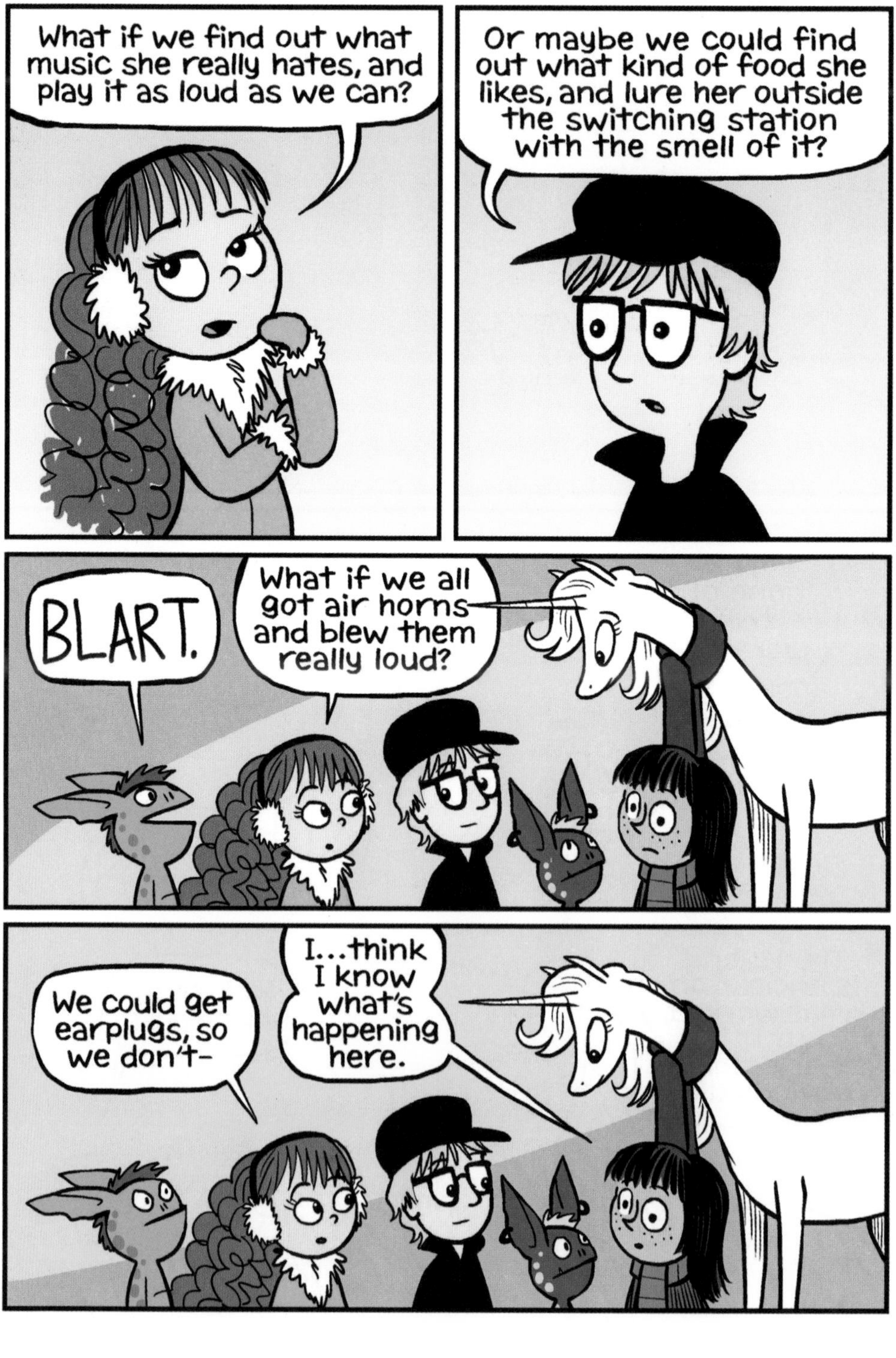
What if we find out what music she really hates, and play it as loud as we can?
Or maybe we could find out what kind of food she likes, and lure her outside the switching station with the smell of it?
BLART.
What if we all got air horns and blew them really loud?
We could get earplugs, so we don't-
I...think I know what's happening here.

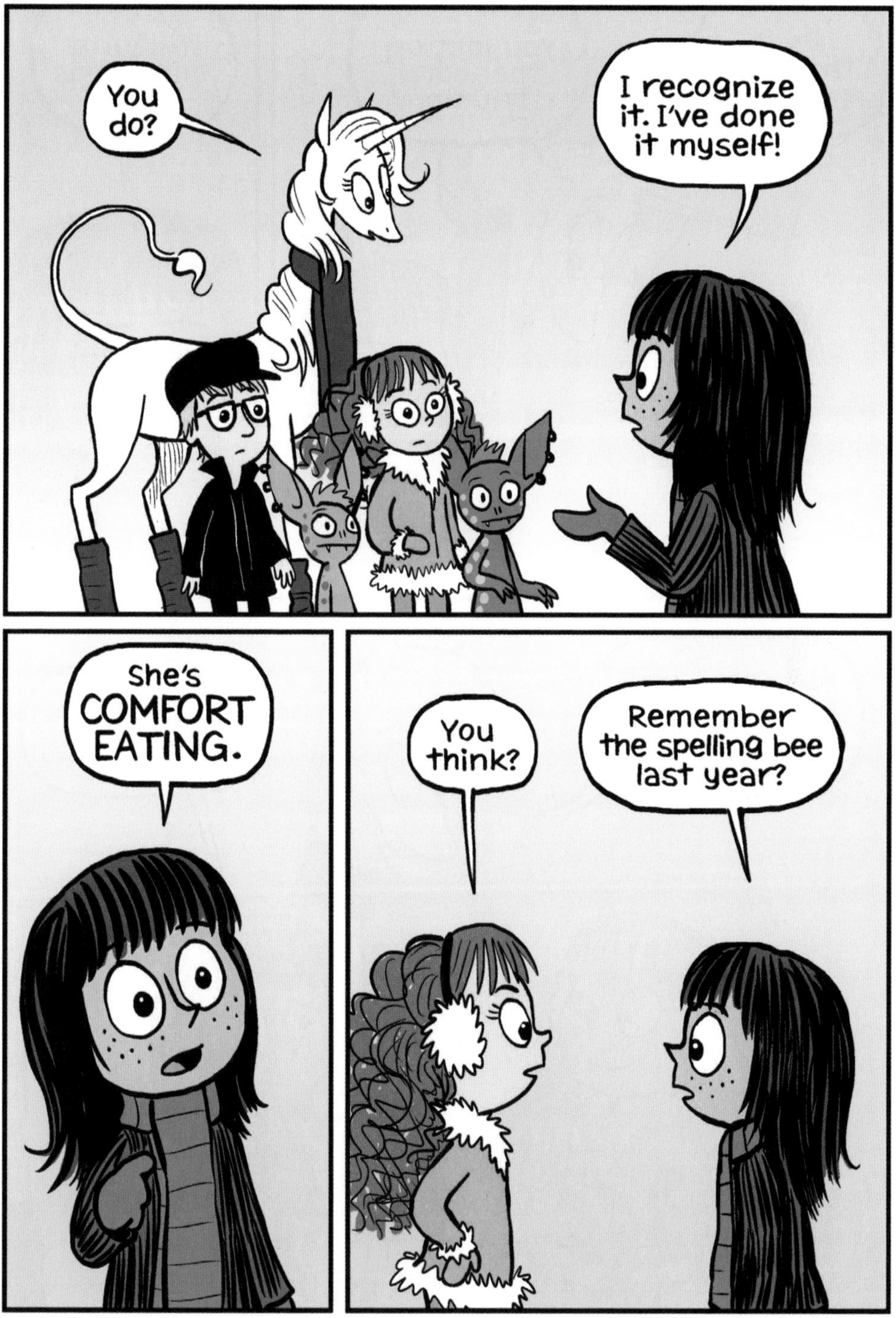
You do?
I recognize it. I've done it myself!
She's COMFORT EATING.
You think?
Remember the spelling bee last year?

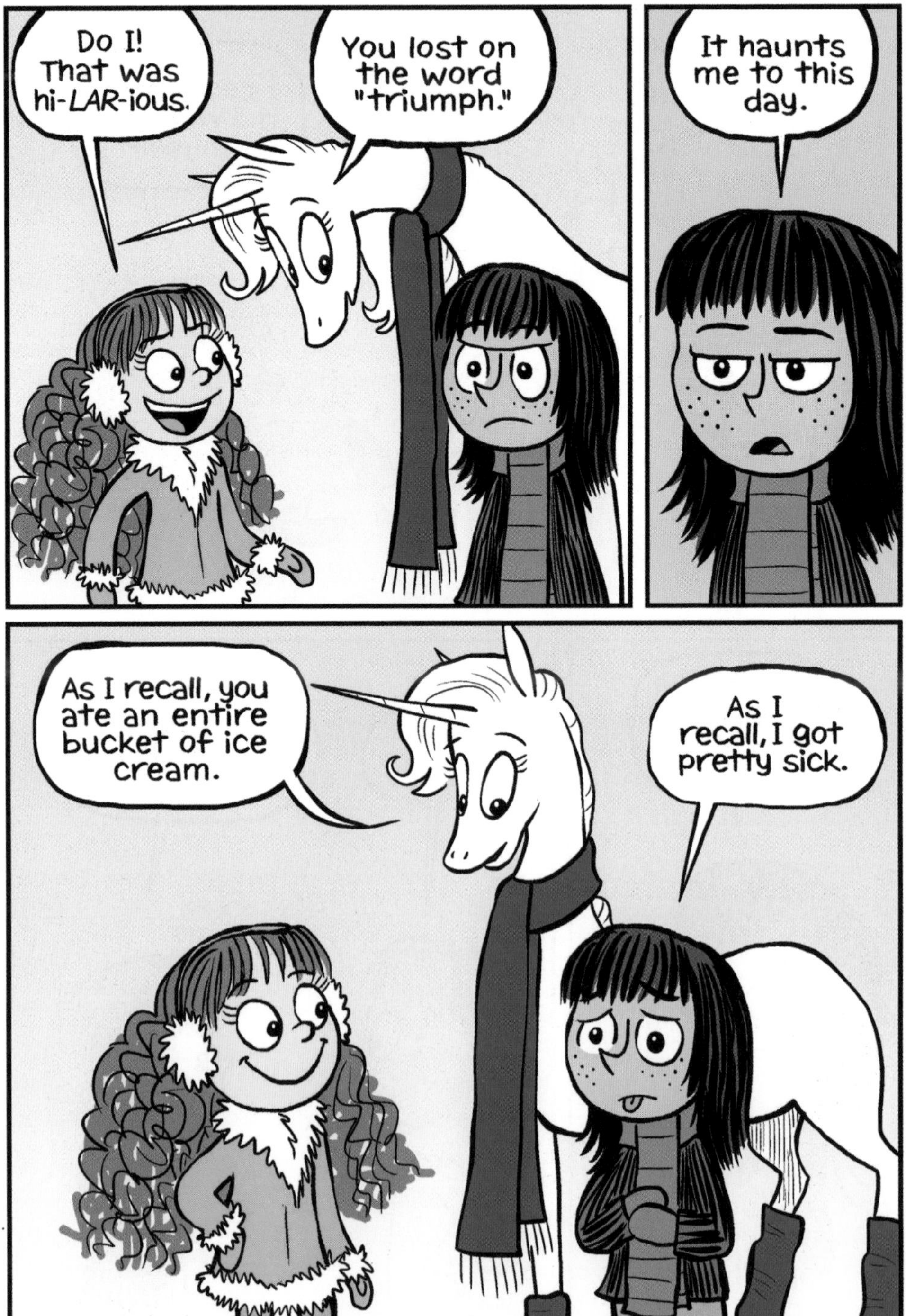
Do I! That was hi-*LAR*-ious.
You lost on the word "triumph."
It haunts me to this day.
As I recall, you ate an entire bucket of ice cream.
As I recall, I got pretty sick.

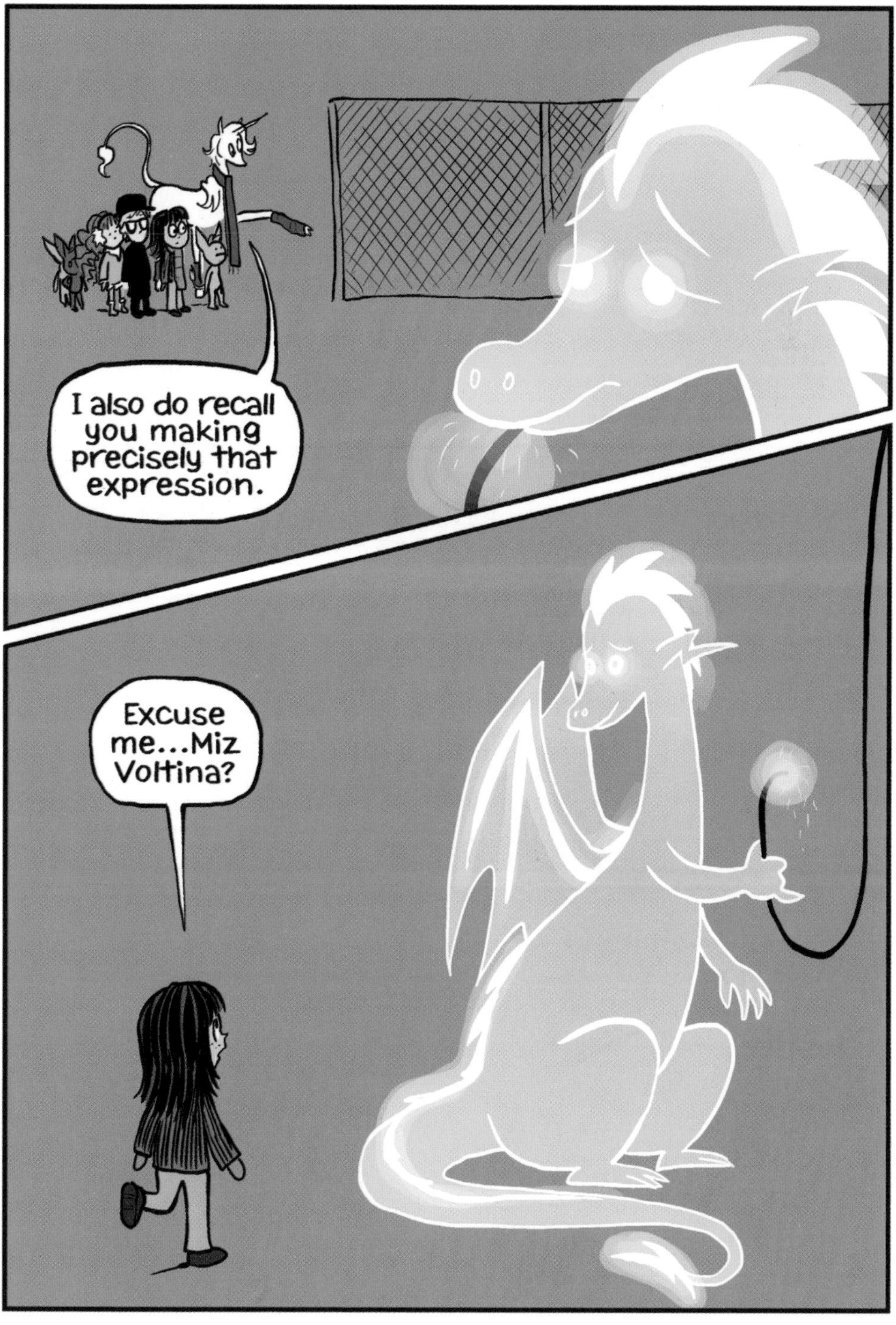
I also do recall you making precisely that expression.
Excuse me...Miz Voltina?

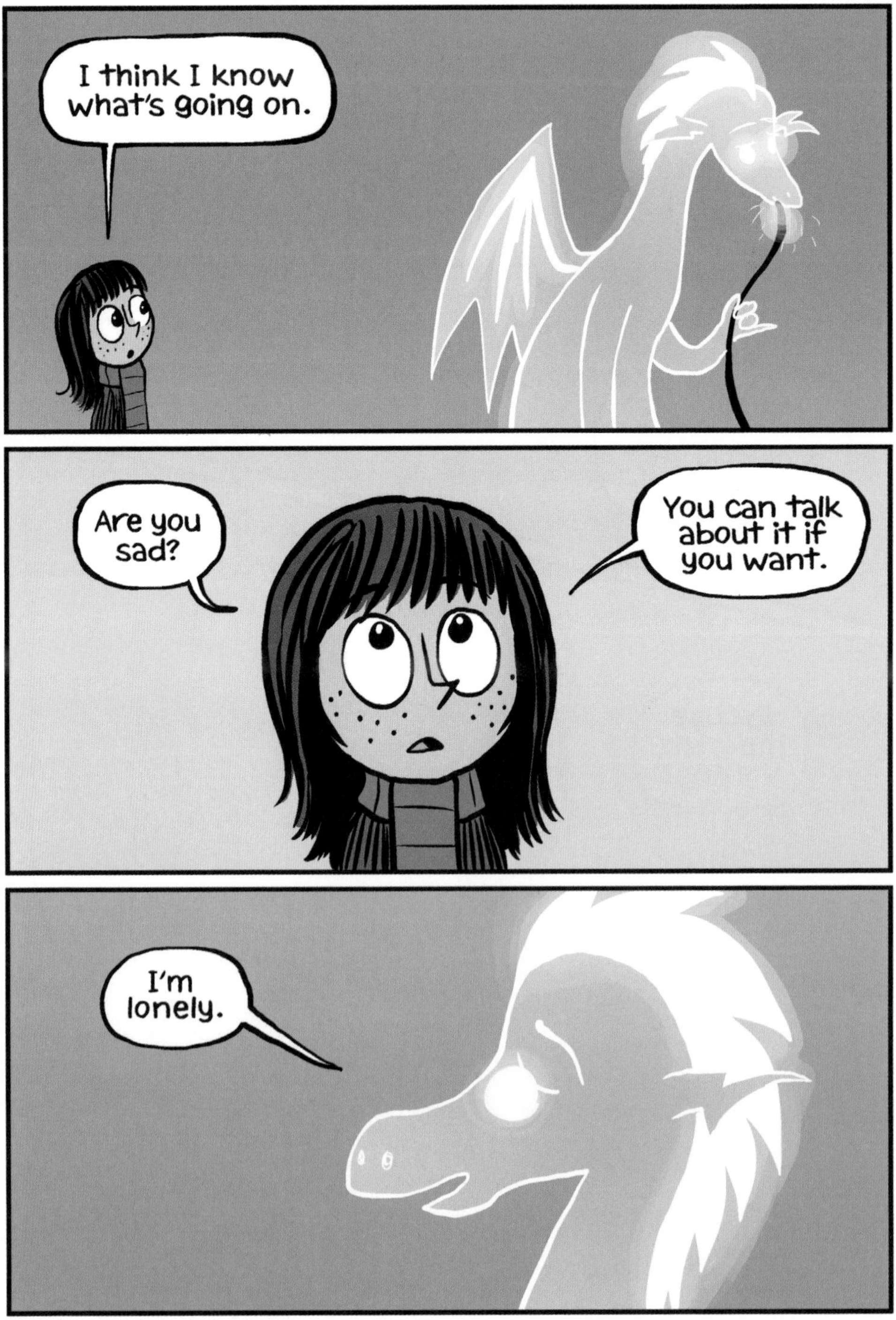
I think I know what's going on.
Are you sad?
You can talk about it if you want.
I'm lonely.

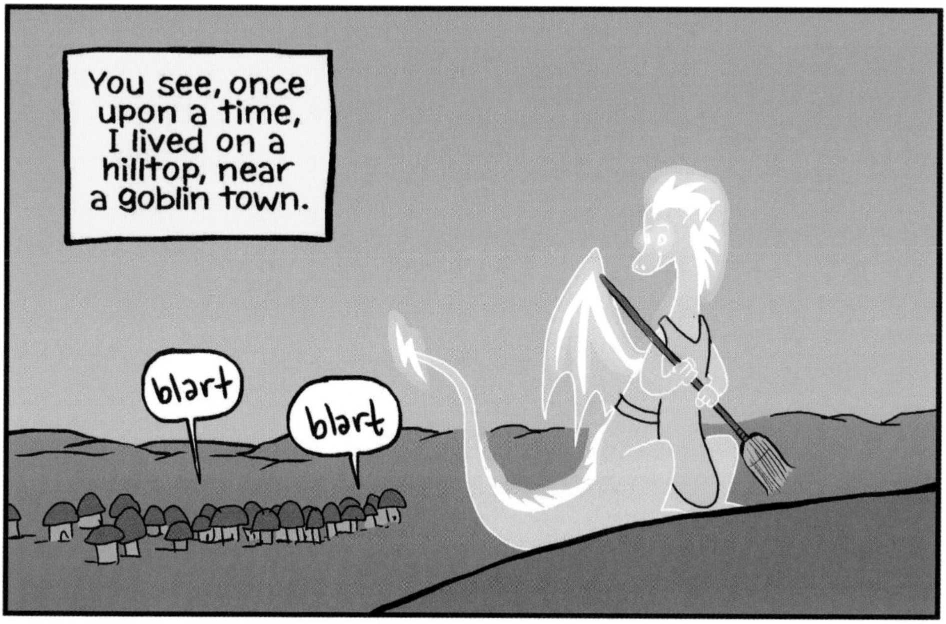
You see, once upon a time, I lived on a hilltop, near a goblin town.
blart
blart

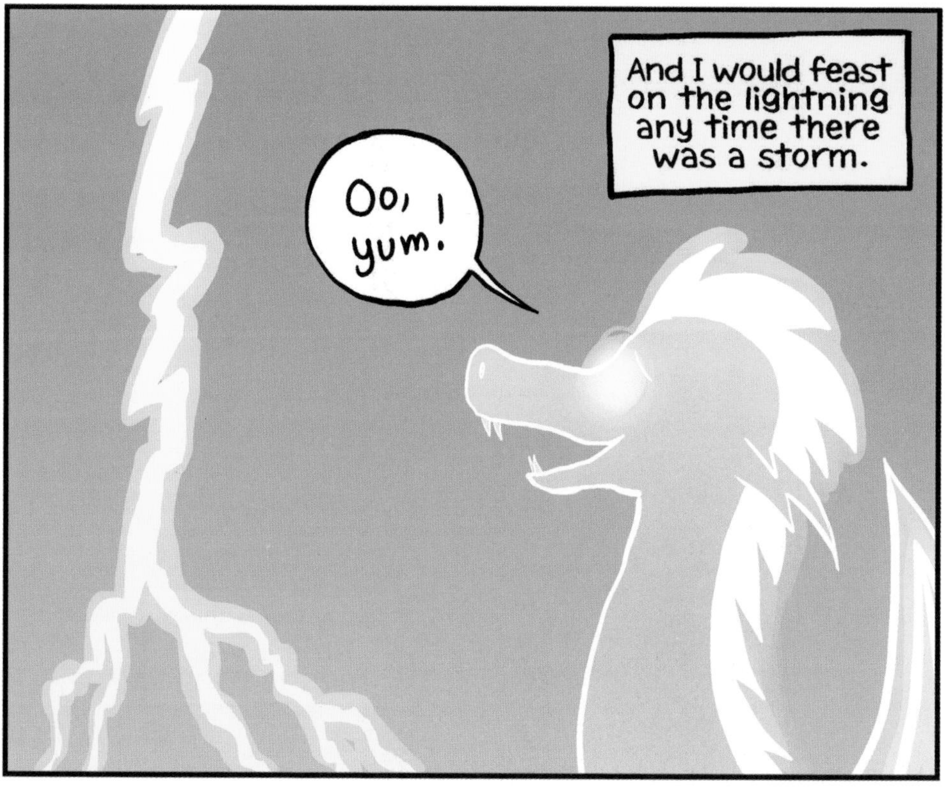
And I would feast on the lightning any time there was a storm.
Oo, yum!

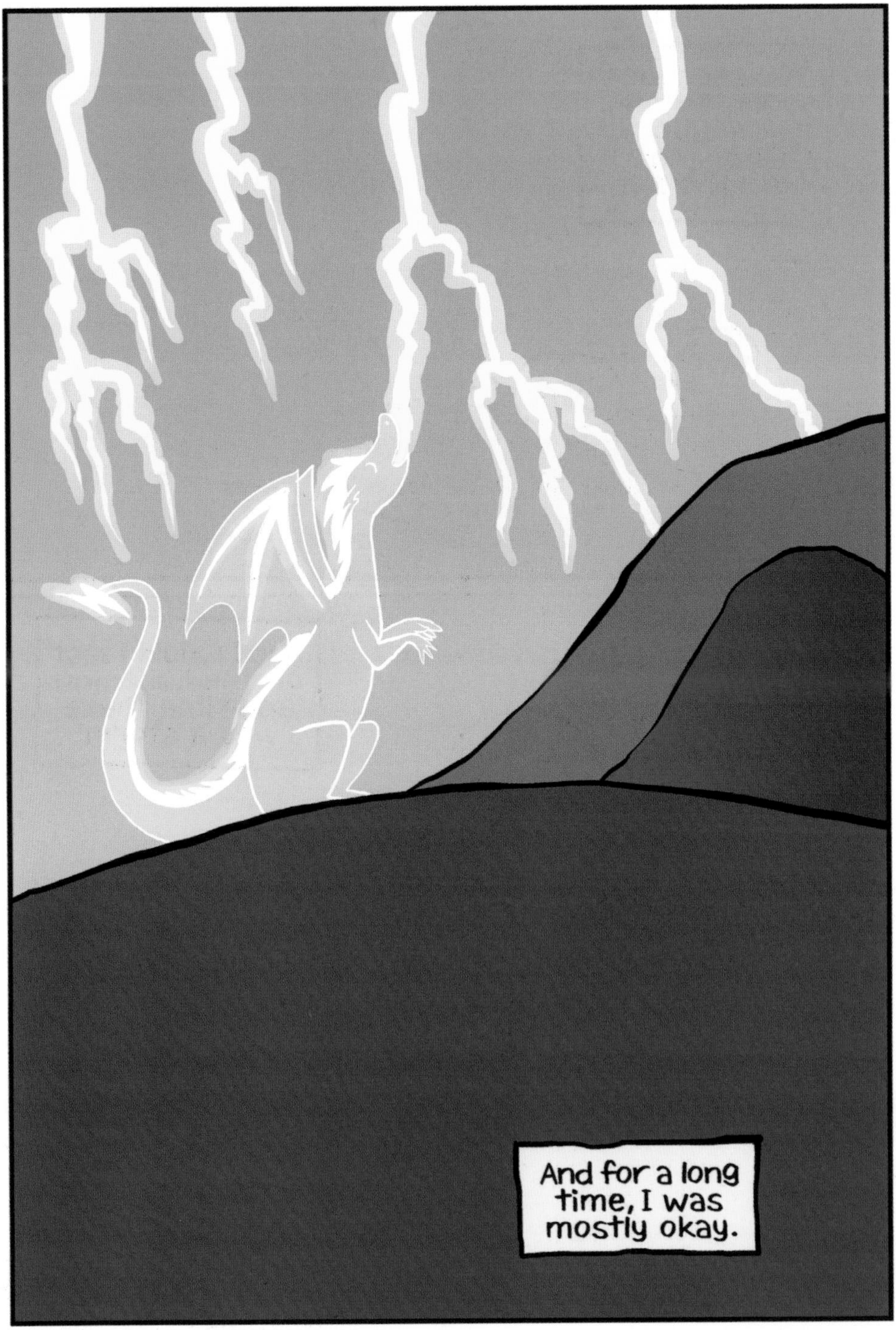
And for a long time, I was mostly okay.

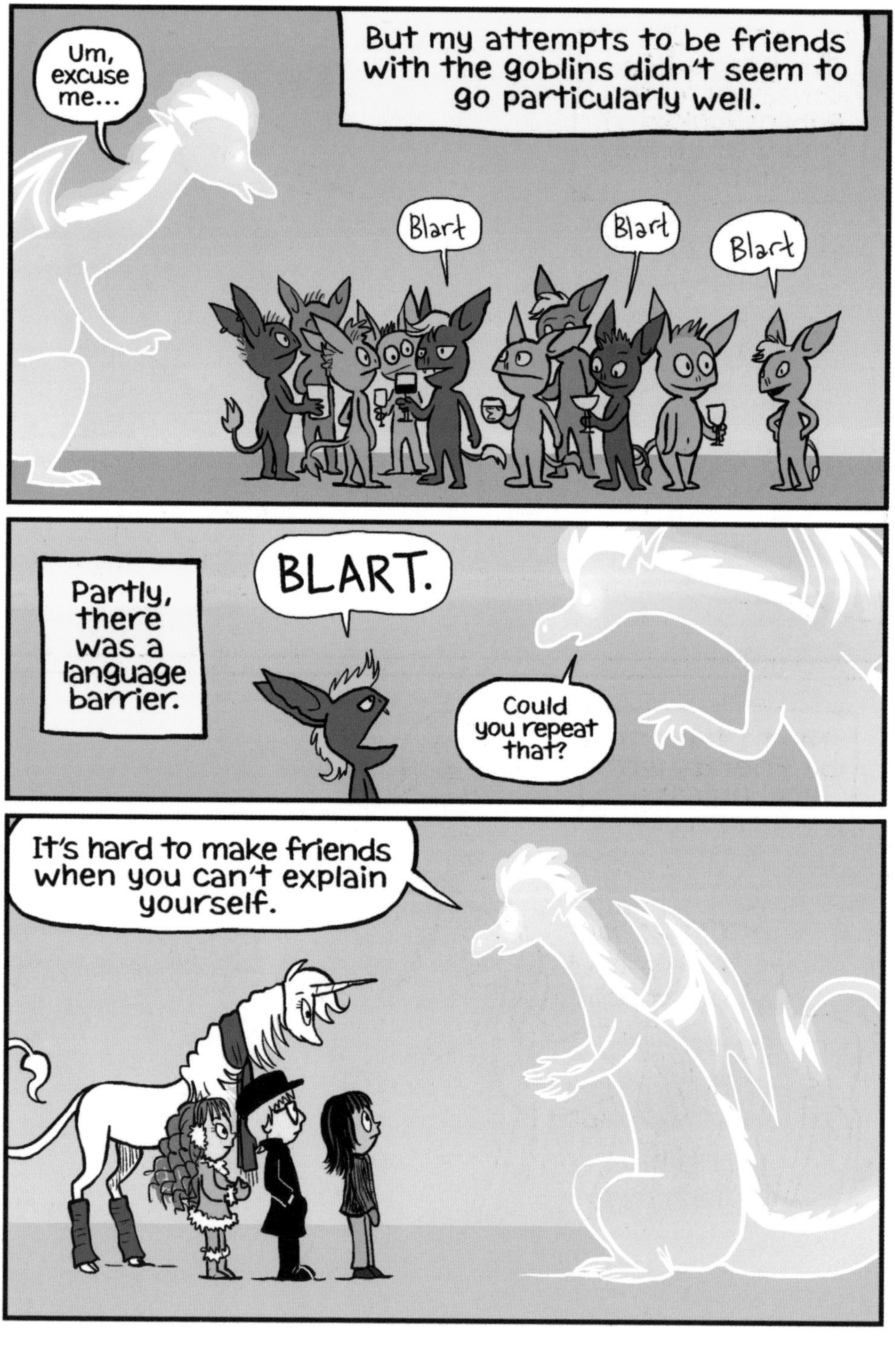
But my attempts to be friends with the goblins didn't seem to go particularly well.
Um, excuse me...
Blart
Blart
Blart
Partly, there was a language barrier.
BLART.
Could you repeat that?
It's hard to make friends when you can't explain yourself.

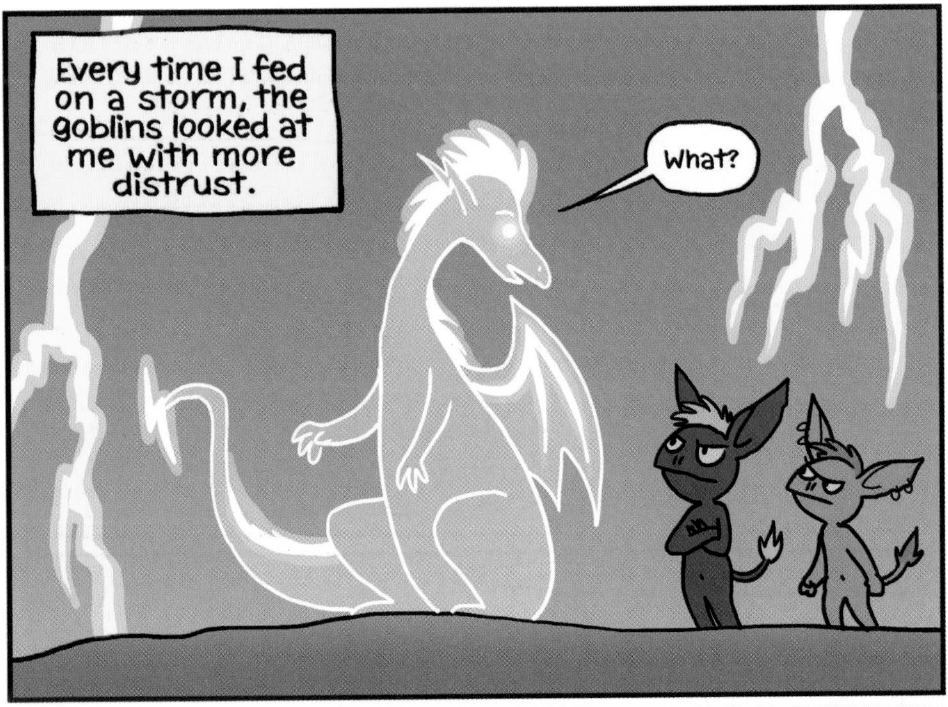
Every time I fed on a storm, the goblins looked at me with more distrust.
What?

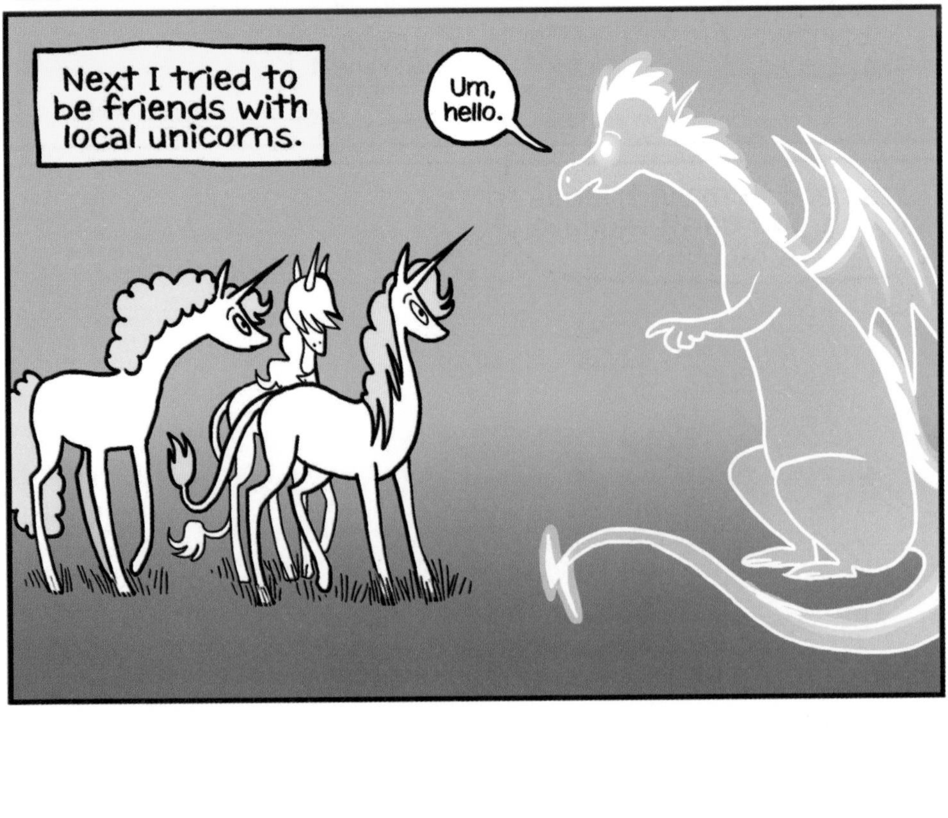
Next I tried to be friends with local unicorns.
Um, hello.

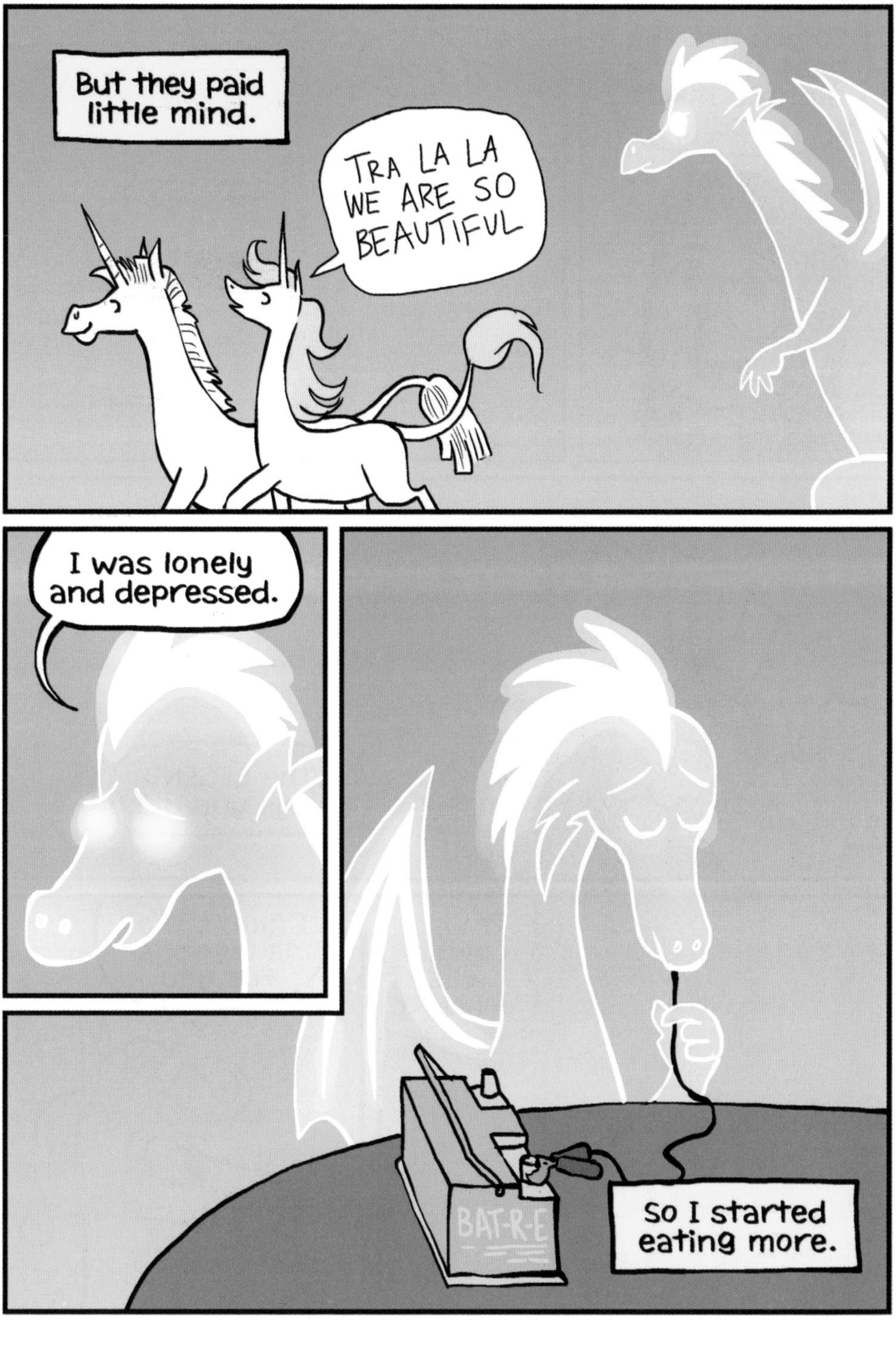
But they paid little mind.
TRA LA LA WE ARE SO BEAUTIFUL
I was lonely and depressed.
BAT-R-E
So I started eating more.

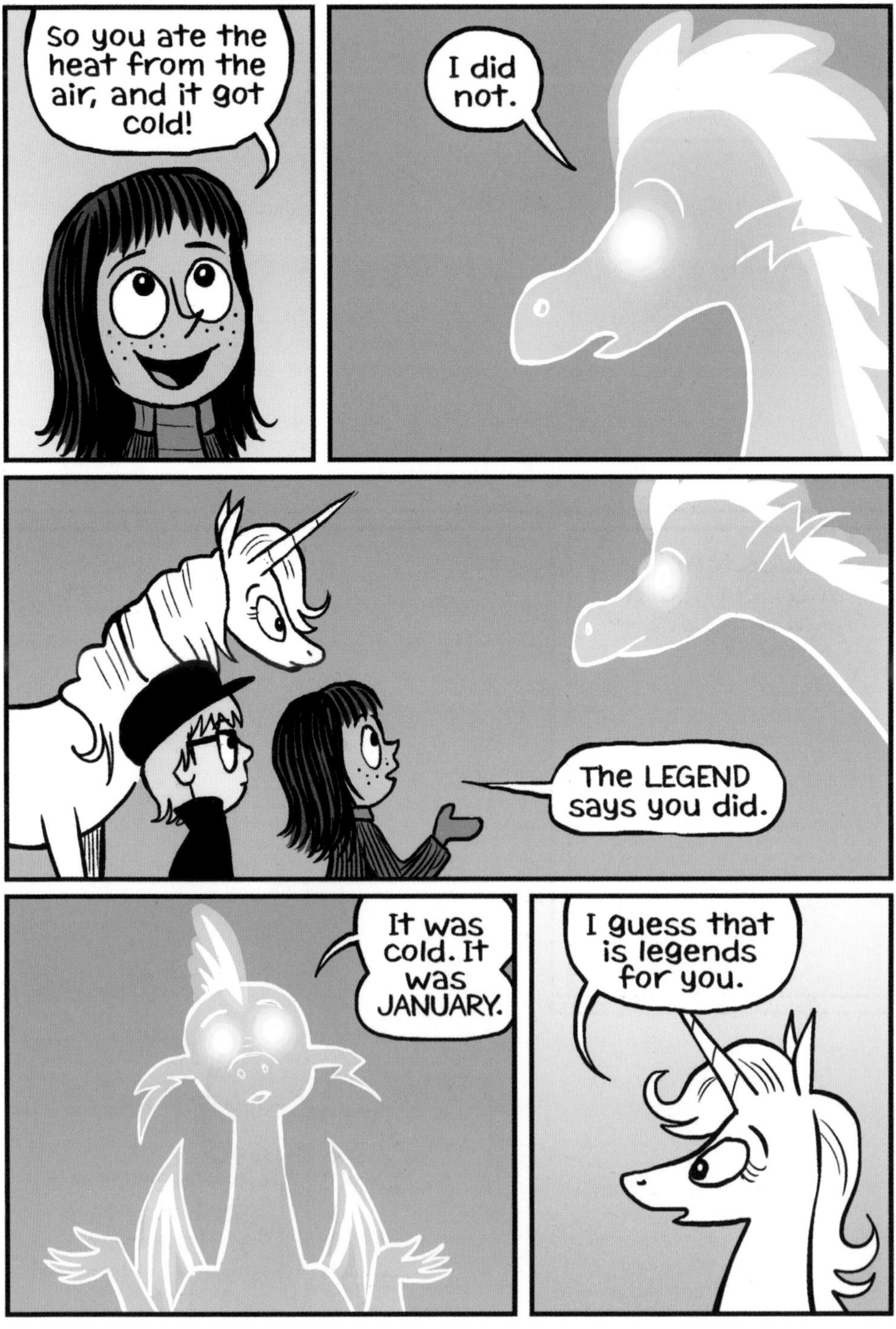
So you ate the heat from the air, and it got cold!
I did not.
The LEGEND says you did.
It was cold. It was JANUARY.
I guess that is legends for you.

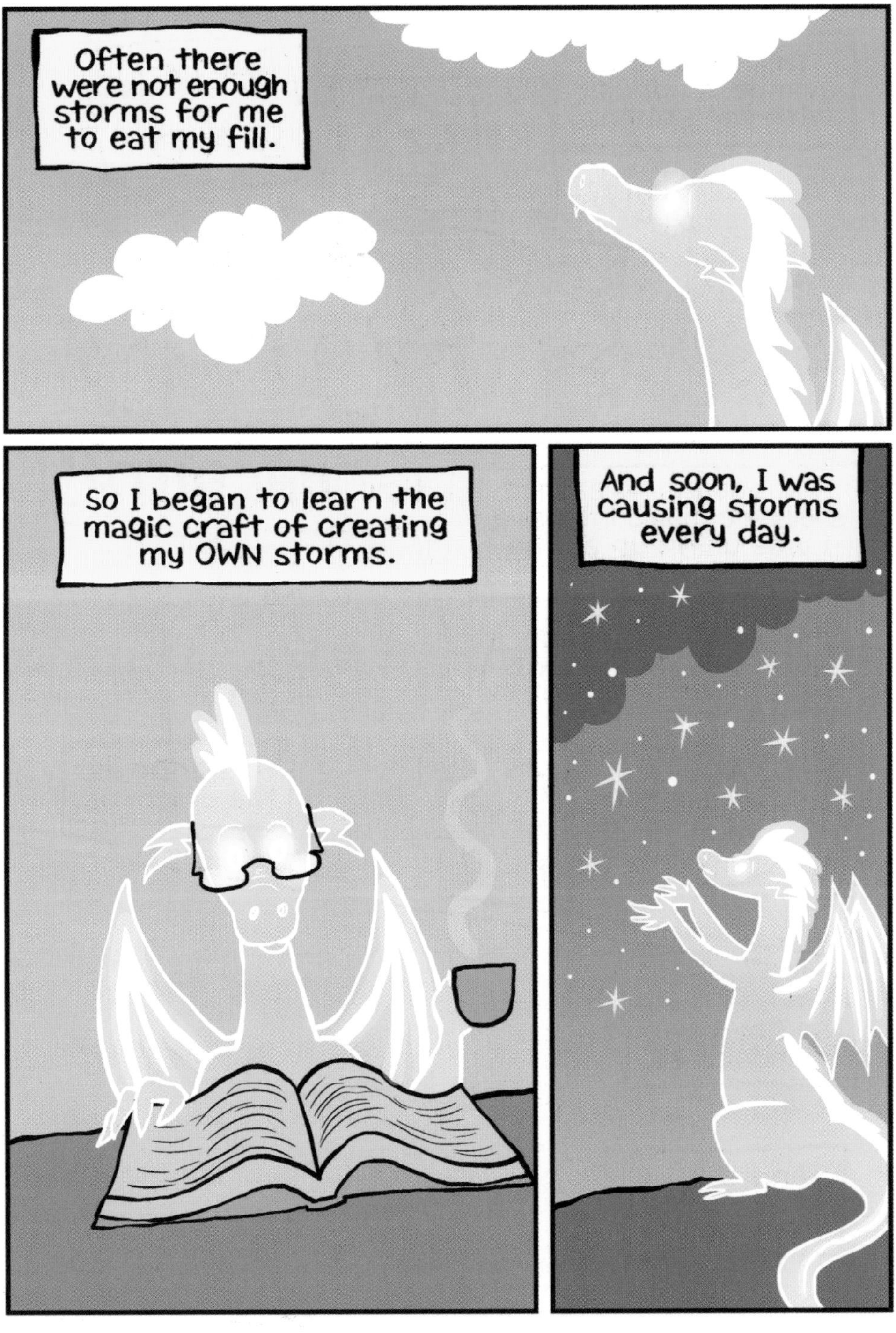
Often there were not enough storms for me to eat my fill.
So I began to learn the magic craft of creating my OWN storms.
And soon, I was causing storms every day.

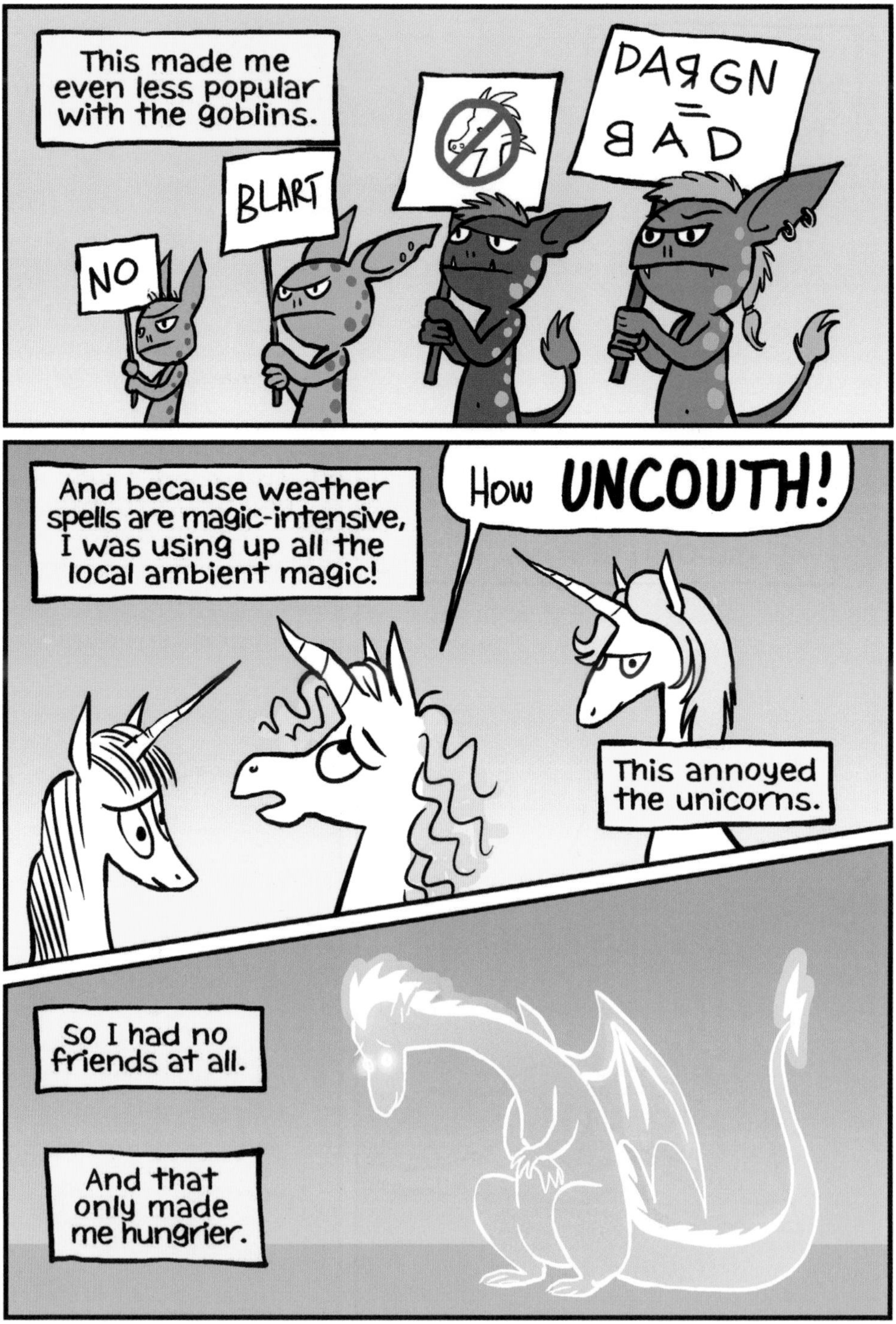

This made me even less popular with the goblins.
NO
BLART
DARGN = BAD
And because weather spells are magic-intensive, I was using up all the local ambient magic!
How UNCOUTH!
This annoyed the unicorns.
So I had no friends at all.
And that only made me hungrier.

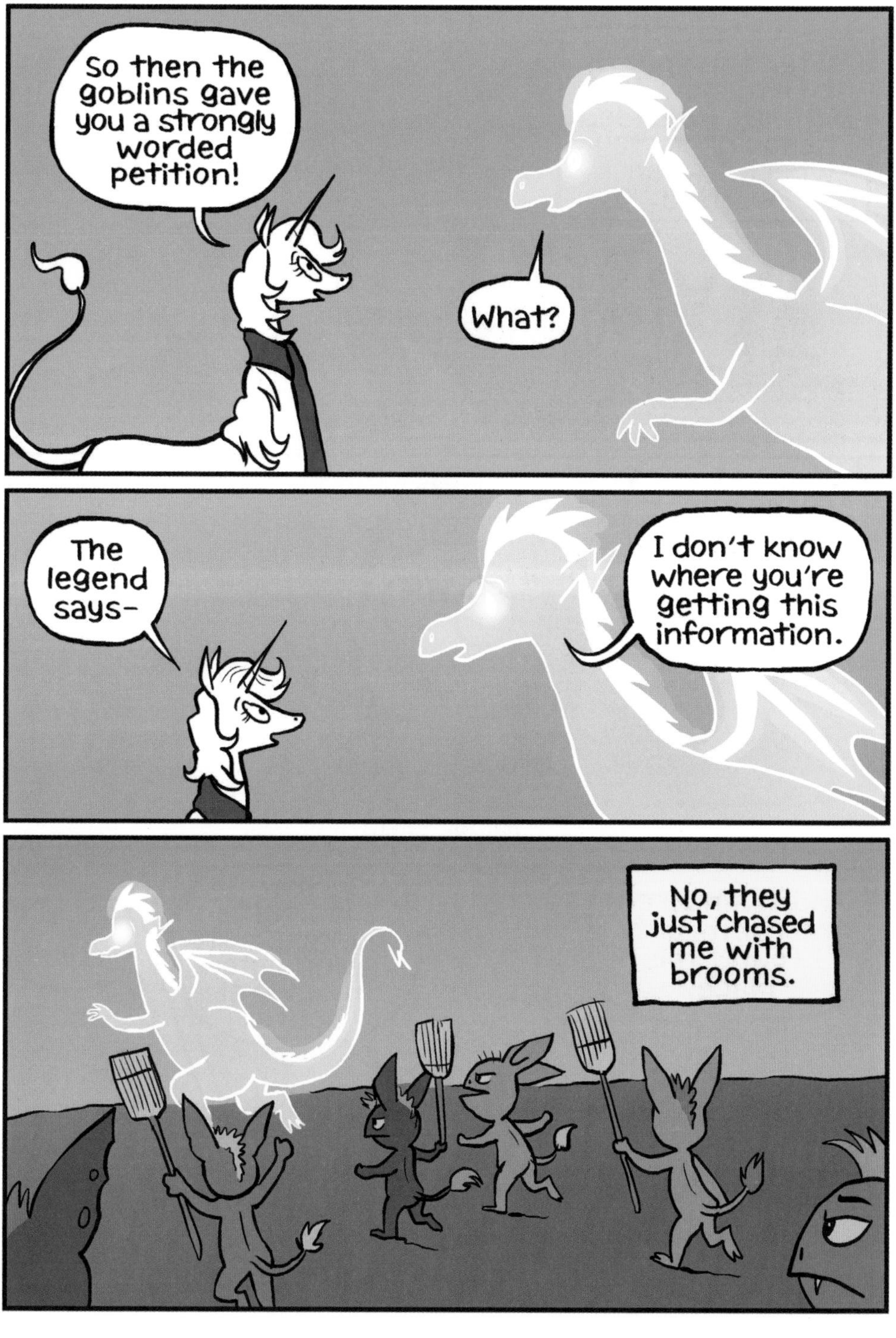
So then the goblins gave you a strongly worded petition!
What?
The legend says-
I don't know where you're getting this information.
No, they just chased me with brooms.

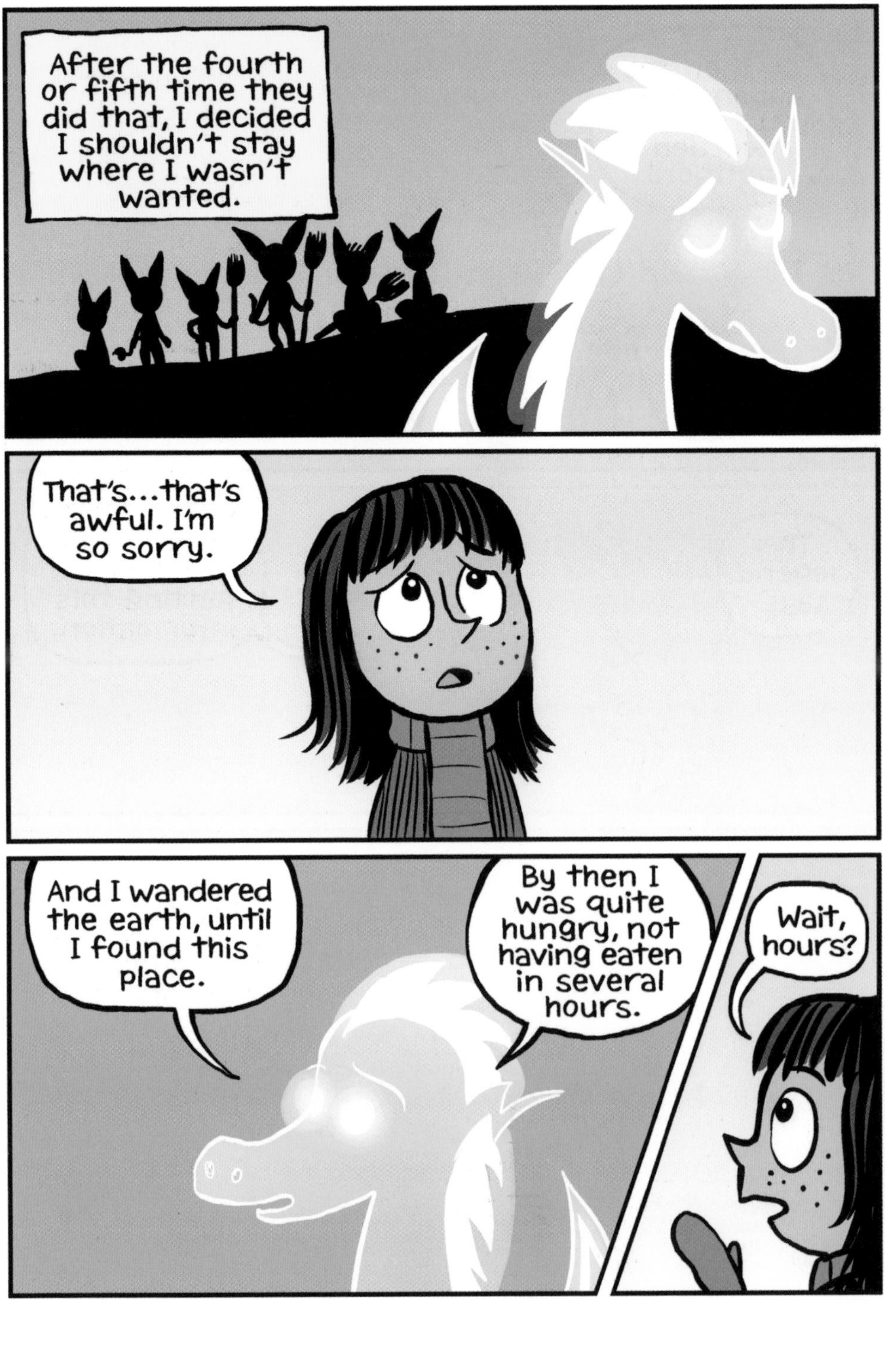
After the fourth or fifth time they did that, I decided I shouldn't stay where I wasn't wanted.
That's...that's awful. I'm so sorry.
And I wandered the earth, until I found this place.
By then I was quite hungry, not having eaten in several hours.
Wait, hours?

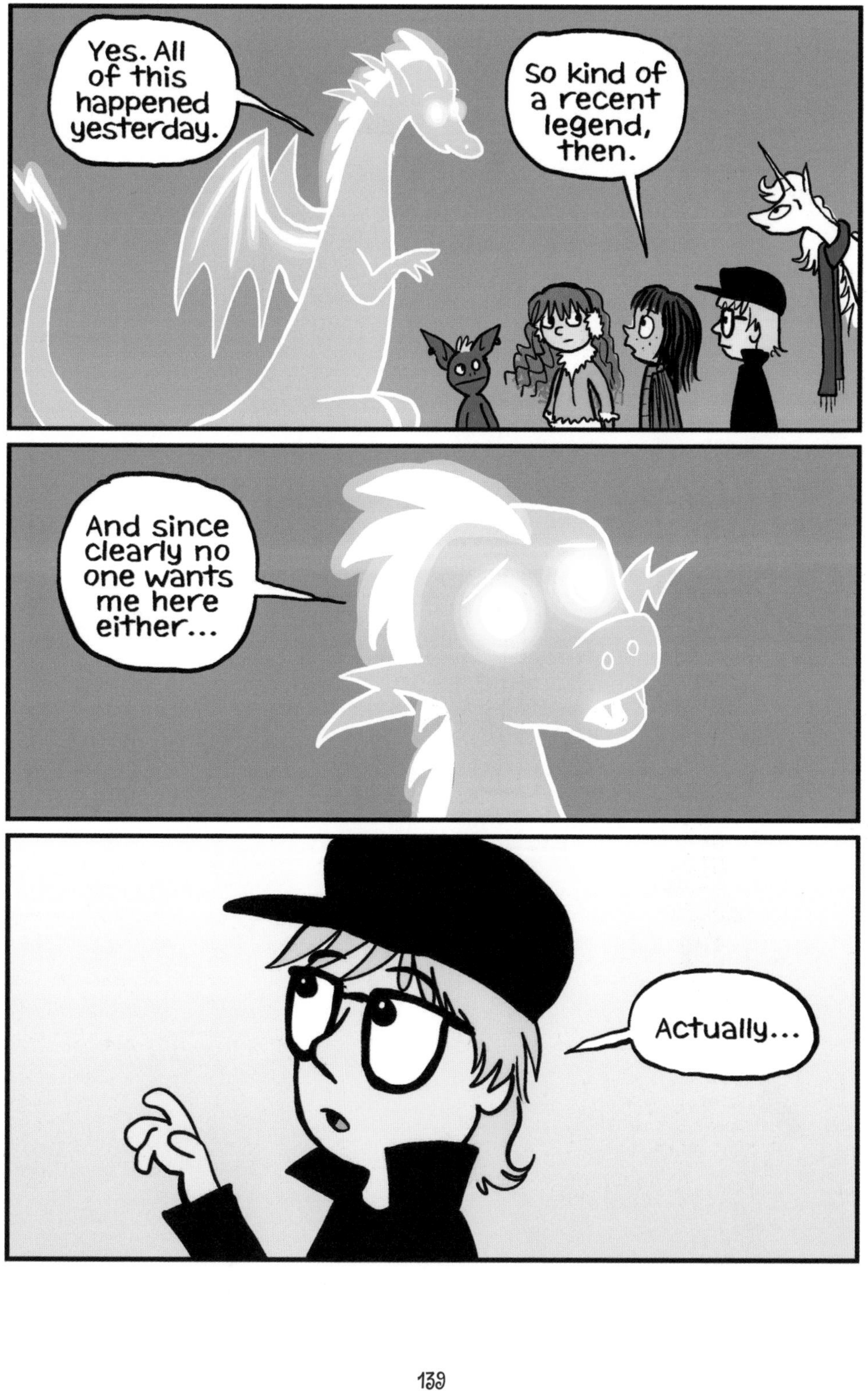
Yes. All of this happened yesterday.
So kind of a recent legend, then.
And since clearly no one wants me here either...
Actually...

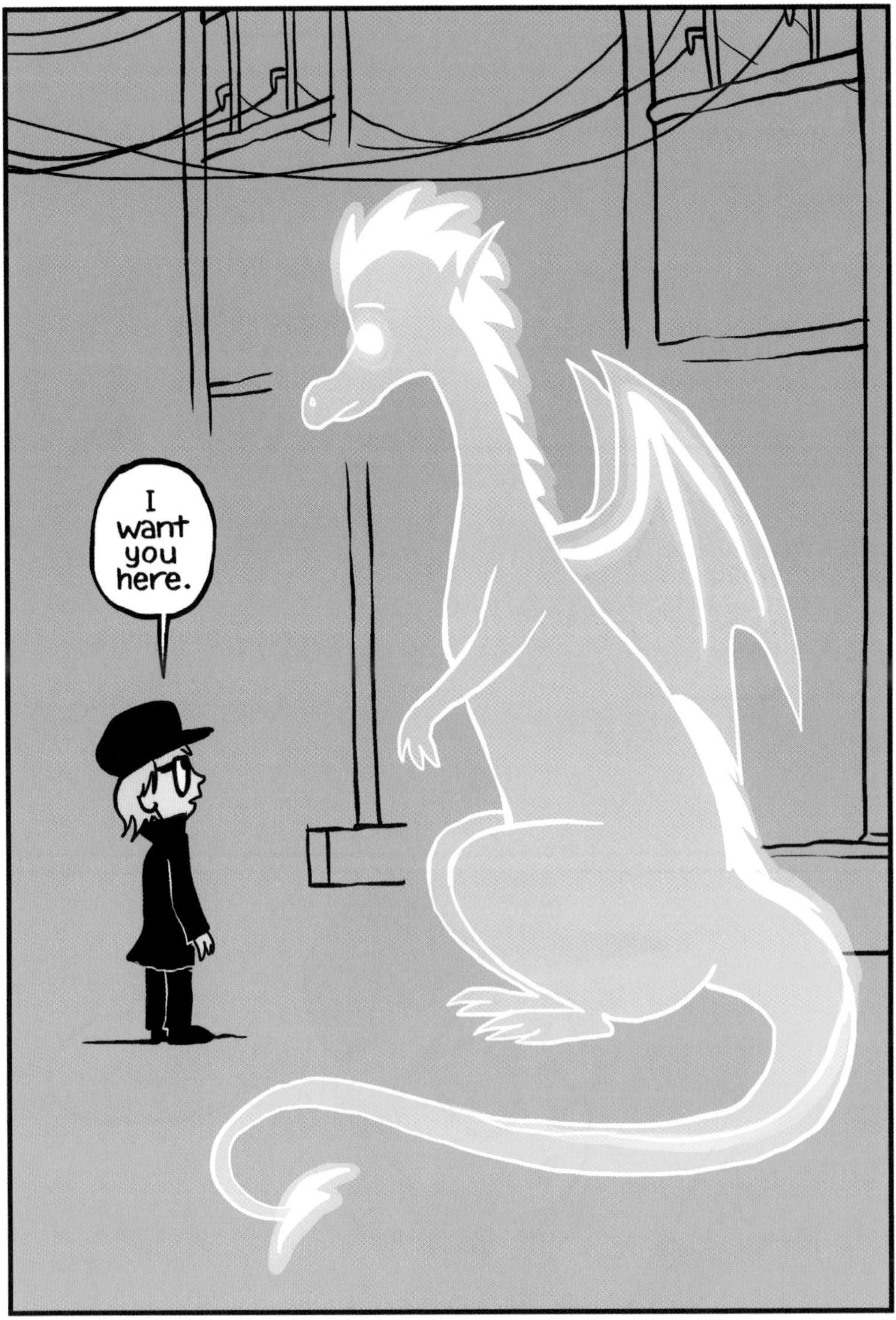
I want you here.

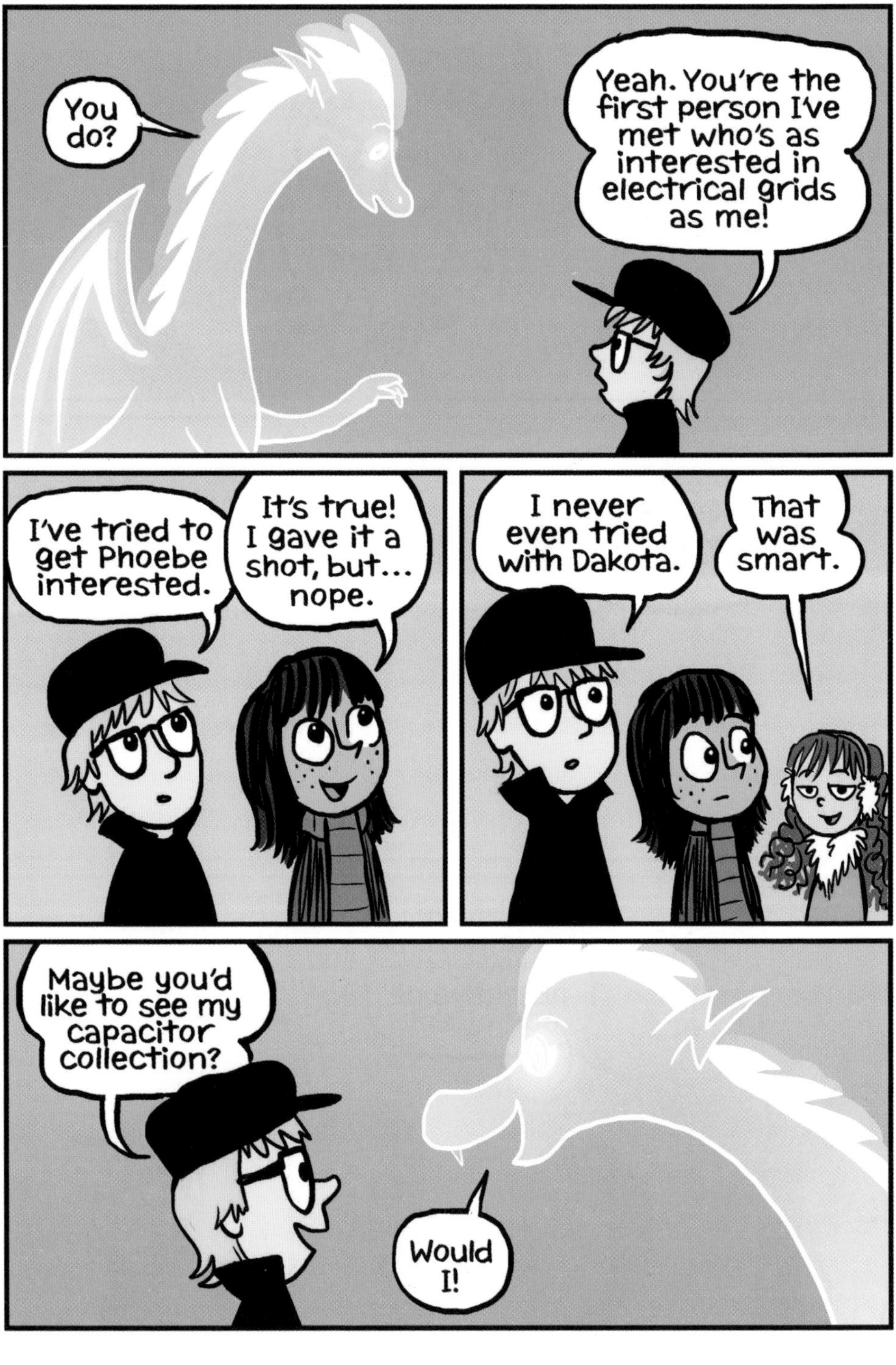
You do?
Yeah. You're the first person I've met who's as interested in electrical grids as me!
I've tried to get Phoebe interested.
It's true! I gave it a shot, but... nope.
I never even tried with Dakota.
That was smart.
Maybe you'd like to see my capacitor collection?
Would I!

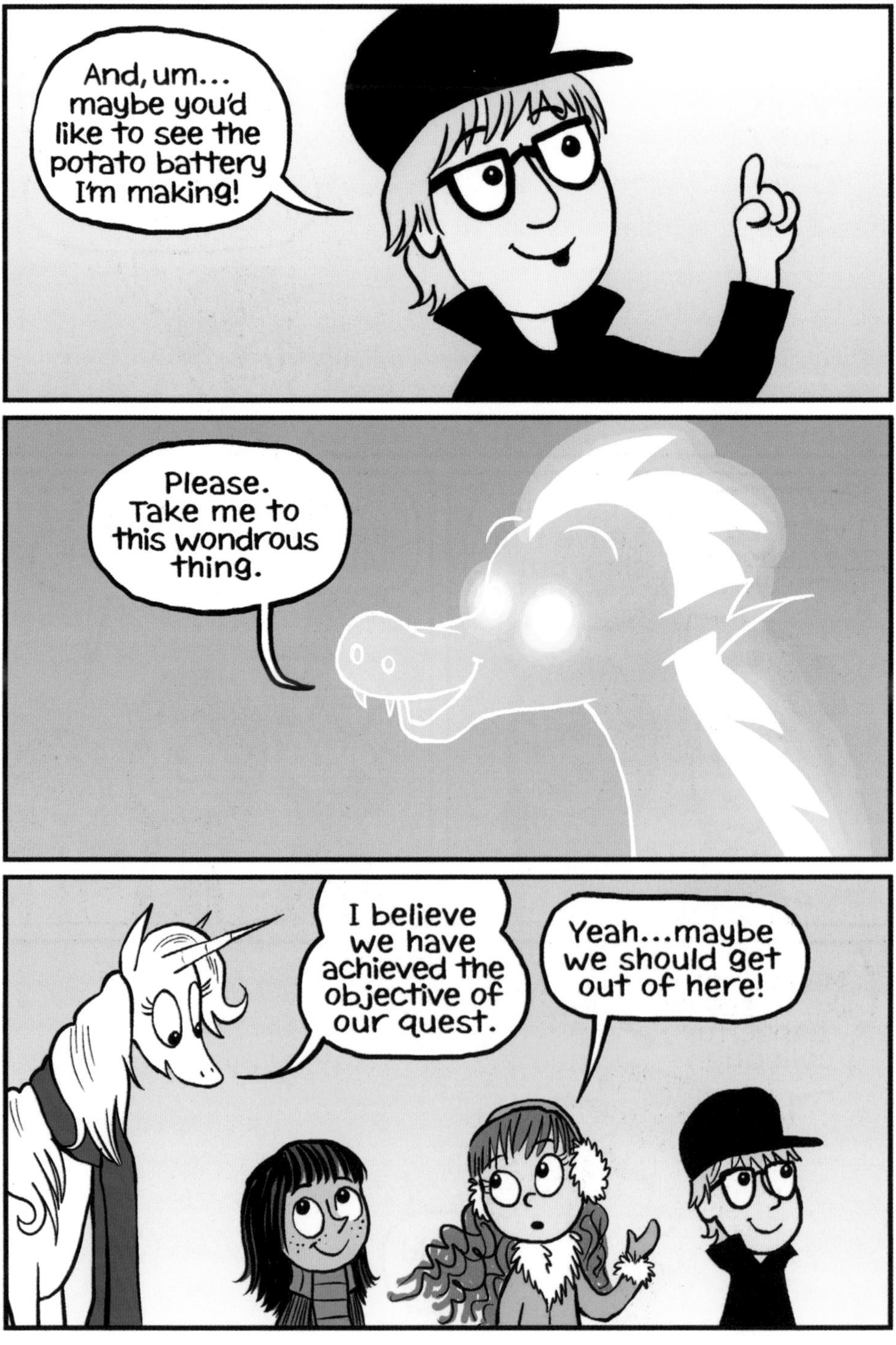
And, um... maybe you'd like to see the potato battery I'm making!
Please. Take me to this wondrous thing.
I believe we have achieved the objective of our quest.
Yeah...maybe we should get out of here!

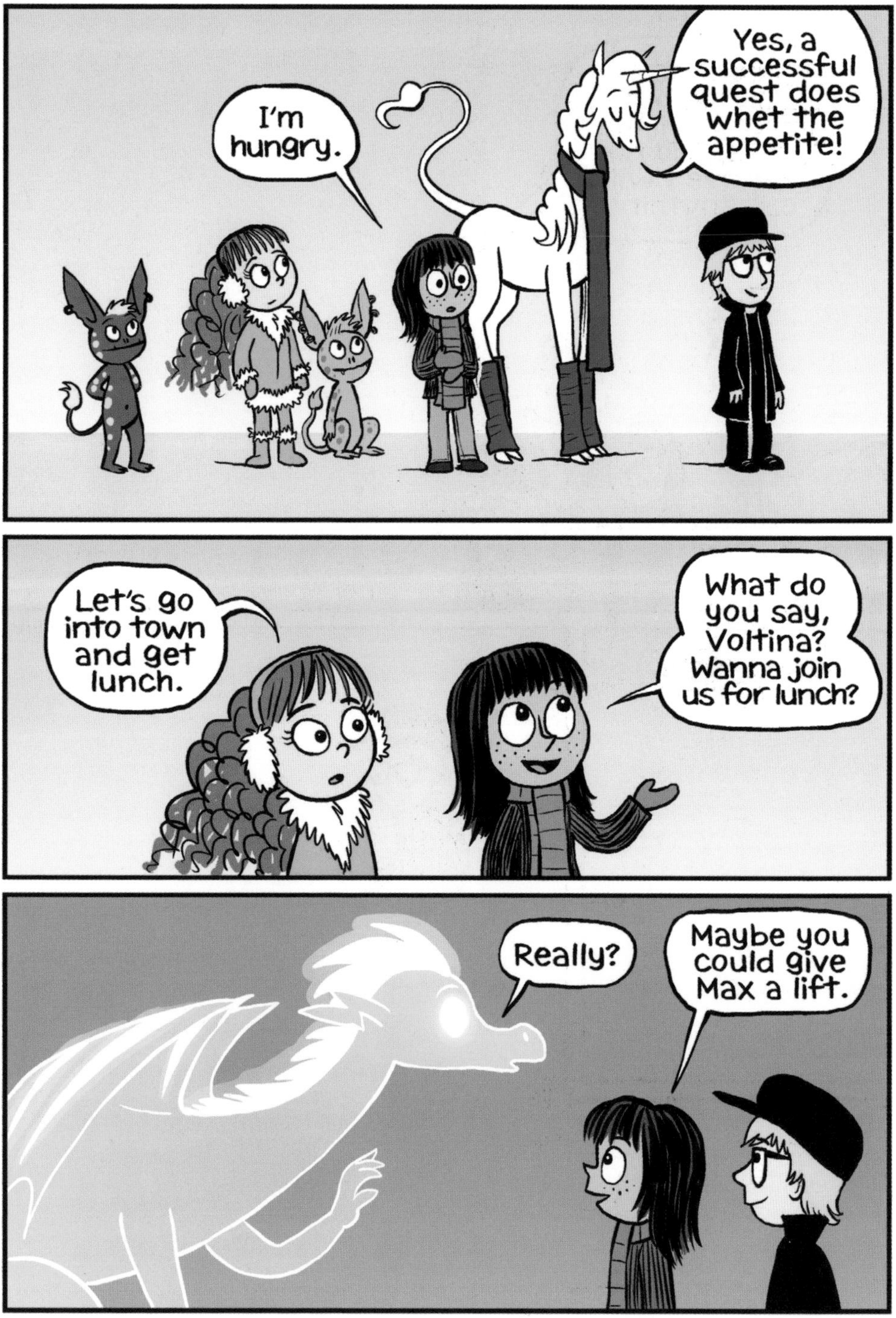
I'm hungry.
Yes, a successful quest does whet the appetite!
Let's go into town and get lunch.
What do you say, Voltina? Wanna join us for lunch?
Really?
Maybe you could give Max a lift.

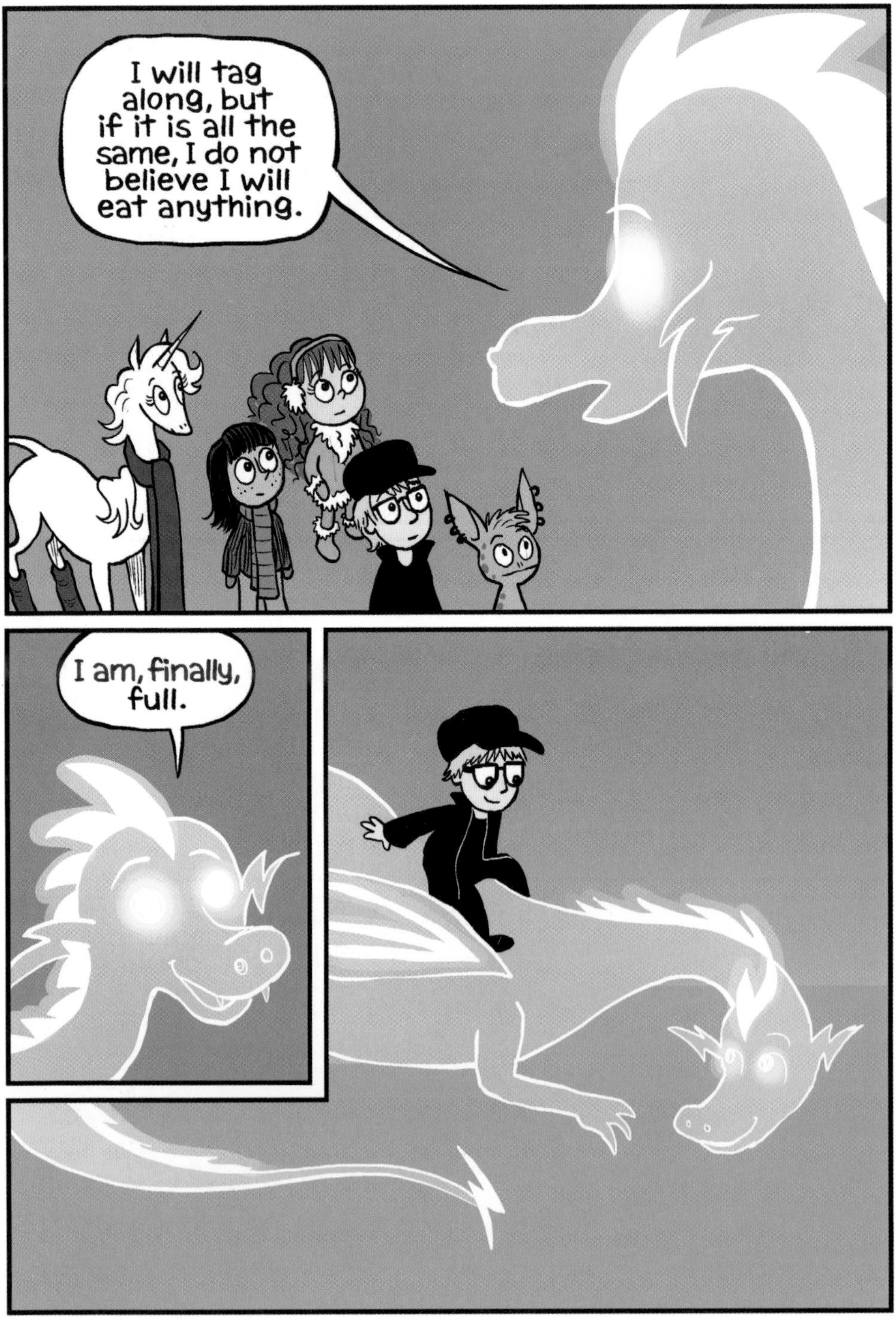
I will tag along, but if it is all the same, I do not believe I will eat anything.
I am, finally, full.

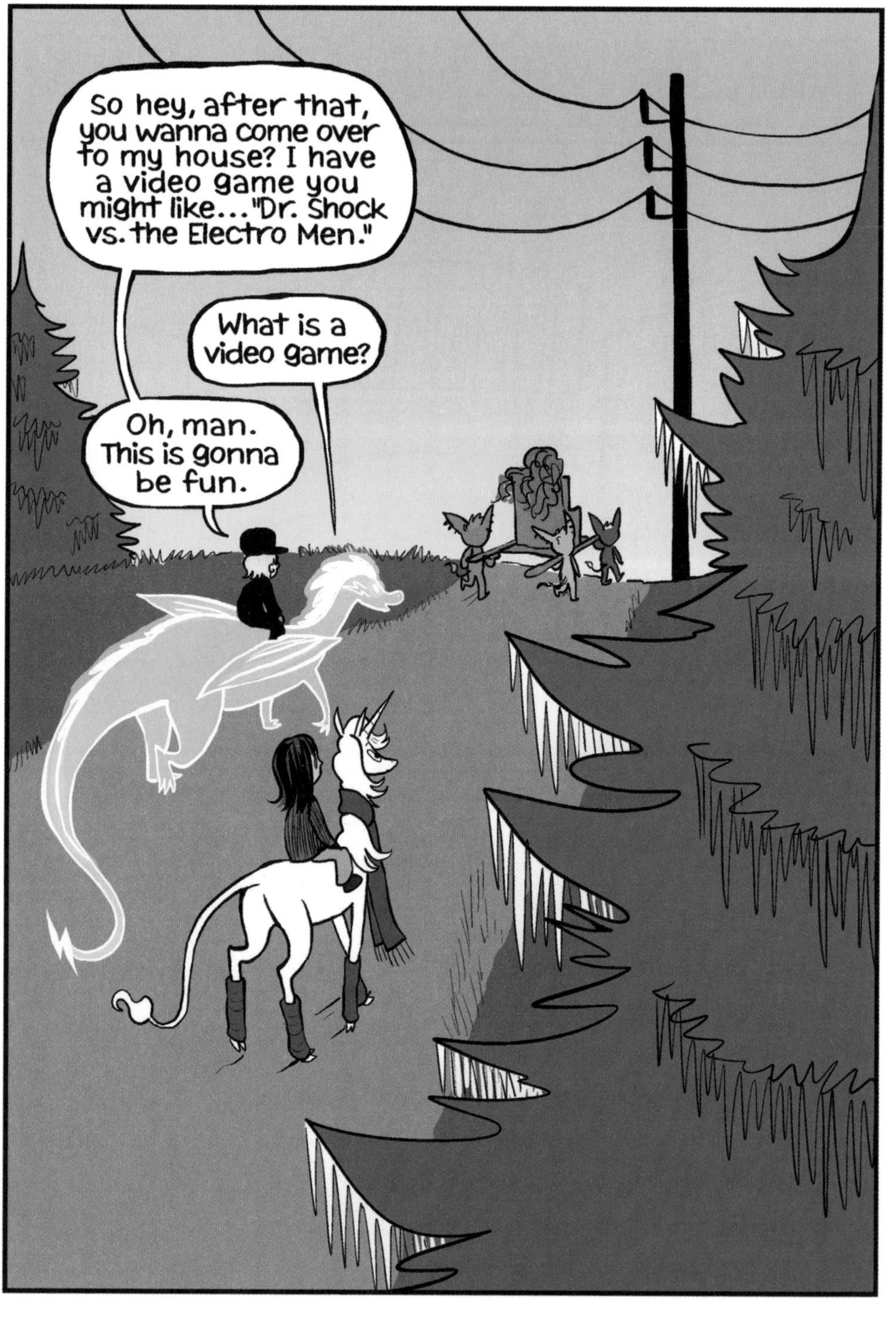
So hey, after that, you wanna come over to my house? I have a video game you might like..."Dr. Shock vs. the Electro Men."
What is a video game?
Oh, man. This is gonna be fun.

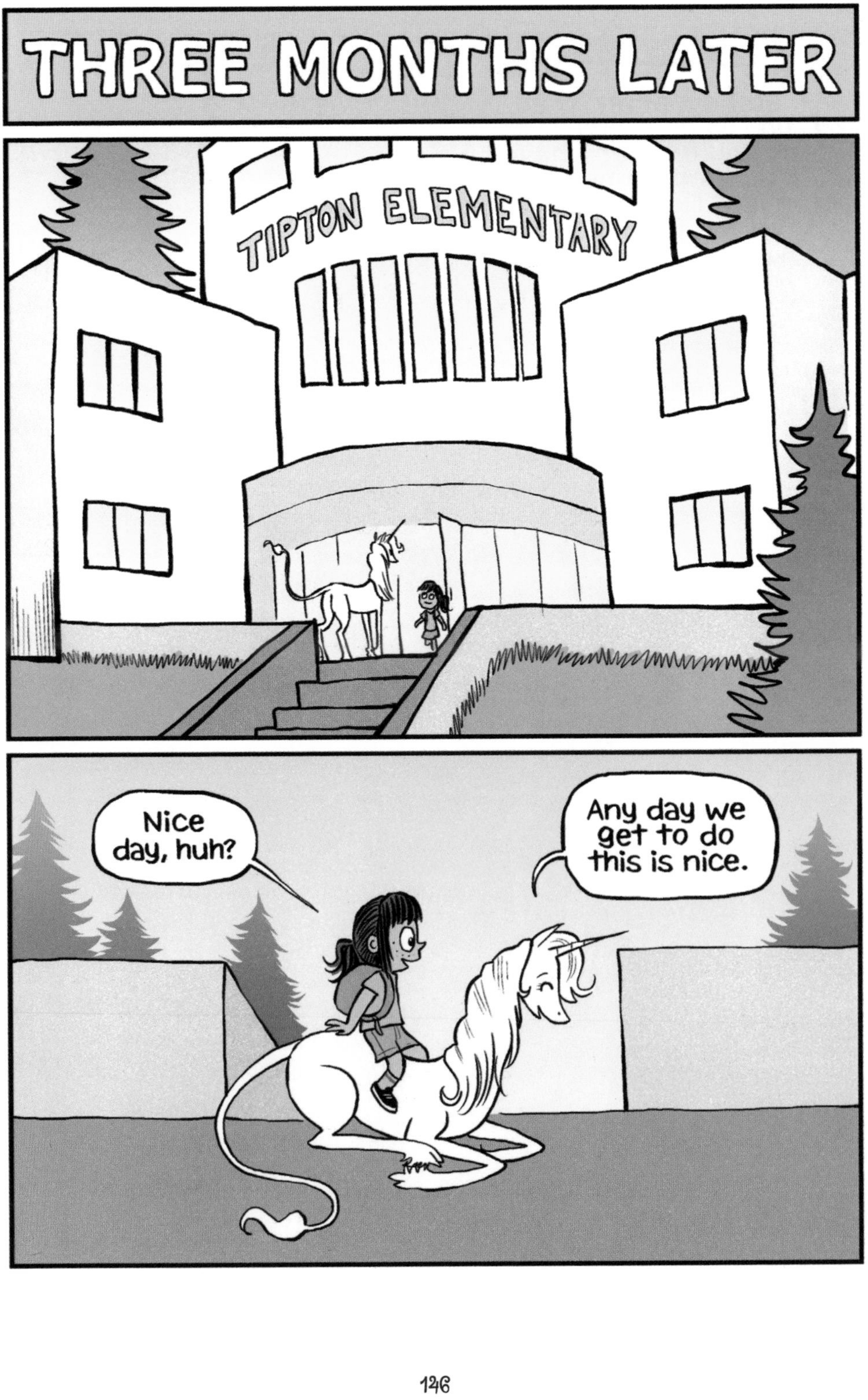
THREE MONTHS LATER
TIPTON ELEMENTARY
Nice day, huh?
Any day we get to do this is nice.

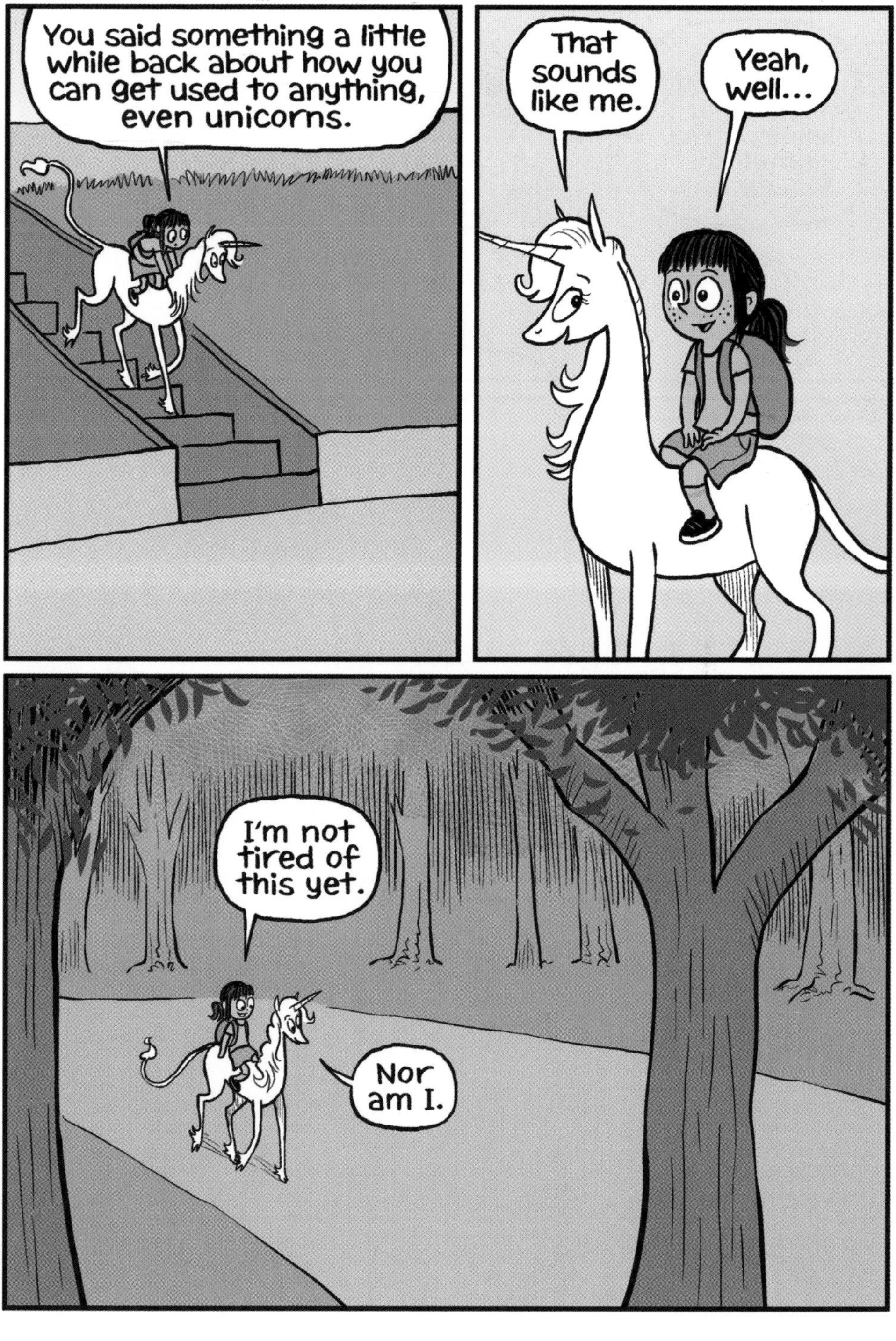
You said something a little while back about how you can get used to anything, even unicorns.
That sounds like me.
Yeah, well...
I'm not tired of this yet.
Nor am I.

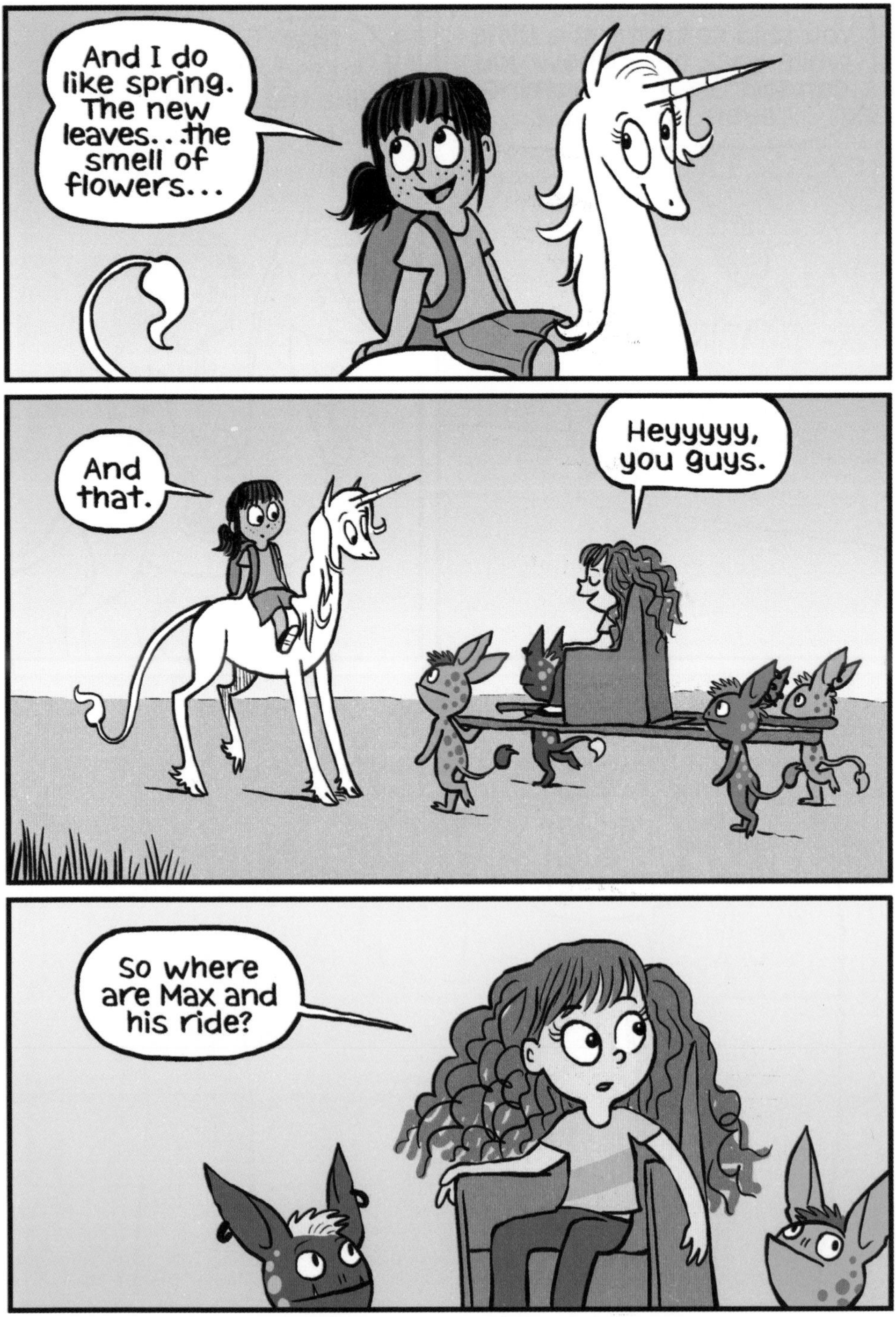
And I do like spring. The new leaves...the smell of flowers...
And that.
Heyyyyy, you guys.
So where are Max and his ride?

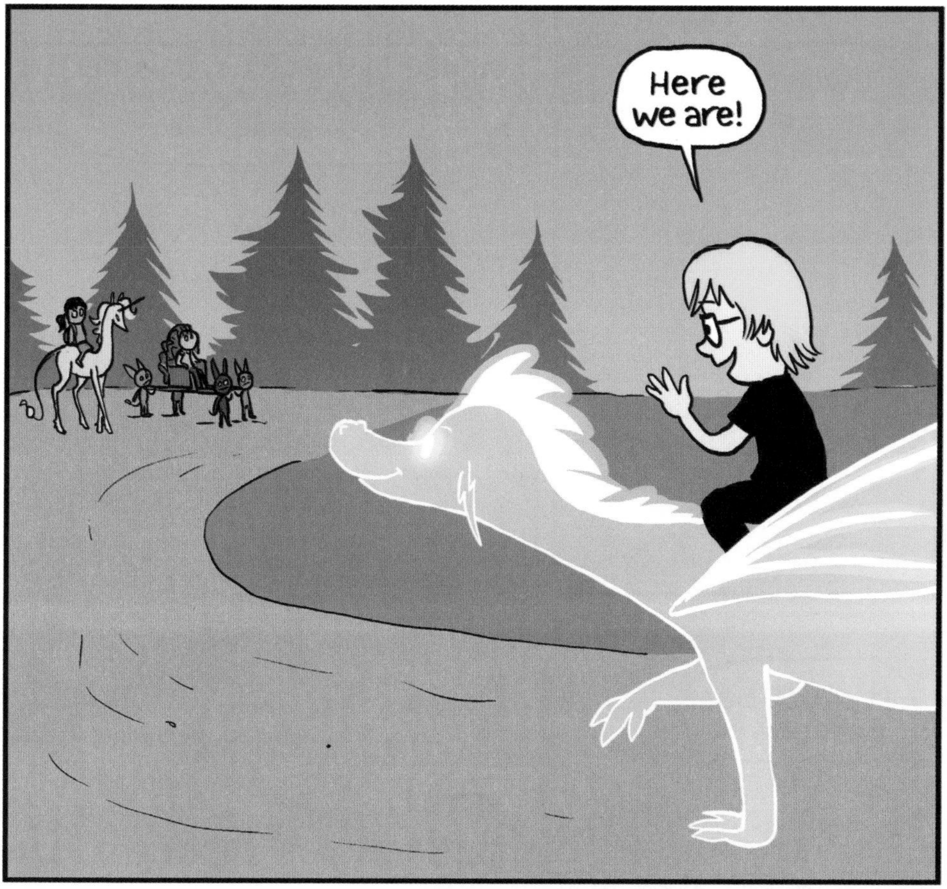
Here we are!

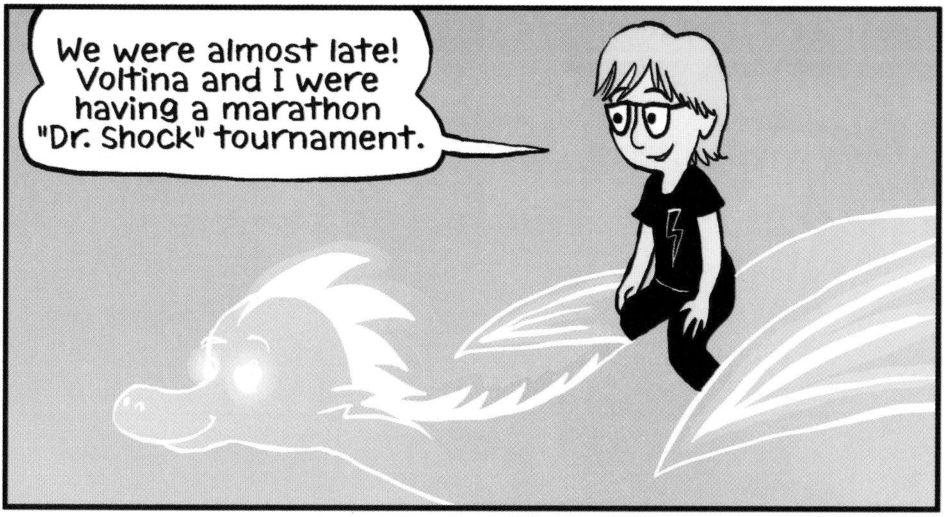
We were almost late! Voltina and I were having a marathon "Dr. Shock" tournament.

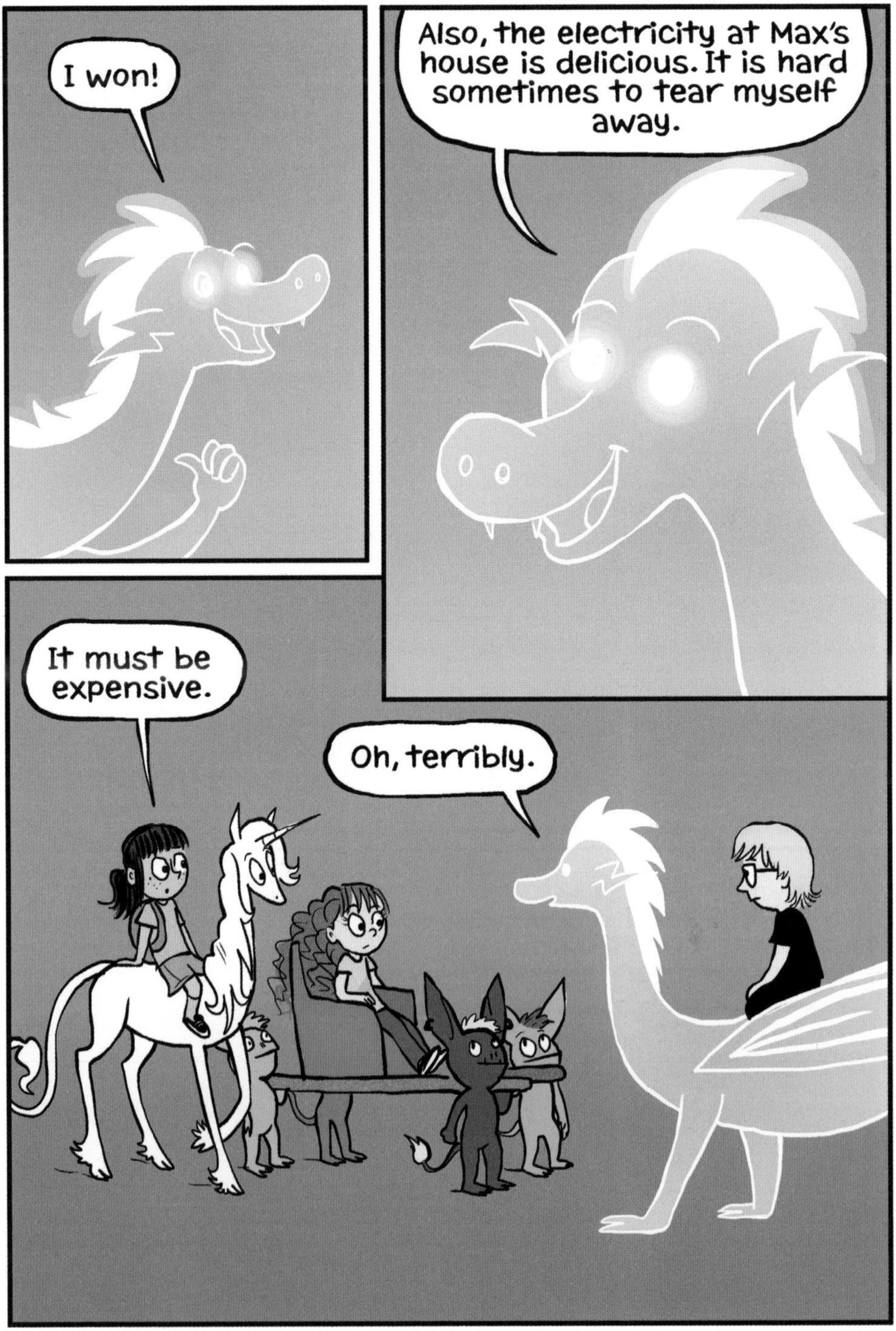
I won!
Also, the electricity at Max's house is delicious. It is hard sometimes to tear myself away.
It must be expensive.
Oh, terribly.

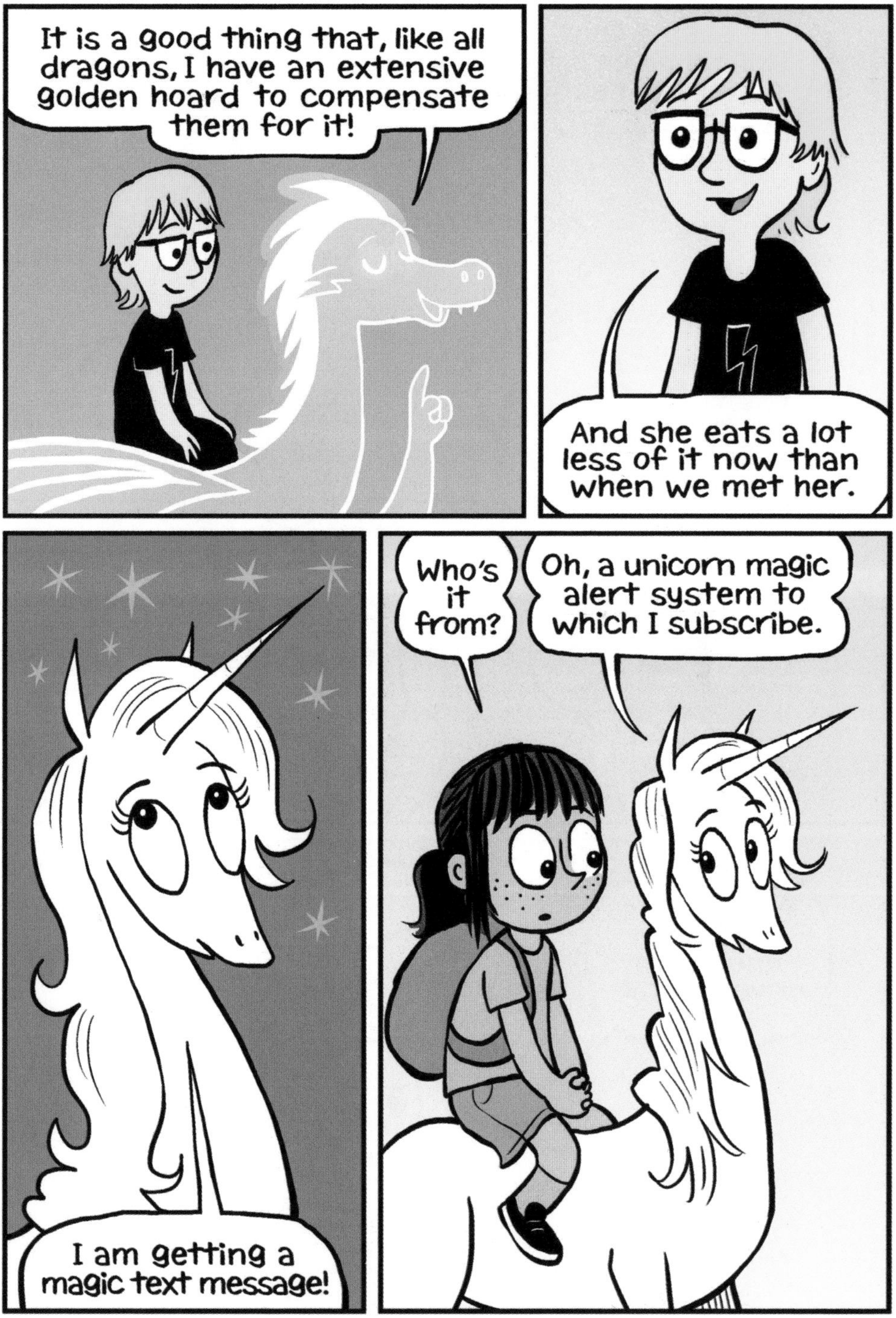
It is a good thing that, like all dragons, I have an extensive golden hoard to compensate them for it!
And she eats a lot less of it now than when we met her.
I am getting a magic text message!
Who's it from?
Oh, a unicorn magic alert system to which I subscribe.

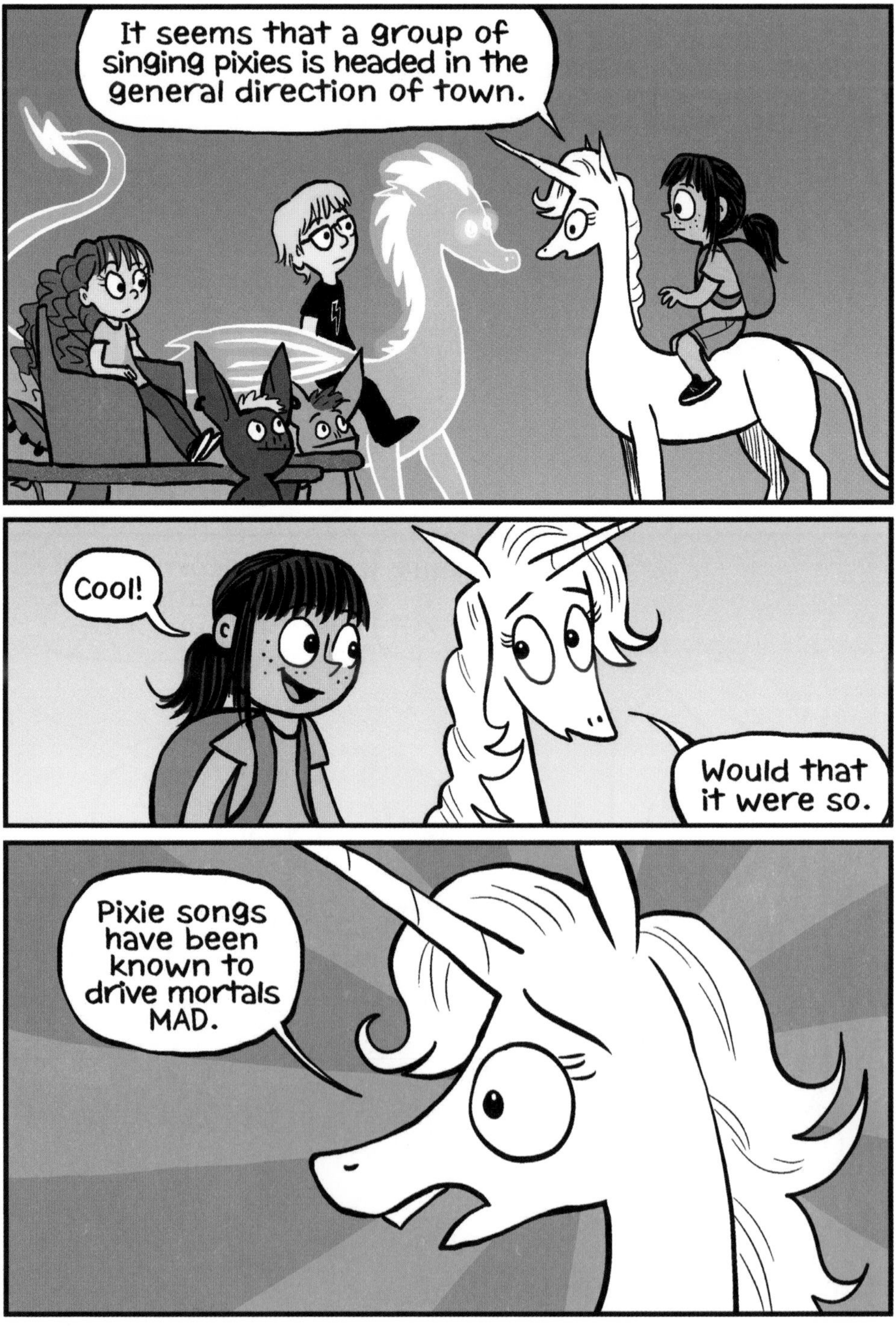
It seems that a group of singing pixies is headed in the general direction of town.
Cool!
Would that it were so.
Pixie songs have been known to drive mortals MAD.

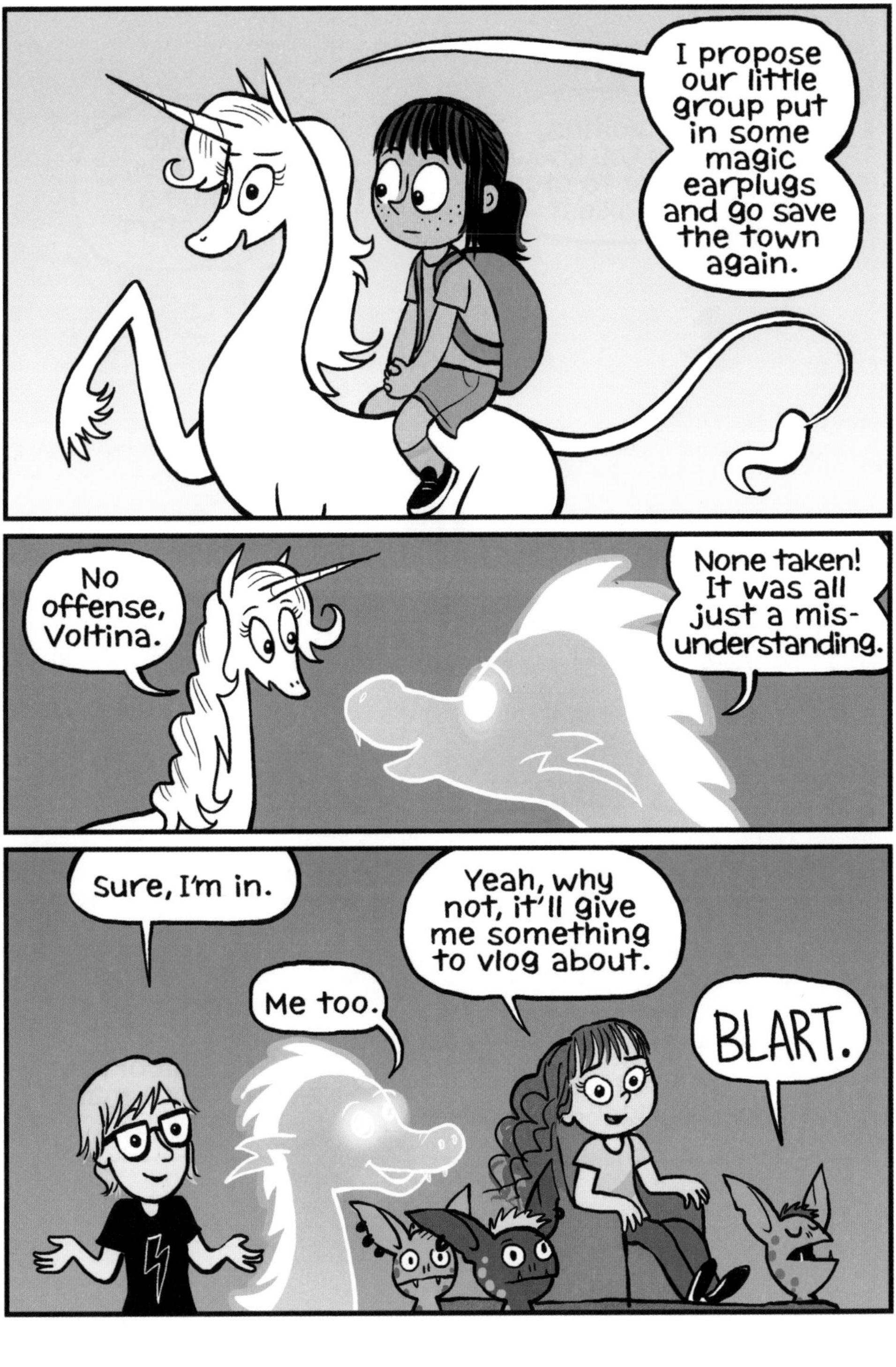
I propose our little group put in some magic earplugs and go save the town again.
No offense, Voltina.
None taken! It was all just a mis-understanding.
Sure, I'm in.
Me too.
Yeah, why not, it'll give me something to vlog about.
BLART.

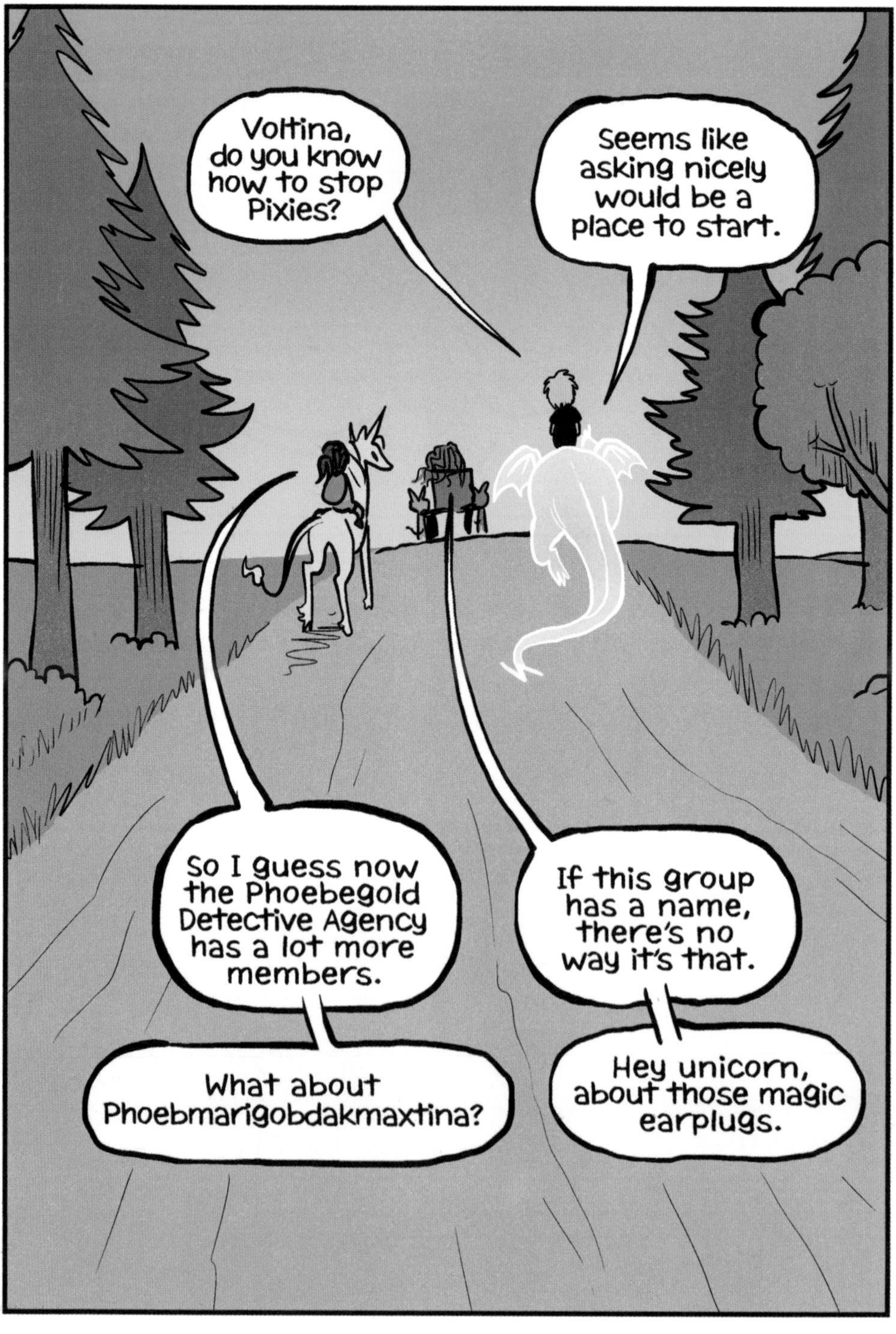
Voltina, do you know how to stop Pixies?
Seems like asking nicely would be a place to start.
So I guess now the Phoebegold Detective Agency has a lot more members.
What about Phoebmarigobdakmaxtina?
If this group has a name, there's no way it's that.
Hey unicorn, about those magic earplugs.

Phoebe and Her Unicorn in Unicorn Theater

Dana Simpson

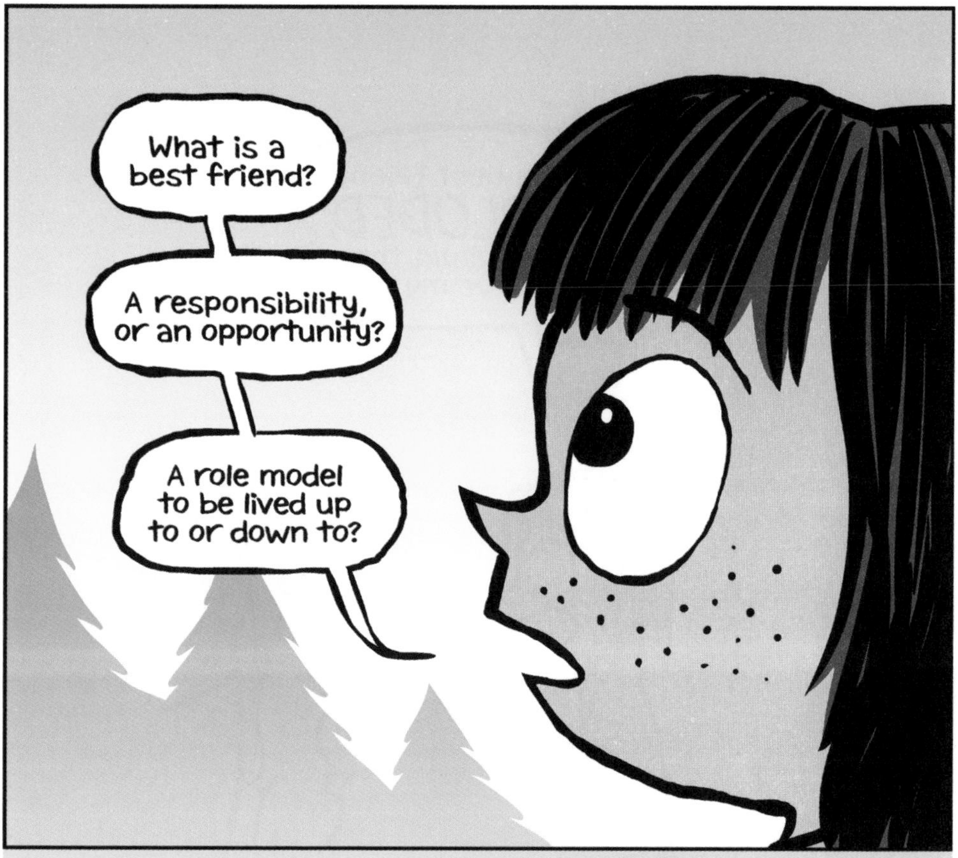
What is a best friend?
A responsibility, or an opportunity?
A role model to be lived up to or down to?

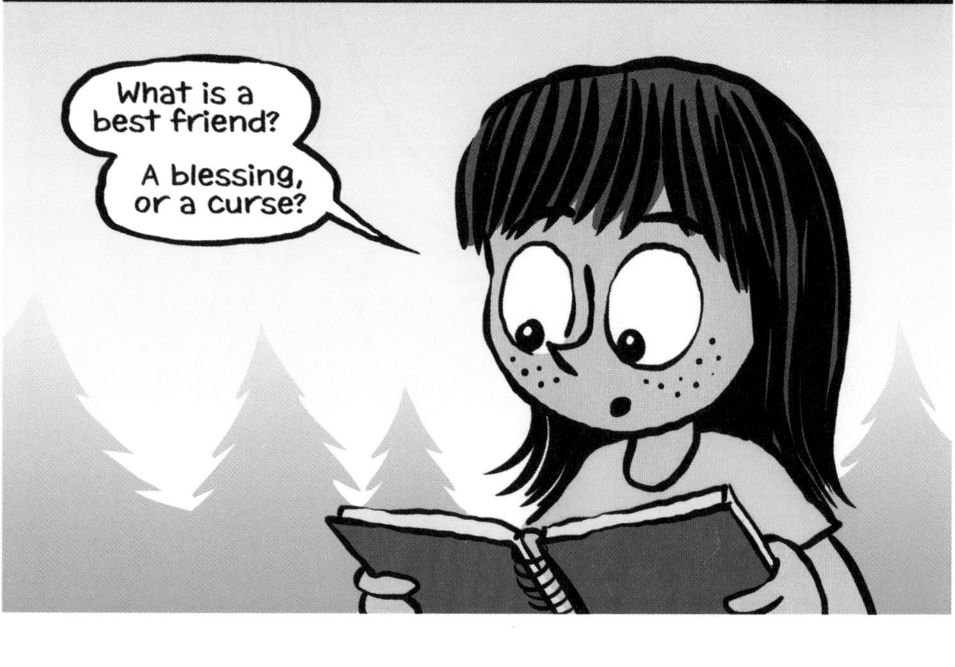
What is a best friend?
A blessing, or a curse?

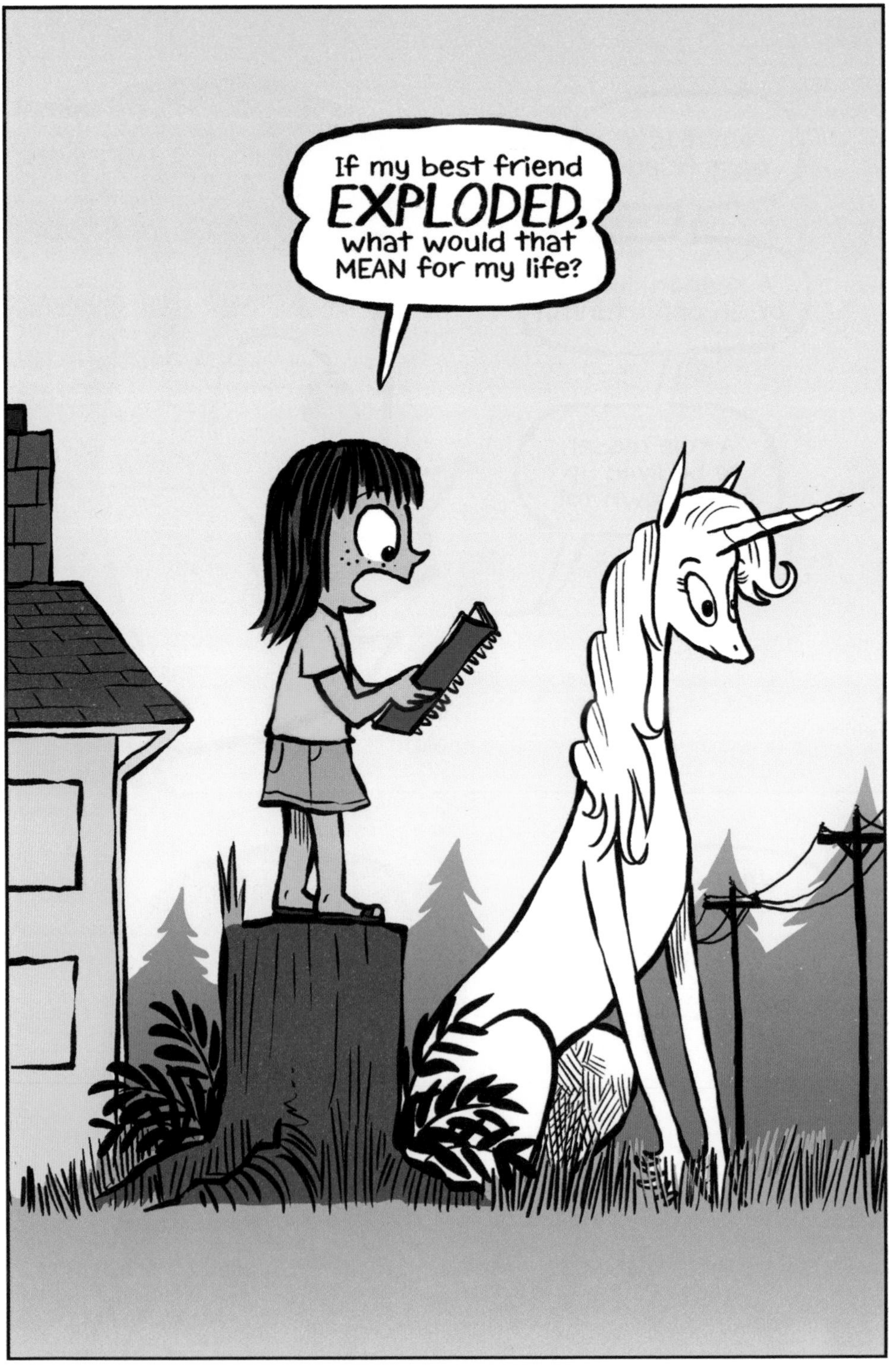
If my best friend EXPLODED, what would that MEAN for my life?

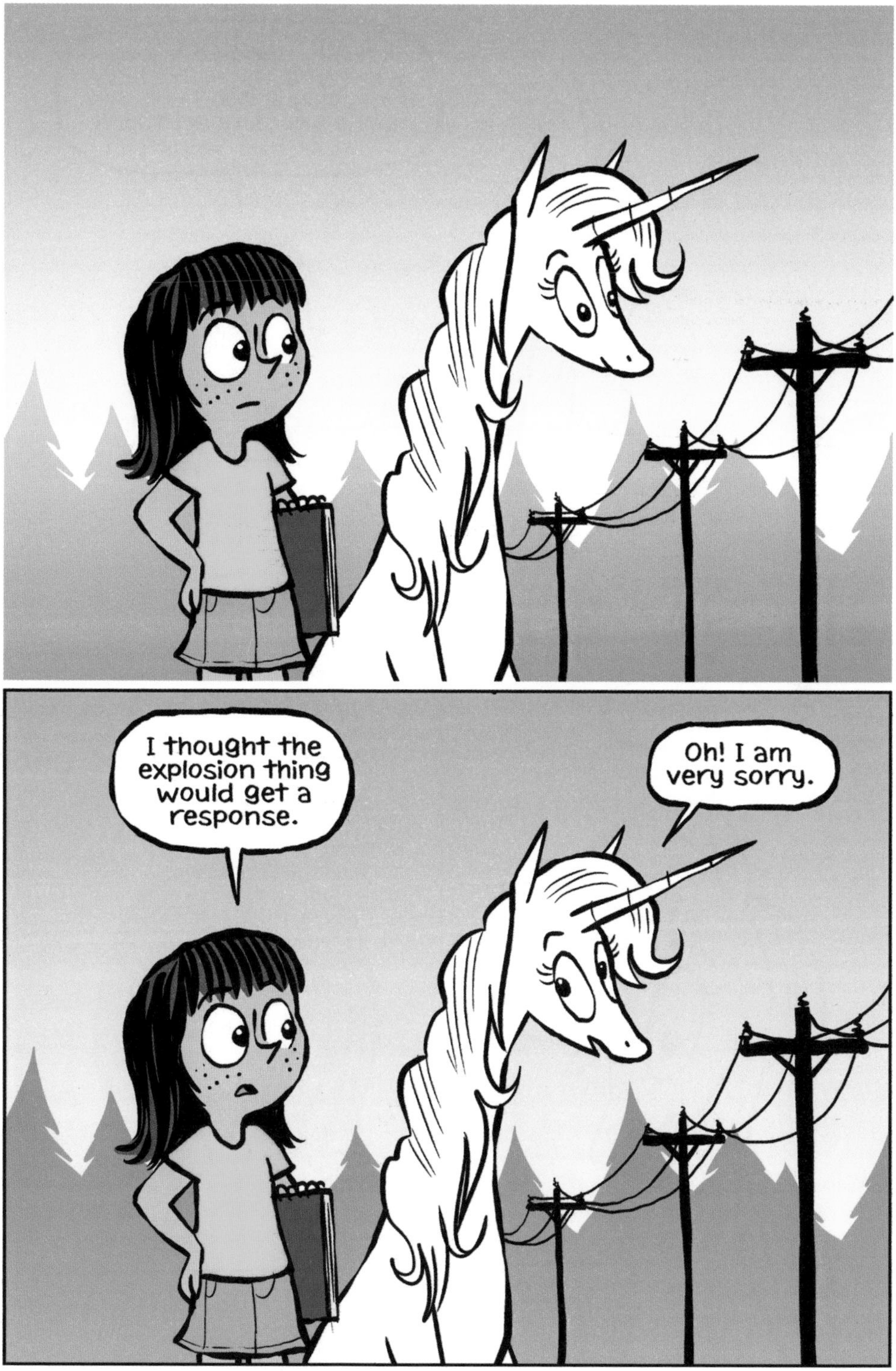
I thought the explosion thing would get a response.
Oh! I am very sorry.

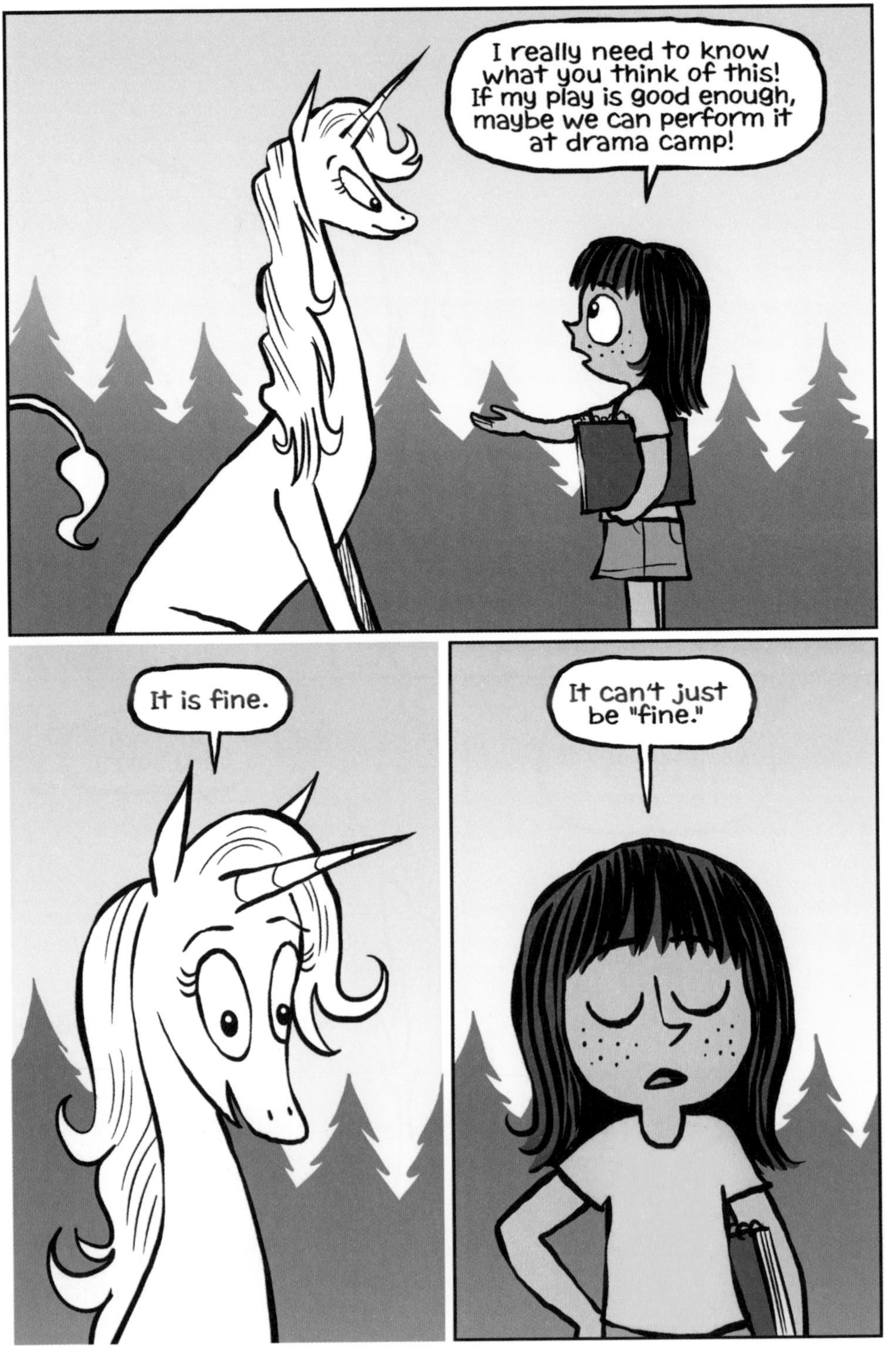
I really need to know what you think of this! If my play is good enough, maybe we can perform it at drama camp!
It is fine.
It can't just be "fine."

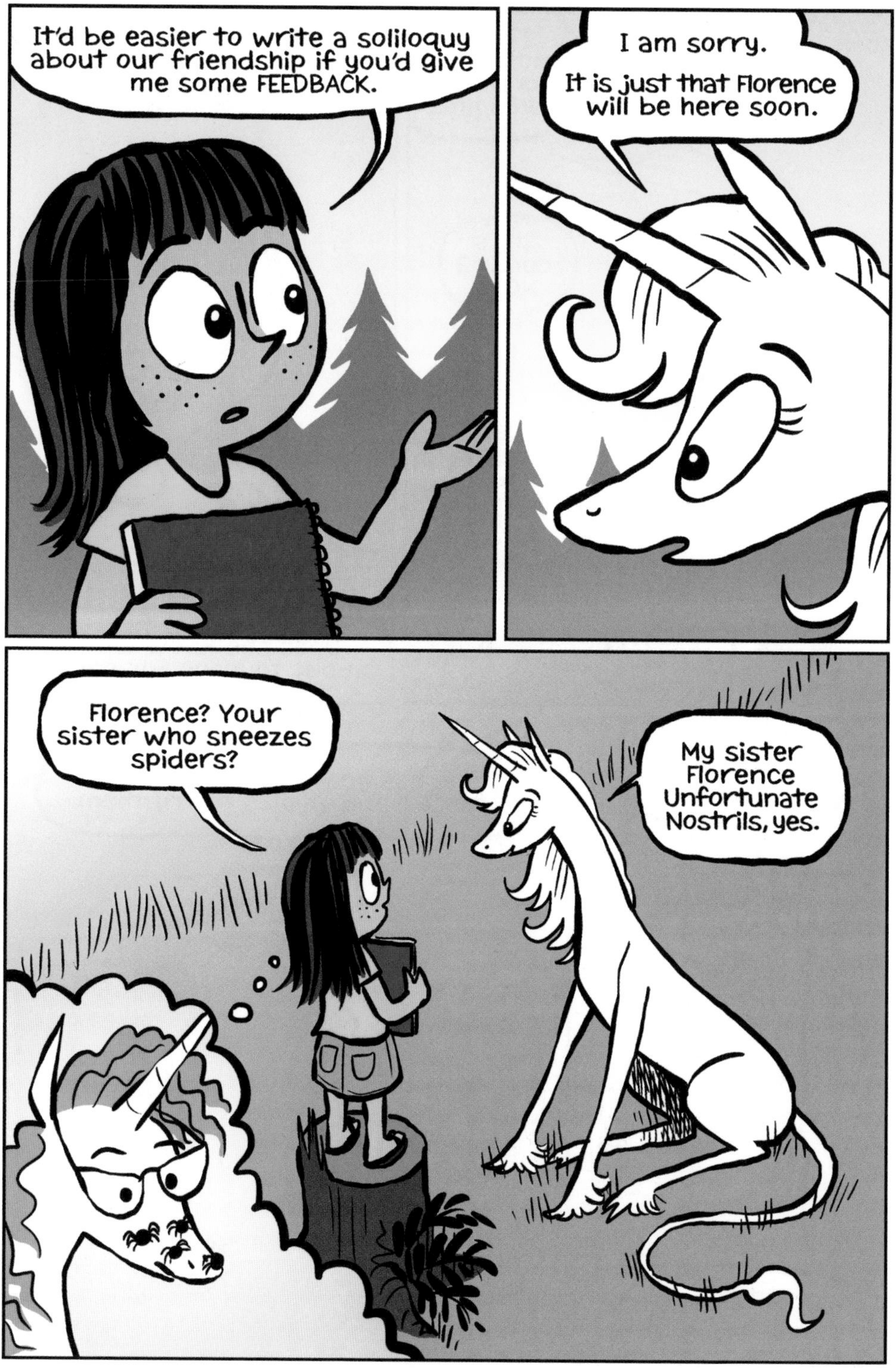
It'd be easier to write a soliloquy about our friendship if you'd give me some FEEDBACK.
I am sorry.
It is just that Florence will be here soon.
Florence? Your sister who sneezes spiders?
My sister Florence Unfortunate Nostrils, yes.

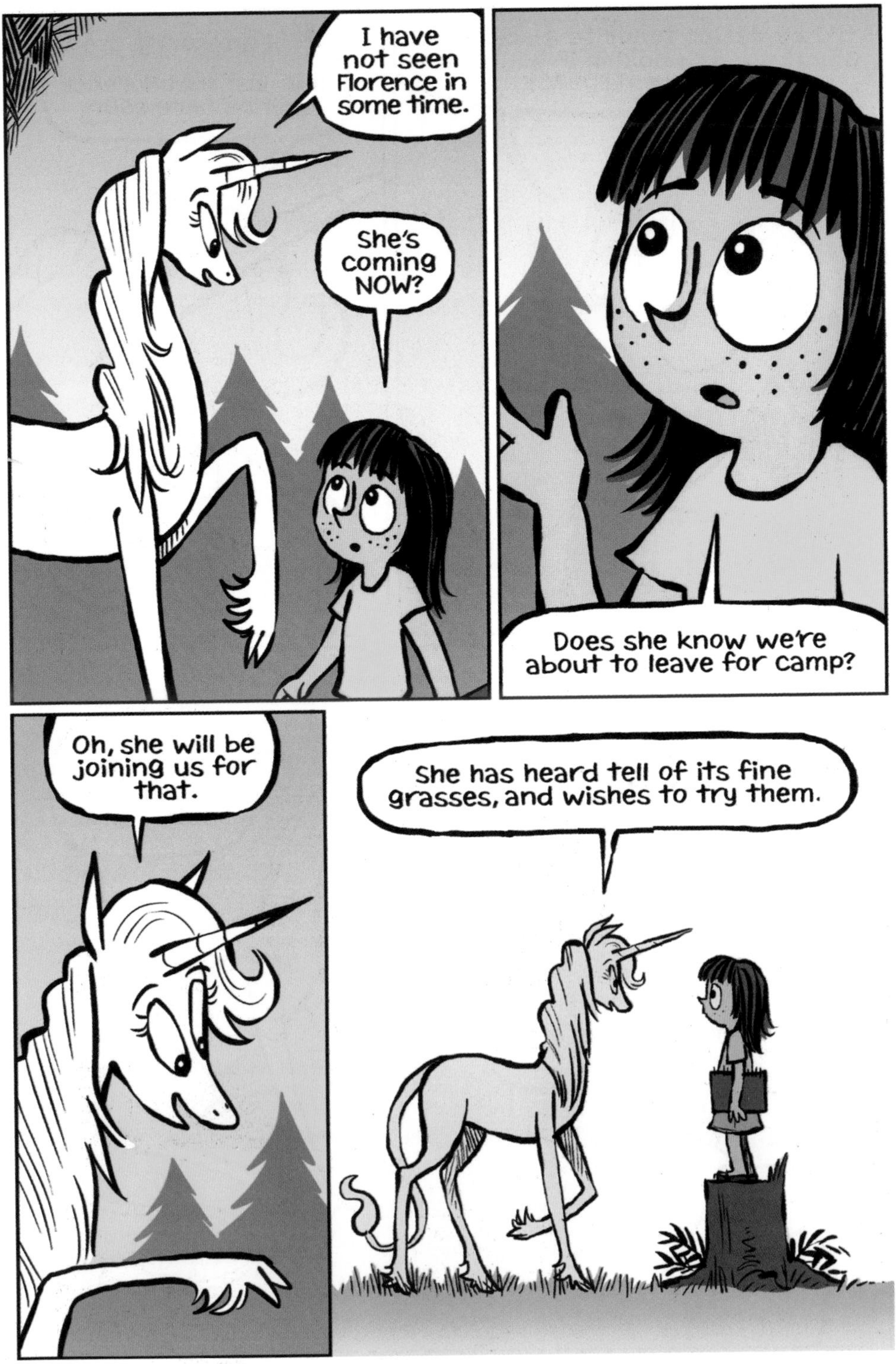
I have not seen Florence in some time.
She's coming NOW?
Does she know we're about to leave for camp?
Oh, she will be joining us for that.
She has heard tell of its fine grasses, and wishes to try them.

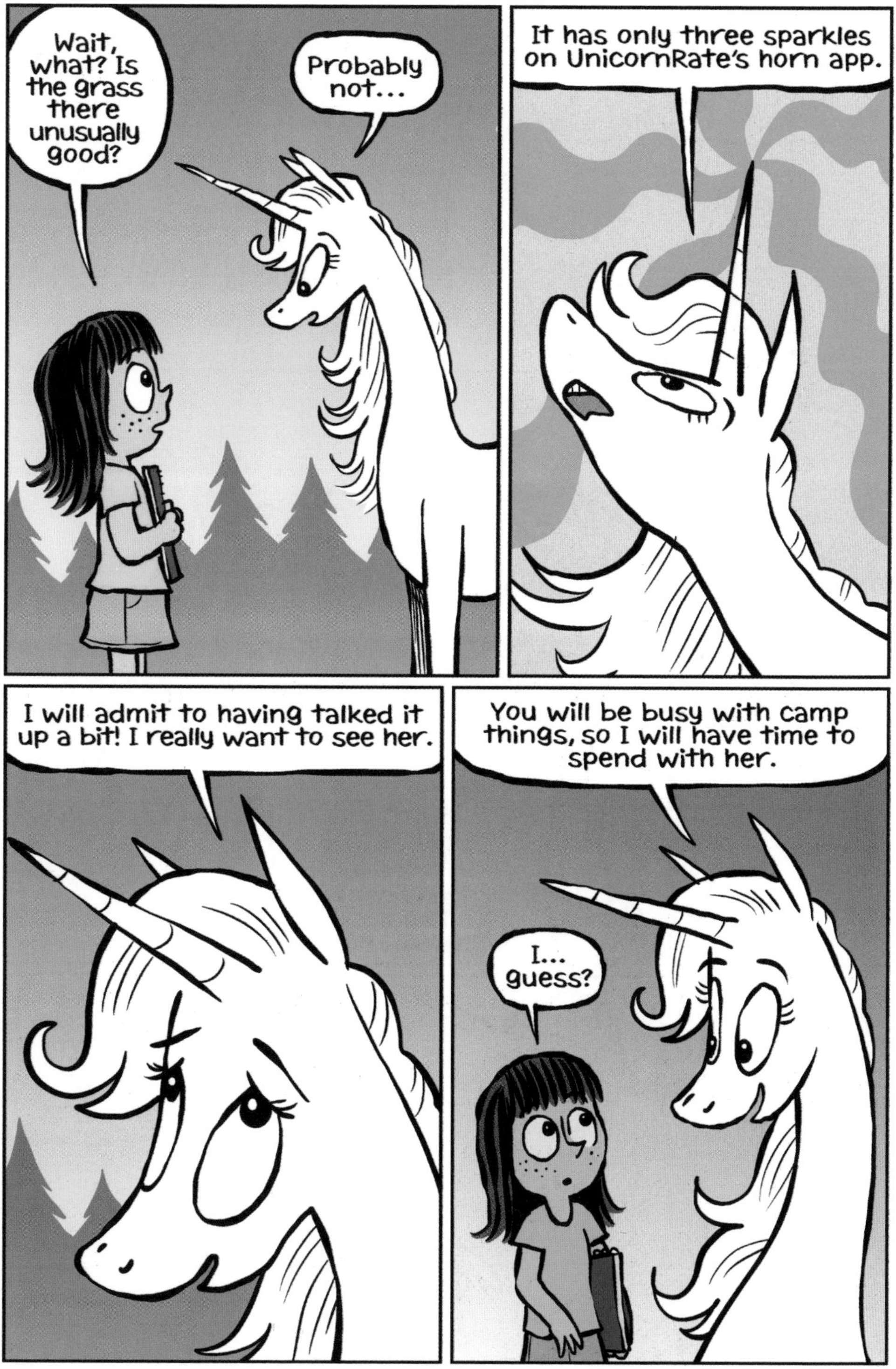
Wait, what? Is the grass there unusually good?
Probably not...
It has only three sparkles on UnicornRate's horn app.
I will admit to having talked it up a bit! I really want to see her.
You will be busy with camp things, so I will have time to spend with her.
I... guess?

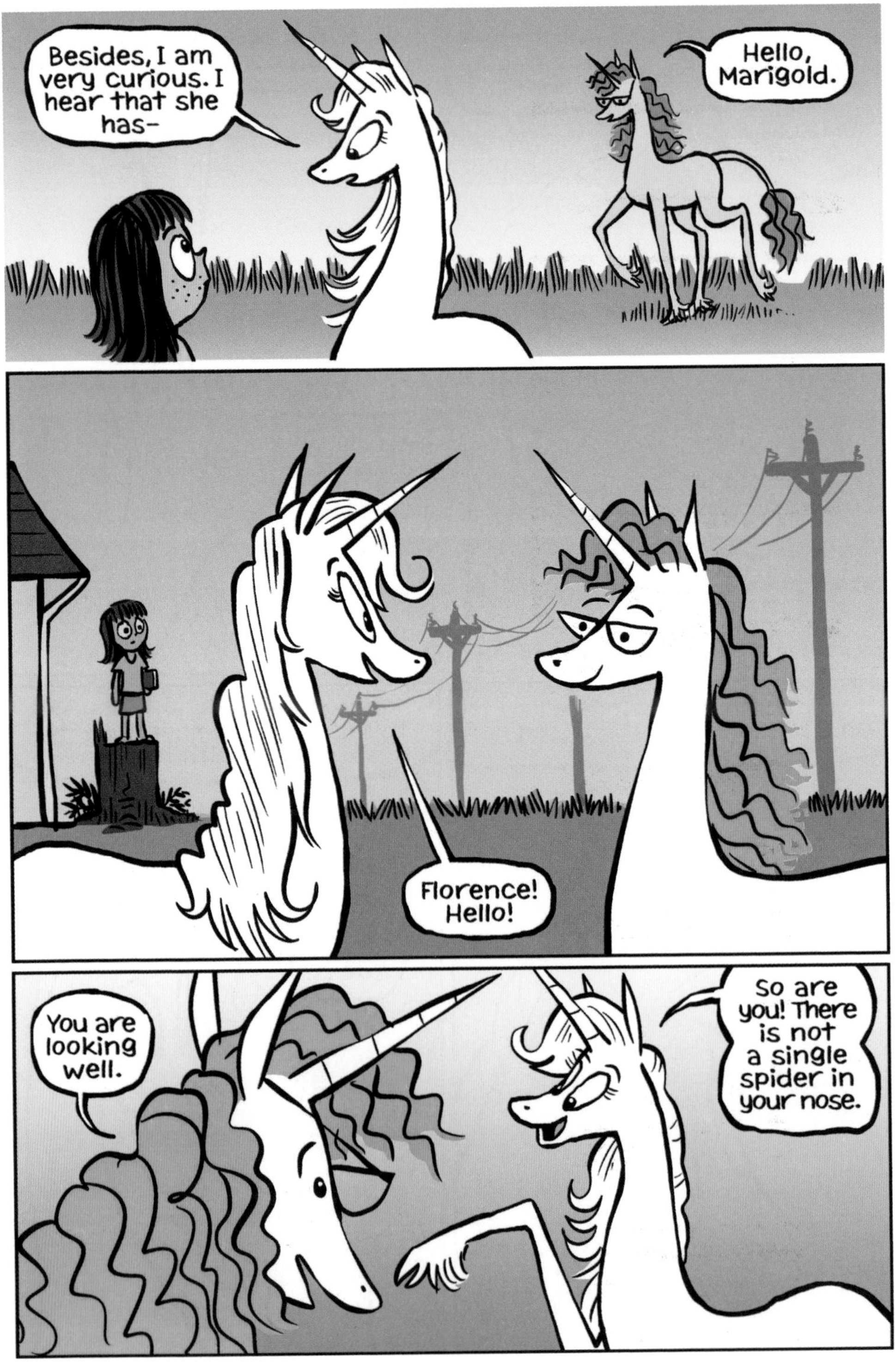
Besides, I am very curious. I hear that she has-
Hello, Marigold.
Florence! Hello!
You are looking well.
So are you! There is not a single spider in your nose.

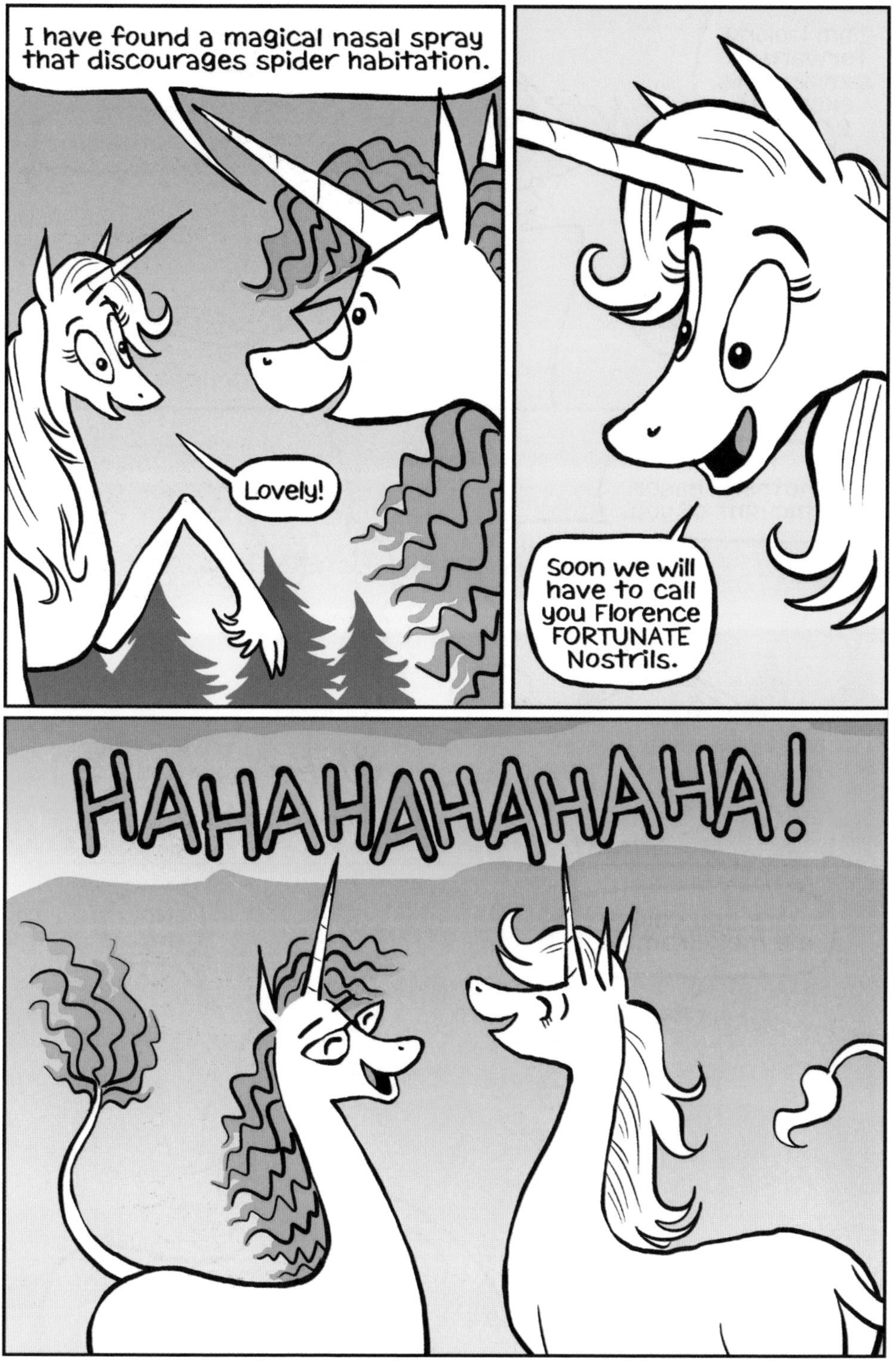
I have found a magical nasal spray that discourages spider habitation.
Lovely!
Soon we will have to call you Florence FORTUNATE Nostrils.
HAHAHAHAHAHA!

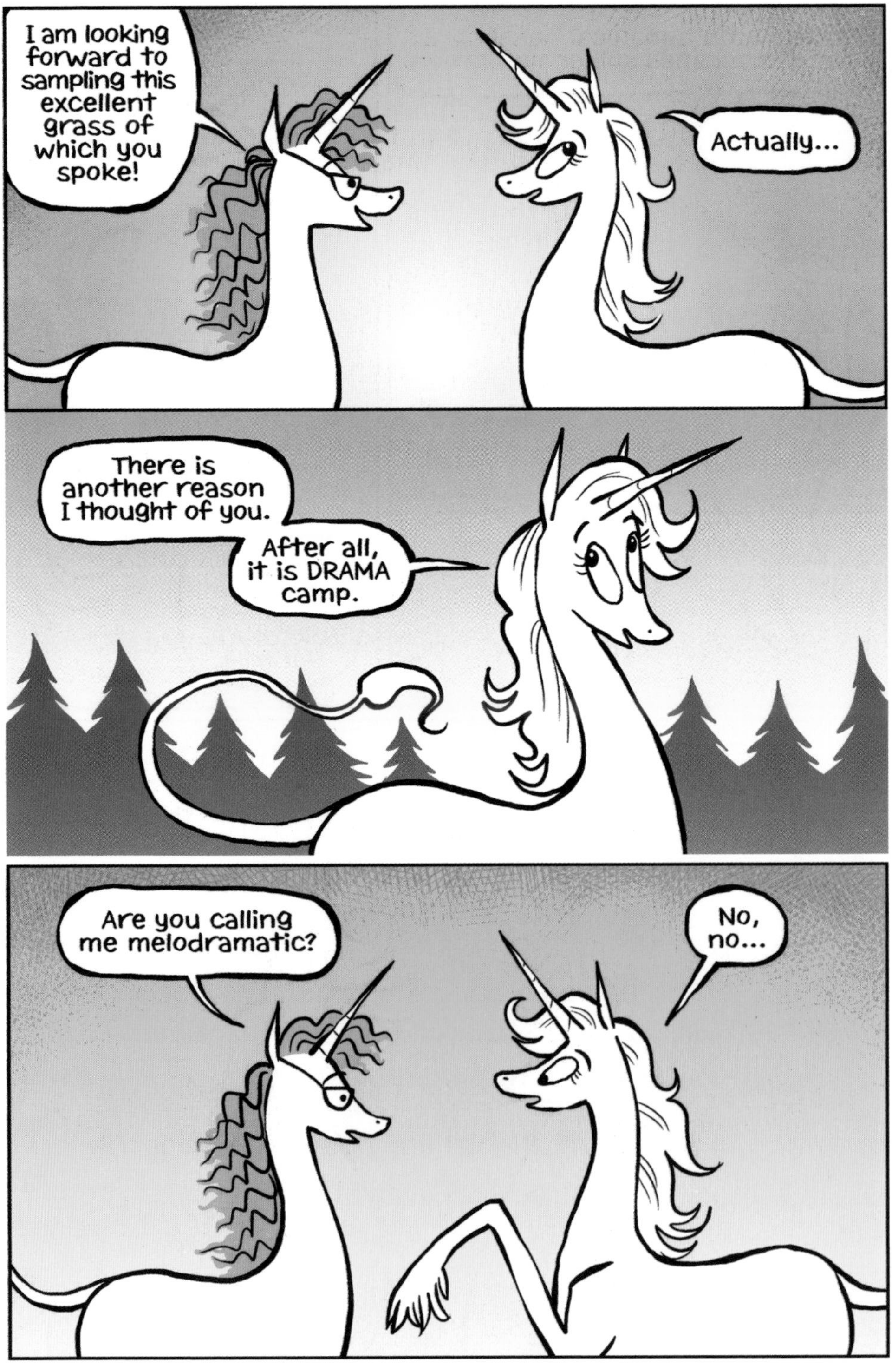
I am looking forward to sampling this excellent grass of which you spoke!
Actually...
There is another reason I thought of you.
After all, it is DRAMA camp.
Are you calling me melodramatic?
No, no...

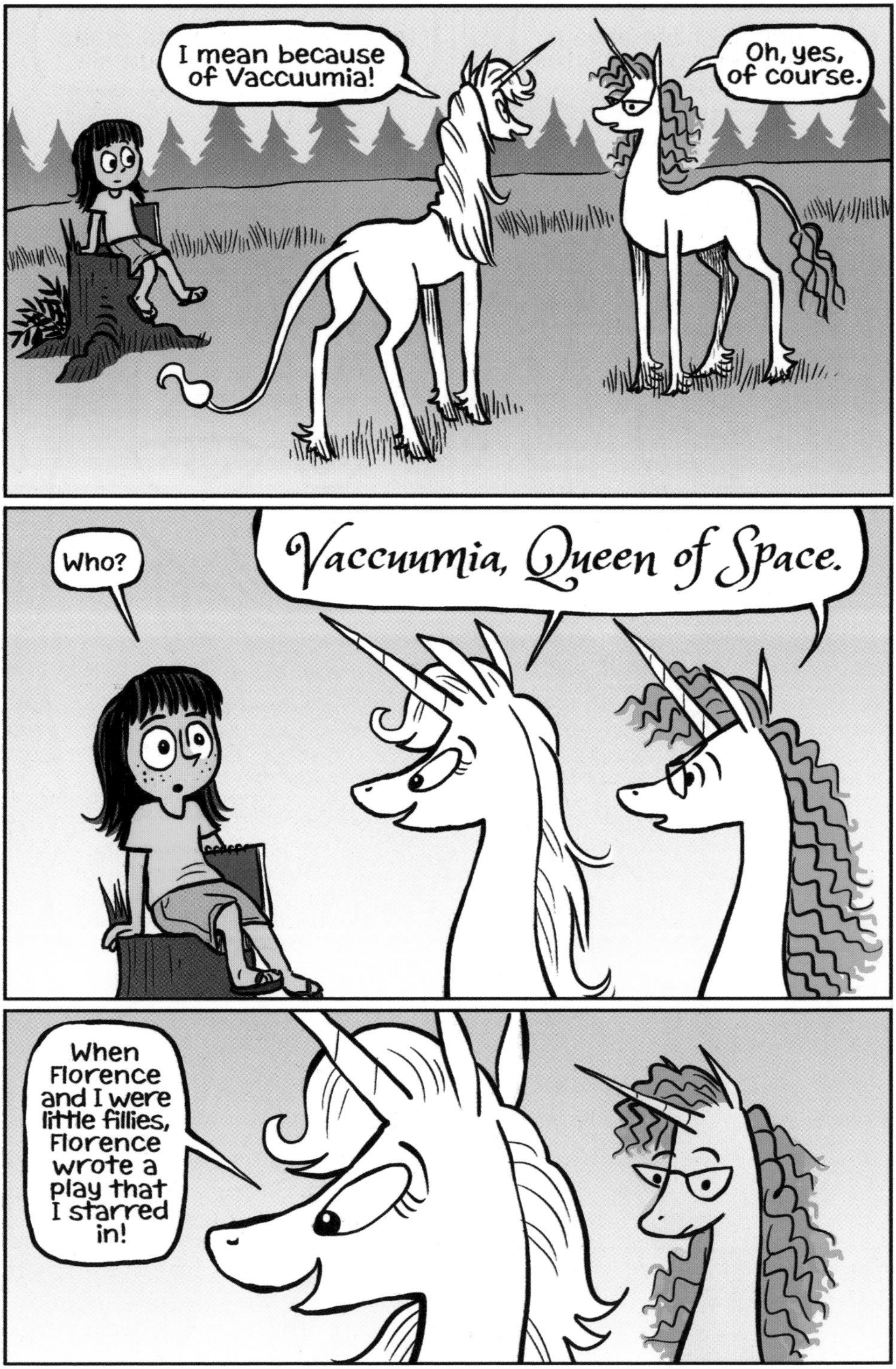
I mean because of Vaccuumia!
Oh, yes, of course.
Who?
Vaccuumia, Queen of Space.
When Florence and I were little fillies, Florence wrote a play that I starred in!

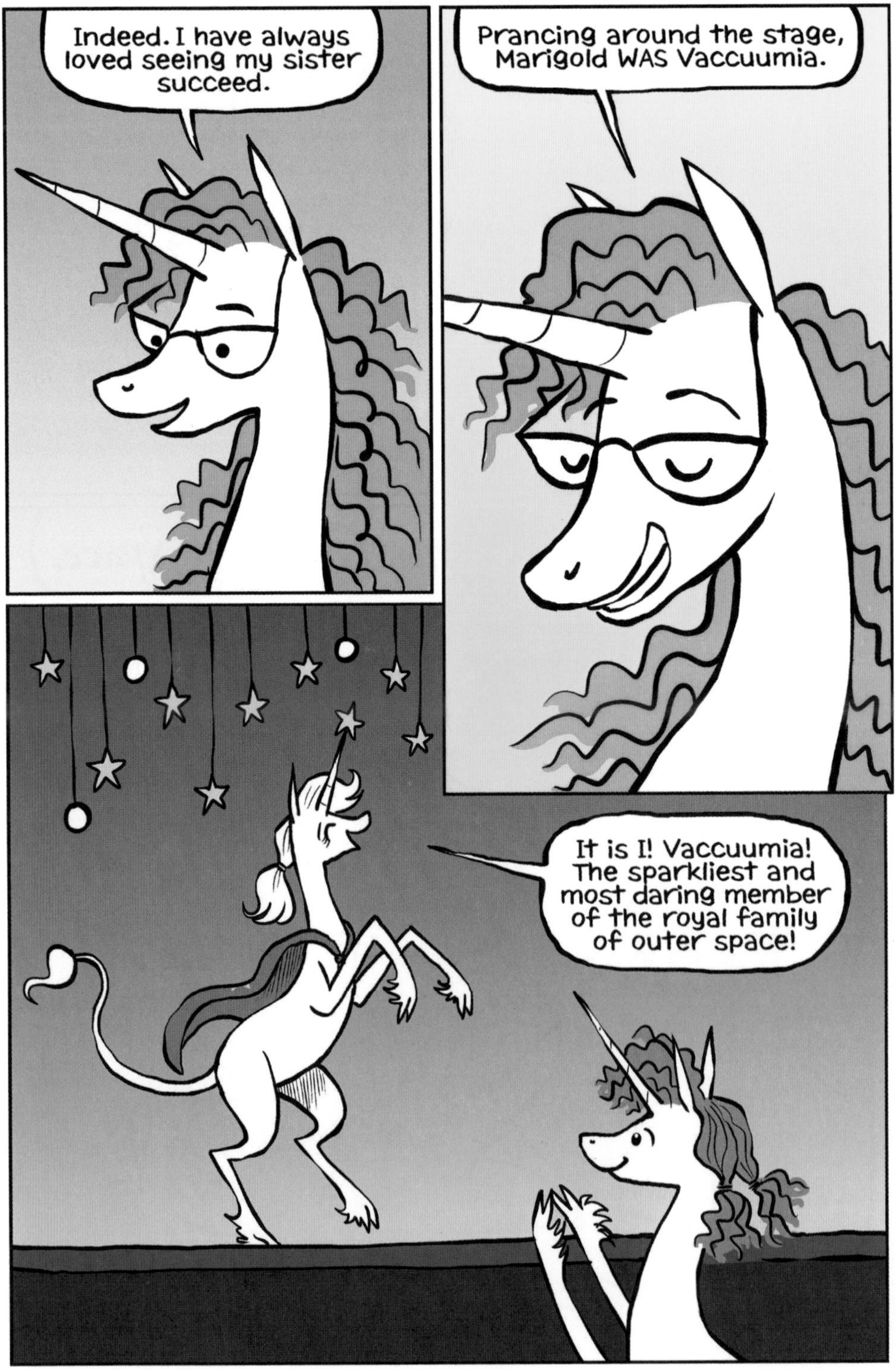
Indeed. I have always loved seeing my sister succeed.
Prancing around the stage, Marigold WAS Vaccuumia.
It is I! Vaccuumia! The sparkliest and most daring member of the royal family of outer space!

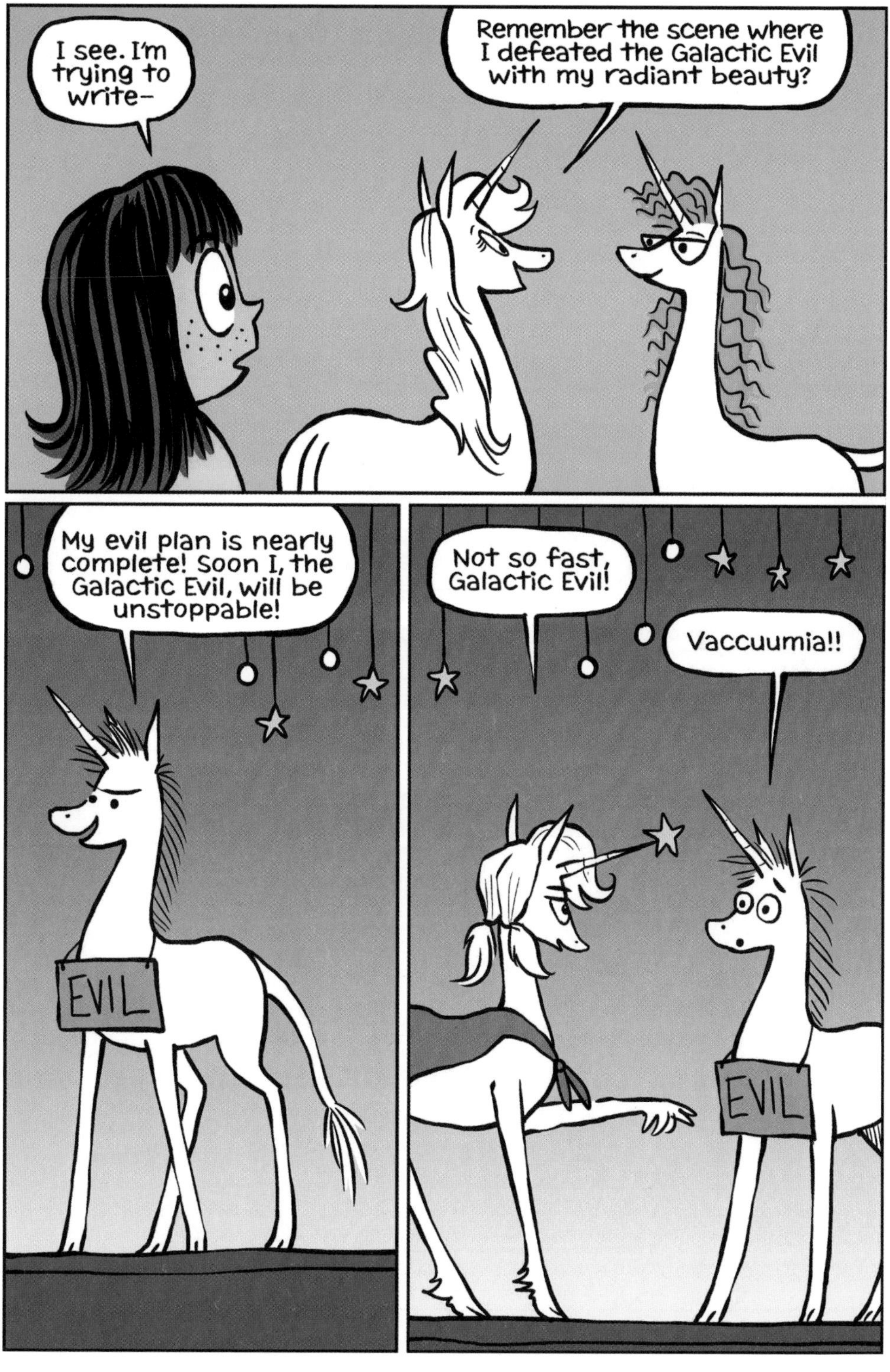
I see. I'm trying to write-
Remember the scene where I defeated the Galactic Evil with my radiant beauty?
My evil plan is nearly complete! Soon I, the Galactic Evil, will be unstoppable!
EVIL
Not so fast, Galactic Evil!
Vaccuumia!!
EVIL

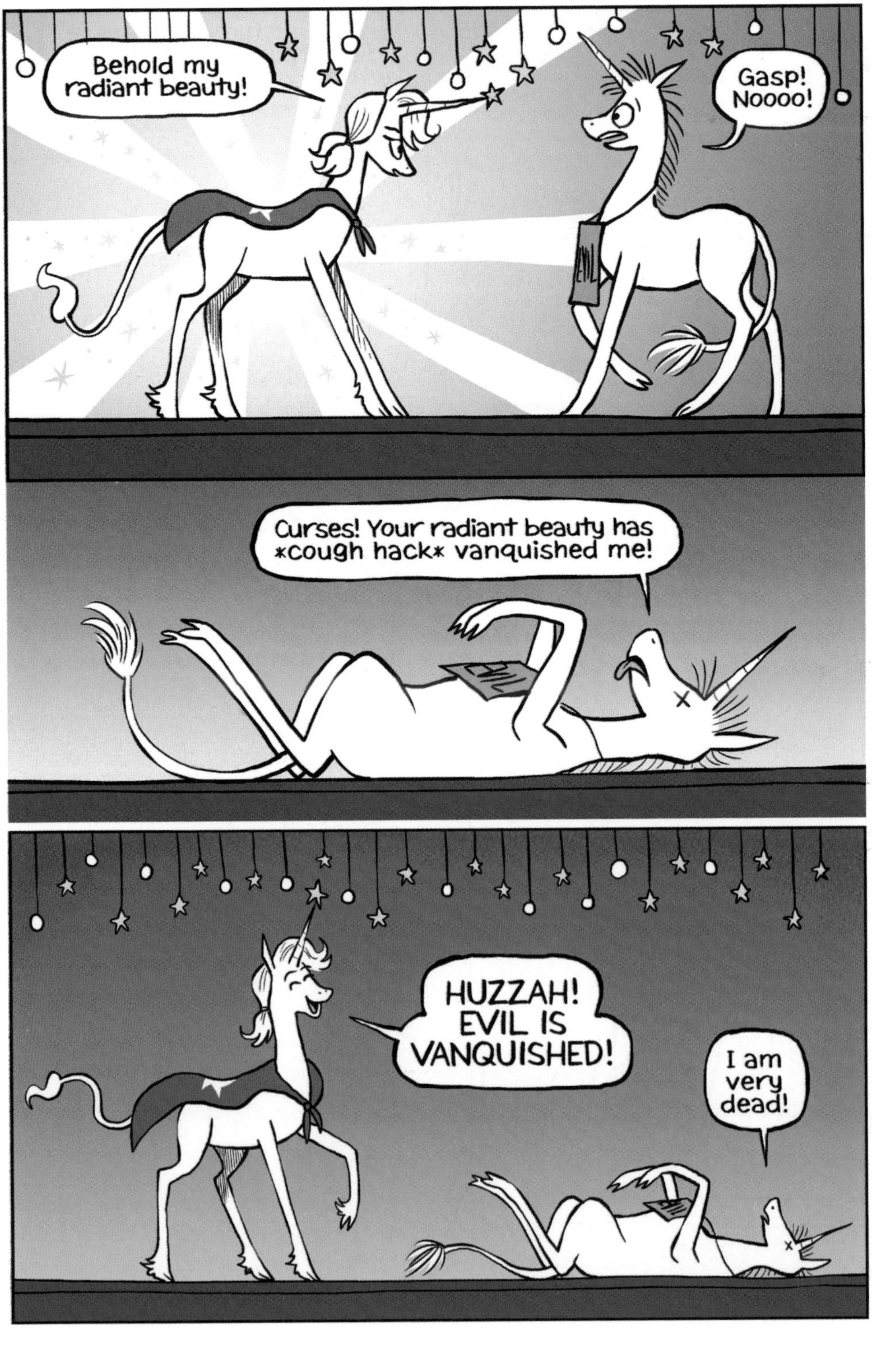
Behold my radiant beauty!
Gasp! Noooo!
Curses! Your radiant beauty has *cough hack* vanquished me!
HUZZAH! EVIL IS VANQUISHED!
I am very dead!

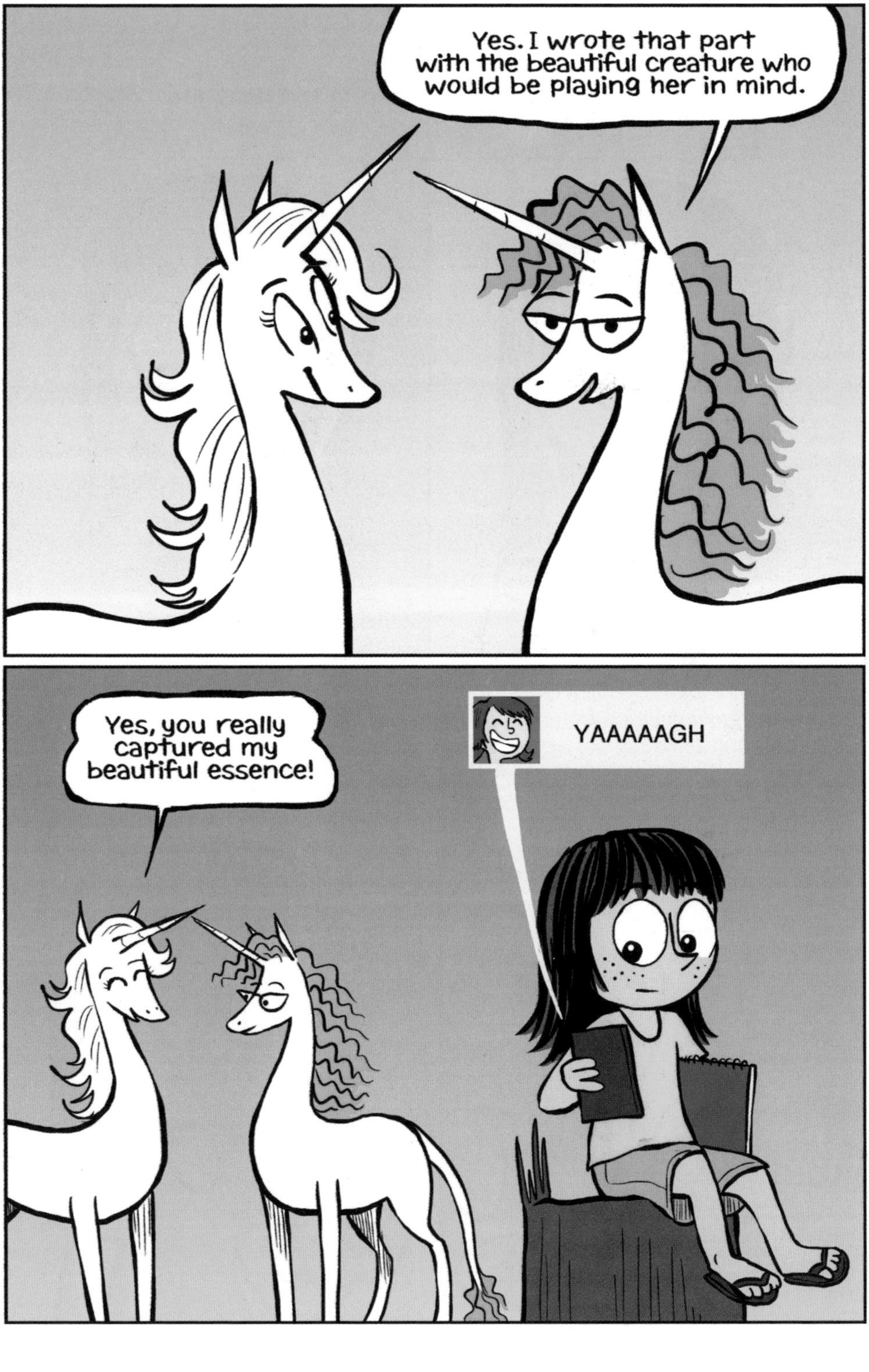
Yes. I wrote that part with the beautiful creature who would be playing her in mind.
Yes, you really captured my beautiful essence!
YAAAAAGH

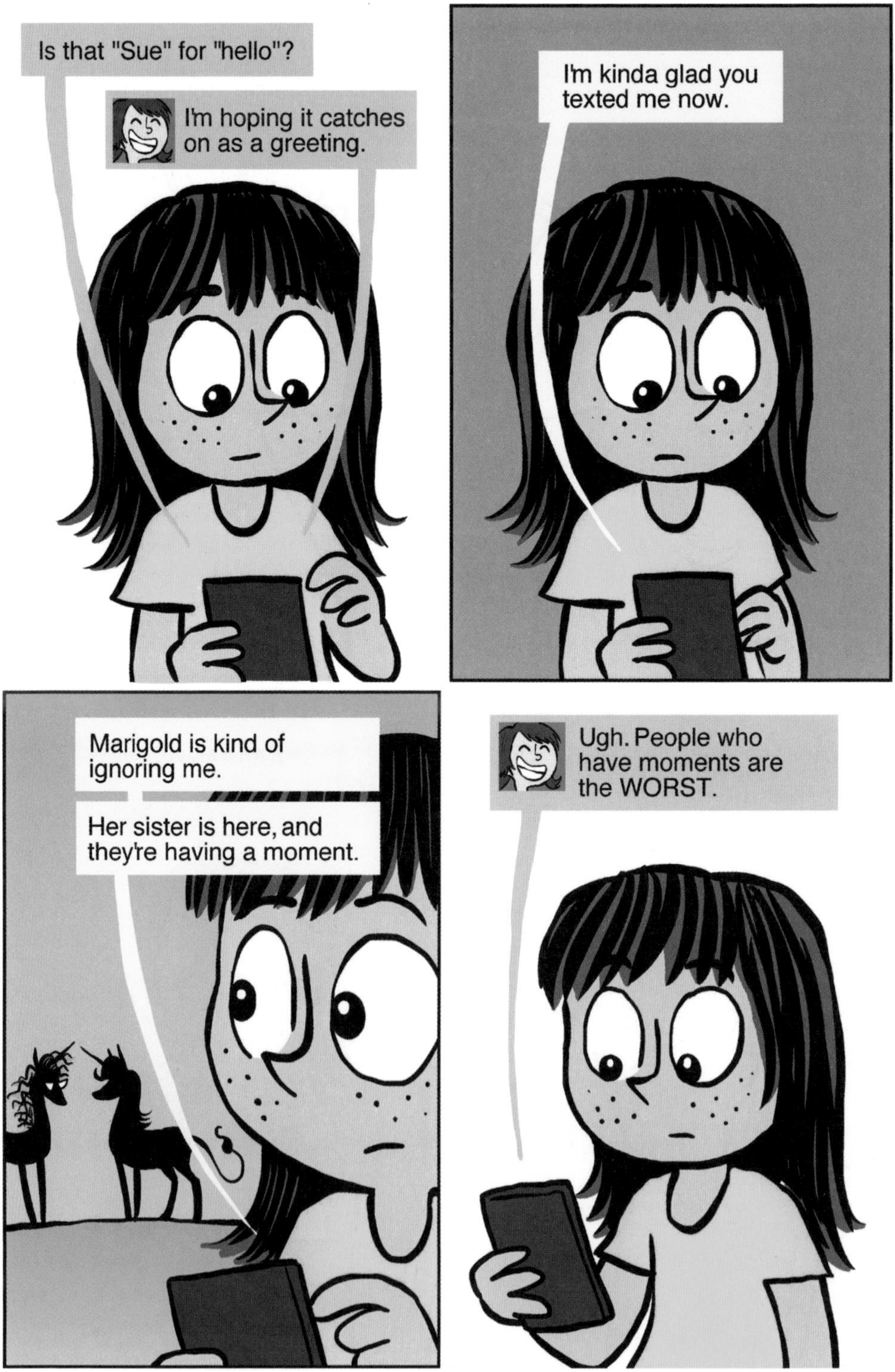
Is that "Sue" for "hello"?
I'm hoping it catches on as a greeting.
I'm kinda glad you texted me now.
Marigold is kind of ignoring me.
Her sister is here, and they're having a moment.
Ugh. People who have moments are the WORST.

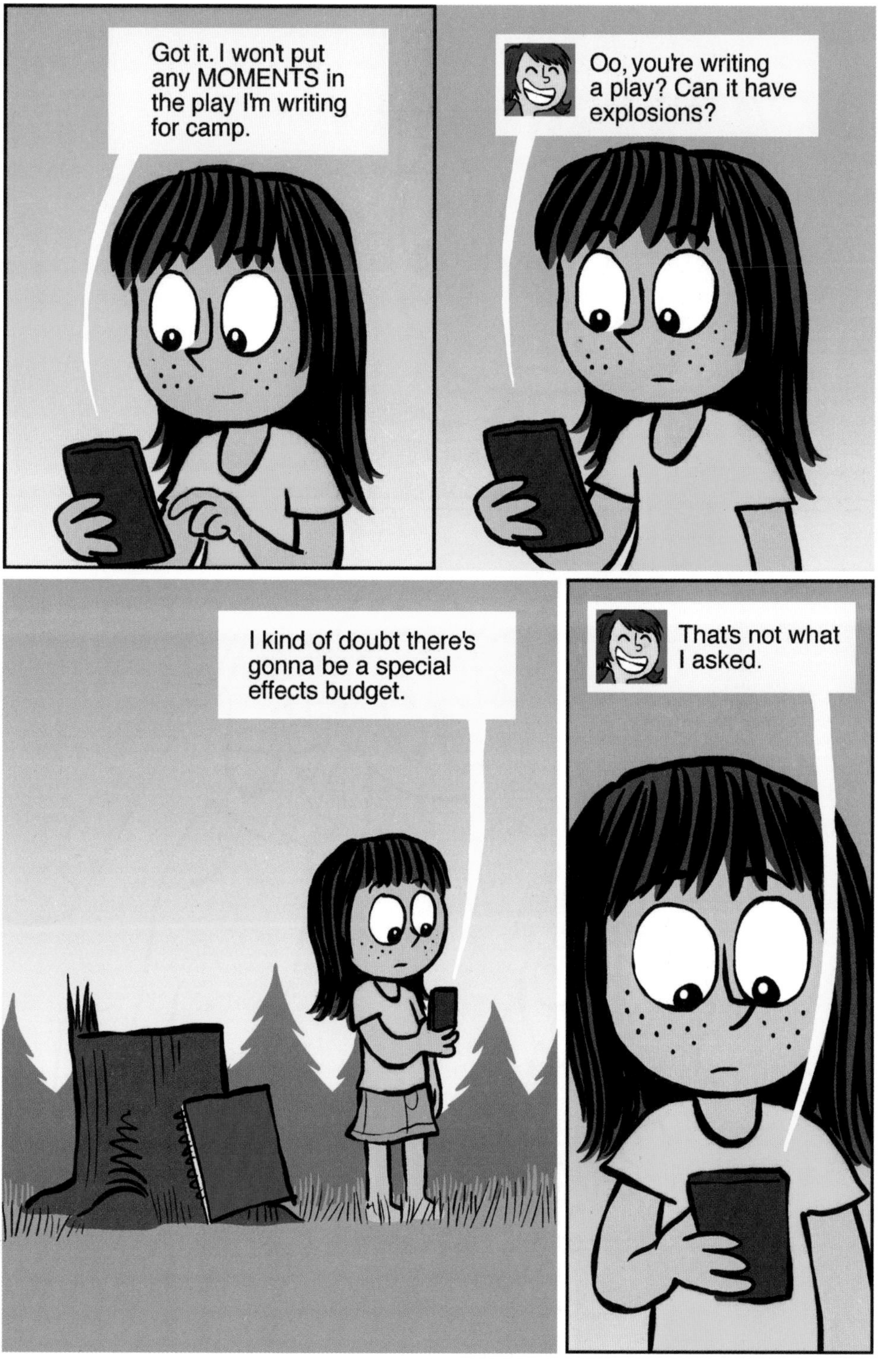
Got it. I won't put any MOMENTS in the play I'm writing for camp.
Oo, you're writing a play? Can it have explosions?
I kind of doubt there's gonna be a special effects budget.
That's not what I asked.

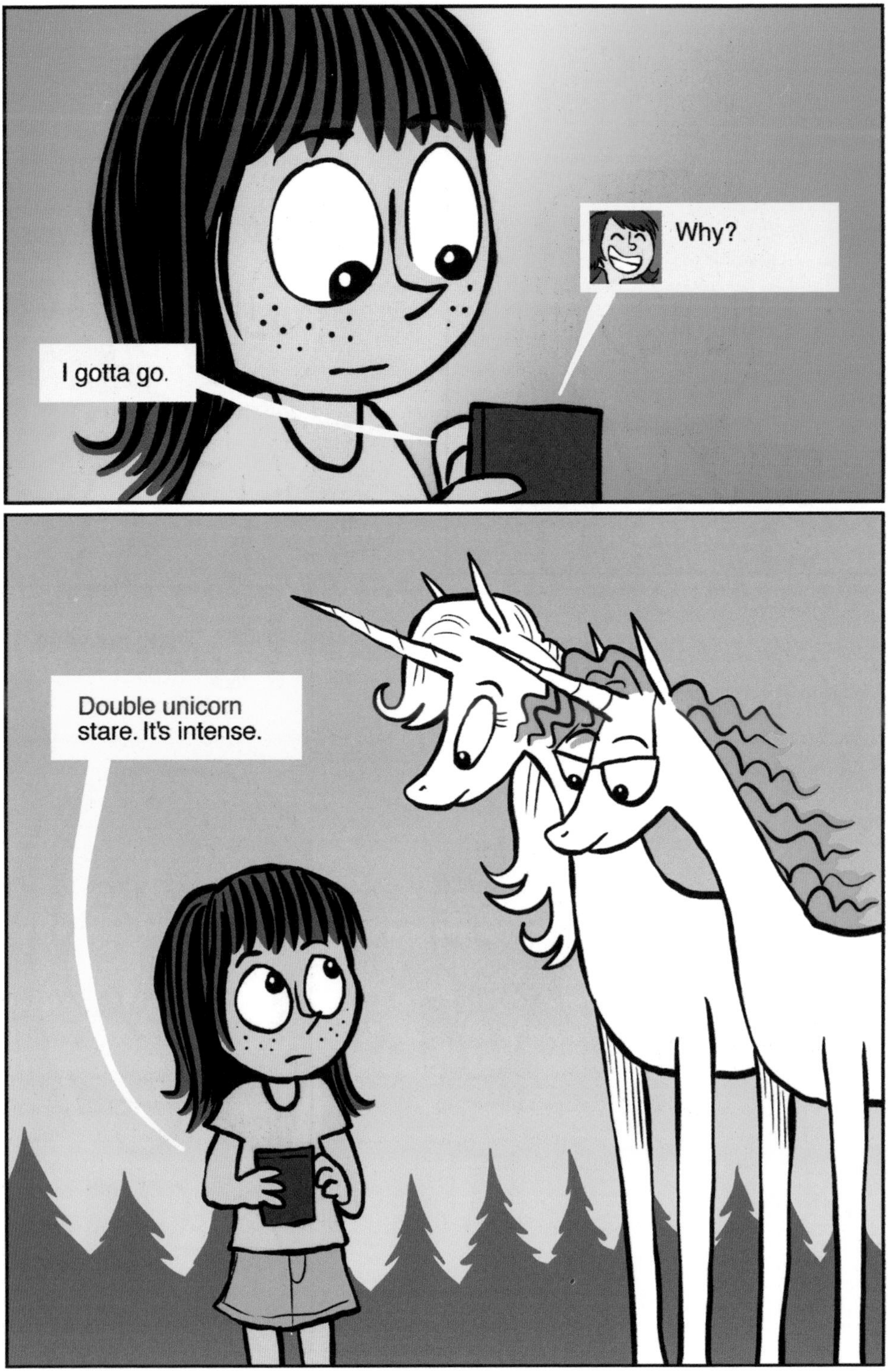
I gotta go.
Why?
Double unicorn stare. It's intense.

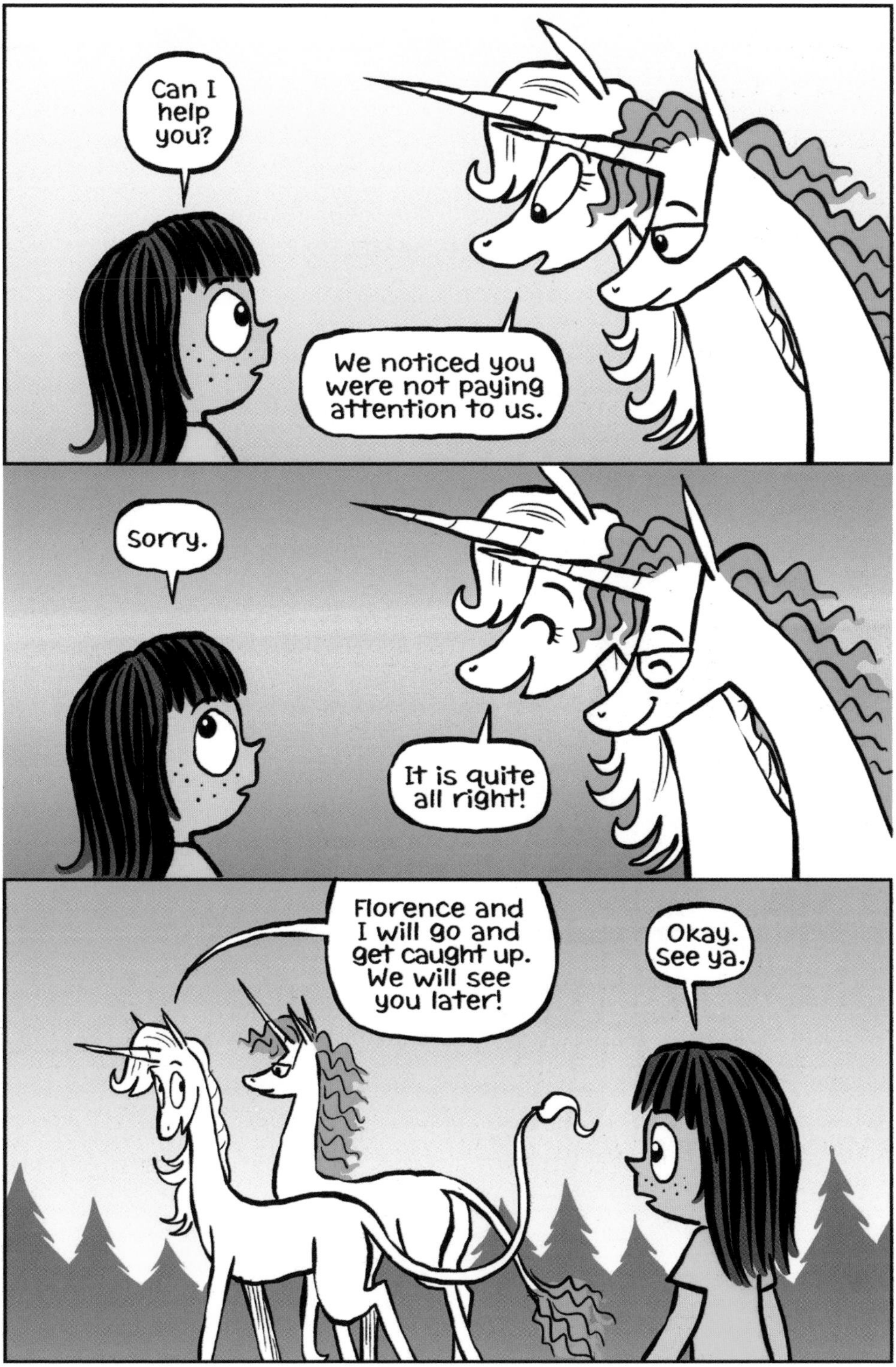
Can I help you?
We noticed you were not paying attention to us.
Sorry.
It is quite all right!
Florence and I will go and get caught up. We will see you later!
Okay. See ya.

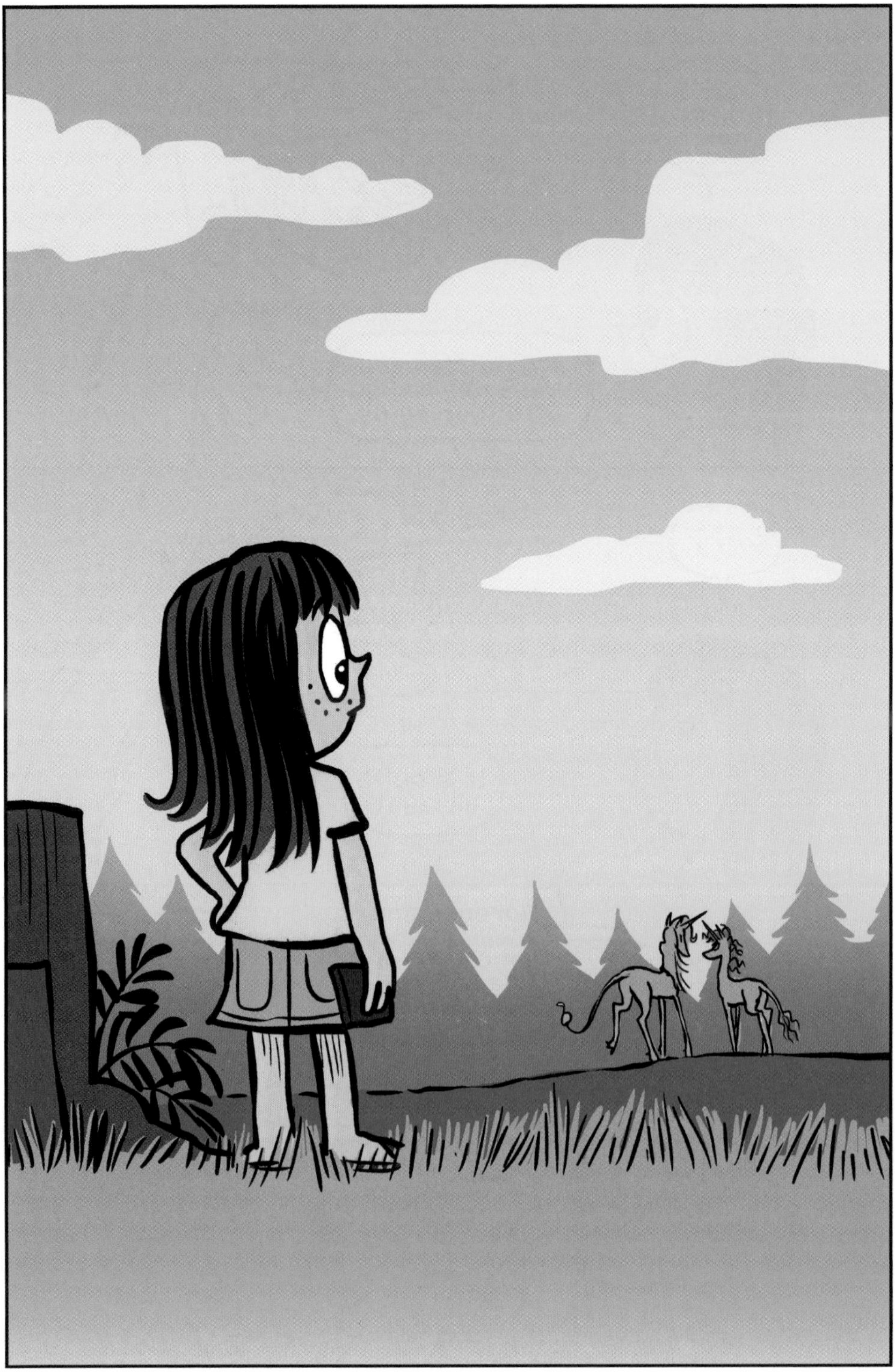

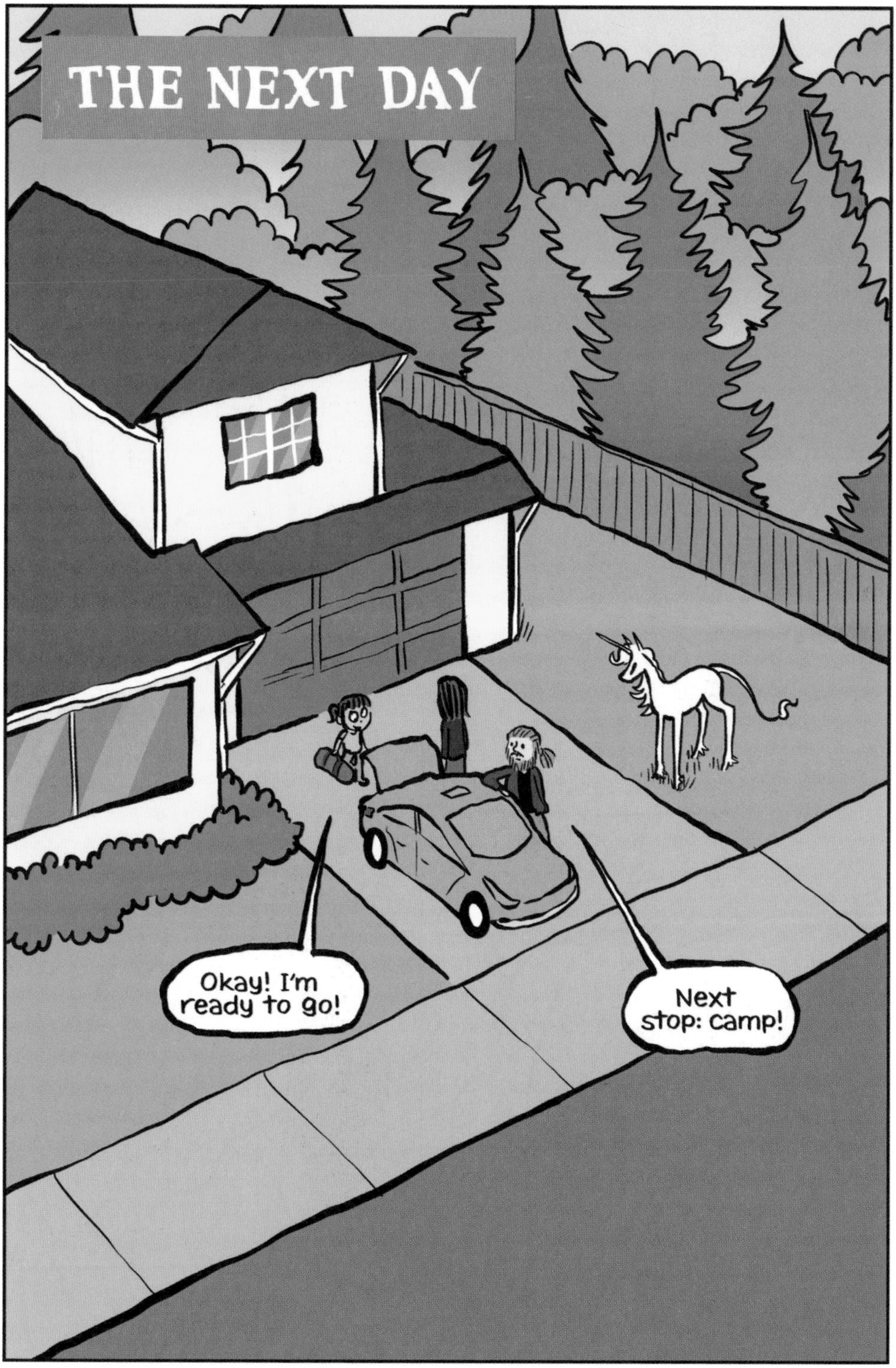
THE NEXT DAY
Okay! I'm ready to go!
Next stop: camp!

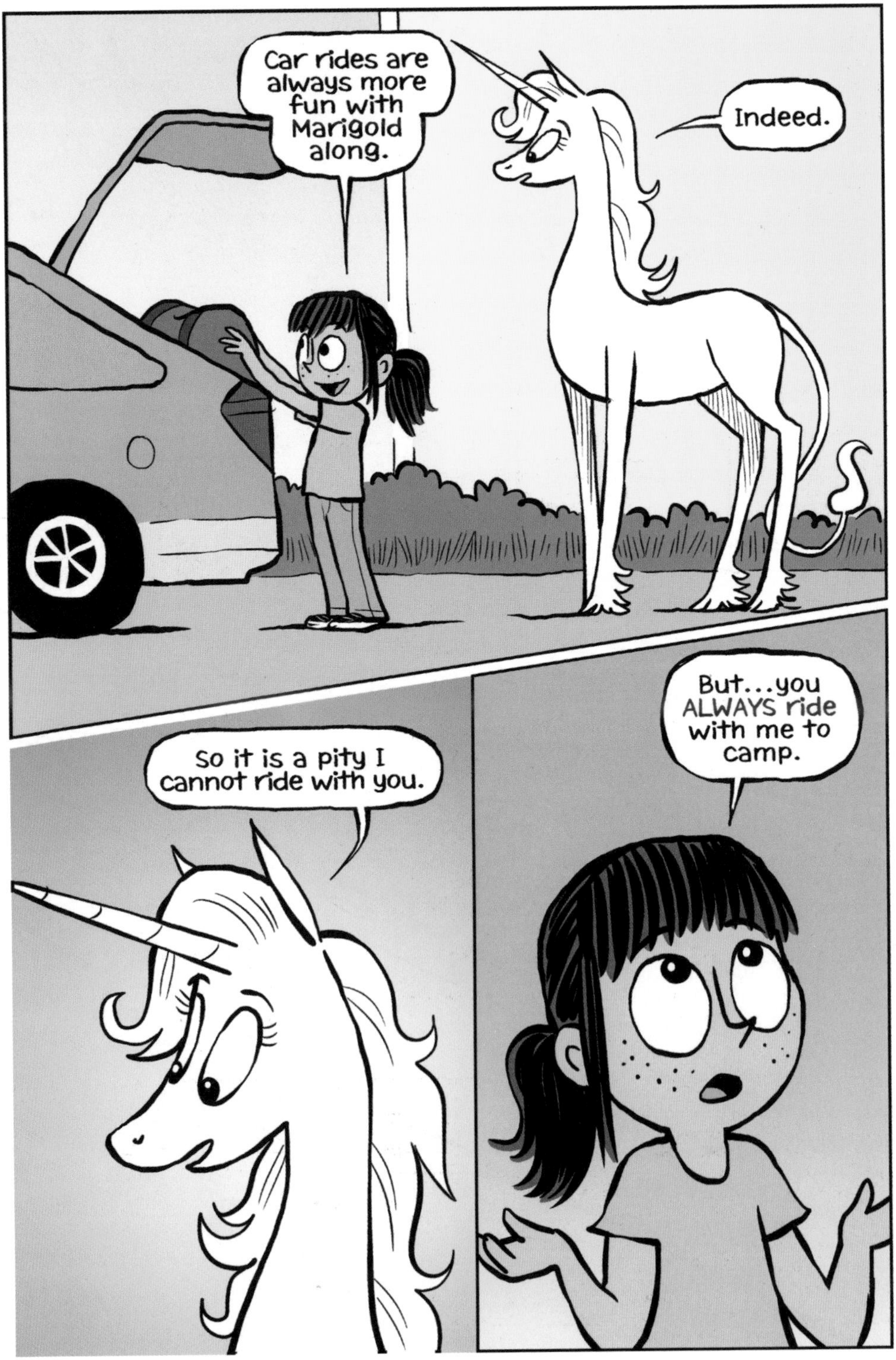
Car rides are always more fun with Marigold along.
Indeed.
So it is a pity I cannot ride with you.
But...you ALWAYS ride with me to camp.

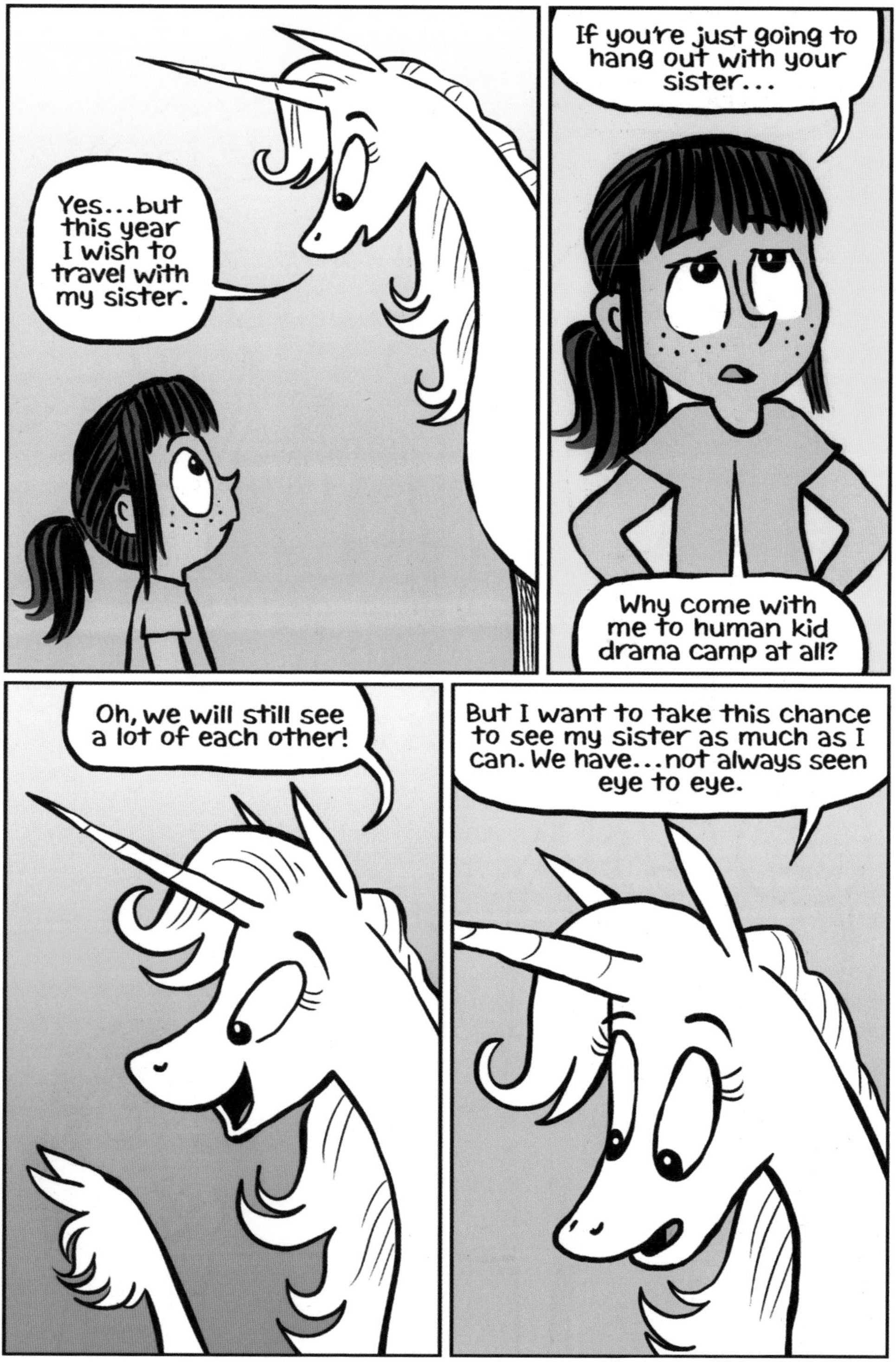
Yes...but this year I wish to travel with my sister.
If you're just going to hang out with your sister...
Why come with me to human kid drama camp at all?
Oh, we will still see a lot of each other!
But I want to take this chance to see my sister as much as I can. We have...not always seen eye to eye.

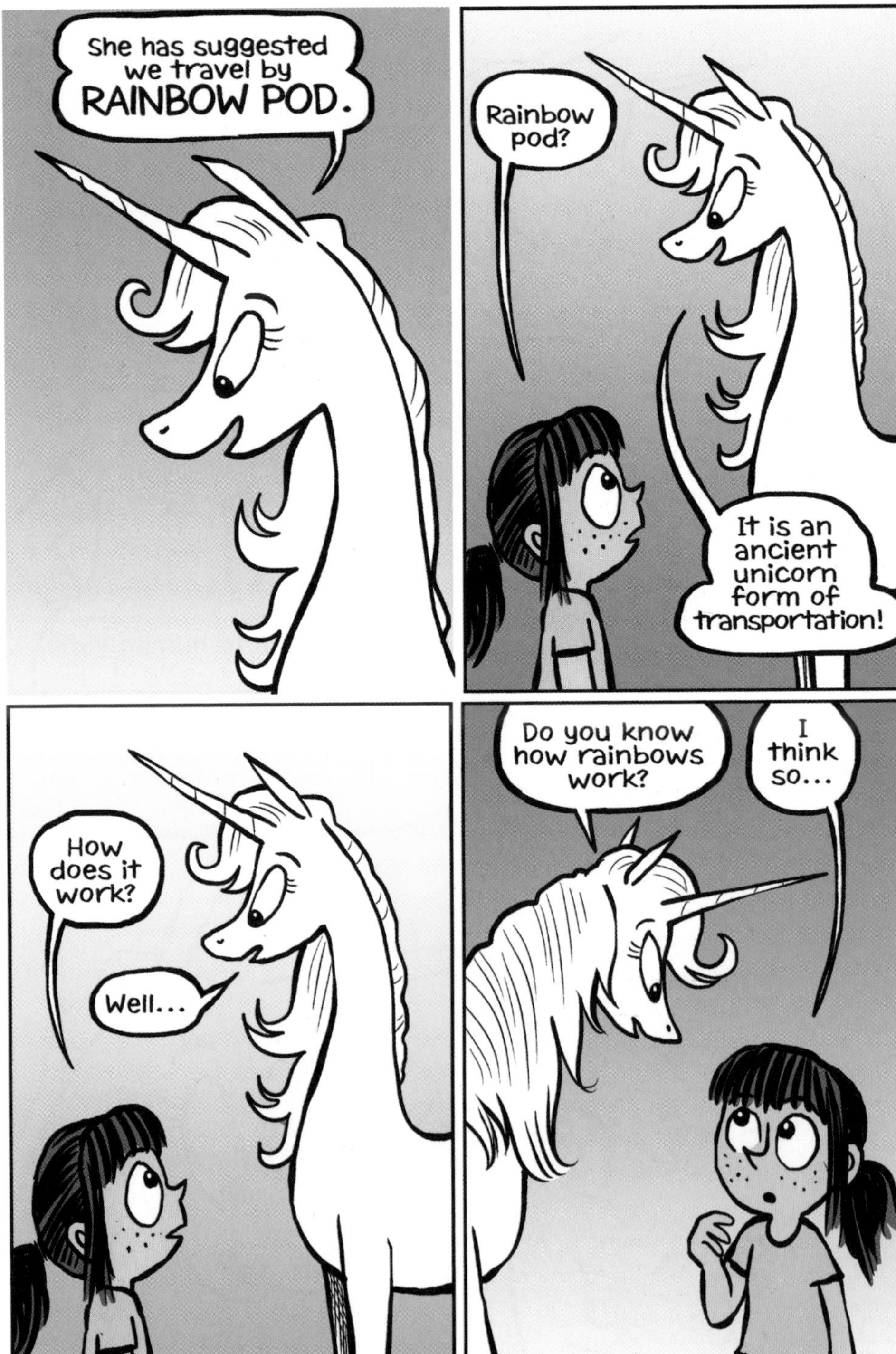
She has suggested we travel by RAINBOW POD.
Rainbow pod?
It is an ancient unicorn form of transportation!
How does it work?
Well...
Do you know how rainbows work?
I think so...

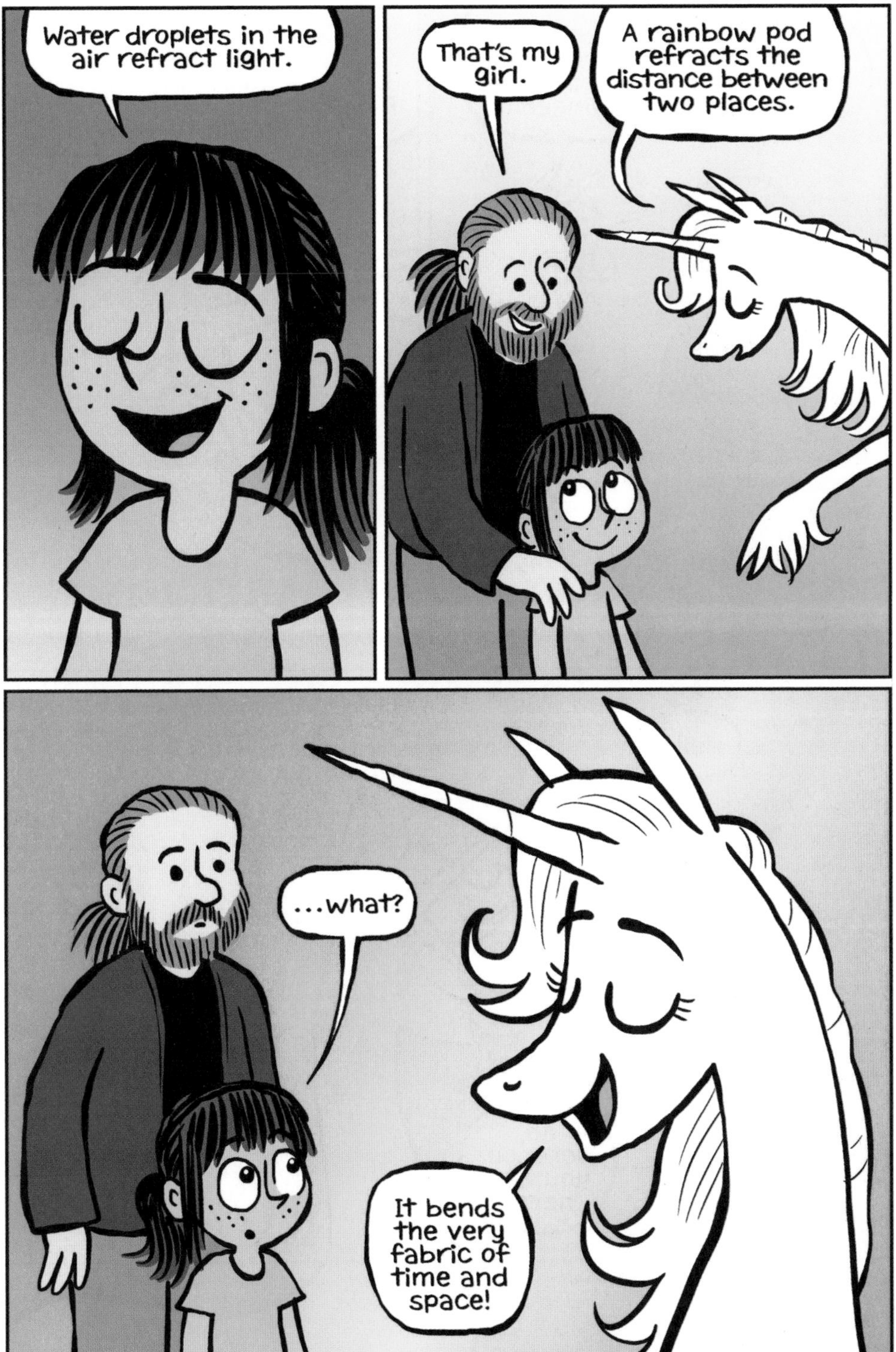
Water droplets in the air refract light.
That's my girl.
A rainbow pod refracts the distance between two places.
...what?
It bends the very fabric of time and space!

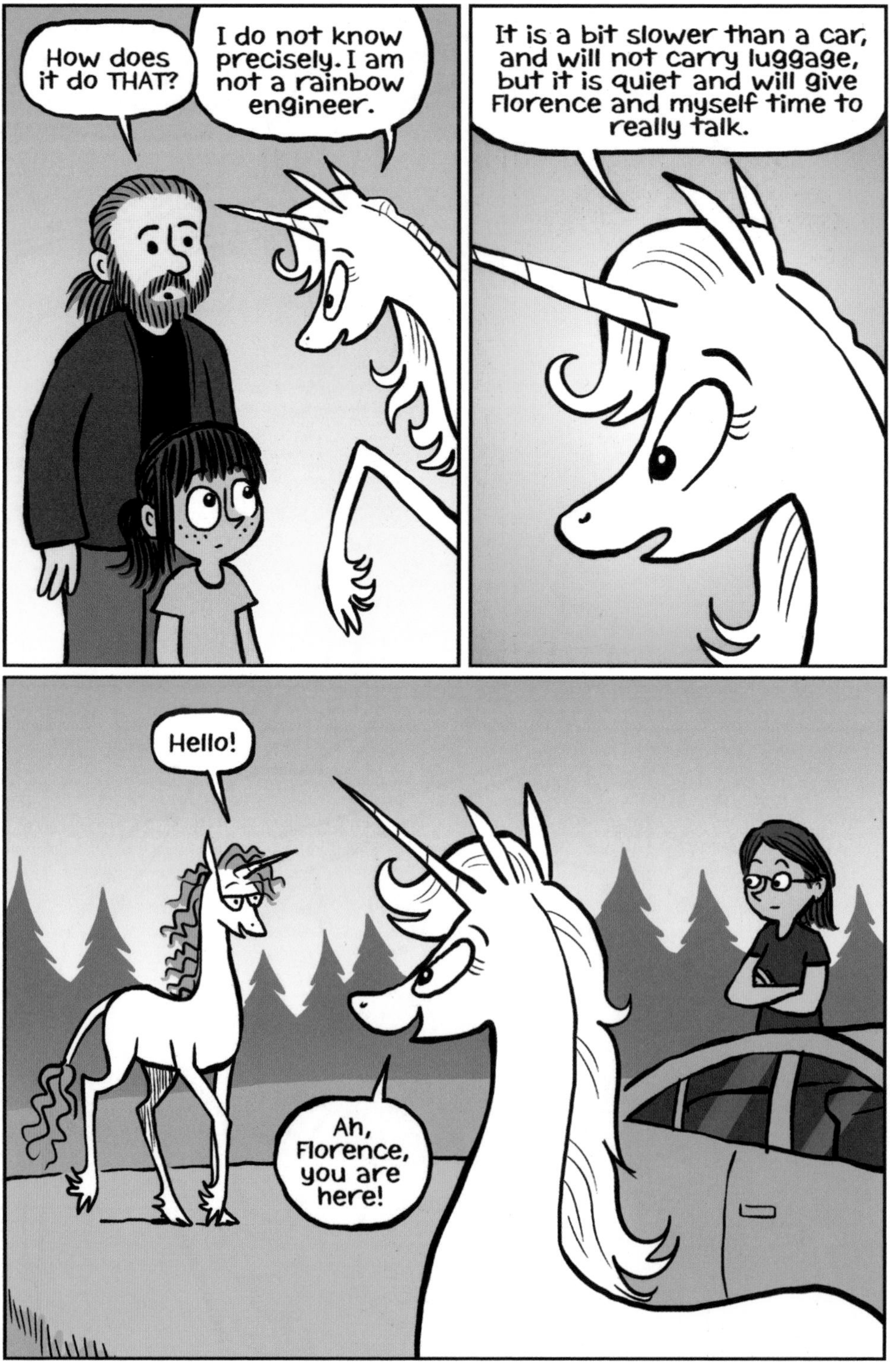
How does it do THAT?
I do not know precisely. I am not a rainbow engineer.
It is a bit slower than a car, and will not carry luggage, but it is quiet and will give Florence and myself time to really talk.
Hello!
Ah, Florence, you are here!

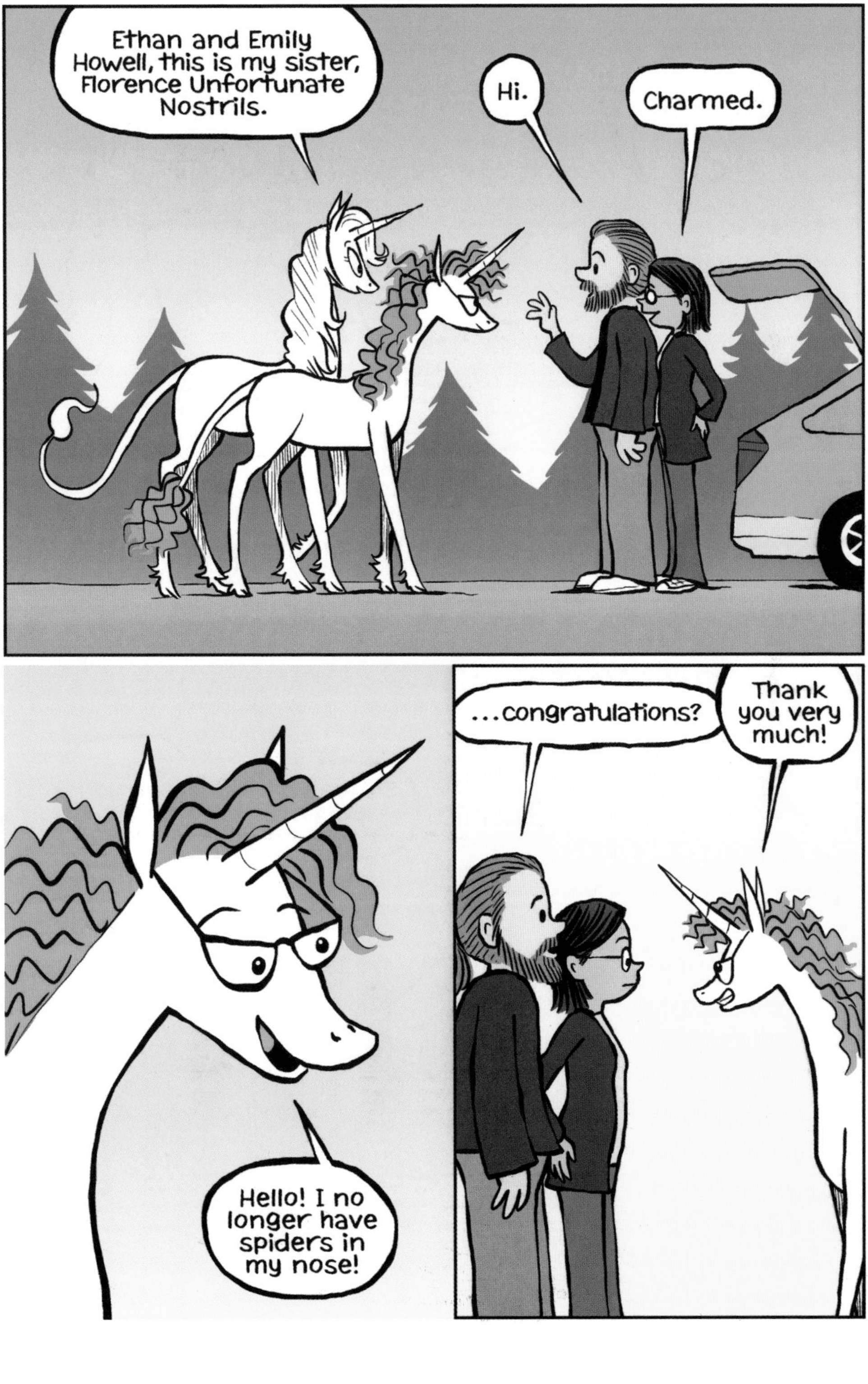
Ethan and Emily Howell, this is my sister, Florence Unfortunate Nostrils.
Hi.
Charmed.
Hello! I no longer have spiders in my nose!
...congratulations?
Thank you very much!

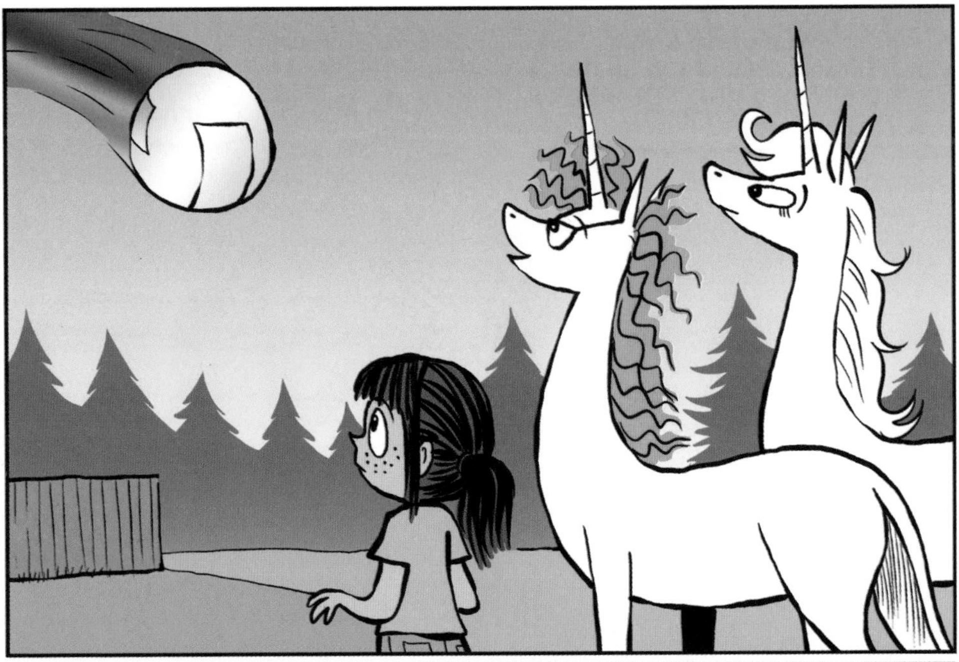

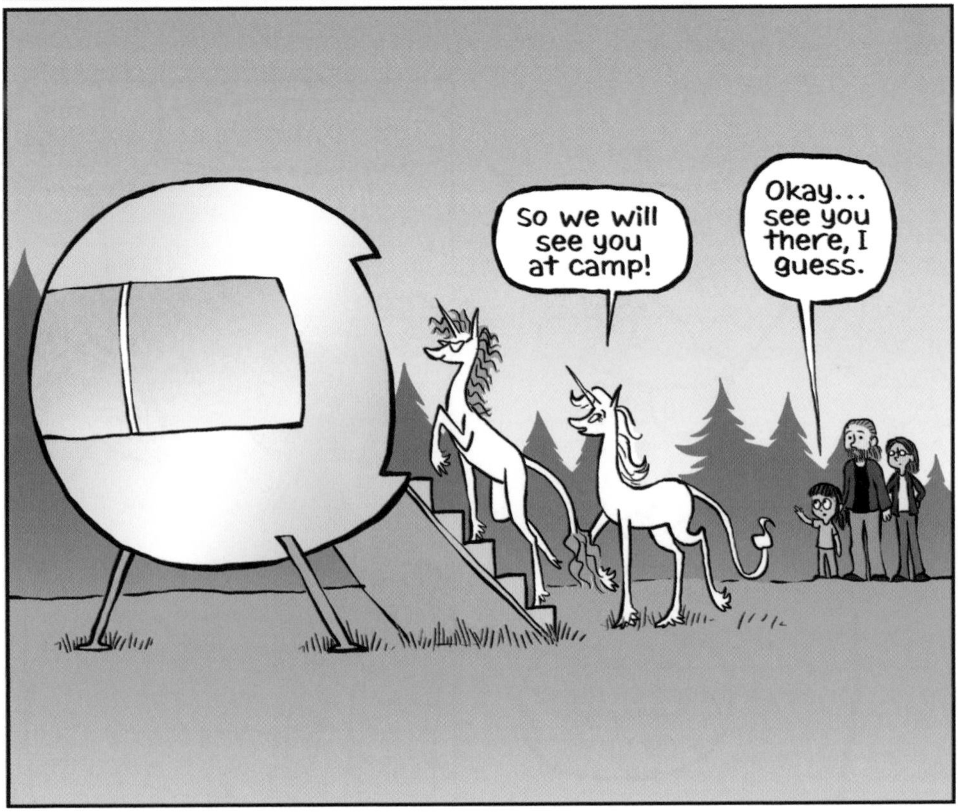
So we will see you at camp!
Okay... see you there, I guess.

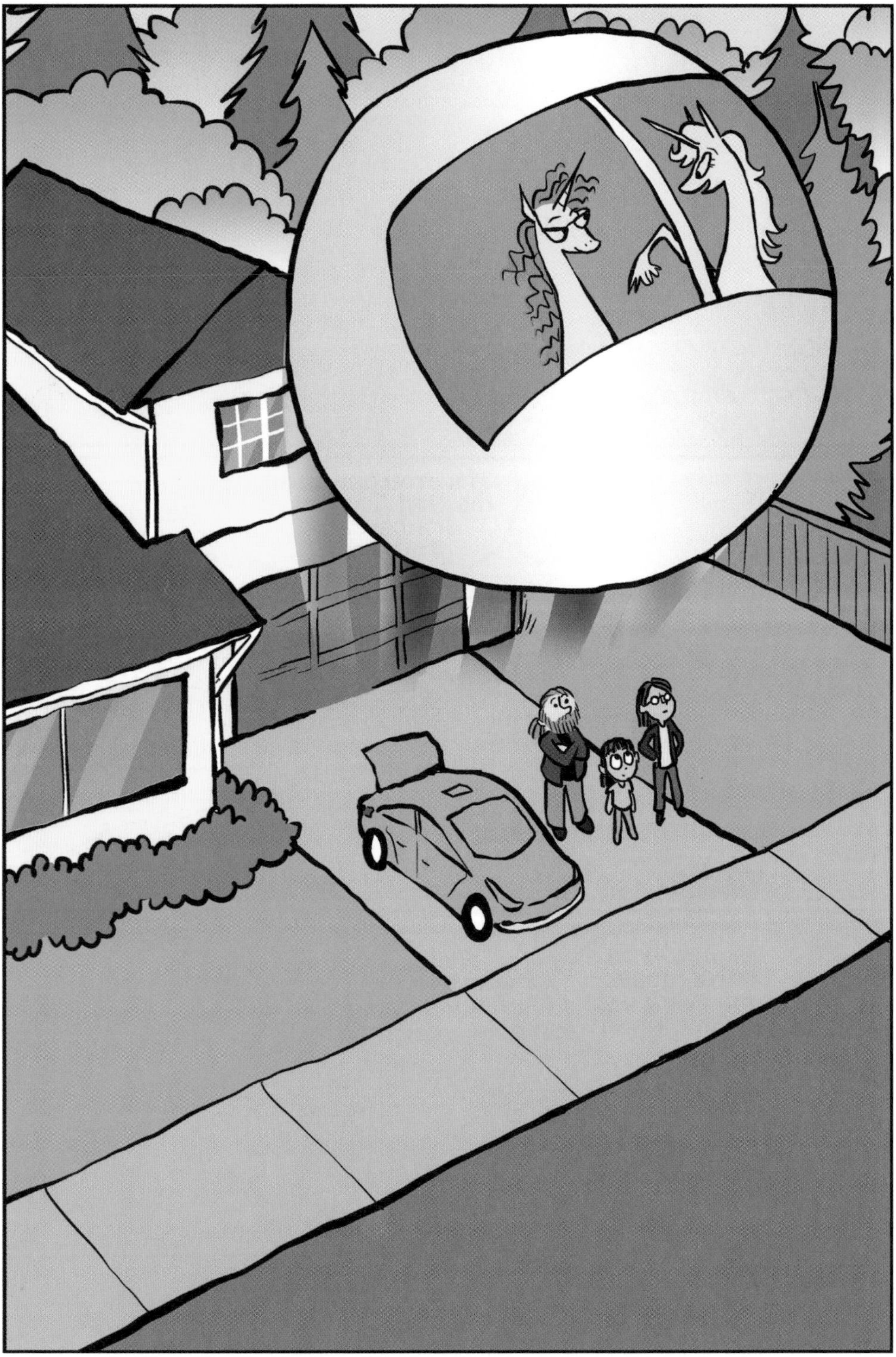

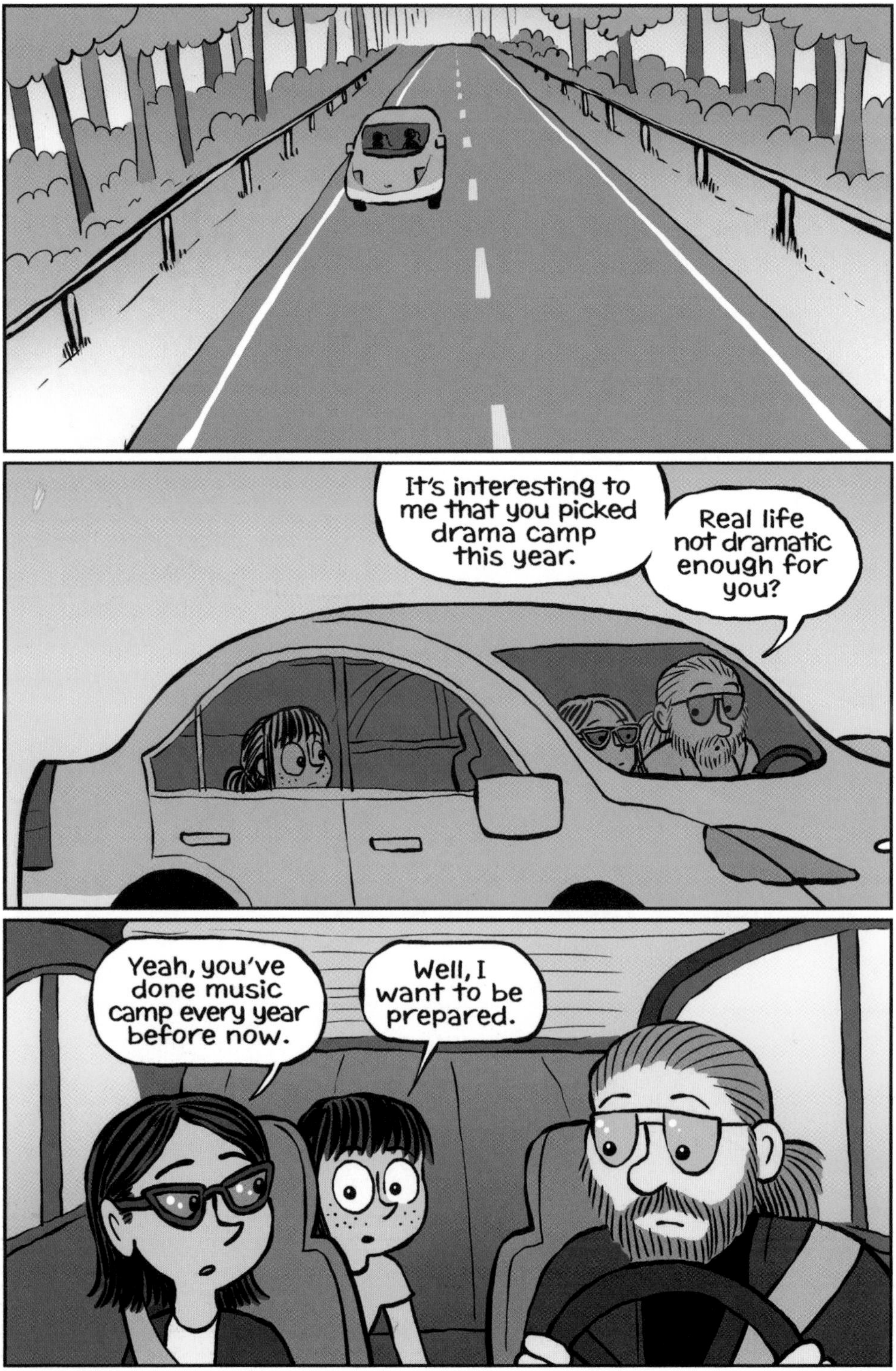
It's interesting to me that you picked drama camp this year.
Real life not dramatic enough for you?
Yeah, you've done music camp every year before now.
Well, I want to be prepared.

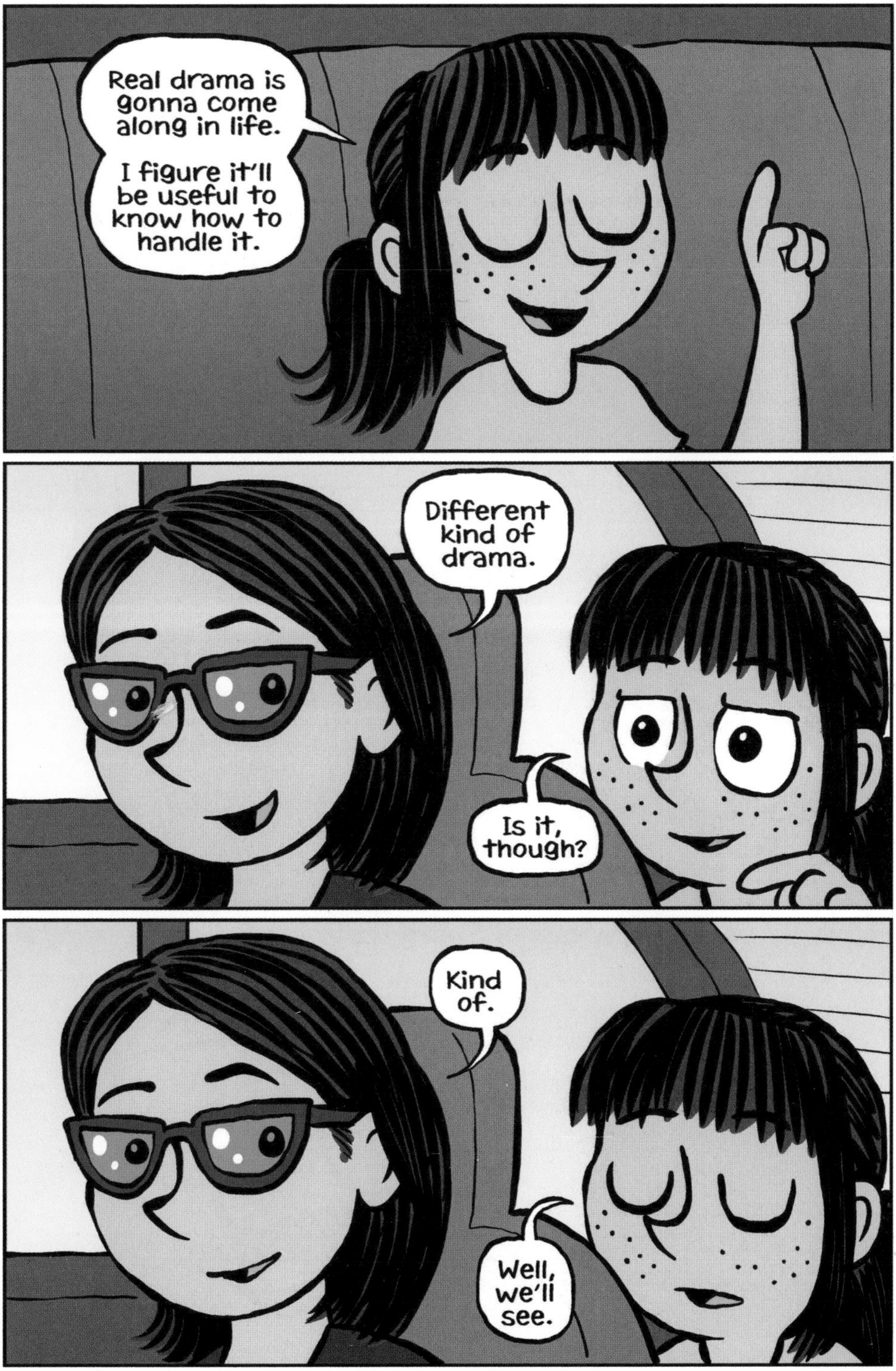
Real drama is gonna come along in life.
I figure it'll be useful to know how to handle it.
Different kind of drama.
Is it, though?
Kind of.
Well, we'll see.

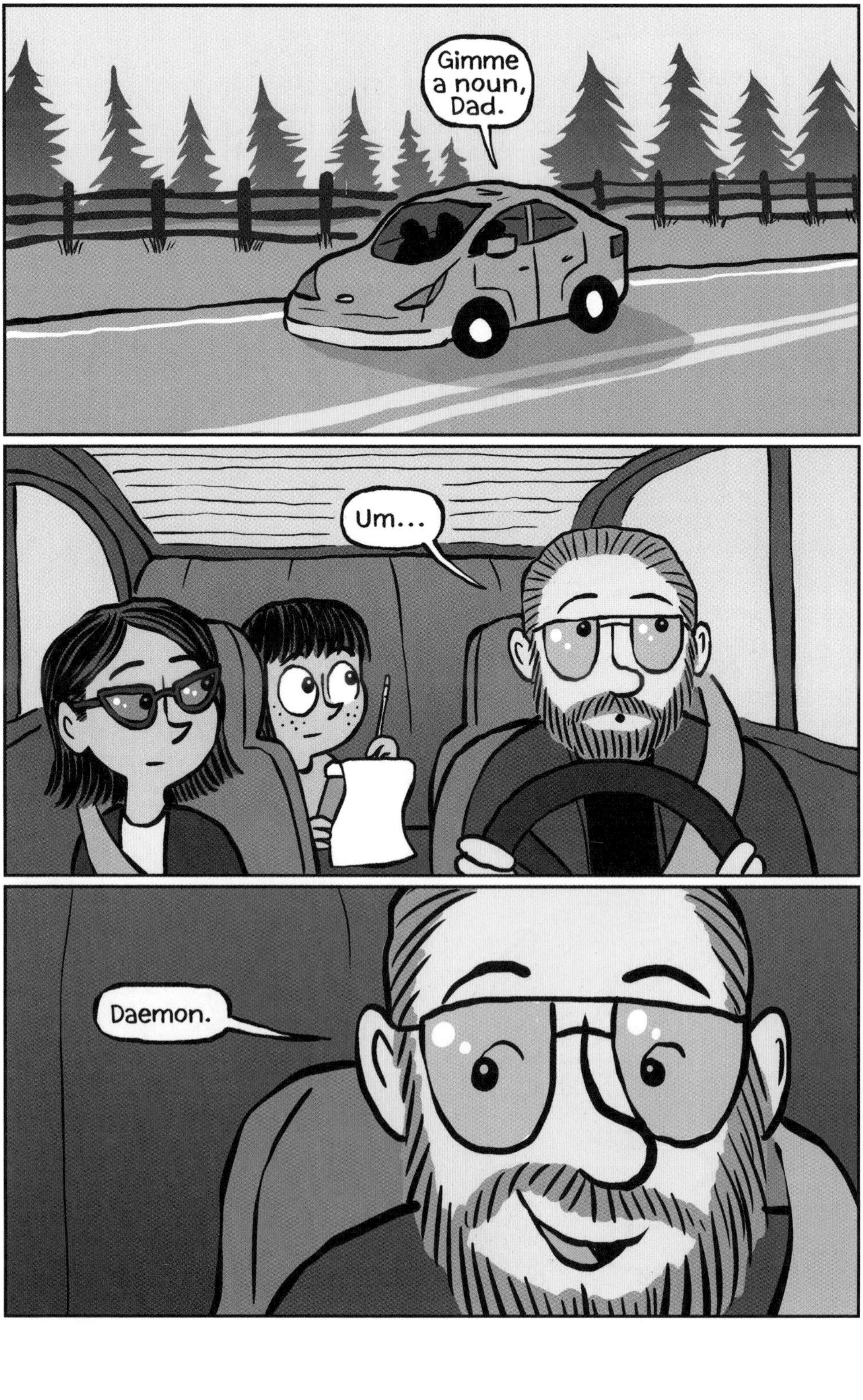
Gimme a noun, Dad.
Um...
Daemon.

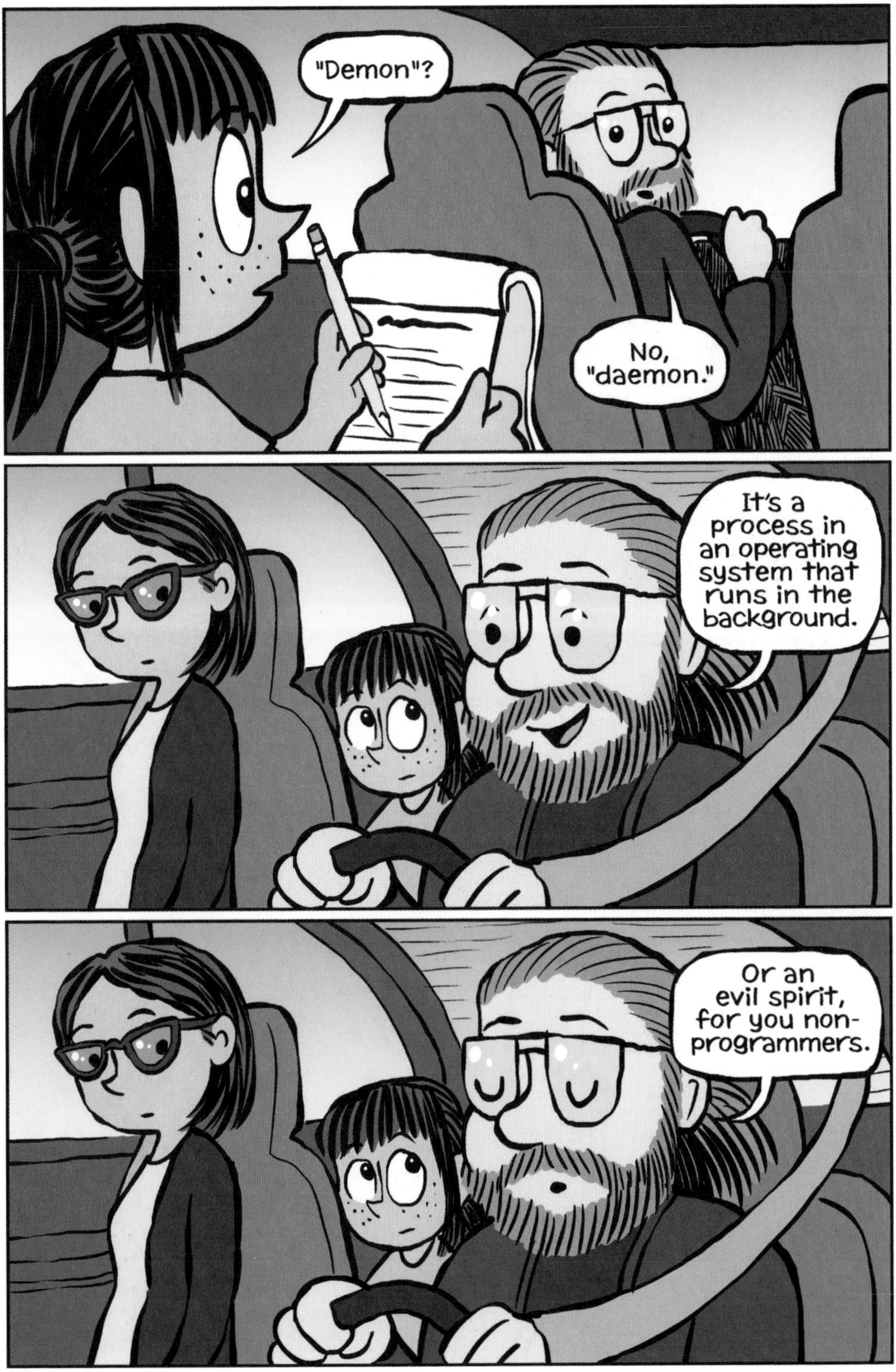
"Demon"?
No, "daemon."
It's a process in an operating system that runs in the background.
Or an evil spirit, for you non-programmers.

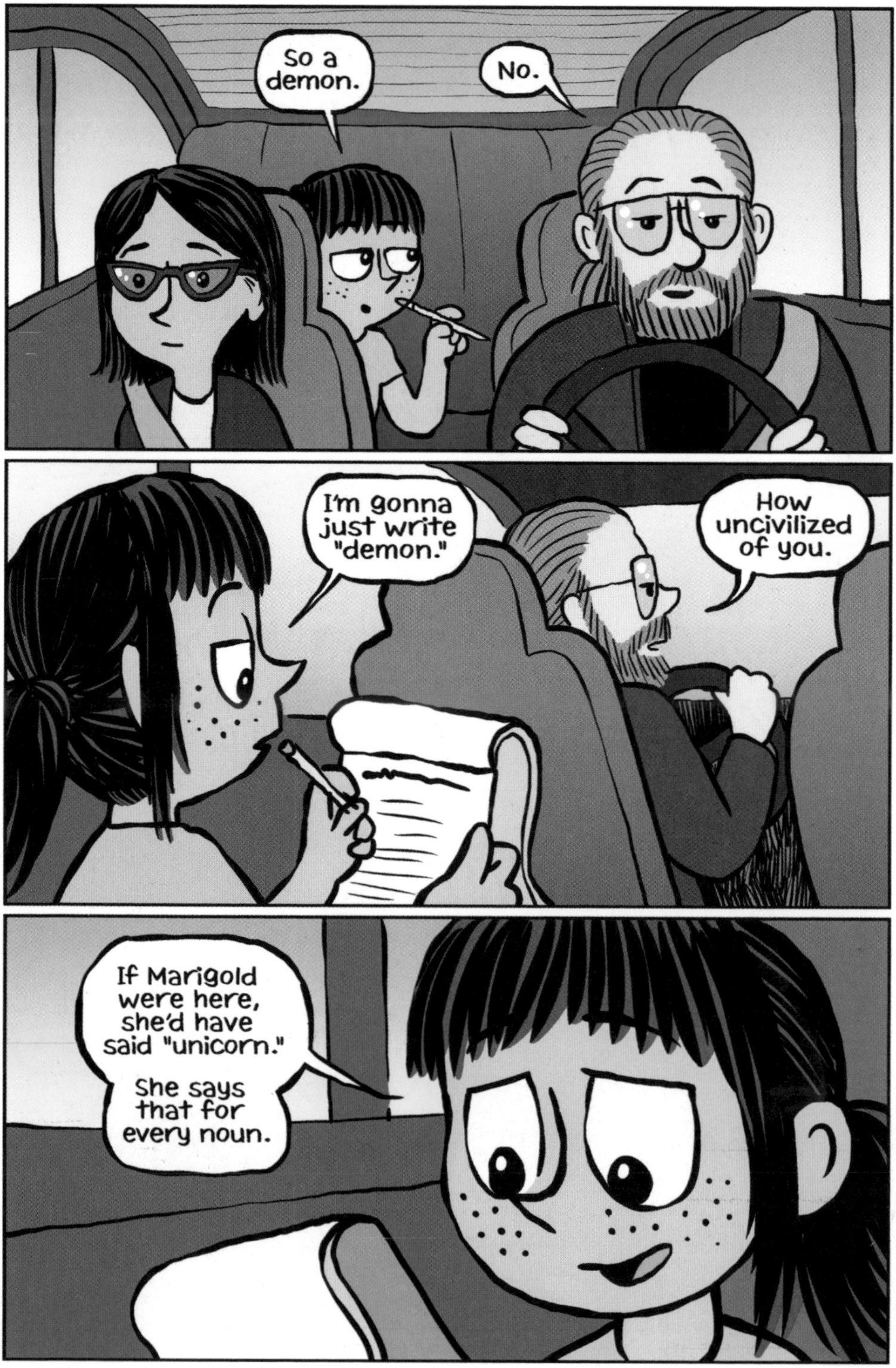
So a demon.
No.
I'm gonna just write "demon."
How uncivilized of you.
If Marigold were here, she'd have said "unicorn."
She says that for every noun.

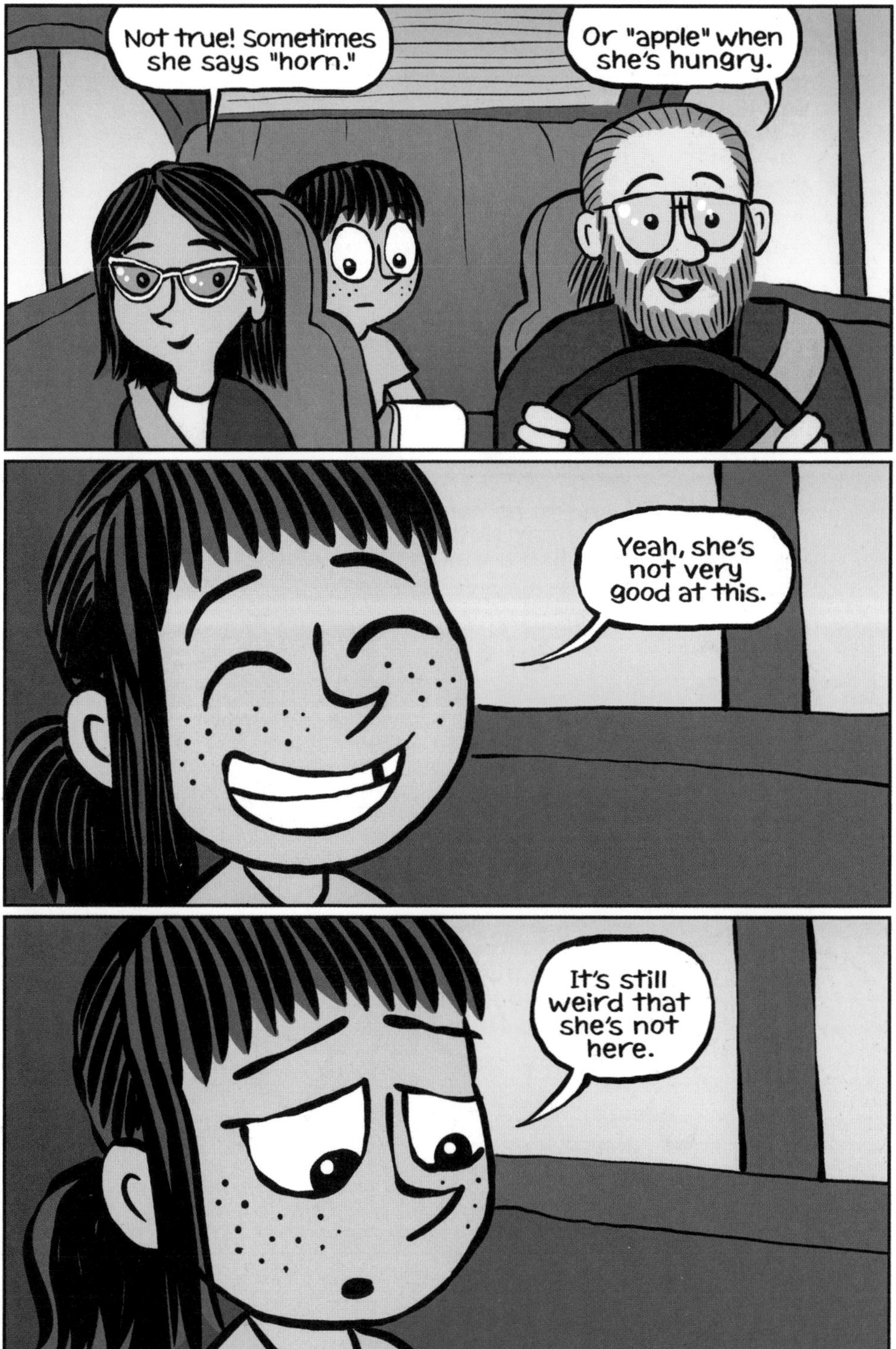

Not true! Sometimes she says "horn."
Or "apple" when she's hungry.
Yeah, she's not very good at this.
It's still weird that she's not here.

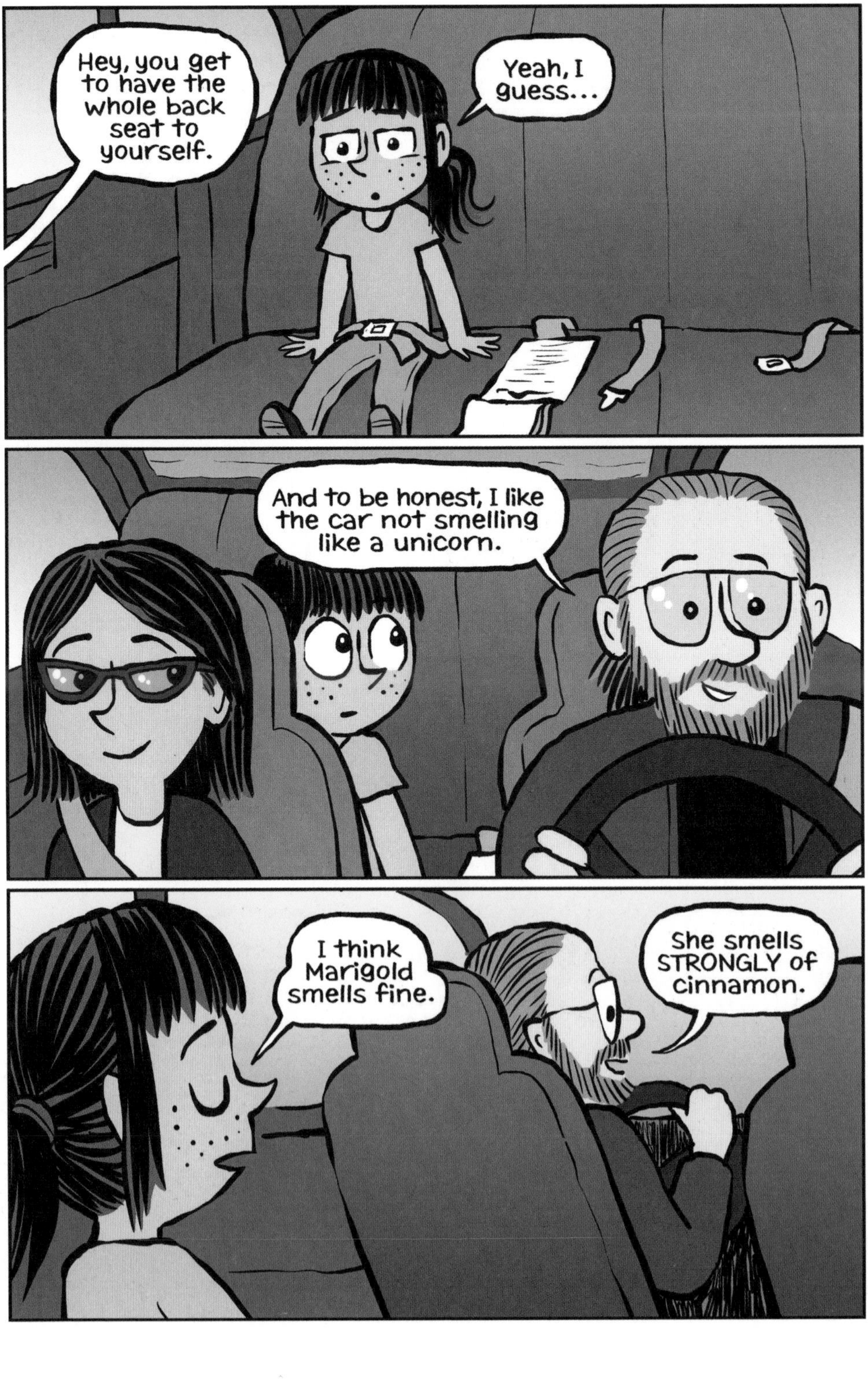
Hey, you get to have the whole back seat to yourself.
Yeah, I guess...
And to be honest, I like the car not smelling like a unicorn.
I think Marigold smells fine.
She smells STRONGLY of cinnamon.

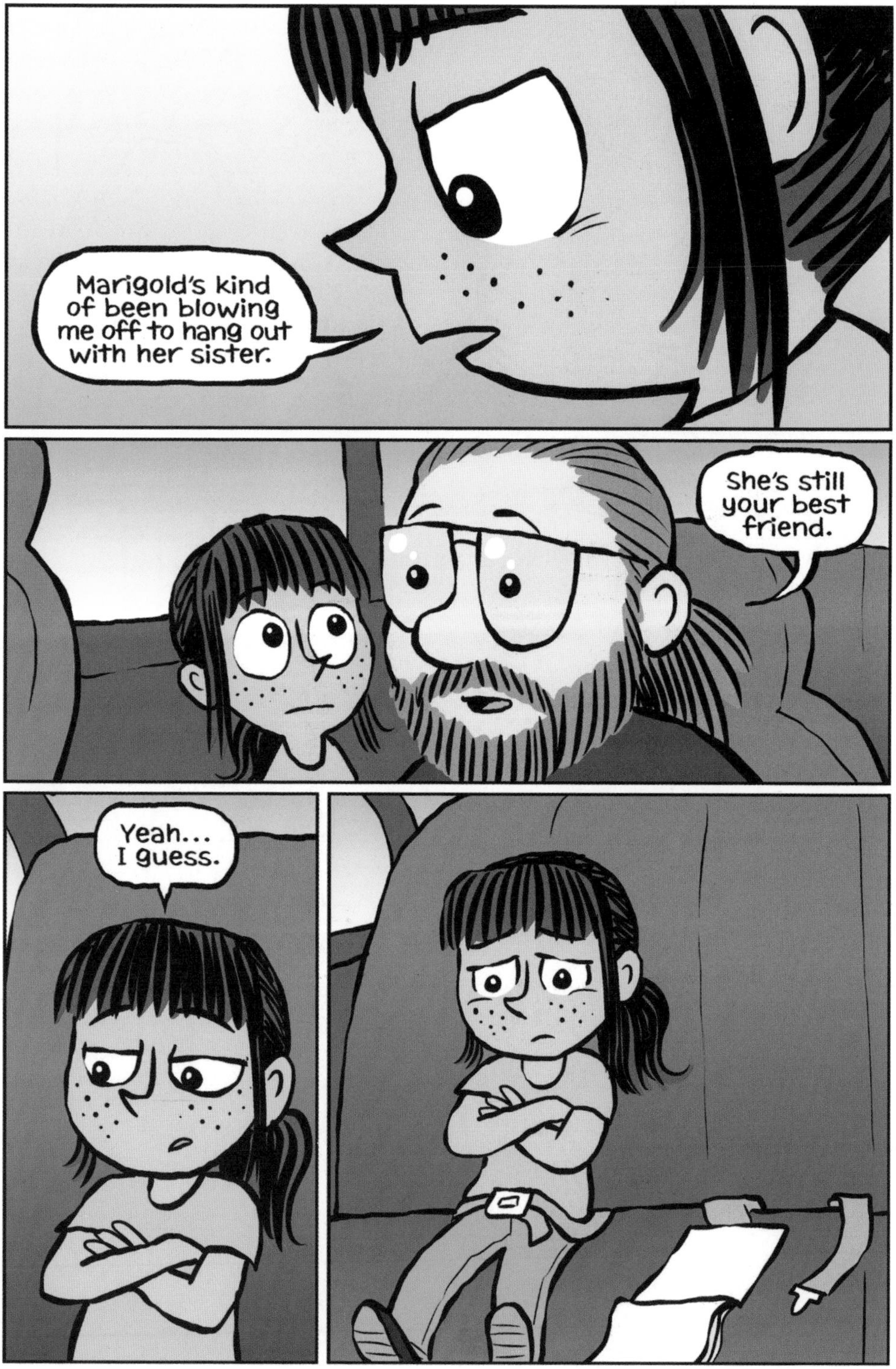
Marigold's kind of been blowing me off to hang out with her sister.
She's still your best friend.
Yeah... I guess.

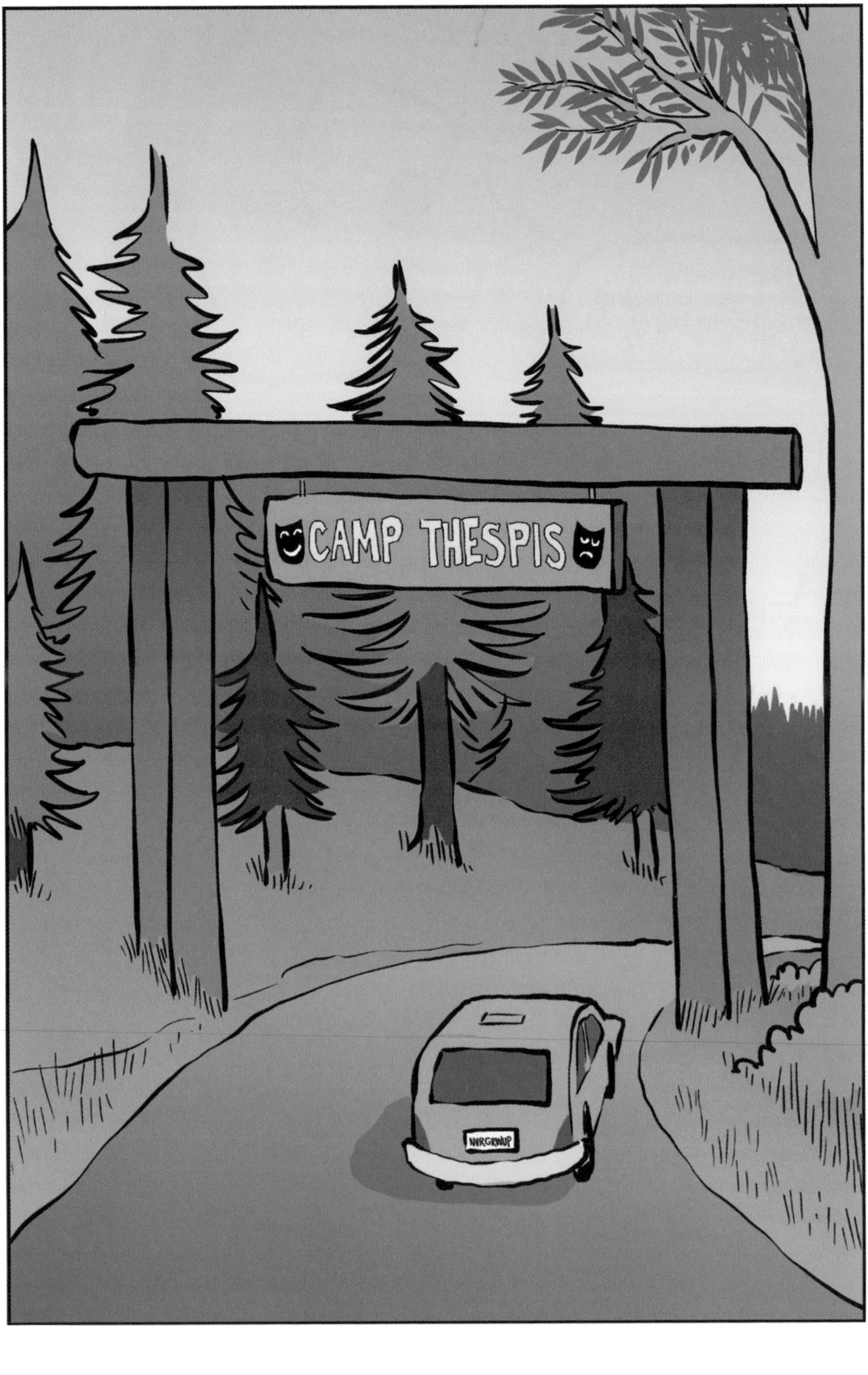
CAMP THESPIS

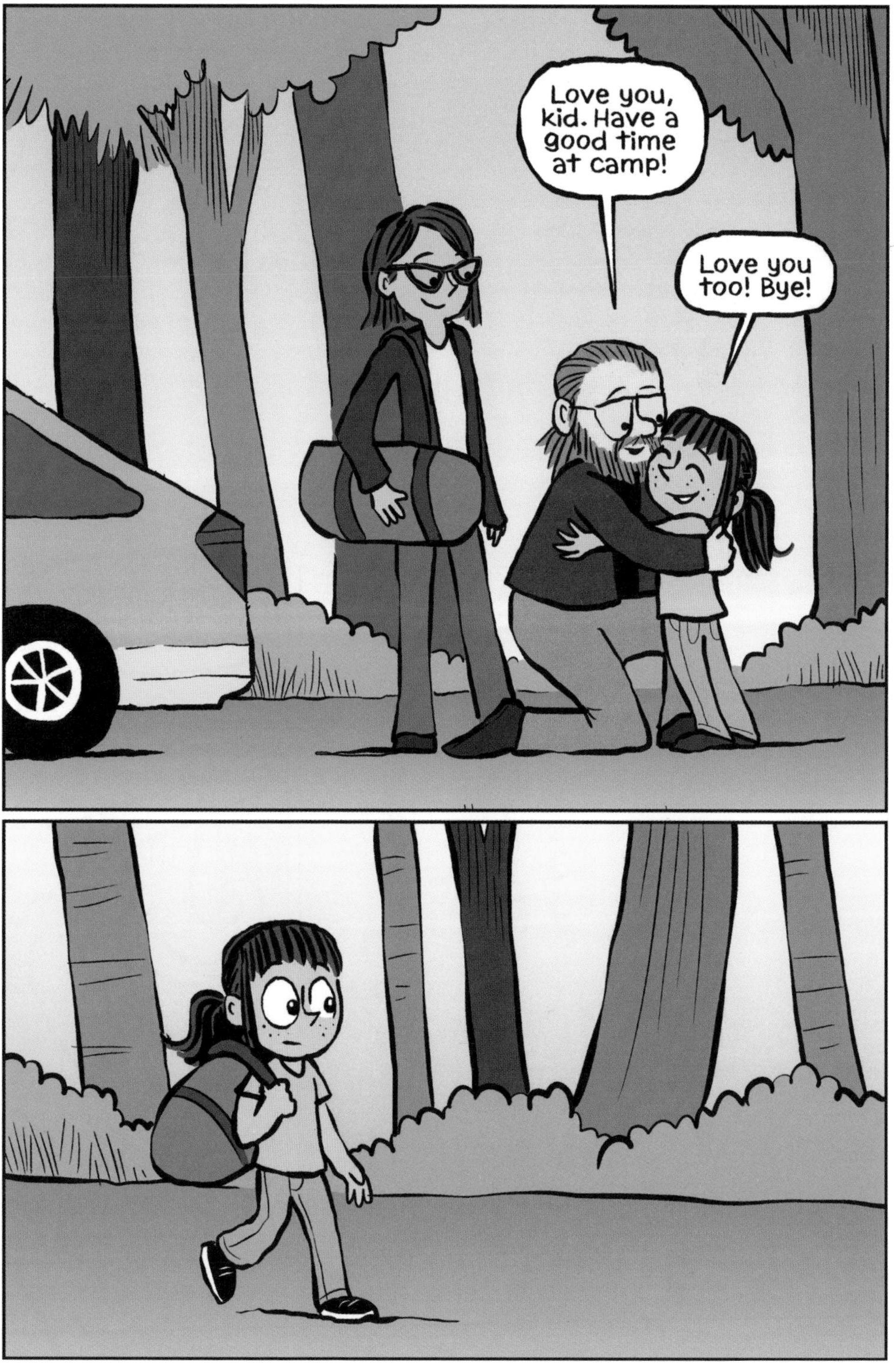
Love you, kid. Have a good time at camp!
Love you too! Bye!

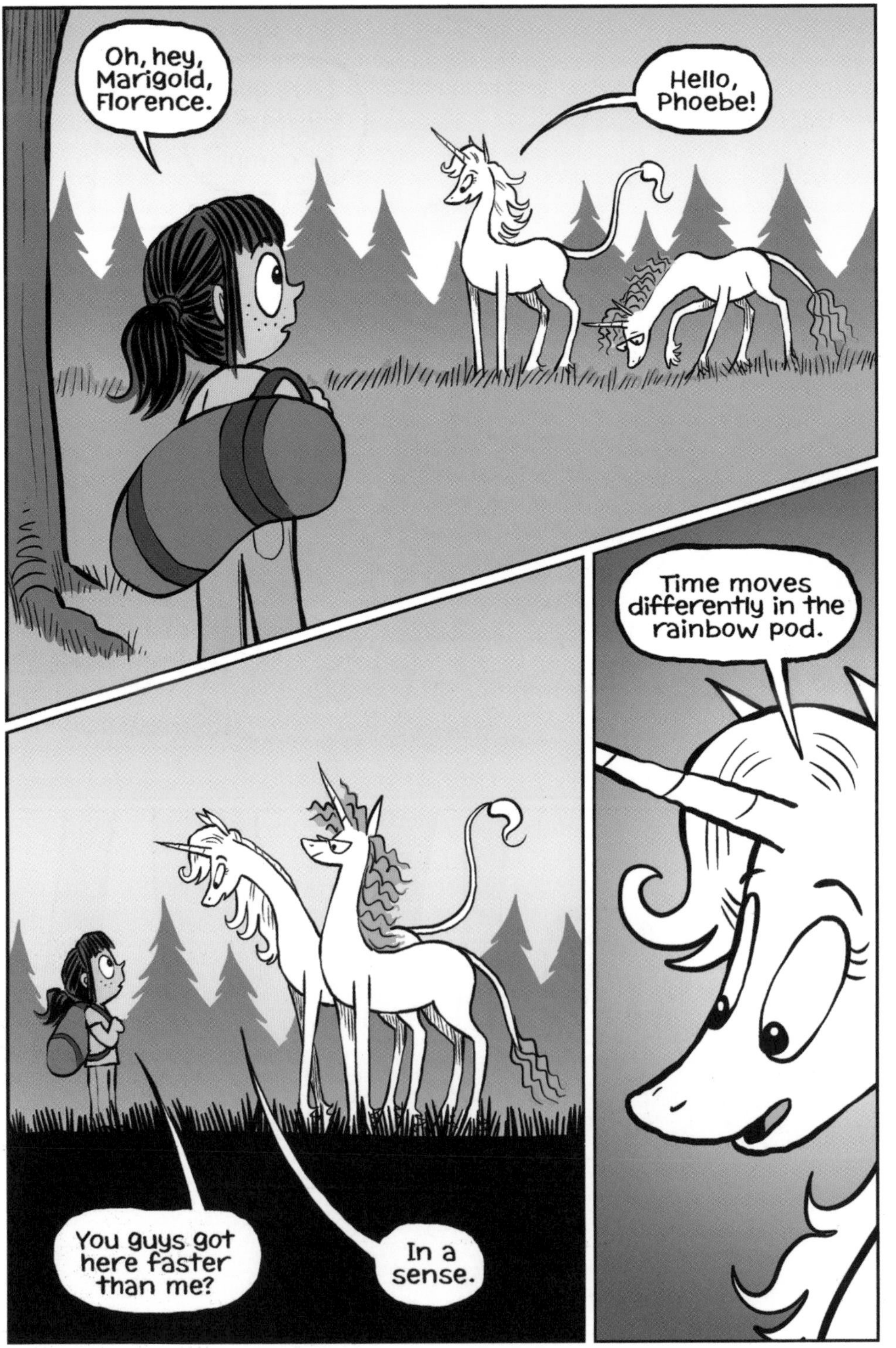
Oh, hey, Marigold, Florence.
Hello, Phoebe!
You guys got here faster than me?
In a sense.
Time moves differently in the rainbow pod.

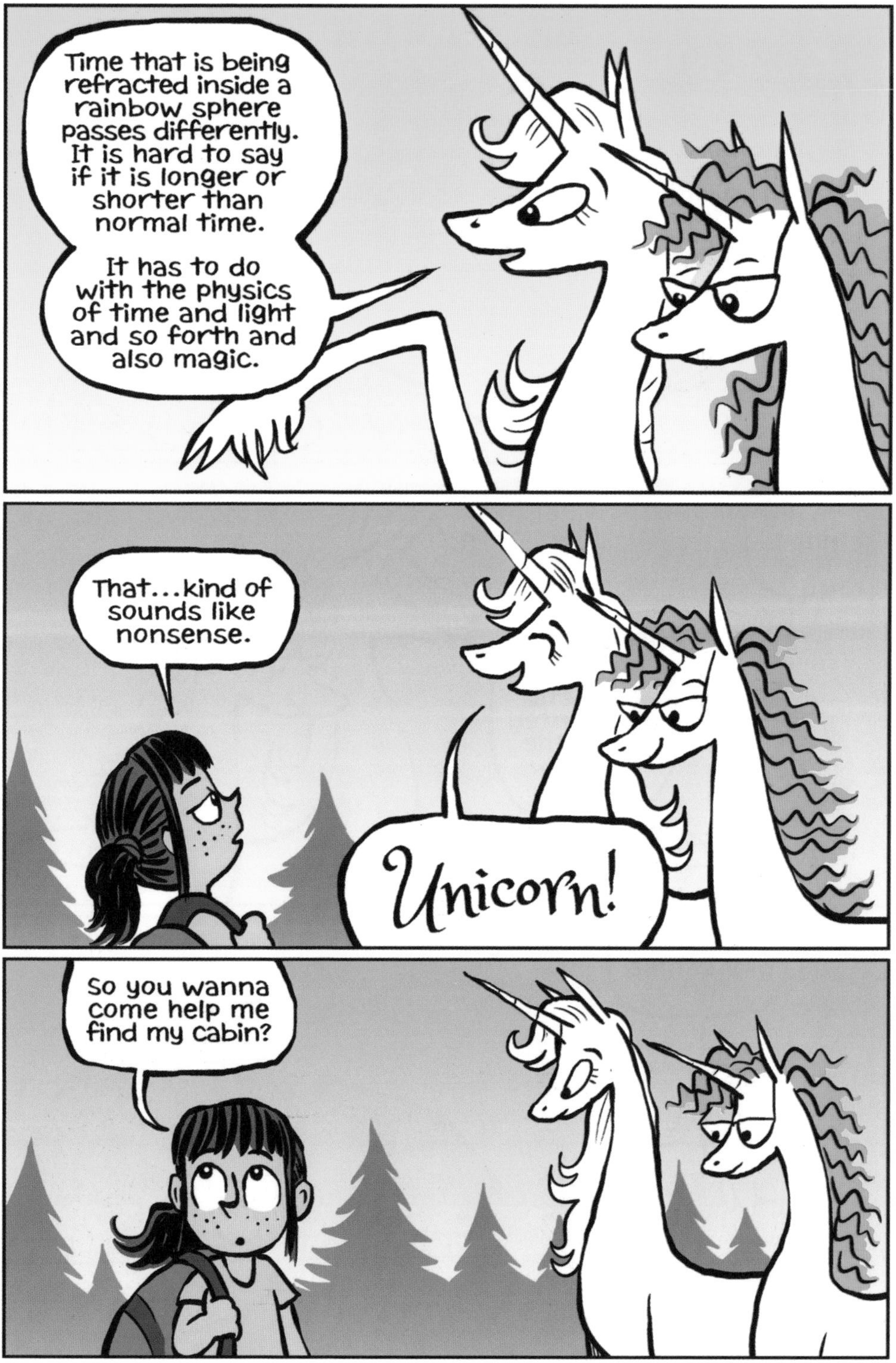
Time that is being refracted inside a rainbow sphere passes differently. It is hard to say if it is longer or shorter than normal time.
It has to do with the physics of time and light and so forth and also magic.
That...kind of sounds like nonsense.
Unicorn!
So you wanna come help me find my cabin?

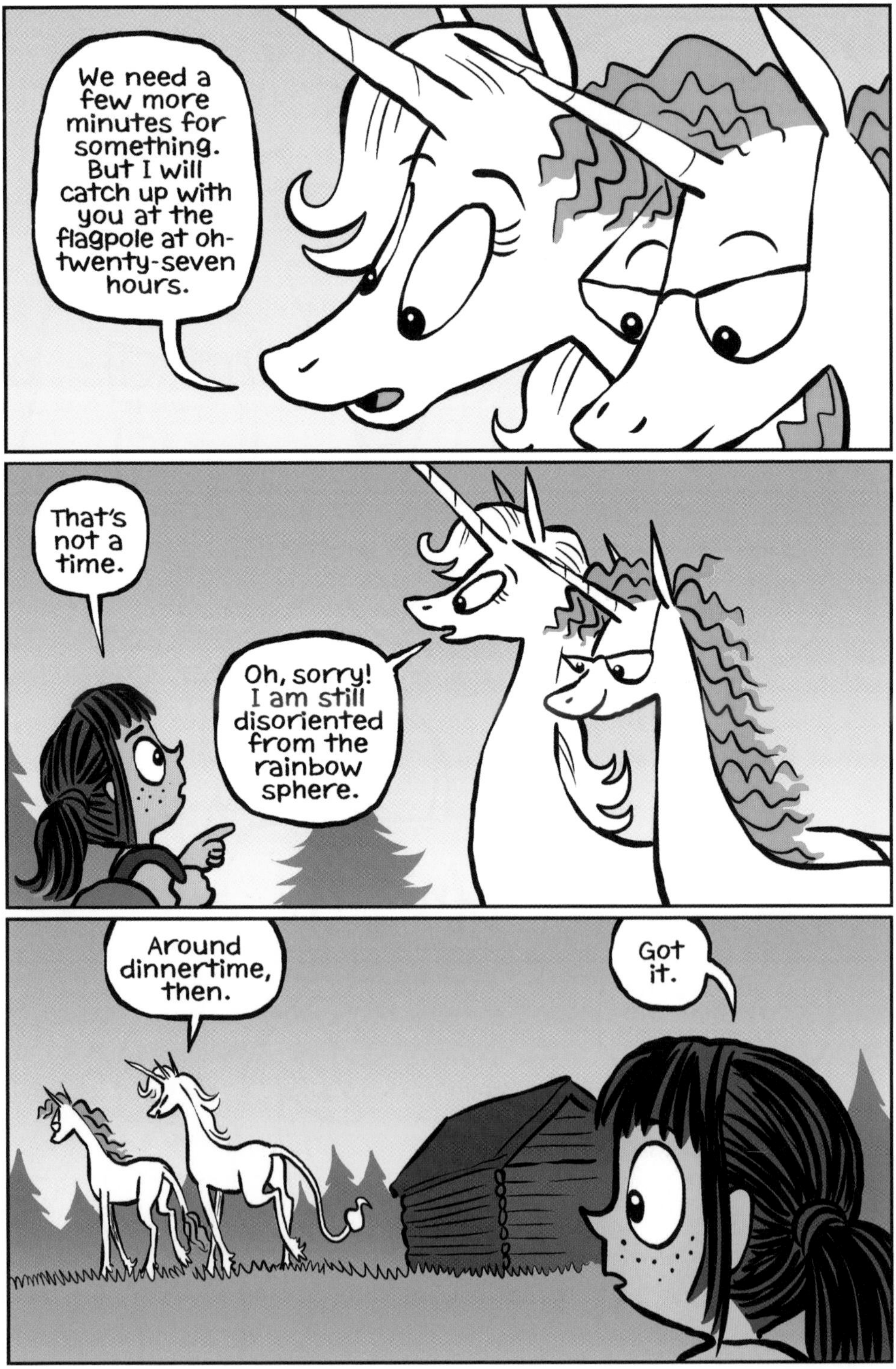
We need a few more minutes for something. But I will catch up with you at the flagpole at oh-twenty-seven hours.
That's not a time.
Oh, sorry! I am still disoriented from the rainbow sphere.
Around dinnertime, then.
Got it.

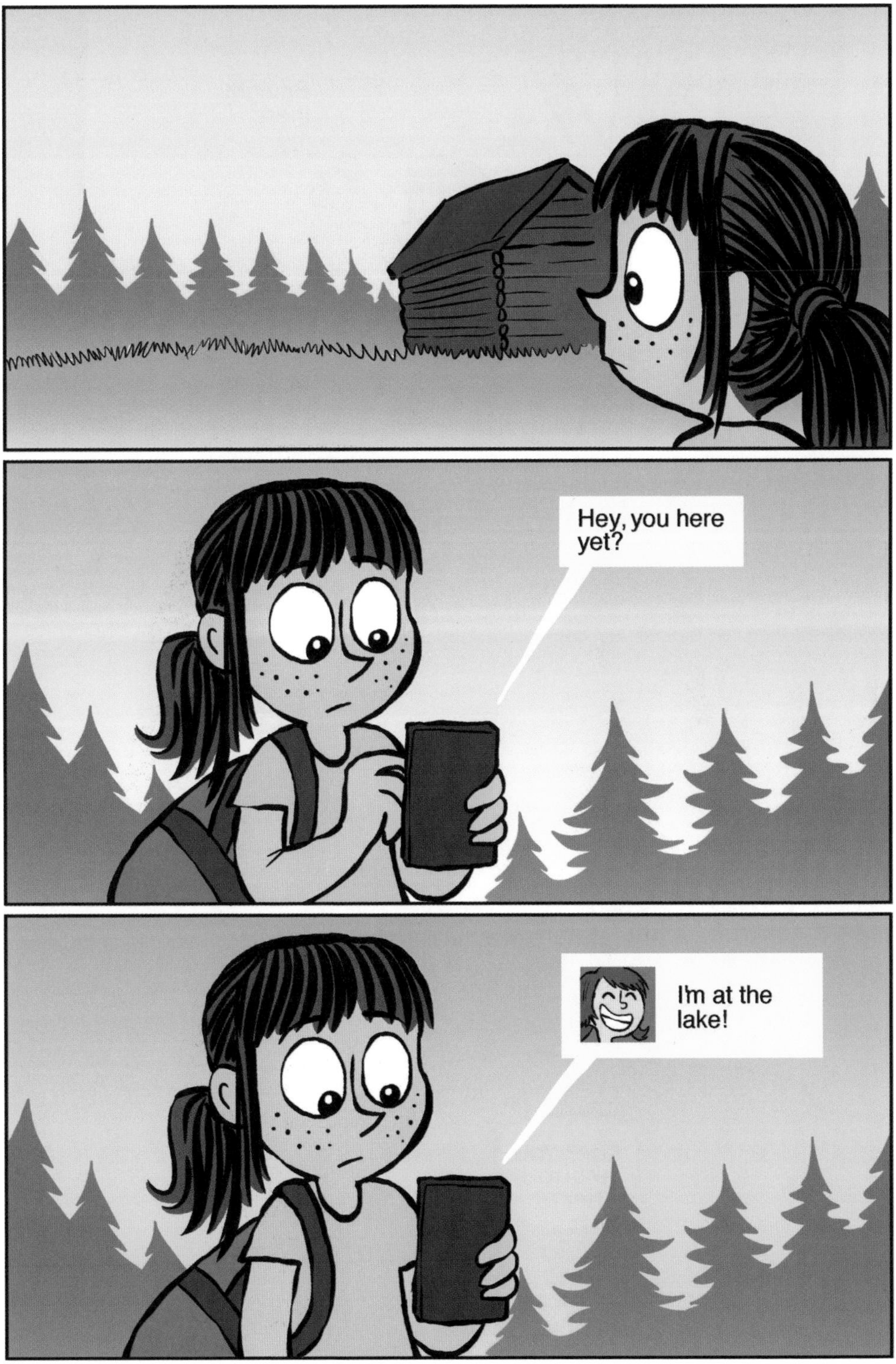
Hey, you here yet?
I'm at the lake!

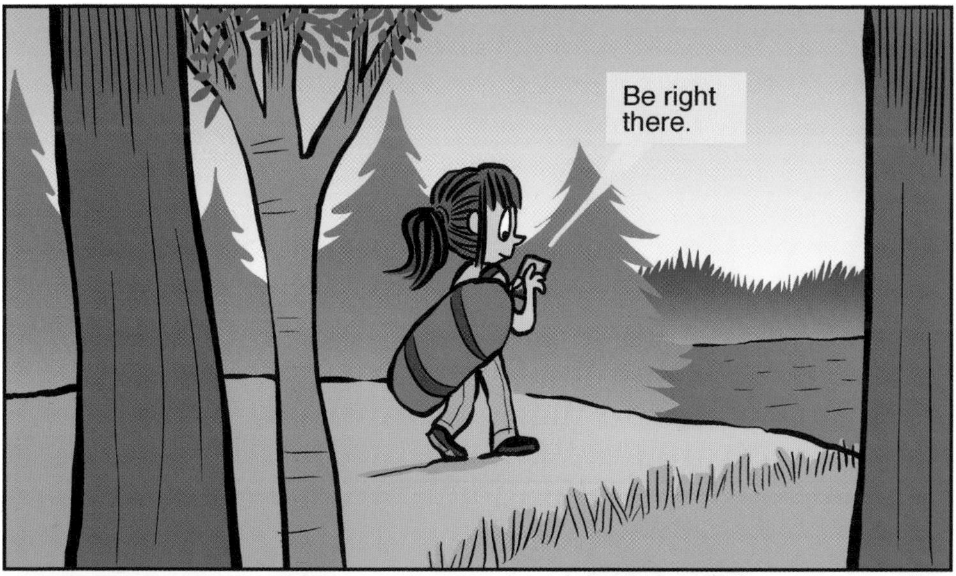
Be right there.

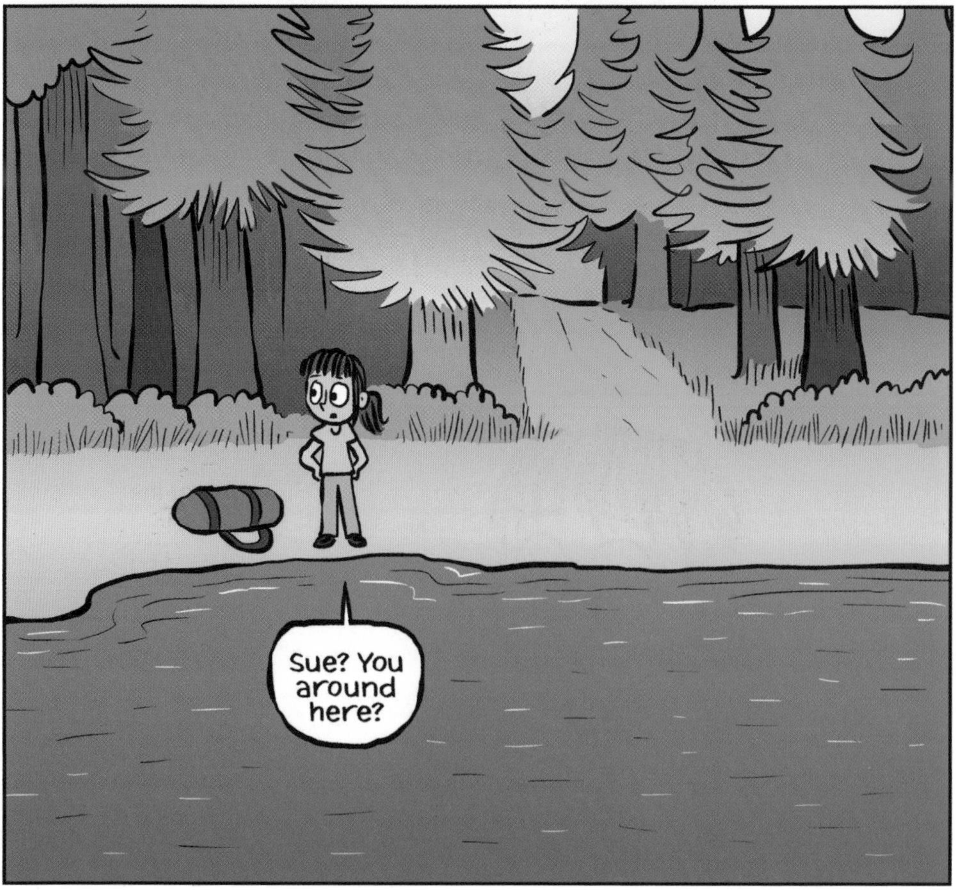
Sue? You around here?

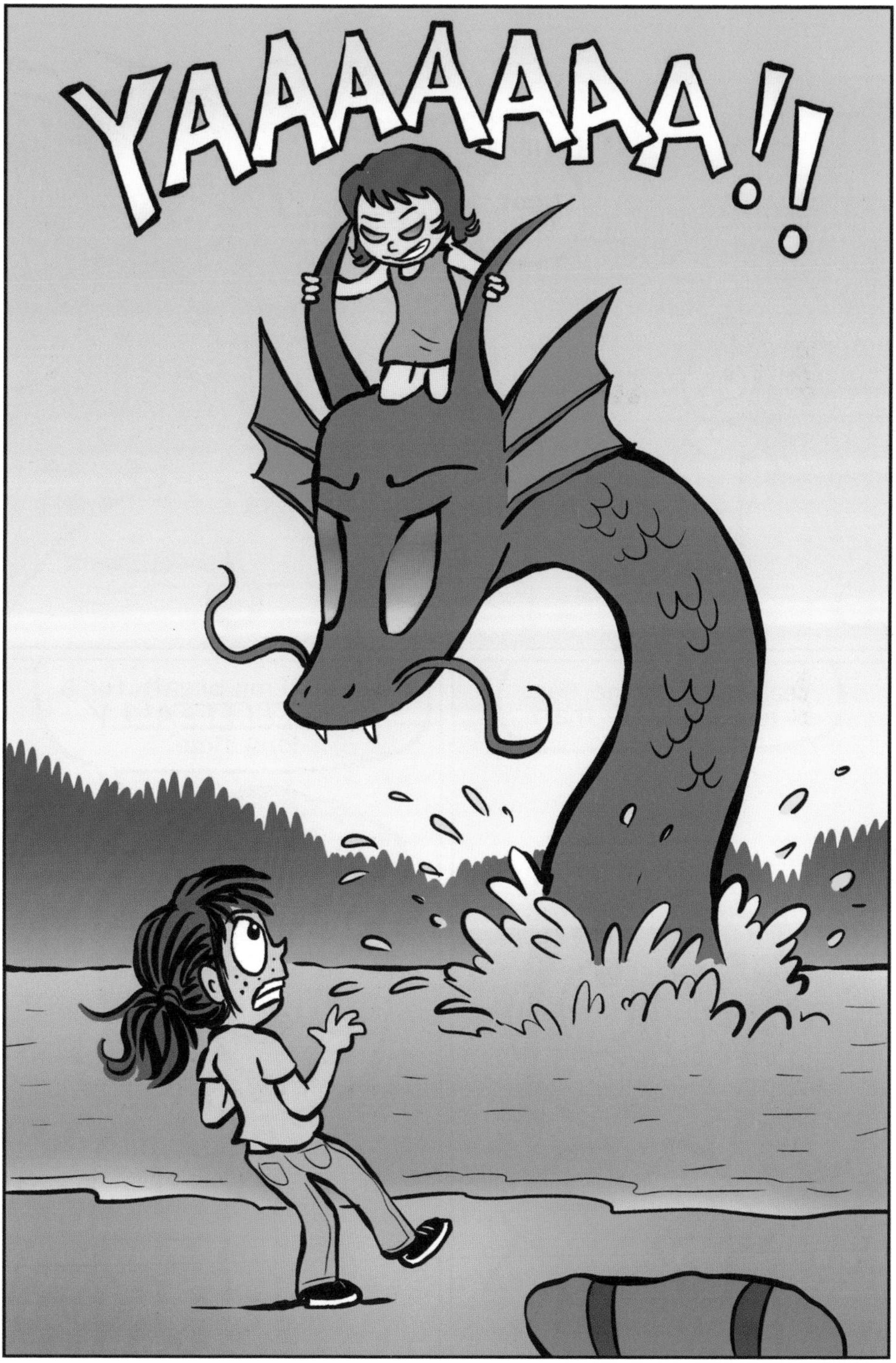
YAAAAAAA!!

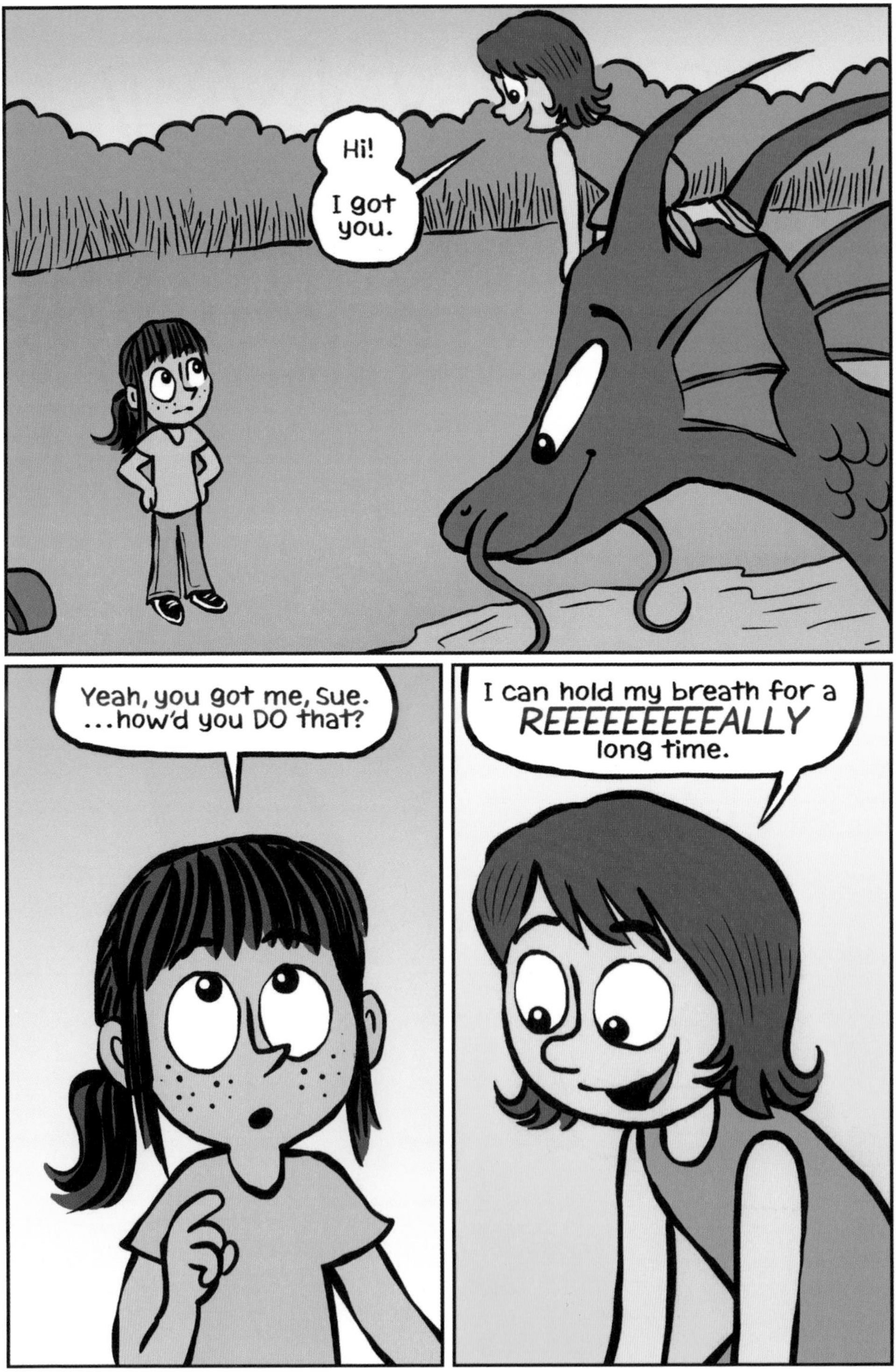
Hi!
I got you.
Yeah, you got me, Sue. ...how'd you DO that?
I can hold my breath for a REEEEEEEEEEALLY long time.

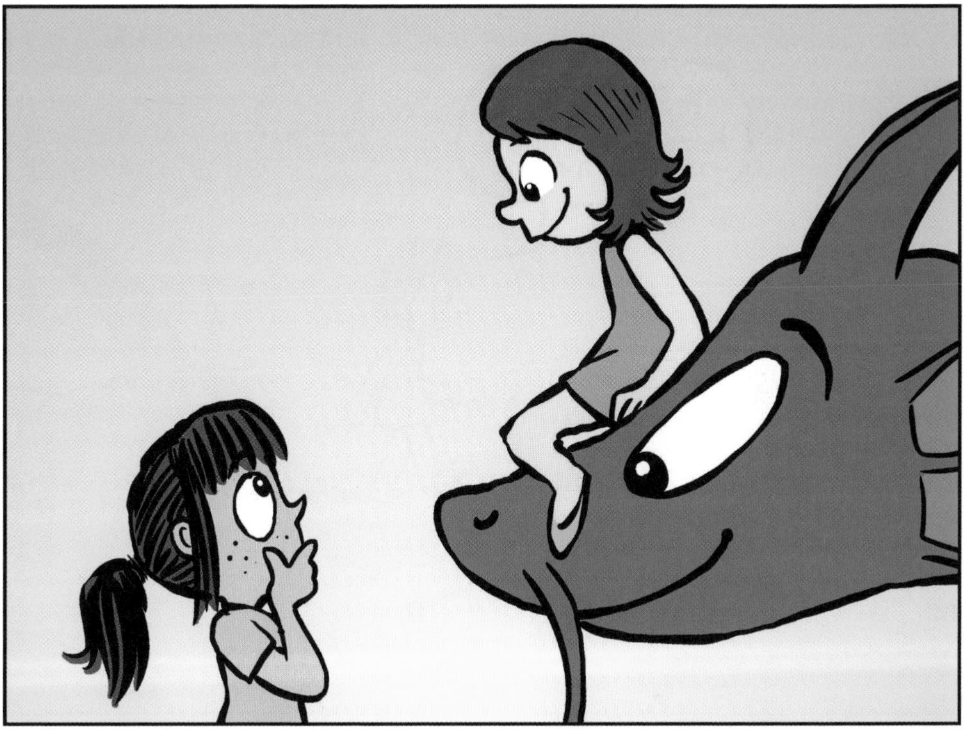

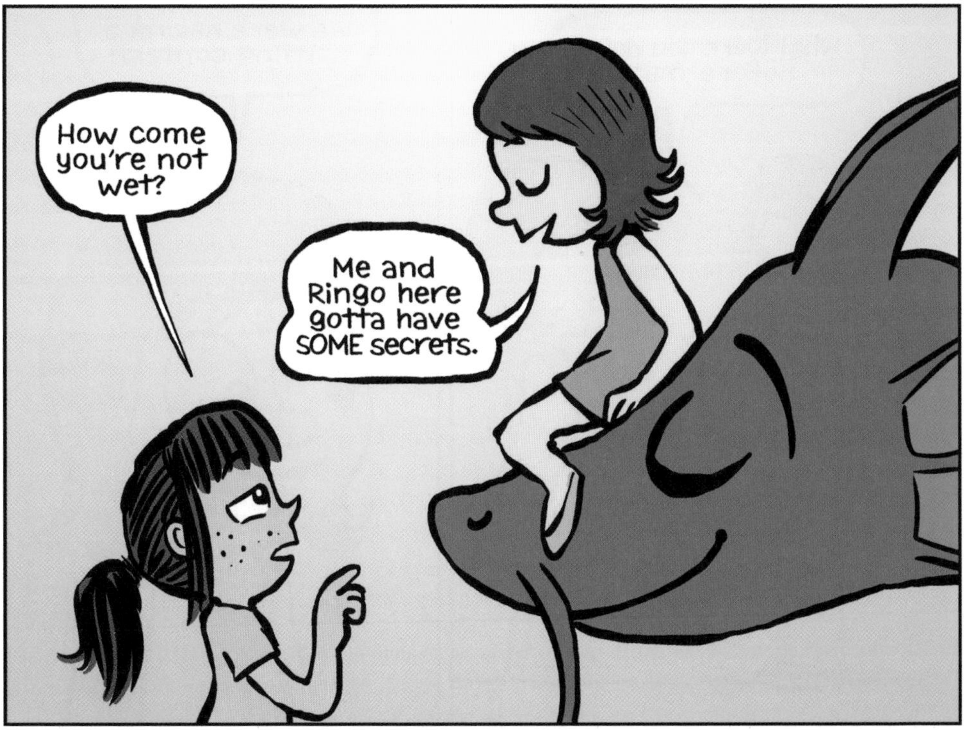
How come you're not wet?
Me and Ringo here gotta have SOME secrets.

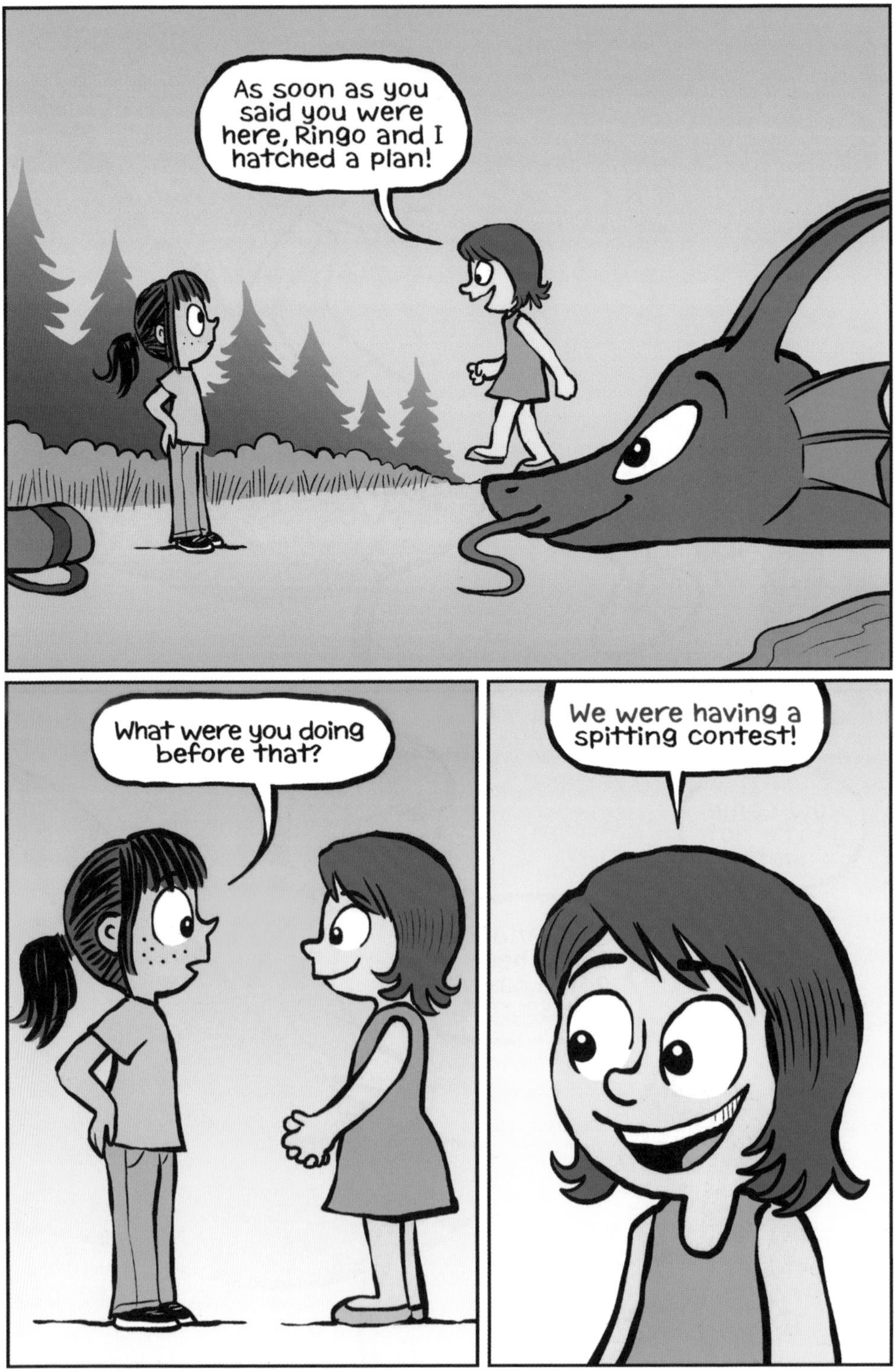
As soon as you said you were here, Ringo and I hatched a plan!
What were you doing before that?
We were having a spitting contest!

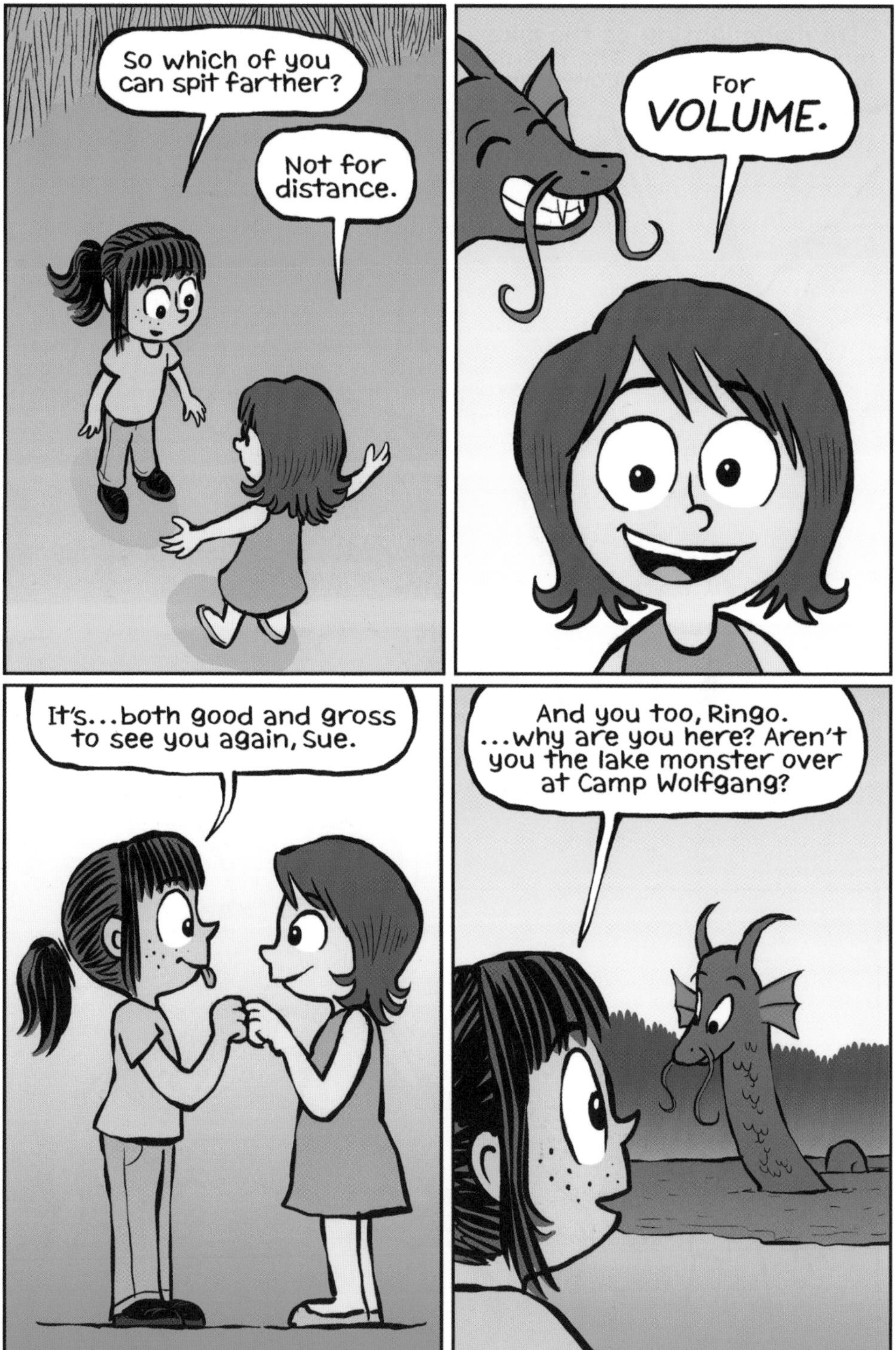
So which of you can spit farther?
Not for distance.
For VOLUME.
It's...both good and gross to see you again, Sue.
And you too, Ringo. ...why are you here? Aren't you the lake monster over at Camp Wolfgang?

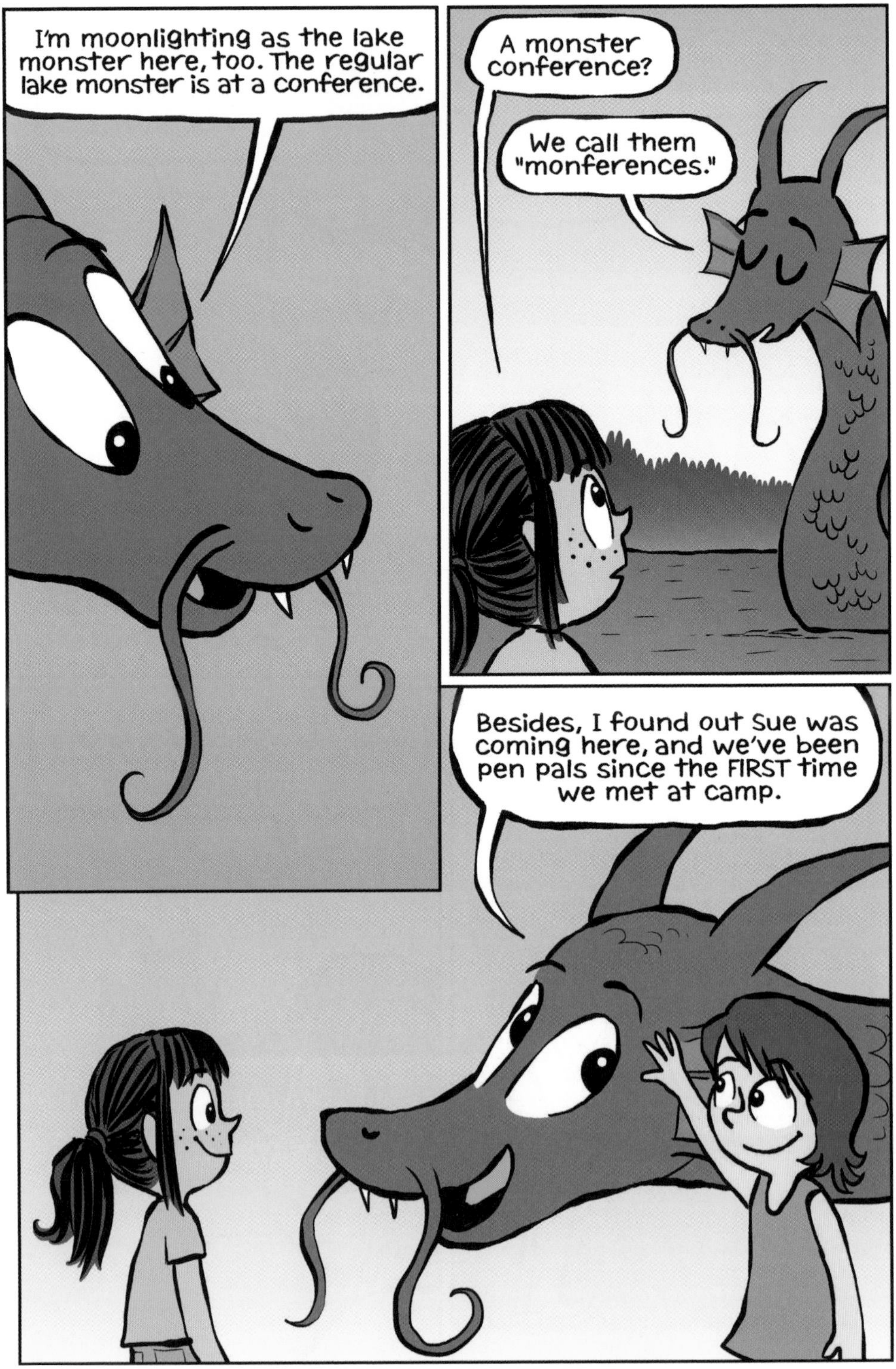
I'm moonlighting as the lake monster here, too. The regular lake monster is at a conference.
A monster conference?
We call them "monferences."
Besides, I found out Sue was coming here, and we've been pen pals since the FIRST time we met at camp.

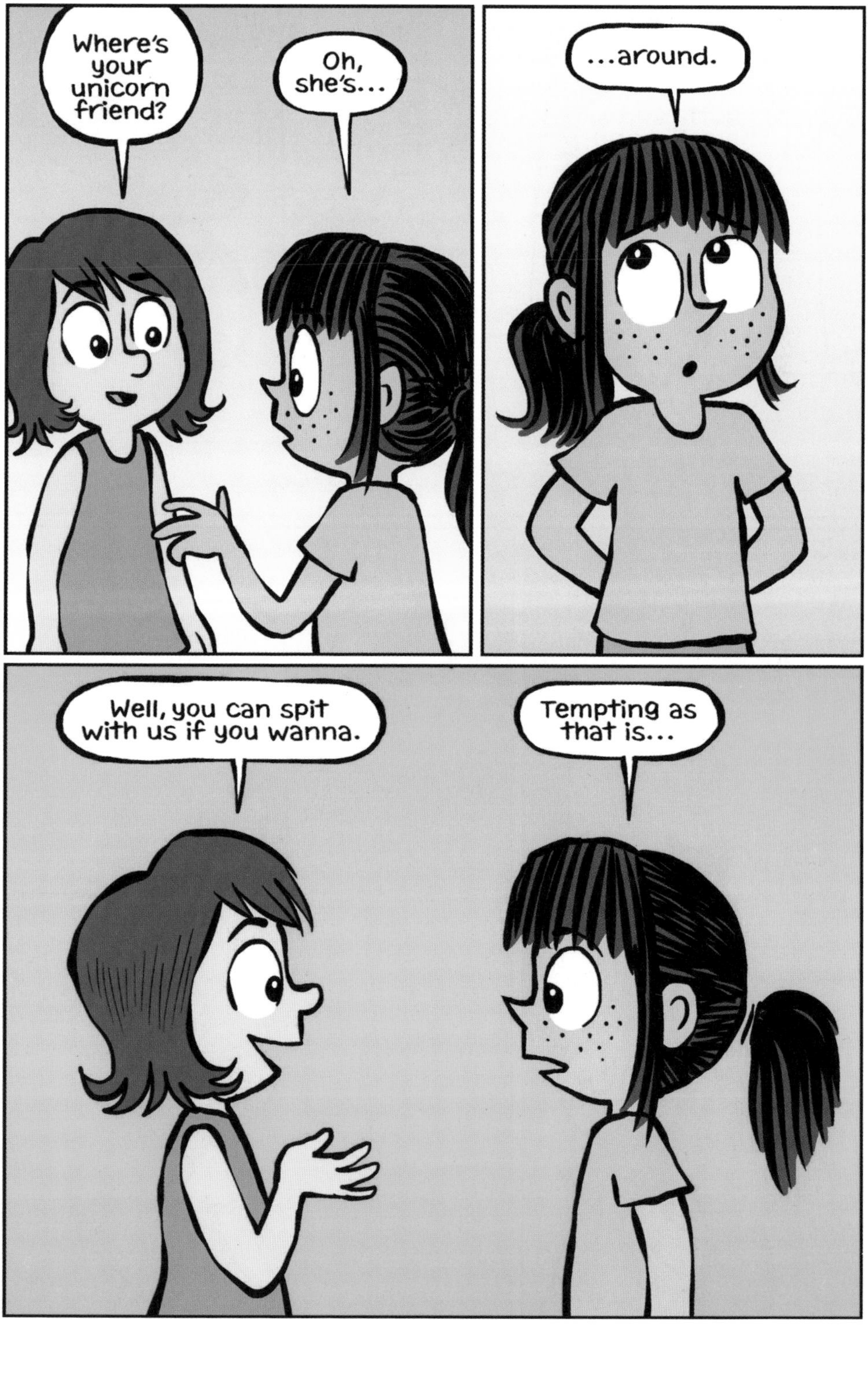
Where's your unicorn friend?
Oh, she's...
...around.
Well, you can spit with us if you wanna.
Tempting as that is...

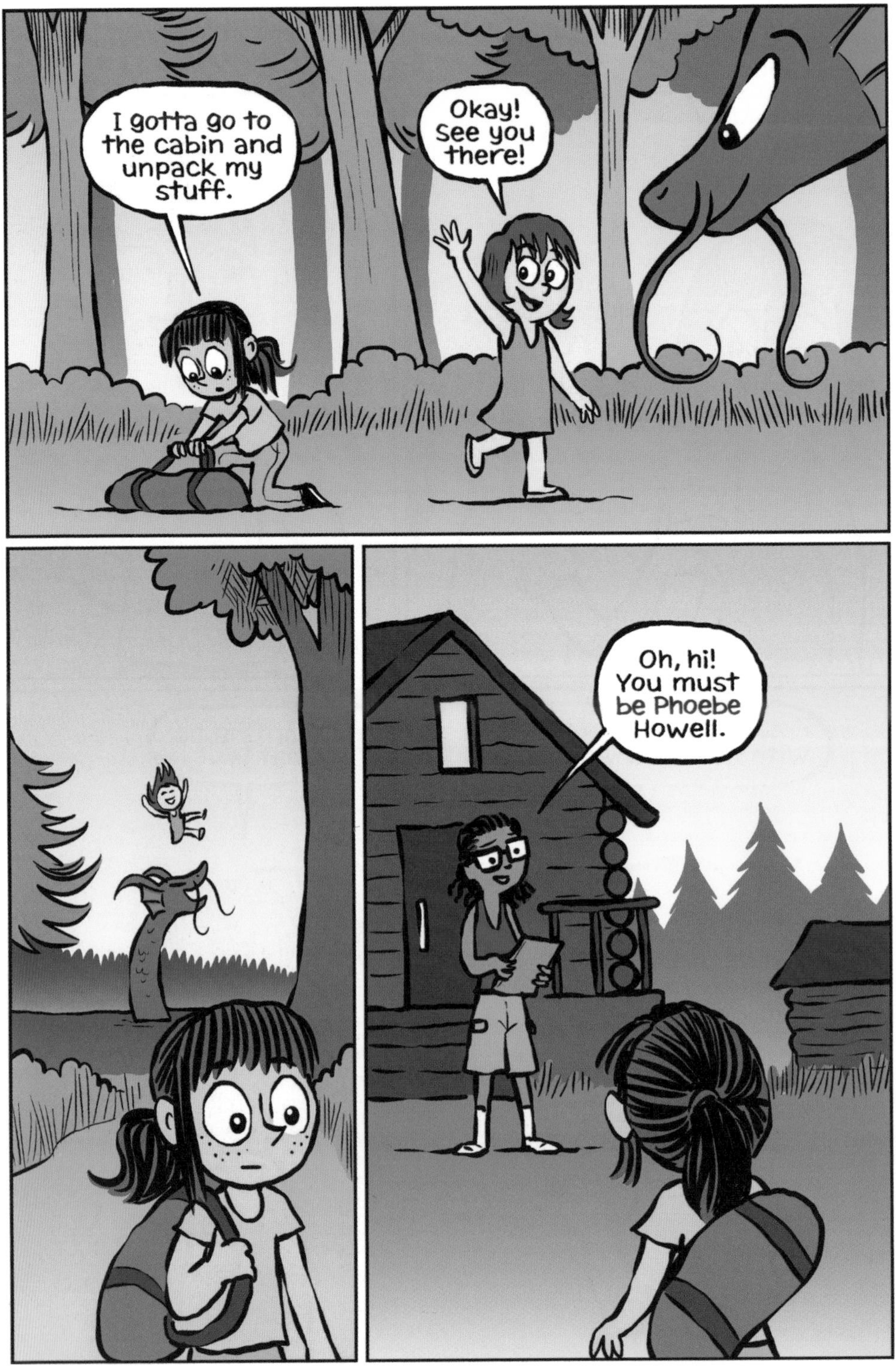
I gotta go to the cabin and unpack my stuff.
Okay! See you there!
Oh, hi! You must be Phoebe Howell.

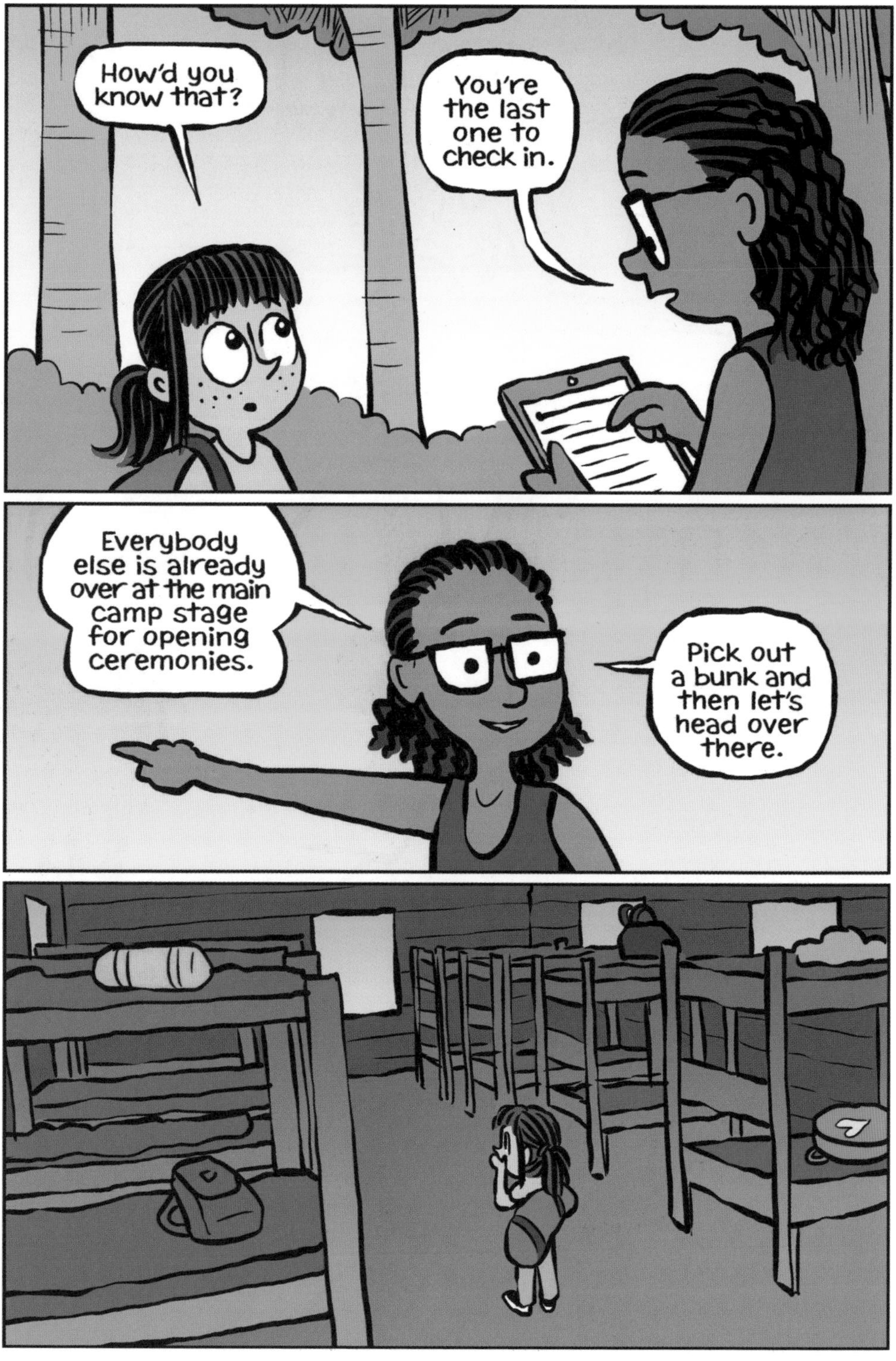
How'd you know that?
You're the last one to check in.
Everybody else is already over at the main camp stage for opening ceremonies.
Pick out a bunk and then let's head over there.

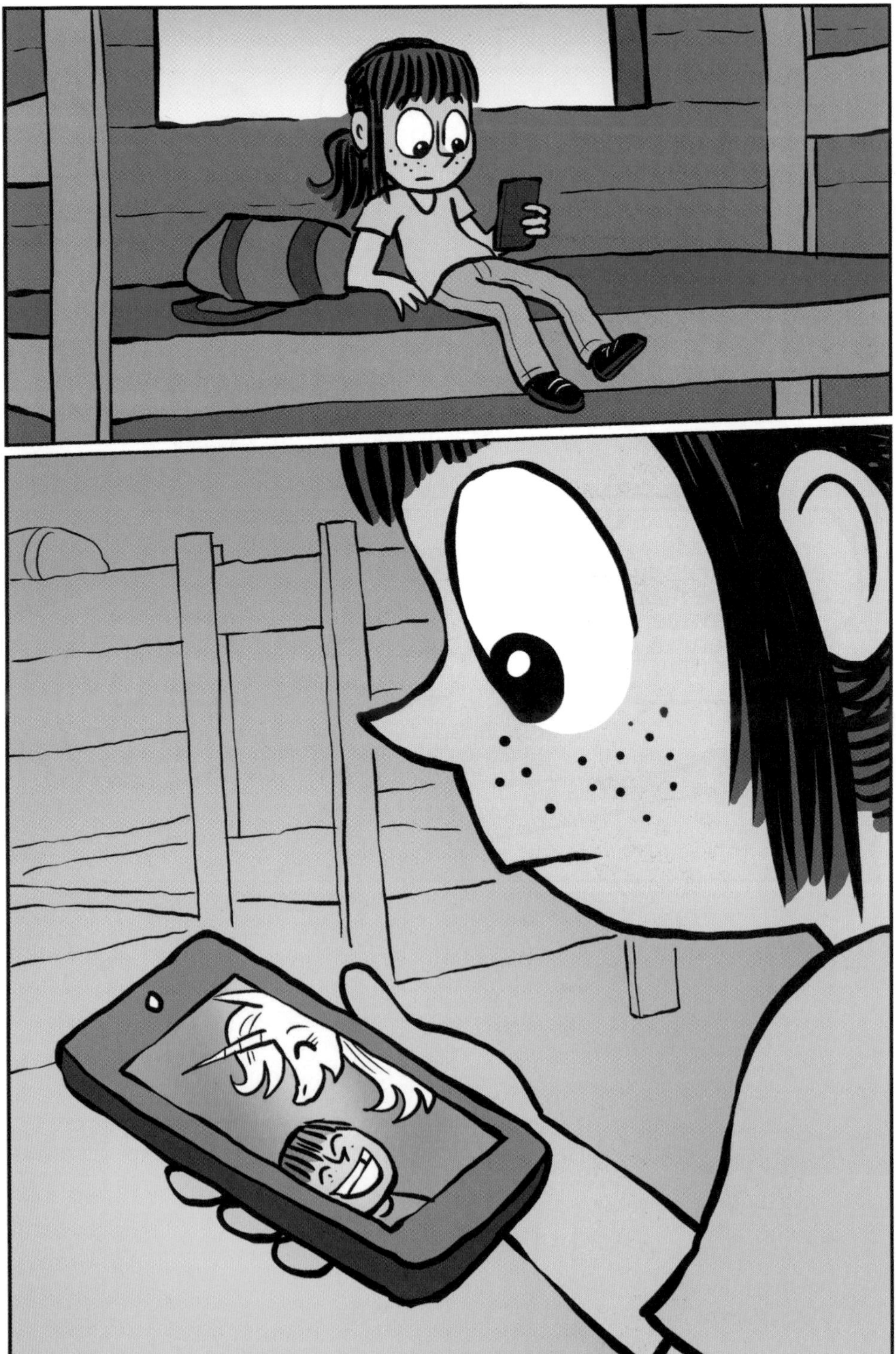

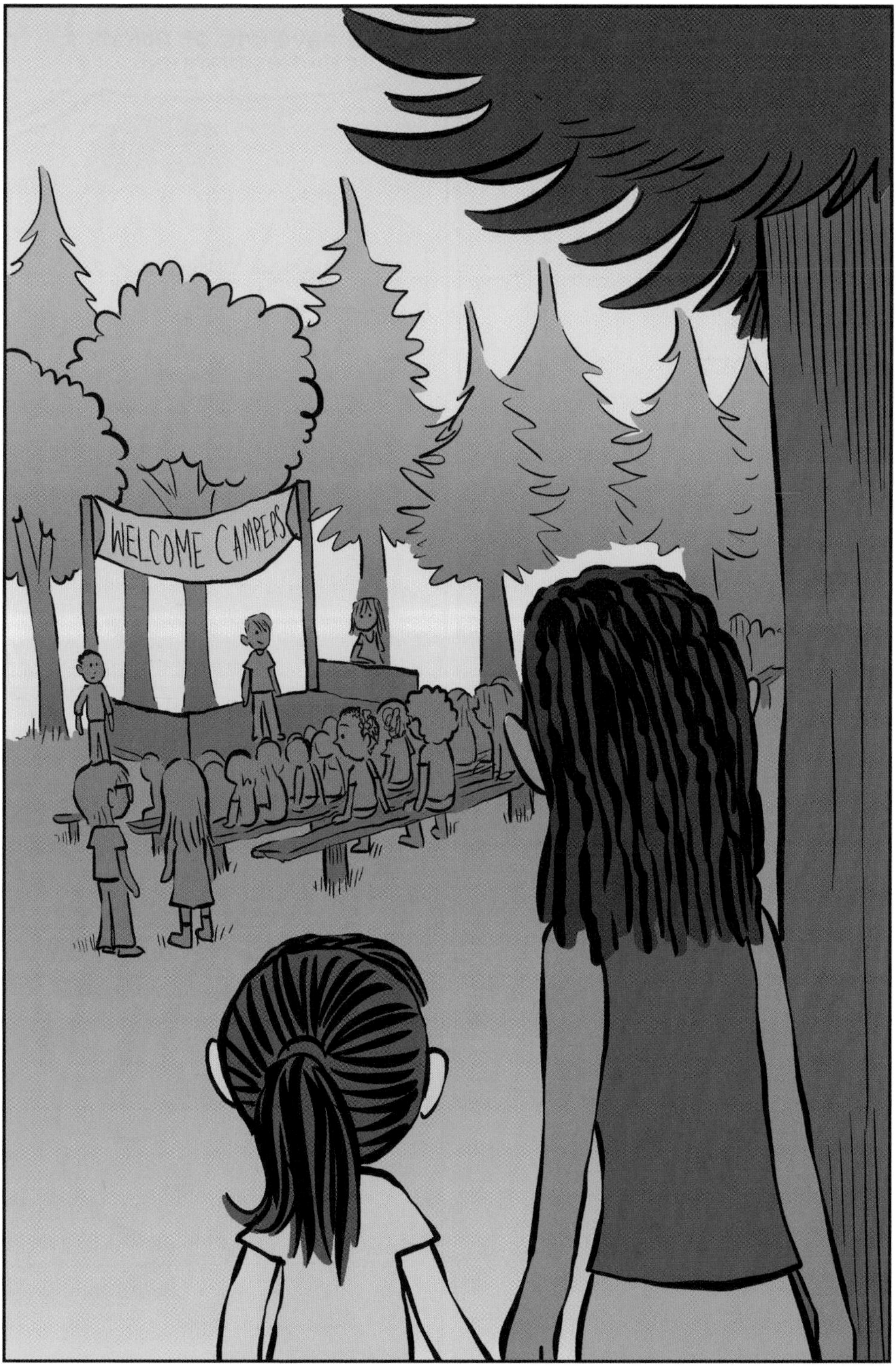
WELCOME CAMPERS

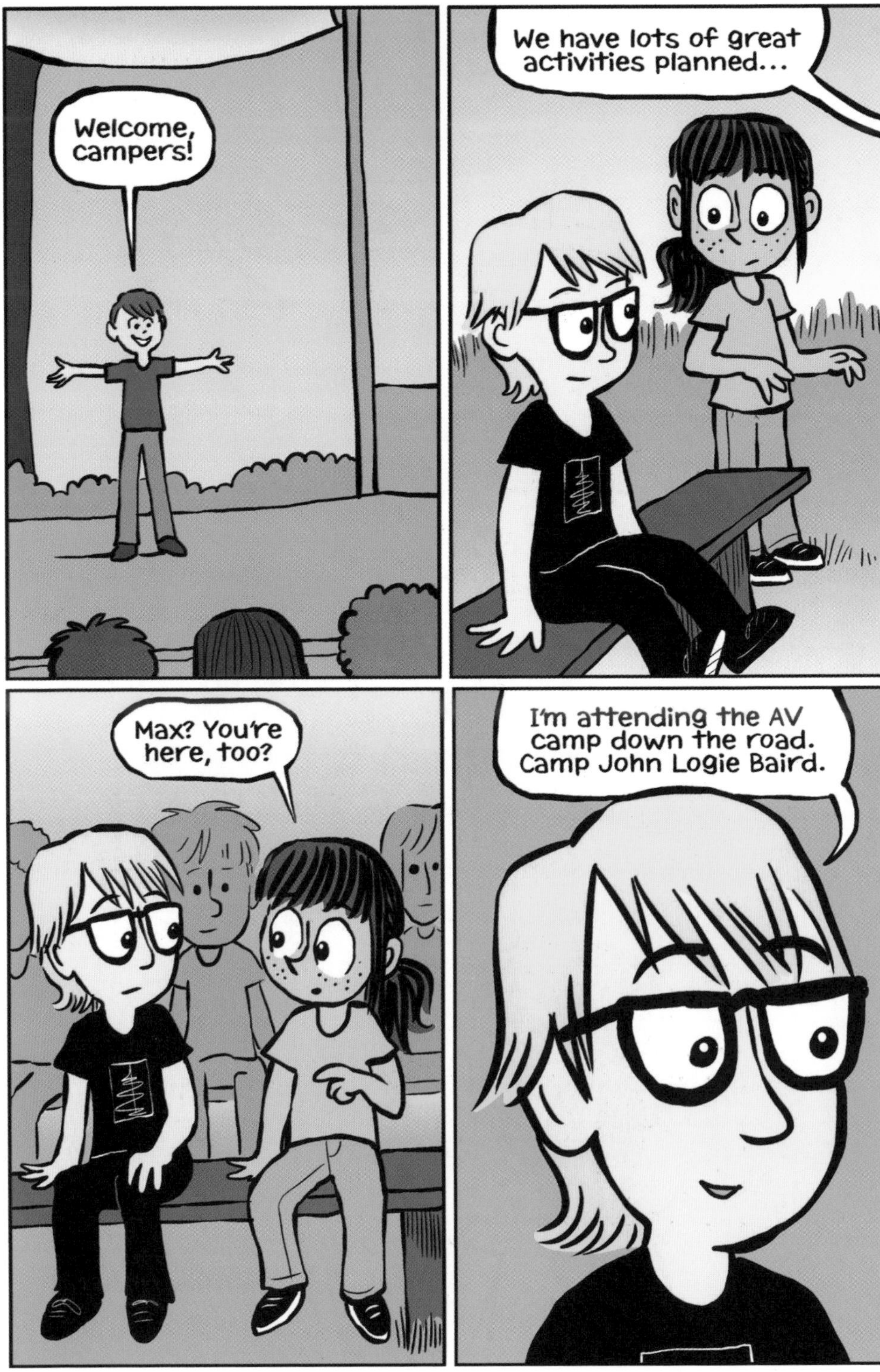
Welcome, campers!
We have lots of great activities planned...
Max? You're here, too?
I'm attending the AV camp down the road. Camp John Logie Baird.

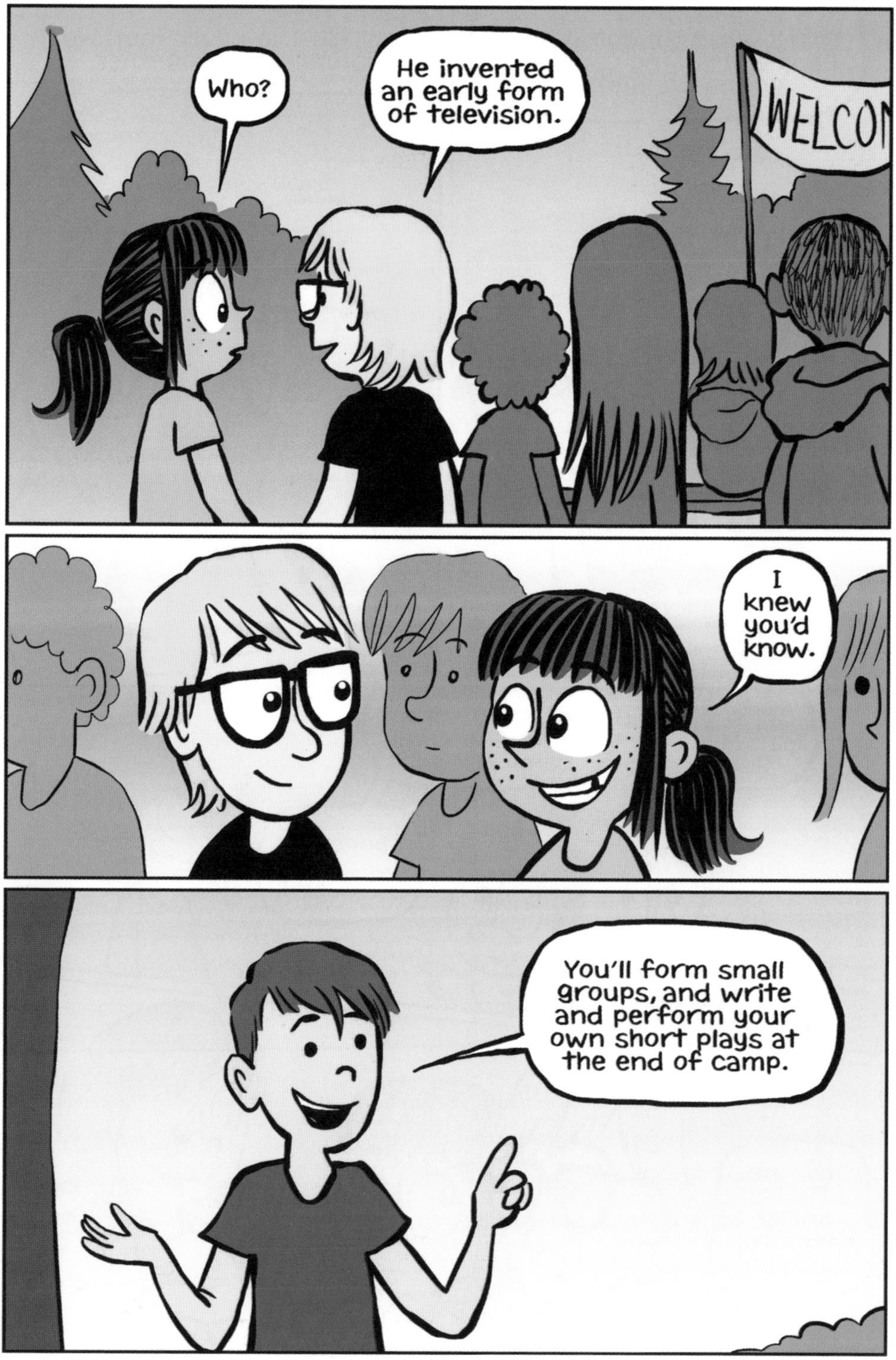
Who?
He invented an early form of television.
WELCOM
I knew you'd know.
You'll form small groups, and write and perform your own short plays at the end of camp.

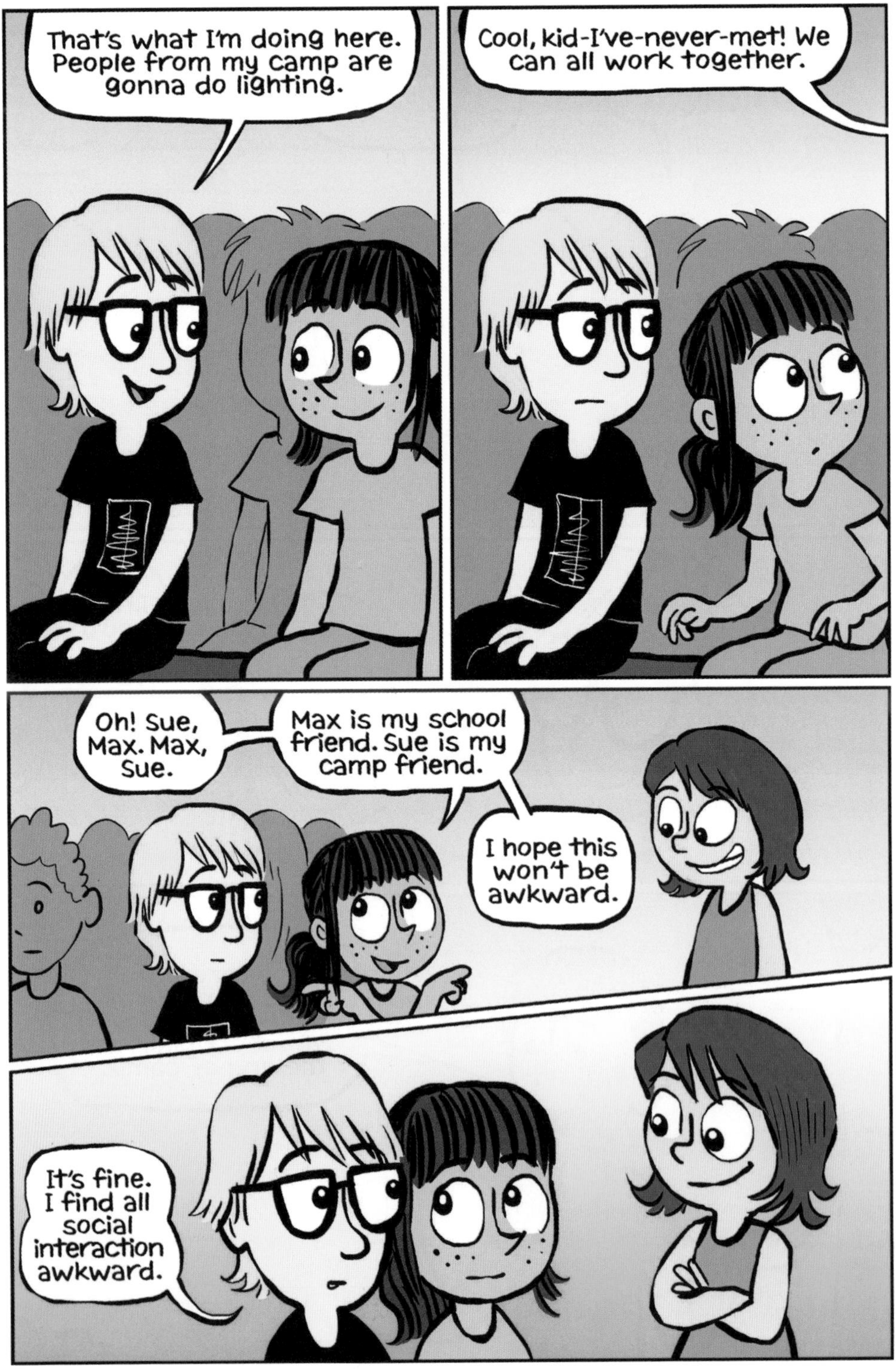
That's what I'm doing here. People from my camp are gonna do lighting.
Cool, kid-I've-never-met! We can all work together.
Oh! Sue, Max. Max, Sue.
Max is my school friend. Sue is my camp friend.
I hope this won't be awkward.
It's fine. I find all social interaction awkward.

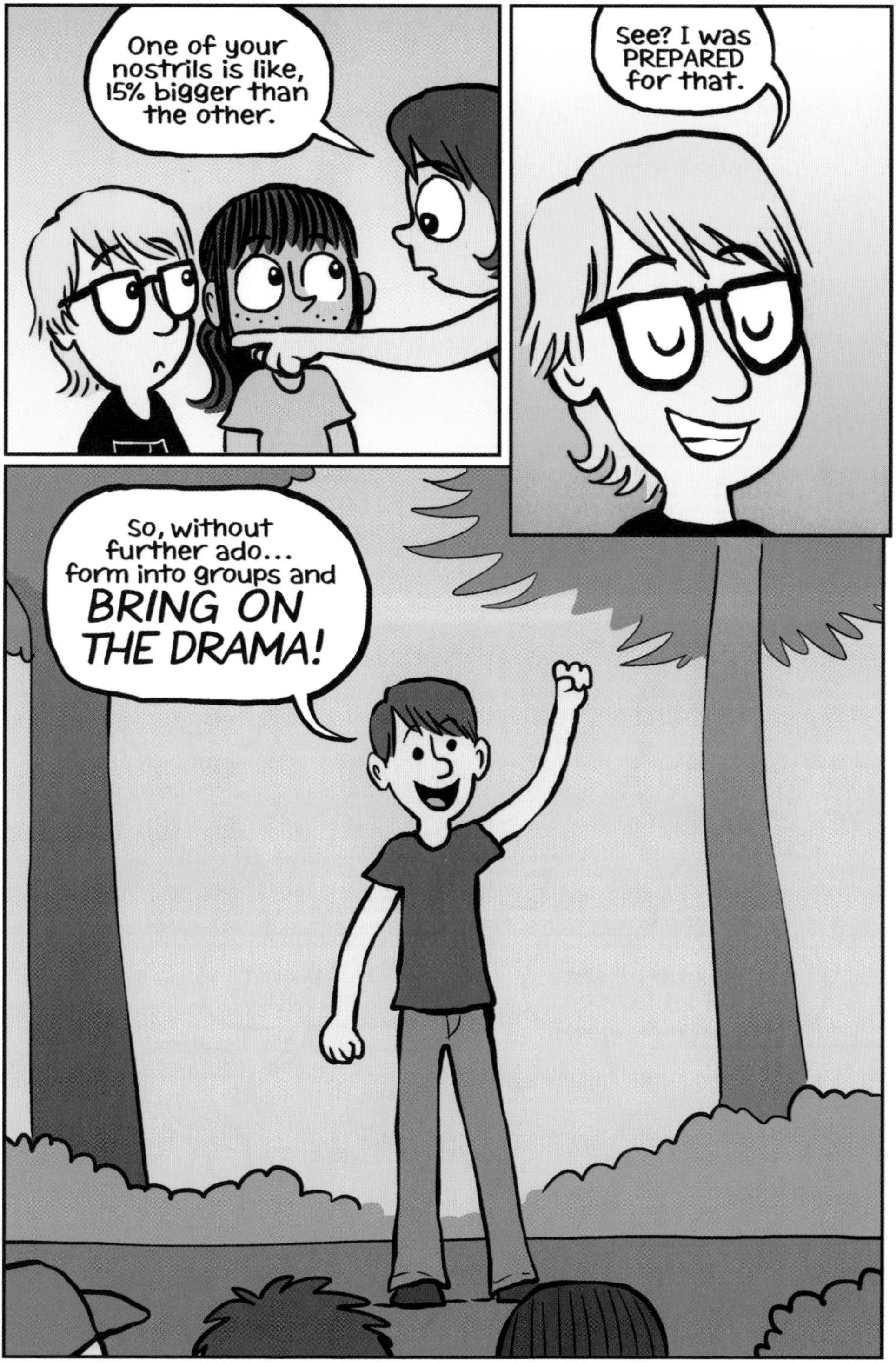
One of your nostrils is like, 15% bigger than the other.
See? I was PREPARED for that.
So, without further ado... form into groups and BRING ON THE DRAMA!

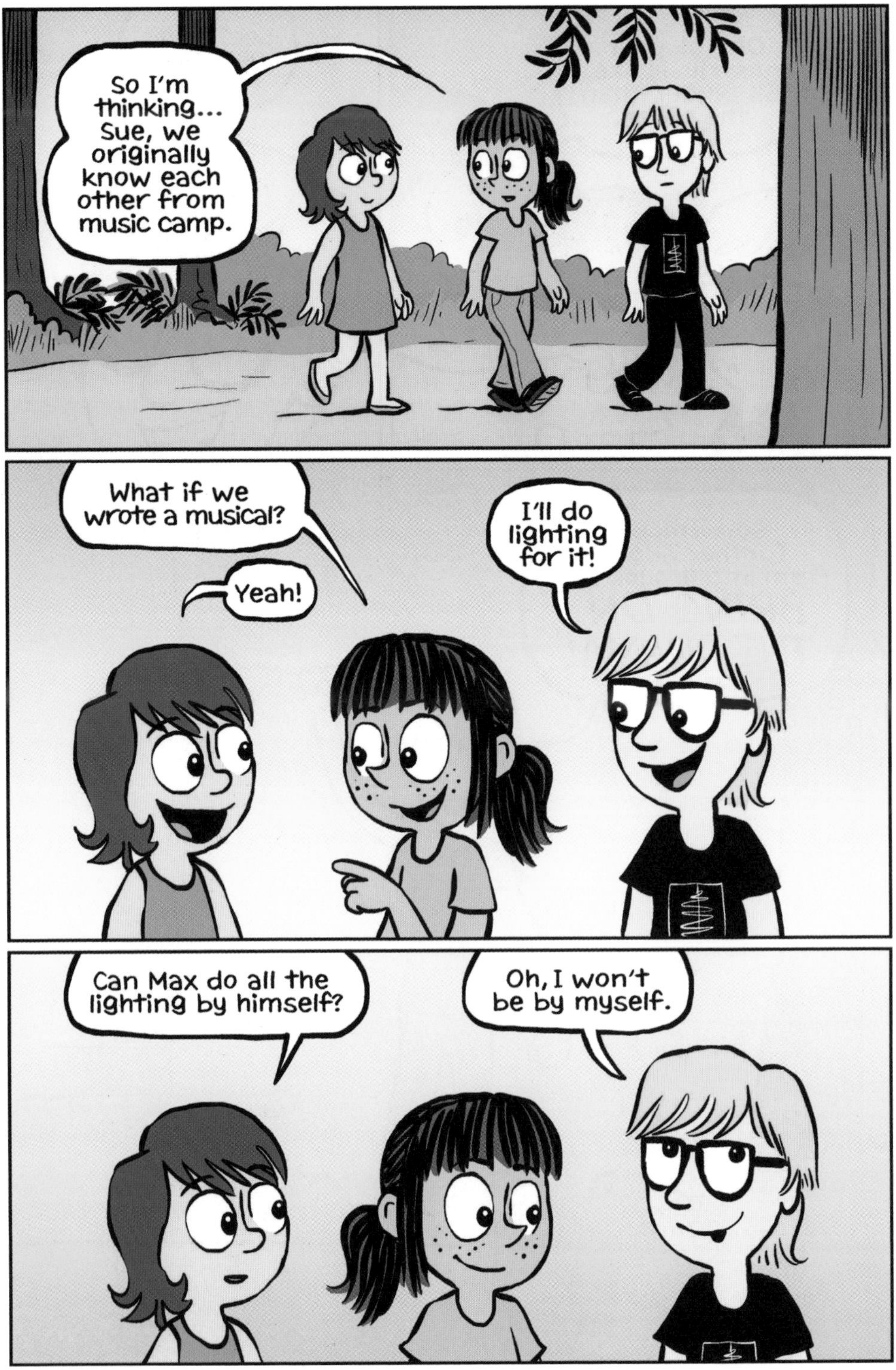
So I'm thinking... Sue, we originally know each other from music camp.
What if we wrote a musical?
Yeah!
I'll do lighting for it!
Can Max do all the lighting by himself?
Oh, I won't be by myself.

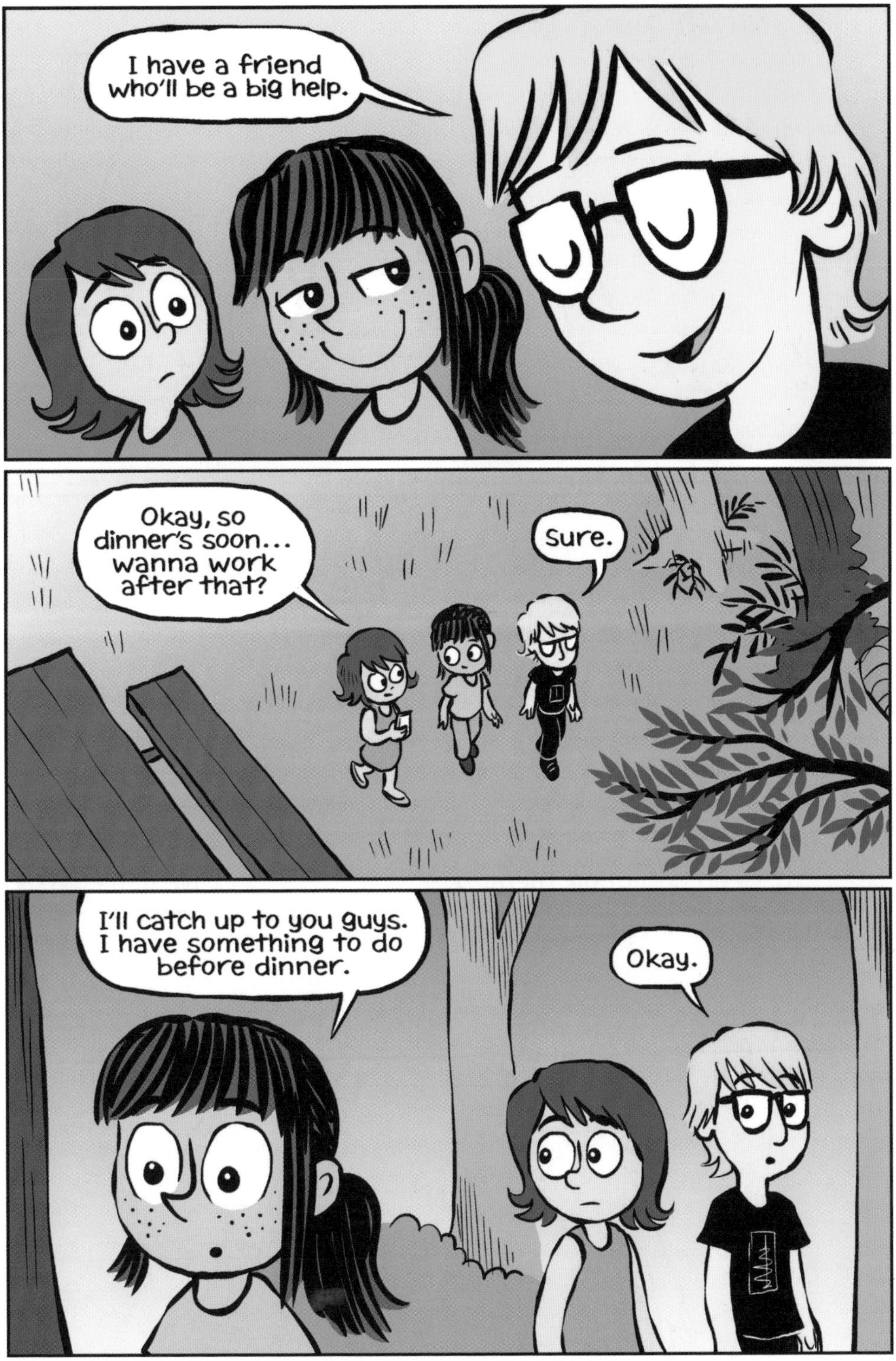
I have a friend who'll be a big help.
Okay, so dinner's soon... wanna work after that?
Sure.
I'll catch up to you guys. I have something to do before dinner.
Okay.

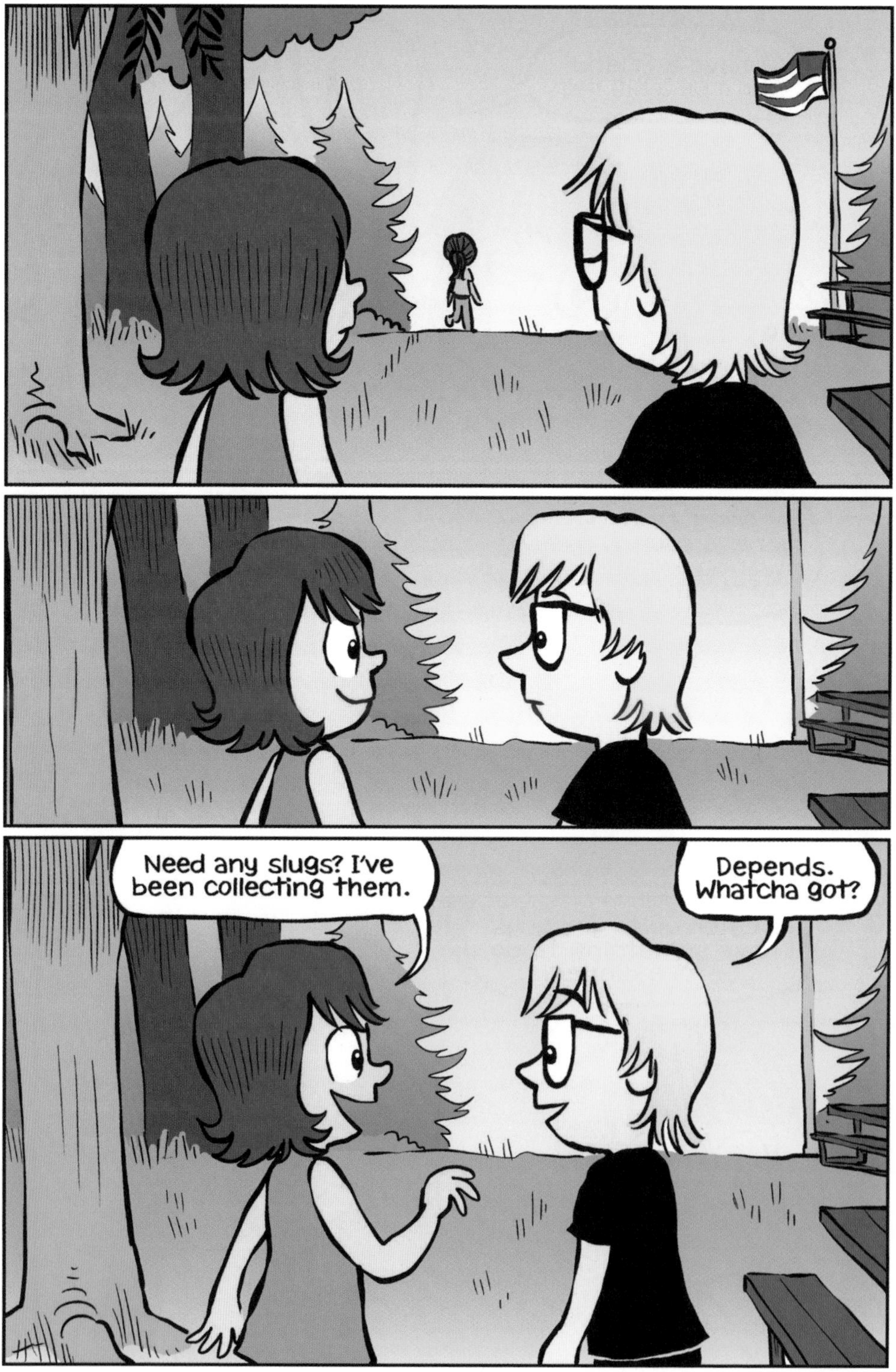
Need any slugs? I've been collecting them.
Depends. Whatcha got?

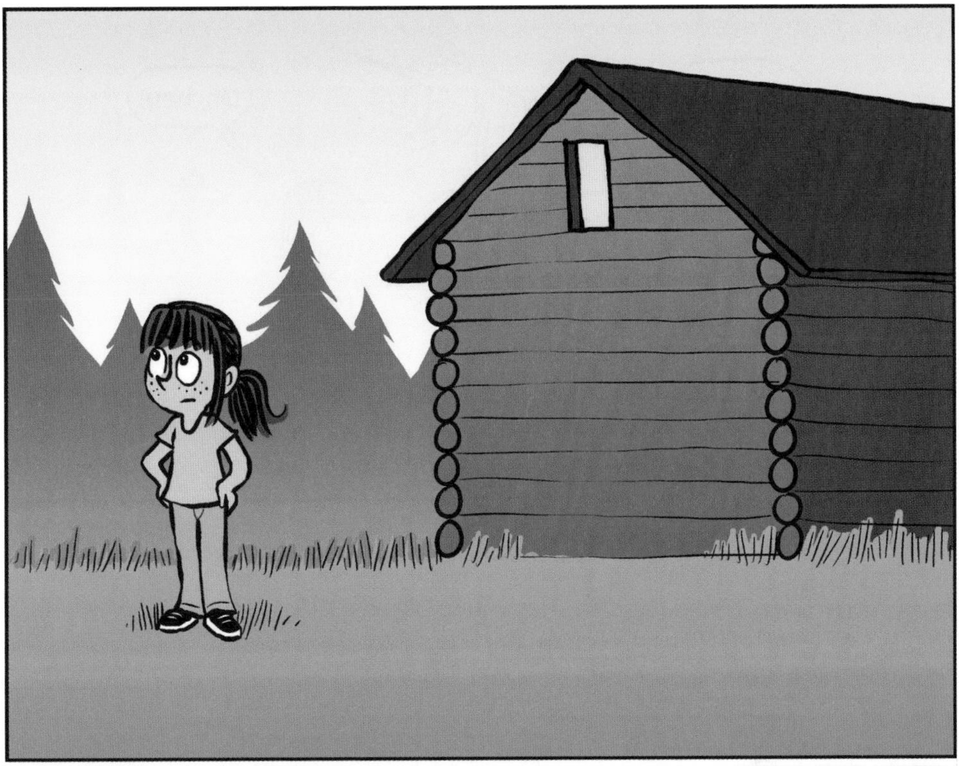

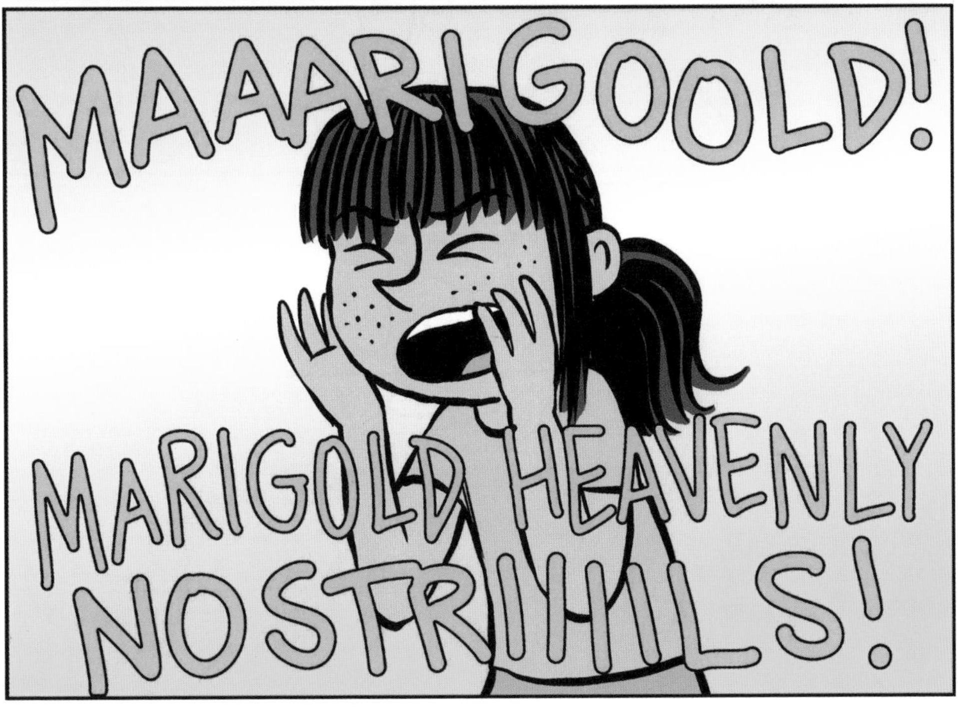
MAAARIGOOLD!
MARIGOLD HEAVENLY NOSTRIIILS!

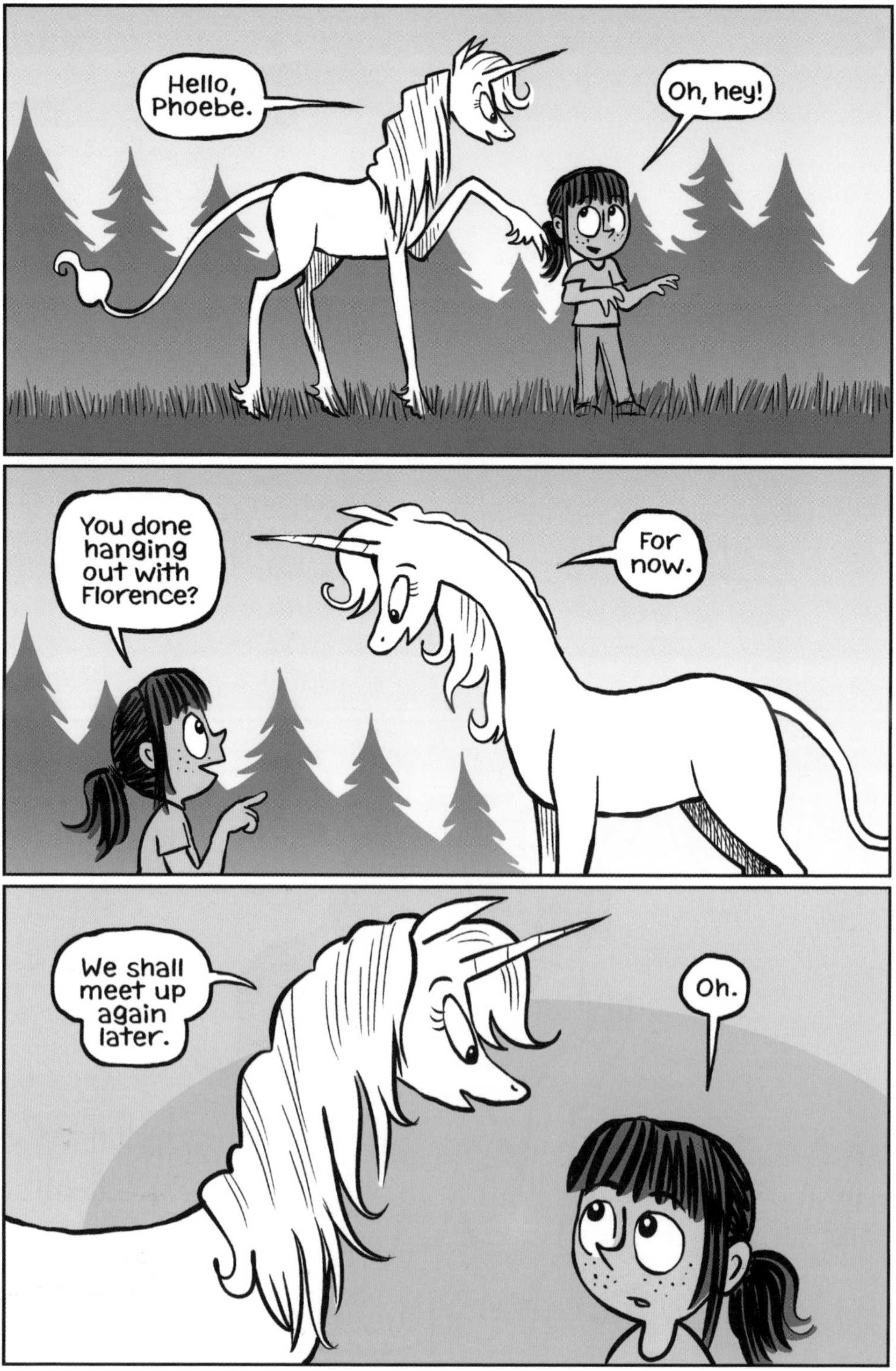
Hello, Phoebe.
Oh, hey!
You done hanging out with Florence?
For now.
We shall meet up again later.
Oh.

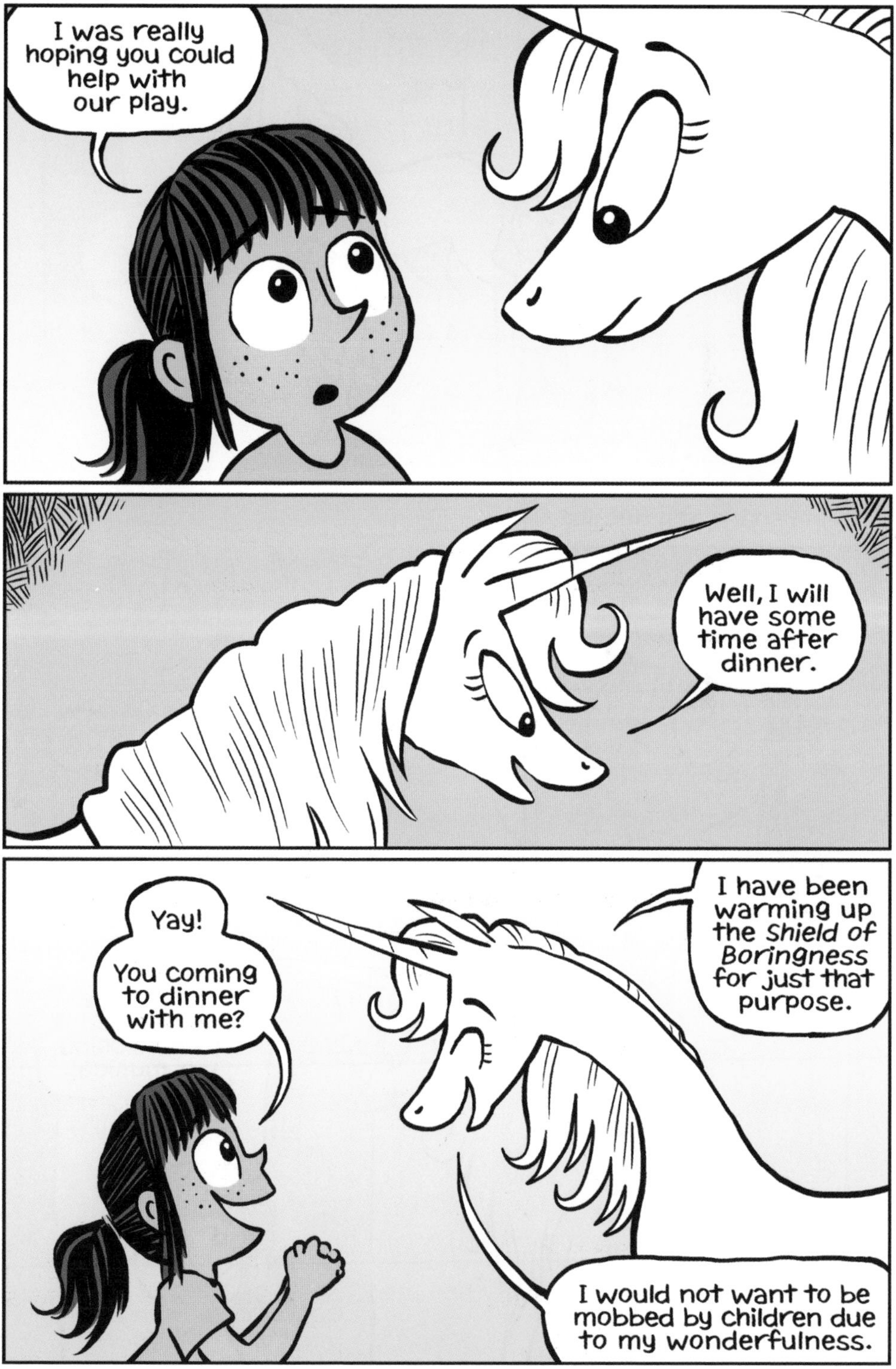
I was really hoping you could help with our play.
Well, I will have some time after dinner.
Yay!
You coming to dinner with me?
I have been warming up the *Shield of Boringness* for just that purpose.
I would not want to be mobbed by children due to my wonderfulness.

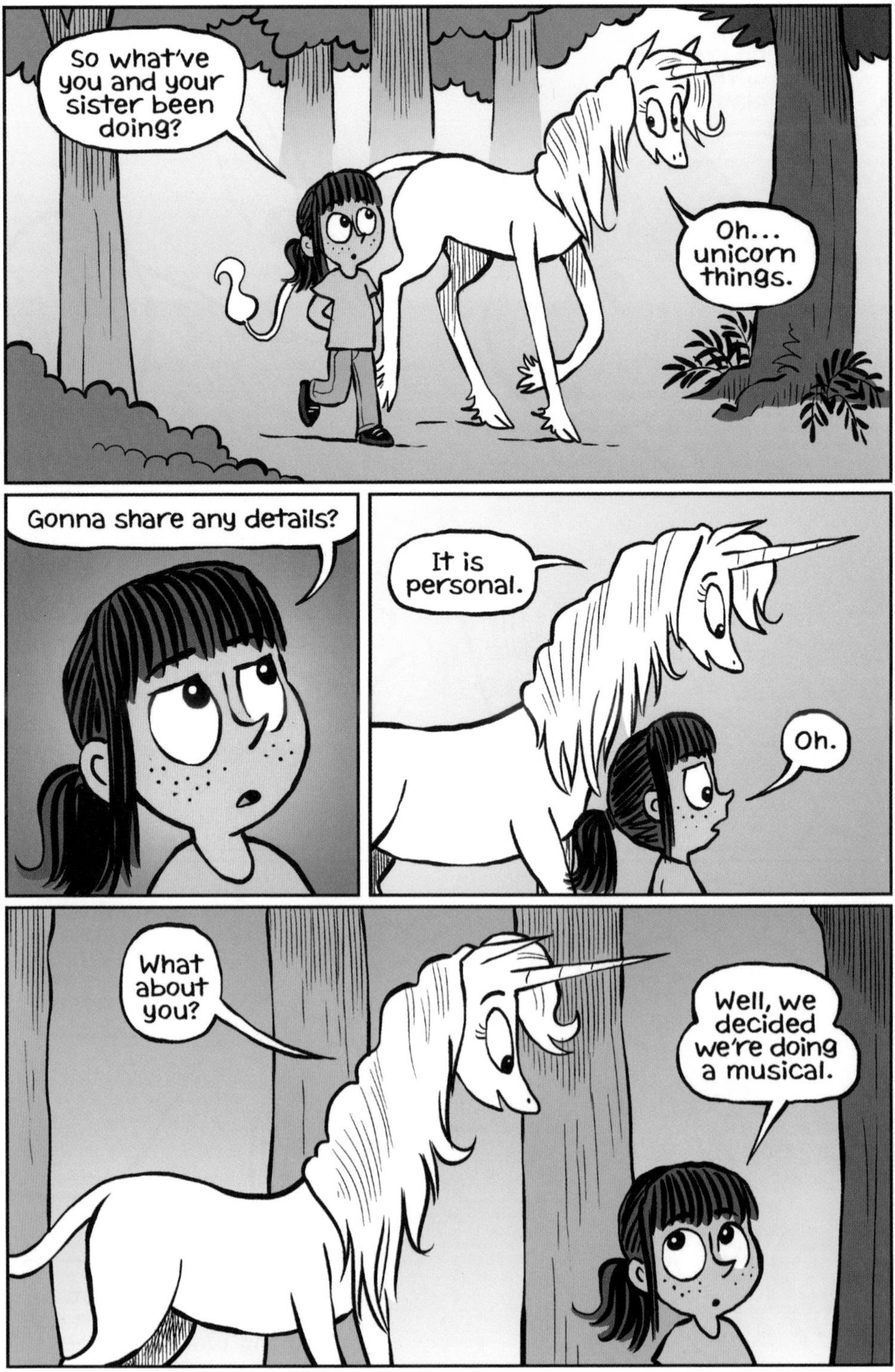
So what've you and your sister been doing?
Oh... unicorn things.
Gonna share any details?
It is personal.
Oh.
What about you?
Well, we decided we're doing a musical.

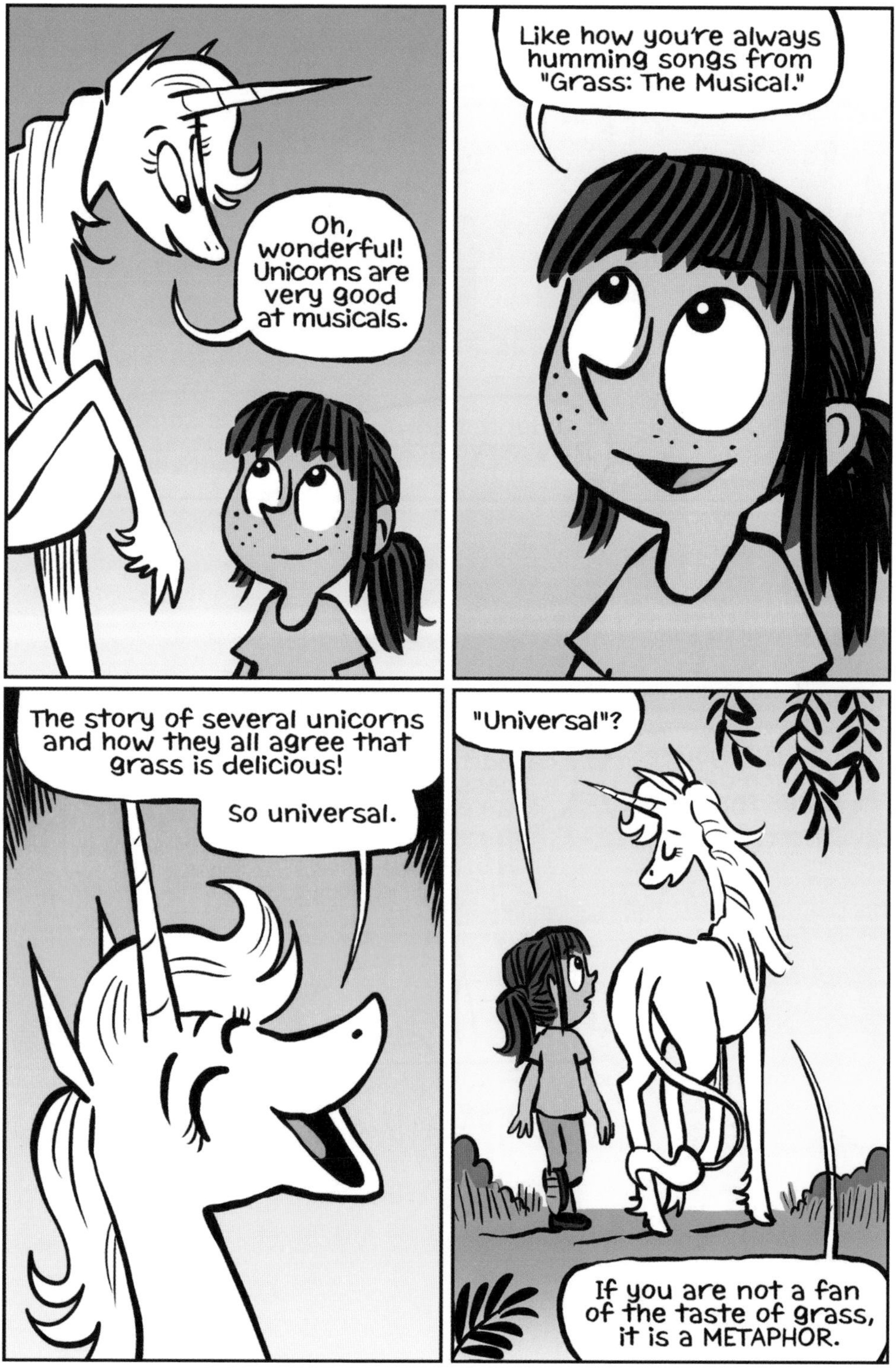
Oh, wonderful! Unicorns are very good at musicals.
Like how you're always humming songs from "Grass: The Musical."
The story of several unicorns and how they all agree that grass is delicious!
So universal.
"Universal"?
If you are not a fan of the taste of grass, it is a METAPHOR.

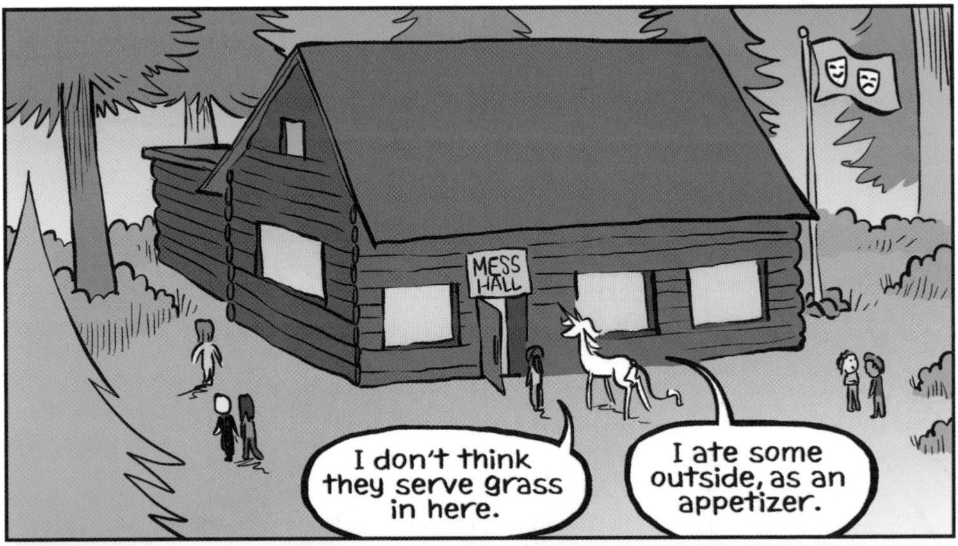
MESS HALL
I don't think they serve grass in here.
I ate some outside, as an appetizer.

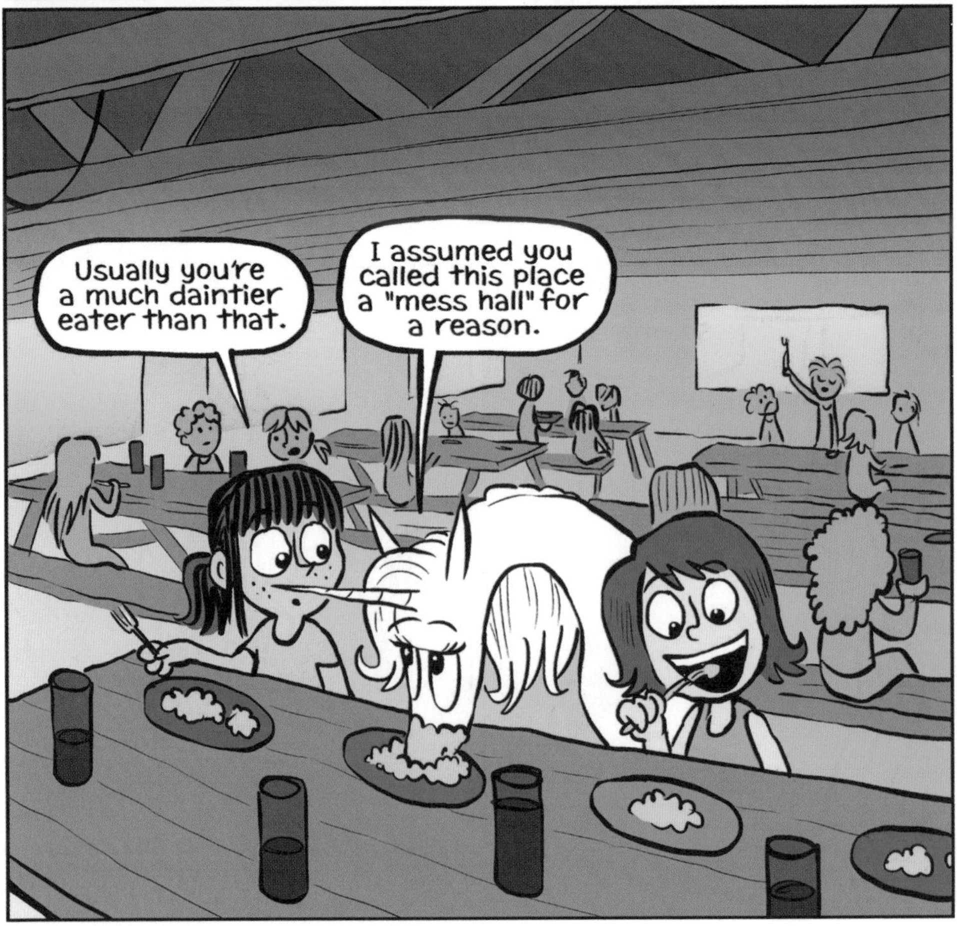
Usually you're a much daintier eater than that.
I assumed you called this place a "mess hall" for a reason.

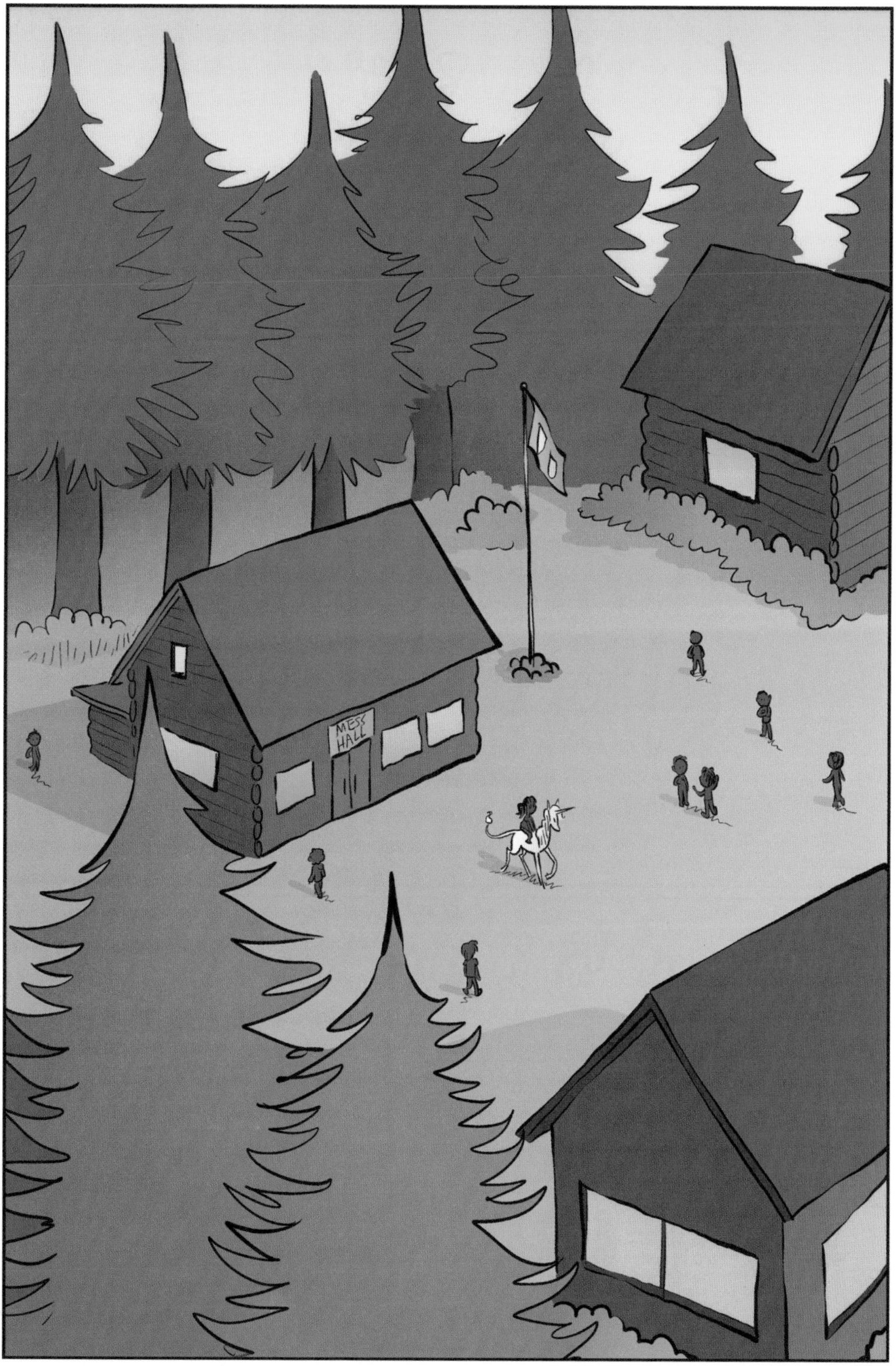
MESS
HALL

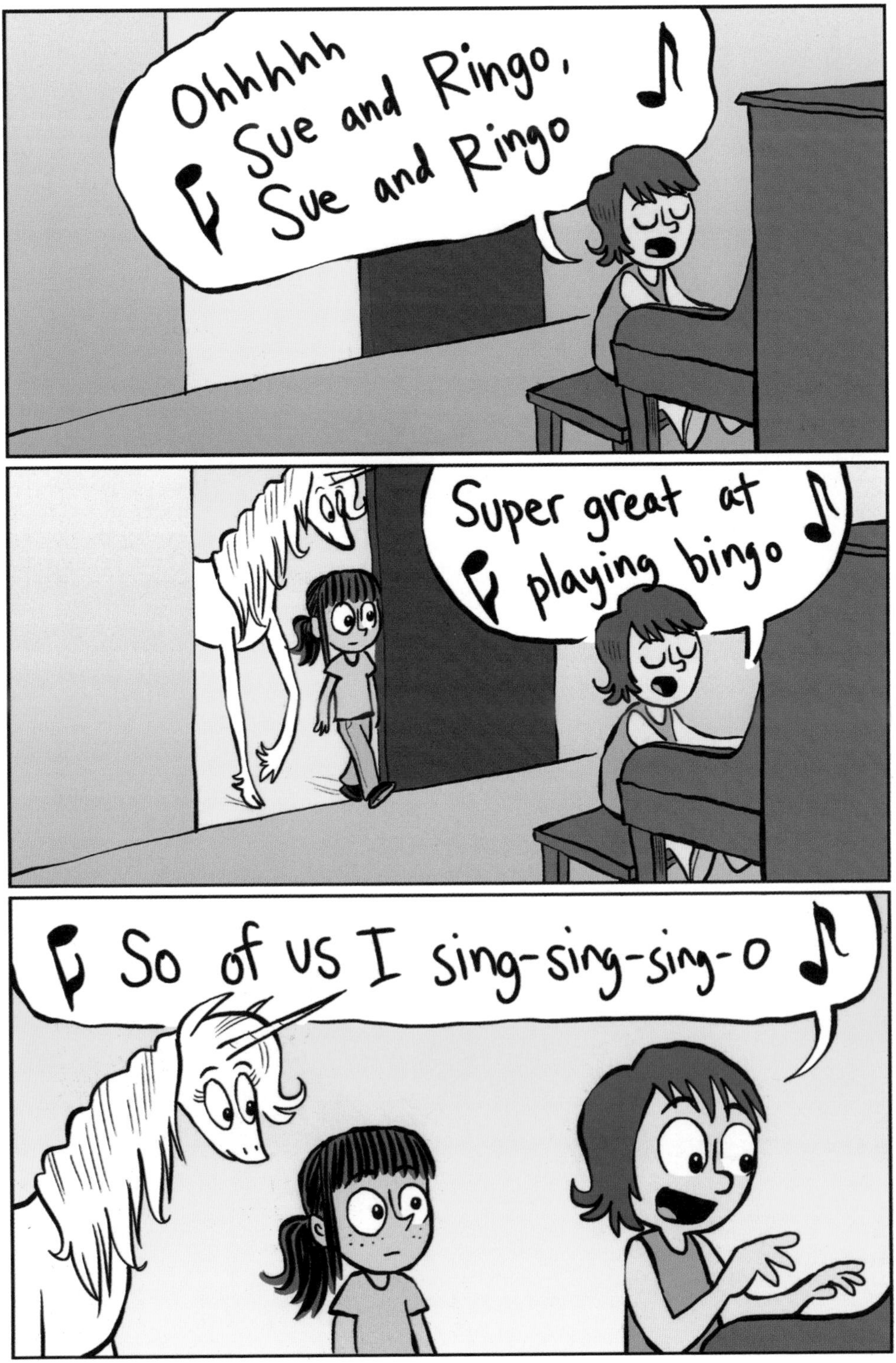
Ohhhhh Sue and Ringo, Sue and Ringo
Super great at playing bingo
So of us I sing-sing-sing-o

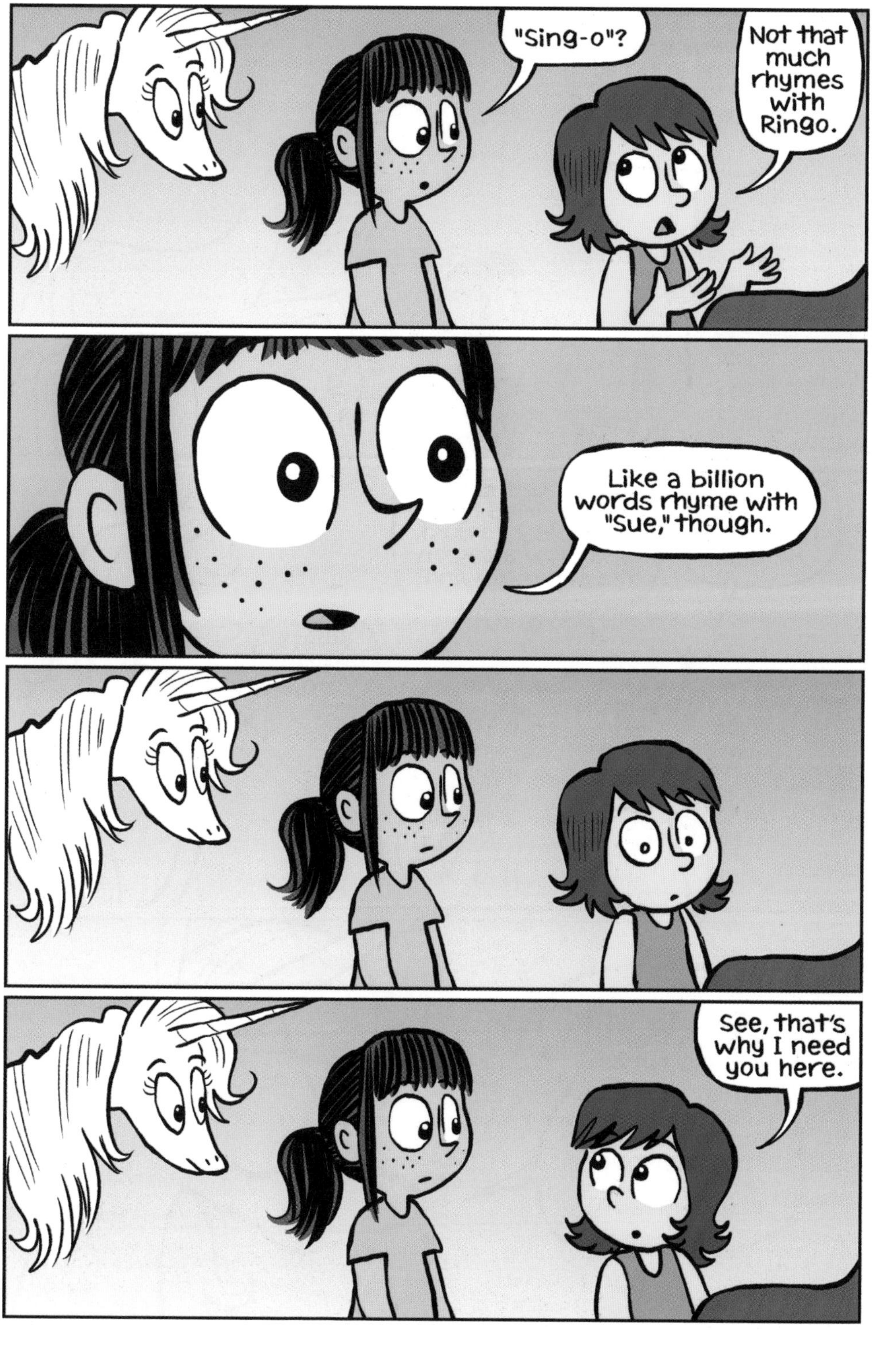
"Sing-o"?
Not that much rhymes with Ringo.
Like a billion words rhyme with "Sue," though.
See, that's why I need you here.

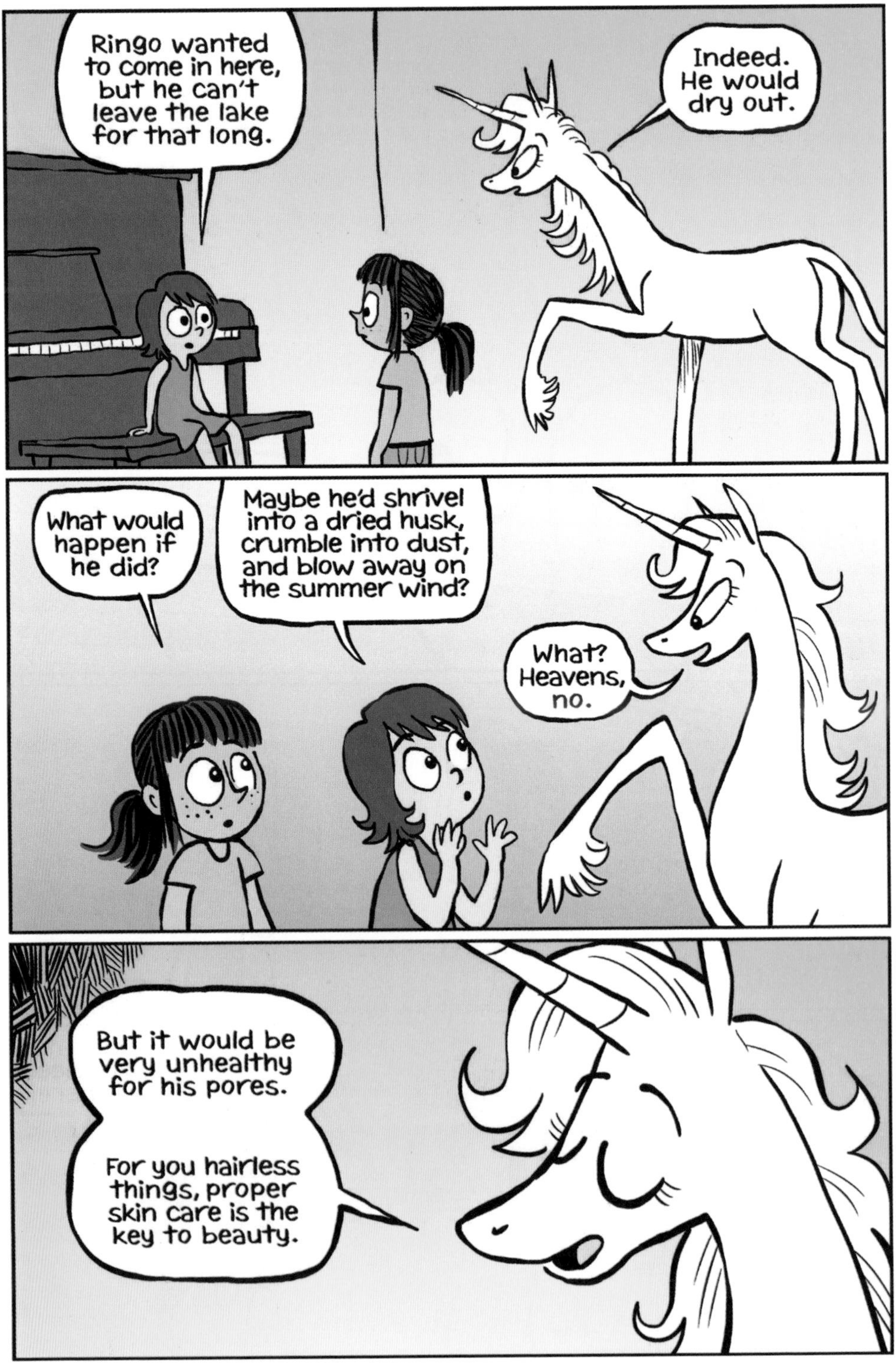
Ringo wanted to come in here, but he can't leave the lake for that long.
Indeed. He would dry out.
What would happen if he did?
Maybe he'd shrivel into a dried husk, crumble into dust, and blow away on the summer wind?
What? Heavens, no.
But it would be very unhealthy for his pores.
For you hairless things, proper skin care is the key to beauty.

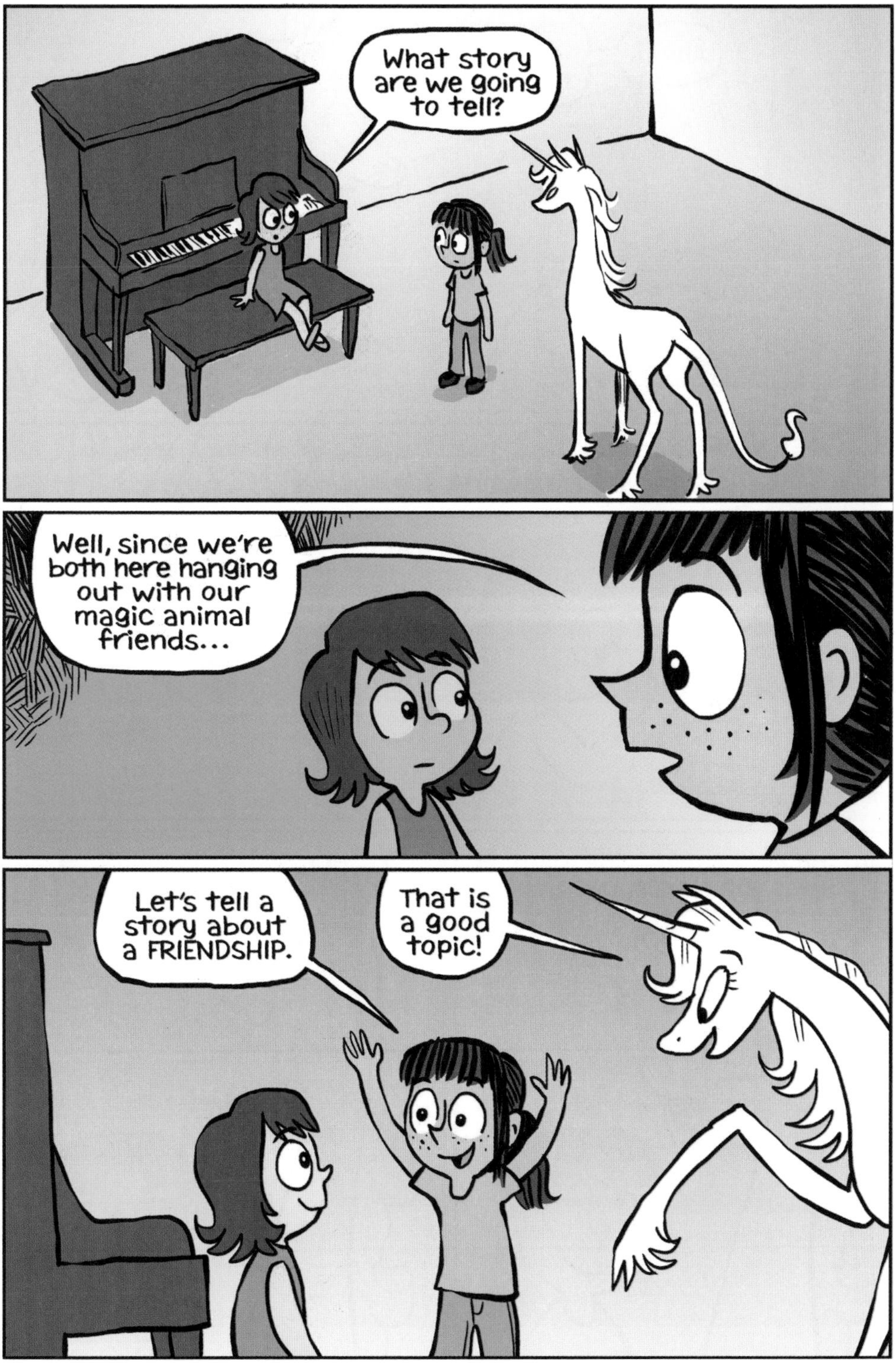
What story are we going to tell?
Well, since we're both here hanging out with our magic animal friends...
Let's tell a story about a FRIENDSHIP.
That is a good topic!

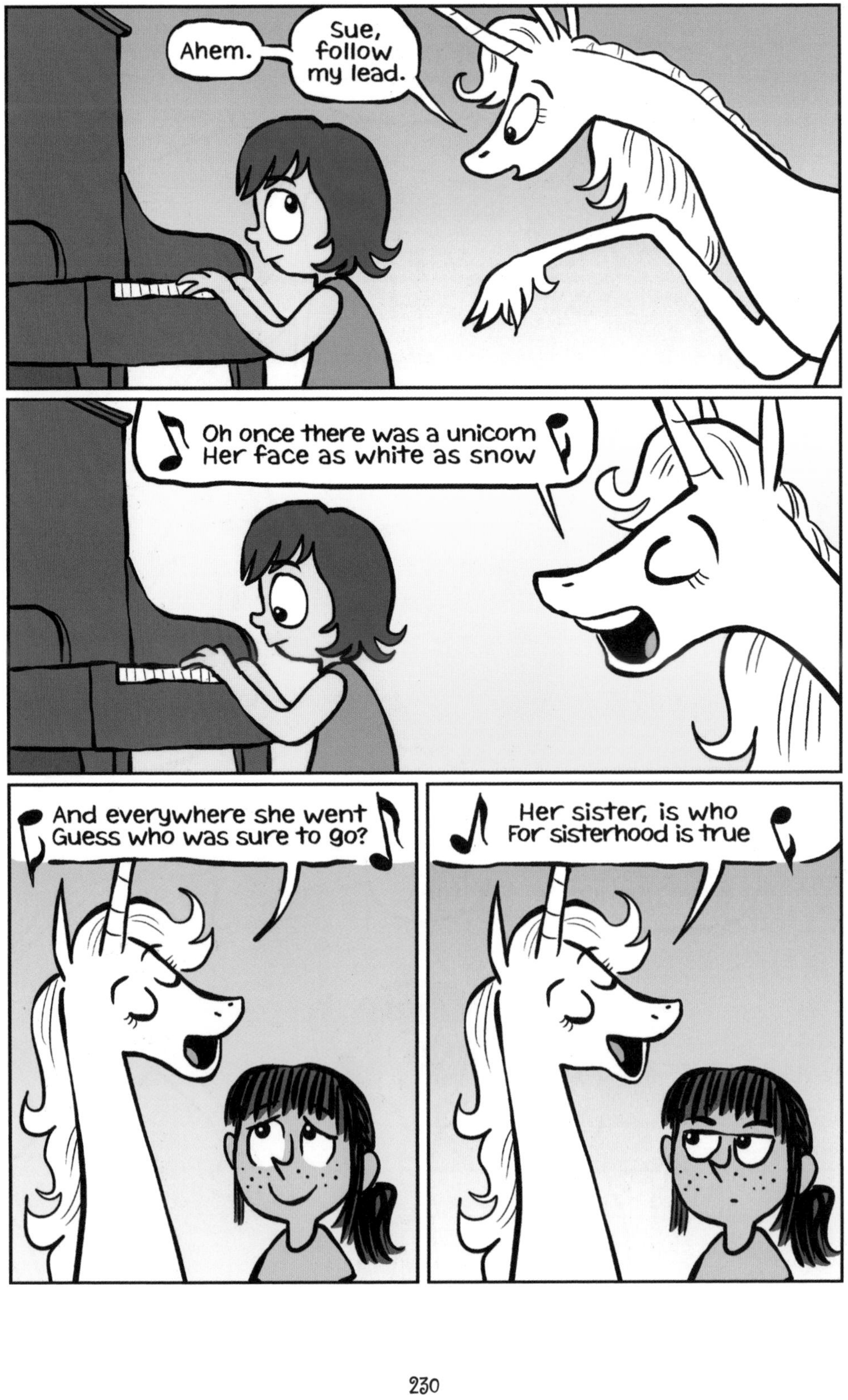
Ahem.
Sue, follow my lead.
Oh once there was a unicorn
Her face as white as snow
And everywhere she went
Guess who was sure to go?
Her sister, is who
For sisterhood is true

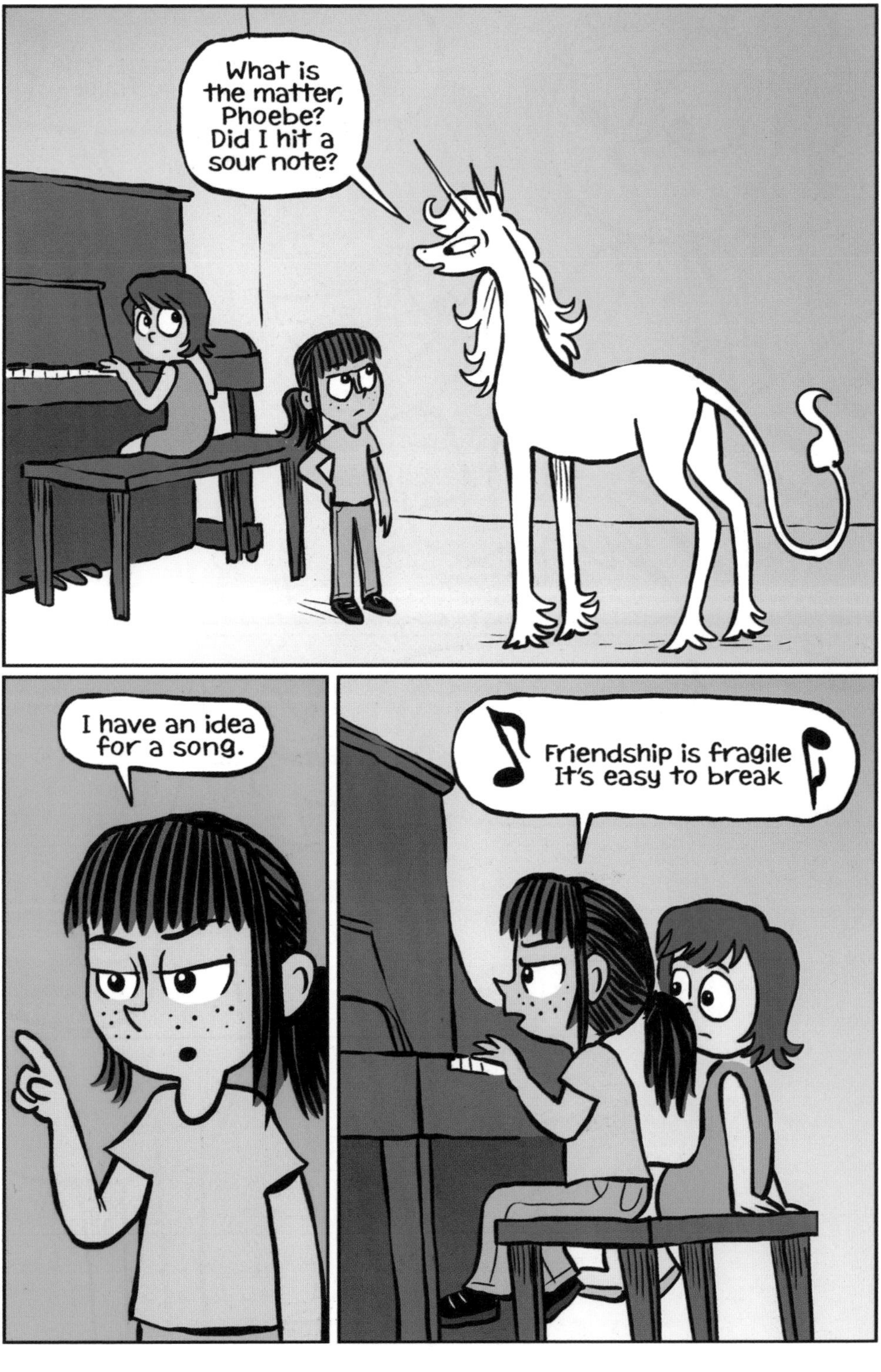
What is the matter, Phoebe? Did I hit a sour note?
I have an idea for a song.
Friendship is fragile
It's easy to break

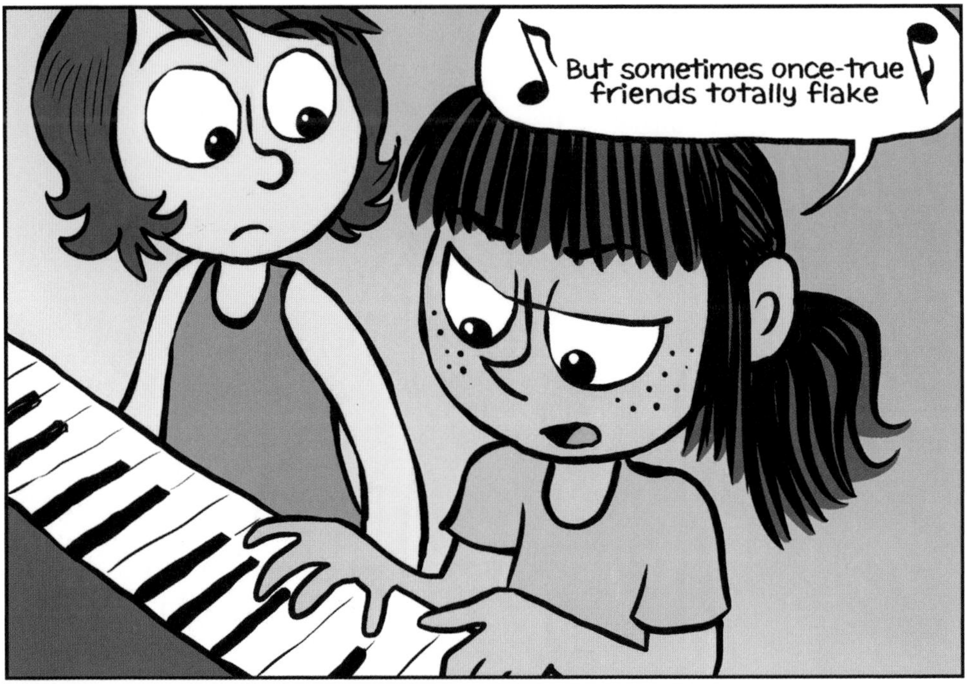
But sometimes once-true friends totally flake

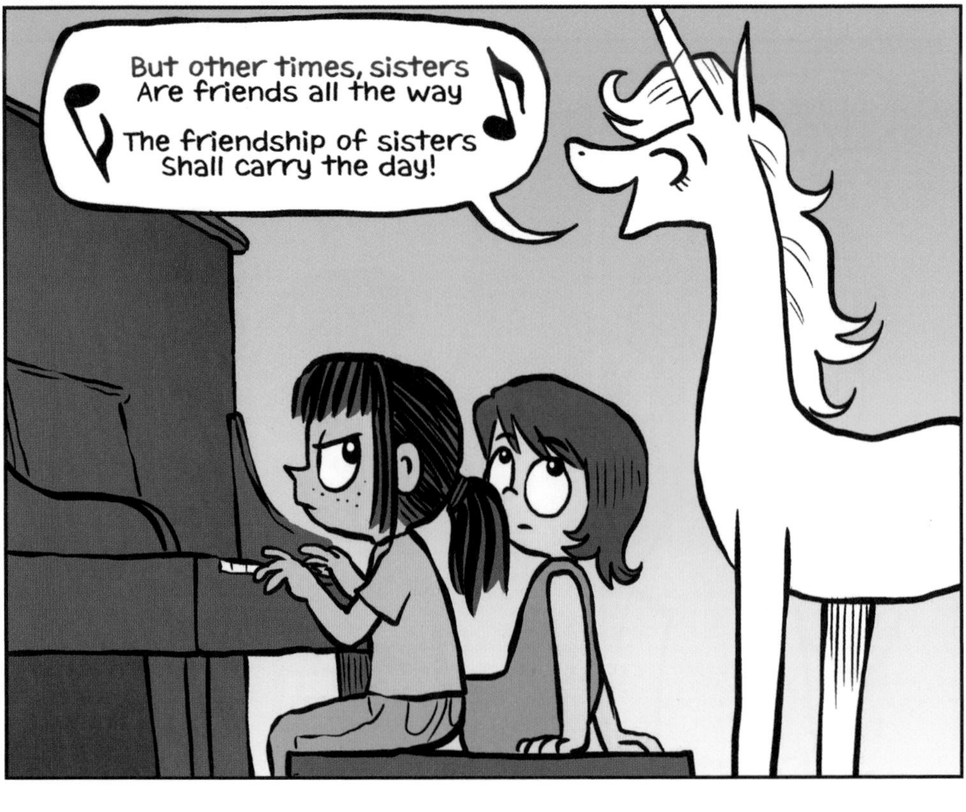
But other times, sisters
Are friends all the way
The friendship of sisters
Shall carry the day!

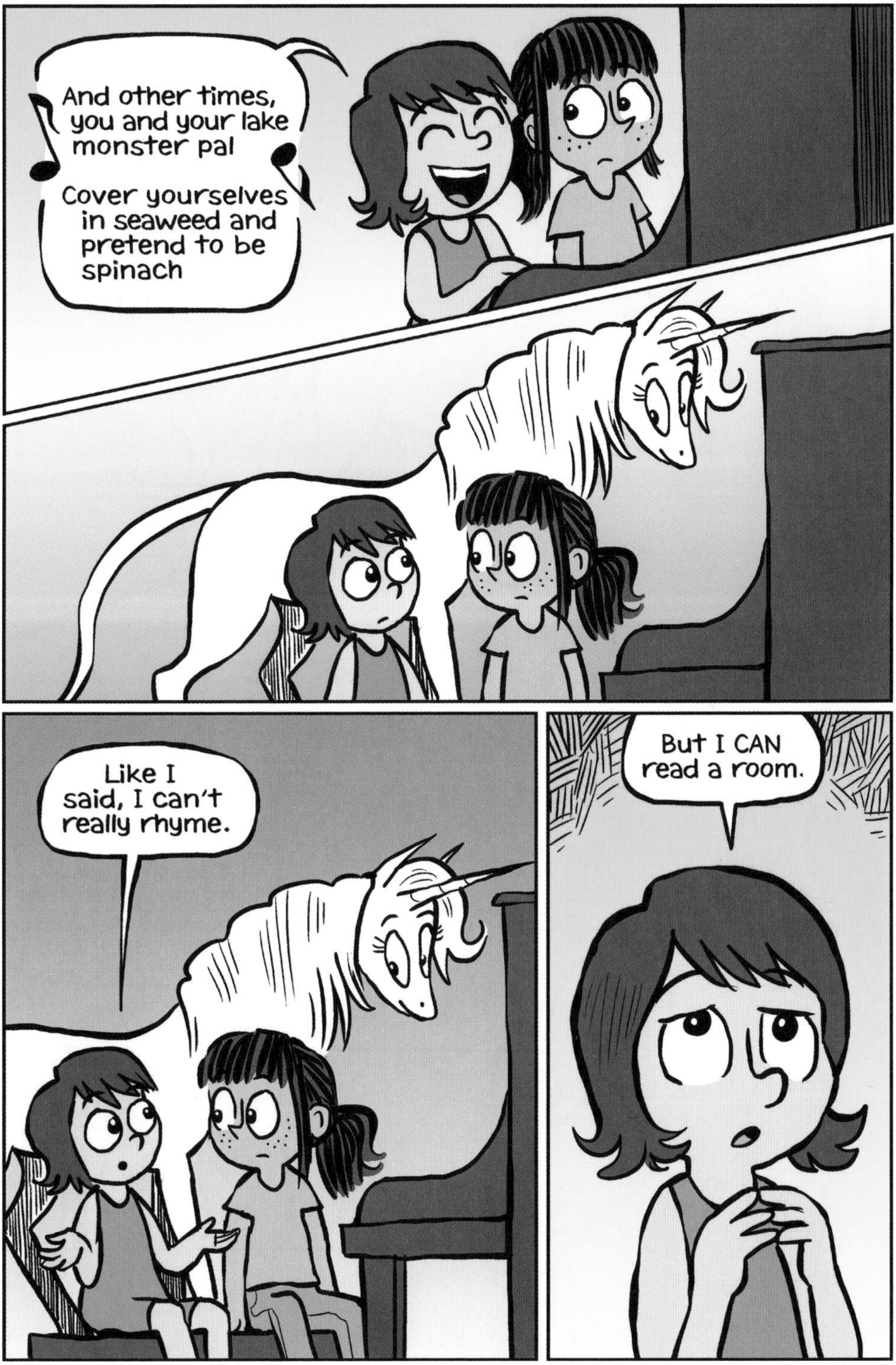
And other times, you and your lake monster pal
Cover yourselves in seaweed and pretend to be spinach
Like I said, I can't really rhyme.
But I CAN read a room.

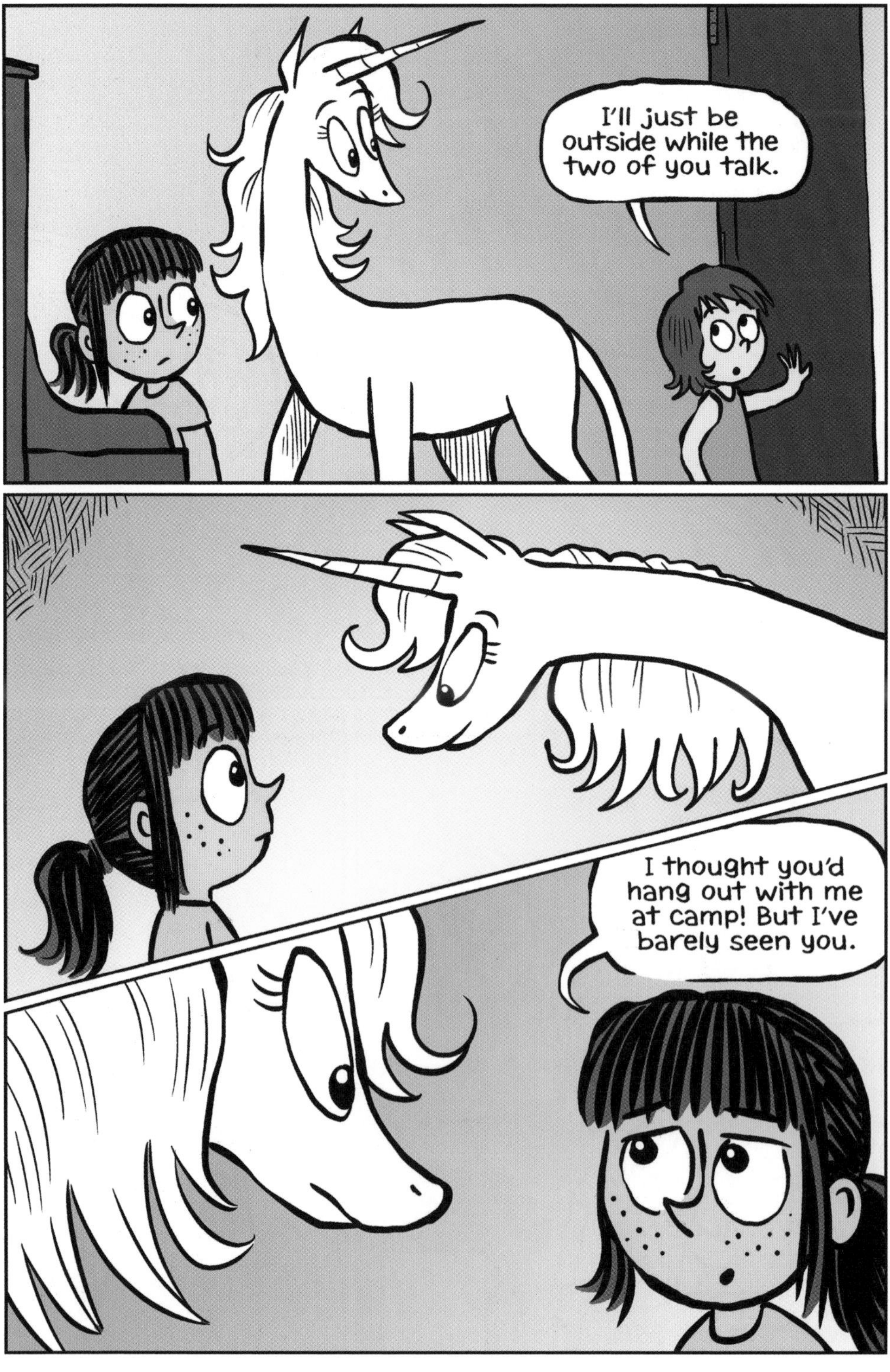
I'll just be outside while the two of you talk.
I thought you'd hang out with me at camp! But I've barely seen you.

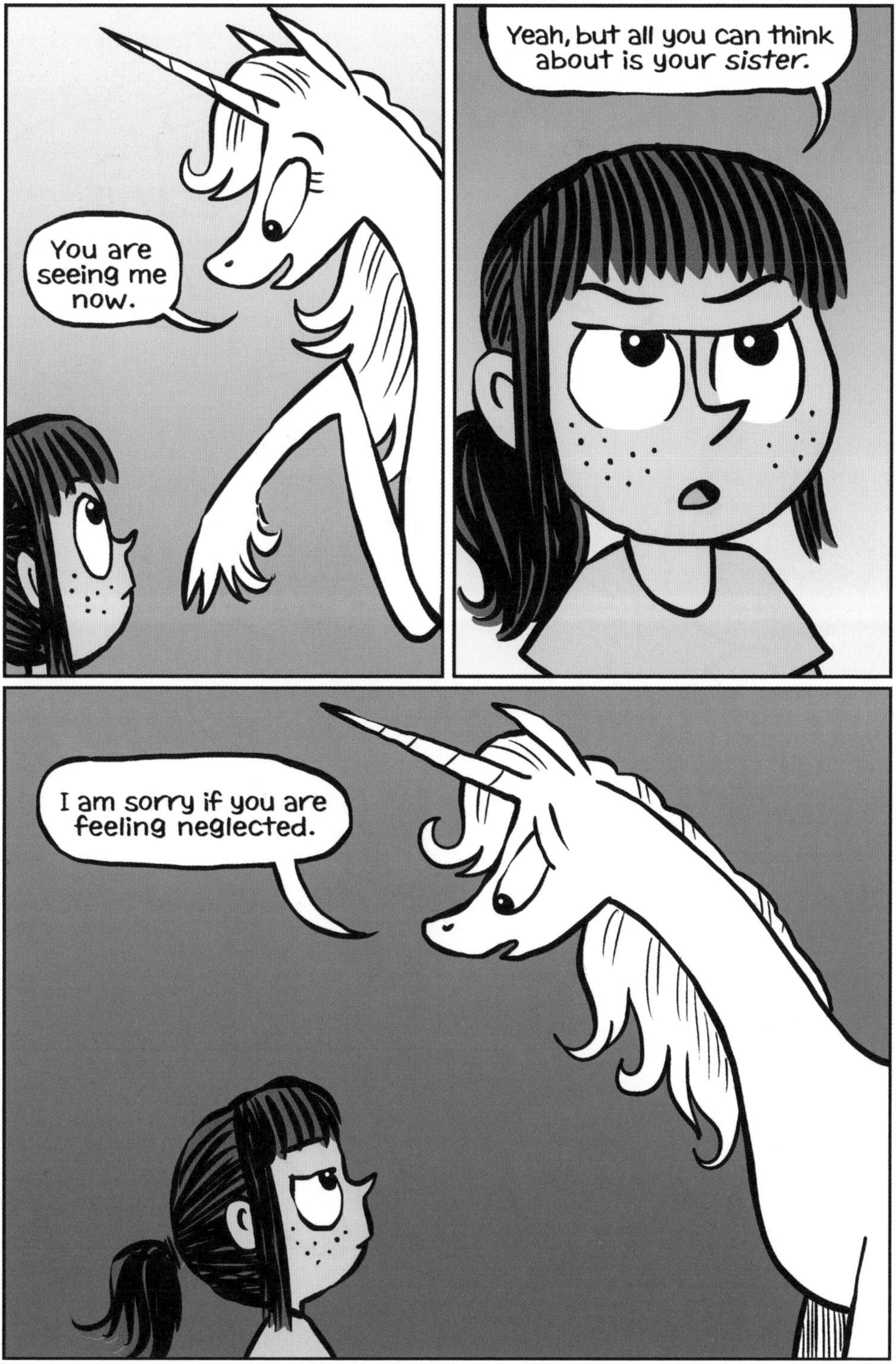
You are seeing me now.
Yeah, but all you can think about is your *sister*.
I am sorry if you are feeling neglected.

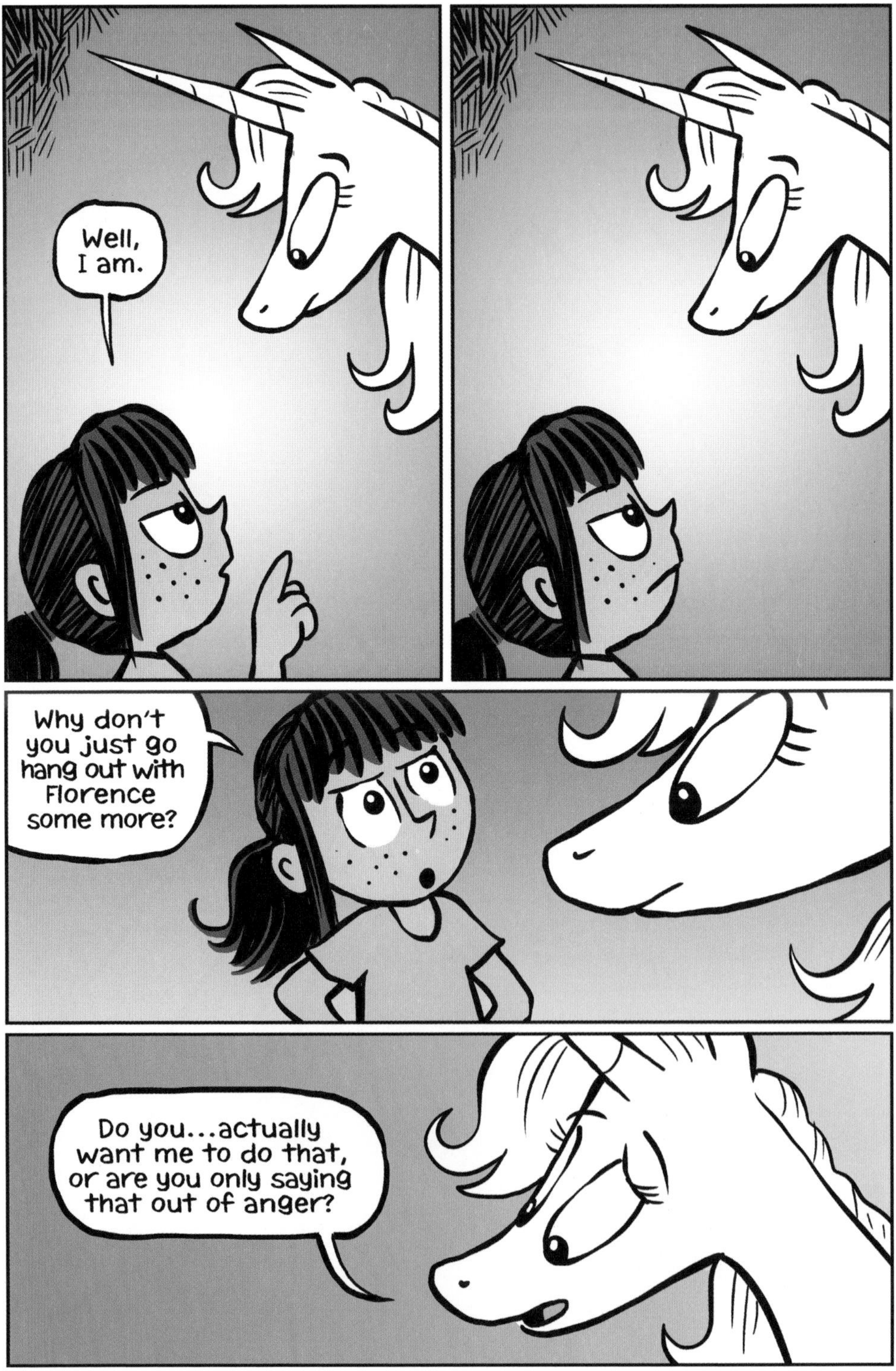
Well, I am.
Why don't you just go hang out with Florence some more?
Do you...actually want me to do that, or are you only saying that out of anger?

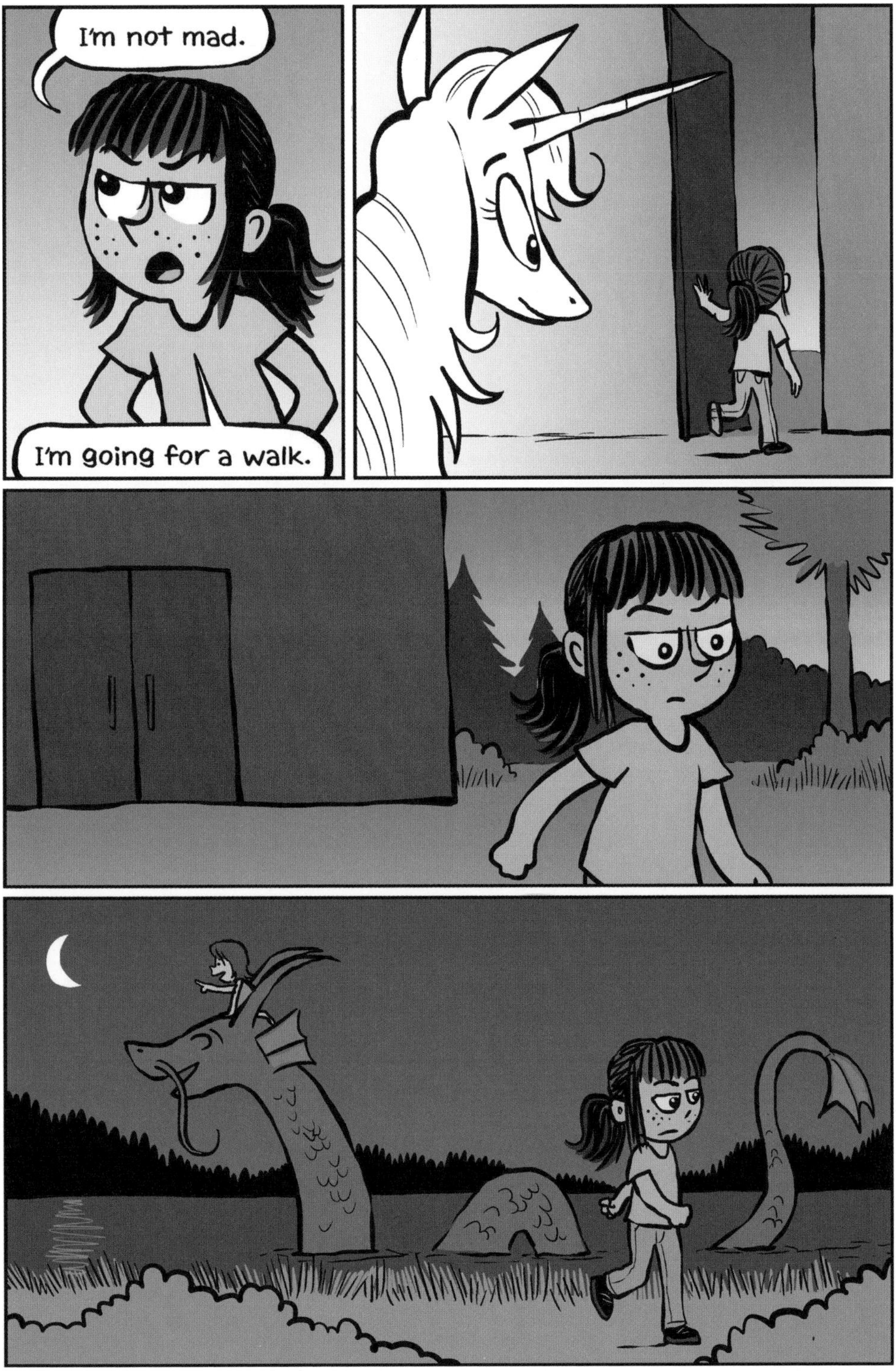
I'm not mad.
I'm going for a walk.

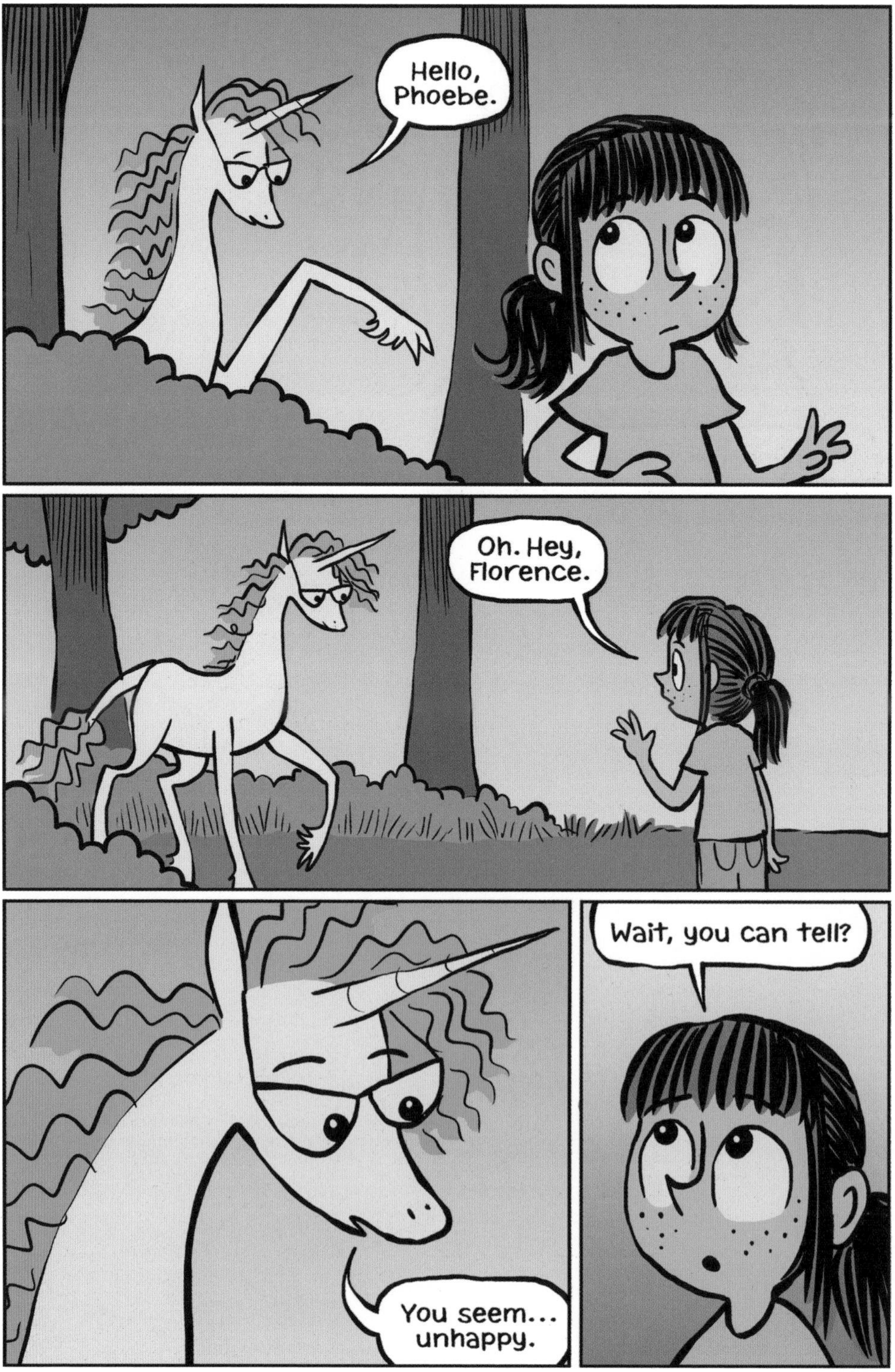
Hello, Phoebe.
Oh. Hey, Florence.
You seem... unhappy.
Wait, you can tell?

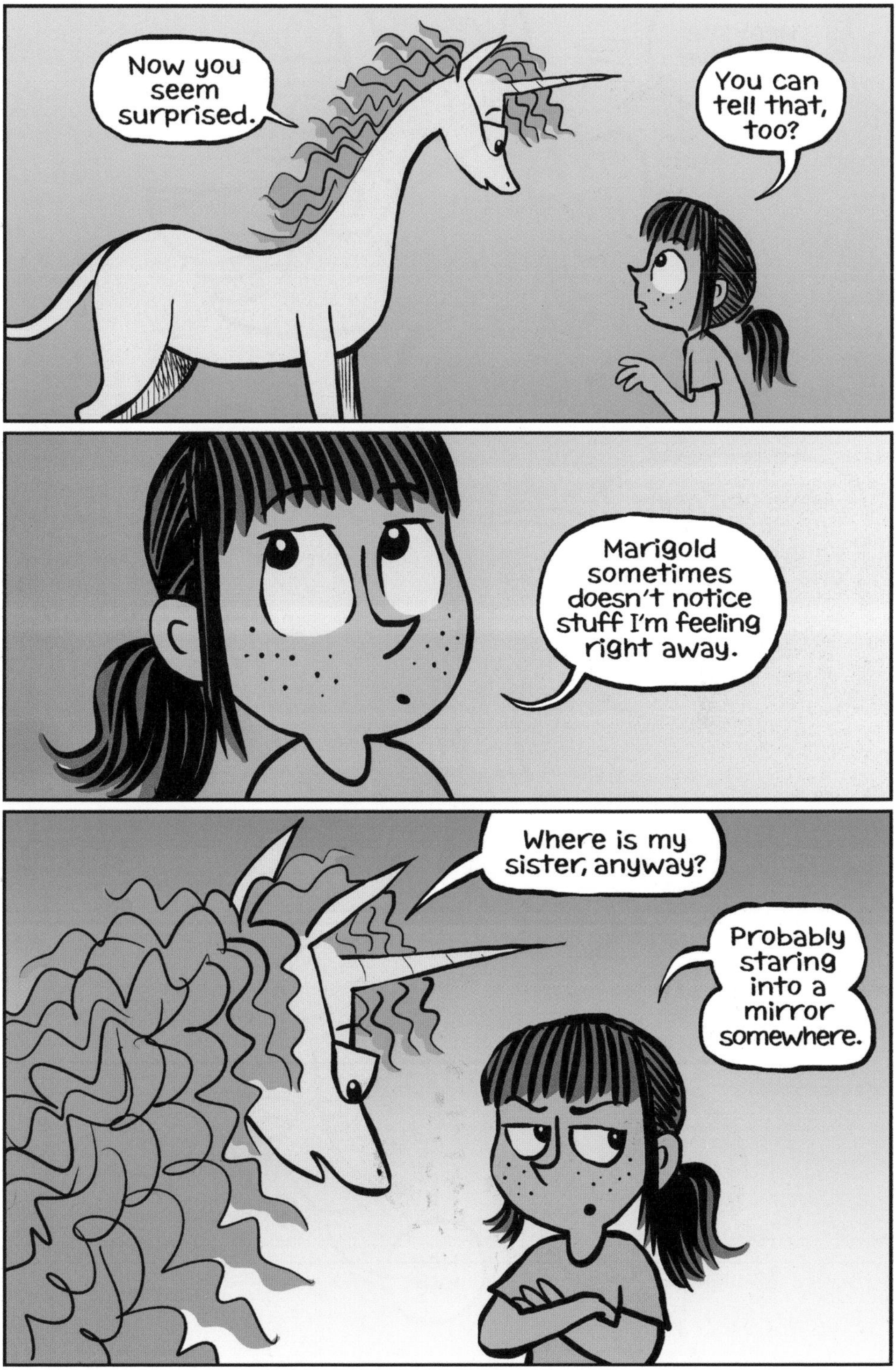
Now you seem surprised.
You can tell that, too?
Marigold sometimes doesn't notice stuff I'm feeling right away.
Where is my sister, anyway?
Probably staring into a mirror somewhere.

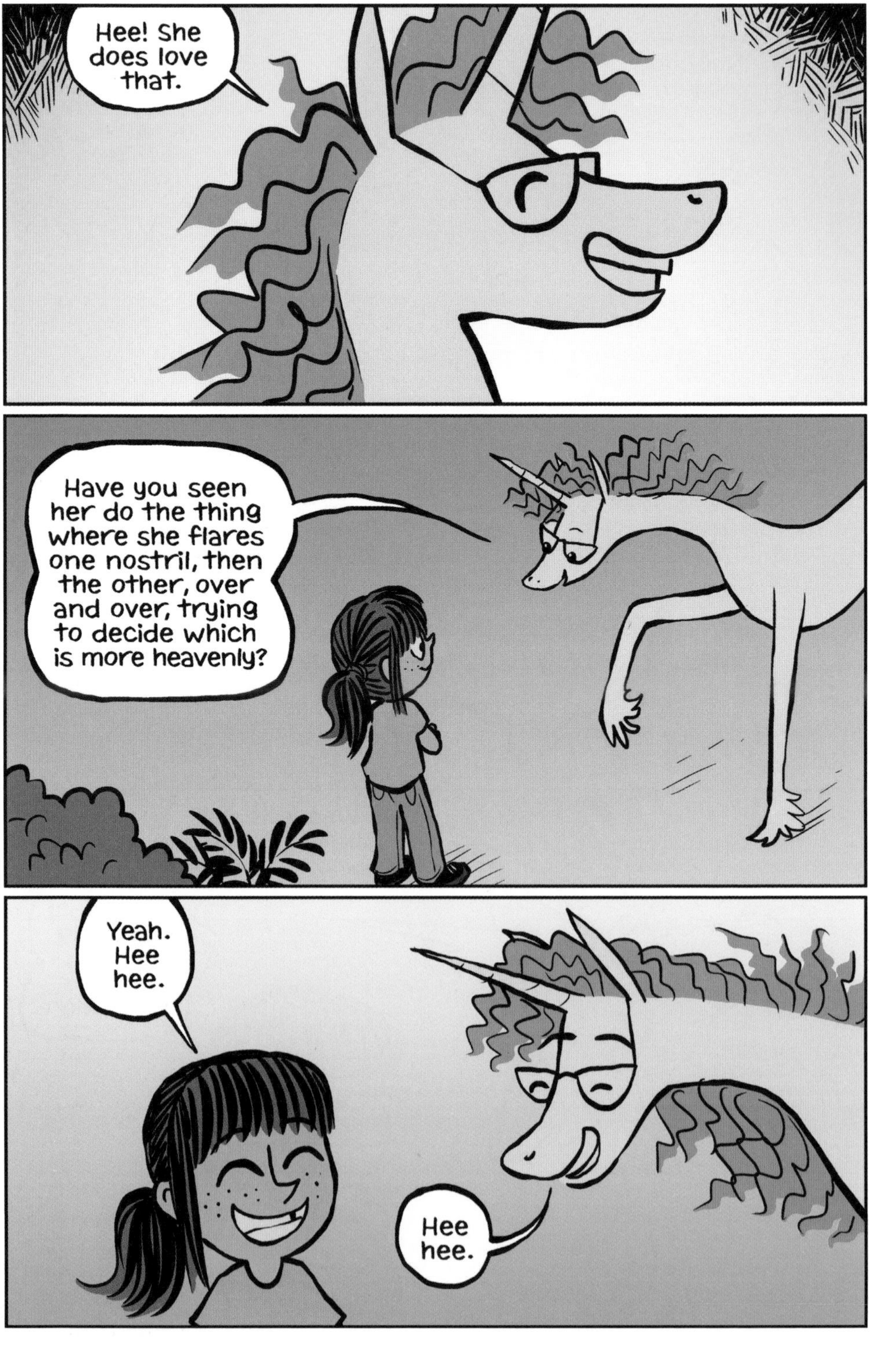
Hee! She does love that.
Have you seen her do the thing where she flares one nostril, then the other, over and over, trying to decide which is more heavenly?
Yeah. Hee hee.
Hee hee.

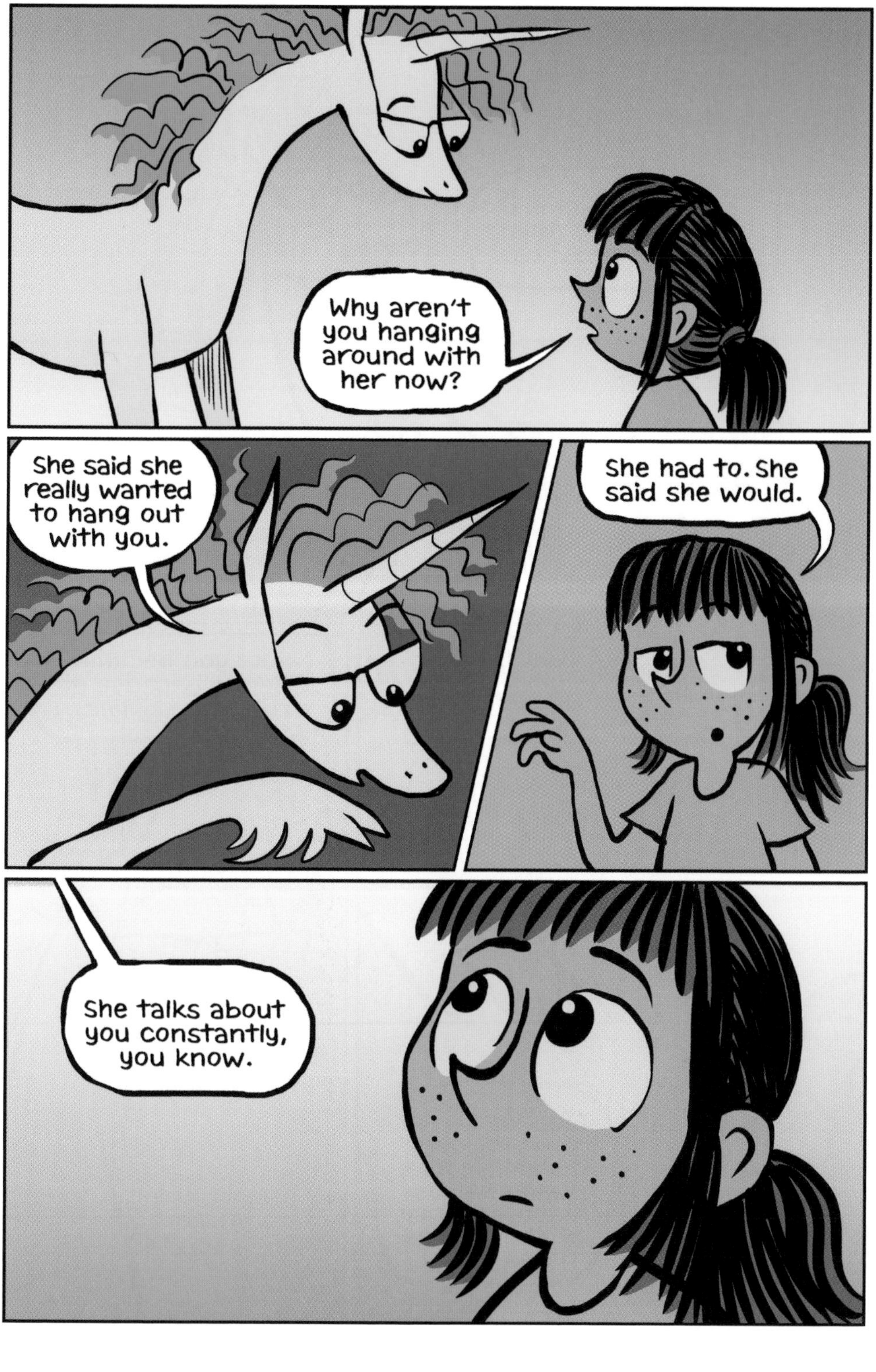
Why aren't you hanging around with her now?
She said she really wanted to hang out with you.
She had to. She said she would.
She talks about you constantly, you know.

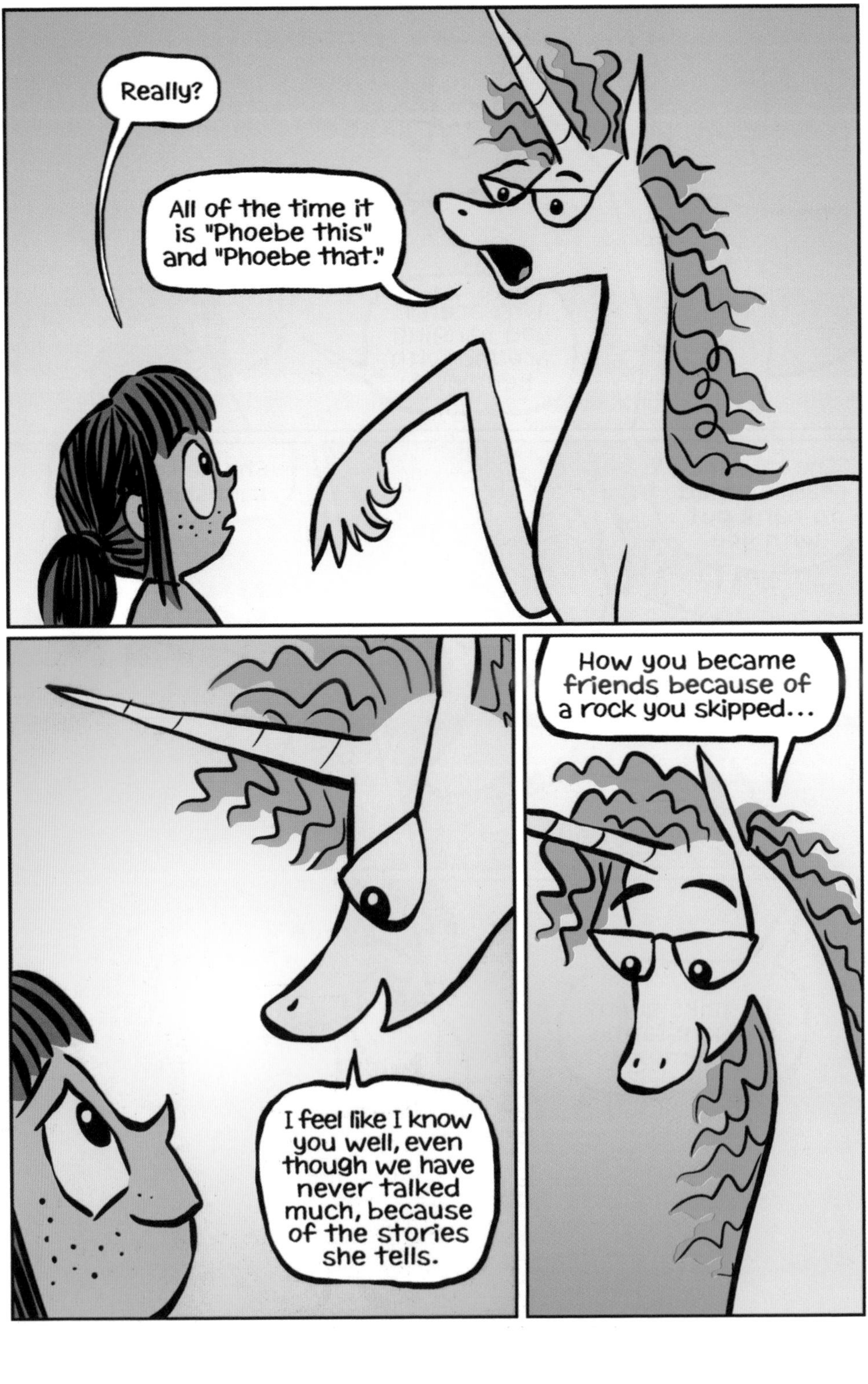
Really?
All of the time it is "Phoebe this" and "Phoebe that."
I feel like I know you well, even though we have never talked much, because of the stories she tells.
How you became friends because of a rock you skipped...

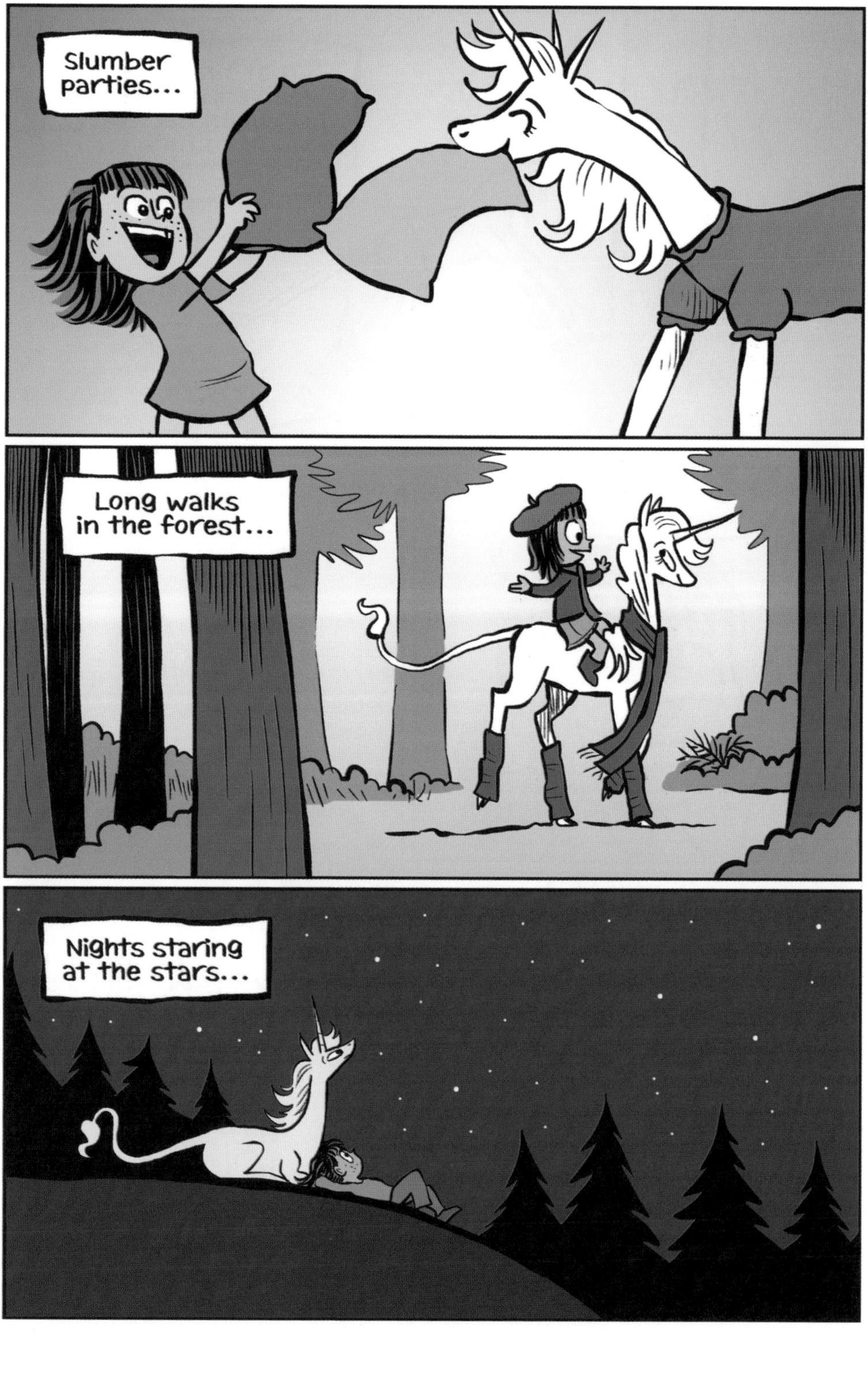
Slumber parties...
Long walks in the forest...
Nights staring at the stars...

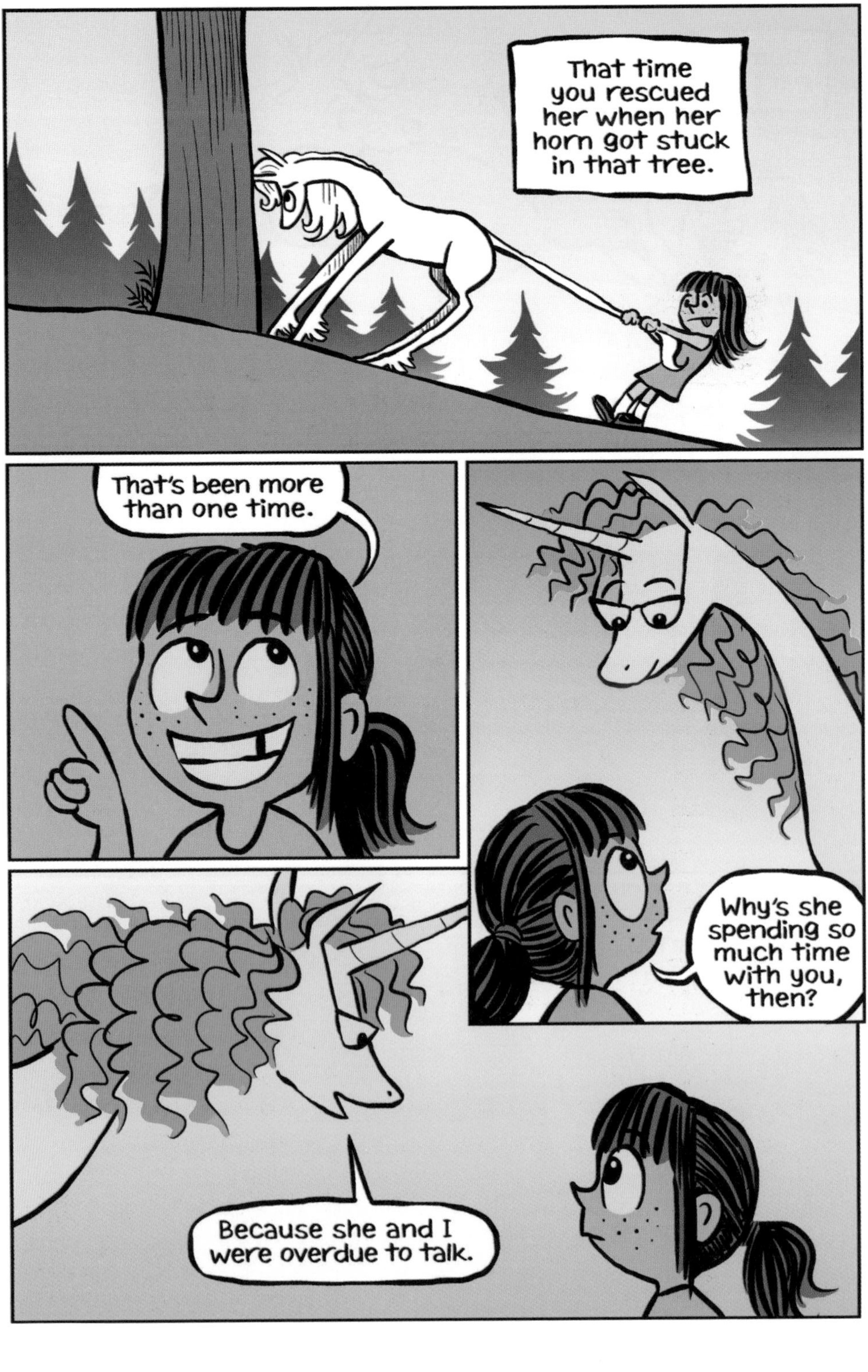
That time you rescued her when her horn got stuck in that tree.
That's been more than one time.
Why's she spending so much time with you, then?
Because she and I were overdue to talk.

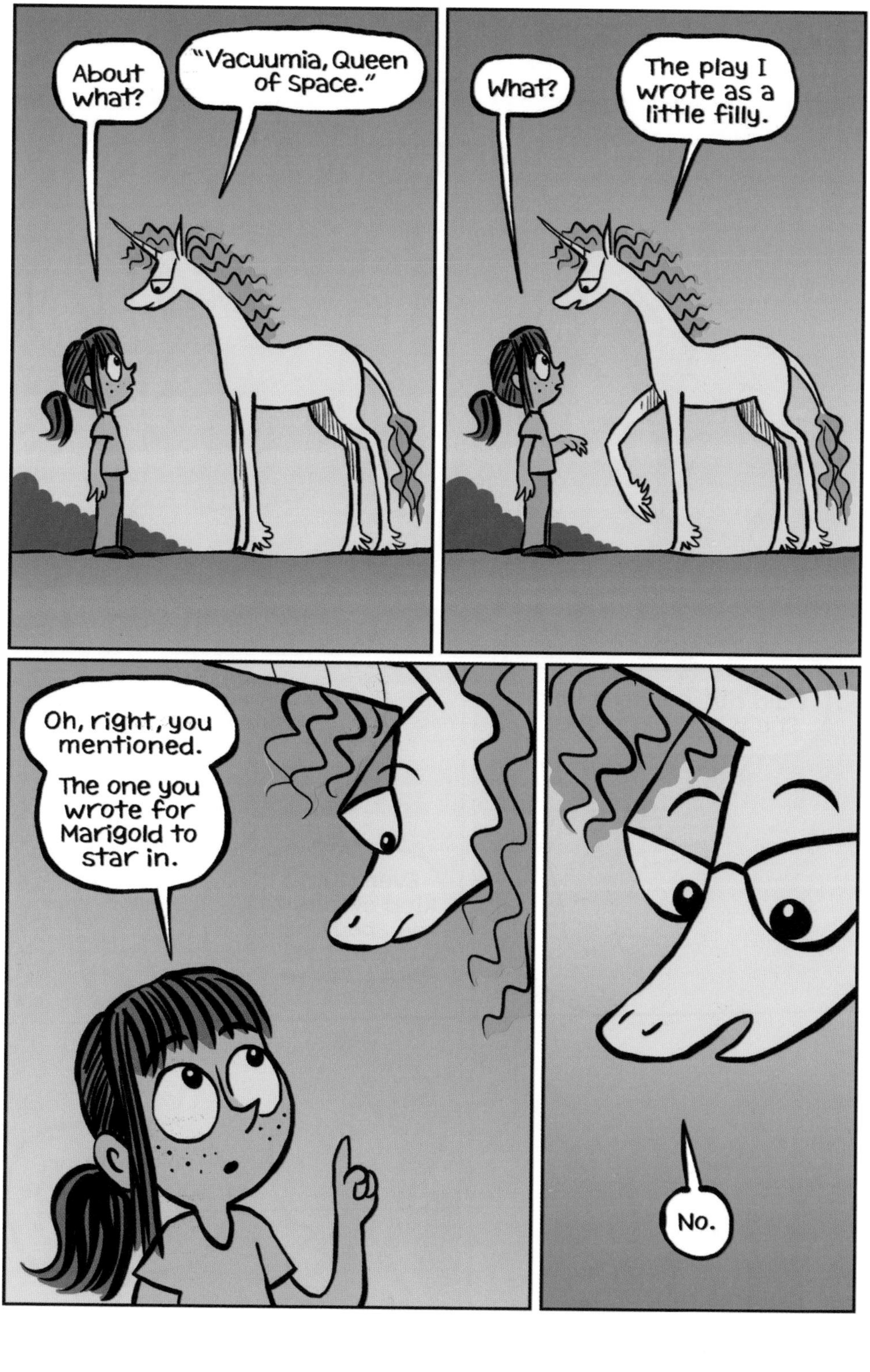
About what?
"Vacuumia, Queen of Space."
What?
The play I wrote as a little filly.
Oh, right, you mentioned.
The one you wrote for Marigold to star in.
No.

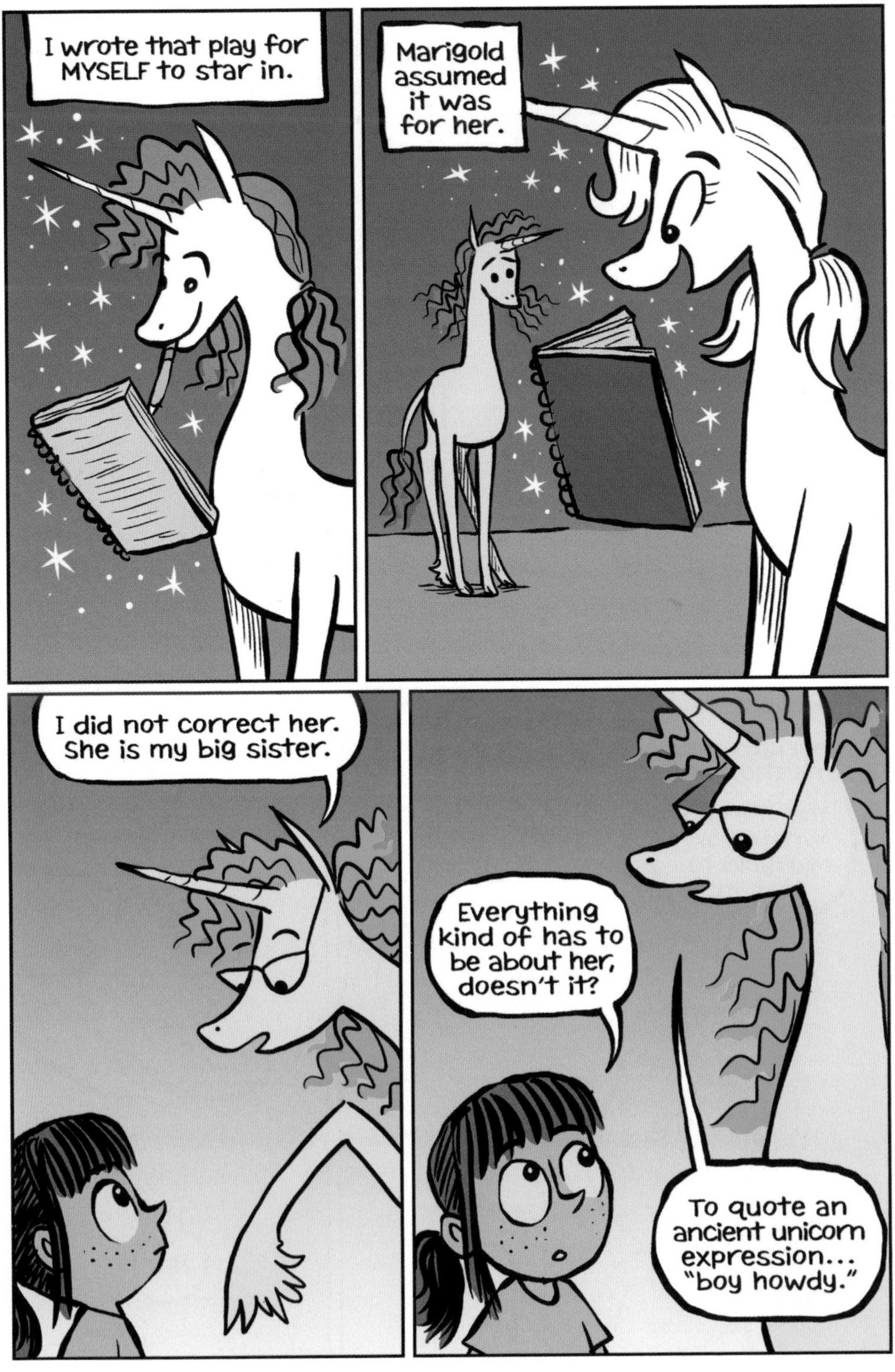
I wrote that play for MYSELF to star in.
Marigold assumed it was for her.
I did not correct her. She is my big sister.
Everything kind of has to be about her, doesn't it?
To quote an ancient unicorn expression... "boy howdy."

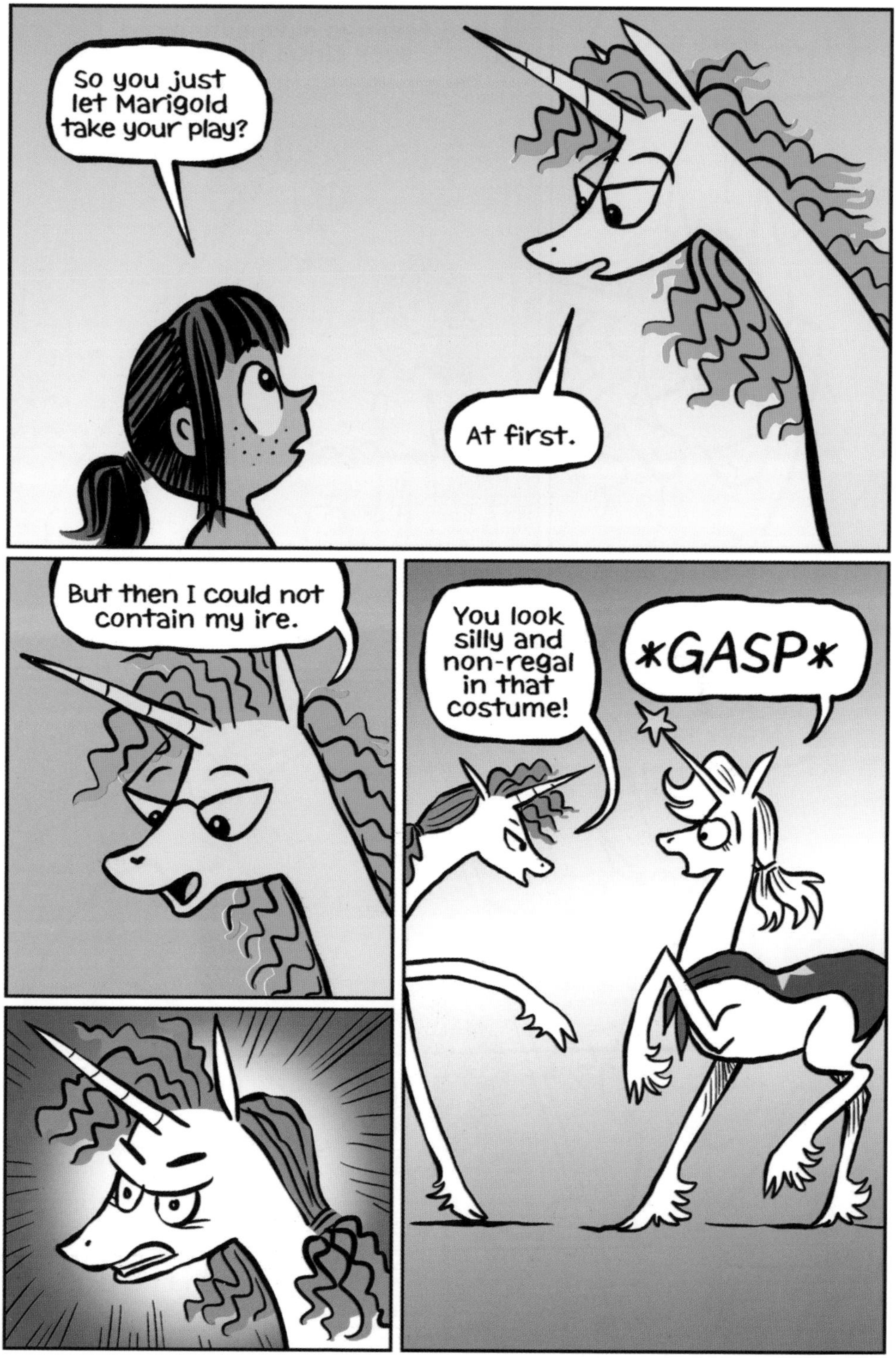
So you just let Marigold take your play?
At first.
But then I could not contain my ire.
You look silly and non-regal in that costume!
GASP

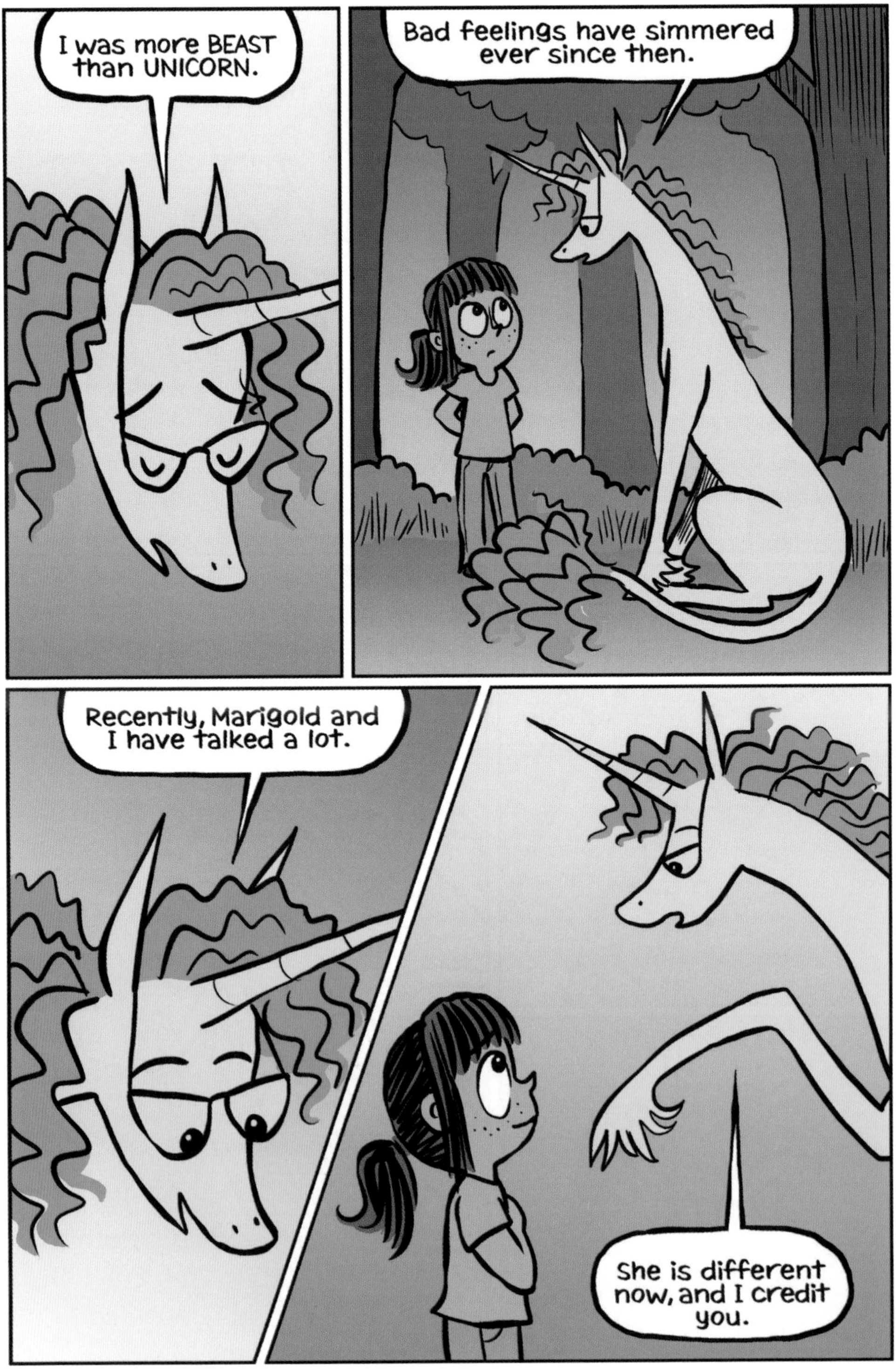
I was more BEAST than UNICORN.
Bad feelings have simmered ever since then.
Recently, Marigold and I have talked a lot.
She is different now, and I credit you.

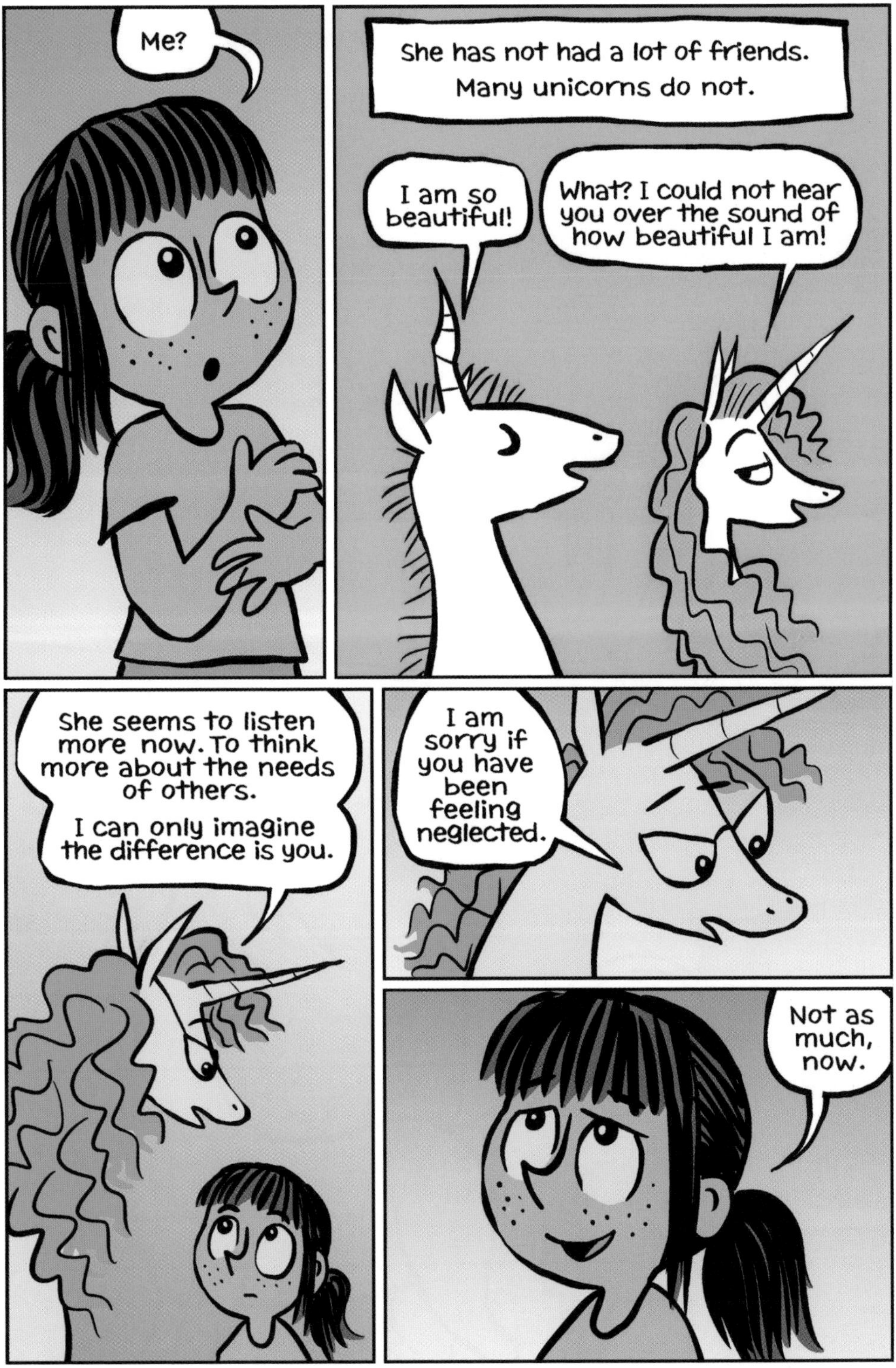
Me?
She has not had a lot of friends. Many unicorns do not.
I am so beautiful!
What? I could not hear you over the sound of how beautiful I am!
She seems to listen more now. To think more about the needs of others.
I can only imagine the difference is you.
I am sorry if you have been feeling neglected.
Not as much, now.

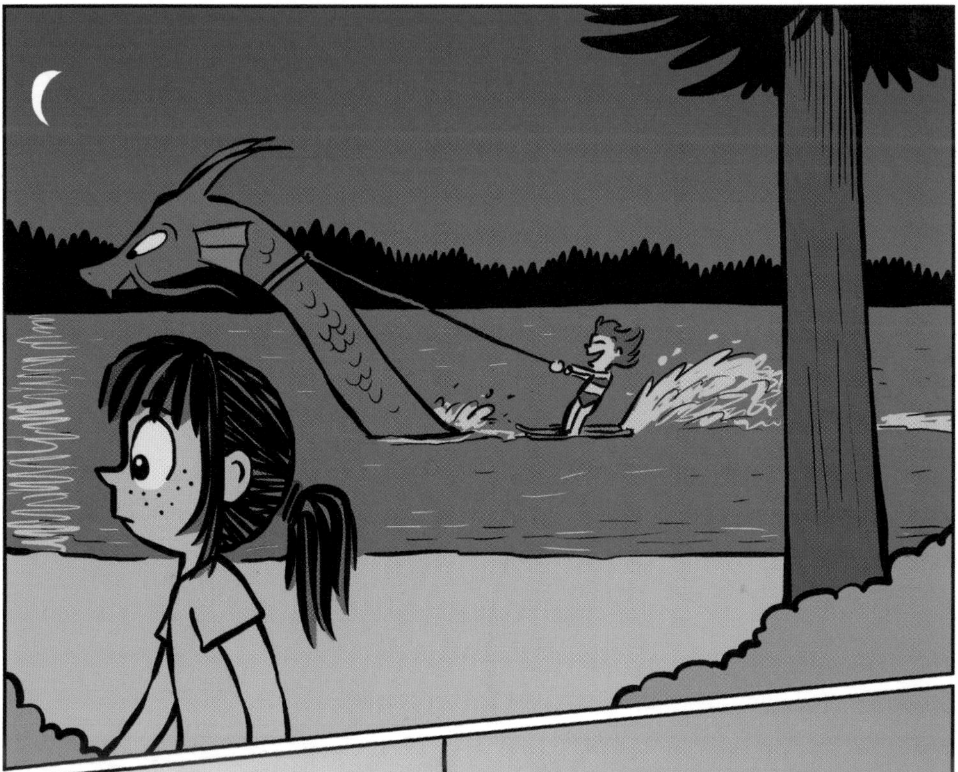

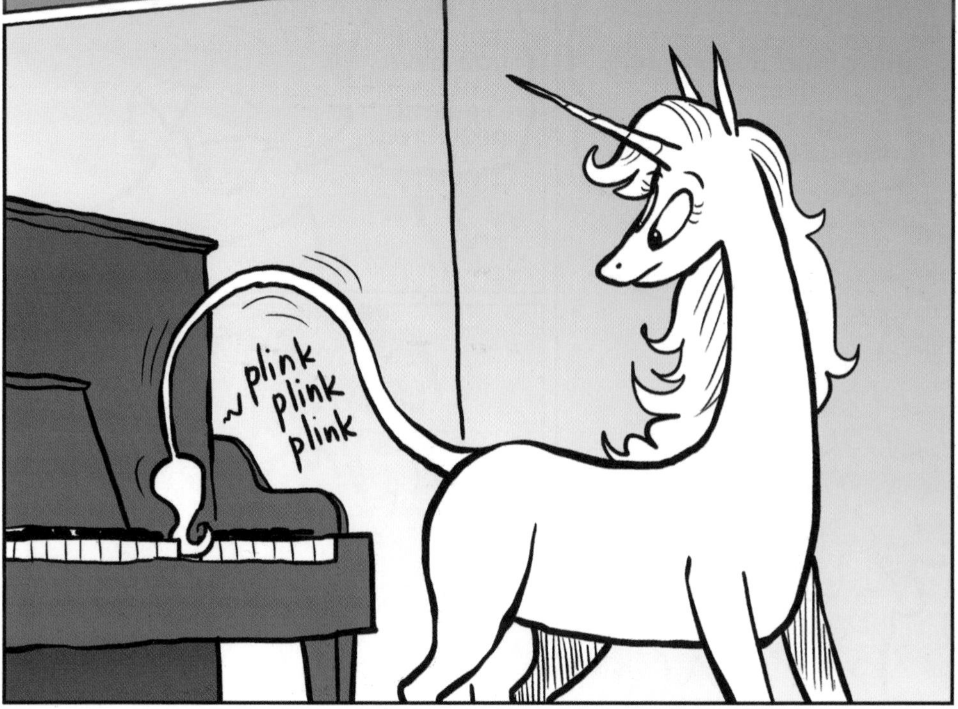
~plink plink plink

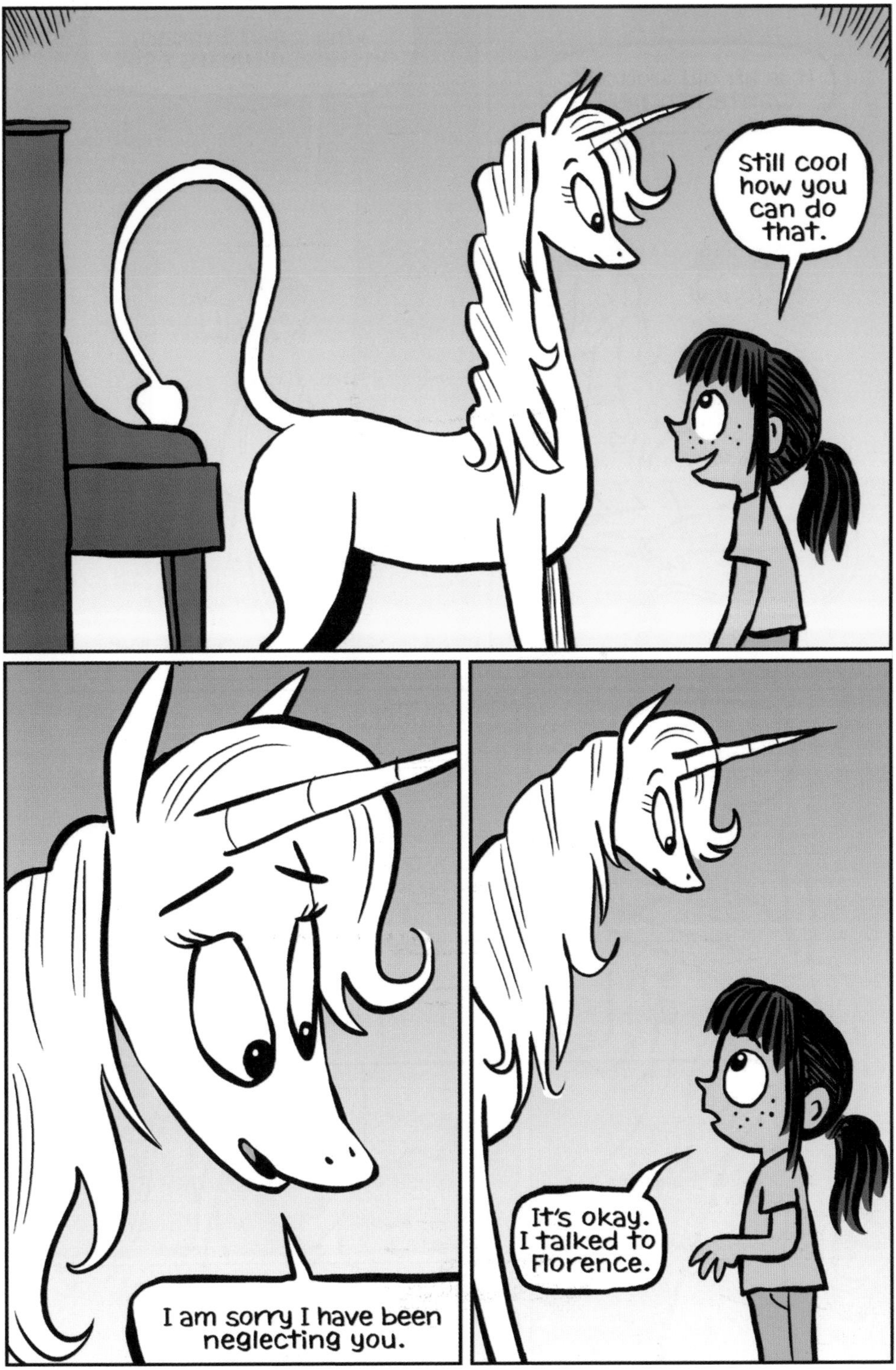
Still cool how you can do that.
I am sorry I have been neglecting you.
It's okay. I talked to Florence.

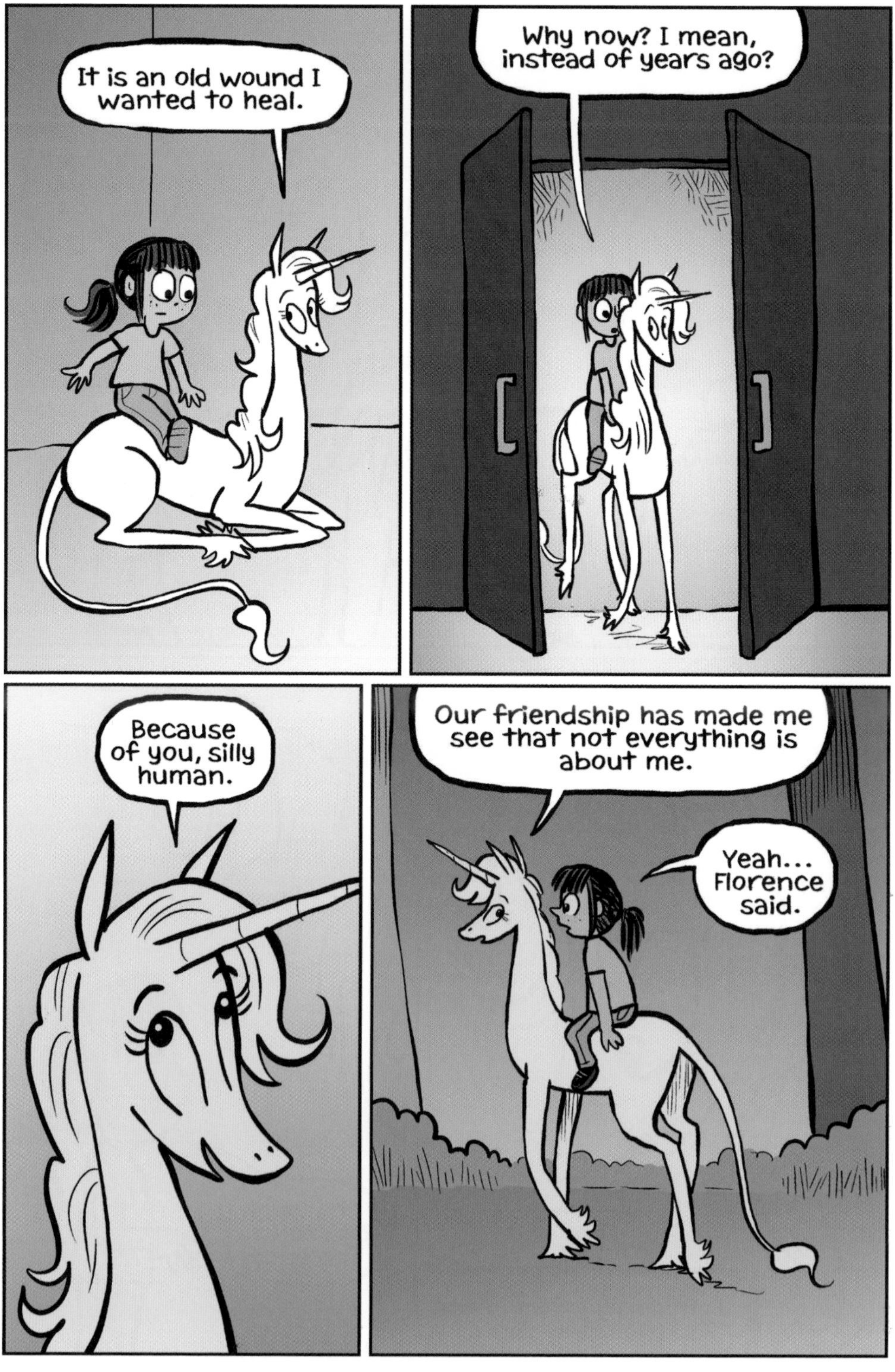

It is an old wound I wanted to heal.
Why now? I mean, instead of years ago?
Because of you, silly human.
Our friendship has made me see that not everything is about me.
Yeah... Florence said.

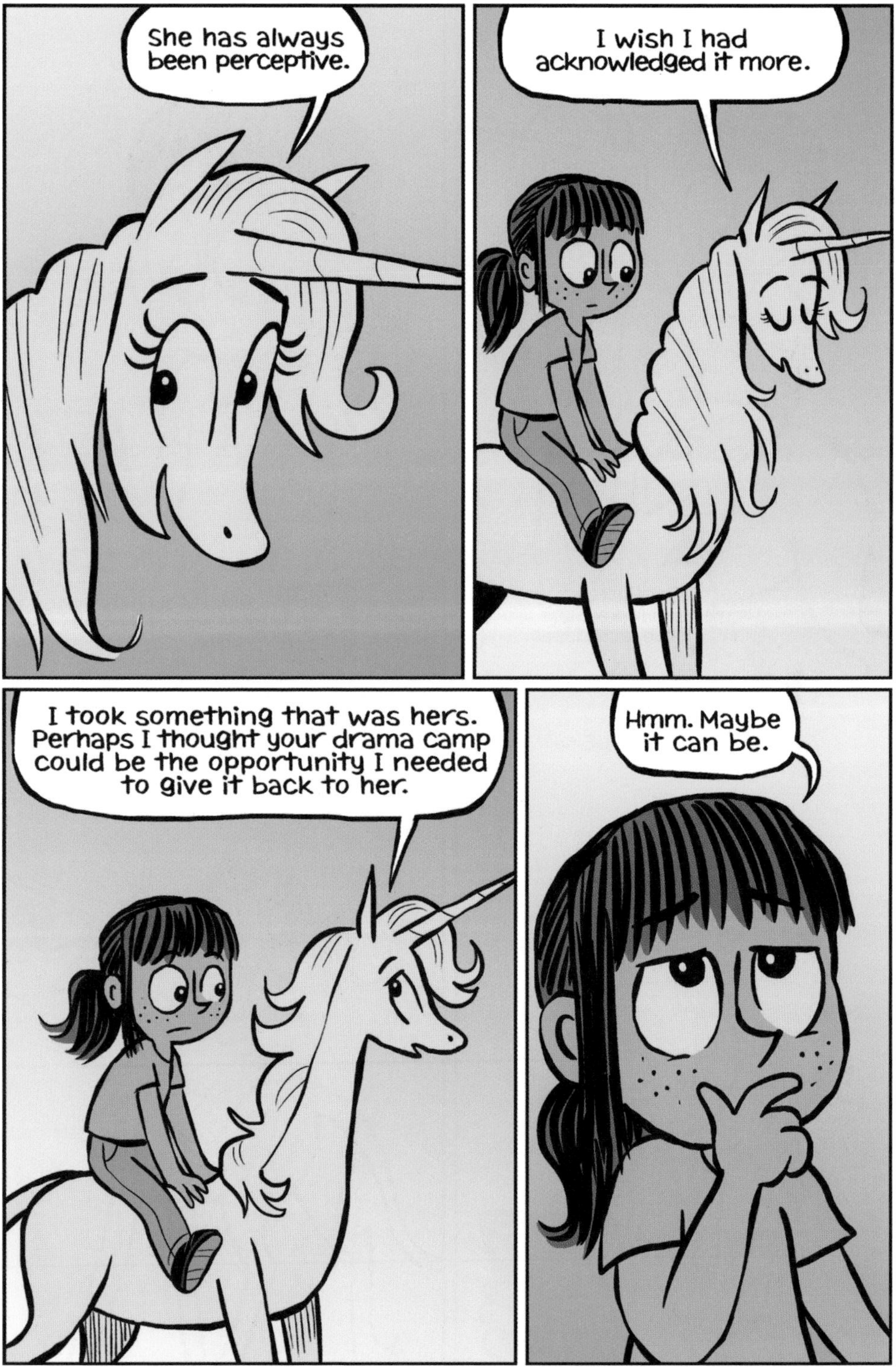
She has always been perceptive.
I wish I had acknowledged it more.
I took something that was hers. Perhaps I thought your drama camp could be the opportunity I needed to give it back to her.
Hmm. Maybe it can be.

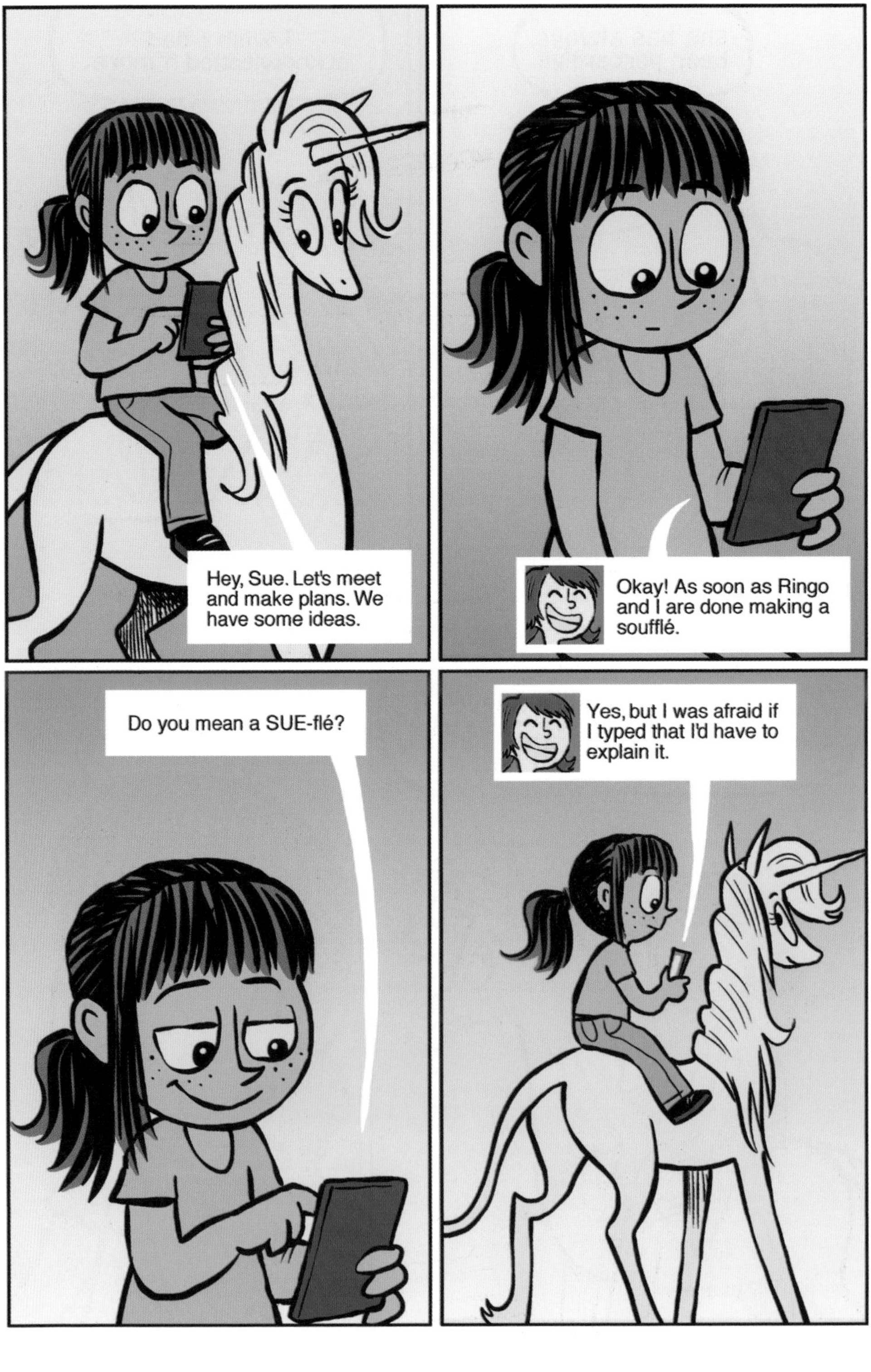
Hey, Sue. Let's meet and make plans. We have some ideas.
Okay! As soon as Ringo and I are done making a soufflé.
Do you mean a SUE-flé?
Yes, but I was afraid if I typed that I'd have to explain it.

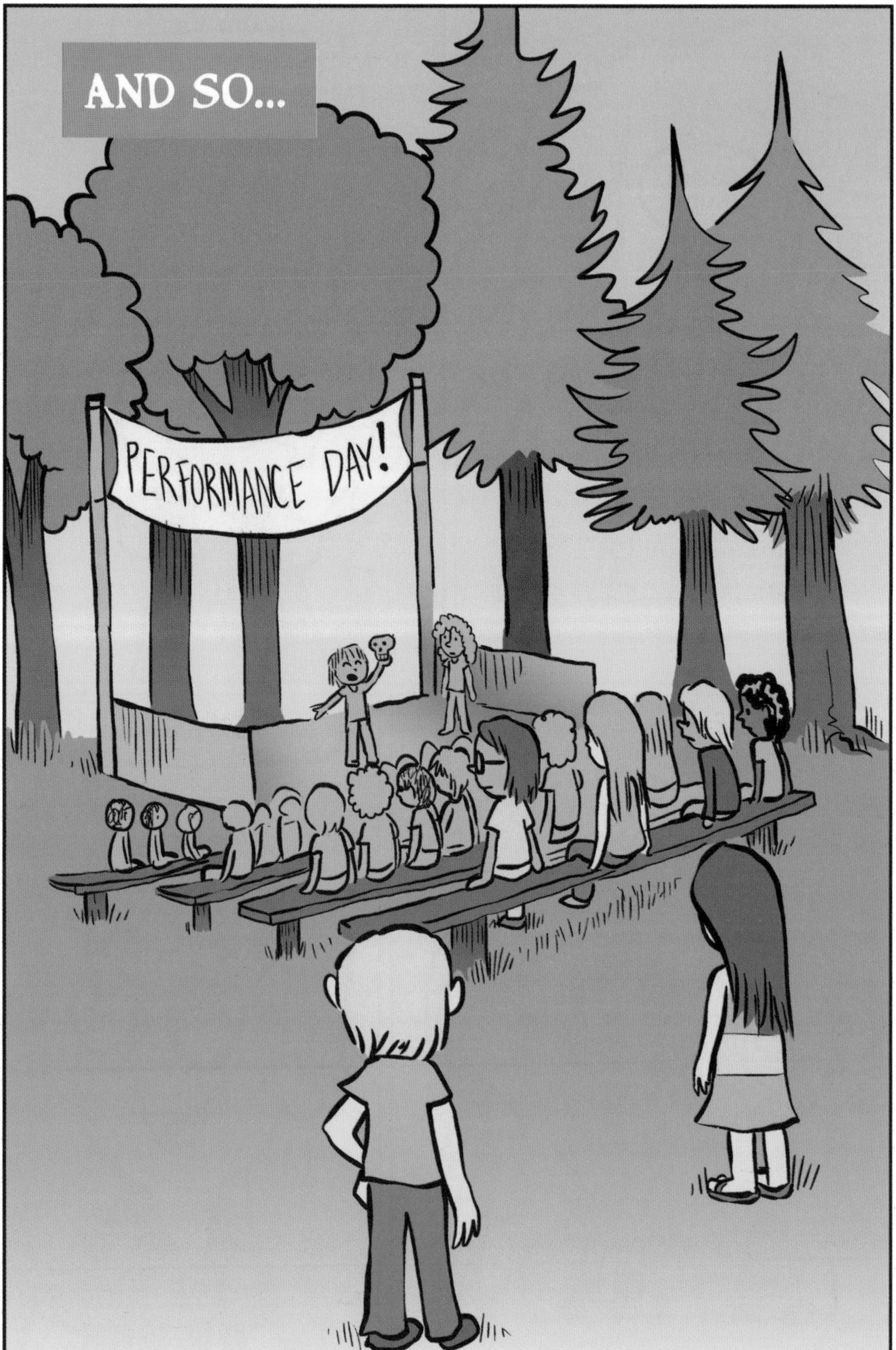
AND SO...
PERFORMANCE DAY!

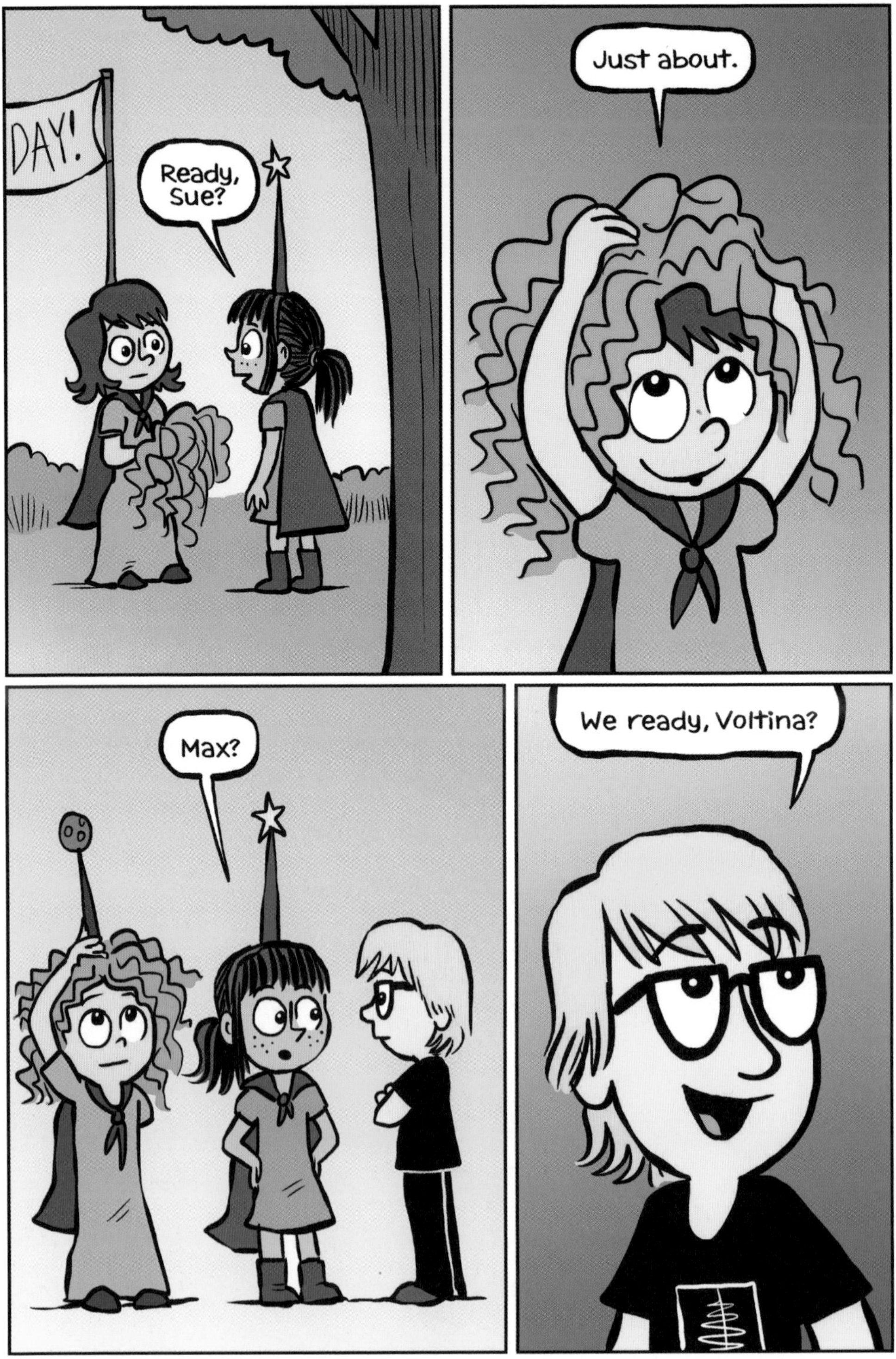
DAY!
Ready, Sue?
Just about.
Max?
We ready, Voltina?

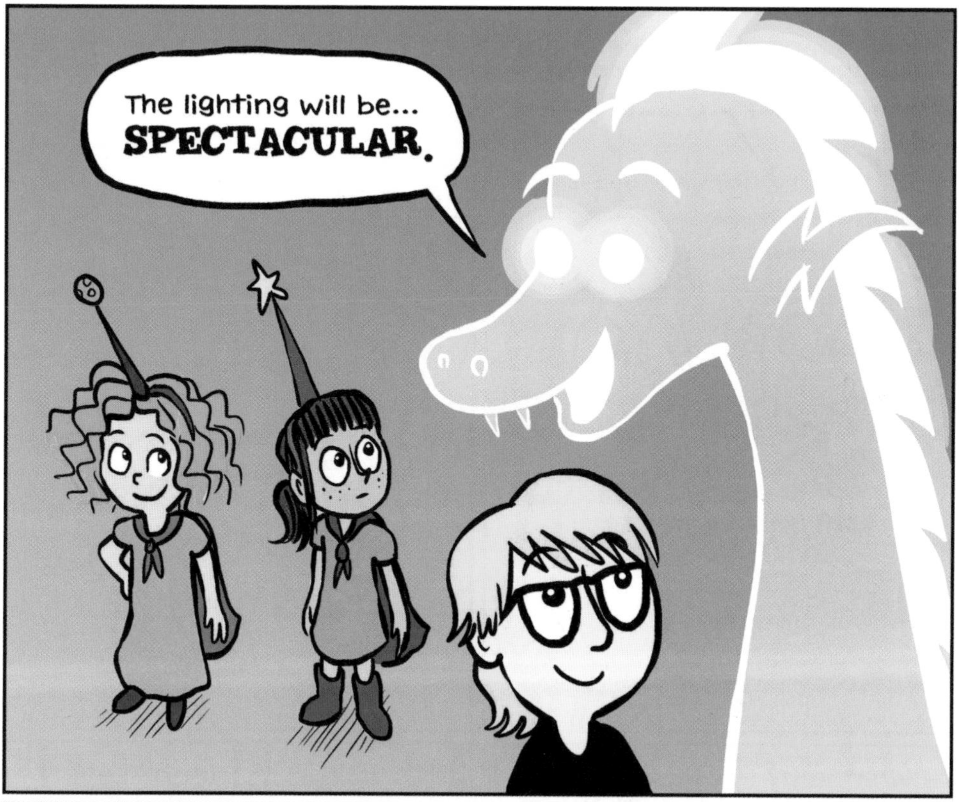
The lighting will be...
SPECTACULAR.

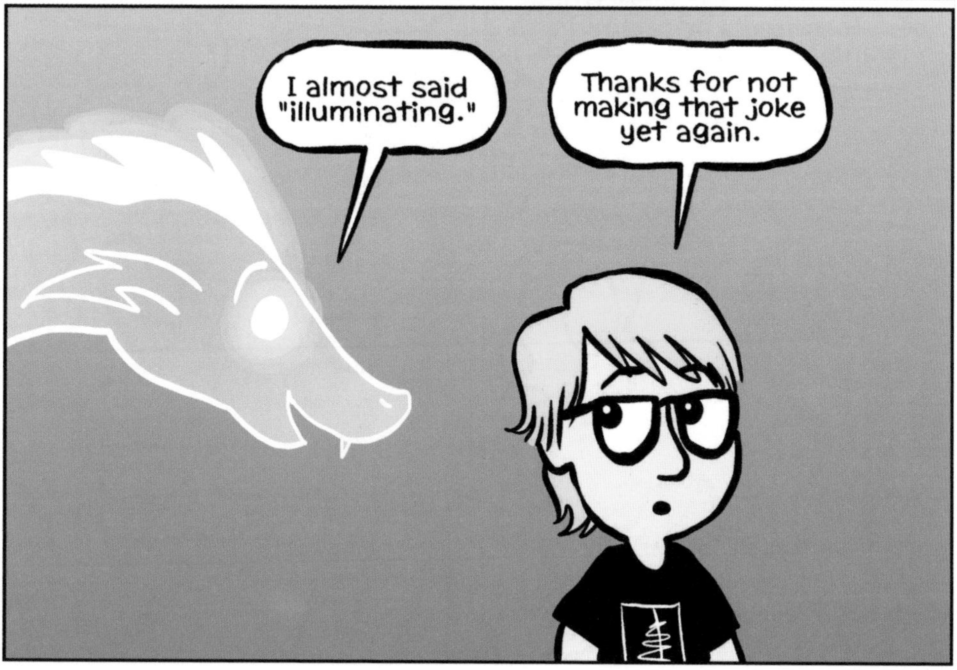
I almost said "illuminating."
Thanks for not making that joke yet again.

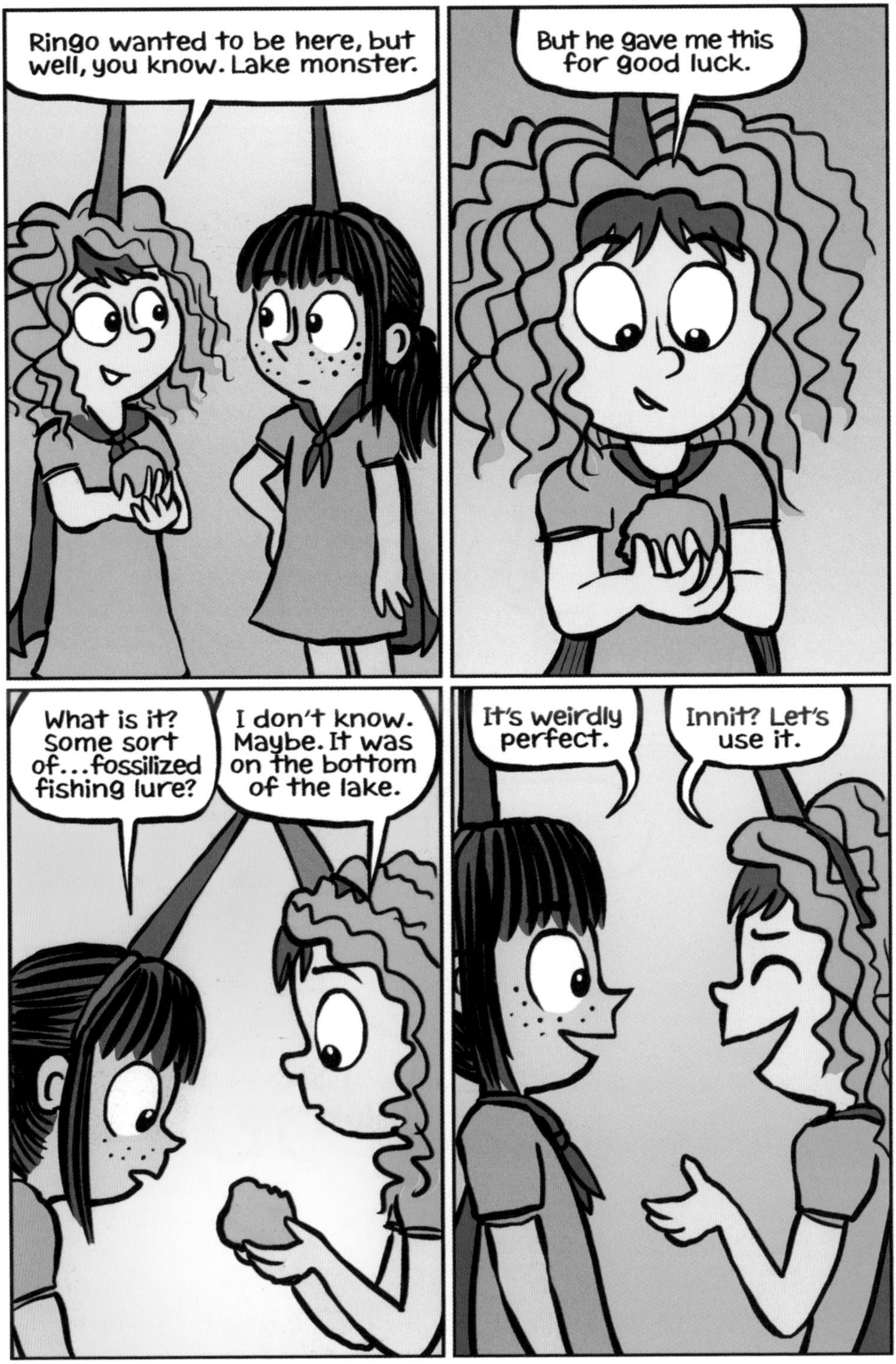
Ringo wanted to be here, but well, you know. Lake monster.
But he gave me this for good luck.
What is it? Some sort of...fossilized fishing lure?
I don't know. Maybe. It was on the bottom of the lake.
It's weirdly perfect.
Innit? Let's use it.

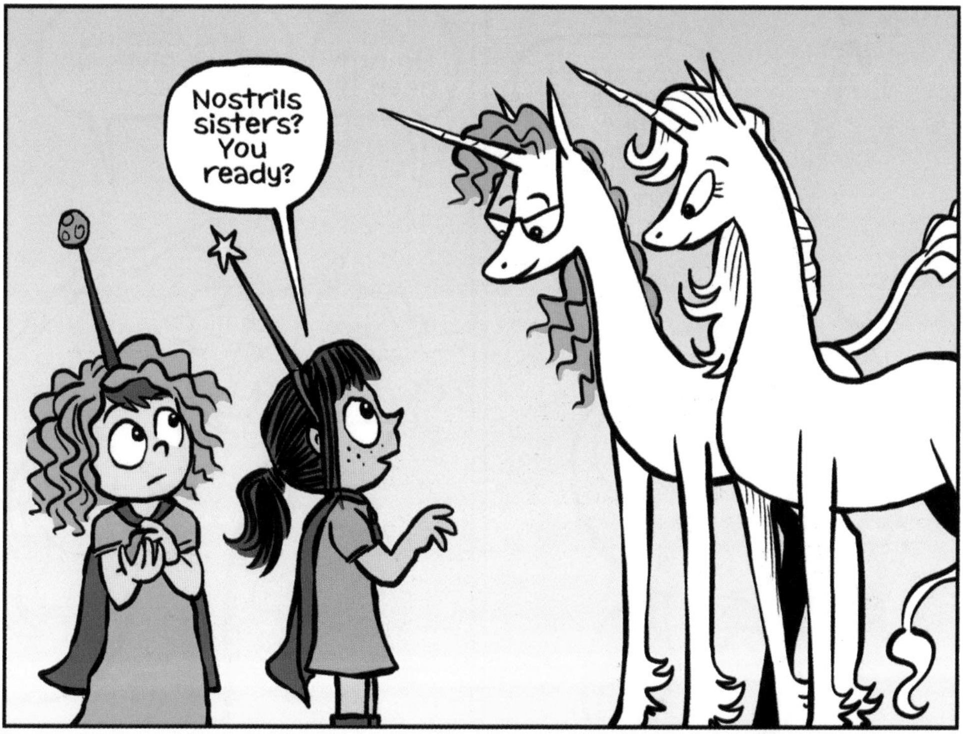
Nostrils sisters? You ready?

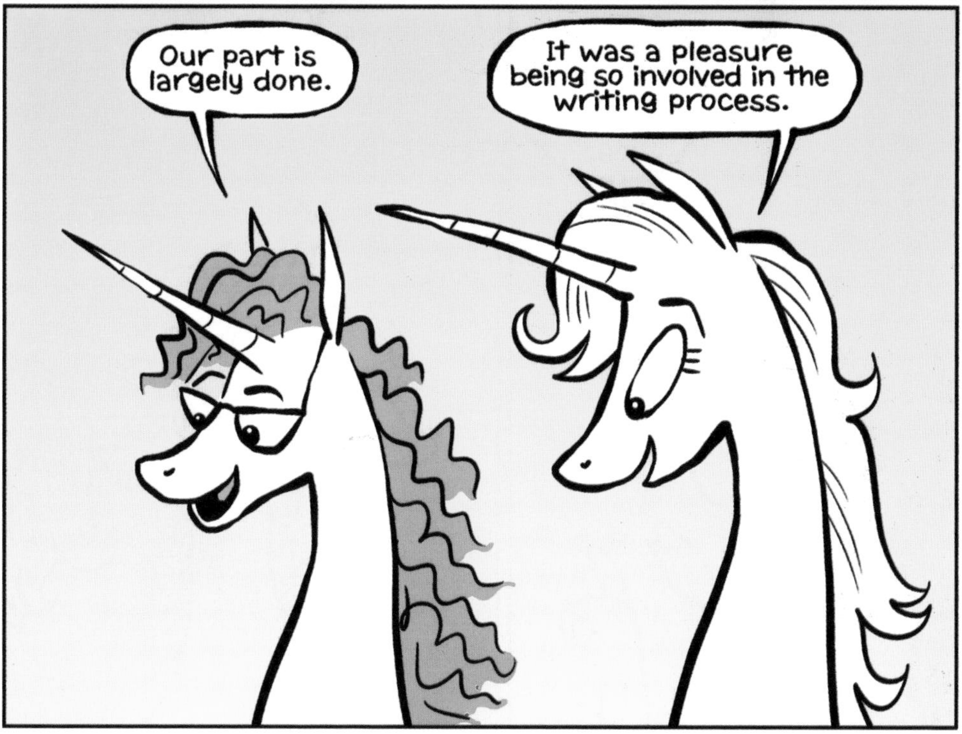
Our part is largely done.
It was a pleasure being so involved in the writing process.

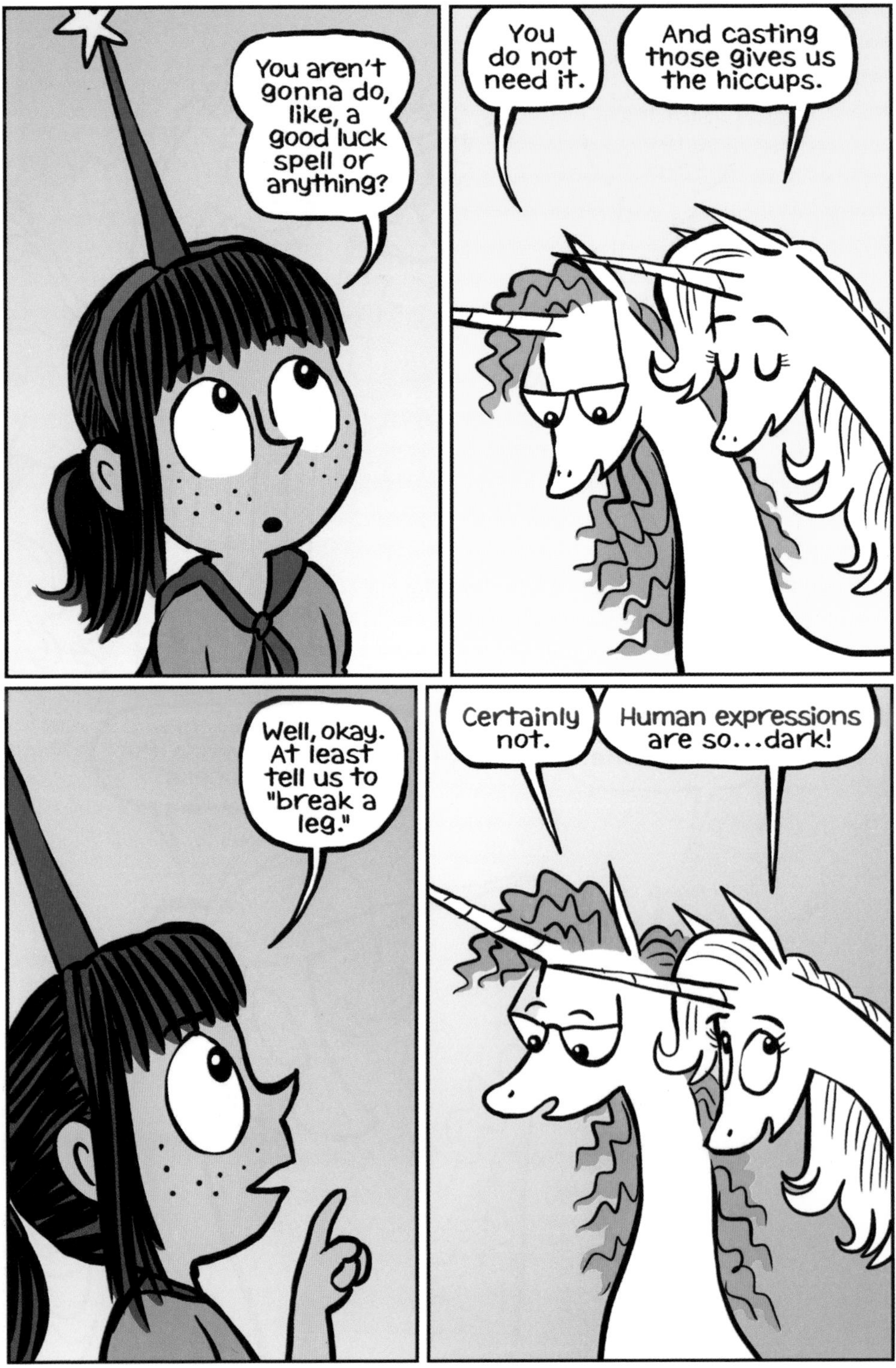
You aren't gonna do, like, a good luck spell or anything?
You do not need it.
And casting those gives us the hiccups.
Well, okay. At least tell us to "break a leg."
Certainly not.
Human expressions are so...dark!

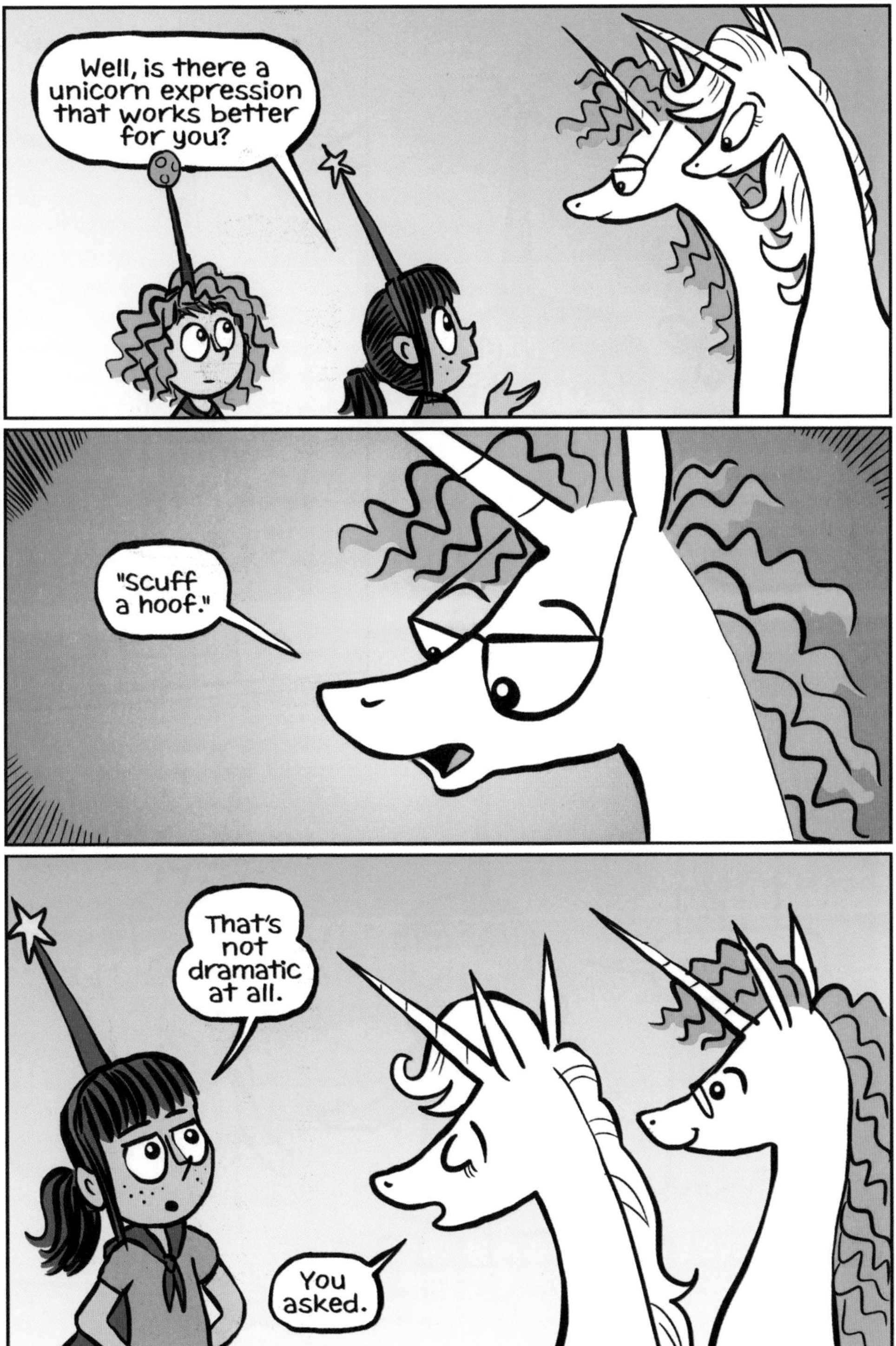
Well, is there a unicorn expression that works better for you?
"Scuff a hoof."
That's not dramatic at all.
You asked.

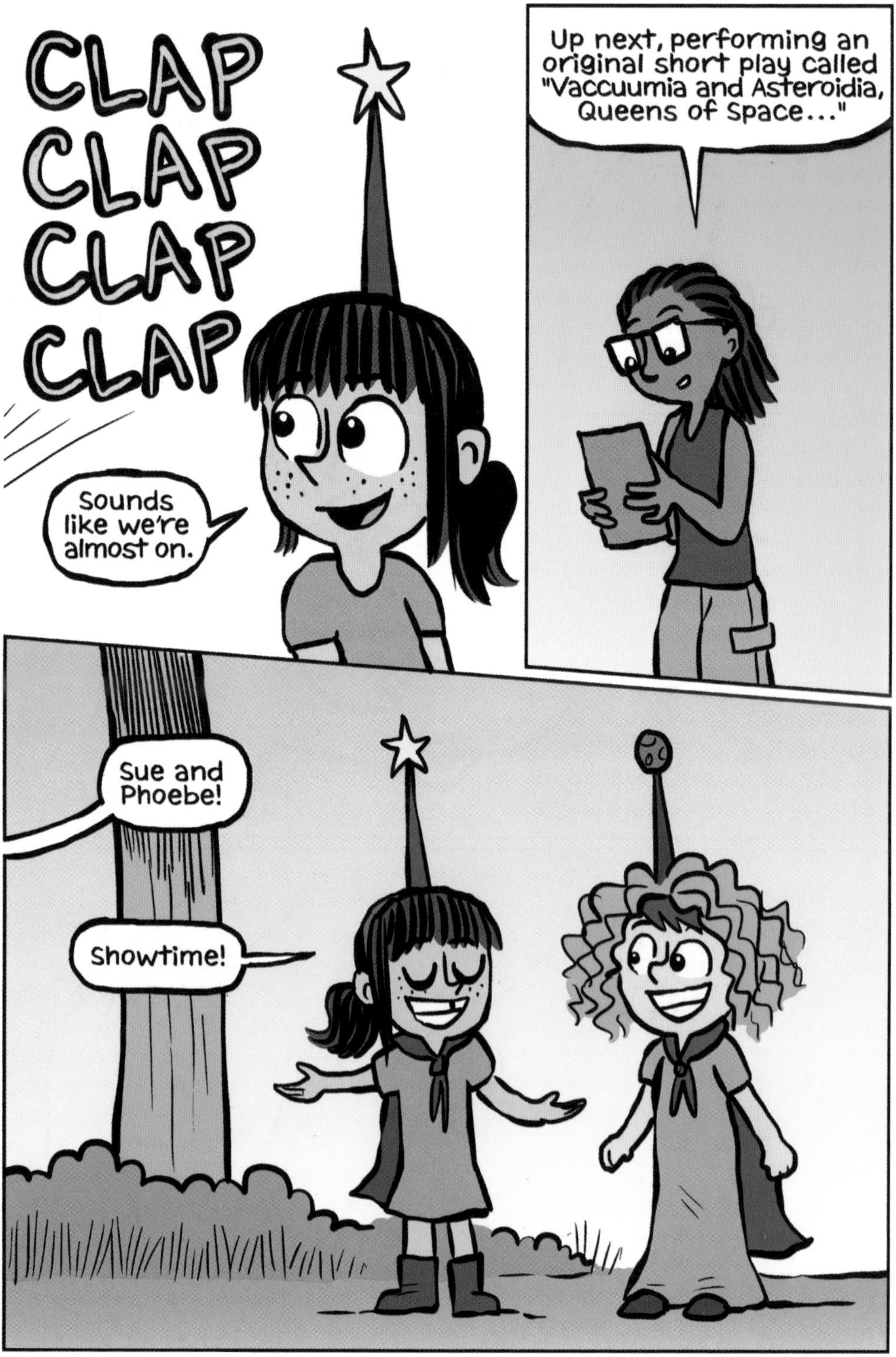
CLAP CLAP CLAP CLAP
Sounds like we're almost on.
Up next, performing an original short play called "Vaccuumia and Asteroidia, Queens of Space..."
Sue and Phoebe!
Showtime!

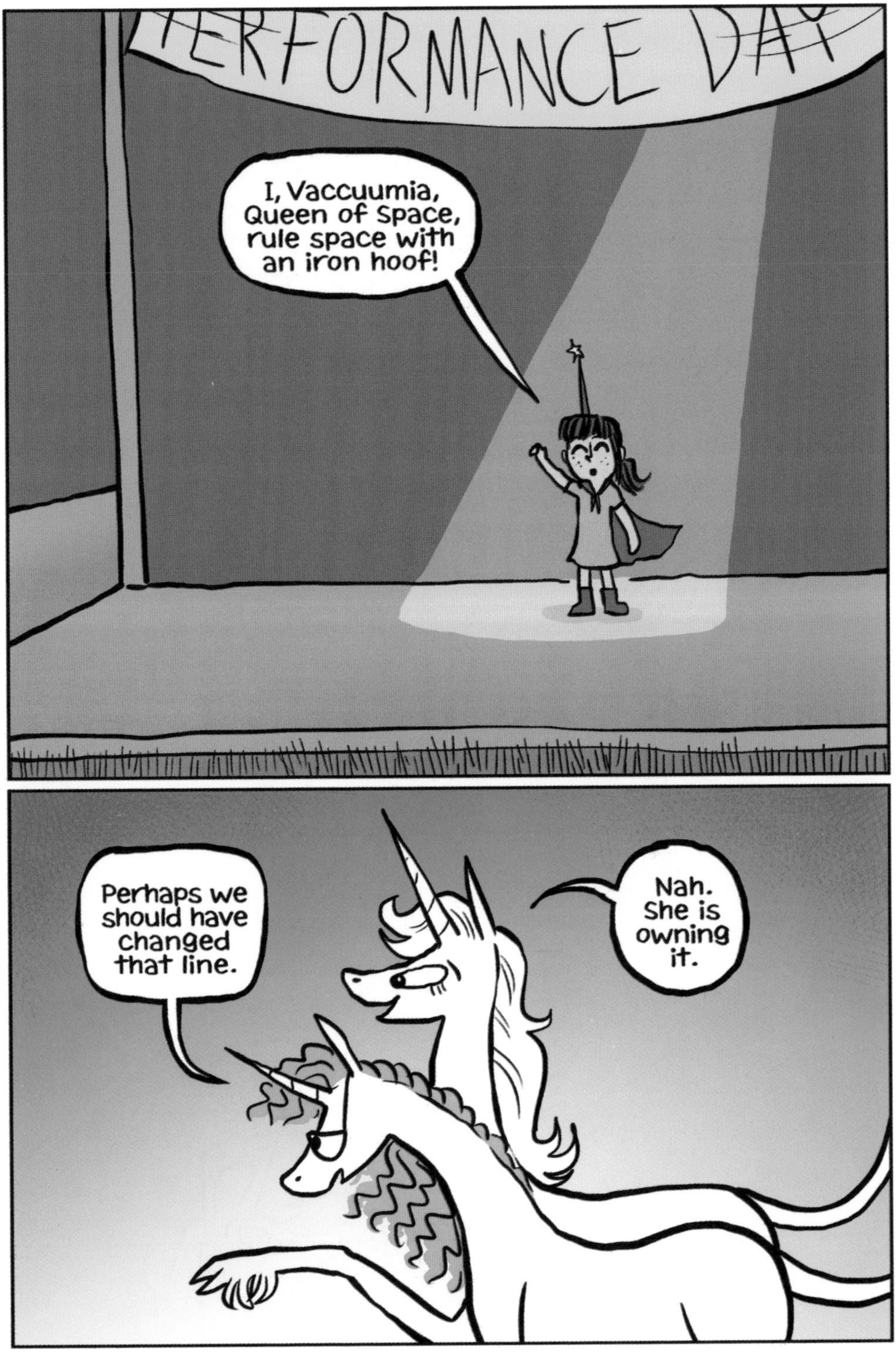
ERFORMANCE DA
I, Vaccuumia, Queen of Space, rule space with an iron hoof!
Perhaps we should have changed that line.
Nah. She is owning it.

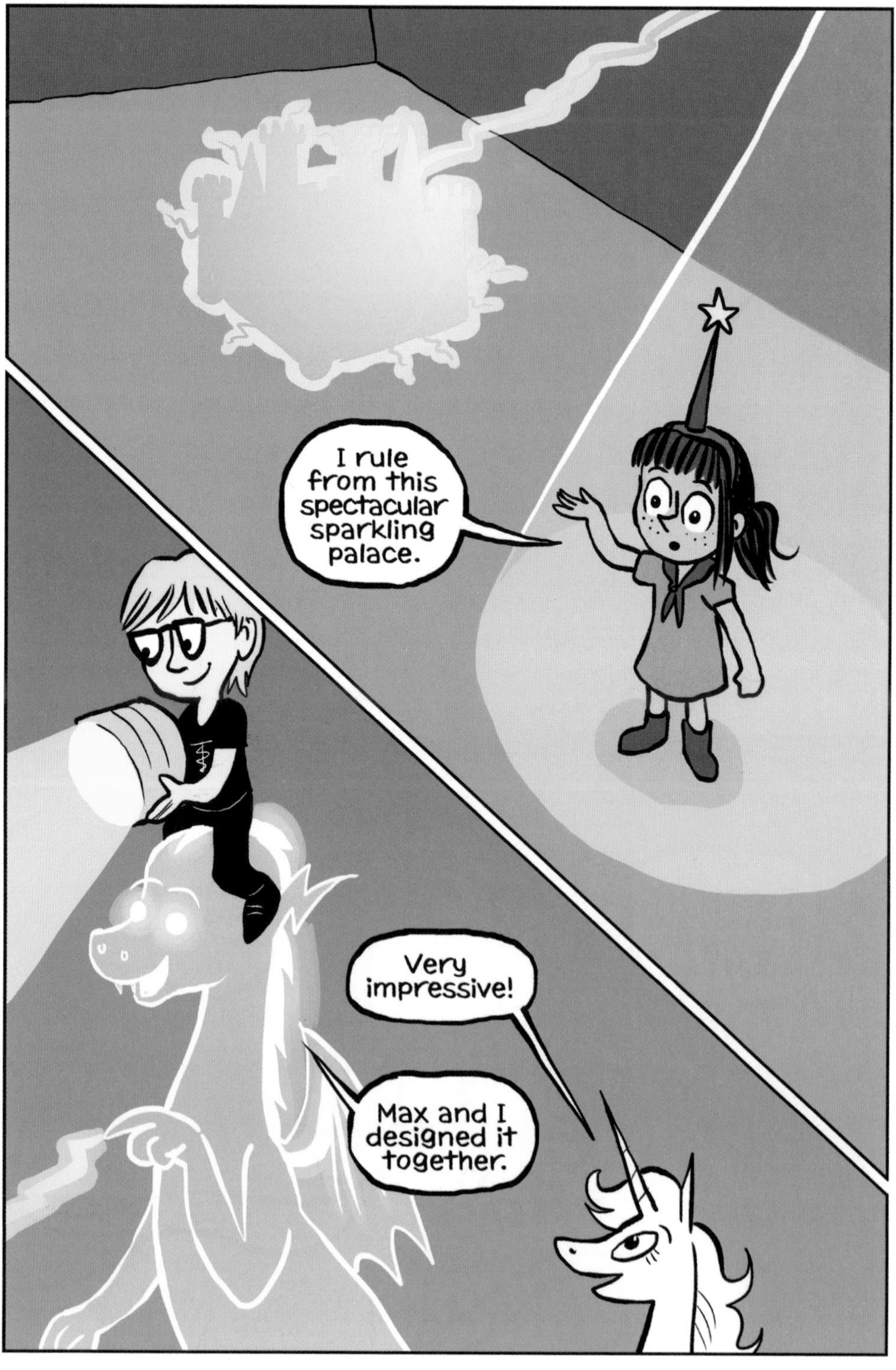
I rule from this spectacular sparkling palace.
Very impressive!
Max and I designed it together.

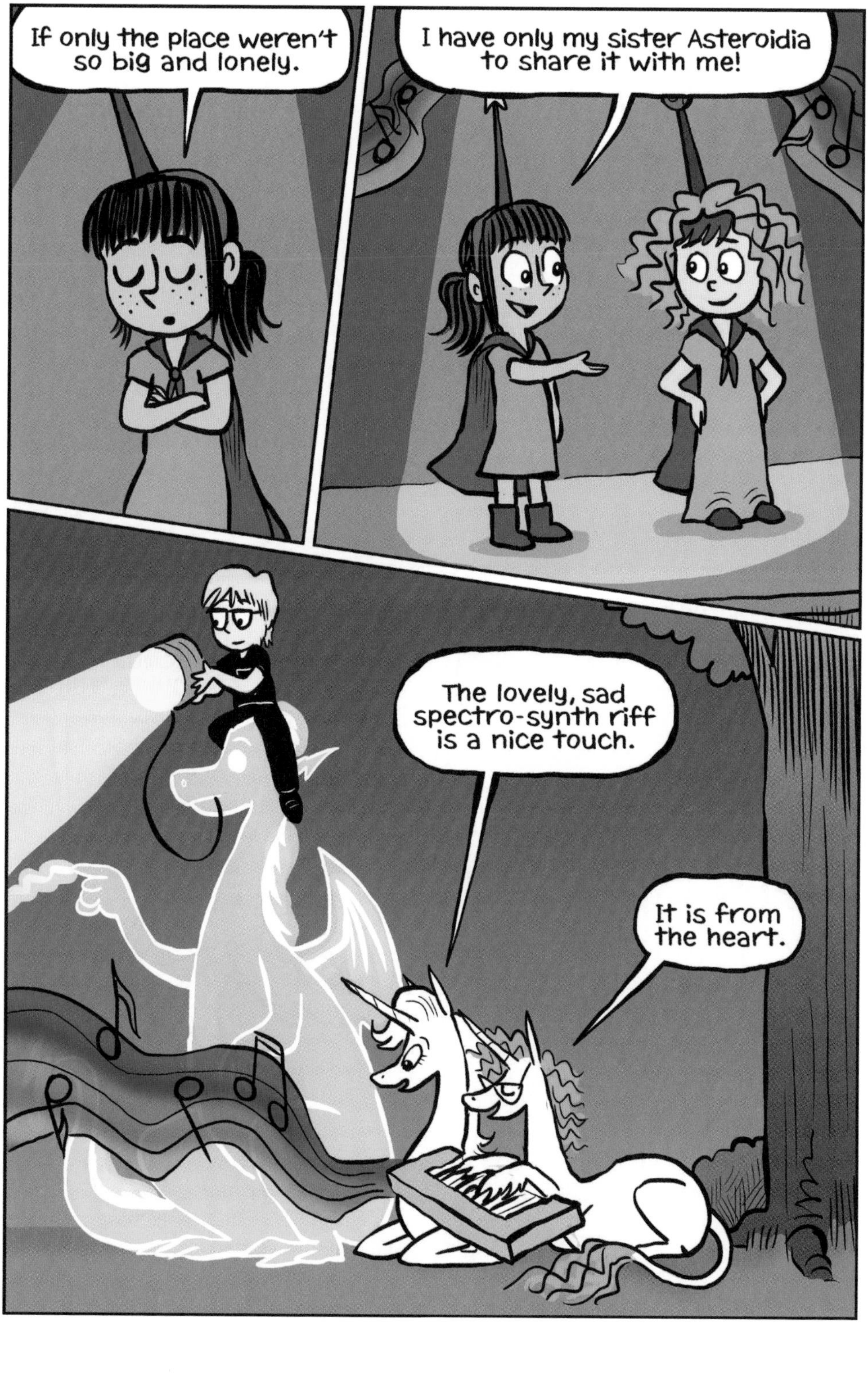
If only the place weren't so big and lonely.
I have only my sister Asteroidia to share it with me!
The lovely, sad spectro-synth riff is a nice touch.
It is from the heart.

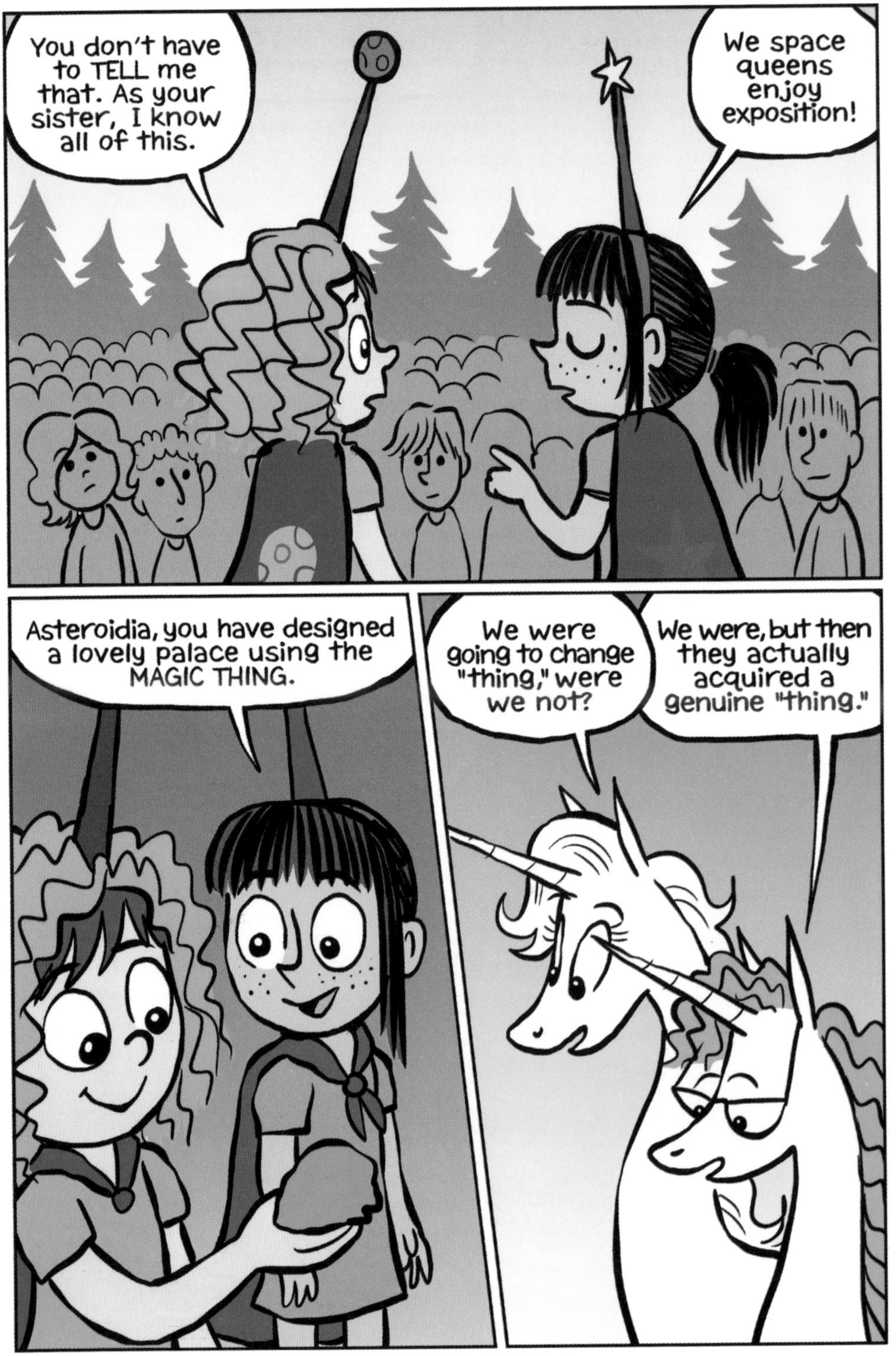

You don't have to TELL me that. As your sister, I know all of this.
We space queens enjoy exposition!
Asteroidia, you have designed a lovely palace using the MAGIC THING.
We were going to change "thing," were we not?
We were, but then they actually acquired a genuine "thing."

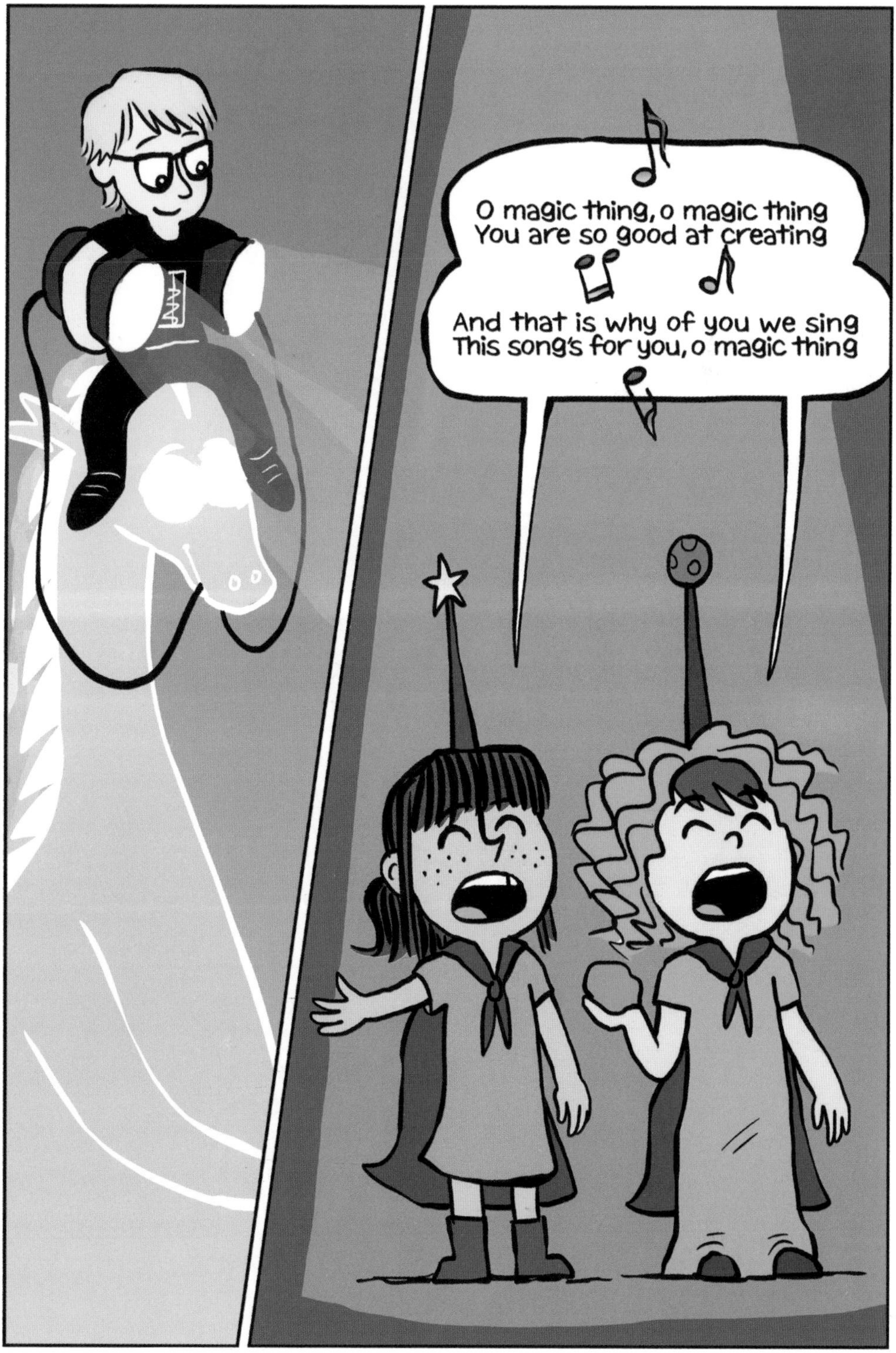
O magic thing, o magic thing
You are so good at creating
And that is why of you we sing
This song's for you, o magic thing

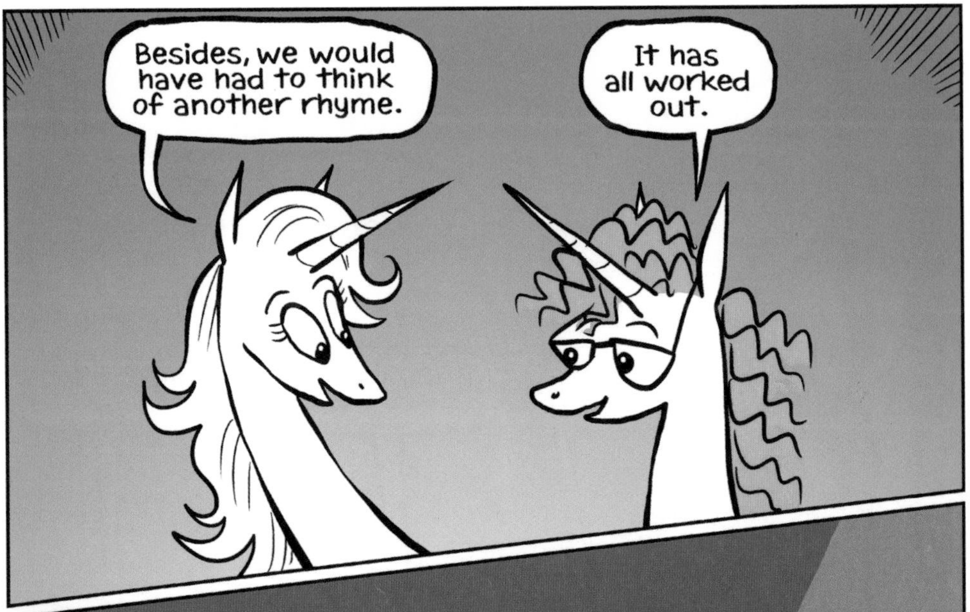
Besides, we would have had to think of another rhyme.
It has all worked out.

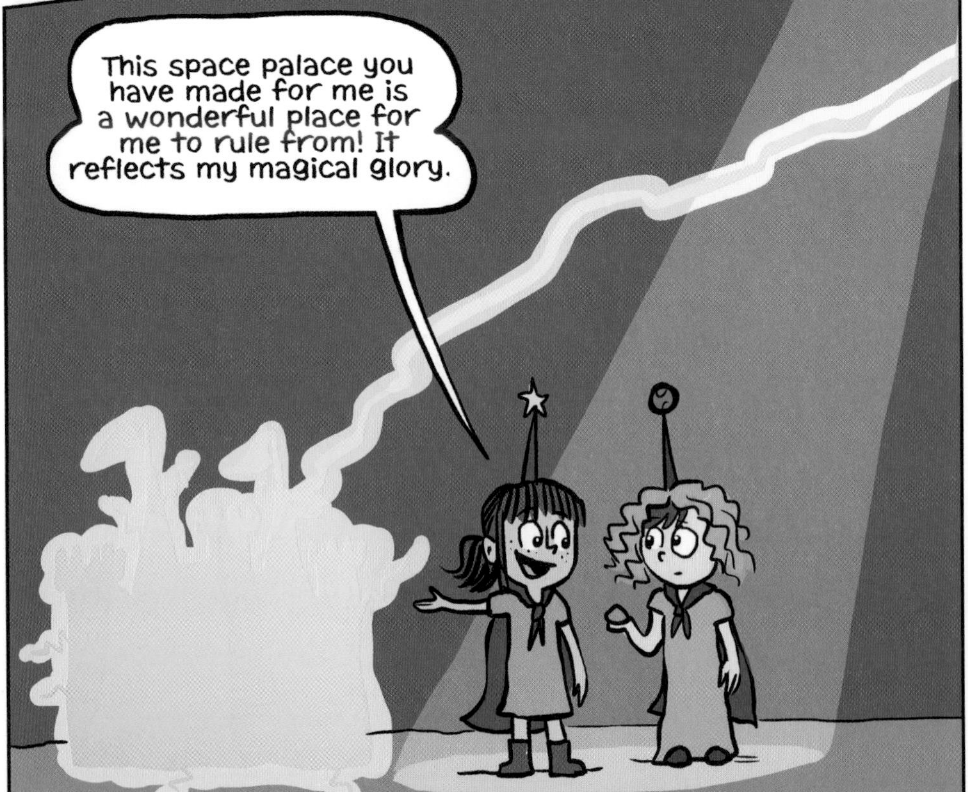
This space palace you have made for me is a wonderful place for me to rule from! It reflects my magical glory.

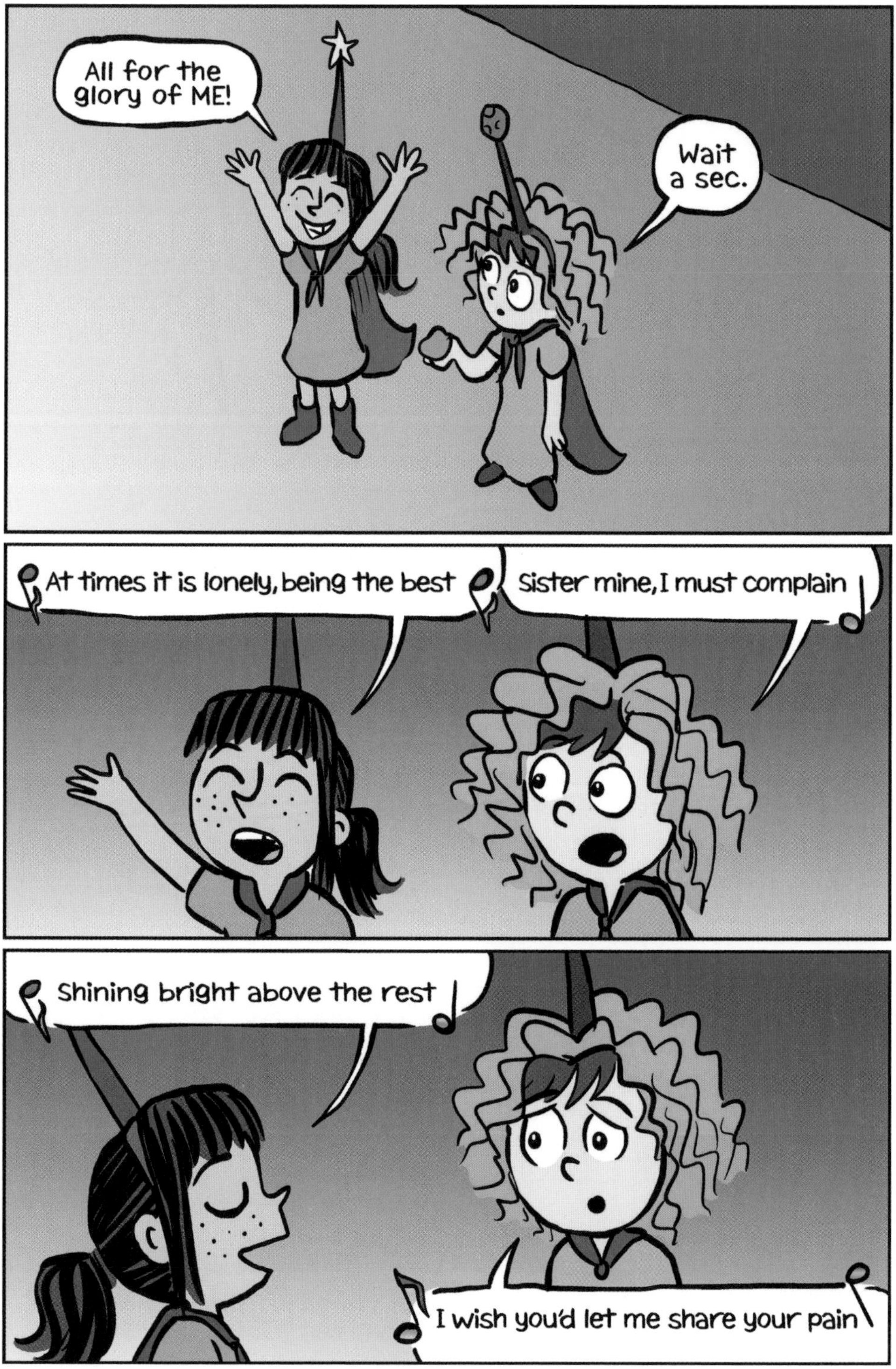
All for the glory of ME!
Wait a sec.
At times it is lonely, being the best
Sister mine, I must complain
Shining bright above the rest
I wish you'd let me share your pain

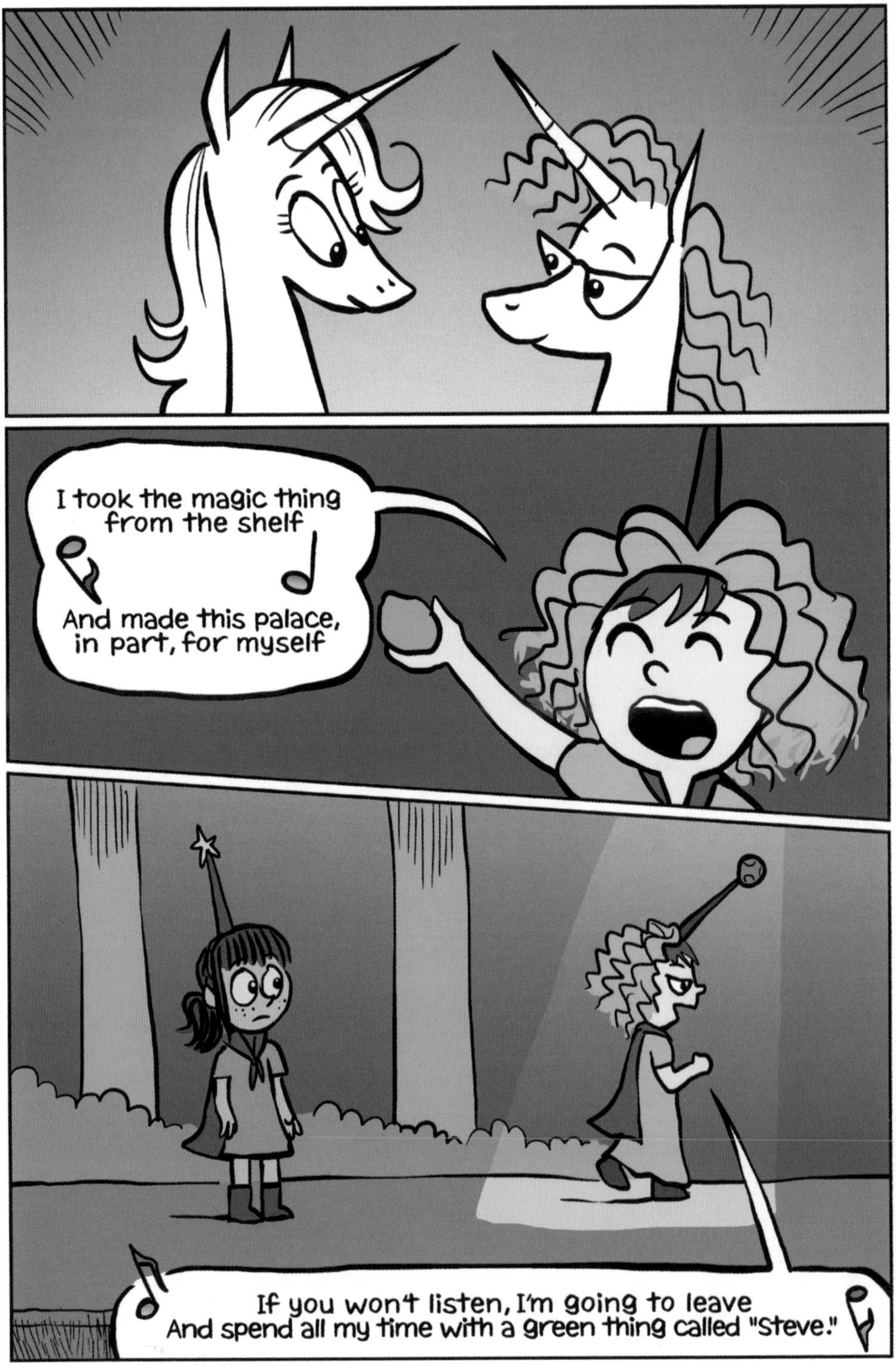
I took the magic thing from the shelf
And made this palace, in part, for myself
If you won't listen, I'm going to leave
And spend all my time with a green thing called "Steve."

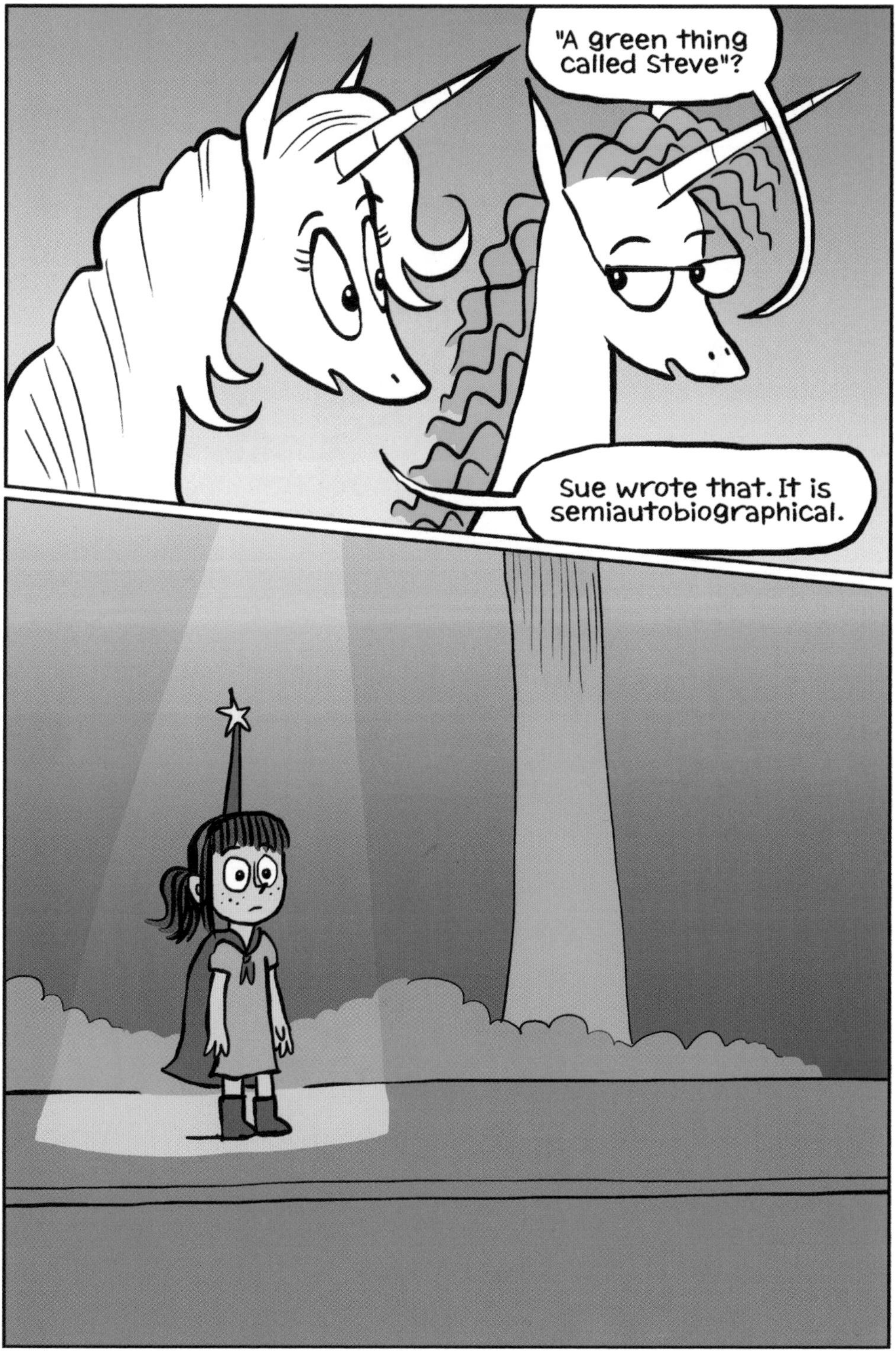
"A green thing called Steve"?
Sue wrote that. It is semiautobiographical.

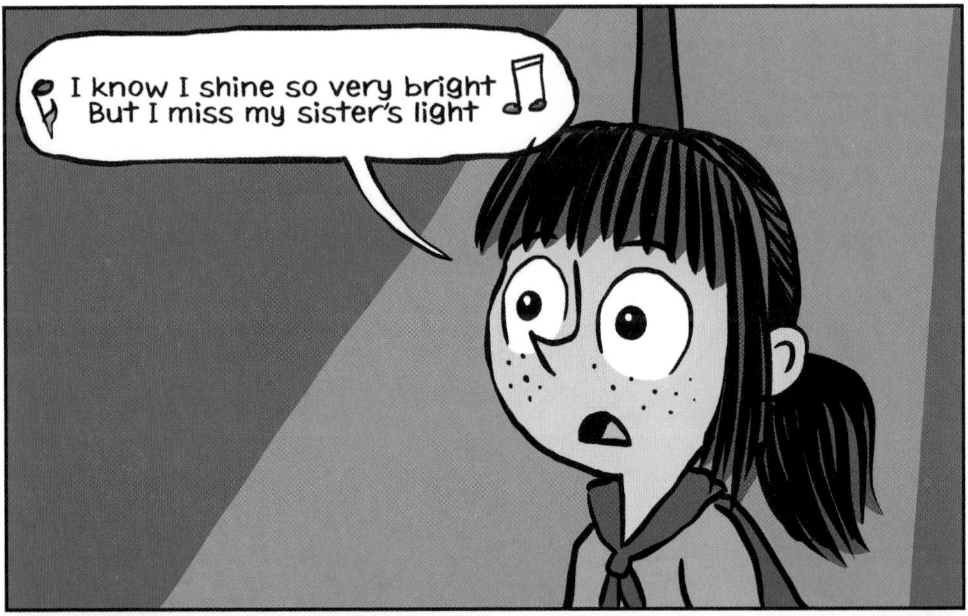
I know I shine so very bright
But I miss my sister's light

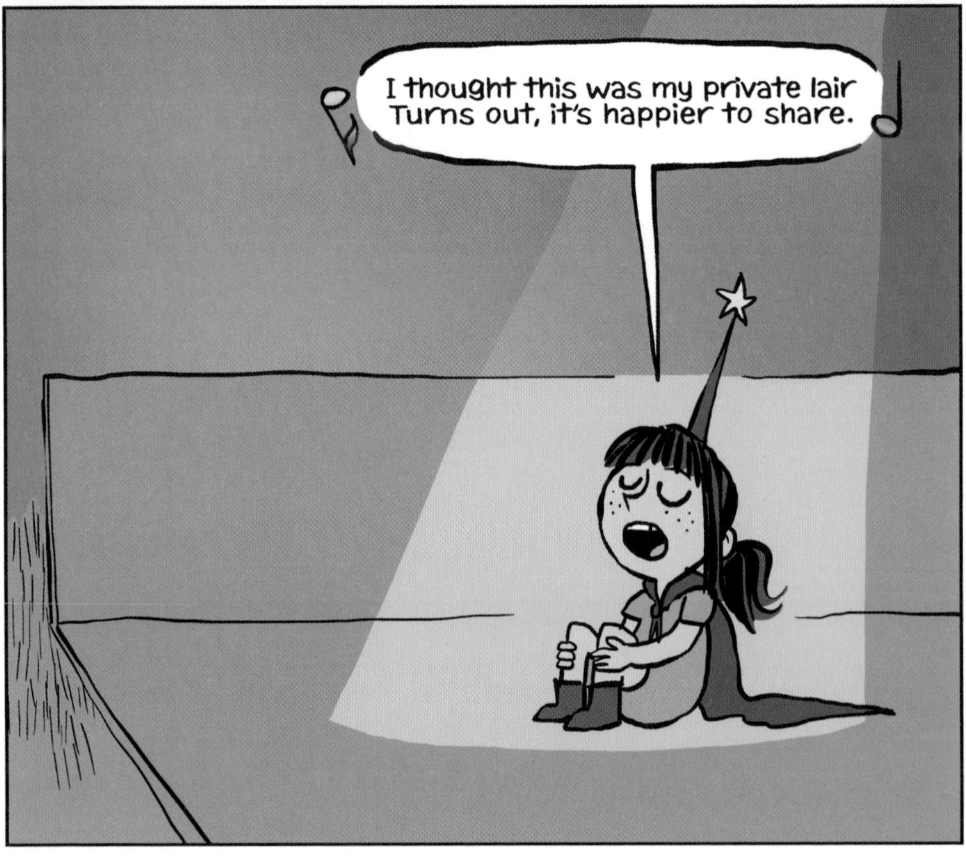
I thought this was my private lair
Turns out, it's happier to share.

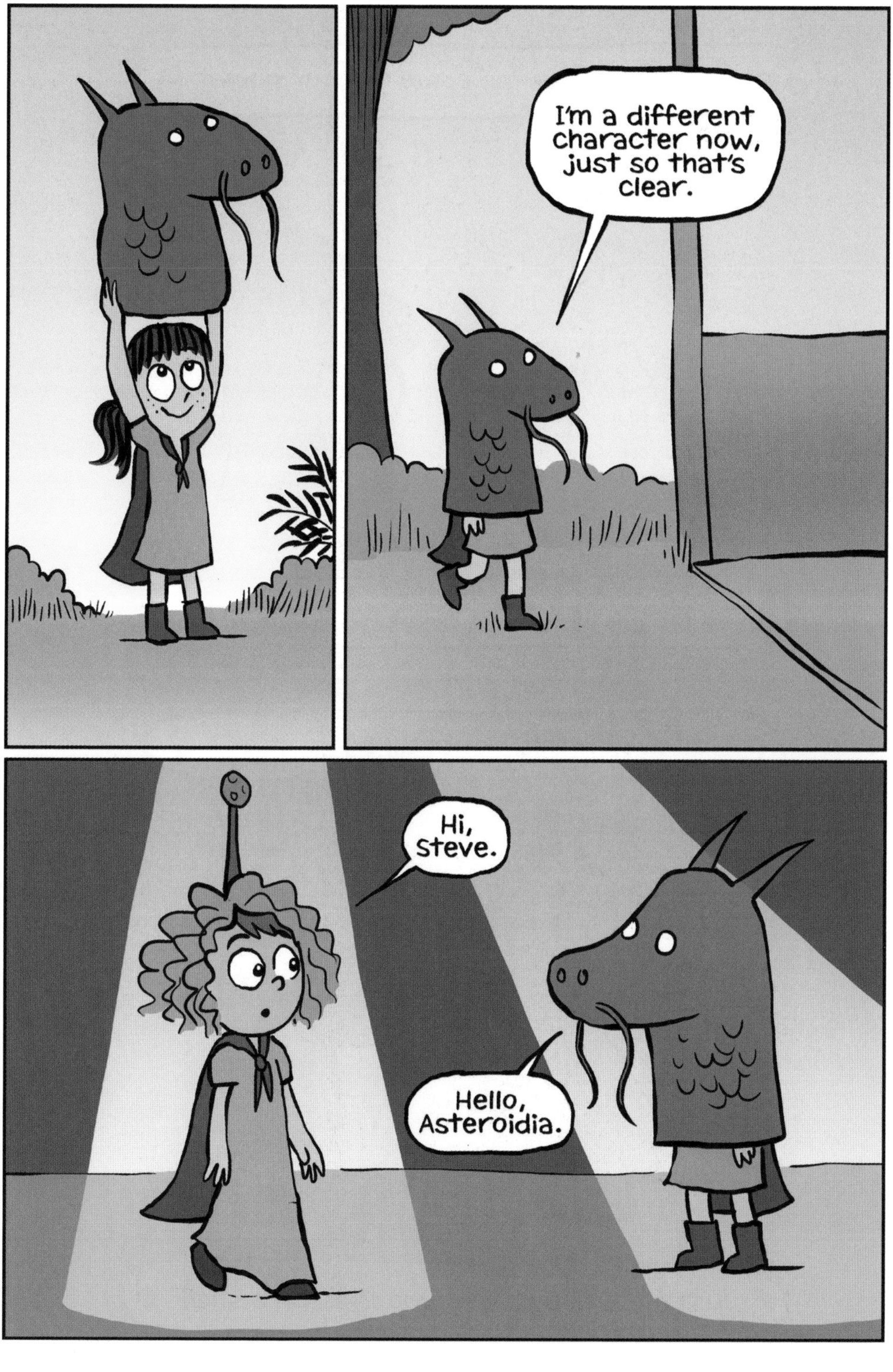
I'm a different character now, just so that's clear.
Hi, steve.
Hello, Asteroidia.

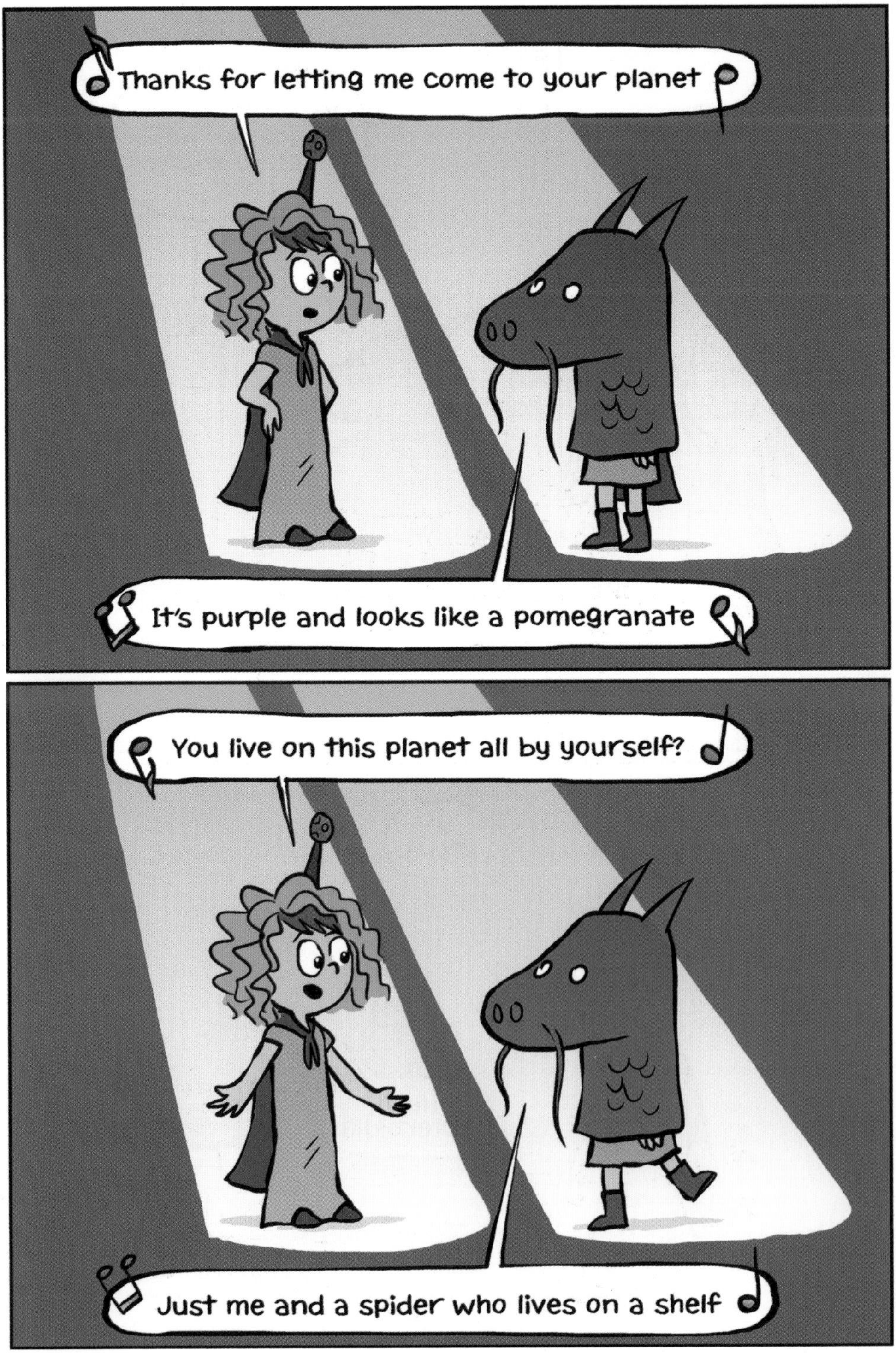
Thanks for letting me come to your planet
It's purple and looks like a pomegranate
You live on this planet all by yourself?
Just me and a spider who lives on a shelf

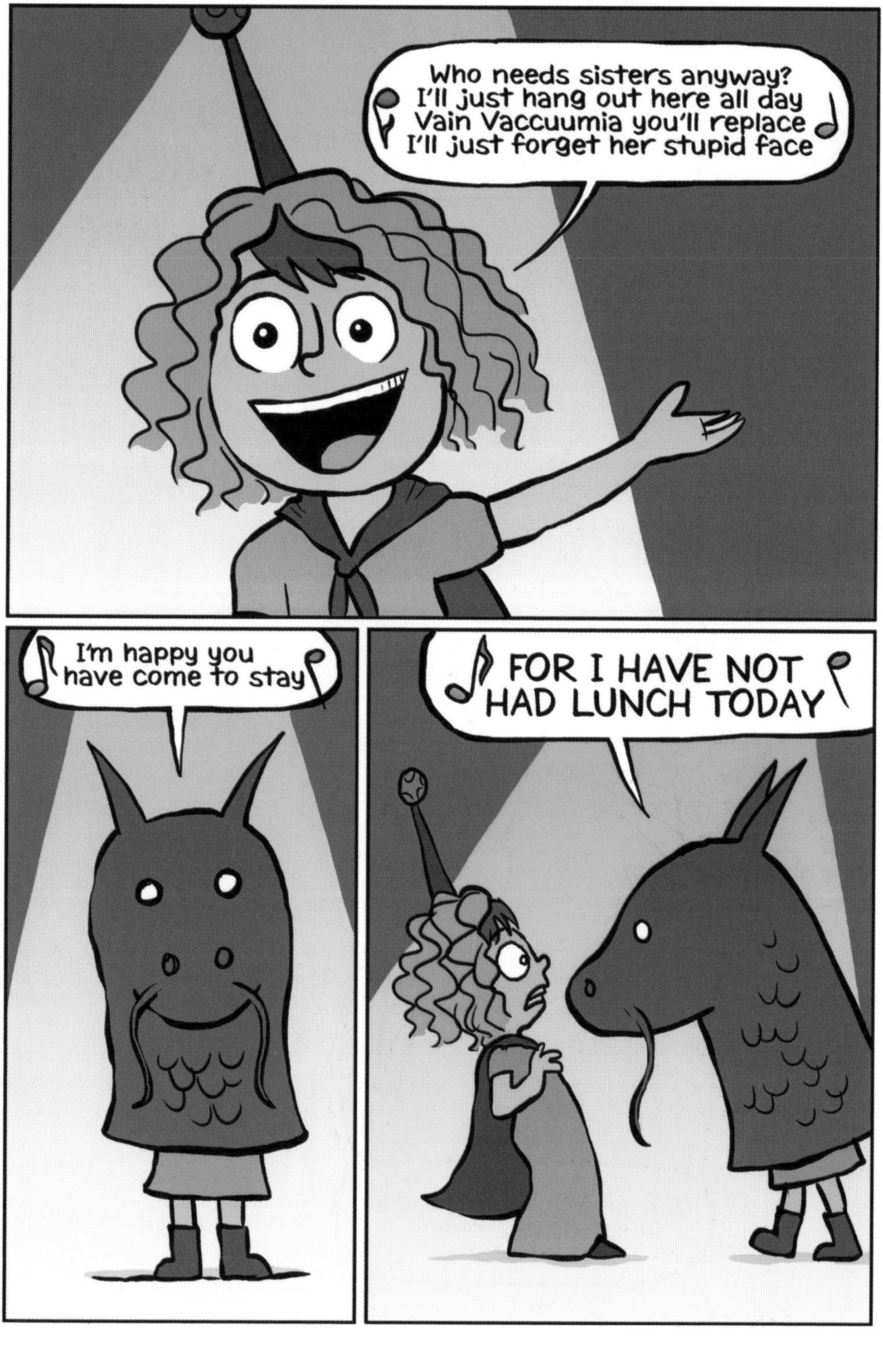
Who needs sisters anyway?
I'll just hang out here all day
Vain Vaccuumia you'll replace
I'll just forget her stupid face
I'm happy you have come to stay
FOR I HAVE NOT HAD LUNCH TODAY

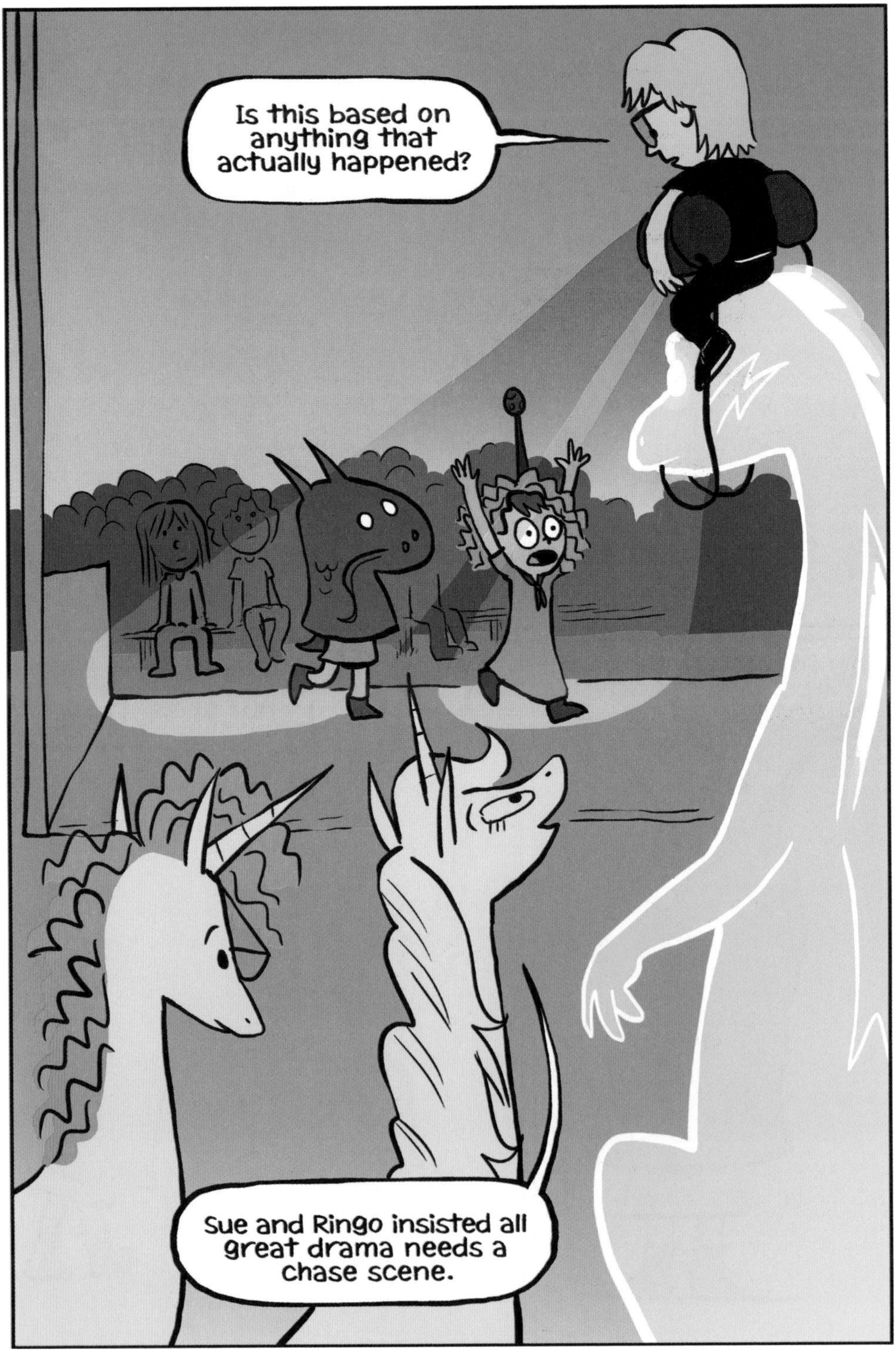
Is this based on anything that actually happened?
Sue and Ringo insisted all great drama needs a chase scene.

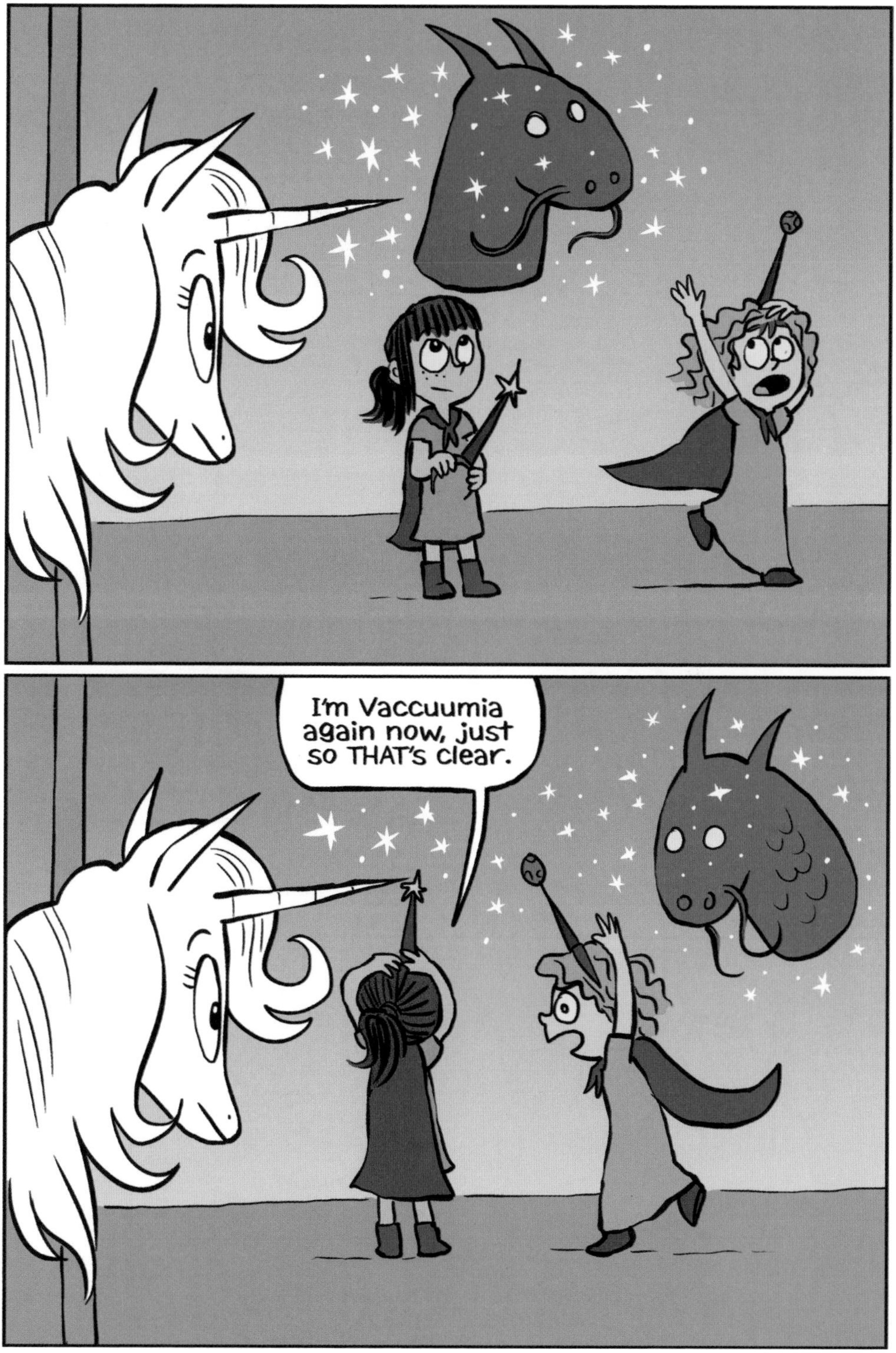
I'm Vaccuumia again now, just so THAT's clear.

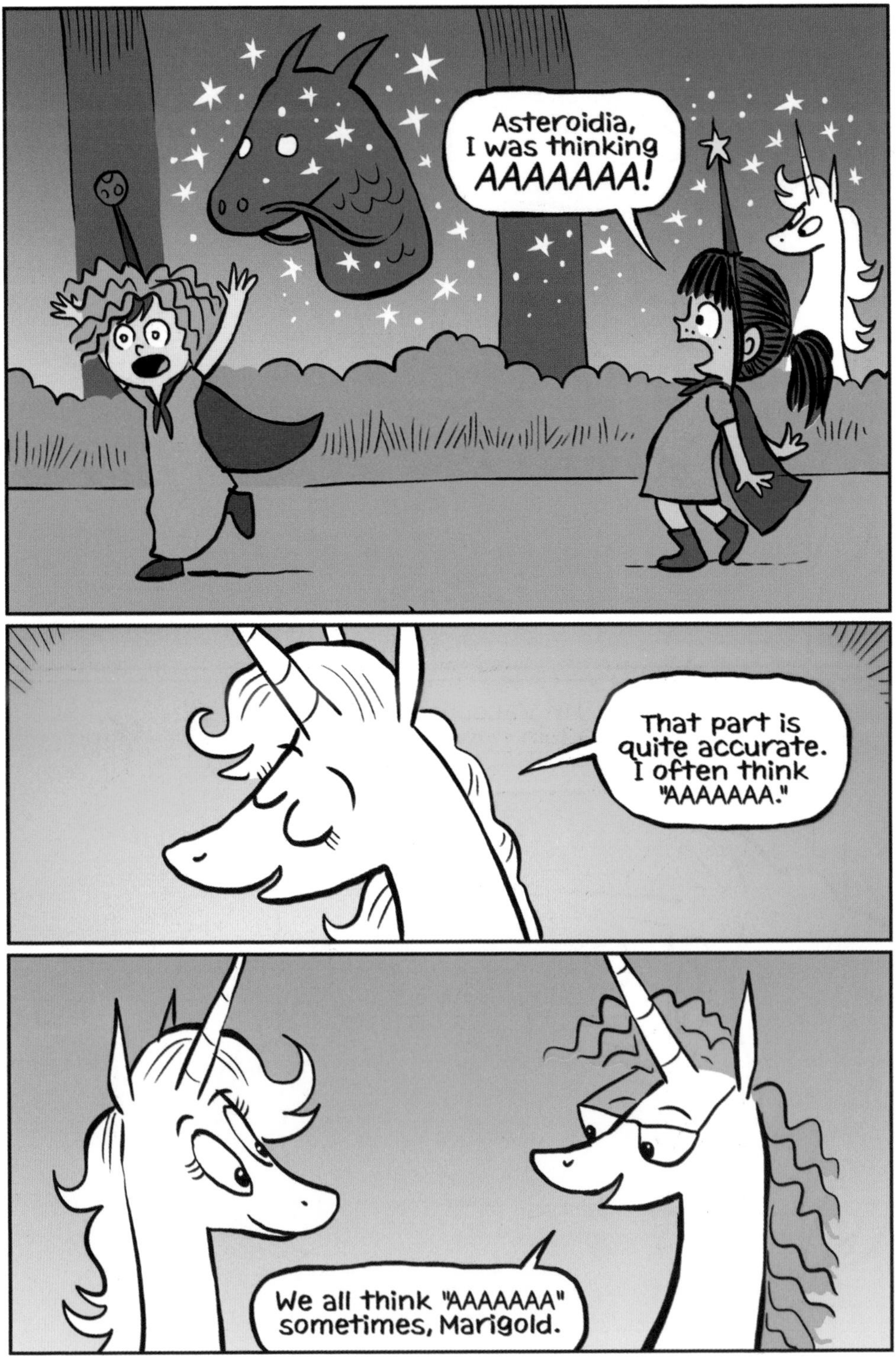
Asteroidia, I was thinking AAAAAAA!
That part is quite accurate. I often think "AAAAAAA."
We all think "AAAAAAA" sometimes, Marigold.

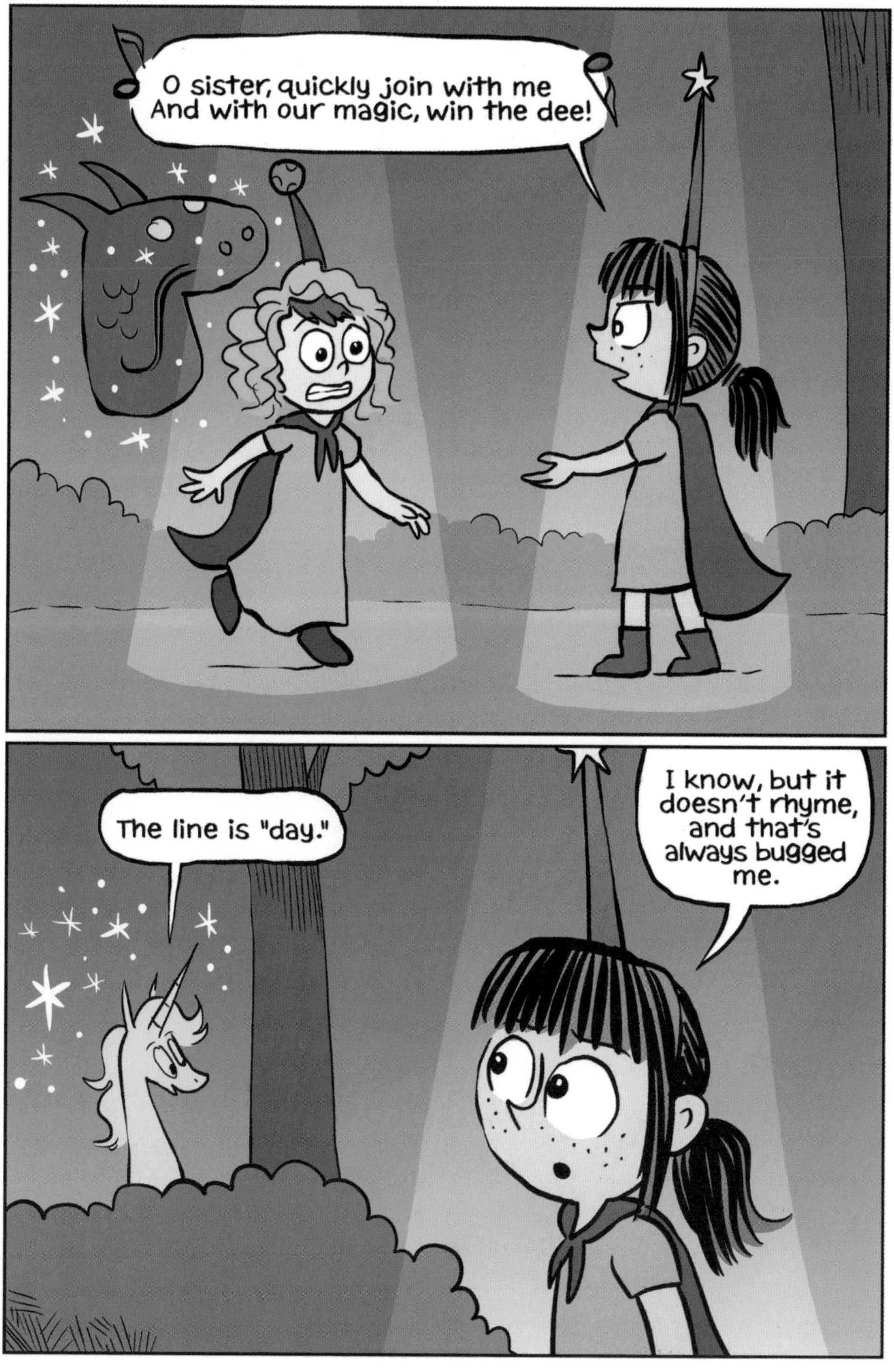

O sister, quickly join with me
And with our magic, win the dee!
The line is "day."
I know, but it doesn't rhyme, and that's always bugged me.

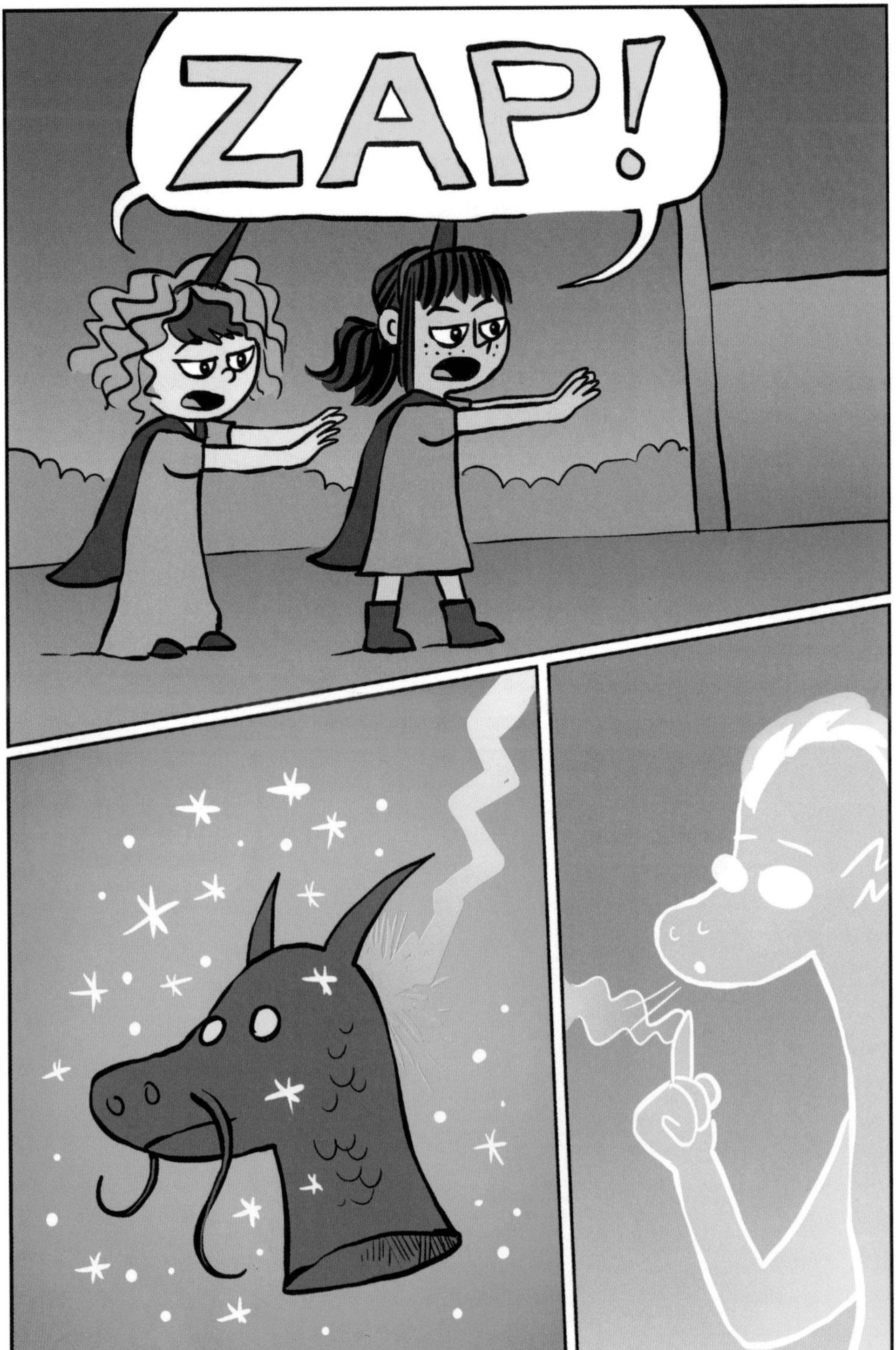
ZAP!

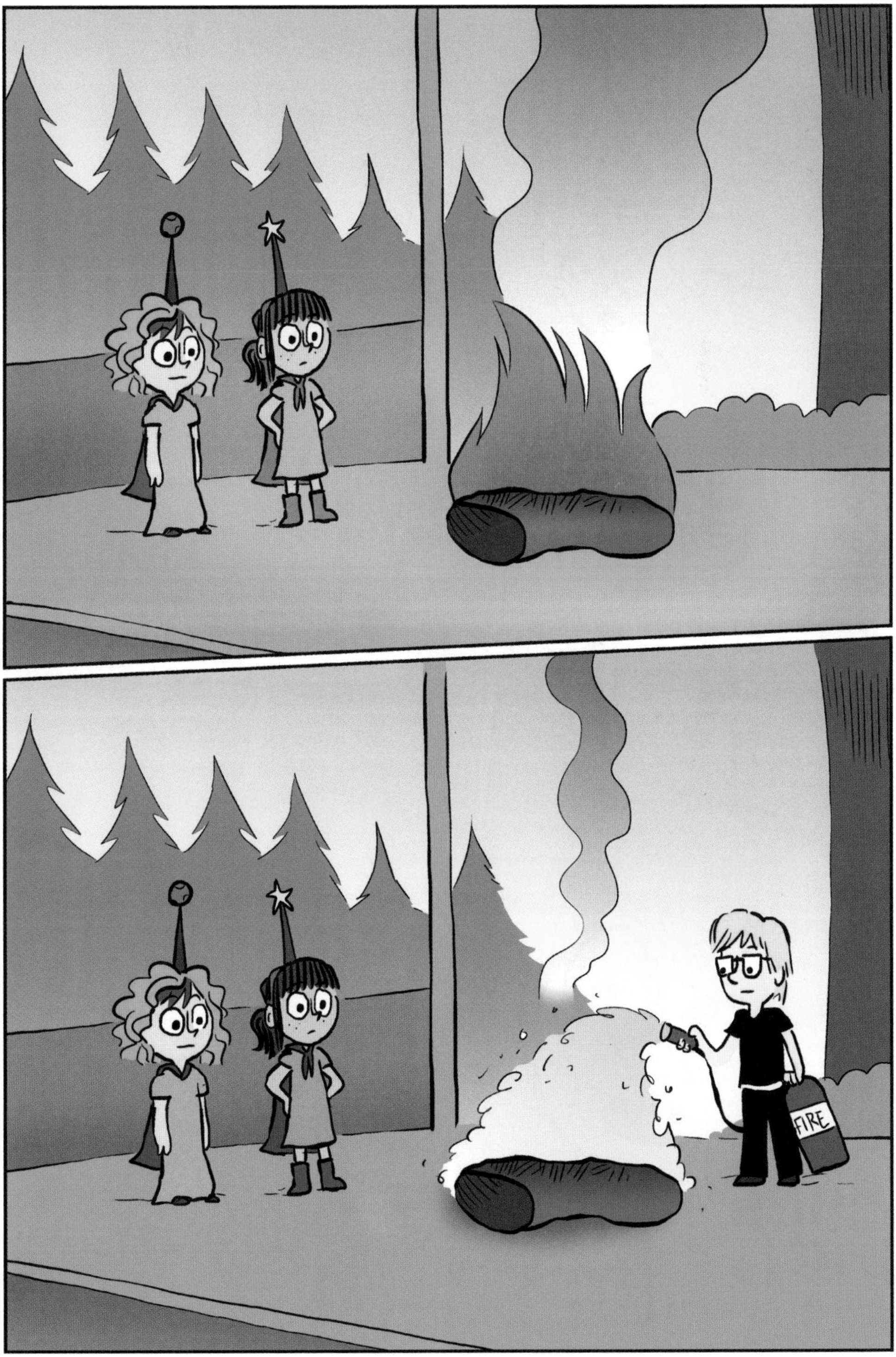
FIRE

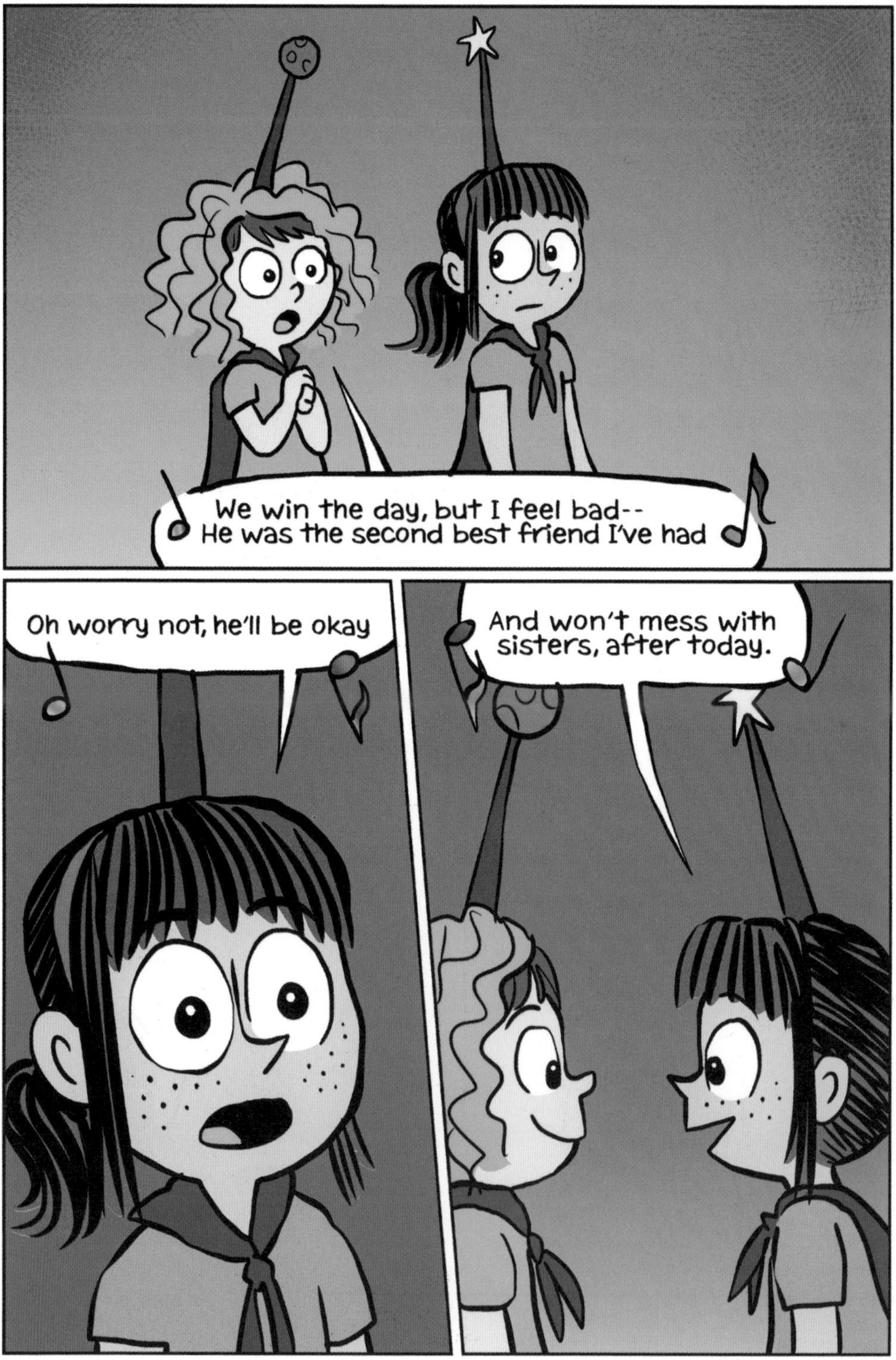
We win the day, but I feel bad--
He was the second best friend I've had
Oh worry not, he'll be okay
And won't mess with sisters, after today.

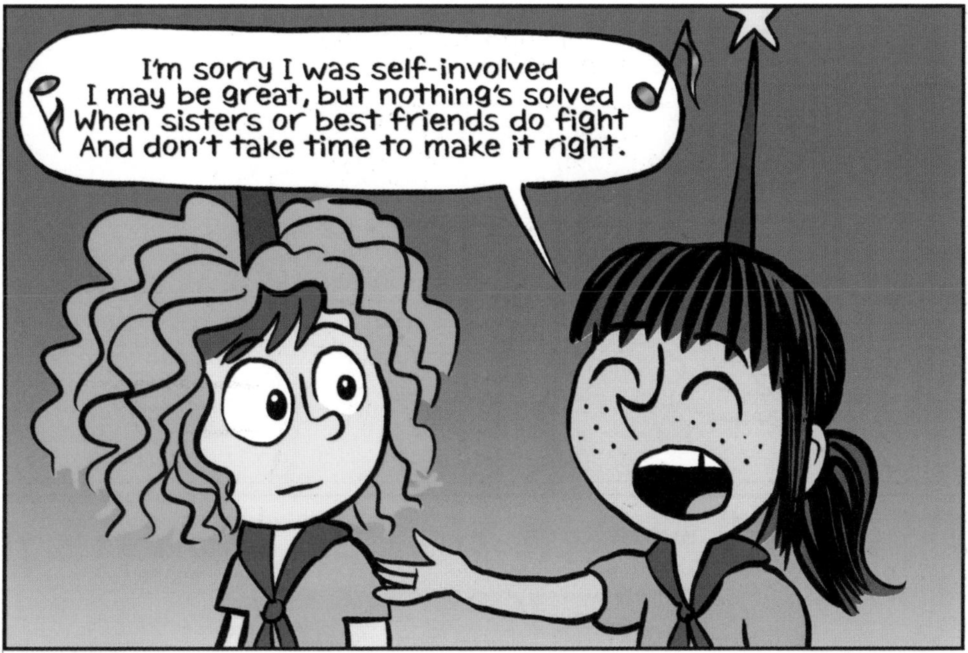
I'm sorry I was self-involved
I may be great, but nothing's solved
When sisters or best friends do fight
And don't take time to make it right.

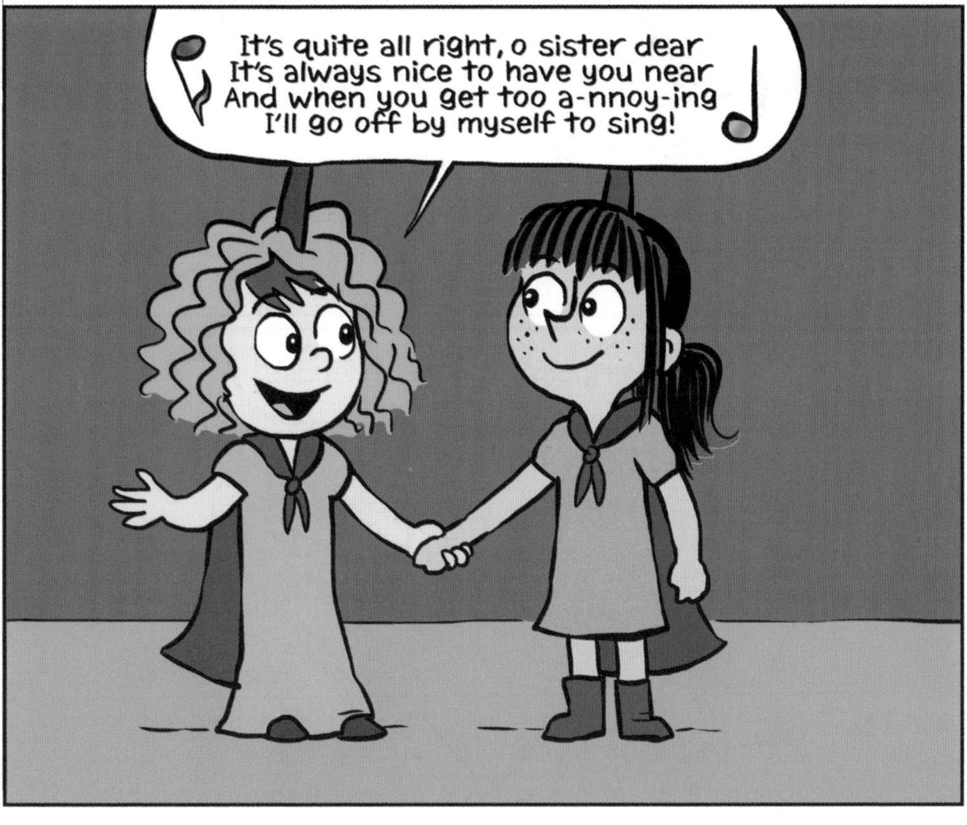
It's quite all right, o sister dear
It's always nice to have you near
And when you get too a-nnoy-ing
I'll go off by myself to sing!

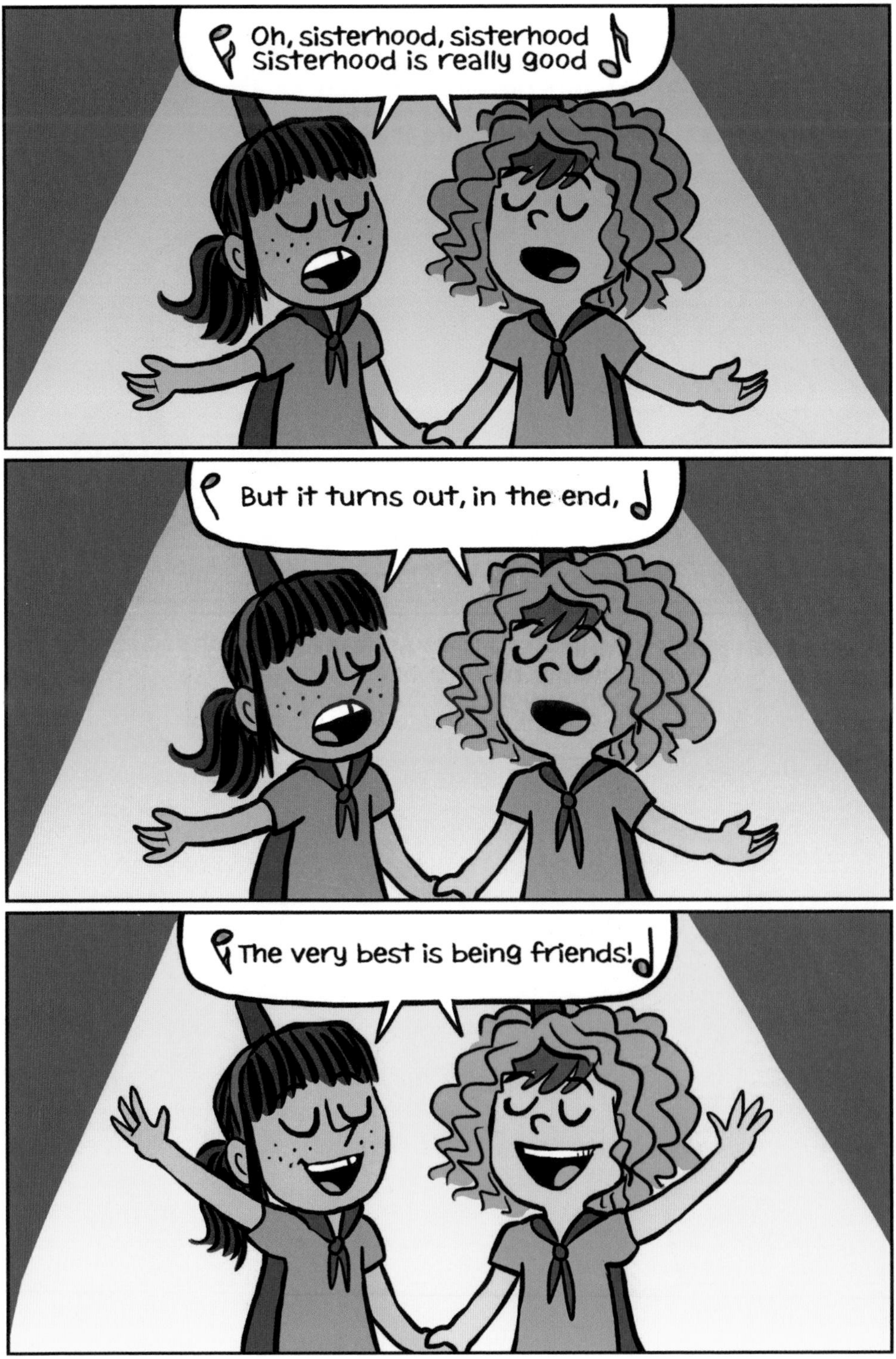
Oh, sisterhood, sisterhood
Sisterhood is really good
But it turns out, in the end,
The very best is being friends!

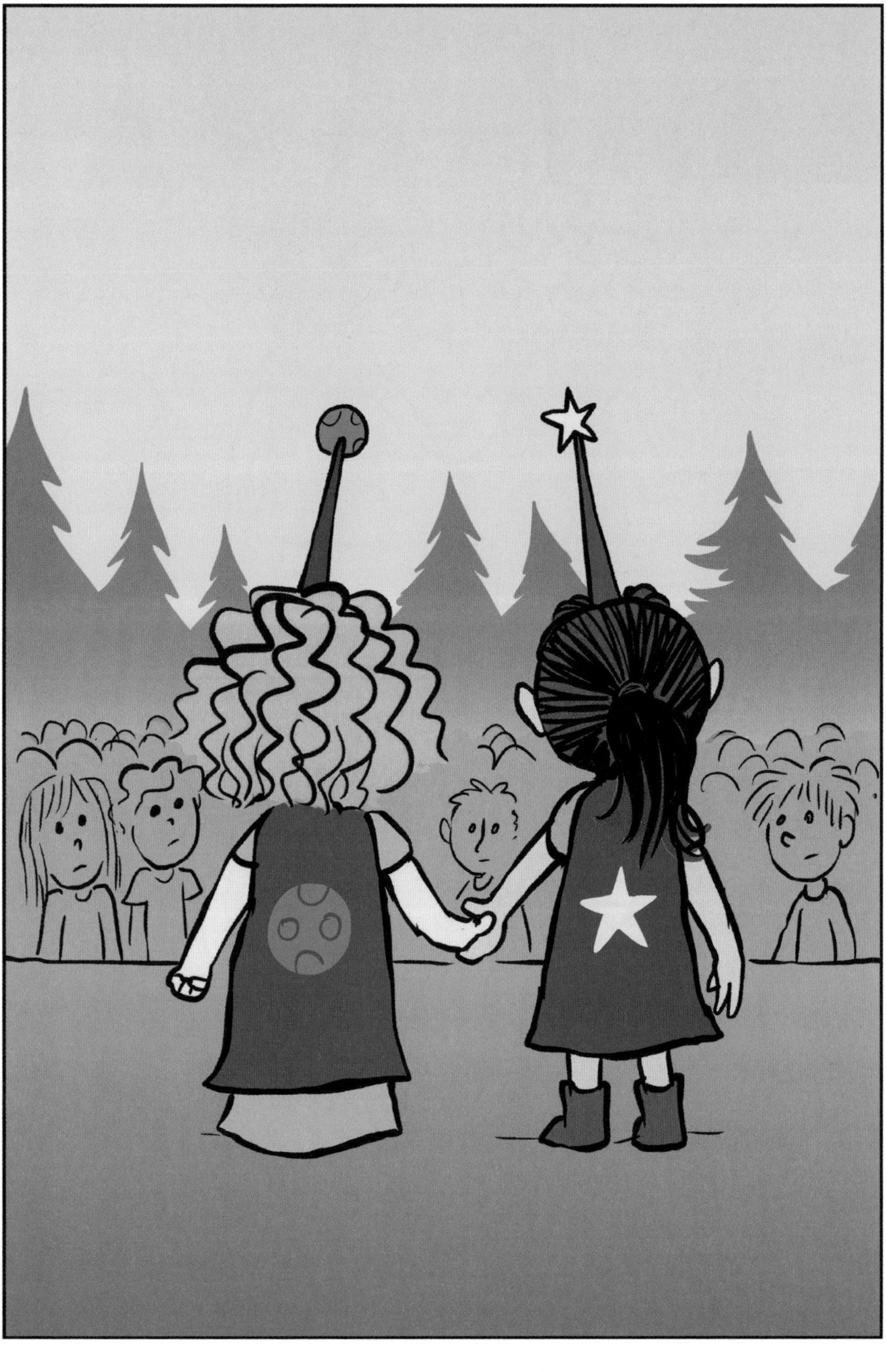

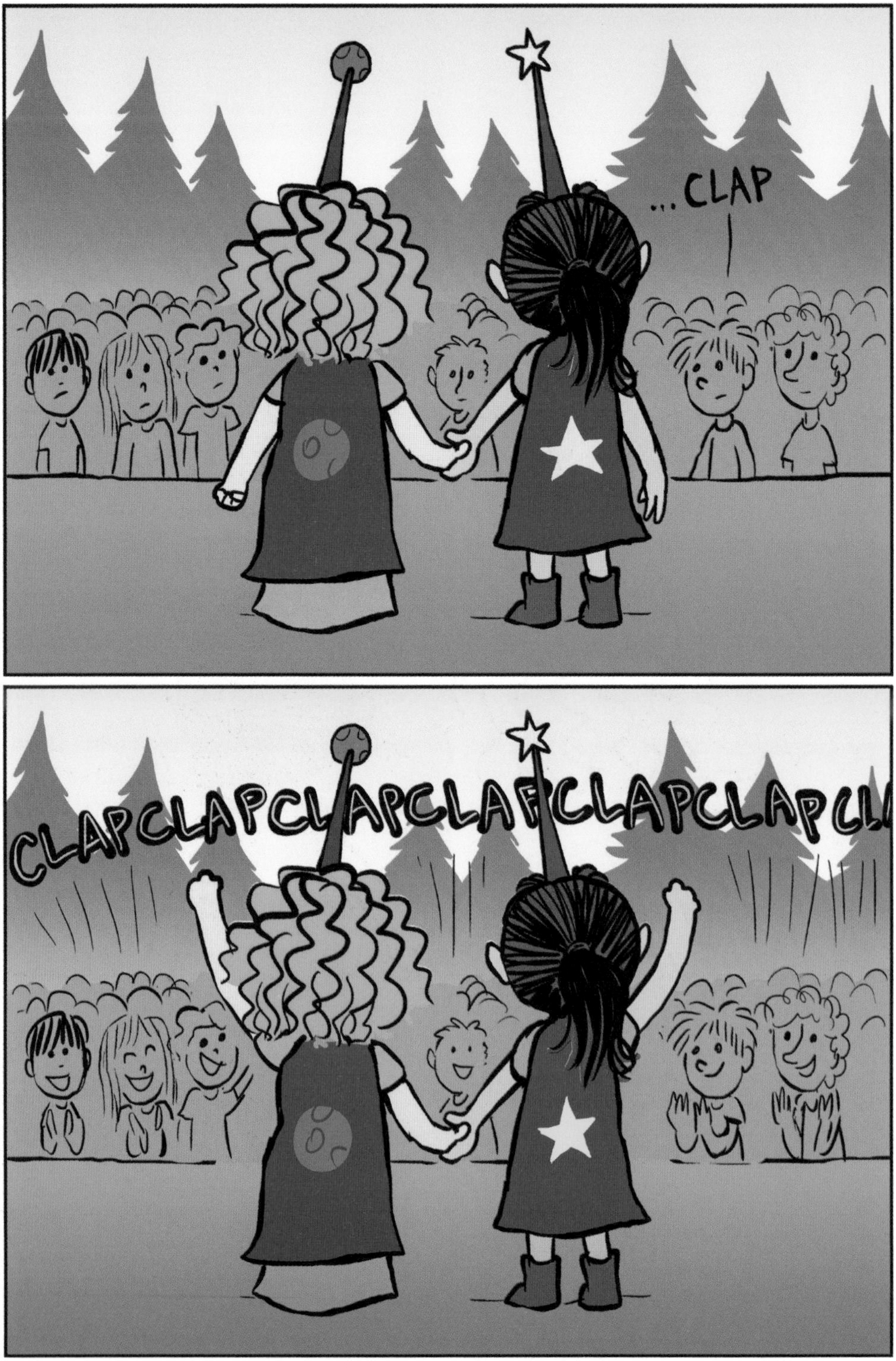
...CLAP
CLAPCLAPCLAPCLAPCLAPCL

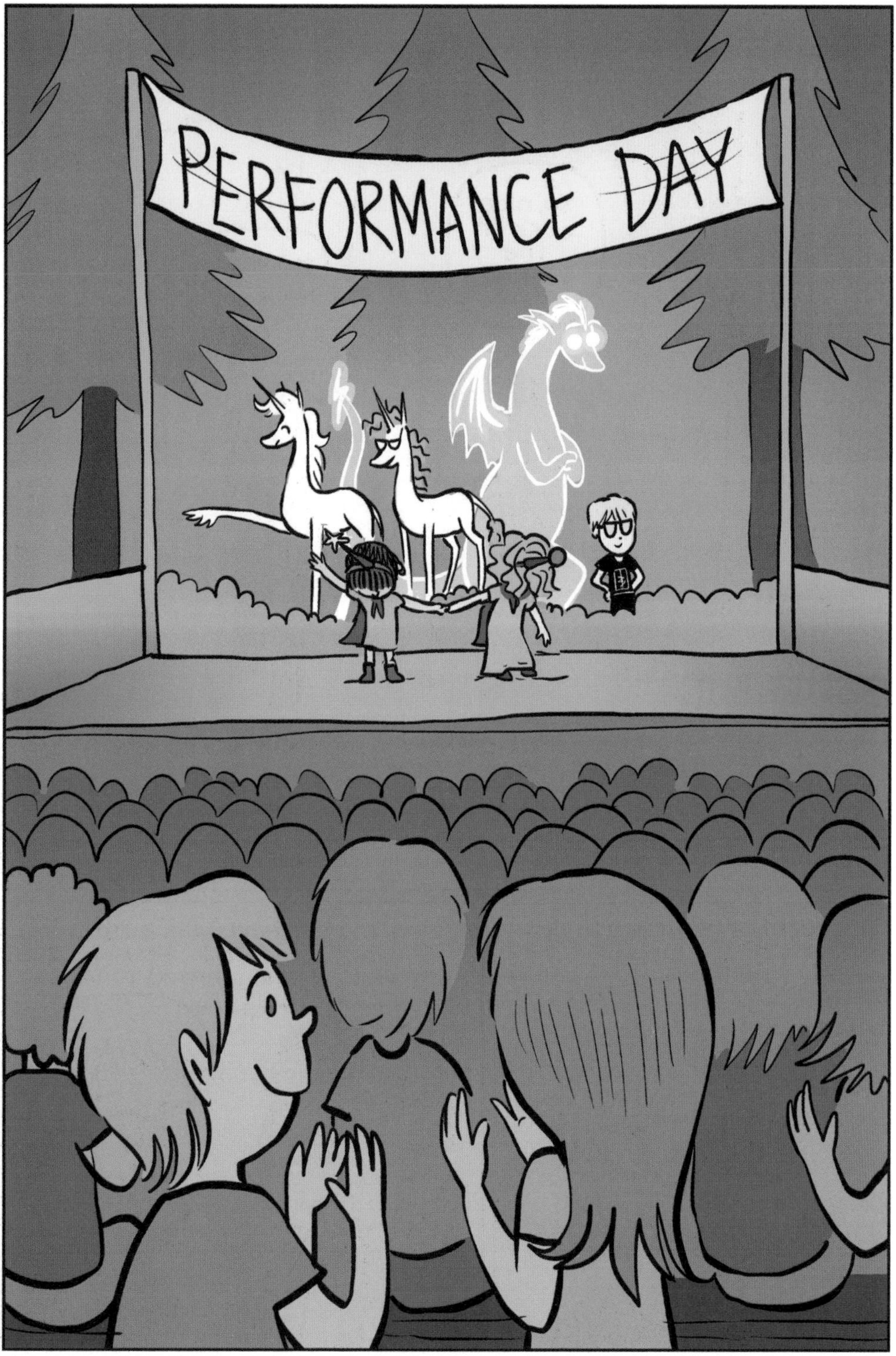
PERFORMANCE DAY

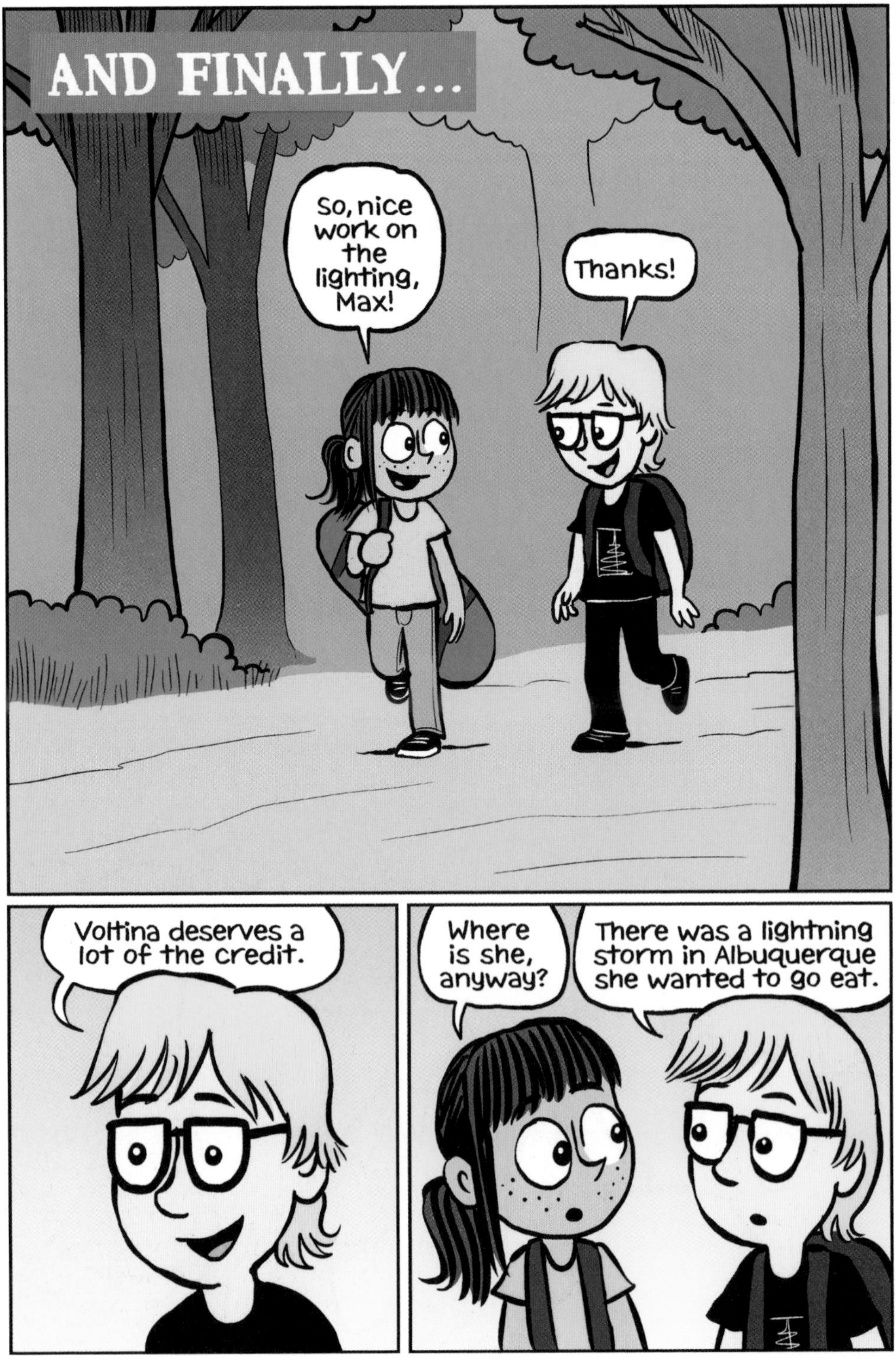
AND FINALLY...
So, nice work on the lighting, Max!
Thanks!
Voltina deserves a lot of the credit.
Where is she, anyway?
There was a lightning storm in Albuquerque she wanted to go eat.

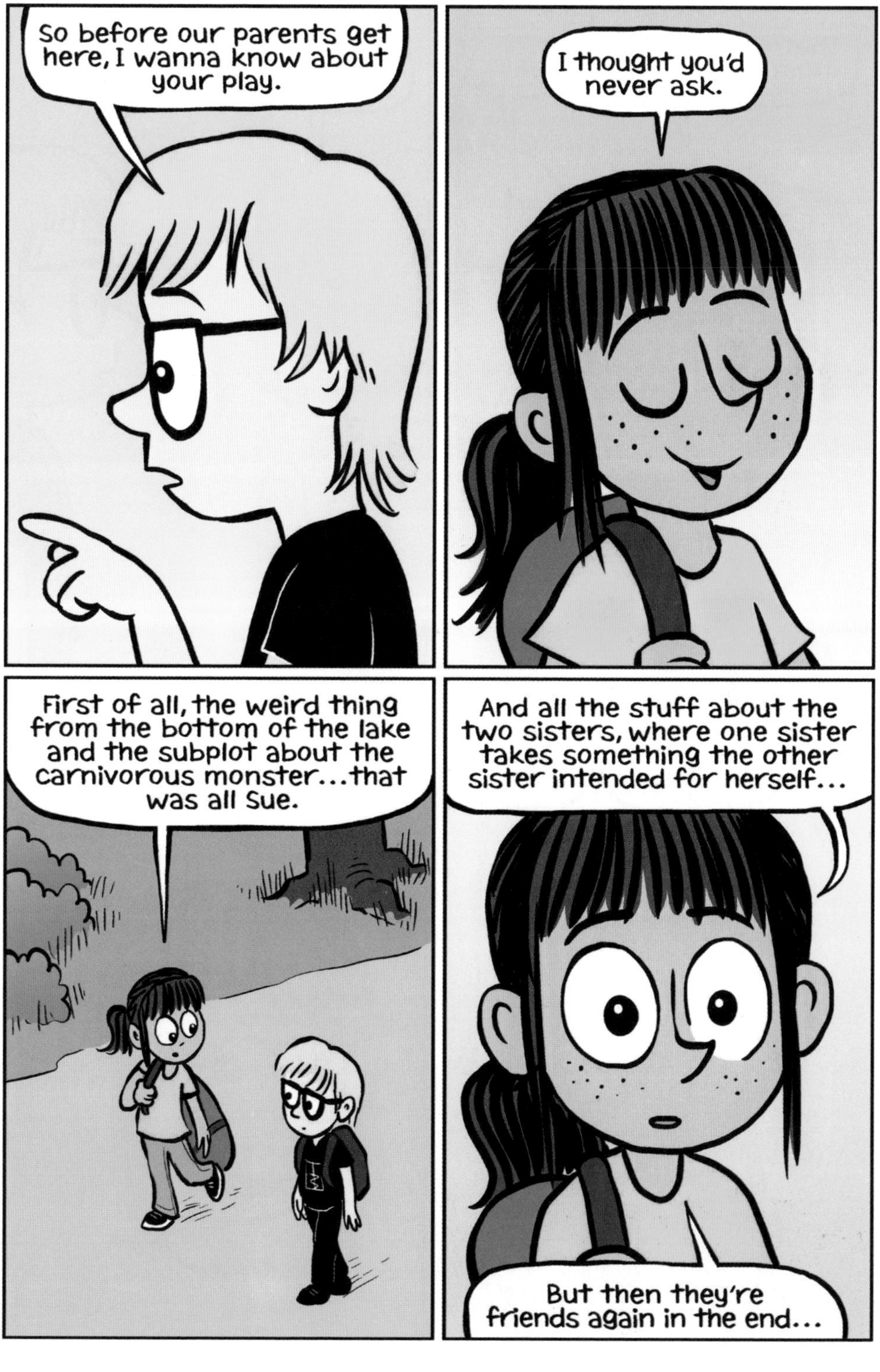
So before our parents get here, I wanna know about your play.
I thought you'd never ask.
First of all, the weird thing from the bottom of the lake and the subplot about the carnivorous monster...that was all Sue.
And all the stuff about the two sisters, where one sister takes something the other sister intended for herself...
But then they're friends again in the end...

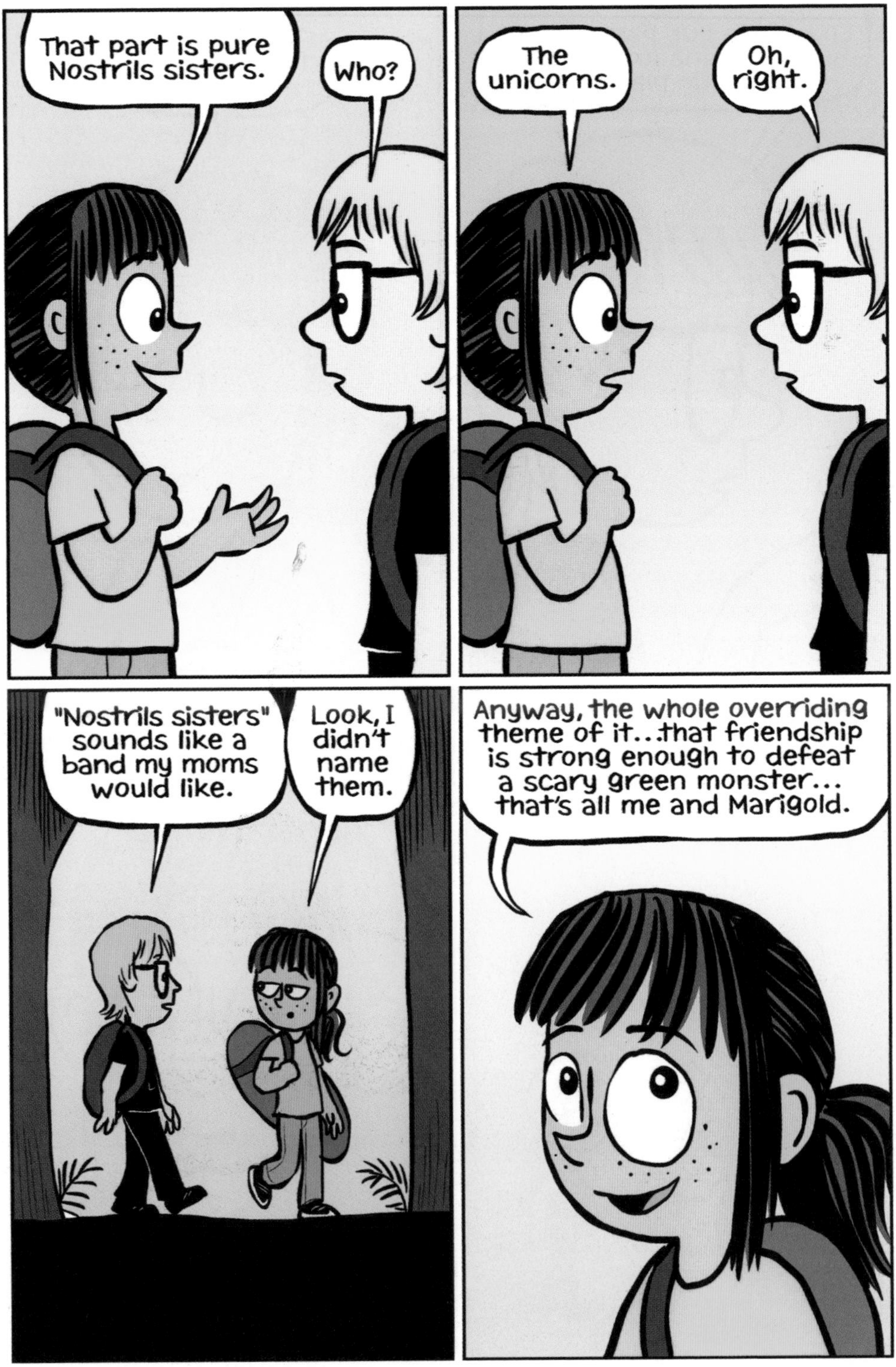
That part is pure Nostrils sisters.
Who?
The unicorns.
Oh, right.
"Nostrils sisters" sounds like a band my moms would like.
Look, I didn't name them.
Anyway, the whole overriding theme of it...that friendship is strong enough to defeat a scary green monster... that's all me and Marigold.

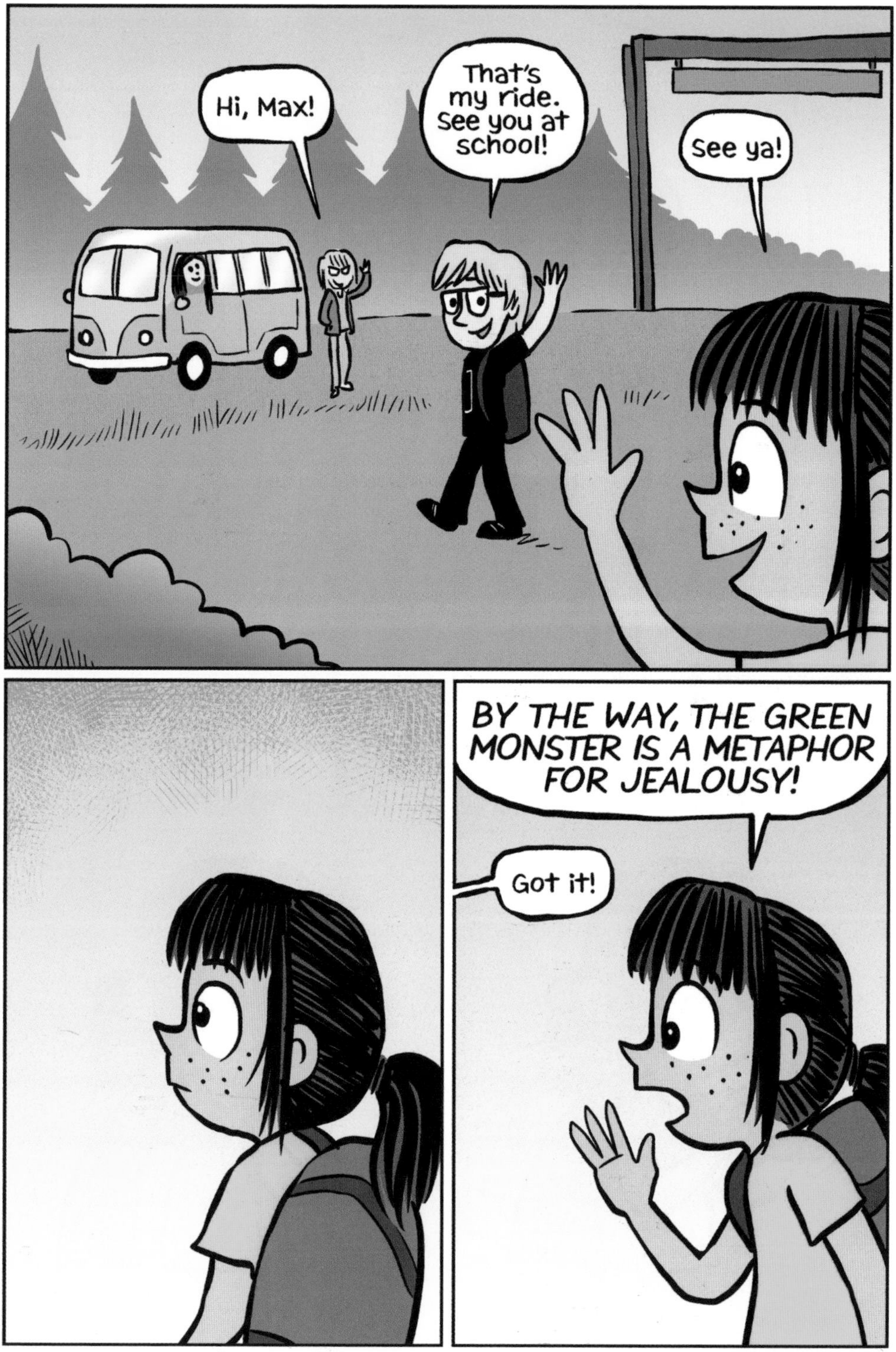
Hi, Max!
That's my ride. See you at school!
See ya!
BY THE WAY, THE GREEN MONSTER IS A METAPHOR FOR JEALOUSY!
Got it!

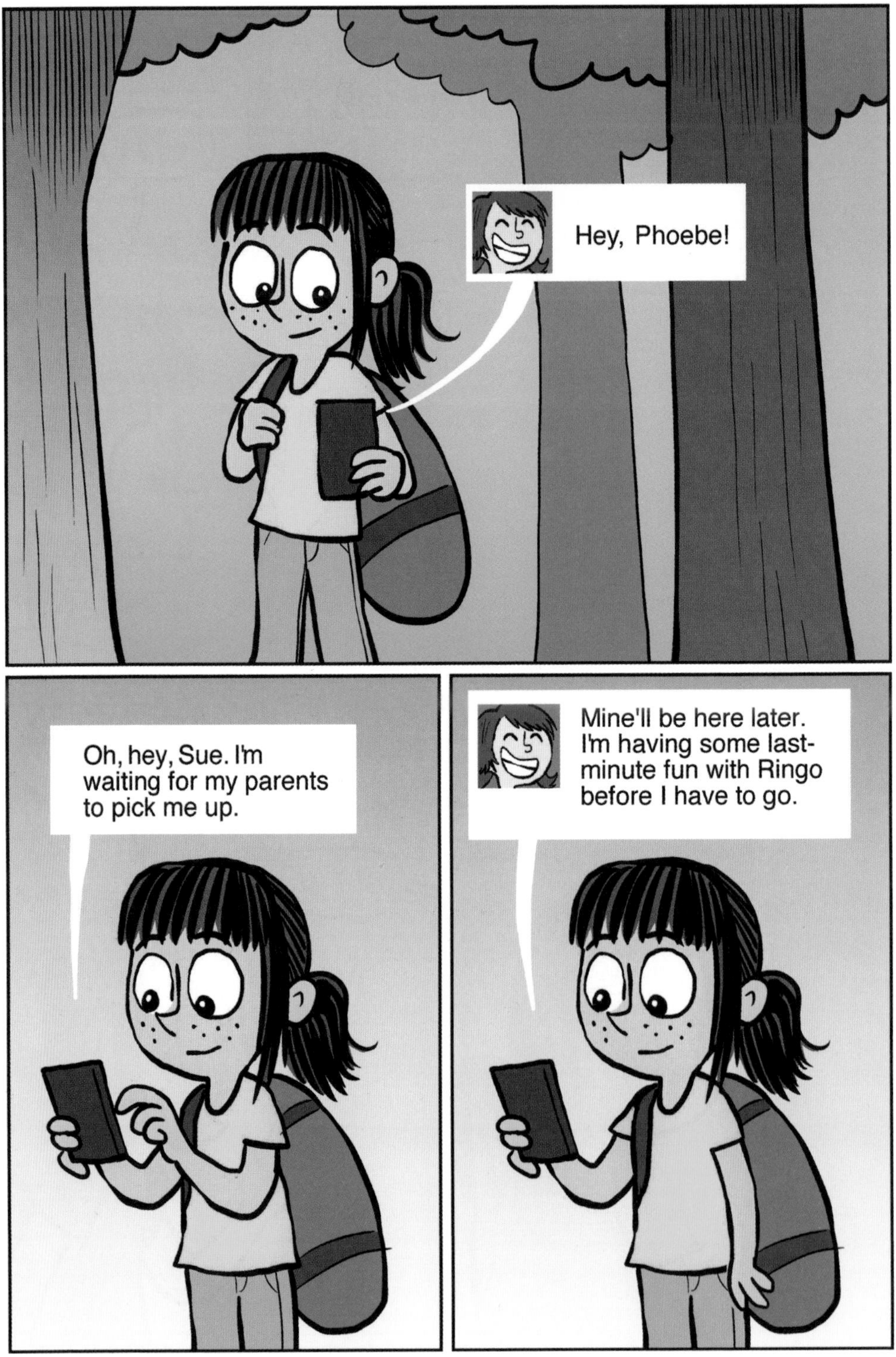
Hey, Phoebe!
Oh, hey, Sue. I'm waiting for my parents to pick me up.
Mine'll be here later. I'm having some last-minute fun with Ringo before I have to go.

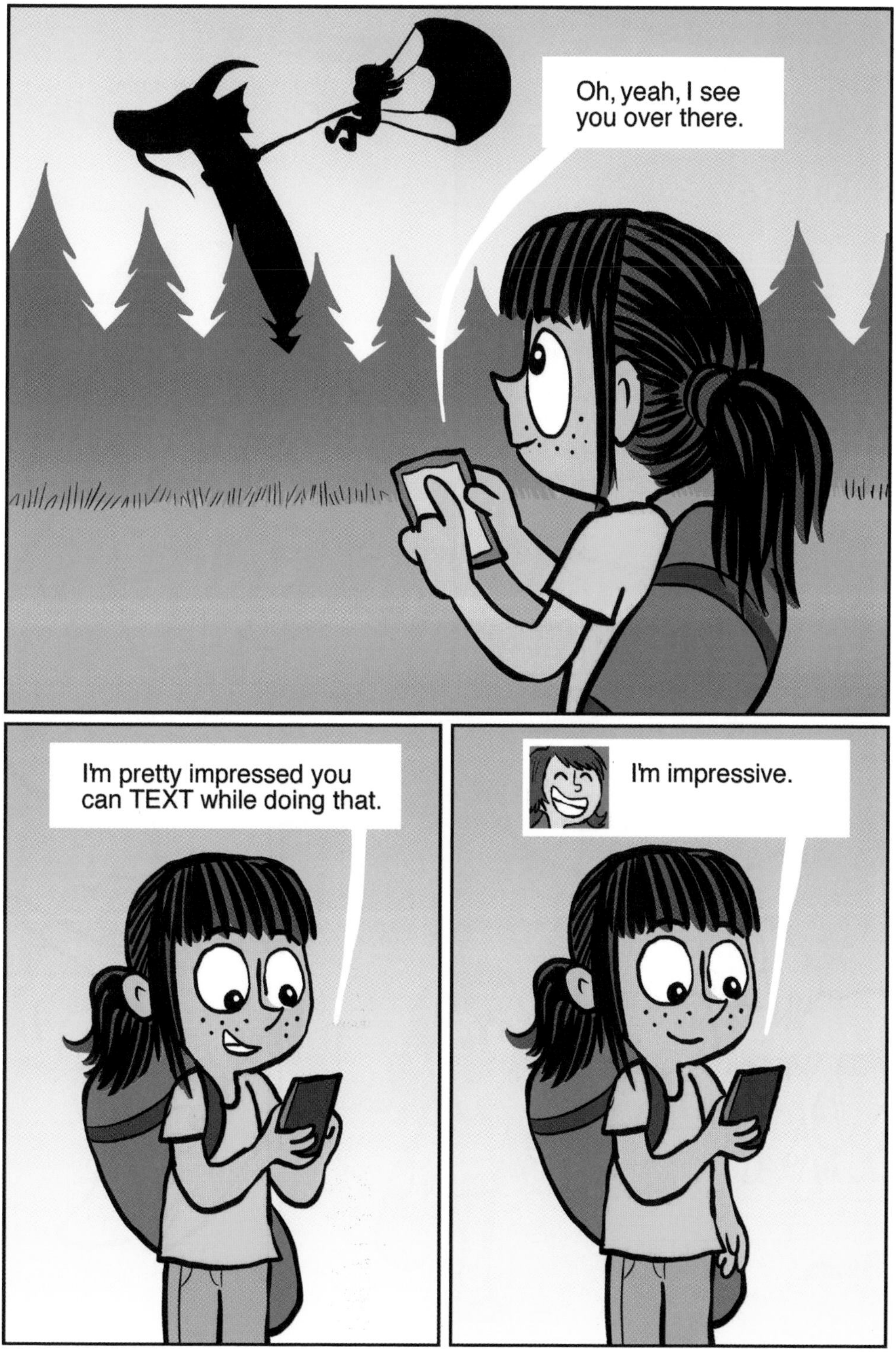
Oh, yeah, I see you over there.
I'm pretty impressed you can TEXT while doing that.
I'm impressive.

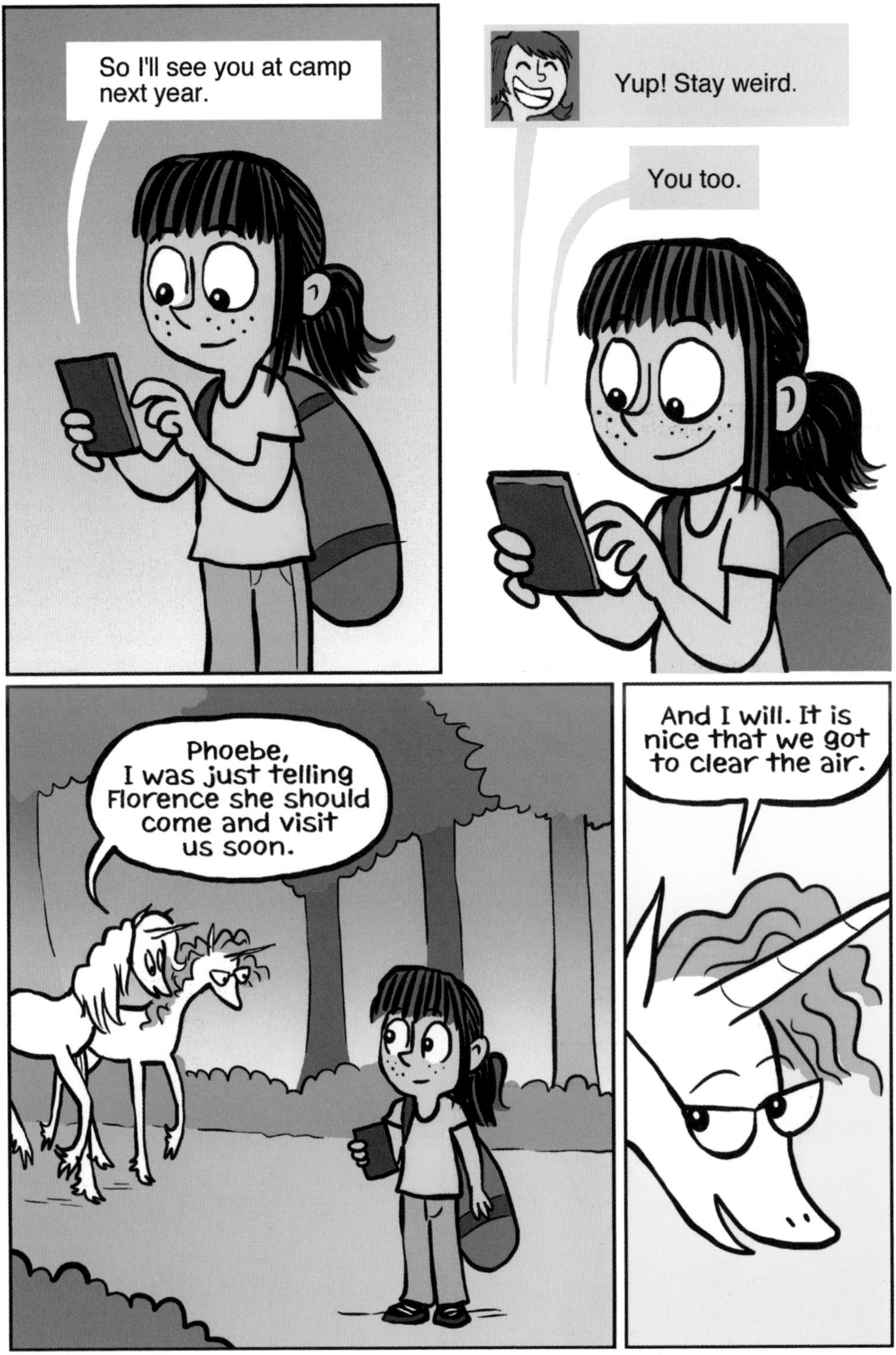
So I'll see you at camp next year.
Yup! Stay weird.
You too.
Phoebe, I was just telling Florence she should come and visit us soon.
And I will. It is nice that we got to clear the air.

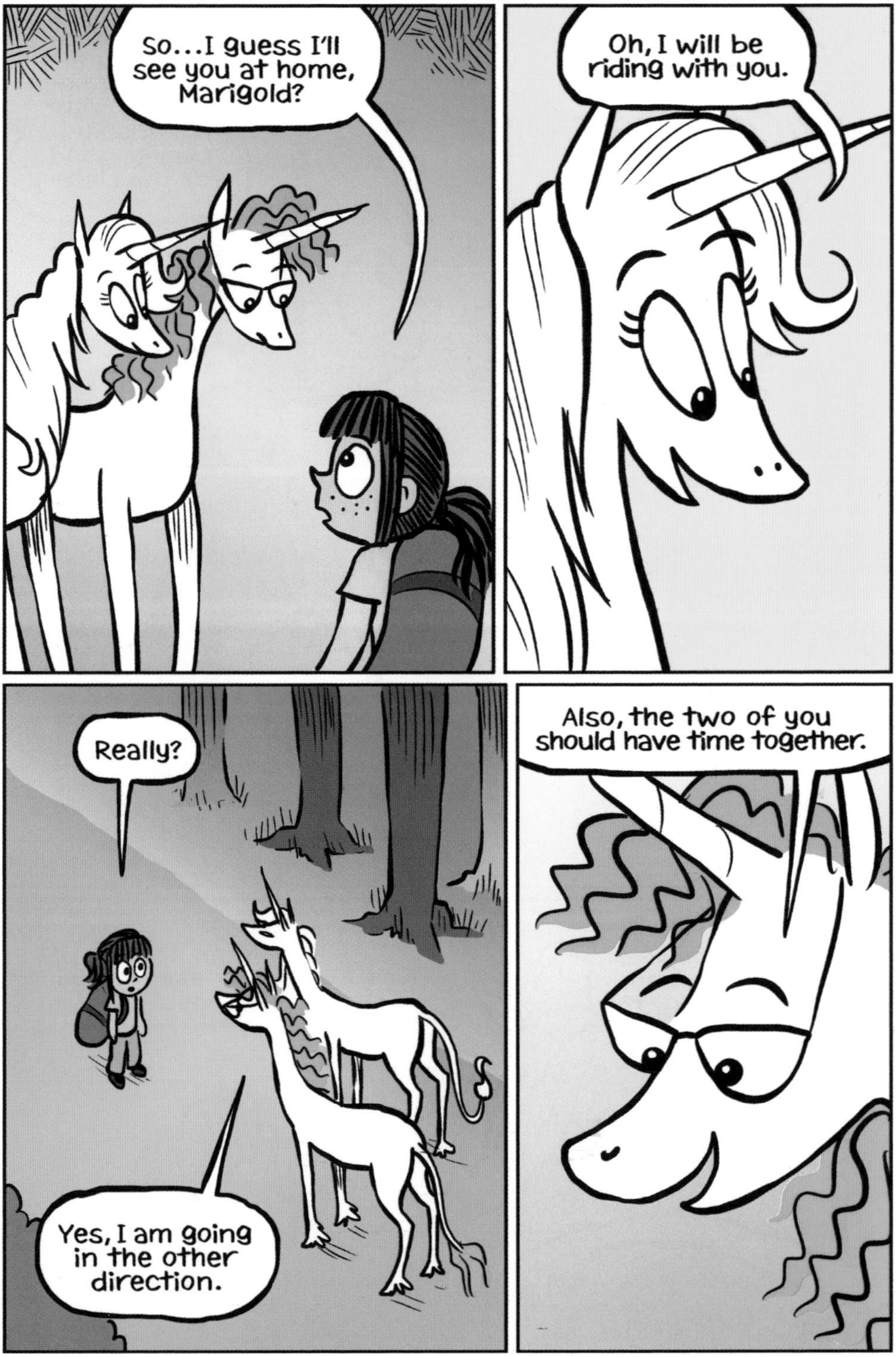
So...I guess I'll see you at home, Marigold?
Oh, I will be riding with you.
Really?
Yes, I am going in the other direction.
Also, the two of you should have time together.

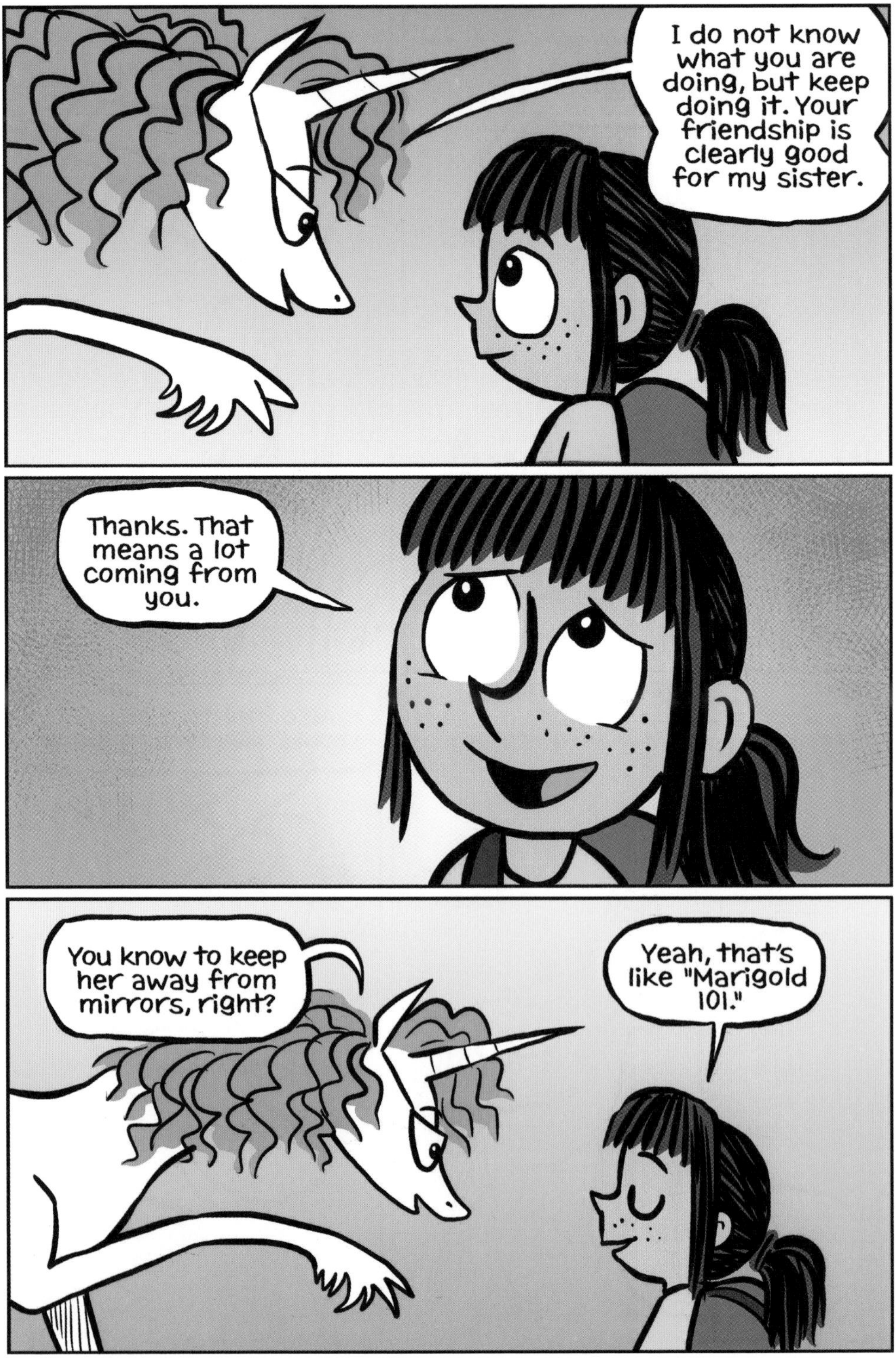
I do not know what you are doing, but keep doing it. Your friendship is clearly good for my sister.
Thanks. That means a lot coming from you.
You know to keep her away from mirrors, right?
Yeah, that's like "Marigold 101."

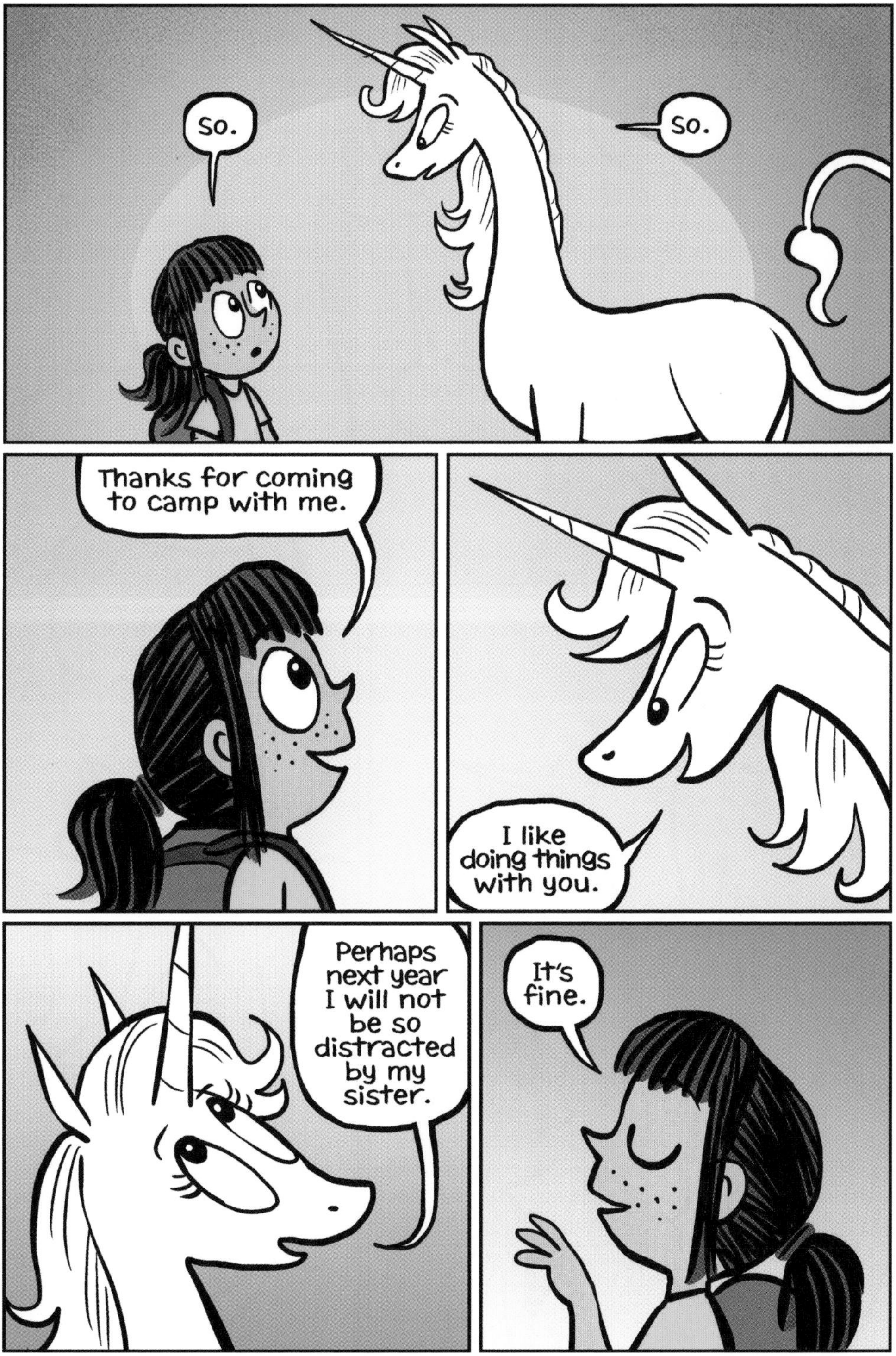
So.
So.
Thanks for coming to camp with me.
I like doing things with you.
Perhaps next year I will not be so distracted by my sister.
It's fine.

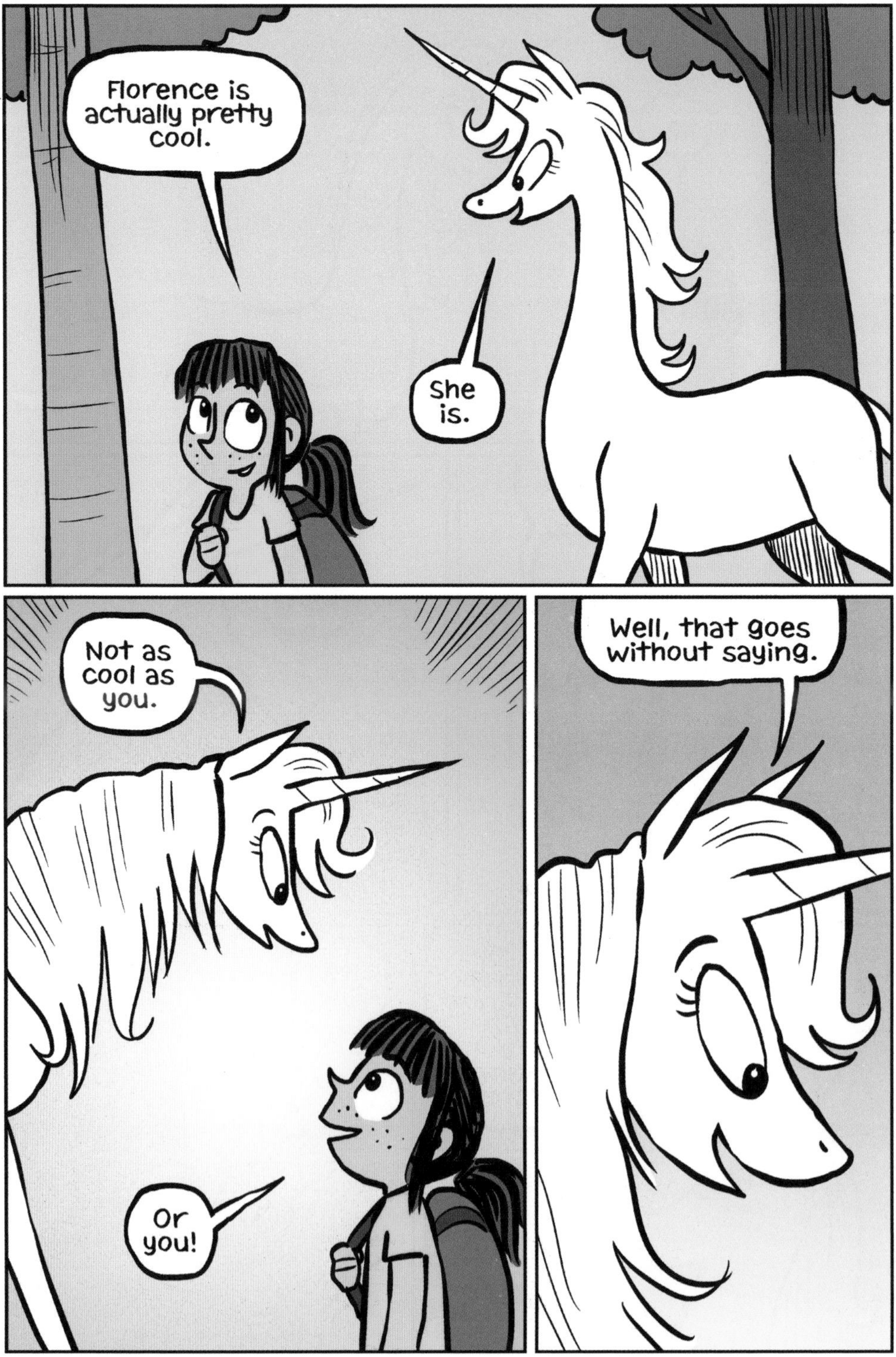
Florence is actually pretty cool.
She is.
Not as cool as you.
Or you!
Well, that goes without saying.

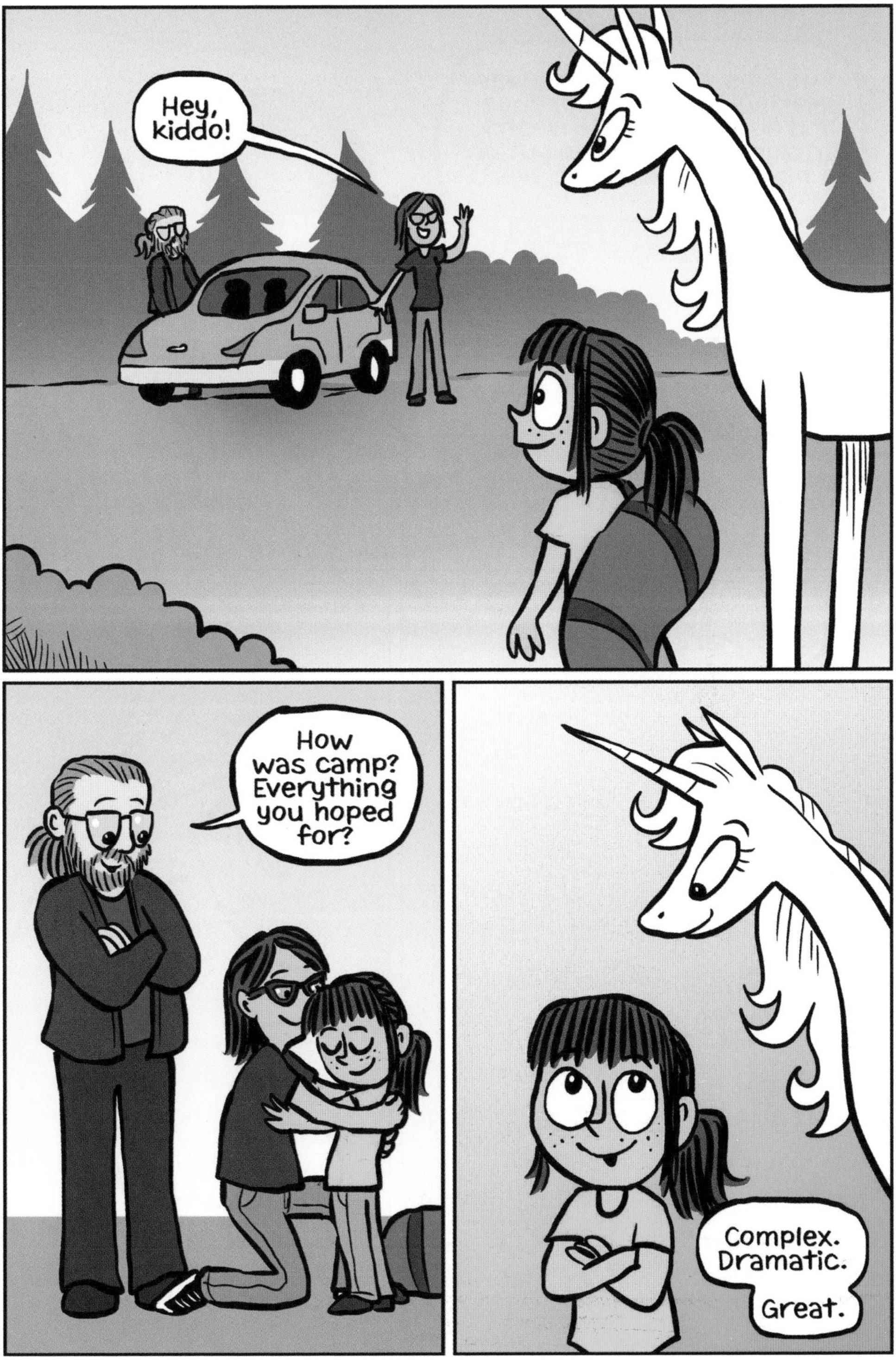
Hey, kiddo!
How was camp? Everything you hoped for?
Complex. Dramatic.
Great.

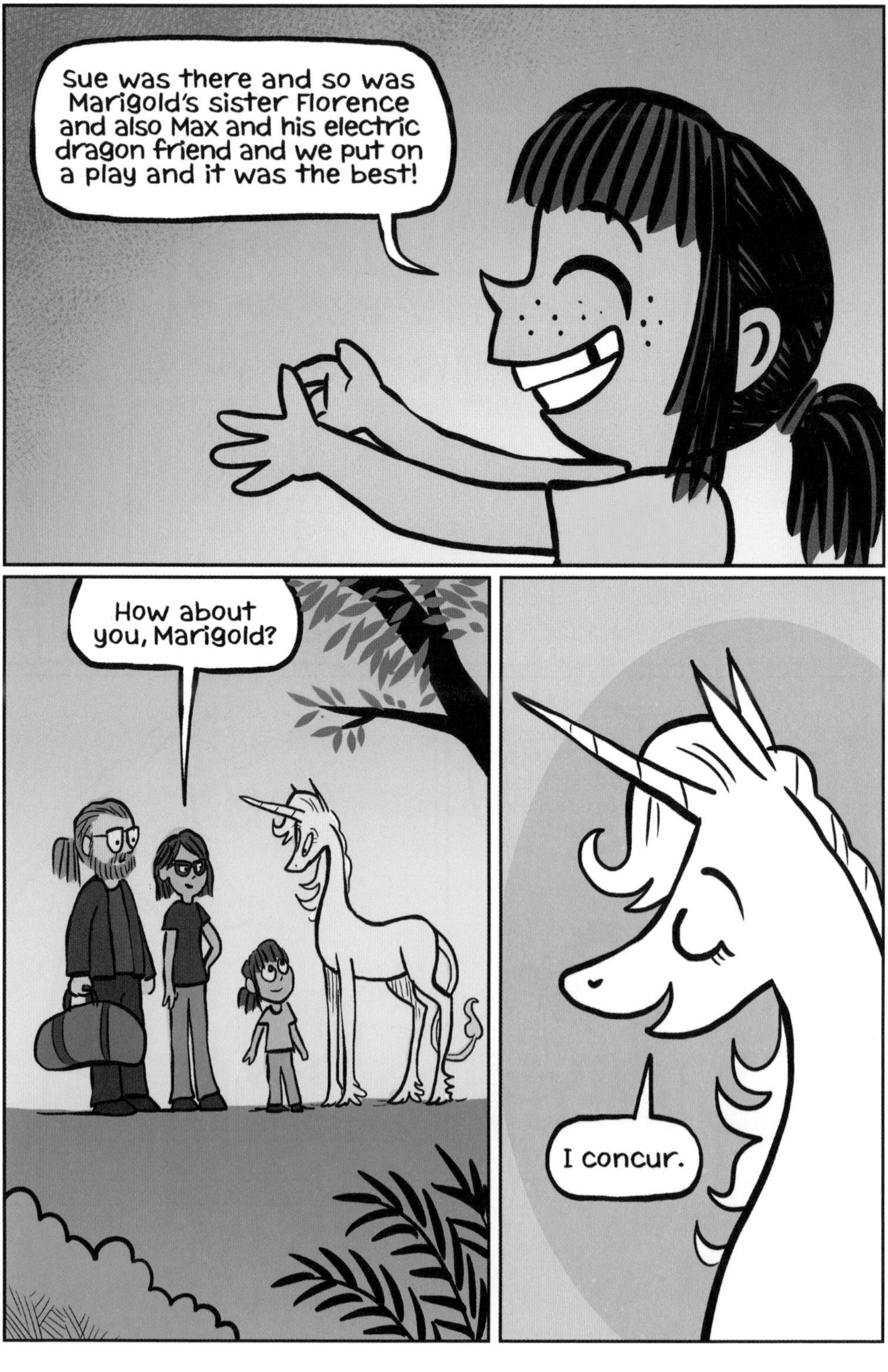
Sue was there and so was Marigold's sister Florence and also Max and his electric dragon friend and we put on a play and it was the best!
How about you, Marigold?
I concur.

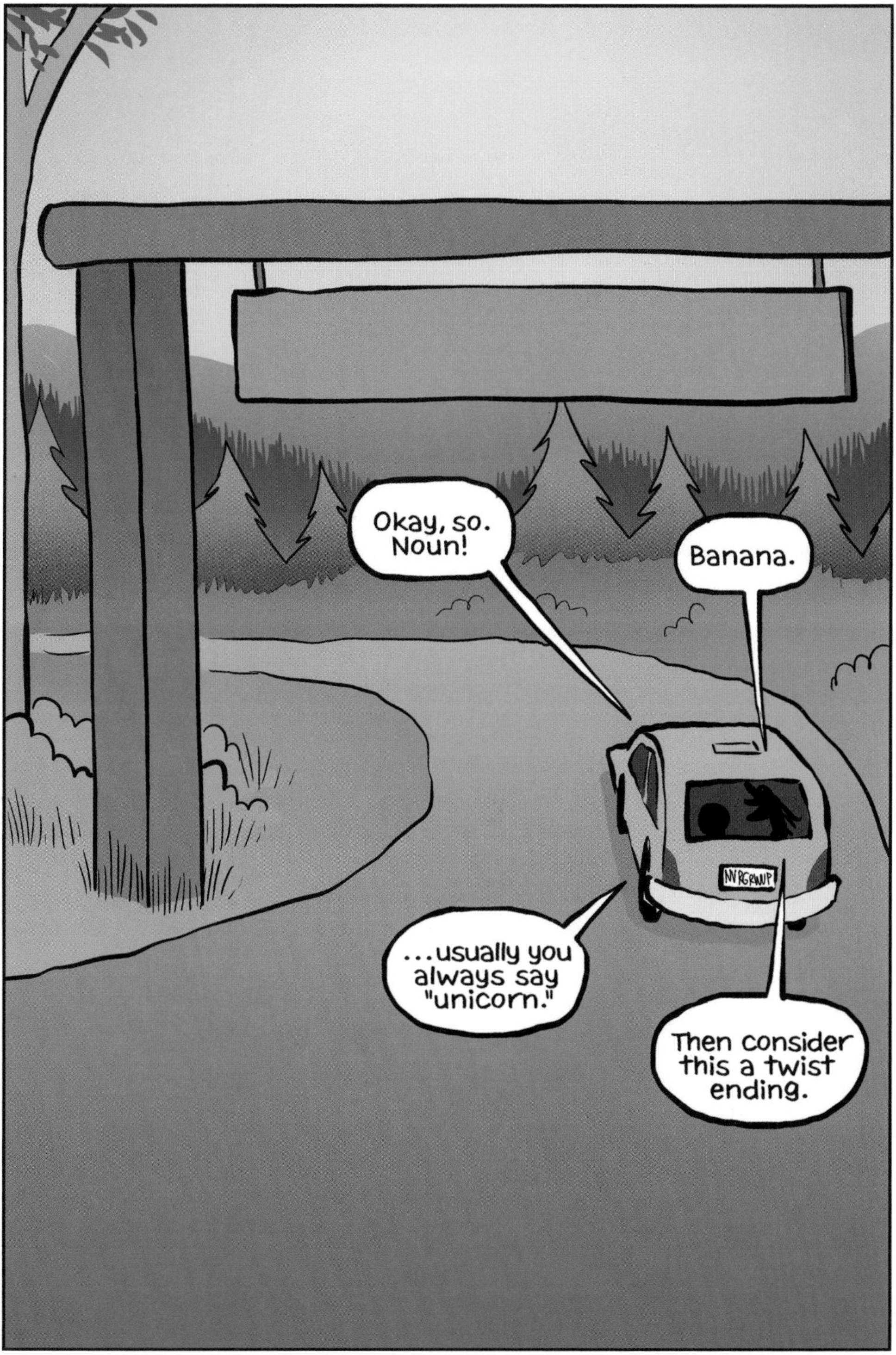
Okay, so. Noun!
Banana.
NVRGRWUP
...usually you always say "unicorn."
Then consider this a twist ending.

Look for these books!

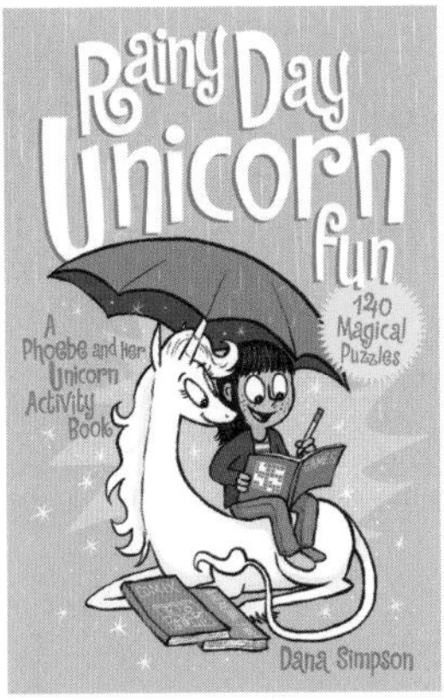
Rainy Day Unicorn fun
140 Magical Puzzles
A Phoebe and Her Unicorn Activity Book
Dana Simpson

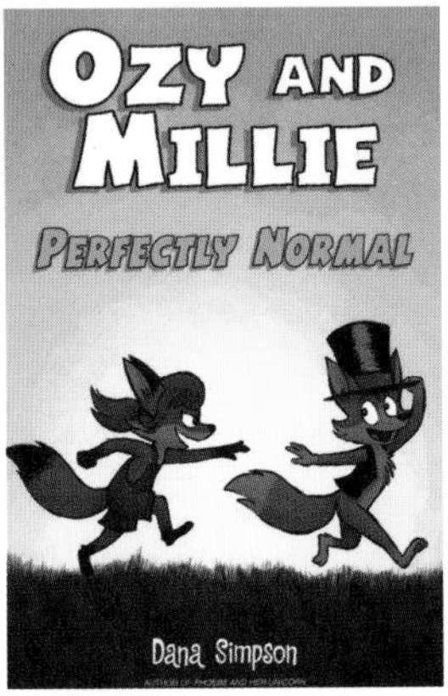
OZY AND MILLIE
PERFECTLY NORMAL
Dana Simpson

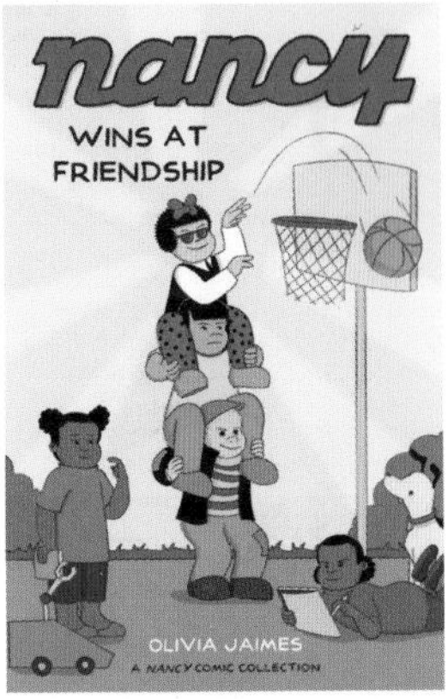
nancy
WINS AT FRIENDSHIP
OLIVIA JAIMES
A NANCY COMIC COLLECTION

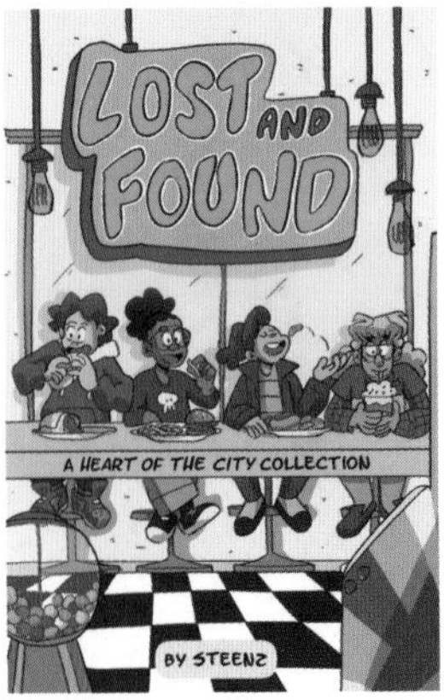
LOST AND FOUND
A HEART OF THE CITY COLLECTION
BY STEENZ

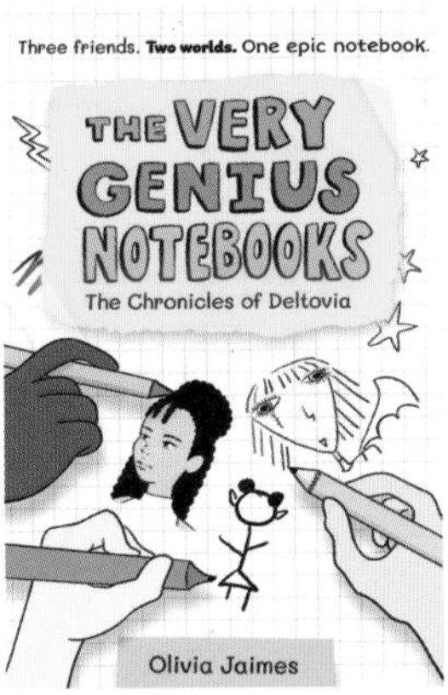
Three friends. Two worlds. One epic notebook.
THE VERY GENIUS NOTEBOOKS
The Chronicles of Deltovia
Olivia Jaimes

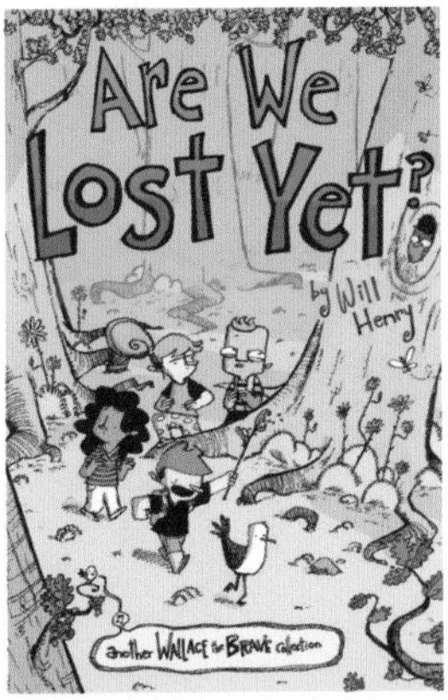
Are We Lost Yet?
by Will Henry
another WALLACE the BRAVE collection

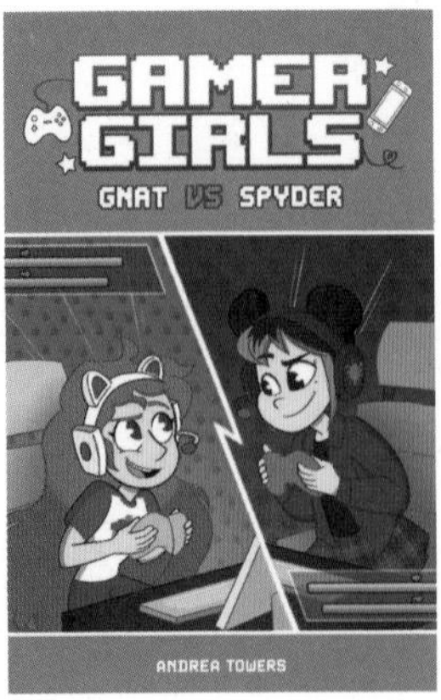
GAMER GIRLS
GNAT VS SPYDER
ANDREA TOWERS

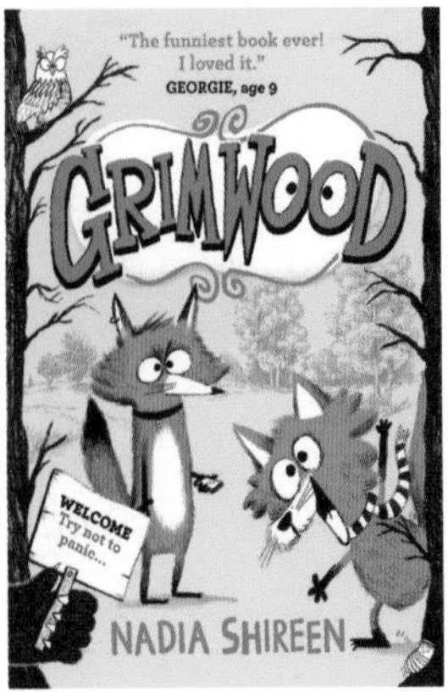
"The funniest book ever! I loved it."
GEORGIE, age 9
GRIMWOOD
WELCOME
Try not to panic...
NADIA SHIREEN

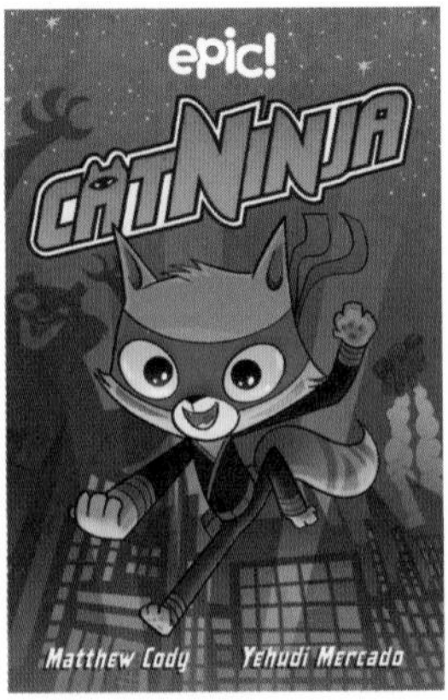
epic!
CATNINJA
Matthew Cody
Yehudi Mercado